THE TUNNELS BENEATH

THE ALDORAN CHRONICLES
- BOOK FOUR -

written by

MICHAEL
WISEHART

Copyright

THE TUNNELS BENEATH is a work of fiction. Names, characters, places, and incidents are products of the author's imagination or are used fictitiously. Any resemblance to actual locales or persons, living or dead, business establishments, or events, is entirely coincidental.

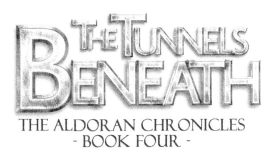

THE TUNNELS BENEATH

THE ALDORAN CHRONICLES
- BOOK FOUR -

Books by
Michael Wisehart

STREET RATS OF ARAMOOR

(Starts 20 years prior to the Aldoran Chronicles)

Book 1 | Banished

Book 2 | Hurricane

Book 3 | Rockslide

Book 4 | Sandstorm

Book 5 | Wildfire

THE ALDORAN CHRONICLES

Prequel | Shackled

Book 1 | The White Tower

Book 2 | Plague of Shadows

Book 3 | The Four-Part Key

Book 4 | The Tunnels Beneath

Map of Aldor – West

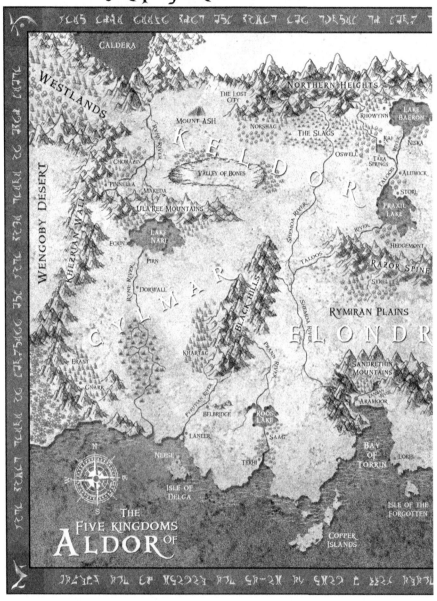

Map of Aldor - East

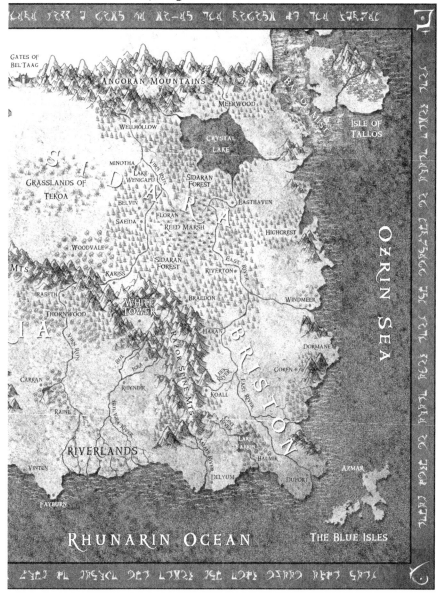

Map of Aramoor

1. LUMBER YARDS
2. THE ROCKSLIDE COMPOUND
3. LANCER CORPS
4. THE GUILD
5. WILDFIRE COMPOUND
6. LANCER BARRACKS
7. SANDSTORM COMPOUND
8. BAYSIDE
9. THE TEMPLE
10. KING'S SQUARE
11. AVALANCHE COMPOUND
12. SHIPPING YARDS
13. THE PIT
14. THE ROYAL PALACE
15. THE GRANARY
16. OLD MERCHANT DISTRICT
17. THE WARRENS

ARAMOOR

Map of Easthaven

Easthaven

1.East Bridge 2.East Inn 3.Mangora's 4.Barracks
5.Sidaran Assembly Hall 6.Overlord Barl's Estate 7.Dockworks
8.Orlyn's Apothecary 9.Harbor House 10.Reloria's Sweet Shop

Map of Aero'set

Aero'set

1. Dormitory 3. Library 5. Shipyard 7. Dining Hall
2. Arena 4. Garrison 6. Arboretum 8. New Wellhollow

Important Notice

NOTE: If you have not yet read the first book in the Street Rats of Aramoor series, entitled *Banished*, you need to put this book down and read it. The characters and storyline in that book play a very important role in this fourth addition to The Aldoran Chronicles.

Chapter 1 | Ty

TY DEFLECTED A BLADE, sidestepped, then deflected another. They were coming so fast, he knew he couldn't stop them. He struck away two more attempts, each getting a little closer. This wasn't working. He could barely see his opponent's weapons. How was he supposed to defend himself when he could barely—

He stumbled while trying to scissor-cross his legs in the snow and went down, losing his sword. He spun over onto his back just in time to see the man standing over him swing. Ty didn't have time to think. He desperately raised his hands and conjured a shield, sending the man's weapons careening to the left.

The man kicked Ty's shin.

"Ow!" Ty released his shield and grabbed his leg. "What was that for?"

Ayrion stood over him, looking disappointed. "I told you. No magic."

Ty heard giggling from the side of the practice ring and turned over. "What? You think you can do better?"

"Of course, yes," Narendi said as she, Breen, and Kraea sat smirking. The Imbatoo princess was wearing her Mzwati robes, with her face covering hanging loosely around her neck. As cold as it was in the Angoran Mountains, especially with snow still covering the ground, Ty was surprised she didn't opt for something warmer.

On the left side of the ring, Ty spotted Bek. The large trapper was decked in his usual fur-lined outfit all the way down to his zabatas, as he called them. Ty had to admit they did look warm. He wondered if the woodsman would be willing to make him a pair. Ty shook his head. *Come on. Focus.*

He turned his attention back to the man in black. He hated weapons practice. He needed to be learning how to use magic with Nyalis, not how to get thrown around like a rag doll by this swordsman, even if he was some kind of weapons master. It wasn't that Ty didn't understand the need to learn how to wield a sword, but so far that was all he'd been allowed to do.

Ayrion held out his hand and helped Ty to his feet. Ty felt more than a little humiliated as he took a moment to stretch and check for injuries before collecting his weapon, which was nothing more than a wooden practice sword. His fingers were cold and numb, which made gripping the sword difficult, so he blew on them until the tips began to tingle.

Their practices were being held inside the Aero'set garrison. Nyalis said that it had been part of a military compound where they trained those set to guard the school. Ty wondered what they had been like.

Ayrion walked over. "Magic is a gift, but if you want to learn how to wield it properly, then you need to understand the basics of what it is you're using it for. What good is a conjured shield if you don't know how to maneuver it? If I had been a real opponent, I would have cut your leg off while you were busy guarding your chest."

"And if this had been a real fight, I would have burned you alive before you got the—"

Ayrion's fist connected with the side of Ty's face, and before Ty hit the dirt, everything went black.

Ty's eyes slowly flickered open to find Breen, Narendi, and Kraea kneeling over him. What were they . . . He remembered the blow and sat up, rubbing his jaw. It felt like someone had crushed it with a sledgehammer.

Narendi shook her head. "Even I saw that coming."

"Where is he?" Ty bellowed, too angry to care how much it hurt to talk.

He twisted around and scanned the practice yard, but there was no sign of the man in black.

"Afraid Ayrion left a while ago," Breen said with a sympathetic sigh as he helped Ty up and over to one of several benches staggered around the practice rings.

Kraea smiled, her fangs quite frightening. "*The dark warrior told them to tell you that if this had been a real fight, you would have been dead half a dozen times over before you got the chance to remember you even had magic.*"

"Ayrion said—"

Ty waved Breen off. "I already heard."

"Oh." Breen looked over at Kraea, and she cocked her head.

Ty was the only one who could hear the draakar, and most of the time he didn't bother translating. It simply took too much time. He attempted to move his jaw around and immediately stopped. The pain was excruciating. "I'm really starting to hate that man."

"You don't have to like him to learn," someone behind them said.

They turned to find Nyalis leaning against his staff next to a large oak at the side of the ring. It had been a couple of days since Ty had seen him, though not for a lack of searching. As big as Aero'set was, Ty could spend the next year exploring the mountain compound and probably not find half of what the magical school held. As it was, they had barely scratched the surface over the last few weeks, having only been inside a few of the more prominent towers near the center.

Nyalis walked over, and the others parted to let him through. He sat down on the bench next to Ty and reached for his jaw. "Hmm. Yes." He shook his head.

"What?" Ty asked, then winced.

"You were definitely hit."

"He knows that," Breen said exasperatedly. "Aren't you going to fix it?"

Nyalis sighed. "I'm growing weary of expending magic to heal the three of you."

"Then tell that sadist of an instructor to quit trying to kill us," Ty mumbled.

"You wouldn't need healing if you'd actually listen."

Ty jumped when he realized Ayrion was standing right behind him. "How did you—" He winced again, cupping his jaw. "Look what you did to me." His words were garbled.

"Hold still," Nyalis said, moving Ty's hand out of the way. He closed his eyes and muttered something under his breath.

Ty felt the familiar rush of icy cold flood through his mouth, and the pain eased. Nyalis released his grip, and Ty slowly opened his jaw, then wiggled it around. The pain was gone.

"How is he?" Ayrion asked, sounding oddly concerned.

"Back to form," Nyalis said, pulling himself up with the help of his staff. "Do take it easier on him, will you? I can't keep wasting my magic on unnecessary healings."

Ayrion looked at Ty. "In his case, I'm afraid it's all *too* necessary. What he knows about the art of defense wouldn't fill the cap on his head." He looked at Ty. "I don't know how you've managed to survive this long."

"With this," Ty said, igniting blue flames from each of his hands.

"Yes, very pretty, but what good is it when you burn yourself out or find yourself with one of those durmas around your neck? Or end up in a place like the one you described in the Riverlands where your magic was unusable?" He turned to Nyalis. "I would guess there are other such places like that around Aldor?"

"There are several, yes. Both here and elsewhere."

Ayrion nodded. "I knew a boy once who could negate magic just by being close, so trust me when I say you need to learn how to defend yourself." He looked at the others. "That goes for all of you."

Kraea growled, baring her fangs.

The weapons master didn't flinch in the slightest. "Yes, that goes for you as well," he said to the draakar. "It wasn't too long ago that you were lying in a pool of your own blood with a witch's dagger sticking from your chest."

"*Don't remind me,*" Kraea said, though Ty was the only one who could hear her.

Ayrion didn't seem to care if she had responded or not. He looked at Narendi. "Our young princess here seems to be the only one of you capable of wielding a weapon in close combat. I must say that your people have my respect. Your skill with the spear is quite advanced."

Narendi smiled, then smirked at Ty.

"Though your sword skills could use some work," he added, and her smile slipped.

"What about Breen?" Ty added. "He can clip the wings off a red flit at fifty paces."

Ayrion looked at Ty's brother, who stood nearly a head taller than he did. "Yes, he does have an uncanny knack for hitting what he aims at, but a bow or a thrown knife are weapons best used at a distance. I'm talking about standing face-to-face with an opponent and surviving. Looking your enemy in the whites of his eyes and walking away without serious injury."

The weapons master took a step back and placed his hands on his sides. "My job, in the short time that I'm here, is to prepare you as best I can." He looked at each of them in turn, then groaned loudly. "I've got my work cut out for me."

"You said *short time*," Breen pointed out. "Are you planning on leaving?"

Ayrion gave Nyalis an odd look. "Now that I've managed to recover my memories, there are . . . obligations that need addressing."

"You have more important obligations here that need tending to," Nyalis said.

Ayrion didn't respond, but he said a lot in that silence. He finally turned and looked at the four of them. "Regardless, my time is limited, so your training will be grueling."

Ty groaned inwardly.

"I can't promise to turn you into expert swordsmen and women, or even that you'll be proficient, but I will do my best to give you the skills you'll need to hopefully survive." Ayrion walked over and grabbed the two wooden practice swords off the ground and turned. "So, who's next?"

That's it? Ty mused. That was all their instructor was going to say to encourage them? That had to be the worst pep talk he'd ever heard.

"I guess I can spot the others," Breen said and walked into the ring to take the practice sword from Ayrion. With a deep breath, they faced off, and the training started up once more.

By the time the afternoon sun had begun to cool as it slipped over the horizon, Ty, Breen, Narendi, and even Kraea were completely winded and barely able to stand. Ty's whole body was covered in bruises and cuts where he'd failed to block or dodge or deflect Ayrion's attacks. He thought one of his knuckles might have been dislocated. The only benefit to the cold was he couldn't feel it all that much.

Ty hated everything about this training. It was terrible. This wasn't why he had worked so hard to find this place, why he'd given up so much. He hadn't risked his life and his brother's countless times over just so he could be beaten and bashed about by some white-eyed know-it-all weapons instructor.

He perked up from the side with the others as Bek finally took his place in the ring. Ty loved watching the hulking woodsman spar. He'd never seen anyone fight with hatchets before, even with wooden practice ones. He spared a quick glance over at the end of the bench where Bek's actual hatchets rested. They were formidable weapons. Each hatchet had an axe blade on the front that tapered to a spike on the back.

The clacking of wood finally drew Ty's attention away from Bek's weapons and back to the ring. Ayrion tended to use two of the practice swords when fighting with the trapper. They had a bond that allowed them to move back and forth almost as one, as if they knew what the other was planning. As talented as Bek was, however, he still didn't hold a candle to the man in black.

Ty took a moment to look at Ayrion's twin blades, where they lay on a bench just beside theirs. He had asked to see the swords back when they had first arrived in Aero'set, back before Ayrion had been instructed by Nyalis to begin training them. The weapons were incredible. Ty had never seen anything like them. He wondered who could have forged blades that beautiful, blades that apparently were indestructible, blades that could actually stand up against a bulradoer's ter'ak.

The loud clap of wood on wood had Ty refocusing his attention back to the ring and the two men inside. Bek was a much larger man, but Ayrion seemed to move like an animal, with the creepy ability to perceive what the other was going to do and counter practically before he did it. There had been no mention of Ayrion having magic, but there were times Ty could almost sense it.

Whoever these Upakans were, Ty was glad Nyalis hadn't taken him there to be raised as a babe. If they were anything like Ayrion, they had to be some of the worst people in the Five Kingdoms to live with, and he should know. He was sure he'd been to nearly every corner of it, and beyond, over the last couple of months. From what Ayrion had said, he and his people began training their children as soon as they were old enough to walk.

"Who's up for dinner?" Narendi asked when the sparring match appeared to be winding down. It seemed she was the only one of them recovered enough to sit up on their own.

"I'm in too much pain to eat," Breen said. "I just want a hot bath, some of Isha's cream, and a soft bed."

Ty turned over. "I don't know how much of it we have left. We've been using it a lot of late."

"We can make more," Narendi said. "We have notes from Isha."

"Yes, but we don't have the ingredients," Ty added. "Isha gave me a few of those wamini plants, but they won't last long."

"There is more," she said.

Ty turned, his neck twinging when he did. "Where?"

"You have not been to the glass house?"

"What glass house?"

She smiled. "I will show you after we bathe and eat."

"I want to eat," Kraea said. *"Something red and warm and juicy."*

Ty's stomach turned.

"What is wrong?" Narendi asked, noticing Ty's expression.

"Just something Kraea said."

Kraea smiled as she stood and stretched. She enjoyed getting under his skin, not that he didn't give it back in equal measure, but her eating habits tended to affect him the most. He could sense her pleasure when she ate, the warm blood sloshing around in her mouth as she tore apart her meals. It had a way of spoiling his appetite.

They left the garrison by way of the south gate and started through the shipyards. Dozens of black dry-docked vessels of all shapes and sizes filled the wide-open space in front of the barracks. Each of the dark ships was decorated with gold trim, beautiful swirling designs along the upper railings.

Ty had to strain his neck to look up at them as they passed. Some were enormous. He had seen large ships before, but he had never really thought about how big they truly were, or how little of them he actually saw once they were on the water.

"You've got to wonder what they used these things for," Breen said. "Most are too big for the river." He pointed at a couple of the smaller ones near the front. "Perhaps those." He glanced back at some of the larger ones closer to the garrison. "I wonder how they got here? Do you think the river was bigger back when this place was in use a thousand years ago?"

Ty shrugged. "Could be."

Breen walked over to one of the smaller vessels and tapped on the side of its hull. "And what kind of wood do you think they used that would have lasted so long?"

Ty shrugged again. "Just one more thing to add to the very long list we need to discuss with Nyalis, if we can ever pin him down long enough to ask him."

"He does seem rather aloof," Breen said.

"What's this aloof?" Narendi asked.

Breen chuckled. "It means he tends to disappear a lot where no one can find him."

"Yes." She nodded. "He is very aloof."

Kraea pranced along beside Ty, quieter than usual. She had grown a little since their arrival, her legs thickening, her horns lengthening. Her scales even looked a deeper shade of red. She wasn't quite the size of her mother, but the way she was growing, it probably wouldn't take her too long. She had gone from the size of a large wolf to perhaps a small pony. She was nearly big enough for Ty to sit on. Not that he would have tried. Kraea seemed real persnickety about being touched. In fact, Ty was the only person she would let touch her.

He could feel a hint of sadness through their link. It was always there, deep in the back of his mind, though he had to admit it wasn't quite as strong as it used to be, fading a little every day. The loss of her mother had been extremely difficult. He remembered what it had been like for him when his mother died at the hands of the spiders. There were still times when he'd find himself tearing up at the thought of her. That sadness was something they shared.

"Finding Nyalis does seem to be rather difficult," Breen said. "But I'm sure keeping up with this place is a full-time task. From what the old wizard said, there used to be hundreds, if not thousands, of people living here. Now there's just us."

Ty hadn't really thought about it until then, but his brother was right. It got him wondering more about how Aero'set worked, how it had been created, where the magic that kept it running came from. Surely it wasn't all being kept in operation by Nyalis? If so, it was no wonder he was getting frustrated with healing all of them.

They took the road south to the main bridge. There was, of course, a closer bridge that ran from the garrison over the river and into Aero'set, but it didn't offer the kind of view that the main entrance did. As was their usual routine, the group stopped to stare out across the impressive white towers, turrets, domes, and bulwarks interspersed around the sea of waterfalls that filled the back corner of this secluded mountain valley.

Aero'set was more than just a school for wizards. It was a city. Perhaps not as big as Easthaven, but certainly more than just a simple mountain village. The white stone was decoratively accented with gold inlay. Several of the domed roofs were gold as well, some even made of glass, all of which reflected the sun in such a way that it filled this corner of the mountain valley with its brilliance. It was truly captivating, made even more so by the colors in the sky from the setting sun. People said the monolithic wall around the capital city of Aramoor was one of the great wonders, but it couldn't be any more impressive than this place.

Both had been created with magic, though it was Ty's people, the Fae, who had been the main architects of Aero'set. Ty felt a small amount of pride at that. It was probably the first time he'd ever thought about the Fae as his people. Even now, the thought felt strangely foreign.

How could a race of beings who created something as wondrous as this place be all bad? As with their lessons on the evils of magic, perhaps what he had been taught in school about the faeries wasn't all that factual either.

"Why aren't we eating?" Kraea asked, standing near the back of the group. *"I'm hungry."*

"Fine," Ty said, turning away from the view. He looked at the others. "We're going. Kraea's hungry."

Narendi smirked. "Kraea is always hungry."

"She's not the only one," Breen said, and they left their spot against the railing and headed across the back half of the bridge and through the main gates into Aero'set.

They made their way along the empty roadways, staircases, and bridges leading toward the center of the school's complex. Several of the towers had interconnecting bridges that rose over a hundred feet in the air. Ty had never been in any of the upper chambers of those towers, so he'd never seen one of the bridges up close. It was, however, on the list of things he and Breen wanted to do.

Narendi, on the other hand, had had enough of sky bridges from the Riverlands to last her a lifetime. She had no intention of going up in any of those towers and had told them as much.

They reached the center of Aero'set just as the last of the colors faded from the evening sky, but instead of finding a town square filled with shops and farmers' carts, the center of Aero'set was comprised of the school's main dormitories. The dorms were constructed of four rather long buildings, each facing inward to form four sides of a square. The main gate leading inside was located at the center of the southernmost building.

All four of the buildings shared a central yard with two crisscrossing cobbled walkways that met in the middle at a large fountain, splitting the open area into four perfect squares. The trees, shrubs, and flower beds were covered in snow, their former glory left to the imagination. Fronting each of the three buildings were covered porches that ran the buildings' full length, allowing those inside to move about without fear of getting caught in the weather.

Not knowing what else to label the buildings, they began referring to them as the north wing, west wing, east wing, and south wing.

Entering by way of the main gate through the south wing, they took the central path across the yard and through the gardens to the north wing, where Nyalis had set up rooms. Ayrion and his companions were being housed there as well, mostly keeping to the common room when they weren't out exploring the greater compound.

Each of the buildings had a crest over the front entrance with some sort of writing on it, but it was in a language that none of them had ever seen—similar to the symbols etched around the traveling mirrors—which meant they had no idea what it said. Breen was the first to reach the porch at the front of their dorm and started up the steps. Torches lined the outer walkways, and if you caught them at the right time of evening, you'd get the chance to see them come to life all on their own. They were too late to see it this time, as the torches were already lit.

Breen grabbed the handle of one of the front doors and pulled it open. Ty followed Narendi in and took a moment to let his eyes adjust to the dim light in the gallery. The windows fronting the courtyard behind them did let in a fair amount of light during the day, but it was softened by the frosted panes of glass. At night, the glass reflected the glow from the three enormous chandeliers that lined the common room.

The gallery was quite large, stretching from right to left. Directly across from the entrance was an enormous stone hearth. It was the biggest fireplace Ty had ever seen, including the ones in Lyessa's home, which were quite grand. No matter the time of day or night Ty happened to be walking by, there was always a welcoming fire crackling inside. Either the wood never burned out or there were invisible creatures walking about, filling them without anyone seeing.

The fireplace had a soft fur rug lying just in front, and on the other side was a couple of sofas, a few chairs, and a table between. And just to the left of the hearth was a corridor that led to an enclosed staircase that wound its way up to the second and third floors.

"How was practice?" Zynora asked as she, Nell, and the kids turned to look from one of the cushioned sofas in front of the hearth on the right.

Ty groaned. "Same as it always is." He glanced around the room to make sure Ayrion wasn't there. "Painful."

"He and Bek went off to bathe," Zynora said with a sympathetic smile. "I'll come by your rooms later and see to your injuries."

Zynora had a gift with helping things heal faster than they normally would. She said it had something to do with her Rhivanni upbringing. It wasn't as powerful as Fraya's healing magic, but when combined with Isha's cream, she was able to keep the four of them in good enough shape to do it all over again the next day. There were times when Ty would have been willing to live with the pain for one day if it meant allowing him to sleep in, or at the very least skip one of his weapons sessions with Ayrion.

Tameel walked in from one of the hallways on the right and spotted them. "Ah, a good evening to you all." He walked over with a cup of something hot in his hand, steam rising from it. Ty wondered if whatever he was drinking was the reason for the old man's seemingly endless cheerful spirit. He also wondered if he could get a cup.

"Dinner should be ready shortly," Tameel said as he sat in one of the high-back chairs near the fire and propped his feet up on the footrest. "Best you wash up beforehand."

Ty didn't have to be told twice. He started across the room for the staircase, Breen, Narendi, and Kraea right behind him. The thought of a hot bath and some of Isha's balm had his feet moving all the faster.

Chapter 2 | Ty

T TY'S REQUEST, Nyalis had assigned them rooms on the upper floor. He was surprised Narendi hadn't balked at the idea of being on the top floor with them. With her aversion to heights, he expected her to request a room on the first floor. Evidently, being close to them was more important than her fear. Ty had asked for the top floor so he could have a better view from the windows, but after seeing the rooms, looking out the windows was the furthest thing from his mind.

They reached their floor's landing. Much like the second floor, it had a small open sitting area with chairs and tables and even a fireplace, though it was nowhere near as large as the one down in the main common room. It was a comfortable-looking setting, no doubt used readily by those who had lived there so many years ago. It still amazed Ty that no matter how long it had been out of use, there didn't seem to be any signs of disrepair or aging: no rotting wood, no worn carpeting, no dust layered across the furnishings. The metal wasn't tarnished, the glass hadn't filmed over. It was like the entire city had just been built.

On either side of the sitting room was a long hallway, one leading to the right and one to the left, housing close to two dozen sleeping chambers each.

Ty paused a moment as he stared down one of the long corridors. "Ever wonder what it must have been like to have lived here when the school was in use? All the people living here, in these very rooms, rushing back and forth between classes." He shivered. "There's times late at night when I can almost feel their presence."

"Okay," Breen said, "if you're trying to put me on edge, well done." He glanced down the hall on the right. "Why did you have to go and say that? Now I'm really feeling strange about the place."

"I wonder how good the people tasted?"

Ty looked at Kraea, who always seemed to be smiling. "Sometimes I really worry about you."

"What did she say this time?" Narendi asked, keeping a close eye on the hallways herself, her spear gripped tightly in her hand.

"Nothing I care to repeat. Come on. That hot bath is calling my name."

They left the foyer and headed down the corridor on the right, their way lit by golden sconces interspersed between the doors. They stopped first at Breen's room, which was about halfway down on the right, which meant his windows faced the inner yard. Across from his was Ty's room, which had a street-facing view of the buildings in the northern sector of the city behind the dorm.

Kraea's room was beside Ty's, but she mainly spent all her time in his, since she didn't like to be left alone. Across the hall from Kraea and next to Breen was Narendi's room.

Ty watched as Breen walked over to his door, stopped, and closed his eyes. A moment later, Breen opened the door, slipped inside, and shut it so fast Ty barely had time to see what it looked like inside. He did spot wooden walls and a warmly lit fireplace on the side, but not much more.

Ty waited as Narendi walked over to stand in front of her door. Like Breen, she closed her eyes a moment, then opened it and stepped inside. Ty looked at Kraea. "You coming with me or going to your own room for a change?"

Kraea turned and looked at the next door down, then sauntered over to Ty's.

"Okay, but I don't want to hear you complaining about the décor."

She said nothing as she waited.

Standing in front of his door, Ty closed his eyes and cleared his mind. A moment later, he grabbed the handle and opened the door. The inside of the room was nearly pitch black and completely encased in stone. A strong damp stench filled his nostrils, and he immediately shut the door and spun on Kraea.

"What did I tell you about changing my room?"

Kraea cackled, the scales on her neck pulsing as she did.

"If you want to sleep in a cave, your room is right over there."

"Fine," she said with a snicker. *"I won't do it again."*

Ty cleared his mind once more, conjuring an image of the most luxurious room he could imagine, which for him was Lyessa's bedroom, or something similar to it. Overlord Barl's estate was the only place he'd ever seen wealthy furnishings. He still remembered how it had felt when he first stepped into the overlord's entryway and spotted the huge chandelier suspended two stories down over the polished marble floors.

Opening his eyes, Ty turned the handle on his door and pushed. The dark, damp cavern had been replaced with polished wood floors, thick plush rugs, a four-poster bed and canopy, and a white stone fireplace with a warm fire beckoning him in.

"I love glamour magic," he said, and waited for Kraea to enter before walking inside and shutting the door. He remembered the first time he'd come across this particular kind of magic during his stay at Zwaneri a Wakale, the ancient temple ruins in the Wengoby Desert. Like the temple, he had conjured his old bedroom back in Easthaven for the first couple of nights, leaving Breen's old bunk for Kraea, who'd decided instead to sleep on the hard floor. However, after having gotten more used to the idea, Ty had decided to experiment.

Unfortunately, the most he could conjure was a rough imitation of Lyessa's bedroom, with a few extra features from her father's study thrown in for good measure. He'd even added a glass dome for a ceiling once, similar to the one in the Sidaran Assembly Hall, but the added light bothered him.

The magic seemed to be more than just glamour, though. It wasn't just a mirage. He could actually sleep in the soft bed, sit in the plush chairs, feel the fibers of the rug between his toes. It seemed real. Thankfully, it didn't transform every little thing on his mind, or he might have woken in the middle of the night to find himself back inside the underground lake, swimming for his life from the water monster.

It seemed to only work from the outside before you opened the door, and only if you focused really hard. Once the room was created, it remained that way as long as you were inside.

Ty pulled off his shirt and yanked off his boots before starting on his trousers, tossing pieces of clothing on the back of the chair and bed and dresser as he made his way to his private bathing chamber. Dozens of candles burst to life as he entered, filling the room with a warm amber glow. At the center of the stone floor was a large rectangular tub that he had envisioned built into the floor itself, one you had to walk down into instead of stepping in. He had read about such things once and decided to add it to his fantasy.

Not even Lyessa had one of those in her bath chamber.

Kraea didn't wait for him to finish undressing and jumped in on her own, sending a wave of water up to soak him from the waist down. "Hey, you're splashing out all the bubbles."

He had gone to a lot of trouble to add that detail, along with herbs like juniper and mint, having remembered Adarra talking about her time soaking with Lyessa and Fraya.

His sister had been right; it was refreshing. He took a deep breath and then removed his long underpants and stepped in. The water was hot, steam rising in the air. Unlike Kraea, who didn't seem all that bothered with things that were on the warmer side, he had to work his way in slowly.

Kraea stared up at him and smiled, but for some reason he didn't feel all that embarrassed anymore about getting naked in front of her. He had at first, telling her to turn around, but after a while, those earlier feelings seemed to fade. Besides, Kraea was more like a pet, albeit one that could talk back and had a mind of her own. He wouldn't have thought twice about getting naked in front of Waddle.

Ty eased his way into the water one foot at a time before working himself down to where he was sitting on the edge with his legs dangling inside. Pretty soon, he was scooting down onto the first step, then the next, and the next, until finally he was up to his shoulders.

"*You humans are so frail with your soft skin,*" she said, shaking her head as she watched him take his time slipping into the new layer of bubbles that had appeared after she had splashed out the first. Even the water seemed to have replenished itself.

"Sorry we can't all be hard and cold like you," he said.

"*You are very pretty for a human, though.*"

He felt a slight blush. "Thank you. I think. And you are very beautiful for a draakar."

"*Stop it,*" Kraea said, "*you'll make me turn red. Oh, wait.*" She raised one of her legs and inspected her scales and laughed. Ty couldn't help but laugh also, and they splashed around in the water for a moment, enjoying the warmth. Ty's skin tingled as the heat thawed his previously numb parts. Unfortunately, that also brought on the pain from all the bruises and cuts he'd suffered at Ayrion's hand.

"Ty, are you in there?" someone from inside his bedchamber called out.

"I'm in the bath with Kraea."

Ty recognized the voice and turned in the tub as Zynora stepped through the doorway with a jar in one hand. "This is quite the room you've created here," she said, glancing around the bathing chamber. "I thought I would come by and get a fresh coat of balm on those wounds before dinner, but I see I've caught you at a bad time."

Ty might not have felt self-conscious around Kraea, but having the old tinker woman staring at him in his bath was certainly reddening his cheeks. "I haven't had a chance to soap up yet," he said, hoping she would take the hint.

Clearly, she didn't, as she pulled up a stool and sat down. "Then I'll wait."

Kraea chuckled. "*You humans and your worries about clothing. You should be more like us draakar. You don't see us worried about covering ourselves.*"

"*That's because you're already covered . . . with scales.*"

Kraea grunted.

Ty grabbed a bar of soap from the side of the tub and quickly lathered himself.

"That is quite the artwork," Zynora said, leaning forward on her stool.

It took Ty a moment to realize she was looking at his markings, which now ran up one arm, across his shoulders, and down the other, tightly knit curves and angles and points, some reminding him of flames, others intricately crafted swords, similar even to that of Ayrion's. There were even a few places, strangely enough, that reminded him of scales akin to Kraea's.

"Where did you get it done?"

"I didn't. They just . . . They started appearing when I first began to use magic, and they've been growing ever since. Each time I use stronger magic, more appear, and it's not a pleasant feeling."

"Interesting. They are very . . . lovely." She finally scooted back and leaned against the wall.

He still had no idea what they meant. The last time he had felt them grow had been during their battle with the bulradoer. He couldn't remember if he'd felt them when he'd expended his magic to bring Aero'set back or not, which was no surprise. Using the key had nearly killed him, so the pain from his mark growing at the time would have been the least of his concerns, though he did notice some further escalation of the designs on the front of his chest. He couldn't help but wonder if they would cover his entire body at some point down the road. He hoped not.

Ty finished soaping, then moved to the other side of the bath with Kraea, looking for some cleaner water to rinse in. Finally, ready to get out, he pointed to one of the wooden pegs on the wall beside Zynora, where several towels hung ready for use. "Can you hand me one of those? And do you mind turning around?"

Zynora laughed. "Son, I'm a healer. I've seen more naked men and women than you can probably count, but if it will make you feel at ease." She tossed Ty the towel and turned.

Ty climbed out and dried himself. He turned to look at Kraea, but she apparently had no intention of getting out and was busy blowing on a wad of bubbles.

"Lie down on the bed," Zynora said as she followed Ty into his bedchamber.

He thought he would be a little more used to this by now, having done it almost every night for the last week, but it still embarrassed him. Carefully, he climbed up on the bed and lay down on his stomach.

Zynora set the jar of white cream on the bed beside him and pulled up his towel to get a better look at his legs. "Not as many today. You must be getting better."

"Or he's taking it easier on us," Ty speculated, then thought better of it. "No, never mind. He doesn't take it easy on anyone."

"Not when what he is trying to teach could save your life," she said, rubbing the cream across the back of his thigh.

Ty shivered. "Your hands are cold."

She chuckled. "I'm old. That's what happens." She spent the next several minutes lathering Isha's cream across every bruise and cut and scrape she could find, and the balm began to do its work. She mumbled the same phrase over and over again under her breath. "*Zintari Folduru. Zintari Freyestra.*"

"Is that magic?"

She stopped halfway through a particularly nasty gash on Ty's left arm. "In a way. It's a prayer for healing." She finished by applying some sort of yellow powder overtop the larger open wounds, then wrapped them. By the time she was done, most of the earlier pain and fatigue had begun to wane. It wasn't alleviated completely, like when Nyalis or Fraya used healing magic, but it was certainly better than anything your average physicker could have done. And by tomorrow, Ty was sure to be back to fighting form. Unfortunately.

Zynora put the lid back on the jar and started for the door. "I'll see you downstairs for supper. Don't dawdle."

Ty waited until the door shut behind her before hopping out of bed. Kraea stood inside the bath chamber and shook herself dry before walking in to curl up in front of the fire.

"Don't hog it all," Ty said, walking over to dry his naked backside in front of the open flames. One of his outfits was lying in the seat of the high-back chair between the hearth and his bed, neatly pressed and folded. He had no idea who was washing his clothes, having not seen any sign of staff, but he really appreciated it.

Just when he finished dressing, there was a knock at the door, and he and Kraea joined the others in the hall. Breen was wearing a freshly cleaned tunic as well, and Narendi had changed into the red woodland outfit she had purchased in Rivertown. Her spear rested over her shoulder. She didn't go anywhere without it. Ty figured she probably slept with it as well. Everything was new and strange and disconcerting to her on this side of the Khezrian Wall, no doubt making her feel more vulnerable than the rest.

"I'm feeling better already," Breen said, moving his arms about. "How about you?"

"Same," Ty said, taking a moment to look at the finger he'd thought to be dislocated, and found that it had straightened. Most of the pain was gone, or at least the sharper, more severe kind. There was still the dull ache that came with having spent most of the day working himself to the bone in the practice ring.

"How are you doing?" Ty asked Narendi, who never seemed to complain when it came to their grueling training schedule.

"I'm hungry," she said, and started down the hall without them.

Ty looked at Breen, and they shrugged.

"At least one of you has their priorities straight," Kraea said, and took off after Narendi.

Ty and Breen chased after the two, catching up just before they reached the open sitting room. Retaking the lead, Ty headed for the staircase and led them down to the common room, only to find it empty. They followed their noses around to a corridor on the right side of the room, which led them to a dining hall, which hosted a long table down the middle and exactly enough chairs for those living there, with the exception of Kraea, whose very large tray of fresh meat was placed at the far end of the room, so the others didn't have to watch her eat.

It appeared the others were waiting on them to arrive, their plates not having been touched. Ayrion was once again at the head of the table on the left. Next to him were Bek and Nel and the two rover children, Taylis and Marissa. On the other side sat the two tinkers, Tameel and Zynora.

The food smelled wonderful, as it always did, and Ty took a seat beside Nel, where there was an empty place setting. As soon as he sat down, the food appeared in front of him, dishes and all. It was just like the feast he and Breen had eaten with Tirana and her people in Karpaath, food magically appearing and then disappearing when they finished. Except here, it wasn't just a single meal—it was every meal. In fact, Ty had found his way down late the previous night to find a warm glass of cream and honey, along with a plate of fresh sticky buns.

Ty never wanted to leave. He loved the magic. He loved the food. "Anyone seen Nyalis today?" He cut into a piece of moist pork and dipped it in apple gravy. "Apart from his brief showing at the practice fields?"

The others all shook their heads.

"Afraid not," Tameel said, chewing on a plump boiled potato that had been soaking in a warm butter sauce. "He's a busy one, that wizard of ours. Always on the go. Like a bee, flitting from one flower to the next, though never stopping long enough to enjoy the smell." Tameel hopped his fork around on his plate, mimicking the movement of a bee.

"I am going to take them to see the glass house later," Narendi said, releasing one of her Imbatoo burps to show her appreciation and enjoyment for the food. She put her hand to her mouth. "Sorry. I forget your customs."

"Think nothing of it, dear," Zynora said, then released a loud belch of her own that had the rest of them gawking. Even Kraea stopped eating on the other side of the room to pop her head up and look.

They all laughed, and everyone began belching on their own just for the fun of it. Everyone except Ayrion, who seemed preoccupied with other matters as he stared blankly at his plate at the head of the table. He hadn't touched much of his food. It was evident that he and Nyalis were at odds about Ayrion leaving. Ty didn't know what it was Nyalis wanted from Ayrion, but knowing Nyalis, it was something he wanted the weapons master to do that Ayrion wasn't all that keen to agree to. Ty knew how that felt and chuckled inwardly. Apparently, he had something in common with the man in black after all.

Ty swallowed his latest mouthful with a gulp from a golden goblet filled with a mildly spiced cider. He couldn't place the fruit, but it was delicious. "I've been trying to find some time with Nyalis for days, but he doesn't appear to want to talk with me. If anyone sees him, please let him know that I've been looking."

He would have tried to say more to him earlier that afternoon at the practice ring, but a broken jaw wasn't very conducive to carrying on a meaningful conversation. Now that he thought about it, he didn't remember ever seeing the wizard leave. After Nyalis had pulled Ayrion aside for a private conversation, the wizard just hadn't been around.

Those around the table agreed to let Nyalis know Ty was looking for him.

Ty didn't know if that would help or not, but it couldn't hurt to try.

"So, you haven't been to the glass house yet?" Bek asked, passing a curious look across the table at Ty and Breen.

Breen shrugged. "I guess not."

"Oh, you would have known if you had," Bek said with a wink to Tameel, who smiled in return.

"Can I go to the glass house?" Taylis asked. The young rover boy was busy stuffing a heaping spoon of pudding into his mouth from his seat between Bek and Nel, while at the same time trying to swallow the previous mouthful.

Beside him, Marissa waved her spoon in the air, sending pieces of carrot flying in front of her plate. "I want to come too." The bright yellow ribbon in her hair was coming unfastened, the bow looking more like a loose knot.

Nel patted the little girl on the head, squishing the bow. "I think we've had enough excitement for one day."

Bek's wife seemed on the frail side, even sickly at times. Ty wondered how she had lost her hair. It was growing back, but it hadn't been growing long. It wasn't much longer than Narendi's, whose dark strands were filling in just enough to cover her scalp. Nel smiled when she caught him looking and even went so far as to rub the top of her head.

"Sorry, I didn't mean to stare." Ty quickly turned his attention back to his plate.

"Did they tell you how it happened?" she asked.

Ty looked up and shook his head.

Nel told them of creatures they called vulraak and their attack on Belvin. Ty had only heard bits and pieces of the story, nothing substantial, so Nel, with Bek, Zynora, and Tameel's help, laid out the story of their battle with Argon and his plague of shadows, and how they had eventually defeated him by following him into his lair and destroying a black crystal holding his essence.

It was an incredible tale, every bit as harrowing as their own had been. It also put Ayrion in a new light, though he didn't stick around for the retelling, excusing himself just after they got to the part where he rescued Taylis and Marissa. As the swordsman left the room, his plate, goblet, and dinnerware all disappeared from the table. Ty wondered where the weapons instructor was going but then got too preoccupied with the story to think more about it, and by the time Nel and the others had finished, Ty had forgotten about Ayrion altogether.

The rest of the dinner conversation moved toward their exploration of Aero'set. Of course, Ty, Breen, and Narendi had been afforded little time to explore, what with training nearly every day, and the times they weren't training were spent resting and recovering. Ty grumbled that he had nearly killed himself to bring this incredible place back into the realm of man, and he wasn't even being afforded the opportunity to see it.

Once the meal was over and their settings vanished, everyone except Ty, Narendi, Breen, and Kraea headed back to the common room to sit in front of the fire and chat. Narendi led Ty and the others out of the dining room, through the common room, and out onto the front porch.

"Where is it, again, that you're taking us?" Breen asked, tucking his hands in his pockets. "Some kind of glass house?"

Narendi smiled. "You will see."

"How was your food?" Ty asked Kraea, who was meandering quietly along beside him down the steps and out onto the snow-covered lane that ran the border of the entire complex. Ty could sense the satisfied swelling of her stomach.

"Savory, as always," she said, licking some remaining blood from her lips.

Ty tried not to let his discomfort at her food show, but he knew Kraea could sense it, and it always gave her no end of pleasure.

Narendi took them across the open yard, past the fountain, and out by way of the southern gate. Instead of taking the bridge across the water, which led into the southern half of Aero'set, she took them left along a road that ran directly in front of the dorm's southern wall. They reached the end, and Narendi started for a small building on the other side of the road, not a stone's throw from the dormitory's southeast tower.

After all the talk, Ty had been expecting something . . . more. The building wasn't much to look at, but Ty could see where it had gotten its name. Its walls were made entirely of glass—even the roof—and the inside looked to be filled with greenery.

Narendi led them around to the front, where there was a sign on the door, scribbled in a tongue none of them were able to read. She glanced over her shoulder and grinned. "Are you ready to see?"

Ty had been ready to see ever since Bek and the others had made such a fuss during supper. "Yes," he said, waving for her to continue.

She turned the handle and flung open the door. "Here we are! The glass house."

Ty looked inside and shook his head, not believing his eyes. He immediately turned and looked at the corners of the building, which weren't maybe ten feet apart in either direction, then back through the door again. This didn't make sense.

Narendi was the first inside, then Breen, Kraea, and lastly Ty. He stepped through the door and onto a brick-covered walkway that led down the center of the enormous glass enclosure. The ceiling was easily a hundred feet off the ground, nothing like the ten- to twelve-foot roof outside. He had no idea as to how wide or long it was since the interior of the building was completely filled with all manner of plant life, but it was certainly larger than the building he had seen from outside.

Soft moonlight spilled down through the glass and filled everything with its pale glow. Lanterns that seemed to hang from nothing, as if suspended by invisible string, marked the way forward into a jungle that lay just before them.

"Incredible," Breen said in awe as he looked up at some of the larger trees rising above the top of the undergrowth. The ground was covered in grass and moss and vines, interspersed with every color of flower imaginable. The brick path wound its way to where the first of the trees began and then disappeared inside.

Ty still couldn't quite fathom how something this immense could have been found inside what looked to be nothing more than a large storage shed. Sure, their rooms used glamour magic, but this seemed to push the boundaries of what was real. This was more like walking through a mirror and ending up in a different part of the world, yet what they were seeing was somehow being encapsulated within this small enclosure.

He had to quit thinking about it. It was making his head hurt.

Kraea shivered. "This place reminds me of *Tulgava Rashuvi.*"

Ty could see how, in a way, all that greenery did feel a bit like the great tree where the live market was held in the Riverlands.

"Come on," Narendi said, and took off down the dimly lit path, quickly disappearing into the thicket.

Ty looked at Breen and shrugged, and they headed in after her.

Chapter 3 | Ty

ONCE INSIDE THE THICKEST of the trees and undergrowth, the moonlight faded, then disappeared altogether, filtered out by the overhanging limbs and vines and leaves. In stark contrast to the bare, snow-covered trees outside, these were still flush with greenery. In fact, if it wasn't for the brick path and the strange floating lanterns, Ty would have thought he was back on his quest, possibly wandering through the parts of the forest surrounding Reed Marsh that the swamp and bog hadn't already claimed for itself.

They had rounded at least three bends with no sign of Narendi.

"Where'd she go?" Ty asked, then shouted down the path. "Narendi! Wait for us."

"I'm here!"

Both brothers jumped as she popped out of some low-hanging leaves on the left, each leaf nearly half the size of Ty. "If I was your enemy, you would be dead," she teased.

Kraea laughed, though it sounded more ferocious than funny.

Ty groaned. The last thing he needed was for Narendi to start acting like

Ayrion. "Get out of there. You don't know if any of that is poisonous."

She took a look at the surrounding plants, shrugged, then walked back onto the path, bumping one of the lanterns with her spear on her way by. It floated forward a few feet, then moved back into place.

"Look at this over here," Breen said. He was kneeling on the right side of the trail.

Ty walked over with the others to see what he was looking at and found a small cluster of shrubs with large purple flowers attached. Most of the large bulbs were closed, but there was one that had opened, revealing a pure white center.

"Do you know what these are?"

Ty took a closer look. They did look oddly familiar, but he couldn't quite place them. With as much tutelage as he'd received from his father on all manner of plant life, not to mention his time spent in Orlyn's apothecary, he would have thought he could have named the beautiful plant. "I'm not sure," he finally admitted.

"They're angelia. Father showed me some illustrations of one in a book years ago."

"It's very pretty."

"They're more than pretty, doofus. They're extinct. No one has seen one of these plants in several hundred years. Their healing properties are said to be quite impressive. People scoured the Five Kingdoms looking for them, especially after the Great Purge. Can you imagine how valuable these were when wielders were no longer allowed to heal? It's why they went extinct."

Now that he mentioned it, Ty did remember hearing about them, though he still hadn't remembered what they looked like. He wasn't the woodsman his brother was. For Breen, forestry seemed to come naturally. Ty, on the other hand, struggled, often losing interest.

Ty had always been a little too carefree, or as his mother had put it, a "free spirit." She had recognized his differences and had encouraged him to let them grow. She was always the one to pull their father aside whenever she thought he was being a little too forceful with his desire to see Ty learn the family trade. Ty's family were gamekeepers, had been for generations. Looking back, Ty wished he had paid a little closer attention when he had the chance.

A small voice in the back of his mind said he needed to take his own advice. An image of Ayrion standing over him, shaking his head with disappointment, had Ty cringing. As much as he hated weapons training, he did see the importance of it, and perhaps if he applied himself a little harder instead of complaining, he might actually progress.

"Ty, you coming?"

Ty looked up, noticing that the other three were all waiting for him farther down the trail. When had they left? He glanced back down at the flower and smiled. His mother was right. He was a free spirit, or at least his mind was, which, under the circumstances, wasn't exactly a good thing. He needed to work on that. Leaving the cluster of angelia, he followed the others deeper into the glass house.

"How far back do you think this goes?" Ty asked.

Breen looked up. "Are we even still in the glass house?"

Or even Aero'set? Ty wondered. He looked at Narendi. "Did you ever reach the back of the room when you were here before?"

"I have not come this far," she said.

"Oh, look at this," Breen announced excitedly as he moved over to the left side of the trail to examine a particular crop of what looked like nettles. "Kalisworth. I've only ever seen it grown on the western shores of Crystal Lake." He grabbed Narendi and pulled her back when she walked over to take a look. "One prick from its nettles will drop a full-grown boar." He took another step back, and she did the same. "I wonder why they would have something like this in here?"

Ty turned and looked at some of the other plants, wondering if they, too, could be dangerous. From then on, they decided to stick to the path, not that they had much choice. The farther in they went, the denser the plants became, the vines and branches seeming to strangle each other to reach the light. The beautiful plants they had seen earlier had slowly disappeared, until there was nothing but vines and thistles and thorns covering everything.

"Anyone else getting the feeling that perhaps we should go back?" Ty asked as the hairs on the back of his neck began to rise. "I don't think this place has an end to it." He noticed Narendi had her spear in hand as she studied the surrounding jungle. He didn't remember her removing it from her back. He really needed to start paying more attention.

A slight breeze rustled some of the leaves on the overhanging vines, causing Ty to look up. At least, he thought it was a breeze. He hadn't actually felt anything down on the trail.

Breen moved up beside him. "Yeah, getting that feeling as well." His brother was also looking up at the sway of the branches.

An overwhelming sense of fear and anger suddenly rushed through Ty's link, and Kraea started to growl. Her shoulders were hunched and her neck stiff as she bared her fangs at the tree line on the left. Narendi's spear rose as she stared at the thick undergrowth. Was there something there?

Breen drew the long belt knife from his waist. It was the only weapon between the two of them. Then again, it was Aero'set. Why did they need weapons? The school was supposed to be a safe haven. Raising his hand, Ty ignited his blue flame so they could better see the surrounding trees.

As soon as the flames burst to life, so did the jungle.

Narendi squealed as a vine shot out from under some brush on the left and grabbed the end of her spear.

Ty spun and released a single ball of fire at the tree line, but not before the vine had yanked Narendi off the path. As soon as her foot touched the soil on the other side, more vines shot out from the trees and latched on to her wrist and ankles and started pulling her up into the branches.

Ty yelled and sent several more balls of fire directly up into the trees just in front of Narendi, hoping to burn the vines apart. Something behind all the undergrowth screamed, producing a high-pitched shriek that had every hair on his body standing at attention. Most of the vines had been burned away, but there were still a few holding Narendi in place.

"What in the flaming Pits was that?" Breen shouted and leaped into the air to grab a handful of vines that Ty hadn't burned and slice them in half. Both he and Narendi landed on the ground, but before they could crawl back to the path, thick tentacles covered in green sprouts reached out of the trees and grabbed them.

Ty unleashed another ball of fire, encapsulating one of the thicker tendrils. Whatever was back there screamed again, so loudly this time that Ty nearly thought his ears would burst. He stumbled but caught himself before he went down and charged straight for the thickest pile of vines, sending blue fire shooting in front of him.

Behind him, Kraea was hissing and barking as she bit down on the closest snakelike arms reaching for her, tearing them off in her mouth. Green goo covered her face after the limbs had been severed. Ty turned around and threw another volley into the surrounding forest, hoping to hit whatever was out there. He then spun back around when he heard Kraea cry out in pain.

A thick vine had wrapped around her neck and was pulling her toward the edge of the woods. She tried stabbing at it with her horns, but they weren't long enough to reach.

Ty sent a single lance of fire into the arm and burned it in two. He turned to help Breen and Narendi but was immediately yanked off his feet and into the air, as several larger vines had dropped down behind him without him noticing. He tried to burn the closest, but they latched on to his arms and held them out to his sides.

Below him, Breen was slashing and cutting as fast as he could. Narendi, on the other hand, had gone completely limp, her body unmoving as the vines and tentacles slowly dragged her body into the underlying brush.

"Help Narendi!" Ty shouted at Kraea.

Things were happening so fast, he didn't have time to think. What magic did he possess? What could he use? "Ru'kasha Kor." The darkness lifted as his night sight burst to life. Unfortunately, he couldn't see that much more than before with how tightly packed the growth of the plants were.

He ignited his hands, and the vines holding them burned away, but before he could do the same to the ones around his chest and legs, something tightened around his head, and it felt like it was going to explode. He couldn't breathe. He tried moving, but the vines were like metal grips around him.

"*Ty!*" Kraea shouted at him through their link.

Ty couldn't say anything back; his mind was slipping. He could hear Breen shouting below, but he had no idea what he was saying.

"*Pintora!*"

A wave of energy shook the entire forest, and even Ty felt it from where he was suspended above the ground. Suddenly, the restraint on his neck loosened, and he felt his breath rush back in. Then, just as suddenly, the vines were gone, and he found himself falling. He hit the dirt with a thud, which knocked the wind out of him all over again.

"What do you children think you're doing?" someone behind Ty bellowed. Ty recognized the voice, and it felt like the wind had been torn from his chest a third time. He rolled over and looked up.

Nyalis stood behind him on the brick path, his face hard as he stared at the four of them. His staff was up and pointed toward the forest, which was still moving. Ty could hear the rustling of the leaves as the vines slowly retracted back within the confines of the darkness.

"Are you trying to kill yourselves before Ayrion gets a chance to? If so, you have picked a rather painful way to do it. Worse, look at the damage you've done to this taeradinium plant. It has been alive since the dawn of the Third Age, and you nearly killed it in a single evening."

"Killed it?" Ty crawled to his feet and staggered back to the path. "It nearly ate us all. Why would you keep something like that in here?" He looked around. "For that matter, where is here?"

Breen helped Narendi back to the bricks after recovering her spear. It was sticking out of the side of one of the trees she had managed to stab before they pinned her down. "This place is a death trap!" Breen barked, turning on the wizard.

"Nonsense. It is perfectly safe as long as you obey the rules, of which there is only one."

"We didn't see any rules," Ty said. "What rules?"

"The one written plain as day on the sign out front."

"We couldn't read it."

"No, of course you couldn't. Fae is taught to every first-year apprentice who walks through those doors, something that none of you are. But while you stay here, here is my rule: Don't open any more doors without my permission." He looked them over one at a time, stopping on Ty. "Is that clear?"

Ty looked at the others, and they all eventually nodded.

"Good. The rule to the arboretum is this: Never, for any circumstance, leave the path without an instructor."

"*What instructors?*" Kraea asked, and before Ty could relay her question, Narendi beat him to it.

"Who are these instructors?"

Nyalis turned and started back up the path in the direction they'd come. "Wizards, of course. Who did you think?"

Ty ran to catch up, his chest and neck aching from where the vines had nearly squeezed the life out of him. He didn't need to look to know he had new bruising. "But . . . there are no wizards . . . except for you."

"Of course, which I guess means you should never leave the path."

"We were *on* the path when they attacked."

Nyalis stopped so quickly that Ty ran into the back of him. The wizard turned. "Are you saying it attacked unprovoked?"

"Yes," Ty said frantically. "We didn't provoke anything. The trees started moving, then *wham*! They attacked. They grabbed Narendi's spear and pulled her off the trail, and we ran to help."

"And up until that point, none of you did anything? Anything at all?"

"No," Ty said frustratedly. Why didn't Nyalis believe them?

"None of you used any sort of magic?"

"Well, when the trees first started moving, I used my fire to see what was happening."

"Ah," Nyalis said and relaxed against his staff. "You conjured your fire."

"Why does that matter? The entire pathway is covered in lamps. There's fire everywhere."

"Not like yours. With magic like that, no wonder the taeradinium awoke."

"What is this taeradinium?" Narendi asked, once again beating Ty to the question.

"A taeradinium is a very old being. They can hibernate for hundreds of years, but then they need to feed."

"They eat humans?" Breen asked. His hand reached for the hilt of his knife. "I've never heard of such a plant. Why would you leave it here?"

Nyalis blew out his lips in a huff. "No, they don't eat humans. They feed on magic."

"Magic?" Ty asked skeptically. And Nyalis thought *their* statement sounded crazy? "How do they do that?"

Nyalis thought a moment. "Probably best you don't know. Suffice to say, it is not a pleasant process. It's even been known, at times, to kill the wielder."

Nyalis looked at the path behind them. "My guess is that the taeradinium was getting close to the end of its hibernation, and when it sensed the four of you, it woke. And when you conjured your fire . . ." He shook his head. "It was like a moth to a flame."

Ty shivered as he thought about it. It reminded him of the swamp creature he'd come across in Reed Marsh. If all they had seen were its tentacles, Ty hated to think what had been lurking deeper in.

Nyalis turned, and they started back down the path once more.

Ty pondered over the wizard's words, and something bothered him. "You said it feeds on magic and not humans. What about Kraea?"

"*Hey, don't bring me into this,*" she said, doing her best to lick as much of the green slime off her face that her forked tongue could reach.

"Why would it have gone after her? Me and Breen both have magic, even Narendi has a type of voda ability, like Gilly . . . but Kraea's a draakar."

"*Way to state the obvious.*"

"Yes," Nyalis said, without stopping. "And as such, she, too, has magic."

Ty looked at Kraea. "She has magic?"

Kraea stopped her licking. "*I do?*"

Nyalis glanced over his shoulder and smiled at Kraea. He looked like he wanted to say more but thought better of it. "It's a different kind of magic."

"What kind?"

"*Yeah, what kind?*"

Nyalis didn't slow. "All in good time." He looked at Ty, who was doing his best to match the wizard's stride. "I hear you have been wanting to speak with me."

Apparently, Ty's comment at supper hadn't been for nothing after all. "Yes. I . . . I want to know when you are going to start teaching me magic. I thought that's why you brought me here. You said I was to start training."

Nyalis stopped once more. "There is more than one way to train, and certainly more that needs training than just your gifts. The instruction you are receiving from Ayrion is crucial to that. Magic takes a lot out of the one wielding it—it can even kill—which means your body must be strong enough to handle it." He tapped Ty on the forehead. "Your mind as well." The wizard turned and continued down the path, leaving Ty to wonder what kind of training could be used for his mind.

They eventually reached the end of the bricks, the glass walls and ceiling appearing as if out of nowhere. Ty wasn't quite the first through the door, but he wasn't the last either.

Nyalis shut the door to the glass house behind them and turned. "I'm sure you will want to see to your wounds, but I would like to show you something first."

Ty's concern about his lack of magical training was quickly curtailed with this new offering from the wizard. He'd been waiting for Nyalis to do something with him for the last two weeks, and so far, this was the most interaction he had had with the man.

"As long as it doesn't involve anything with plants," Breen said.

Nyalis smiled. "You won't find them where we are going." He turned and started back up the road toward the south gate leading into the dorms.

Ty and the others followed close on his heels as he took them back across the yard and into the north-wing common room. Ty felt a little disappointed, having thought Nyalis was going to take them some place they hadn't been before, some place brimming with magic and mystery.

Bek and the others turned and watched as they headed through the common room and down the main hall, past the grand staircase leading up to the next floors, and all the way to a set of doors at the back. The doors led to a covered walkway that spanned the water behind the dorm and over to a building just behind, one that Ty had yet to explore.

It was a large rectangular building. A second set of double doors opened when Nyalis waved his staff in its direction, and they headed inside. The building appeared to be an enormous dining hall, nearly the size of one of the dorm's wings. It was certainly large enough to seat all the students at once, unlike the dining room where they had been taking their meals. Though the building was nearly as tall as the dorms, there didn't appear to be any upper floors, as the singular room was open all the way to the rafters.

Six enormous chandeliers burst to life as they started down the main aisle between several rows of tables and benches. Long stained-glass windows rose on either side of the room, letting some of the pale moonlight in from outside. The glass was a mosaic of beautifully painted images, one for each window.

Strangely enough, the way the moonlight reflected through the shards gave the images the appearance of moving. Ty stopped to get a better look, the others doing the same. Nyalis, however, did not, and he continued on to the other side.

The first window was of a tree with a long trunk and brilliant leaves that seemed to be swaying from an unknown breeze. Some of the leaves actually appeared to be falling. Ty looked at Breen, and Breen nodded that he could see it too. The second window was filled with rich blue water with several large white whales swimming inside. Their tails swished back and forth slowly as they paddled themselves up to the glass.

"Come on," Nyalis called from farther up. "You'd think you'd never seen spelled glass before."

"The windows are moving," Ty said excitedly as he and the others rushed to catch up. "Was that what you wanted to show us? It's incredible."

"Hardly," Nyalis said, not even giving the glass a second look. "Now stop dawdling. We've still got a ways to go yet."

The front of the room boasted several rows of ornate windows, each row a little smaller than the one under it, crowned with an arch at the very top.

Their steps left a hollow trail behind them as they passed through the empty hall. It left him wondering what it must have been like when the place was full of people. Did these enormous tables fill with food like the ones in the dormitory? That would have been quite the spectacle.

They exited through a side door on the left, walked down a short corridor, and then out onto a bridge that crossed over to another rectangular building with a tower in front. The cold wind caught Ty off guard, and he pulled his cap down over his ears as he spared a passing glance behind him, spotting the back of the north wing of the dormitories. He thought he could see his bedroom window.

From there, they headed north, or as north as the maze of roads and bridges would allow, crossing from one spit of land to the next. The buildings grew farther apart the closer they got to the back of Aero'set, and Ty's excitement mounted, his imagination running wild with possibilities. Where could Nyalis be taking them? They were inside a school for magic. What incredible parts of it had they yet to discover?

"The last time you discovered something, it nearly ate us," Kraea growled. *"I wouldn't be so keen to do it again."*

"Aren't you even the littlest bit curious?" he responded. *"This place was built by faeries and wizards. Can you imagine all the amazing things we could find? The traveling mirrors were created here."*

"Yes, and look how well that turned out for us. We left my mother to die and walked right into the arms of your precious White Tower."

"That wasn't the mirror's fault."

Ty glanced over his shoulder at Breen and Narendi. Breen was preoccupied staring up at the buildings, some of which were connected with sky bridges. Narendi, on the other hand, looked worried, her head shifting back and forth as her eyes scanned each new building.

They crossed several more bridges that spanned some of the smaller falls at the back. The frosty spray from the water, which left a notable chill in the air, dampened the sides of their faces as they passed. The pools of water joined with others to form larger streams in and around the towers. It was beautiful and cold. Ice formed around the sides of the walk where the water struck, making the edges slippery.

Ty grew more anxious with every new building they passed and every new bridge they crossed. The mountain peaks loomed ahead of them. If they didn't get to where they were going soon, they were going to find themselves face-to-face with the Angoran cliffs.

Several times, they climbed winding staircases up to the next level of falls, and then up even further. Pretty soon the last of the buildings were behind them as they reached the outer edge of Aero'set, where they found a single set of stairs hewn out of the mountainside itself and leading up as far as Ty could see. The stone steps reminded him of the ones he and Breen had climbed down to reach the Maze.

"Where exactly are you taking us?" Ty asked as they stared at a set of large stone steps behind Nyalis.

"You'll see," was the only reply he received.

By the time they reached the seventh or eighth landing, Ty was winded. Breen and Narendi were breathing heavily as well. Nyalis, on the other hand, didn't seem all that affected. The wizard was a mystery.

"Not much farther," Nyalis said, having only stopped to rest his feet for a few moments before continuing.

Ty looked up, but all he could see was more rock. He wondered if they were going to climb all the way to the top. He took a moment to blow on his hands, stuffing them in his pockets to try to keep them warm. They were getting stiff.

"*I hate the cold,*" Kraea said.

Ty could feel her shivering through their link. Her scales were like ice when he rubbed up against them.

Narendi scooted up beside him. "Where are we going?"

"No idea," Ty said with a shrug, and she moved back beside Breen, keeping as close to the mountainside as she could and as far from the edge as possible.

"And here we are," Nyalis said, stopping on one of only a few landings left before they reached the peak. This particular landing opened behind one of the main falls that poured down off the mountain to the school below.

Ty stepped back out from behind the water and looked down over the side, immediately wishing he hadn't. It was a very long drop down. He hadn't really noticed how far they'd climbed, too preoccupied with what lay ahead.

Before Ty could ask Nyalis where *here* was, seeing as how there was nothing there but more steps leading farther up, the wizard turned and walked behind the falls, then right through the wall.

Ty's jaw dropped, and he, Breen, and Narendi stared wide-eyed at the face of the rock. Narendi backed away from where she had been pressing against it, as if afraid it was going to swallow her as well.

"Did you see that?" Ty asked.

"*See what?*" Kraea asked, circling around to the front. "*I wasn't looking. Hey, where's the wizard?*"

As soon as she said it, Nyalis walked back through the mountainside, and she jumped.

"Are you waiting for an invitation?" he asked. "Or do you prefer to stand out here in the cold?" The wizard turned and walked back through the mountain once more.

Ty walked over and cautiously lifted his hand to touch the moist rock where the wizard had disappeared. His hand vanished. He quickly yanked it back out to find it was still there. He looked at the others and smiled. Now this was what he had been waiting for. Magic! He had no idea where it led, but he wanted to find out, so he closed his eyes and stepped through.

Chapter 4 | Ty

A TINGLING RUSH OF WARM AIR struck Ty in the face, and he opened his eyes. He was standing in a wide-open chamber, maybe one hundred feet across. Stone pillars lined the outer wall, supporting the mountain of rock overhead. On the other side of the cavern was a set of stone steps leading about twenty feet up the back wall to a hewn-out platform holding five stone seats. They were much larger than any Ty had ever seen, more like thrones. Each was fashioned from the same white stone as the buildings in Aero'set, and like those buildings, they were covered in decorative designs.

As remarkable as the pillars, platform, and stone seats were, they were hardly the most unique aspect of the room. Across the cavern, thin strands of pulsing white light tinged with blue slithered across the floor. Each intersected at various points to form a maze or some complex design Ty didn't recognize, beginning at the center of the chamber and stretching to the outer walls.

There was something about the place that made the hairs on Ty's arms stand on end. He couldn't put his finger on it, but whatever it was, it was powerful. He felt different, something stirring inside. Stepping out of the way to give the others room to enter, Ty was careful where he placed his feet, so he didn't accidentally step on one of the pulsing lines.

"They will not harm you," Nyalis said from near the center of the room, about the time Breen and Narendi walked into the cavern behind him.

Ty turned and stared at the wall behind him, waiting for Kraea. *"Come on. It doesn't hurt. You can walk right—"*

Kraea's head poked through.

"See?" Ty said, trying not to laugh. She looked silly, standing there with just her head showing, like a trophy mounted on a hunter's wall.

Kraea looked around the room, then stepped the rest of the way inside. *"It's warm,"* she said, and released a soft throaty growl, much like a cat's purr.

"What is this place?" Breen asked, turning in a complete circle to take it all in.

Narendi had her spear in her hands, but after seeing that there were no enemies lurking within, she hooked it back over her shoulder. "It is like the archive of the Wazeri. A very big room."

Ty knelt down to get a closer look at the pulsing lines. He held his hand over one, and the glow brightened his palm. He tapped it with his finger. It pulsed a little brighter for a moment, then returned to its original state. Seeing that he hadn't been hurt, he risked putting his hand inside. The warm pulses were like blood running through a vein.

"What's it feel like?" Breen asked, standing behind him. Narendi and Kraea walked over as well.

"It's like a heartbeat. As though the mountain were alive."

"That is a more accurate statement than you know," Nyalis said, his voice echoing off the surrounding rock.

Ty turned and pointed at the five throne-like chairs behind the wizard. "What are those?"

Nyalis turned. "Those are reserved for the Empirium, the heads of the wizard order, and before that, they were used by the ruling members of the Fae, prior to the Faerie Wars. Aero'set was built by the Fae with the help of the newly formed wizard order, and because of this, the Fae allowed one seat to be held by humans. Aerodyne himself used to sit there." Nyalis frowned. "Back before his descent into madness."

Ty felt a chill run through him. He was standing in the very place that the Dark Wizard had once stood. He stared up at the seats, suddenly wondering which one had been Aerodyne's.

"Come." Nyalis beckoned them closer. "There is a great history to this place. A history that needs telling."

Ty left his spot near the entrance and the pulsing line he'd been studying and started for the center of the cavern. Breen, Narendi, and Kraea followed him across.

As they drew closer to the wizard, Ty could see that all the lines converged at a single point, a circle that had been cut into the stone floor directly under where Nyalis was standing. The pulsing white lines stopped on the outside of the circle and disappeared beneath the rock. The center was nothing more than a flat piece of stone, probably ten feet across, with no engravings or markings of any kind to set it apart from the rest of the floor.

"You say you want to learn how to use magic, but in order to do so, you first need to understand where it comes from."

Ty stopped just outside the circle. "You said it was in me."

"Yes, well, that might be an oversimplification. It is in you. It's in all of us . . . Well, those gifted with wielder abilities."

"You also said it was different for me."

Nyalis slowly stroked his long white beard. "True. While the rest of us were born with magic. You were born *of* it. Magic took part in your conception, as it does with all of the Fae, but that is a discussion for another time. What I wish to discuss now isn't how you received your magic, but where it originated."

"From the Fae," Breen said.

Nyalis waved it off. "Another oversimplification. To be more precise, it came from their realm, but now that the realm of the Fae has been resealed and the faeries themselves vanquished, why is it still here?"

Ty hadn't really thought about it, but that was a good question. If the faerie had brought the magic with them, why didn't it leave when they did? "You told me once about lines of power that run throughout Aldor."

Nyalis smiled. "You were listening."

"Is that what these are?" Ty asked, looking down at the floor.

"In a way . . . a very small way. The faerie realm lives and thrives on magic. It is in the very soil and rock that is the foundation of their world. That is why most wielders require transferal crystals to be able to use those powers. They are but shards of the faerie's home world, tiny fragments of a much larger source of power." He looked at Ty. "Can you feel the magic flowing throughout this place?"

"I feel something, something very old." Ty reached out with his magic to see if he could find what it was that had him so unnerved. Not being able to pierce through the rock, he finally released his web. "I don't know."

Nyalis motioned them forward. "Come, stand here," he said, pointing down at the circle. "I think it best I show you." He combed his thick brows to the side with his thumb and smiled. "You will like this, I think."

Ty and the others cautiously stepped over the glowing bluish-white lines and into the circle with Nyalis. Kraea was the last to enter, not quite as eager as the others. However, once inside, Nyalis tapped the butt end of his staff on the stone, and the crystal fashioned into the top of his staff flared to life with a golden glow. "Make sure to stay within the circle," he said.

Suddenly, the stone beneath their feet began to tremble. Narendi yipped and grabbed Ty's arm as the platform began to lower, carrying them downward into the bowels of the mountain. It reminded Ty of the time outside of Gilly's home, when he had lowered himself down the stone well using the water inside.

He looked up and watched as the hole above them grew smaller and smaller and then eventually disappeared altogether, and yet their descent continued. The veins of pulsing light that had disappeared around the edge of the circular platform were now running down the walls of the tunnel, lighting their way. The walls were fashioned from the same greyish rock as above—lighter in some areas, darker in others. Every so often, they would pass through a few layers that had a red sheen and then a couple that were a pale yellow.

The farther down they went, the stronger that feeling in the back of Ty's mind became. Something was waiting. The feeling was so strong that his own magic was reacting to it. He could feel its heat warming inside him as it came to life.

"How deep does it go?" Breen asked.

"Quite a ways," Nyalis said, a grin on his face, as though he had a secret he couldn't wait to share. "You are about to see what few humans ever have—none living, that's for sure. Well, except for me, of course. Stand here, near the center, while I raise the barrier."

Everyone quickly moved away from the edge of the circle and huddled near the center, boxing the wizard in.

"You don't need to get that close."

Ty and Breen moved back a step or two to give the wizard some room, and Nyalis walked over to the side of the platform as it continued into the depths. He raised his staff, and the crystal at the top brightened once more. "*Suethian Duwanite.*"

A golden light shot up from the edges of the platform about a foot over Ty's head, then disappeared. Ty thought the incantation sounded familiar. "That's the same incantation you used in Meerwood, isn't it?"

Nyalis reached out with his hand, and it looked like he was going to grab some of the stones as it passed, but as soon as his fingers neared the edge, the barrier brightened around his hand. He pulled his hand back, and the light disappeared. "You have a very good memory, my boy," he said as he turned. "That was indeed the same protection spell I used in Meerwood, but on a much smaller scale, of course."

Whatever was below them seemed to be reaching out for Ty. He could almost hear it, as though it was calling to him. The magic inside him was rising, taking even more concentration on Ty's part to hold it back. Before he could say anything, Nyalis raised his arms out to the sides and smiled. "Welcome to Meeisredon, the heart of Aero'set."

The platform suddenly dropped away from the well of rock above, and they found themselves hovering over an enormous chamber at least several hundred feet deep. Pulsing veins of bluish-white light branched out from the tunnel above to form an incredibly intricate web across the surrounding stone.

Everyone crowded to the center of the platform to gawk. No one wanted to get too close to the edge, especially Narendi, who was presently gripping Ty's arm tight enough to leave a bruise.

Nyalis hit the invisible barrier with his staff. "There is no need to fear. You are quite safe. Come, take a look."

Assured he wouldn't fall off, Ty started for the edge, a hand held in front to find where the barrier began. As soon as his fingers pressed against the invisible wall, the barrier glowed softly, and he released it. It was solid, but he still didn't feel safe enough to press against it. Either the cavern below was much warmer than the one above, or the strange reaction his magic was having to the place made him feel that it was. Either way, Ty found himself needing to shed his coat as he stared out over the edge and down across the incredible landscape.

Pools of pale blue water sparkled and shimmered around the rocks below, filled by falls that plummeted off the higher formations above. It was like a miniature Aero'set inside the mountain, but one that didn't seem to need a moon or even a sun to stay lit.

The strange, overbearing feeling Ty had sensed while in the cavern above was a hundred times stronger down there, strong enough now to nearly take his breath. His magic kept wanting to react, to be released.

"You feel it, don't you?"

Ty turned to find Nyalis staring at him. "What is it?" Ty asked. The closer they got to the rock formation below, the stronger it became. He could hear a slight buzzing in the back of his head, almost like the sound of a flitting bee as it moved from flower to flower, except the lower the platform went, the louder the bee became. By the time the stone had settled into place within a wide platform between two smaller falls, Ty could barely hear anything else.

"What's happening to me?" Ty cupped his hands to his ears. His head felt like it was going to explode, as if an inferno of magic burned inside him, begging to be released. He turned to see that Nyalis had gathered everyone over to the side of the platform, but as soon as Ty took a step in their direction, he ran into another invisible wall. "What's going on?" he shouted over the buzzing.

Nyalis's lips were moving, but Ty couldn't hear what he was saying over the deafening hum.

Kraea's voice broke through the noise. *"The wizard says to let it go, Ty. Release your magic."*

"No! I don't know what it will do." Ty was suddenly lifted about ten feet into the air. What was happening to him?

"The wizard says you need to do it now."

The floodgates broke. A blinding light exploded from his body, so bright he had to close his eyes. The heat of his magic flooded through him, the same way it did when he conjured his fire, except this time his entire body was the tinder.

He wanted to move, but his arms remained outstretched to his sides as the magic continued to pour from him. He could hardly breathe; the force was all-consuming.

Just when he thought it was sure to devour him altogether, the light began to dim, and the heat cooled as he was slowly lowered back onto the stone platform below. He opened his eyes. His magic had permeated the surrounding rock and crystal formations, causing them to glow even brighter, so much so that he almost needed to squint when looking directly at them.

Ty dropped to his hands and knees, fighting for his next breath of air. Breen was the first to him, then Narendi, and they tried to help him up.

"Are you hurt?" Breen asked, inspecting Ty for injuries.

Ty managed to get his feet under him, wobbly as they were. "I'm fine. I think." He looked past them and over to where Nyalis was inspecting one of the larger crystal formations near the falls on the left.

The wizard finished his examination and turned with a smile. "Yes, yes. He is fine. Better now than he was a moment ago, I assure you."

"What was that?" Ty demanded.

"The same thing that happens to all faeries who come down here. You bonded with your homeland. Although, I must admit I wasn't expecting something quite that . . . powerful. I suspect it has something to do with this being your first time."

"First time for what? What do you mean, I bonded with my homeland?" Ty looked around the monolithic chamber. "Are you saying that we are in the realm of the Fae?"

Breen and the others turned as well and looked at the wizard.

Nyalis laughed. "I would hope not. Knowing how they feel about faelings, you would probably be dead by now if we were. No, we are not in the faerie realm . . . but we are standing on a small piece of it."

They all looked down at the moist crystalline stone and the bluish-white veins running throughout. Narendi hastily stepped back onto the circular platform. Breen looked like he wanted to but also didn't want to leave Ty. Kraea, on the other hand, lay down on the wet rock and rolled over. *"I like it here."*

"I would expect so," Nyalis said, and she and Ty looked over at him. Sometimes they forgot that Nyalis could hear Kraea as well. "The draakar are not originally from our realm. They were brought over when the faerie first broke through. So, like Ty, you should feel some sort of connection to this place."

"Am I going to . . ." She looked at Ty. *"I won't glow like he did, will I?"*

Nyalis chuckled. "No, my dear. You don't need to worry about that happening. Only a faerie can connect to their homeland like that. Your connection has already been made." And he turned and looked at Ty to clarify that he meant their connection. "It's a bond that will continue to grow as long as both of you are still alive."

"You mean I'm going to have to listen to her incessant droning for the rest of my life?" Ty asked.

Kraea rolled over from where she'd been lapping up the water in one of the smaller pools. *"And I'm going to have to put up with his constant whining?"*

Nyalis shook his head and sighed, then turned and stared up at the large crystal on the right. "There are several such deposits like this one that the Fae buried across the known world. They make up the Pentarium, a network of ley lines that feed magic throughout the realm of man, making it possible to be used here. Even though there are several such places throughout Aldor and beyond, there were only two as large as this one here, which is why the faeries decided to build Aero'set here. The other is—"

"The White Tower," Ty said.

Nyalis nodded. "Yes, the Tower is the source for the second deposit. Some even say it is larger than this one."

"Why did the faeries bring them here?" Breen asked, keeping a supportive arm around Ty's waist.

"They needed that connection to their own realm in order to retain their magic. I believe they had intended to grow these deposits until they managed to completely transform our realm into theirs."

"How much would have changed?" Breen asked. "Are you saying

everything up there would eventually have looked like this down here?" He glanced around the room. "Don't get me wrong, this is pretty and all, but I'd hate to live in a world of nothing but stone and crystal. No trees, no grass, no good rich soil." He shivered. "I couldn't even imagine such a place."

"Never to feel the warm sand under my feet?" Narendi frowned. "I don't like these faeries."

Nyalis chuckled. "As bad as their intentions were, the faeries did manage to give us a great gift. They gave us the best of both worlds. While we still have our lush grasslands, thick forests, and burgeoning seas, we also have our magic as well, hidden deep within the foundation of our world but ebbing up into the life around us. If our leaders did not fear its use as they do, that magic could be used for the betterment of all."

The wizard stared out at the surrounding formations. "I remember the golden years of magic, after the Faerie Wars, back when the Wizard Order stood for the highest ideals of man. They used their gifts for everyone, back before Aerodyne lost his way. It was an incredible time to be alive. So much prosperity. Kingdoms at peace. The gift of healing alone made it a time to treasure. Great explorations." Taking a deep breath, he turned back around. "Daydreaming of what once was isn't going to fix the problems we face now. Come." He headed back to the circular platform. "We have accomplished what we needed to."

"That's it?" Ty asked, just now getting enough strength back to move on his own. "What about all of this?"

"What about it?" Nyalis asked. "It's not going anywhere."

"Then what was the purpose of bringing me down here?"

"The purpose was so that you could connect with the true source of your magic in a way you have not been able to before, to discover a valuable piece of your heritage. You are half faerie, which means there will always be a part of you that needs this place, that needs that connection. I believe it will also help stabilize your use of magic, and possibly strengthen it. More importantly, now that you have been made aware of its presence, you will have the charge of keeping it safe." He looked at the others as well. "That goes for all of you. You are now the custodians to one of the greatest secrets of our world."

Breen groaned. "Great. Just what I always wanted. It wasn't like we didn't have enough to worry about already."

Nyalis smiled as Breen and Ty started for the platform. "Oh, I almost forgot." Nyalis raised his hand as if to stop them, but then released a fist of air that hit Ty in the chest and threw him backward into the nearest pool.

Ty was so stunned that he didn't even have time to hold his breath before he went under. The water wrapped around him like a blanket, warm but soothing. It left his skin tingling. He kicked up with his feet and broke through the surface, coughing up water. He swam to the edge and crawled out with Breen's help. "What was that for?" he demanded, his boots sloshing against the stone as he stomped back toward the platform.

"That was for your benefit." Nyalis pointed at Ty's arm. "Check your wrapping."

Ty pulled up his sleeve and removed Zynora's now-soggy bandaging. The deep cut from his spar with Ayrion was gone. In fact, so were the newer abrasions he'd acquired during his battle with the tree monster in the glass arboretum. He lifted his shirt and stared at the spot on his chest where he was sure had been a bruise from the taeradinium vines, but there was nothing there, not the faintest mark.

"These waters can be a source of healing to the Fae. Another possible reason for your people's long age, I believe."

Breen started for the pool.

Nyalis waved him off. "You're wasting your time, I'm afraid. The waters will not work on you. Unless, of course, you have some faerie blood we don't know about."

Breen blew out his lips and turned back around. He looked at Ty and shrugged sheepishly. "Thought I'd give it a try." Breen's head shot up. "We could take some with us. Bring a skin to fill next time."

Nyalis chuckled. "Doesn't work like that. Outside of this place, the water is no different than what you'll find pouring down the side of the mountain. In fact, it's the same water. There's a small fissure in the rock that funnels a portion of it down to fill what's here."

With nothing else to look at, they followed Kraea back aboard the circular platform. Nyalis repeated his protection spell, and with another tap from his staff on the stone, the platform rose into the air, causing Narendi to once again latch on to Ty's arm.

Ty stared down at the rock and crystal formations below until their platform shot back up into the hole at the top of the cavern and everything vanished from sight. Of all the interesting things he had been hoping Nyalis would show him of Aero'set, a piece of his own homeland had not been on the list. It was beyond anything he could have hoped to see. Even now, he could still feel his connection to it, lingering in the back of his mind like a passing thought.

He hoped that this new connection didn't present any new challenges for him to face. He had enough to handle as it was.

Chapter 5 | Ty

HE TEMPERATURE COOLED further the higher the platform rose, so Ty pulled his jacket back on, not that it did much with his clothes soaking wet from his unexpected dunking.

They reached the top of Meeisredon, where the stone seats for the ruling members of the Fae sat, and made their way across the cavern with its maze of pulsing bluish-white lines. Once on the far side, Ty stopped and turned, looking up at the platform. He had been wanting to see something unique and strange, and Nyalis had certainly shown him that.

Before they stepped through the wall, Nyalis raised his hand and conjured a large ball of golden fire above their heads. Ty could feel the heat wafting down around him. The wizard whispered something, and a gust of wind shot from the fire and encircled Ty. It was warm, almost too warm, and the heat began to steal his breath.

A moment later, the fire disappeared, and his clothes were dry.

"Wouldn't want you catching your death of cold, now would we?" Nyalis said as he lowered his hand and then marched through the hidden entrance at the front.

"No, I guess not," Ty said, inspecting his now-dry shirt before following him out. On the other side, Ty could feel Kraea's hesitation. She'd been enjoying the warmth of the cavern, especially the one below, and didn't want to go back out in the cold. *Are you coming? Or do you plan on getting left behind? For all we know, the entrance might seal up once we're gone.*

Kraea grumbled but eventually stepped out onto the moist landing behind the falls. She growled as the frigid mountain air cascaded down around them, freezing all of them to the bone. Well, almost all. Nyalis stood on the first step, waiting. He didn't seem all that affected by the frigid air. In fact, his robes were barely moving. "If you're that cold, then do something about it."

"Like what?" Ty shouted over the roar of the falls. "You didn't exactly give us time to pack something warmer."

"Think, boy. You have magic. Use it."

What could he do? It wasn't like he could control the weather, could he? He could gather the wind to him, but not exactly stop it. Conjuring his fire wasn't going to help. There was plenty of water there to manipulate, but how would that help?

Nyalis sighed. "Your shield. Conjure your shield. Ayrion tells me you used one while fighting with the bulradoer, and I've seen you create a full shield inside the Sidaran Assembly Hall. You encased yourself in it, remember?"

"You mean the bubble? That was Mangora, not me."

Breen cleared his throat. "Actually, you conjured one for us in the underground cavern."

"That was more a manipulation of the water than a shield. Remember what happened when I tried to create a pocket of air under the water? It shot back out." Ty shivered as an image of the water monster appeared, and he quickly pushed it away. "Fine. Stand back. I'll give it a try."

The others moved away, huddling near the edge of the steps as Ty gathered the wind. It wasn't like he had to work very hard at it. It was strong enough to nearly send him over the side of the cliff. He focused on hardening it around him like he had with his shields. He could feel it growing, expanding. He could almost see it as he focused on shaping it around him like a cocoon. It was working. The wind coming down from above was no longer striking his back. The sound of the water was dimming. He was doing it.

Nyalis raised his hand. "Just make sure you don't—"

A gust of wind whipped down over the ridge and struck Ty's shield, and he nearly lost his breath as it latched on to his shield and flung him through the air and straight for the edge of the cliff. He released an embarrassingly high-pitched shriek as he saw it coming, unable to stop himself.

Kraea roared and raced after him, but not before Nyalis raised his staff. Ty hit an invisible wall at the edge of the landing and stopped. Ty was so flustered he'd forgotten to even release his magic, and as soon as he did, the shield vanished. He dropped to his hands and knees, panting as the wind funneled around him. Quickly, he crawled away from the edge and back against the mountain's face.

"Well, that was quite entertaining," Nyalis said with a gulp, looking a little pale himself. "And what did we learn from this experience?"

Ty pulled himself back up to his feet with Breen's help, his heart pounding. "I learned that if I keep listening to you, I'm going to wind up dead."

Nyalis chuckled. "I tried to warn you."

"You didn't try hard enough," Breen said angrily, then looked at Ty. "What happened? Didn't the shield work?"

"Oh, it worked," Ty said. "It worked so well the wind just about carried me off the side of the mountain." He took a couple deep breaths. "It's the same problem I had against the bulradoers' fists of air. If my shield wasn't angled, the strike would throw me."

Nyalis raised his finger. "Quite right. So how would that apply here?"

"It doesn't," Ty said, his teeth chattering against the cold. "There's no way to predict which way the gusts will come."

"True. And when they do come, where is the safest place to be?"

"Here, against the mountain," Narendi said, her back pressed as tight to the rock as she could get, Kraea standing alongside her.

Nyalis smiled. "Good." He turned to Ty. "So what does that mean?"

Ty didn't know, and was growing more than a little frustrated, especially with his friends standing there half freezing to death. Still, this was what he had been waiting for, what he had spent the last months risking his life for. To be here and to learn magic from an actual wizard.

Nyalis's thick brows lowered. "Think, boy. What keeps a sail from blowing away during a strong gust of wind?"

"The mast," Breen said.

"Correct. The only way the sail works is when it is held by a mast. In your case, you were the mast."

"Yeah, and I nearly died!"

"So to keep that from happening again, you will need to lash your shield to a sturdier mast."

"Like what?" Ty turned and looked at his brother. "Breen?"

Nyalis groaned and walked over and grabbed the top of Ty's head and spun it around. "That," he said, pointing at the face of the rock with his staff.

"The mountain?"

"Exactly! Do you think you could find something more stable than a mountain?"

"But how do I lash the air?"

"The same way you are doing anything with it. Magic, of course."

Ty rolled his eyes. "I know that, but how?"

"Does it really matter?" Breen asked, blowing on his hands. "We're freezing to death. If we wait any longer, we won't make it back down." He put one arm around Narendi, who was wearing nothing more than her Mzwati robes, and pulled her close. "I say we wait till we get back to Aero'set, then you can play with it to your heart's content."

"No better time to learn than when it counts the most," Nyalis said, and looked at Ty. "Now, try."

As much as Ty had been wanting Nyalis to teach him magic, this wasn't exactly what he'd had in mind. But seeing that he wasn't going to budge, Ty stepped over to the rock face and reached out and gathered the wind, but only a small amount this time. He focused, and it hardened into a disc not much wider than the size of a barrel lid. "Now what?" he asked.

"Now lash it to the rock."

"How?" He took the small shield and pushed it against the side of the rock, but it didn't do anything but form a barrier between his hand and the mountain. He pulled back, and the shield came with him. "I don't understand what I'm supposed to be doing."

"Think," Nyalis said, walking over to inspect Ty's progress. "You have taken a permeable thing and made it impermeable."

"What?"

"You have taken something you shouldn't be able to touch and have made it hard enough to stop a bulradoer's fire. It shouldn't be that much more difficult to take it and connect it to something."

"It is if you don't know how." Ty shoved it up against the side of the rock once more. *Come on. Lash.*

Nyalis sighed. "You are trying to force the two together. It won't work like that. This is why they would never let me teach. It's one thing to use magic; it's quite another to tell someone else how to do it." He thought a moment. "Perhaps my example of the sail was not the best to use in this situation. It's not so much trying to tie the shield to something as it is trying to stick it to something. Think of a cobbler's glue. Your shield is the boot, your magic is the glue, and the mountain is the sole. Now fasten the two together."

Ty blew on his hands, which had gone almost completely numb, his entire body trembling from the cold. Why couldn't Nyalis just put his own shield around them while Ty worked? Ty turned to press his shield up against the rock once more, this time imagining his magic being brushed onto the shield like glue on the bottom of a boot before pressing it against the sole. He forced the two together. He had no idea if it was working. He was too afraid and too cold to even move to find out.

"Well?" Nyalis asked. "Give it a tug."

Ty took a deep breath and, gripping with what little strength he had left in his fingers, he jerked back on the shield. It didn't move. In fact, he nearly went down when his fingers slipped from the edge.

Breen was there behind him to hold him up. "Did it work?"

Ty turned and smiled. Breen smiled as well.

"Well, what are you waiting for?" Nyalis asked. "Applause? Expand your shield before our Imbatoo princess's lips turn even bluer."

Ty switched his focus to the shield's shape as he reached out with his rather stiff fingers and pulled the mountain air to him. He hardened it around him, expanding the invisible barrier as he did. It worked. He opened the front, making sure the rest was good and lashed before expanding it around the entire group. As he did, it grew very quiet inside the bubble, the howling wind reduced to a dull moan.

Nyalis smiled as he felt along the edge of Ty's creation. "Excellent. Now let's do something about the cold, shall we?" He raised his hand once more, and a small flame appeared. He sent a faint trace of wind to circulate the warmth of the fire throughout, then released it. Unlike Mangora's circular shield or the bubble Ty had created inside the underground lake, this one wasn't completely airtight. A small amount of air seeped in from the bottom, where it rested across the top of the steps.

Ty's skin prickled as the numbness faded and the feeling returned. "Can we leave now?" Ty asked. The moon overhead was bright, bathing the side of the cliff in pale light, including the stairs leading down.

"Of course," Nyalis said. "Lead the way."

Ty looked at Narendi. "How are you?"

"Better than you will be if you don't get me down from here."

Ty nodded and started for the steps. He walked straight into the front of his shield and bounced off with a grunt.

He heard chuckling behind him, and he turned to find Nyalis with a sheepish grin on his face. "Did you forget something?" the wizard asked.

Ty turned and looked at his shield, then shrugged.

"It's still lashed to the mountain, isn't it?" Nyalis said.

"Yes."

"So how do we get down?"

"By unlashing it?"

"Sounds about right."

"But if I release it, what's to stop the wind from pulling us over?"

"The fact that you aren't unlashing all of it. So as you move ahead, you will expand the front and decrease the back."

"I don't know if I can do all of that at the same time."

Nyalis smiled. "It's like walking. When you first begin, you have to concentrate on placing one foot in front of the other, but after a while, you no longer think . . . you simply do. The more you work with magic, the more capable you will become. Pretty soon, lashing a shield will be as easy as breathing."

"Well, right now, breathing seems mighty hard."

Nyalis sighed. "Concentrate. You can do it."

Ty focused on the glue between the shield and the mountain, doing his best to cut away the strands of it at the back of his shield. It took a while, but he finally managed to free the back of the shield far enough for them to make it down the first couple of steps before Kraea's snout struck the front, and they stopped. She turned, and her eyes narrowed.

"Sorry," he said, then focused on the back of his shield, releasing the strands of magical glue. Once again, they started downward, this time only stopping every couple dozen stairs. Pretty soon, he was managing the flow of unlashing and lashing fast enough that he didn't need to look at what he was working on. He was able to keep his eyes ahead and still concentrate on keeping the shield moving.

They stopped a couple more times when something caught him off guard and broke his concentration. The first was Narendi tripping over one of Kraea's paws; the second was Breen trying to ask Nyalis about something to do with his room. Both times were enough for Ty to lose focus and miss the unlashing, causing one or more of those at the front to careen into the wall.

By the time they reached the bottom of the stairs, Ty had worked up quite a sweat, but the lashing was notably easier than it had been at the top. All thought of where they had been and what they'd seen had vanished, replaced by a strained weariness that had him wanting to crawl into bed and sleep for the next three days. In fact, if given the choice, he would have probably chosen a day of training with Ayrion than go through another one of Nyalis's lessons. The man was a terrible teacher. And at least with the weapons master, Ty didn't have to fear dying in the middle of a lesson.

The moon was nearly at its peak by the time they made it back to the main entrance of the dormitories, having returned by a different route than the one they had gone. Nyalis wished them all a good night, then crossed over the bridge and disappeared down one of the streets leading south through the city.

"That was quite the experience," Breen said offhandedly as he, too, watched the wizard vanish out of sight. He yawned. "I don't know about you lot, but I could use some sleep."

"I want a hot drink," Narendi said and quickly headed through the southern wall.

"*I'm with her,*" Kraea added and followed Narendi into the inner courtyard. "*Some warm blood will do very nicely on the throat.*"

Ty shivered at the thought, then he and Breen followed the two across the snow-covered path to the front entrance of the north wing. This time, Ty held the door as the others walked in.

"We were wondering if you were going to be returning tonight," a voice said from the shadows.

They all turned to find Ayrion and Bek sitting at a small table near one of the windows on the left. Bek was smoking his pipe while Ayrion sipped on a drink.

"Best you get to bed," Ayrion said, setting down his tankard. "We have a long day of training tomorrow."

Ty groaned. The man was as bad as Nyalis. "You can't give us a few extra hours? Nyalis had us traipsing all over a mountainside tonight." Ty didn't say more as to where they had been in case Nyalis didn't want them to know.

"In combat, your opponent isn't going to care if you got a proper night's rest. He's going to try killing you one way or the other." He looked them over, then finally sighed. "Fine. But I expect you to be there by ninth bell."

"Thank you." Ty and the others turned and headed for the stairs. He could hear the faint whispers of Ayrion and Bek's conversation starting up once more as they headed up. The climb took longer than it should have, Ty's legs twinging by the time he reached the top landing. He wished he'd requested a room on the ground level.

They headed down the corridor on the right to their respective rooms, Kraea joining Ty at his. "Goodnight," he said to the others. Breen and Narendi wished him the same.

Ty shut the door behind them and turned. The fire was still crackling warmly in the hearth. His clothes were also still strewn across the chair and bed, including the towel he'd dried off on. Too tired to even think about picking them up, or even undressing, Ty walked over and sat down on the side of the bed facing the fire. He did manage to get his boots off, while Kraea curled up on a rug in front of the hearth. She was breathing heavily before Ty had made it under his covers, apparently too tired to get that warm drink after all.

The last thing he remembered was thinking about the rock and crystal formations inside Meeisredon and how they had made him feel when he'd touched them with his magic. There was no mistaking the bond between them. He wondered what the real faerie realm must be like.

"Wake up," a voice in his head called to him, pulling him from the darkness.

Ty opened his eyes slowly, one at a time. He got one look at Kraea staring at him from across the bed and pulled his covers up over his head. "Go away."

"Get out of bed, or I'm going to crawl up there with you."

Ty groaned. "You're too big."

"Fine," she said and stuck her two front paws up on the bed beside his legs. The tips of her claws poked through the quilt.

"Hey, now look what you've gone and done." Ty rolled over and kicked her legs off the edge, then sat up to take a look at the damage. "It's a good thing these sheets are magical. You're a flaming menace."

Kraea grinned. *"Now get up. I'm starving."* She took a few steps back and then stretched, her red scales glistening in the firelight. Ty had to look twice, but Kraea actually seemed . . . bigger. The horns on her head were nearing the top of his seat by the fire. Had she always been that tall? *"What are you looking at?"* she asked.

"You look . . ."

"I look what?"

Ty shook his head. "Never mind." He looked down at his clothes, the same ones he'd been wearing the previous night. He was honestly too tired to worry about changing. He doubted anyone would notice anyway. He walked over and opened the shutters to the large window beside his bed and light struck him in the face, causing the dull ache in the back of his head to suddenly shift to the front. "I hate this place."

"No, you don't."

"No, I don't, but a few more weeks of this and I could grow to." He stared out the window at the large dining hall behind the dorms, letting his eyes adjust to the light pouring in. It looked bigger from the outside.

As incredible as Aero'set was, there was still something missing.

"You're thinking about it again."

Ty turned away from the window. "Thinking about what?"

"*Home.*"

He sighed. She was right. He had been thinking about home. Aero'set was an incredible place—beautiful—but he missed the Sidaran Forest. He missed the East Inn on Performance Night. He missed working in Master Orlyn's apothecary and spending time with Lyessa. He especially missed his cottage on the outskirts of town. No matter how realistic his magical bedroom was, it just didn't compare to the real thing.

Most importantly, he missed his family.

He couldn't imagine how worried they must be. It had been several months since he and Breen had left on their quest. Had they given up on them? Did they believe they were dead? The more he thought about it, the more he realized how much he wanted to go home. He couldn't believe he was even contemplating it, especially after having worked so hard to get here, but now that he had finished his quest, there was nothing he wanted more than to hold his father and sister in his arms. Well, that and kiss Lyessa.

"*If I had a choice,*" Kraea said, "*I would do the same.*"

Ty looked at the draakar and smiled. "I'm sorry. I didn't mean to be insensitive."

"*You were thinking about home. How is that insensitive?*"

"I'm sure it brings up difficult memories for you." Ty walked over to his nightstand and buried half his head in the bowl of water on top. It was just cold enough to wake him up but not enough to make his headache any worse. He grabbed the folded towel beside the bowl and dried his face. "You know, I don't think I've ever asked where home is for you." He turned. "Where did you come from? Are there others of your kind?"

He thought he remembered the Live Market owner mentioning something about where he had captured Kraea and her mother, but Ty didn't remember where that was. No, wait, it hadn't been Dalibor who had said it. It was Mangora. She said something about the draakar and the arachnobes coming from—

"*The Caldera,*" Kraea said. "*The draakar live on the western side, and the arachnobes live on the eastern side closest to the Shroud.*"

Ty sat down on the edge of the bed and pulled on his boots. "The what?"

"The great mist."

"What's that?"

"It's what separates us from them."

"Them? Them who? The arachnobes?"

"No. The cursed."

Ty shook his head. "What cursed?"

"I don't know. It's just what Mother always said. 'Never go into the mist, or the cursed ones will get you.' Not that we had to worry that much, since the mist was on the arachnobes' side of the Caldera. Only draakar on the hunt would dare venture there."

Ty was going to have to mark that down on his ever-growing list of things to ask Nyalis, if he ever saw him again. Then again, after what had taken place last night, he wasn't sure he wanted to, at least not right away.

"Come on," Kraea said, heading across the room for the door, her claws clicking on the wooden floors where the rugs didn't reach. *"Let's eat."*

Ty blew out his lips and stood, feeling a little lightheaded as he did. "I'm coming." He hoped whatever the dining room was serving was strong. Even with the extra couple of hours of sleep, he was definitely going to need it if he had any hope of making it through another day with their beloved weapons master.

Chapter 6 | Ty

HE AIR SEEMED SLIGHTLY warmer than the previous day as Ty, Breen, Narendi, and Kraea stepped out the back of the north dormitory and started across the covered bridge to the school's main dining hall—the same route they had traveled through with Nyalis to Meeisredon. Ty was ready for winter to be over. Unfortunately, as high as they were in the mountains, it seemed there would still be a couple of months of snow left to endure before then.

By the time they reached the far side of the bridge, the frosty winter air had set Ty's teeth to chattering, and he quickly pulled on his stocking cap and gloves. He waited for the others to do the same, which took several minutes since Breen had to set down their lunch basket to get his on. It wasn't exactly correct to call it a "lunch basket" since it didn't contain their lunch, but a late morning snack of mostly leftover fruit from breakfast. Ty hoped it would be enough to get them through Ayrion's grueling lessons until they broke for lunch.

He handed Narendi a spare cap for her bald head. After the first day of practice out in the snow, she had exchanged her Mzwati robes for the woodland outfit she had purchased in the Riverlands. Ty thought it a wise decision, as her Imbatoo clothing had been created for desert conditions and not snowdrifts. She did seem much happier in the new outfits, even though she wouldn't say it out loud. Ty had caught her on more than one occasion admiring the red lining of her cloak.

Breen grabbed the basket just as Kraea leaned her neck over to sniff around the lid.

"I hate this cold," she grumbled.

"Yes, I know," Ty said. *"You've told me a dozen times already."*

Kraea blew out her lips.

Having forgone their usual southern route to the garrison by way of the main gate and up through the shipyard, Ty headed into the dining hall and out the left exit, taking them across the northeastern side of the city. It was a shorter trek than the southern route but also more tedious with the extra staircases. And since they were running behind to meet Ayrion in the practice fields, this was the most direct course. It helped that the buildings in this part of the school were much more sparsely placed near the main branch of the falls.

Unlike Easthaven, whose river skirted the outer edge of the city, leaving a flatter area in the middle suitable to build on, Aero'set had been nestled amongst the lower cliffs of the Angorans, making it necessary to place buildings wherever a flat-enough space could be created and required the use of many winding staircases and bridges to navigate.

The dormitory was located on one of the largest landmasses in the center of the city that didn't have water running through it. The farther south in Aero'set one went, the fewer stairs and bridges were required and the more compact the buildings became.

Once through the eastern quarter, they headed over the river and into the garrison by way of its eastern gate. The terrain flattened rather quickly on that side of the river. A small copse of trees bordered most of the eastern side, shielding the school from sight of the open grassland that lay between the surrounding mountains. Those grasslands made up the bulk of the Valley of Needrin. Despite Aero'set's size, it only took up the top-left corner of this hidden valley.

Ty could hear the clacking of practice swords echoing through the empty garrison as they made their way toward the practice field, passing the stables on the right, which were half built into the mountainside. Ayrion and Bek were in one of the rings, already working through their morning routine. Ty wondered how late the two had stayed up talking. Neither had been at breakfast. Or had they skipped breakfast and been out here sparring the entire time?

The practice field in back of the garrison butted up against the mountainside. Most of the field was left open for running routines, but there were a few trees around the border to provide shade. Breen placed their basket under one of the benches at the back, and they all took a seat to watch. Kraea scraped away as much of the snow beside the bench as she could with her claws and tail before settling down to watch the impressive display of skill.

"Have you ever noticed how quickly Ayrion moves?" Ty asked the others, a topic he'd wanted to broach for the last couple of weeks but hadn't quite been sure how.

"Yes," Narendi said. "It's called skill. Something you are sadly lacking."

Ty rolled his eyes. It was more than just skill. He could feel it. There was something about Ayrion that had always unsettled him. He could normally sense wielding. He could even see it if he used his web, but with Ayrion, it had always felt different. Ty had tried several times but was still unsure as to whether their instructor was indeed a wielder.

Curiosity once again getting the better of him, he reached out with his magic and sent a small web of it across the practice field. He could easily sense Breen's and Narendi's magic and Bek's lack of it, but once again, Ayrion eluded him. There was something there, but he wasn't sure what. If Ayrion was a wielder, then his magic wasn't like any Ty had felt before.

"He's probably watching more than just Bek's hatchets," Breen said, breaking Ty's concentration enough that he dropped his web. "You heard him. He told us to watch everything. The slightest movement in the shoulders or hips can signal where your opponent plans to strike next." Breen chuckled. "For faerie's sake, the man's been doing this since he was barely old enough to speak. He can probably tell what you're going to do by the way you blink your eyes."

Ty continued to watch the exchange inside the ring, a little disappointed in his brother's ready acceptance of the swordsman's abilities. He was about to address it when his brother's words sank in, and he turned. "For *faerie's* sake?"

Breen shrugged sheepishly. "I don't know. I just came up with it."

Ty thought about it a moment, then chuckled.

"Who's first?"

Ty turned, startled to realize the ring had grown quiet.

Ayrion was looking at the four of them, and before Ty could think of what to say, Narendi was off the bench and unhooking her spear. "I am first."

Bek walked over and took her spot on the right side of the bench.

"Have you been out here long?" Ty asked.

Bek's face was lathered in sweat, some dripping from the hair peeking beneath his fur-lined cap. "Long enough," he said, wiping his face with his sleeve.

Realizing this might be his best chance to find out something about Ayrion, Ty nodded toward the practice ring, where Ayrion and Narendi were just facing off. "You seem to know him pretty well. Does he have any weaknesses? One side worse than the other, a dodgy knee, limited vision out of either eye?"

Bek laughed. "If he does, I haven't found it. The man's half faerie if you ask me." Bek's brows lifted as he realized what he'd just said. "Oh, I didn't mean any offense. Just a figure of speech."

Ty waved it off. "None taken. I would have said the same a few months ago. I've only just recently learned of my . . . well, sordid heritage." Before Ty could bring the topic of Ayrion back up, Bek continued.

"What was that like . . . learning you were part faerie?" He shook his head. "Sounds strange just saying it. The idea that I'm sitting here talking with a Fae is . . ."

"Yeah, *strange*," Ty echoed. "Can't really think of a better word. I don't remember what it was like, honestly. I've been too busy trying to stay alive to really give it much thought, I guess. I don't really feel any different. Well, maybe a little."

"That's because you *aren't* different," Breen chimed in. "You're the same obnoxious little brother you've always been. Apart from that white hair, of course." He stared at Ty's cap and the hair sticking out from it. "Still trying to get used to that."

Ty smiled and turned back to the ring, hoping to draw the conversation away from him and back to their instructor. Narendi and Ayrion were deep in the middle of their match. Narendi was doing a good job of holding her own, her spear spinning left and right as she threw back Ayrion's advances as fast as she could while trying to get in a few hits of her own. She was fast and kept her stance low to the ground while maintaining incredible balance, something Ty certainly needed to work on. She moved with such precision, her spear seemed like an extension of her arm.

Ayrion was always one step ahead, but no more.

"So what's his story?" Ty asked Bek. "You've spent the most time with him."

"Actually, I haven't known him all that long."

Ty turned. "Long enough to know something about him, surely. All we know is that he's Upakan, loves to wear black, and is a faerie-lovin' maniac with those blades." He had to be careful how he approached the topic of whether Ayrion had magic. Wielders in Aldor often kept such things hidden for good reason, and he didn't want to out something that perhaps the others didn't know. On the other hand, not knowing was driving him crazy.

"He's also a loyal friend," Bek added. "Doesn't say much, but when he does, you'd be wise to listen."

"Is he always so . . . serious?" Breen asked. "I'm not sure I've ever seen him crack a smile."

Bek stared at Ayrion from the side of the ring. "It's tough to say. There're two sides to the man. As I'm sure you've been made aware, he lost his memories during the battle between Elondria and Cylmar."

"We heard," Ty said. "He really didn't remember anything after that?"

Bek shook his head. "Not a thing."

"Apparently he didn't lose all his memory," Breen added. "From what it sounds like with your battle against the shadow people, he didn't lose any of his fighting abilities."

Bek thumbed his chin. "That's true. Unfortunately, once his memories returned, he seemed to pull even deeper into himself. He's not as talkative as he used to be, like he's carrying the weight of the world on his shoulders. He hasn't spoken much of it, but I think there were some pretty awful things that took place during that last battle, things he's still trying to deal with." He looked back out at the practice ring. "To be honest, I miss the old Ayrion."

Ty turned back to the ring. This wasn't exactly going the way he had hoped, though he was learning some interesting things about the man. He studied the way Ayrion moved, tracking the way he countered before Narendi had a chance to attack. Surely he wasn't the only one to suspect there was something more. "Any idea on how he does that?"

"Does what?" Bek asked. "Fight?" The big trapper chuckled. "When you figure that out, let me know."

Ty pointed toward the ring. "Watch the way he anticipates her moves. No one's that good."

Bek chuckled. "He's Upakan. I think they all do that. Had the unfortunate luck of running into a couple of Upakans in Minotha. I have to say, they are a people I certainly wouldn't want to face in battle."

"I'm telling you, there's something more to it." Ty couldn't believe how far the others were willing to go to overlook their instructor's clearly unnatural gifts, or was he simply making more of this than he should? No, there was something about Ayrion that Ty just couldn't shake. He could feel it in his bones.

"Watch this," he said as he leaned over and grabbed an apple out of their basket. A voice in his head warned he was probably going to regret this, but he ignored it. He *had* to know. He waited until Ayrion's back was to them and then threw the piece of fruit straight for the back of Ayrion's head.

"What are you—" was about all that Breen got out before the apple struck and Ayrion stumbled forward, barely blocking Narendi's overhead strike.

Everyone on the bench froze, especially Ty. That wasn't what was supposed to have happened.

Ayrion spun around, his eyes scanning the bench, stopping on Ty. Ty stared in disbelief, too stunned to even know what to say. Ayrion was supposed to have spun and caught the apple. Or cut it in half with his sword. Or dodged it with his back still turned. It never even occurred to Ty that he would actually hit the weapons master with it.

Ayrion's eyes narrowed as he raised his hand and slowly motioned for Ty to join him in the ring.

Ty gulped. Well, this was a terrible way to start the day.

Breen sighed. "What were you thinking?"

"I thought . . . I thought he'd . . ."

Breen shook his head. "Don't expect me to help you out of this one."

Ty could sense Kraea laughing as he stood from his seat. Bek handed him one of the practice swords from the rack beside their bench and smiled empathetically. "Good luck. Wouldn't want to be you right now."

Ty grimaced. He didn't want to be him right now either. Why had he thought to press the issue? Why hadn't he just left well enough alone? Slowly, he made his way out into the ring, passing Narendi on his way, who gave him an exasperated look and a snort. He wasn't sure if it was for his stunt or the fact that her time in the ring had been cut short.

Ty would have been more than happy to let her keep going. He looked at Ayrion, who was waiting in the middle. "I'm . . . I'm sorry about that. I thought . . . I thought you would have caught it. Or something." Even saying it sounded ridiculous.

"Caught it? And how was I supposed to do that with my back turned?"

Ty shrugged. "I . . . I've seen the way you move. It's like you know what we're going to do before we do it. I thought maybe you had . . ." Ty shook his head. "Never mind. Sorry."

Ayrion motioned for Ty to take his place across from him, and Ty hesitantly moved into position. His wooden practice sword betrayed the quivering of his hand as he held it up, nervously awaiting Ayrion's punishment. He was sure to be bruised for days.

"No magic," Ayrion said, and Ty nodded, bending his knees slightly for balance as he awaited what was sure to be a—

Ty barely got the chance to flinch before his sword was flying from his hand. He'd been too worried about what Ayrion was going to do to him to make sure he had a tight enough grip on his sword.

Before Ty could move to retrieve the fallen weapon, Ayrion lunged with a shout, and Ty stumbled backward into the snow. Ayrion's sword stopped in front of Ty's face and Ty gulped, his eyes wide and staring up at the wooden edge of the blade hovering a few inches from his nose.

Ayrion drew the weapon back and held out his hand. Ty took it, and

Ayrion pulled him up. "Your weapon is your life. You lose one and you're likely to lose the other. Now get your sword, and this time, hold on to it."

Ty rushed over and retrieved the fallen weapon, wiping the snow off the handle with his cloak to dry the grip. His fingers were stiff from cold, making it even more difficult as he walked back over to the center of the ring and returned to his fighting stance. This time he focused on his grip, watching Ayrion intently for any sign of movement, hoping to anticipate his opponent's first strike, like he'd been taught.

He stared at Ayrion's wooden blade, but more importantly, he watched Ayrion—his shoulders, hips, feet—for any sign of movement.

There it was!

Ayrion's foot shifted. Ty also caught the slight lift in his elbows, signaling a strike to the right side. Quickly, he raised his blade and deflected the strike, but as soon as their swords touched, Ayrion's was already up and circling to the left. Ty immediately shifted his stance as he'd been taught and deflected the blow, but he ended up spinning too far. Ayrion took advantage of the opening and kicked Ty's leg out from under him while his body was angled sideways.

Ty's back hit the packed snow, but this time he managed to keep hold of his sword and blocked Ayrion's attempt to drive home his point. As soon as he batted Ayrion's sword away, he rolled over and onto his knees to block another attempt for his head. Their swords clacked, the echo reverberating off the side of the mountain behind them. Ty smiled. He couldn't believe he'd managed to hold Ayrion off this long.

Ty swung for Ayrion's legs, hoping to force a retreat, but Ayrion batted the attempt away and unleashed a sudden barrage while Ty was still on his knees. The strikes were coming too fast and from every side at once, it seemed. He couldn't block them all. He couldn't even see them. With everything he had, Ty fought to keep his sword moving, to block the flurry of blows, but the weapon's master was too skilled. A single crack to the knuckles sent Ty's sword flying.

Ayrion stopped and took a step back, and Ty dropped onto his back in the snow, clutching his fingers until the pain began to dull. Ayrion looked down at him a moment, then up at the others. His eyes narrowed. "I can see I'm not going to get much out of you today. With eyes that tired, it's a wonder you can even see out of them. We are through for the day."

Ayrion walked out of the ring, and Ty turned over to watch him go, half expecting him to turn around and say he was only joking. Bek met Ayrion at the edge, and they started back toward the barracks.

Ty's hand was twinging, and feeling slightly vengeful, he decided to attempt one final test. He raised his good hand and gathered some wind.

"*That's a very bad idea,*" Kraea said through their link, sensing his intentions.

"*Quiet,*" Ty said, waiting until Ayrion had walked under one of the taller oaks. As soon as the weapons master neared the trunk, he sent a small fist of air hurtling toward the upper snow-filled branches. The air struck the upper limbs and sent a cascade of snow plummeting down for Ayrion's head.

Just before it hit, Ayrion stepped to the right, and the snow thudded onto the ground between the two men. Bek looked up at the branches and scratched his head, wondering what had happened. Ayrion, on the other hand, looked directly at Ty and winked.

Ty's mouth gaped as Ayrion turned and kept walking. *He knew!* And what's more, he *did* have magic. Which meant he had to have known about the apple as well. *But why didn't he stop it?*

Maybe he didn't want the others to know. Did all Upakans have magic? If so, what kind of magic was it? Could he sense what was around him, like Ty could when he used his web? Was that why he was so good with his blades? But even being able to sense what was around you couldn't give you the kind of skill Ayrion had, so it couldn't be just that.

Though Ty's head was swimming with questions, he did at least feel vindicated.

"*Best you keep that knowledge to yourself,*" Kraea said. "*It's not yours to tell.*"

Breen walked over and helped Ty to his feet, since Ty was finding it rather difficult with what felt like another broken knuckle or two. Ty pulled off his glove to see the damage. His first two fingers were red and swelling.

"Let's get back to the dorms," Ty said, cradling his hand. "I need to see if Zynora can help me with this."

"Can't say you don't deserve it," Breen said with a sigh. "Stupidest thing I've seen you do in some time. Still can't figure out what you were thinking."

"Him, thinking?" Narendi laughed.

Breen smiled. "Guess you have a point."

Ty thought about telling them what he'd discovered, but one look from Kraea and he kept his mouth shut. She was right. It wasn't his secret to divulge.

"Let's go get those fingers looked at," Breen said as he placed their weapons back on the rack and grabbed their basket.

Ty nodded, and the group started back through the practice rings toward the main garrison. "Thankfully, my hands are numb enough to cut the pain."

"You should use the spear," Narendi said.

Ty grunted. "He'd wallop my fingers just as easily with that."

"Not the way the Mzwati hold it."

Ty shrugged. The last thing he wanted to think about at that moment was fighting. They had been given their first free day, and his mind was already racing with ways they could spend it. They took the eastern gate out of the garrison and went back the same way they had come earlier.

Zynora wasn't in the common room when they arrived like she normally was, but they did find Nel playing with Taylis and Marissa. She told them that Zynora was in her room and pointed them in the right direction. Ty had seen Breen's, Narendi's, and Kraea's, but none of the others. They headed up to the next floor and down the left side corridor, stopping at the second room on the left.

Breen knocked, since Ty couldn't, and they waited.

"Coming," Tameel called from the other side of the door. A moment later, the handle turned, and the door opened.

Ty looked beyond the old tinker and into the room. It wasn't at all what he expected.

The room was tiny with wood slate walls, floor, and roof. There was a small potbelly stove in the corner and two cots on either side with shelves above each. Zynora sat at a small table with two chairs on the opposite side from the stove, sipping on a cup of what smelled like mint tea.

"Welcome to Ol' Lerra," Tameel said, "or as close to the old wagon as we could think up, I guess."

Ty turned and looked at the others. "Uh, I don't think we're going to all fit inside."

"We'll wait for you downstairs," Breen said, eyeing the tinker wagon curiously.

They left, and Ty stepped inside. The room jostled from side to side as his weight offset the bed of the wagon. It was so realistic. There was even a set of windows at the front. He wondered briefly, if he opened them, would he see the driver's seat?

"What can we do for you, young man?" Zynora asked, blowing on her tea. "Or do you prefer Fae? Young Fae?" She smiled. "Never thought I'd find myself asking someone if they preferred to be called a man or not. If you would have told me a year ago that I'd be lathering a faerie's backside every night, I would have laughed in your face." Her brows lowered curiously. "You have finished rather earlier today, haven't you?"

"Ayrion said he was giving us the day off to rest."

She pursed her lips. "Doesn't sound like him. But he's had a lot weighing on his mind these days." She looked at Ty's hand, which he was still cradling, and motioned him over to the cot on the right side of the wagon. "Come, let's see to that wound."

He walked over and took a seat on the edge so as not to completely rumple the covers on top, then held out his hand.

"Ooo. Yes, that's a bad one," she said.

Tameel grabbed a jar of Isha's cream from the second shelf and plopped down in the seat on the other side of the table.

Ty placed his hand on Zynora's lap carefully as she scooped up a small bit of the white balm from the jar. She rubbed it gently around the injured knuckles until everything was covered, then closed her eyes and whispered her prayer. Ty could feel the cream and whatever magic she was infusing into him take effect.

He knew it wouldn't heal everything on the spot, but it would certainly give it a good start. He could already feel the throbbing beginning to ease.

"Best you don't use that hand today so it will be ready tomorrow."

Ty nodded as he stood. "Thank you." He started for the door.

"I suggest you take Ayrion up on his offer and get some rest," Zynora said.

Ty stopped at the door and turned with a smile. "I will."

Tameel pulled the unlit pipe from his mouth and chuckled. "Who do you think you're fooling, boy? You're as likely to go climbing into bed as I am to take on one of those flaming bulradoer."

Ty grinned and then walked out. He found the others in the common room downstairs, standing in front of one of the large fireplaces. Taylis and Marissa were playing some form of hide-and-seek while Nel read on the sofa.

"We've got the whole day," Ty said excitedly, flexing his fingers so the others could see they were at least partly back to full use. "Where do you want to go?"

Breen looked up and smiled. "I've got an idea."

Chapter 7 | Ty

TY FOLLOWED BREEN OUT of the dormitory by way of the main gate and then across the bridge to the white rotunda on the other side. The rotunda was a building they passed every time they took the southern route to the garrison. The circular tower was several stories tall and boasted a soft blue dome that blended so well with a clear sky it almost seemed invisible. From a distance, the building reminded Ty of a layered cake with white and gold frosting.

Each level of the building was surrounded by a row of evenly spaced windows; however, only the upper-floor windows had glass. Those on the main floor were nothing more than window-shaped indentations in the wall. Each indention housed a different animal that had been cut to perfection from the same stone as the building, but unlike the building, the animals had been so meticulously painted that they almost looked real.

Ty was rather partial to the black-winged falcon whose resting place faced the dormitory. The detail in its feathers was incredible: white highlights in its dark wings, the black spots and stripes on its underbelly, even the different shades of yellow around its beak, eyes, and feet. Its wings and tail were extended, and its short, curved beak was stretched wide, as if in the middle of a hunting cry. The longer Ty looked, the more he thought he could see the bird's eyes move.

The rotunda had four entrances, one on each cardinal face of the building. Unfortunately, all the doors leading in were locked, and with no glass in the windows on the first floor, they had no idea what was inside. Each entry connected to a walkway wide enough that perhaps a single cart could move down the center without running over those walking at the sides. The walkways led to other buildings or bridges or clusters of buildings. It was one of the few places they had explored since their arrival—what little they could from the outside—mainly because it was the closest to the dorms, and they hadn't found much time to do any sightseeing farther out.

They normally took the walkway around to the southern door of the rotunda, which crossed another waterway and then headed south toward the city's main gate. This time, however, Breen took them to the road on the eastern side that led to a peninsula with two bridges and the convergence of two streams, one of which ran directly in front of the dorms.

The bridge on the left crossed over to a small island with a mill, but Breen took the bridge that led straight ahead and into the lower third of the city.

"Where are we going?" Ty asked.

"I found this place a couple of nights ago."

"You've been out exploring without me?"

Kraea cleared her throat.

"Without *us*," Ty amended.

"I'm here too," Narendi said.

Breen sighed. "I couldn't sleep."

They reached the end of the bridge and started for the side of one of the largest of Aero'set's buildings. It wasn't quite as large as the dormitories, but certainly more so than anything else Ty had seen so far, at least in circumference. It was shaped like an amphitheater.

They had passed by the front of it almost every day on their way south to the main gate, but so far, they hadn't found the time to stop and take a closer look. At least, *Ty* hadn't been able to yet. Apparently, his brother had been out gallivanting through the city without him.

A wide covered portico surrounded the lower levels of the amphitheater, so those waiting to get inside didn't have to do so in the weather. There were numerous open archways leading to the covered walkway from the outside, and Breen took the closest. They didn't have to walk far before he directed them through a doorway that took them through a short corridor and into the seating area of a large arena.

"Wow!" Ty stepped out of the corridor, stopping on the landing. "It's even bigger on the inside."

The stairs led down to the edge of the arena, while other stairs behind them led up to even higher seating. The center of the complex had been dug out, which placed the stadium floor another twenty or thirty feet below the lowest row of seats.

A glance behind him told Ty they were only about halfway up the gallery. "How many people do you think this place holds? And what do you think they used it for?"

"Competitions would be my guess," Breen said.

"Between wizards?" Ty asked. "I can't imagine what those must have been like."

Breen shrugged. "We'll have to ask Nyalis when we see him next."

The floor of the arena below looked to be covered in sand, but something about it didn't seem right, though Ty couldn't put his finger on why.

"Where's the snow?" Narendi asked.

Ty's head shot up. *That's it!* There was no snow. He tilted his head to see grey winter clouds passing over the arena's open-air roof, but unlike the rest of Aero'set, the stadium was completely dry, no snow or even slush in sight.

"Must have one of those invisible barriers," Kraea said, looking up through the top of the arena.

"I think you're right," Ty said.

"Right about what?" Narendi asked.

"Kraea thinks there might be one of those invisible protection spells over the arena."

They all looked up.

"Could be," Breen said. He stared upward a moment, then walked over to the nearest bench and ran his hand across the stone. He looked at his fingers.

"Surprisingly clean. You would think that after a thousand years, this place would have at least gathered some dust."

Ty looked back up at what he thought was an invisible ceiling. "Let's find out." He raised his hand and drew on his magic, feeling the warmth tingling up his arm just as his hand ignited in blue flame. He could sense Kraea's excitement through their link. She was always very keen on him using his fire; she almost seemed drawn to it. He raised his hand and sent a ball of fire racing into the air. It rose up over the seating and out toward the center of the stadium and continued to rise above what looked like the top of the arena. "Maybe we were—"

The fireball hit something and vanished, immediately extinguished.

"Huh. I guess you were right," Ty said to Kraea.

She grunted, letting him know how foolish she thought he was for having ever doubted.

"There must have been great battles that took place down there," Narendi said, staring down at the arena floor.

Ty looked down as well. "I doubt they were doing battle."

"Then what is this competition you speak of, if not to test one's skill with the spear?"

"I'm sure there was more to the wizard games than fighting," Breen said, then pursed his lips. "At least, I would hope so."

Ty shrugged. "I say we keep looking."

Breen turned for the exit. "Where to next?"

"I don't know," Ty said, following his brother back through the enclosed corridor and out into the open-sided portico that surrounded the enclave. "Have you explored any other parts of Aero'set without us?"

Breen sighed. "No. This was as far as I got."

Ty looked to the right where they had entered, but not wanting to retrace their steps, he headed left instead. "I say we keep going."

He continued around the outside of the arena until they reached the main entrance, an enormous archway with a wide set of stairs that led down to the road they took almost every morning on the way to the garrison.

Ty didn't take the stairs down, however. Instead he continued around to the other side of the arena, stopping at an opening about three or four doors down from the main entrance that let him get a better look around. The eastern side of the arena had been built into one of the lower cliff faces, and directly above that, resting firmly on top of the cliff, was a building shaped similarly to the main dining hall just north of the dorms. The main difference was that this building's roof was made entirely of glass and had a large tower connected to it at the back that held one of the skybridges Ty and Breen had been anxious to see.

Ty pointed to the top of the cliff. "There. Let's go see what that is."

Narendi frowned at the prospect of once again being forced to such heights.

Breen pointed to a staircase that led up the mountainside, but it was one they couldn't reach from the arena. "Looks like we'll have to head back down to the main road and take it around and up."

Narendi groaned. "I say we look at one of those buildings down there." She pointed to a single rotunda at the base of the arena stairs.

"We can look at that on the way back to the dorm," Ty said and headed back to the arena's front entrance.

Narendi huffed but chased after him.

They exited from the main entrance and walked down the wide staircase to the southern road, which led to one of the city's main crossings. The road to the right passed through the main gates of Aero'set. The smaller road on the left headed to the bottom of the cliff face and the stairs leading up to their destination.

Ty took the left street, passing under a set of twin towers that were connected by another sky bridge before they finally reached the first of the stairs. It was a very long and very arduous trek up, and by the time they reached the top, Ty was more than winded. It wasn't nearly as high up as Nyalis had taken them when they had gone to see the Meeisredon and the Pentarium, but from this vantage point, he could see most of the school. Again, he was struck by the size of the place.

"It's higher than I thought," Breen said, looking out over the water-filled landscape. "Impressive."

Ty could see the entire city all the way to the garrison. It appeared that the majority of the school's buildings lay to the north, many built right into the side of the mountains, spaced perfectly between the falls coming down from the peaks above. To the south, there was the small village that was nestled into the lower woodlands. The structures looked out of place with their common stone and cedar siding, wood shingles, and thatched roofs, but they would have looked right at home in Easthaven.

Narendi remained several feet back from the edge, even though it had a waist-high stone wall, just close enough to see over. Kraea's claws clicked on the pavers as she made her way around to the front of the enormous building behind them. She could see over the short wall, but Ty could sense that doing so forced her to crane herself at an angle she found uncomfortable, and she wasn't interested enough to keep looking.

"This one's open."

Ty heard a hinge squeak and turned. "Wait, Kraea, don't go in there." He ran around to the front and found he was too late, her tail whipping out of sight as she slipped through one of the doors. *"You heard Nyalis. He said we can't open any doors without his permission."*

"What is it?" Narendi asked, joining him at the front with Breen following just behind.

Ty pointed at the slight opening in the door. "Kraea went inside." He walked over to the front and peered in. He couldn't see much, as the door was only cracked wide enough for Kraea to slip between. He whispered through the opening, his voice echoing inside the open hall. "Kraea, we can't go in there. Nyalis said—"

"Nyalis said you couldn't open any more doors without his permission," she said through their link. *"And I didn't. The door was already open."*

Ty looked at the others. "Well, she's got a point."

They both looked at him funny, and he blew out his lips. He had once again forgotten they couldn't hear her and was forced to repeat what she had said.

Breen pinched his chin. "I don't know about this."

Ty thought it over and then slipped through the doors himself before Breen could stop him.

Inside the building was a single open room even larger than the main dining hall, with white stone and long windows on either side, though most of the natural light came from the enormous glass ceiling. Ty stared up in awe, wondering how something like this had been created.

The room was at least three stories tall and filled with shelves that stretched all the way to the ceiling. Walkways spanned the spaces between at various levels, and each level had a full balcony with at least two ladders connected to metal rails that ran the full length of the shelves. Tables and chairs and places to read and study were tucked all around.

"Are those all books?" Breen's voice echoed off the stacks as he and Narendi cautiously made their way to where Ty was standing. "How can there be so many? I thought BookBees was incredibly well stocked. Master Townsend would dance the high step if he saw this."

"Forget Townsend," Ty said, still gawking up at the innumerable number of books. "Imagine what Adarra would do."

"Probably faint," Breen said.

Narendi lowered her spear. "There are more records here than what a hundred Wazeri could ever devise in a hundred lifetimes."

Ty and Breen had seen the Imbatoo's histories. All the books and scrolls that the Wazeri had written and collected over her people's long heritage probably wouldn't have filled the bottom row of just one of these shelves. It was truly one of the most incredible sights Ty had ever seen, even more than the glass ceiling, which Narendi was presently gawking at.

"Come, look at this."

Ty could hear Kraea clicking across the dark marble floors somewhere ahead. "Don't run off without us," Ty called out, not having to speak too loudly since his voice carried rather efficiently throughout the massive library. He made it halfway down the first row of shelves before the echo of his words finally faded.

"What is she doing?" Breen asked as he and Narendi followed Ty through the towering stacks of books toward the other side of the room.

"She wants us to see something."

"What?" Narendi asked, her spear still in hand.

"No idea."

They reached the other side and found an enormous stone archway leading into the grand tower Ty had seen from the outside. The columns on either side of the arch were covered in green vines that wound up and around the full length of the opening. Tiny violet flowers poked through the greenery, creating a vibrant contrast to the white stone underneath. As beautiful as the archway and flowers were, they didn't hold a candle to the tower itself, or more importantly, what was in it.

The tower rose at least twice as high as the hall behind them, nearly every inch filled with inlaid cases of books. It had to be at least ten stories high. Ty craned his neck to see the top. From what he could tell from standing on this side of the archway, the dome of the tower was also made of glass. Light spilled down across the books on the left side. Stairs encircled the tower, leading from one floor to the next, all the way to the top.

Even more incredible, each level had its own water feature: a fountain that poured out of the mouth of a large sculpted creature mounted just under the balcony of the floor above it. The water fell into a trough that ran along the inner perimeter of each level, which fed the next sculpted fountain below. Ty wondered idly where the water went once it reached the bottom.

"Why can't we hear it?" Narendi asked.

Ty pursed his lips, realizing she was right. The fountains were silent. They all stared at the water for a moment, listening intently but hearing nothing.

"I say we take a look," Breen said. "Besides, that sky bridge has to be up there somewhere." Before Ty could respond, Breen stepped inside. He suddenly spun back around with a wide grin on his face. His mouth started moving, but nothing came out.

Ty looked at Narendi. She looked as confused as he did.

"What is he doing?" Kraea asked. *"He looks ridiculous."*

"I don't know." Ty stepped through the archway, and the sound of water hit him, and he froze. He turned and waved Narendi and Kraea through.

"Why didn't you answer me?" Breen asked.

"We couldn't hear you," Ty said. "We could see your mouth moving, but there was nothing coming out." He turned and raised his hand out toward the center of the arch, but he didn't feel anything. He then closed his eyes and released a small web of his magic, letting it lie across the opening. There was something there. "It's faint, but I can sense magic."

"It must be one of those sound spells," Breen said, "like the one Mangora used before performing the Sola de Blanava on the bloodstone."

Ty shivered at the memory. He took a step back through the arch, and suddenly the sound of the falling water ceased. He stepped back through, and it returned. He smiled. "I bet it's used to keep from disturbing those out in the stacks." The outer perimeter of the shelves in the main building was filled with tables and chairs and places for those inside to read and study. Ty looked up at the glass dome above. "Let's go up."

Narendi frowned. "Must we?" She stared up with a nervous gulp.

"I guess you can stay down here if you like," Ty offered.

"I think that's wise," she said, turning to scan the room. "I can keep watch down here." She moved out to the center of the tower and started to sit, but then caught herself. "What's that?"

Ty turned. She was pointing to an empty spot in the inlaid shelves that divided the trough of water on the first floor, directly across from the foot of the stairs. It looked like an open doorway between the inset shelves of books. He started for it, just ahead of Narendi, but soon realized it wasn't an open door at all but a mirror reflecting the books in the room they were already in. The mirror looked familiar.

"It can't be." His heart leaped as he spotted the runes surrounding the ancient wooden frame.

"Is that—"

"Yes," Ty said, before his brother could finish. "It's one of the traveling mirrors. Nyalis said the Mirrors of Maon had been created in Aero'set. I guess it's no coincidence we would see one here."

"Where does it go?" Narendi asked, carefully touching the edge of the ancient frame.

"I have no idea."

"Can you read the names?" Breen asked.

Ty's hand automatically reached for his pocket, but the little pouch with the silver compass wasn't there. He'd turned it over to Nyalis, along with the key, the first day they'd set foot in Aero'set. Ty shook his head. "I can't read it, not without the compass. And even then, I doubt I'd be able to. Remember, the compass only showed us the names of the mirrors that would direct us to the next missing part of the key. When we were up in the great tree at the Live

Market, the compass didn't show me the names on any of the other mirrors, only the one we needed to take us to Wellhollow."

"The Live Market? We can go there?"

Ty turned as Kraea slid over beside them to get a look at the tall piece of glass. "I'm afraid not."

"But we could look for my mother?"

"What is she asking?" Breen asked.

"Kraea wants us to use the mirror to go back to the Live Market and look for her mother." He turned to Kraea. "Even if she somehow survived that fall, she wouldn't still be there. It's been weeks. She would have tried getting as far away from that place as possible. Besides, I can't read the name of this mirror. And even if I could, I'm not sure I could even remember the name of the mirror in the Riverlands."

"Shuta Ningiwa."

Ty looked at her. "You remember the mirror's name?"

"Of course. How else would I get back to her?"

Ty could feel Kraea's frustration, which covered an even stronger sadness, but he didn't know how to help her. Maybe he could speak with Nyalis about it the next time he saw the wizard. Of course, he had so many, many things to ask Nyalis that a request to go back to the Riverlands would probably get lost in the pile.

Breen looked back toward the staircase on the other side. "How about we go take a look at that skybridge?"

Ty turned and followed him over to the start of the stairs. Kraea came as well. Narendi, however, took her seat on the floor at the center of the tower so she could see everything at once. She made sure to keep her eye on the mirror, seeming to not want to turn her back on it.

Ty, Breen, and Kraea headed up the stairs, stopping on the first landing and the balcony that wrapped around the second floor. Instead of heading up the next flight of stairs, Ty followed Breen over to one of the falls of water pouring down from the sculpted creature's head above. Depending on which angle he looked at the statue, Ty could see similarities to Kraea. He turned and looked at her.

"If you say it looks like me, I'll bite you," she said.

Ty kept his mouth shut.

"You know," Breen said, stopping to stare at the water as it poured into the trough at the bottom of the inlaid shelves. "This seems like a really stupid thing to put in a library. What's to keep it from damaging the books? I'm surprised half these tomes aren't filled with mold." He grabbed a book from off the bottom shelf, closest to the water, and opened it.

Ty glanced over his brother's arm. The book looked surprisingly dry. Not a touch of moisture anywhere. Ty grabbed one of his own to examine. Just like the other, the book was quite dry, the pages still loose and pliable, not stiff and brittle or wet and soggy as one would expect. The title read: *The Rise of the Horned Tower and the Fall of Sindoratti*. He placed the book back on the shelf and moved around to the other side of Breen where the water was pouring down from above.

He stuck his hand into the fall, half expecting it to be just an illusion, but instead he found it every bit as wet and cold as it should be. "Huh. I thought it might be a glamour."

Breen stuck his hand in also. Kraea stuck her neck out and lapped at it with her tongue. After a couple of tries, she gave up.

"Doesn't work," she said.

Ty looked at her. "What doesn't work?"

"The water is no good."

"What do you mean?" Ty cupped his hand to try some, but as soon as he removed his hand from the falls, the water disappeared. "That's strange." He stuck his hand in once more and tried again, only to find that once again, there was no water in his hand.

Breen tried as well. "Maybe it *is* a glamour." He leaned down and attempted to scoop it out of the trough only to get the same result. "Guess we know why the books don't seem to be harmed."

Ty took a step back and smiled as he admired the ingenuity of the falls, then turned and leaned out over the railing to call down to Narendi. "You need to try the water. It's delicious." He winked at Breen, and they started up the stairs to the next landing, Kraea right beside them.

Ty stopped once more to quickly stick his hand in the trough to see if it was the same on the second level, and sure enough, it came away dry. He didn't stop again except to take a quick look down with each new floor that they reached.

"There's something wrong with the water," Narendi called up as they reached the next landing.

Ty looked over the railing. "We found it quite refreshing. Maybe you should try the water on the second floor."

They climbed all the way to the ninth floor before Ty stopped again, this time more to catch his breath and rest his legs than to take another look over the side, though he did do that as well. He didn't see Narendi. He wondered if she had attempted the stairs leading up to the water on the second-floor balcony or not. Looking down, it seemed a greater distance than it had from the ground looking up.

"Only one more floor to go," Breen said, pointing to the next set of stairs. "I see a door up there."

Ty nodded, and they headed up the final set, reaching the top to find that there were no books on this level. The only thing above them was the glass dome. The clouds had thinned just enough for the sun to punch a few of its rays through the glass. Ty was surprised by how much warmer it was at the top.

I like it up here, Kraea stated and slowly stretched out on the floor inside the sun's rays.

Ty ignored her and followed Breen over to the door and tried the handle. He didn't think this would count so much toward not opening a door since they were already inside. He twisted the handle and was yanked forward as a strong gust of wind nearly ripped it out of his hand. Ty's hair would have been all over the place if he hadn't been wearing his winter cap.

The initial gust died down, and they stared out at a long bridge that connected the tower to a building that had been partially carved out of the mountain behind them.

Breen looked at Ty with a grin a mile wide and started through. He'd barely stuck his foot outside when Narendi's panicked scream filled the tower behind them.

"Ty!"

Chapter 8 | Ty

TY SPUN AND RAN FOR the balcony, Kraea just ahead of him. He heard the door behind him slam shut, and his brother reached the railing almost before he did. The sound of steel and wood filled the tower as they looked over the side. They were too high up to see Narendi clearly, but they could tell she was fighting for her life.

"We're coming!" Ty shouted as he ran for the stairs. "Hold on!"

His brother reached the steps before him, and they both bolted down, hopping two or three at a time as they raced to the bottom. Breen's legs were longer and stronger, and he pulled ahead of Ty.

"Kraea, go help her!" Ty shouted as he bounded down the steps as fast as his legs would take him. Who could possibly be down there?

Kraea was much faster than either Ty or Breen, and she barreled down the stairwell in front of them, sprinting from one landing to the next as she circled toward the bottom. Ty could hear her claws digging into the stone as she began to pull away from them. As Ty reached the third landing from the bottom, he heard the draakar roar, and he could taste blood through their link as she sank her teeth into whatever was down there.

"Hurry!" she shouted back up at him.

Ty reached the second-floor balcony and spared a quick glance over the side as he ran for the final set of stairs. The bottom of the tower was filling with what looked like . . . children. Wild, angry, well-armed children climbed over each other to reach Narendi and Kraea, who were fighting to hold them back, being forced partway up the first flight of stairs as they did. A small group broke off and started for the archway leading from the tower into the main building. Ty panicked. If they got outside the library and into the city itself, Ty doubted the others could ever stop them.

Where were they coming from? The only thing down there was . . . the mirror. Had Narendi somehow opened it? He discarded the notion, deciding it was more important to figure out a way to shut it off. He turned to Breen. "Go help the girls!" He shoved his brother forward and then turned to the open arch and raised his hands. He drew the wind, readying a fist of air to fling into the fighters.

The open doorway into the main part of the library was directly across from where Ty stood on the second floor, which meant he couldn't use the air or he'd risk flinging them into the main part of the library himself. Instead, he formed a shield in front of the arch and fused it to the stone. He hadn't had much practice other than the trip down the mountain with Nyalis, but he did what he could, forming a barrier that they hopefully couldn't get through or over.

The air shield hardened just as the children reached the entrance. They hit the invisible barrier and bounced off. Immediately, they began beating on it with their spears and clubs and short swords. Ty felt a swift flash of relief. His magical glue had held.

Once he was sure it would hold them in, he turned back to the fight. The bottom of the tower was filling with enemy combatants. They had to be coming from the mirror. But how was he going to shut it off? He leaned over the rail and sent a fist of air down into the middle, and a pile of small forms flew across the room. It was all he could think to do. He didn't exactly want to send fire down and kill a bunch of children. He also didn't want to risk open flames inside the library.

He shot another volley down into the mass of bodies trying to reach the stairs, which scooped out another swath, sending them cartwheeling across the room. Some didn't get back up as quickly this time. He sent another wave, then another, but there were so many by now that he couldn't keep up.

Breen and Narendi were swinging weapons as fast as they could. Kraea, beside them, was bashing kids with her tail and snapping them up in her jaws if they got too close. Ty tried not to let her thrill of the hunt get to him as he raced down to help. He didn't like the idea of killing children, but when children were about to kill you, survival instincts kicked in.

"Get down!" he roared, and as soon as they dropped to the steps, he hit the front of the enemy ranks with a wide blast of hardened air, which succeeded in clearing the stairs all the way to the bottom. A few of those close enough to Narendi and Breen managed to get spared the hit, and they immediately jumped on them. One of them sank his teeth into Narendi's arm, and she screamed, then headbutted him and kicked him back down the steps.

Breen snatched two of them off their feet and threw them over the railing.

Drawing his sword, Ty bounded down the rest of the way, finally close enough to realize that they weren't children after all. They were grown men— very, very short, deadly men. Were they fighting pygmies?

Ty raised his arm to gather another fist of air, and something hit him in the shoulder. He felt like he'd been kicked by Waddle and was suddenly flung back against the wall. Pain flooded through him, and as soon as he managed to catch his breath, he screamed. An arrow was sticking out of his left shoulder. His mind raced. Everything was happening too fast. Why was there an arrow sticking from his shoulder?

He looked up just in time to see a sword swinging for his neck. His good arm shot up before he had time to think, and he deflected the pygmy's blade with his own, ignoring the injury from earlier that day. Its pain was hardly worth considering compared to his shoulder. He twisted, anticipating the next blow, and then slashed the man's throat. Warm blood splashed across Ty's face, and the little man slumped to the floor.

Ty stared in horror. It was the first time he'd ever killed a man in such close proximity. Ayrion would have been proud. Ty had defended himself and neatly dispatched his foe. However, all Ty wanted to do was retch. Defending himself, and killing, with magic granted precious distance from those it harmed. Taking a life with a blade in his own hand somehow felt more real.

Ty looked up to see that the pygmies had managed to scale the wall of books and were crawling over the railing on the second floor, boxing them in. If he didn't do something, they would all surely die. He turned, ignoring the pain shooting through his arm and chest, and hit the entire lot with a wall of air. Desperation fueled his anger, which stoked his magic to burn hotter. He wanted to unleash his flames. He could feel Kraea's desire for him to do so through their link, but he held back. Not here. Not with all these priceless books and the mirror.

Ty spun at an enraged cry from Narendi. The mass of pygmies had managed to rip her spear from her hands, and she was now cutting them back with her swords. She moved faster than Ty had ever seen her move, every motion fluid and deliberate. If the brutal training sessions with Ayrion had taught him anything, it was just how much work went into fighting well and what a decent swordsman looked like. Narendi was incredible, every bit as skilled as Lyessa.

Breen took a knife to the arm, and in response punched the little man responsible so hard in the face that Ty winced. His brother stumbled up the steps, and Ty ran down to get him, his own fear and anger blunting the pain of the arrow in his shoulder. He unleashed another barrage of hardened air into the growing numbers coming up the steps, giving the other three a chance to regain their footing.

The respite didn't last long, as the bottom floor was now swimming in pygmy warriors rushing toward them like waves about to break over rocks, and they were the rocks.

"We need to shut off that mirror!" Narendi shouted.

"No!" Breen said. "We need to go higher! If we can get to the door at the top, maybe Ty can seal them in."

Ty tried to decide which they should do—or could do, for that matter.

"*Behind you!*" Kraea yelled.

Ty spun to find another group of pygmies rushing down the stairs at them. They must have climbed over the railing once more while his back was turned. He hit the first couple rows with another fist of air and sent them flying backward, some over the side of the rail, but more were climbing up right behind them. There had to be something else he could do. Turning, he reached for the closest thing he could find—the water in the troughs. He'd battled a cave monster with water. He could do it again. Sending his magic up and out, he connected with all the water within the tower at once, and with a shout, he pulled it to him.

Nothing happened.

"Curse this flaming magic!" He swept his sword up to block the first of the next wave, his arm moving by reflex. He tried to think about the lessons he'd been taught, the routines Ayrion had put them through—stance, block, move, eyes open.

Hang it!

He just needed to keep swinging as fast as he could. He dropped the first attacker, his sword going straight out the man's back. He'd barely pulled it free before the second was on him.

Ty fought to keep the pygmy's blade away from him long enough to gather more air. He hit the next three with a fist and squashed them against the wall.

Kraea howled behind him as one of the archers hit her from the other side of the tower. A shaft was sticking out of her back, but thanks to her thick scales, it didn't penetrate far. Ty could sense the arrow was more of an annoyance than an actual injury.

He quickly raised a shield as more arrows flew their way. "Get behind me!" he shouted, holding the shield in place as another barrage flew across the room. Narendi and Breen rushed past him and up the stairs to meet the next wave of those climbing over. Ty was forced to retreat up the stairs himself, Kraea fighting beside him to keep the closest of the pygmies back.

More poured over the railing on the second landing, preventing Ty and the others from escaping up the stairs. They were surrounded. Ty continued swinging his sword, holding his shield as best he could as the pain of the arrow through his shoulder threatened to break through his defenses. He set his jaw. As long as one hand was taken with the shield and the other his sword, he didn't have a way to use his fists of air. But if he dropped his sword to form one, the pygmies would overrun him before he had time to gather enough wind to be effective.

Above him, Breen was barely holding off three on the right side while

Narendi did the same a few steps higher. Blood soaked his brother's left arm where he'd been slashed.

Ty blocked another barrage of arrows with his shield, then swung low with his sword to stop an attempt at his legs. He twisted too far, and his swing created an opening for a second assailant, whose spear grazed his leg. He screamed and nearly went down but managed to wedge his shield against the steps to keep from tipping over completely. Ayrion's voice in the back of his mind berated him for not paying closer attention to their training.

Kraea roared and spun, hitting the men in front of Ty with her tail, flinging them back over the railing.

Breen gave an enraged shout, and Ty turned to see that two pygmies had managed to grab his arms and were restraining him enough for a third to close with a sword.

"No!" Ty shouted, and dropped his sword long enough to grab a fistful of air and hurl it up the steps at the pygmies, but he wasn't fast enough. The short man thrust his sword through Breen's side, and Breen dropped with a loud cry. Ty's fist of air knocked the men back far enough for Narendi to scramble down to Breen's aid and finish them off.

Ty turned, realizing just how desperate their situation was. There was no escape. They were cut off from help. If they were going to get out of this mess, they would have to do it themselves. That desperation ignited something inside of Ty, his magic burning to the surface. He spun and hit the pygmies behind him and those above with another wall of air, giving him just enough room to limp his way up to his brother. Kraea was there beside him, slapping men off the steps with her tail and plunging her claws and teeth into as many as she could reach.

Ty raised his shield and stopped another volley, then sent a fist of air into the archers, scattering them and their bows in the process. His anger seethed to the surface, his magic boiling in its wake. He felt stronger than before. A disconnected part of his mind wondered idly if it had anything to do with being this close to the Pentarium. He decided to try something desperate, one last attempt before he called on his fire and sent the tower and its books to the Pit.

"Get behind me!" he shouted, and drove his magic up through the center of the tower. He gathered all the air he could from inside the building, then reached for what was outside. He could feel it all, and he called to it. *Come to me!*

He'd never attempted anything like this before. He had no idea if it would work—or if he was about to kill them all.

There was a loud crack from above, and the tower's glass dome overhead shattered into a thousand pieces as Ty pulled all the air within his grasp straight down through the tower's throat. Books swirled in a vortex, ripped off their shelves in the wake of his magic. At the last second, he raised a shield and leaped back toward the others, covering them as he drove the glass and wind straight into the pygmies below. The tower shook with the force of the hit.

Everything went silent.

After a few moments, Ty finally lowered his shield. What awaited was one of the most horrific sights he had ever witnessed. The last time he'd seen this kind of death had been during their battle with the arachnobe army, and that didn't even begin to compare. The first and second floors were covered in blood and worse. Pieces of bodies lay everywhere. Then the smell hit him, strong enough to taste—a coppery scent of blood and the stench of entrails.

Ty's stomach churned. Breen lay propped up against the water trough, pressing his wadded-up tunic over the stab wound in his side. He looked like he was about to empty his guts. Narendi actually did, and Kraea barely hopped out of the way in time. Narendi wiped her mouth, then turned to Ty. There was fear in her eyes.

Kraea seemed giddy at the sight of so much carnage, but even she seemed to hesitate when looking his way. Ty could feel it through their link. It didn't exactly feel like fear, more like concern.

Ty's head spun. It was too much to take in. He'd just saved their lives, but he hated how he'd done it. It wasn't like they'd had many options. Why were they looking at him like he might do something worse?

The soft scrape of feet caught his attention, and Ty dragged himself over to the railing and looked at the massacre below.

There were survivors, though he didn't know how. Perhaps they'd been under the staircase when the glass and wind had struck. However they had managed to escape, they didn't appear to be interested in fighting anymore. He could hear cries of fear and pain and rage as the pygmies that were still alive stumbled toward the mirror.

The small band reached the glass and started through to what Ty could only guess was some sort of jungle. Without warning, a blinding flash of lightning shot through the mirror, and the few survivors were consumed.

Ty screamed, and time seemed to slow as he fought to raise another shield. The lightning bounced from the mirror and struck the railing in front of him just as his shield snapped into place. The impact sent him flying backward into the others, and he landed on top of Breen. Breen grabbed his side and moaned in pain.

"What in the fires of Aran'gal happened here?" roared a voice from below.

Ty's head lifted. "Nyalis?"

"Ty? Is that you?"

"Yes! We're up here."

Nyalis's staff clicked sharply on the marble below, and then on the stone steps as the wizard rushed up to them. He frowned as he was forced to pick his way through the dead to reach them.

"Why is it I can't turn my back around here before the four of you have gone and stuck yourselves in the fire again?"

"You act like it's on purpose," Ty said.

Nyalis inspected the arrow sticking out of Ty's shoulder and cocked one of his bushy brows. "Sometimes I truly wonder how you've managed to survive this long. Watching out for you has become a full-time endeavor."

"Don't worry about me," Ty said, trying to push Nyalis off. "Breen's been stabbed."

The wizard looked up sharply and moved over to Breen. After examining the wound, he helped Breen lie down and placed a hand over the injury. His hand glowed with a soft golden light, and Breen relaxed as the magic flowed into him. Once Nyalis had finished with Breen's side, he returned to Ty.

"Hold still. This is going to hurt." Nyalis grabbed the arrowhead from behind and muttered something Ty didn't understand. As soon as he did, the shaft snapped in two near the exit of the wound. Nyalis then moved around front and grabbed the remaining part of the arrow by the fletching. "You ready?"

Ty gritted his teeth. "Just do it."

Nyalis yanked the arrow free, and Ty cried out. Just as things were starting to spin, Nyalis's hand began to glow once more, and he placed it under Ty's shirt and on the wound. An icy chill poured through the hole, filling his shoulder with a soothing coolness. The pain lessened but hadn't vanished altogether before Nyalis moved on to examine the wound on his leg. When he was done, Ty's leg ached far less than it had before, but it still throbbed. Nyalis then returned to Breen.

Ty pulled his shirt away far enough to see the flesh of his shoulder was mended, but he could still feel some pain when he moved his arm. "I wish Fraya were here," he moaned.

"You and me both," Breen said, his teeth clenched tight. Breen's beloved was incredibly gifted when it came to healing. When Fraya used her abilities, it was like the injury never happened. There was no lingering pain afterward. Ty wondered if it was more difficult for Nyalis to perform healing because it wasn't a natural gift of his. At least, he didn't think it was. Ty had never thought to ask the wizard what type of wielder he was. He seemed to be able to do everything.

He opened his mouth—and then shut it. Now probably wasn't the best time to ask.

Nyalis spent a couple minutes on Narendi, who had sustained several smaller cuts and blows to her waist and on her back that would bruise terribly, then moved over to Kraea, who was busy trying to get her teeth around the arrow sticking from the scales on her back. Nyalis reached out with his magic and yanked the shaft out of its resting place without even touching it. Ty wasn't sure if he used wind or some other form of magic Ty knew nothing about.

Nyalis placed his hand over the scales where the arrow had been lodged, and once again his hand began to glow. A moment later, he removed his hand, and the injured scales were sealed.

"I'm going to sleep deep tonight after all of this." Nyalis sighed as he turned and shuffled over to the railing. He looked down at the gory sight below, then up at the shattered dome and shook his head. "Does someone want to tell me what happened here? I thought I was clear about you not opening doors without my presence."

Ty looked at Kraea, but she purposefully kept her head turned to keep from catching his eye.

"To be fair," Ty said, "we didn't exactly open the door. It was already cracked, and when we saw all the books, I figured, how dangerous could it be in a library?" He started to chuckle but stopped when he saw the others weren't smiling with him.

Nyalis's eyes narrowed as he looked down at the four of them. "Yes, I'm sure you were thinking the same thing when you decided to walk into the arboretum. You thought, hmm . . . how dangerous can a bunch of plants be?"

Ty stiffened at the reprimand. "What I want to know is how an army of bloodthirsty pygmies nearly managed to breach Aero'set. You might be upset about us being here, but if we hadn't been . . ." Ty pointed toward the arch and his quickly rigged blockade. ". . . they would have made it into the greater city, and then we'd have likely never gotten them out."

Nyalis turned and pursed his lips as he studied Ty's handiwork. "It seems my lessons haven't fallen on deaf ears after all." He looked up. "You want to explain what happened up there?"

Ty looked up. "I'm not quite sure what happened. We were about to be overrun, so I reached for as much of the wind as I could and pulled it down through the tower. I didn't mean to shatter the dome like I did. And I certainly wasn't expecting . . ." He looked out at all the dead and blanched.

"It was either you or them," Nyalis said. "As difficult as it might be, you will need to look beyond this. I'm afraid there will be far worse things ahead for you to face."

Ty's heart sank at those words. He had wanted justification for their actions—acknowledgment that they hadn't been defying Nyalis's instruction, but that was not the kind of consolation he had been hoping for.

Nyalis frowned at the large hole. "It's going to take me days to construct a new ceiling. That one held fast for over a millennium, but after a single day of coming in contact with you, it is lying in pieces all over the tower."

"Would you have preferred I used my fire?"

Nyalis's eyes widened. "You wouldn't have."

"I nearly had to. I tried the water first, but that crazy stuff can't be budged."

"Yes, it was spelled to keep from damaging the books," he said, glancing up and down the stairwell. "Though it seems you've done quite enough damage anyway." Nyalis looked at the four of them and eventually smiled. "Still, I am relieved you are well."

"Who were these people?" Narendi asked. "I have not seen their like before."

"No," Nyalis agreed, "you wouldn't have. They are the Gopee. They live in the southern jungles southwest of Cylmar, just on the other side of the Khezrian Wall. They are a very violent sect. Cannibalistic. They believe strongly in the power they can obtain when eating another's flesh, especially an enemy. They believe that eating their flesh will grant them all the strength and skill of that person."

"Sounds like the Tallosians," Ty said with a cringe, "the way they wear the scalps of their enemies because they believe they will acquire their skills if they do."

"I suppose," Nyalis said, also frowning at the thought.

"Why were they here?" Breen asked. "How did they get through the mirror?"

Nyalis lowered his head. "Yes, well . . . I might be partly to blame for that. Ever since Aero'set's return, I've been testing out mirrors across Aldor to see which ones are still viable. It just so happened that theirs was one of those still functioning. Unfortunately, this particular mirror was being used in some form of death ritual. The Gopee were claiming it as holy ground and had built a shrine around it. Apparently, my appearance only stirred the hornets' nest, and when they saw I had magic . . . well, you can imagine how hungry they got . . . literally. Before I knew it, I was being swarmed by at least half of the entire war party, who just happened to be performing said ritual before going to battle against another tribe."

"The other half must have found their way in here," Ty said.

Nyalis ran a hand down his long white beard. "Bad timing all around."

Ty had a hundred different questions he needed to ask, but the only one he could get out was: "Do any of these mirrors lead to Easthaven?"

Breen looked up, faint hope in his eyes.

Nyalis smiled sadly. "I'm afraid not."

Ty's shoulders sagged. "As wonderful as Aero'set is, and it is an incredible place, we'd like to go home. We need to let our family know that we're still alive. It's been months without any word. They probably believe us dead by now."

Breen nodded in silent agreement.

Ty looked at Narendi and had a thought. "Would this mirror be able to take us back to the mirror at the Khezrian Wall, or do they only connect with certain other mirrors? We could take Narendi home."

Narendi turned, excitement on her face, but it was quickly replaced with determination. "No. I will not go home. I stay with my husband."

Ty rolled his eyes but didn't argue. Instead, he waited for an answer from Nyalis.

"To the question of whether this mirror will take you to the one at the Khezrian Wall . . . the answer is yes. As long as you know the name of the mirror you are wanting to reach and the name of the mirror you are stepping through, then you can get there. But as for you leaving Aero'set, I do not advise that yet. You still need more training with Ayrion. And with him about to leave on a quest of his own, you need to spend as much time with him as you can before he is no longer available."

"Ayrion's going on a quest?" Ty asked, anxious to hear about where the sword master was going and why.

"Yes, but we can discuss that later. Right now, I think it's time we leave this tomb. My nostrils are already starting to burn."

Nyalis was right. The stench of death was overwhelming. Ty lowered his shield across the archway, and they stepped through. Once inside the main part of the library, Nyalis turned and raised a shield of his own to keep the smell contained to just the tower and then created a permanent funnel of air, which he attached to the bottom floor, that directed most of it up and out the now-open roof. Ty didn't get to see exactly how the wizard had made it, but he could tell it was a more complex weave than his simple shield.

"I'll have to put up a temporary ward across the top to keep the weather out," Nyalis said with a sad shake of his head before marching them all out of the library and shutting the door behind them.

"When will Ayrion be leaving?" Ty asked, partly because he was curious about the new quest, and partly because he wanted to know how soon they might be able to make their way home.

"Sooner than he realizes," was all Nyalis said as he walked them around the side of the library and started down the steps on the face of the cliff.

Ty followed close behind, anxious to get back to the dorms to find out more about this new expedition. Anything to take his mind off of what he'd just been forced to do. He shivered. He had a feeling he wouldn't be sleeping much the next few nights.

Chapter 9 | Ayrion

AYRION STARED OUT THE window of his second-floor bedroom inside the dormitory's north wing, which overlooked the central yard in front. The yard was covered in snow, decorated with a spiderweb of footprints. Most of the prints were restricted to the footpaths that crisscrossed at the fountain in the middle of the yard, but branching out from there was a myriad of smaller prints, no doubt created by Taylis and Marissa as they enjoyed being taken out to play during the day.

Without a regular routine for school, and not wanting to risk exploring any farther than the protective walls of the dormitory after what had happened to the half-faerie and his friends in the arboretum, the children spent most of their time divided between the common room and the snow-filled courtyard. Ayrion felt sorry for them. So much tragedy had befallen them over the last few months, from losing their family and friends to being dragged from one horrific battle to the next. It was a wonder they were still sane.

There were times that he questioned his own sanity. Especially now, with the return of his former memories. He lifted his hand and smiled at the raised flesh on his wrist in the shape of an X, a brand he had borne proudly to recognize his status as a reject, one of the unwanteds. His eyes teared as thoughts of Reevie and Sapphire, Bull and Tubby, Mouse, Petal, Squeaks, Muriel, and even Collen and Gustory the bard came flooding back. So many memories he had thought lost forever now fought for dominance against those he had more recently acquired.

He wondered how Master Fentin and Mistress Orilla were doing, whether they were still working their orphanage. It had been longer than he'd like to admit since he found the time to go by and visit. They wouldn't be able to keep a place like that running for much longer. They were getting along in years. They'd been old when he was a child running through the streets. Then again, his younger self would have thought Ayrion was old had he seen himself right now.

Ayrion felt aged, not just in body but in spirit. He was in his midthirties, but he didn't feel a day under fifty. This last year, especially, had really taken a toll.

He felt broken now that he had regained his memories. It was as though there were two people living inside him, both vying for the same body. They were the same, but different. They were both capable of fighting, both held that same sense of honor and duty, but Jair, or the new Ayrion, seemed a little more laid back. He tended to smile more, had even been known on occasion to crack a joke.

But with these new memories had come a mountain of anguish, pressing him to the point that even breathing became difficult at times. He was the Guardian Protector, and he now finally knew what that meant. Memories of that last battle outside of Belbridge plagued him, memories of Dakaran and Valtor's betrayal. He could see clearly King Rhydan's face covered in blood and dirt as he stared up at Ayrion in horror, realizing he'd been betrayed by his own flesh and blood.

Ayrion clenched his fist, his knuckles whitening with anger as he relived those last few moments before he had lost it all. The betrayal was no less deep for Ayrion now. He had spent his later years in the palace, and Dakaran was almost like a brother to him. Even though Ayrion knew Valtor's role in all of this was no small thing, Dakaran had still agreed to it.

Closing his eyes, he took a deep breath to slow the pounding of his heart, attempting to steer his thoughts elsewhere. One mercy was that he now knew he hadn't left a wife and children behind. It had been one of his greatest fears during the time of his lost memories.

Still, he had left someone very dear.

He pictured Amarysia. Remembered her beauty and kindness. He wondered what she must have gone through when she was told of his death. How she must have suffered. Worse was the thought of Dakaran using this as an opportunity to get what he had always desired: *her*.

Again, Ayrion squeezed his fists tight. His focus shifted, and he thought about Barthol. Had his friend survived the battle? He remembered kicking Barthol down the back side of the cliff just before Valtor's guards shot him with crossbows.

Barthol had been one of his closest allies since Ayrion was fifteen years old. He chuckled at the memory of the first time they'd been introduced, of Commander Tolin—or at that time, *Captain* Tolin—thinking to break Ayrion by sticking him in with the outcasts of Room Eleven. It was the most beneficial mistake Tolin had ever made, and the friendships born that day had lasted a lifetime. Ayrion smiled as he thought about that rowdy lot—Barthol's intimidating size, Gellar's thick red beard and three eyebrows, Fipple's topknot that he was always careful to keep hidden, Waylen's ferocious appetite and merriment, and of course Mjovic's missing hand, which led to those who loved him to call him Stumpy.

There were times Ayrion wished he could go back to those days. Things were simpler then, though his fifteen-year-old self would probably have disagreed.

Ayrion stared out the window at the snow drifting down across the lawn and wondered what his next move should be. He wanted nothing more than to pack his weapons and bags and ride for Aramoor, but Nyalis had other plans. Ayrion didn't know what those plans were, since the wizard was even less forthcoming than himself, but he was sure they would involve some form of unpleasantness, no doubt a very arduous task. It was most likely why the old wizard had yet to divulge what they were, for fear Ayrion would take off.

The world was shifting, and not in the right direction, which meant he needed to turn his focus to what mattered, and that was Aramoor. He couldn't let the White Tower take control of the capital. If that happened, Aldor would likely be lost. Word had spread, even to Belvin and Wellhollow, that Dakaran was now sitting on his father's throne, and that he had not only ordered the execution of Cylmar's overlord and his family, but had disbanded the kingdom altogether, swallowing it up as he expanded Elondria's borders.

How he had managed to do that without the Provincial Authority's consent, Ayrion didn't know. He wondered what the other overlords were going to do about it. Were they too scared of the Tower to stand up against the throne?

Ayrion's musings halted when he spotted movement at the south gate. It was the faeling and his friends . . . and Nyalis. He wondered where they had gotten off to. The sun was already beginning to set as the grey clouds darkened overhead. He had hoped his students would have taken him up on his suggestion of using the day off to catch up on some sleep.

He didn't like singling Ty out during their sessions, but the young man needed to learn. The boy had talent, raw as it was. If he'd devote even a portion of the effort to his training that he expended trying to get the wizard to teach him some new magic, he could become quite a skilled fighter. He had the instincts . . . if he'd only use them.

His brother wasn't quite as agile, but his ability to hit a target with anything you put in his hand, and possessing the size and strength of a bear, made up for what he lacked. Ayrion wished he knew more about Breen's unique talents so he could help him develop a style that complemented them.

The Imbatoo princess, on the other hand, was already very skilled with the spear and sword. Ayrion could tell she had been training since she was young. Though her people's own style was not quite as focused as the Upakans, she was a force to be reckoned with.

As for the draakar, Ayrion didn't know how to work with her. Teaching skills to a two-legged human was much different than a four-legged creature. Balance, the way she moved—everything was different. He had yet to adapt his usual training methods to suit her. She really needed the instruction of another draakar.

Ayrion watched the small party trudge across the snow-covered walk toward the north wing. They were moving slower than usual. He turned and headed for the door, scooping his swords off his bed and slinging them over his back as he strapped them to his front with practiced motion. He wasn't about to be caught meandering around the magical school without protection.

He turned and spared a passing glance around his room to make sure he hadn't left anything before heading downstairs. After the wizard had told them that they could form their room to whatever they so desired, the first image that came to Ayrion was his assigned room in the palace, but then he remembered how much more comfortable his room at Sandstorm Manor had been. It wasn't the most lavish of bedchambers, not like that of the king and queen, or even Dakaran's, but Ayrion was never one for extravagance and much preferred a simpler design. Plus, the bed had been much softer.

Ayrion had been quite intrigued the first time he'd tried the room. Opening the door to find his old chambers waiting for him was magic beyond anything he'd expected to see in his lifetime. The large four-poster bed with purple-and-black pillows rested at the back of the room, and long deep-purple curtains framed the windows. Every detail had been met, details he'd thought forgotten, like the brush on the dresser beside the set of whetstones for his blades.

The room even had the secret chamber in the corner that opened when you pulled on the sconce beside it, and the view from the side windows actually looked out over the trees and yard on the side of the manor, though unlike the real manor, there were no kids playing in the trees. It was impressive, to say the least, and he would have been lying if he said he hadn't been tempted to try another room, like the royal bedchamber, just to see what it was like and how much detail his mind could recall, but so far, he'd restricted himself to what was most familiar.

Shutting the door, he made his way down the hall past Bek and Nel's room. He couldn't hear Taylis or Marissa inside, so they must already be downstairs. He then passed Tameel and Zynora's door. Most nights he would join them for a spot of tea before heading to bed. He'd laughed the first time he'd walked into their room and found he was once again standing in the back of Ol' Lerra.

He headed down the wide staircase, his hand sliding across the smooth wooden banister. He could hear the playful banter of the kids before he reached the bottom landing. Stepping into the common room, he found Zynora and

Nel chatting quietly in front of the fire, Zynora with a cup of warm tea and Nel with her yarn and what looked like the beginning of a stocking cap.

Ayrion barely made it into the room before he was tackled by a wily little monkey with a bright yellow ribbon hanging sideways in her hair. He untangled Marissa's arms from his leg and picked her up. She smiled, and after giving him his usual kiss on the cheek, began to play with his beard, which he'd actually managed to trim that morning, having woken early, troubled by thoughts of what Nyalis might want to discuss with him.

After hearing the quest the two brothers had been sent on, Ayrion shuddered to think what the wizard might expect from him. Whatever it was, Ayrion was going to have to be firm in his rejection. He didn't have time to go galivanting around Aldor collecting unknown artifacts. He had more important things to worry about, Dakaran's betrayal rising to the top of that list.

"Not so scratchy," Marissa said with a smile as she gave him another kiss, this time on the clean-shaven part of his cheek.

He couldn't help but smile at the rover girl. It was hard not to. She was the perfect distraction to derail his typically dour mood. "And I see you've managed to once again nearly pull the bow out of your hair."

She reached up and tried to adjust the ribbon, but it wouldn't budge, apparently more determined than she was. The attempt was quickly forgotten when she noticed the dragon etched on his sword.

"Kraea," she said, patting the hilt.

Ayrion chuckled. "No, not Kraea. Those are dragons." At least, they were supposed to be. It wasn't like he or anyone he'd ever heard of had actually seen a dragon, other than depictions. According to legend, they'd disappeared a thousand years ago, during the banishment of magic. From what the stories said, most had been hunted to extinction before then. Their blood was apparently very valuable.

The front doors to the common room opened, and everyone turned to see Nyalis step inside, trailed by the faeling and his friends. Ayrion stiffened when he saw the state they were in. They had holes in their clothing, gashes that could have only been made by blades, and they were covered in blood.

Zynora and Nel gasped when they saw them, which caused Bek and

Tameel to turn from their game in the corner.

"What happened?" Ayrion asked.

Nyalis waved dismissively. "Everything is fine. We can discuss it later. No need to frighten the children."

"The *children*?" Zynora said, frowning at the wizard. "One look at the four of you, and *I'm* frightened."

Marissa squirmed in his arms in an attempt to reach the old wizard, so Ayrion set her down. She and Taylis rushed over and stood in front of the old man, waiting.

Nyalis looked down at them and grinned. "Oh, alright." He raised his hand and whispered something, and a flourish of colorful sparks flew into the air, forming various shapes of animals that began to hop, gallop, or fly around the room. The two kids chased the light creatures over to the fire, where they watched the animals dive into the flames and disappear.

They turned and clapped their approval, the adults smiling as they watched. Ayrion, however, wasn't to be distracted with the wizard's magic and pulled Nyalis aside. "Is this something I need to be worried about?" he asked, keeping his voice low so the children wouldn't hear. "They look half dead, blood and gore pasted on them like grave diggers after a battle. What in the faerie-loving blazes is happening around here?"

Nyalis patted Ayrion's arm. "As I said, it is nothing for you to concern yourself with. We can discuss it this evening once the children are in bed."

Ayrion's lips tightened as he turned to look at the four stragglers standing just inside the doorway. He didn't want to sit around waiting to hear why they were covered in death.

"I'm going to take the children up to their rooms to wash for supper," Nel announced. By the anxious looks on everyone's faces, Ayrion wasn't the only one who didn't want to wait. She walked over to grab Marissa's hand and told Bek, "You can fill me in later."

Bek smiled. "Thank you."

"We don't want to go," Marissa groaned, attempting, and failing, to pull out of Nel's grip.

Taylis crossed his arms. "It's not fair. You all get to hear all the good stuff. Why can't we listen?"

Bek looked at the boy and pointed toward the stairs. "Because we don't want you waking us up in the middle of the night trying to crawl in our bed."

"But—"

"No buts," Bek said. "Now scoot. The sooner you bathe, the sooner you can eat."

Taylis's eyes lit up, and he took off running for the stairs, nearly knocking Marissa over on his way.

As soon as Ayrion could no longer hear footsteps or the giddy excitement of Taylis as he shouted for Nel and Marissa to hurry up, he turned to Nyalis. "Okay, the children are gone. What happened?"

Nyalis calmly proceeded to recount how he'd been testing the traveling mirrors and had ended up at one of the pygmy tribes on the other side of the Khezrian Wall. "Did you know their written language is very similar to the old Gaopic writings in the—"

Ayrion cleared his throat. "I think we're getting off topic."

Nyalis studied the surrounding faces. "Right. Well, I'll turn the rest of the story over to our rather headstrong band of trouble gatherers. Seems everywhere they go, misfortune finds them, like lightning to a tree."

At a look from Breen, Ty picked up the story from there, describing the incredibleness of the library, if that was even a word, and the tower, and the spelled water, and the stone creatures feeding the water, and the winding staircase to the top, and the glass dome, and the—

"As interesting as that all is," Ayrion finally interrupted, "how about getting to the part that has you all standing here covered in guts?"

Bek, Tameel, and even Zynora all nodded in agreement.

"Get to the good stuff, lad," Tameel said with a wink.

Ty frowned but finally went on to describe the battle they had fought. The other three added in their copper's worth, making sure Ty didn't forget anything, especially the important roles they each played and the wounds they had suffered, which had indeed been grave. It was a wonder they had survived. Ayrion found he was almost proud at how they had handled themselves. It seemed his training had paid off in some small way. At least the faeling hadn't lost his sword, and from the way he told it, had wielded it with some small amount of accuracy.

Ty finished by mumbling something about using the glass dome of the tower to destroy the pygmy army.

Before that really had time to sink in, Nyalis spoke again. "By the time I was able to reach the mirror and make it through, I found a room full of pygmy corpses. After I imparted some much-needed healing, we came straight here." He looked around the room. "So, if there are no further questions, I believe these four would greatly appreciate a hot bath and some new clothes."

Tameel wrinkled his nose. "I believe we would be happy to see that as well."

Zynora took a couple of steps forward as she looked the four over. "Will there be any need of my services? Should I get the cream?"

Ty rolled his shoulder, and Ayrion caught a faint tightening of his mouth as he did. "I think we are fine," he said. Ty pulled back part of the torn garment and rubbed at a spot on his upper shoulder. "The wounds have healed."

"Food and rest is what they need," Nyalis said, waving them toward the staircase. "They will be right as rain tomorrow."

"Good," Ayrion said. "We have another long day ahead of us."

His students visibly wilted and then slogged across the room and up the stairs. If they weren't going to listen to him, then they would have to face the consequences. He hadn't given them the day off to go battling pygmies. He had wanted them to catch up on some sleep. They needed to rest if they were to keep up their training. Though, he was quite proud of the way they had apparently handled themselves, and thereby prevented a bad situation from getting a hundred times worse.

Bek walked over. "A bit hard on them, weren't you?"

"Not hard enough, if you ask me," Ayrion said, keeping his eye on the wizard, who was speaking with Tameel and Zynora. "Nyalis was right about one thing. Wherever those four go, trouble follows."

"You're one to talk."

Ayrion smiled. "Fair point." Trouble never seemed to have any problem tracking him down either. "Still, we've only been here a few weeks, and they've almost died twice. If anything, it looks like I need to push them more. They'll never be Upakan, but if I can at least ram enough training in them to keep them alive, then I will have accomplished something. My days here are numbered. I need to help them as best I can in the time I have left."

Bek shrugged his broad shoulders. "You're the weapons expert, not me. Just saying, those four looked like they've been through the Pits and back."

Ayrion nodded but didn't say anything further.

Bek took a puff on his pipe, sending rings of smoke to swirl over his head. It had a sweet smell, one Ayrion had grown accustomed to over the last several months, as both Bek and Tameel enjoyed their pipes every evening.

Ayrion watched the wizard, judging by the slow backward sliding of Nyalis's feet away from the tinkers that his conversation with Tameel and Zynora was nearing its end. Ayrion needed to have a word with him before he up and disappeared again.

"So, where do you plan on going?" Bek asked.

It took a moment for Ayrion to process the question as he watched the wizard finish his conversation and turn for the door. "Umm, Aramoor. If you'll excuse me, I have some business to discuss with the wizard while I have the chance."

Bek pulled the pipe from his mouth. "Just don't ruffle his feathers. He might appear like a friendly sort, but I get the feeling he's not one to trifle with."

"Neither am I," Ayrion said as he started across the room.

Nyalis turned before Ayrion managed to reach him and smiled. "No, I have not forgotten that I owe you a conversation."

Ayrion slowed. The crazy old man had eyes in the back of his head. "I would appreciate some more clarity," he said, walking with Nyalis over to one of the front windows to talk in private.

Nyalis sighed. "Tonight, I promise. I will come for you after supper." Nyalis started to turn, but Ayrion stopped him.

"What about this mirror? How safe are we? What's to stop others from coming through and infiltrating the school without us knowing?"

"There are wards that guard the mirrors from entry."

Ayrion stiffened. "*Mirrors*? There are more than one?"

Nyalis smiled. "A great many more."

"Well, that's terrifying. We nearly had a foothold situation, and you're telling me there's more of these flaming things?" He didn't think the wizard was a fool, but so many potential entries into the school seemed awful foolish to him.

"Using a mirror is not as easy as walking up and stepping through," Nyalis said, his voice teetering on frustration. "If one desired to gain entry, they would first need to know what the mirror was, then they would also have to know how to use it—which would require them to be able to speak the ancient Fae tongue, as well as know the name of one of the mirrors inside the school—plus the name of the one they are hoping to travel through, and that's if the mirror is still working." Nyalis shook his head. "The possibility of any of those happening, let alone all of them, is infinitesimal. And like I said . . . there are wards."

"Somehow that doesn't exactly fill me with confidence. I'm guessing travel to and from the school was done regularly, using these so-called mirrors?"

Nyalis nodded, waiting with thinly veiled impatience for Ayrion's point.

"Then it seems to me that this would be an ideal way for someone to invade, which apparently just occurred, and I shudder to think what might have happened if Ty and his friends had not been there at the right moment. We might have lost Aero'set in a single day. What's to keep a more dangerous adversary—say, the White Tower—from doing the same? I'm sure they have competent-enough wizards there to figure out the mirrors' uses."

Nyalis face hardened, and Bek's warning echoed in the back of Ayrion's mind. He might have pushed the wizard too far.

"First of all," Nyalis said, his hand tightening around his staff, "the pathetic excuse for wielders that are being produced by the Tower are anything but wizards. True wizardry takes a lifetime of study to master, not a few weeks learning how to conjure fire or weave an air shield. There is only one wizard still remaining, and you are looking at him. Second, Aero'set was much more than just a school. It was a haven for all wielders. It was a city unto itself, and as you've seen from the garrison outside, it employed its own military. They were one of the deadliest fighting forces in all of Aldor. Their sole purpose was the protection of the school and its people. You couldn't find a more dedicated or braver unit of warriors."

Ayrion wasn't exactly sure where Nyalis was going with all of this. "That's all well and good, but it means nothing in the here and now. There is no battle-ready fighting force here to protect this place. There's only us. Clearly, that's not enough."

Nyalis took another deep breath and then smiled. It seemed out of place and had Ayrion even more worried. "I will talk about it more after supper," Nyalis said, "but for now I have a few errands to complete." He started to turn, then stopped. "Oh, and you might want to set a few extra places at the table this evening."

"A few extra places?"

Nyalis turned and made a quick exit instead of answering. Ayrion shook his head. The crazy old man. You never could get a straight answer out of him. Frustrated, Ayrion turned back to the others to find them quietly chatting near the grand fireplace on the right, no doubt discussing recent events. Ayrion didn't see the need to interrupt, so he walked over to his usual nook on the left and sat down at the table, where his half-finished game of batmyth from the previous night sat waiting, the pieces still in place from where he and Bek had left off.

Ayrion didn't like sitting there without an opponent and was about to head up to his room when the front door suddenly opened. Ayrion looked up, wondering what Nyalis had forgotten, then jumped from his seat and drew his sword when he realized there were too many to be Nyalis.

Chapter 10 | Ayrion

IVE PEOPLE STEPPED INTO the entryway and began to brush the snow from their cloaks. Ayrion lowered his sword when he spotted the brown bear's head riding on top of the man in front.

"It's really starting to come down out there," Ozlin Beartooth announced in his typical booming manner. "A man could catch his death." He swatted the arms of his bearskin coat and patted the snow from the thick braid of hair hanging from his chin. "It's a farther jaunt across that valley than what I remembered, or maybe I'm just getting older by the day." He looked up and frowned when he saw Tameel and Zynora standing over near the fire. "Well, are you going to come greet your guests or just stand there enjoying the flames while we freeze to death over here?"

"If you'd give them a chance to open their mouths, my dear, I'm sure they would." Hanani wiped the snow from her fur-trimmed dress and cloak and tapped her boots on the rug in front of the door. Ozlin's wife stood nearly as tall as he did, with hair just as thick and just as red. Behind them were three men, each covered in fur and leathers like Ozlin—the magistrate's personal guard, by their bearing.

"True guests would have given us fair warning of their arrival," Zynora said with a harumph. "They wouldn't have simply shown up at mealtime, covering our entrance in snow."

"Tongue as sharp as ever, I see," Ozlin said with a deep belly laugh. "So, how are my old friends? To be honest, when we didn't hear from you over the last few weeks, I was beginning to think this place had swallowed you up." He spotted Ayrion over at the side with his sword in hand, and his smile dropped, his jaw tightening. "Though I have a feeling it would have spat *you* back up."

Ozlin clearly hadn't gotten over the death of their beloved oracle, or the fact that Angioma had passed on some form of her gift to Ayrion before she slipped away. Ozlin still held Ayrion at least partly responsible for her passing, if only because there was no one else at whose feet he could lay his anger.

Ayrion allowed it to a point. The man's town had just suffered a great loss, not just with the death of their seer, but also all who'd perished during the skirmish with the Black Watch and the Bulradoer. If Ozlin needed to vent his frustration, Ayrion was fine with him doing so on him, as long as it didn't interfere with Ayrion's work.

Ozlin turned to Tameel and Zynora and smiled. "Did I hear someone mention something about a meal?"

Zynora grunted as she began to gather their coats and place them on a table near the door. "Don't think for a moment we believe this was unplanned."

Ozlin patted his stomach. "Are you saying we purposefully left Wellhollow in time to arrive for the evening meal, which would then force us to bed down here for the night as opposed to attempting the walk back through the dark?" The man grinned sheepishly through his whiskers.

She gave him the eye, the same look she used to give Ayrion when she suspected him of pinching an extra biscuit when she wasn't looking. "That's exactly what I'm saying."

Ozlin grinned. "Well, you'd be right."

"Come," Tameel said, waving the party over. "Warm yourself by the fire. Supper will be ready shortly."

Tameel's statement struck Ayrion as he recalled the wizard saying nearly the exact same thing. How had Nyalis known?

Ayrion replaced his sword, but instead of heading upstairs like he'd planned, he moved closer to the fire, where the others were doing their best to dry off, and listened in on the conversation. He doubted Ozlin would have made the trip all the way from Wellhollow just to partake of their food. Then again, the magistrate had been there the first day they arrived in Aero'set. He had seen what the school had to offer. Still, the rugged mountaineer never seemed the greedy sort, so whatever his reasoning, Ayrion wanted to hear it.

"Things have been interesting around here, to say the least," Tameel said. "Why, not an hour ago—"

A bell chimed, interrupting Tameel's statement to let those in the dorm know that supper was to be served. Ayrion had spent considerable time during their first few days in Aero'set trying to find where the bell was located or where the sound was coming from. He had finally given up the search, resigned that it clearly had something to do with magic, as did most things in Aero'set.

"Ah, I recognize that sound," Ozlin said, turning to his wife. "You will see for yourself, my dear, that I speak the truth." He looked at Tameel and Zynora. "She did not believe me when I told her that the food appears by magic."

The older couple smiled in return as Ozlin anxiously directed Hanani across the common room to the doorway on the left, leading back toward the dining area. His guard remained a step or two behind, their heads swiveling back and forth as they kept an eye out for any possible signs of danger.

Ayrion chuckled. If they only knew.

Before Ayrion had made it halfway down the hall, Taylis and Marissa darted past and shot into the dining room ahead of him. They were in their seats before he made it through the door. The long table was decked out as it normally was—golden candelabras lining the center, with greenery and flowers placed between. The settings had all been assigned in perfect order, with five extra places, filling more of the table than usual. Aero'set, it would seem, was not surprised by the sudden arrivals.

Ayrion took his usual spot at the head of the table on the left. He wasn't quite sure how he had ended up with it, other than he wasn't part of a pair— Tameel sat with Zynora, Bek with Nel, Marissa had Taylis, and Ty, Breen, and Narendi tended to sit together, which left a spot on one side open for him and one on the other for the wizard, if Nyalis was kind enough to grace them with his presence. Ayrion could have counted the number of times he had on one hand. Of course, there was the draakar, but she typically kept to her corner in the back, where she spent most of her time chewing on the raw bones and sinew of whatever uncooked creature the dorm provided.

Ty, Breen, Narendi, and Kraea were the last in, and the others quieted. The four certainly looked better than they had an hour ago now that they had washed and were wearing a new change of clothes.

The three smiled when they spotted the guests.

"Master Ozlin, Mistress Hanani." Ty was the first to walk over and shake their hands. His brother and the princess followed behind. Instead of shaking Narendi's hand, Ozlin attempted a formal bow, his wife doing the same, both looking ridiculous.

"Princess Narendi," Ozlin said in greeting. "It's good to see you again."

Narendi shook her head and tried to get them to stand. "No. You embarrass me. Please." She motioned for them to take their seats.

"Oh, I almost forgot," Ozlin said, turning to Breen. "I believe these are yours." He waved to one of the three men who had accompanied them, and the man handed over a long thin bundle. Ozlin unwrapped it and held out several long black arrows.

Breen's face brightened.

"I found as many as I could," Ozlin said, "before we discarded the bodies. Don't know if that's all of them or not, but better than nothing, I guess."

Breen took the arrows excitedly. "Thank you for looking. I was afraid I had lost them for good." Breen had mentioned to Ozlin after they had recovered Aero'set that he was missing several arrows that needed to be found if possible. Ozlin thought he was crazy and told him he could make more, but after Breen explained their value, namely that they had magical properties, Ozlin agreed to look. Ayrion wondered if they had anything to do with his uncanny ability as a marksman.

Ozlin and Hanani took their place down the table from Ayrion on the left, their men directly across from them on the right.

"What brings you to Aero'set?" Breen asked as everyone found their places.

Ozlin shared a peculiar look with his wife before answering. "We are here to visit. I haven't been able to get away as oft as I would wish. So much to do in Upper Wellhollow after the battle, you know. Besides, Hanani does not believe me when I tell her that this place has food that just appears on your plate without being prepared and rooms that shape to your imagination."

"It is quite remarkable," Narendi said to Hanani with a smile.

Ayrion stared down the table at the empty dishes, all waiting to be filled. It looked like everyone was ready.

"I want to go this time," Taylis said, raising his hands.

"No!" Marissa shouted, snatching at his arms. "It's my turn."

Nel looked at Taylis. "Marissa's correct. It's her turn. You got to go at breakfast."

Taylis lowered his hands disappointedly. "Fine."

Bek placed his hand on Marissa's head. "Go ahead."

"Watch this," Ozlin said, poking his wife. His face beamed as he stared at the empty spots down the middle of the table.

Marissa raised her hands and clapped loudly three times. On the third, the table suddenly filled with food—dishes and platters and bowls of all shapes and sizes appeared out of nowhere, the smells filling Ayrion's nostrils with delight. He wasn't one for outward bursts of emotion, but he couldn't help but enjoy the thrill of excitement on their guests' faces.

Hanani gasped, and Ozlin slapped the top of the table. "See! What did I tell you! Food that just appears without anyone's help." He grabbed a leg of lamb from a platter in front of him and took a healthy bite, juice dripping into his beard. "Here," he said, holding it out to her. "Try it. You'll not taste better, I assure you."

Hanani scooped a lock of hair back over her shoulder, then leaned forward and took a small, dainty bite. Her eyes brightened, and she smiled at those around the table who had paused to watch.

"Well?" Ozlin asked, waiting for confirmation.

She looked to be getting frustrated by the attention from her husband. "It appears you were correct, my sweet. That is the perfect leg of mutton."

Ozlin grinned victoriously.

The three men who had accompanied them began snatching food off the trays and stuffing their faces like there was no tomorrow. Ayrion stared. The people of the mountains were hardly known for their couth, but this was bordering on the absurd. They splattered the table with half of what they were trying to fit between their jaws.

Hanani's eyes began to water, and she quickly wiped the tears before they streaked her cheeks. And it was no wonder. If any of Ayrion's men had acted in such a manner, he would have been wholly embarrassed as well.

"Is something wrong?" Tameel asked. "The food is excellent, I grant you, but I have yet to see it bring someone to tears."

Hanani looked up and smiled. "You have no idea how much this means to us."

Ayrion leaned forward and looked at Ozlin. Now, he was curious. Clearly, something was troubling them. "This wasn't just a social visit, I take it."

Ozlin stared at the perfectly cooked piece of meat in his hand, then set it down on his plate with a heavy sigh. "You are correct. We haven't come solely to visit." He looked down the table at all the eyes staring his way and hesitated. Hanani laid her hand on his arm and nodded for him to continue.

"I'm embarrassed to bring this to you," Ozlin said, "especially after everything you've done already in saving our town from the Tower, but I'm afraid we are facing another threat. One of our own making."

Ayrion could already tell where this was going. "You're running out of food."

Ozlin looked perplexed. "How did you—"

"It wasn't hard to deduce by the way the two of you were fondling that piece of meat." He turned and looked at the three men opposite the magistrate, who had barely taken time to breathe as they continued to clean their plates. One look from Hanani, though, and all three stopped, even going so far as to wipe their bearded mouths with the provided dinner cloths.

Tameel leaned forward. "How bad is it?"

"With the passes buried by the avalanche, we have no way off the mountain."

"I'm sorry about that," Zynora said. "It is a problem laid solely at my feet."

"Hardly," both Ozlin and Hanani said at almost the same time, before Ozlin continued. "If it weren't for your intervention, it's doubtful any of us would be sitting here today. But as it stands, it has come at a difficult time."

"Our hunters hadn't yet finished filling our meat stores for the winter," Hanani said. "And we still needed several trips back down to Lower Wellhollow to purchase grain."

Ozlin nodded. "If we ration carefully, we can last another few weeks, perhaps a month at best. But even that will be barely enough to keep all alive. There was tremendous damage, as you know, to many of the homes during the battle from those cursed black wielders. Many of our people find themselves without shelter in one of the worst times possible."

Ayrion waited to see if Ozlin would get around to saying what it was he wanted, but he had a feeling the man was too proud to ask for charity, and before Ayrion could say anything, Zynora beat him to it.

"Then you should bring your people here," she said.

Ayrion tensed. They were having a difficult enough time trying to keep up with the small group they had. They would never be able to keep an entire town, small as it was, safe. There would be people wandering all over the school, unleashing who knows what on top of them. For once, Ayrion hoped the wizard would make an appearance and put a quick stop to it.

Ozlin took a moment to look at those gathered around the table. "We . . . we had only thought to ask for food and any supplies you could offer. We hadn't considered . . ." He turned to Hanani, who seemed to be contemplating Zynora's suggestion as well. Her eventual smile and nod seemed to assure her husband that it was a welcomed decision. Ozlin turned. "Our people are not beggars, though. We are men and women of the mountain. We work for what is ours."

"And no one here would suggest otherwise," Zynora chimed in.

Ayrion had to slow this conversation down before they started bringing people over tonight. "We can't promise anything right now," he said, cutting in as quickly as possible. "Not until we first speak with Nyalis. As the caretaker of this place, it will be up to him as to what needs to be done. To be honest, as wonderous as this place may seem, it can be just as deadly."

The excitement on Ozlin and Hanani's faces vanished. "Deadly?" Ozlin looked at Ayrion. "Has something happened?"

Those gathered turned to look at Ty and his friends.

Ty lowered his glass. "There might have been a couple of incidents."

Ozlin leaned forward, placing his elbows on the table. "And by incidents, you mean . . ."

"I mean we may or may not have come close to dying on two separate occasions."

"Three, if you were to add nearly falling off the side of a cliff," Narendi added.

Ayrion cocked his brow. That was one he hadn't heard about. It must have been during their trip up the mountain with Nyalis.

Ty went on to explain the two deadly encounters, doing his best to not make it sound as gruesome or worrisome as it really was. Ayrion would have preferred he not hold back. Ozlin and Hanani needed to see how serious it was.

Once Ty had finished, Ayrion continued. "The truth is, we don't really know what all dangers this place holds. The two attempts that have been made at further exploration have both resulted in near catastrophes. I'm just not sure how safe it would be to bring your entire community over without some sort of strict regulations at least. So as I said, best we speak with the wizard before getting your people's hopes up." Ayrion looked toward the open doorway into the corridor beyond. "I was hoping Nyalis would have joined us this evening, but it appears he is needed elsewhere. I promise you I will discuss your need with him to see what options are available to keep your people fed and sheltered."

Hanani laid a hand on her husband's arm. "I think it would be wise for us to wait to see what the wizard has to say. The last thing we need is to subject our people to an even worse situation than the one we are facing now."

"Don't know how it can get much worse than slowly starving to death," Ozlin grumbled.

"We won't let it come to that," Ayrion said. "Give me tonight to speak with Nyalis, and I assure you he will have a solution." At least, Ayrion hoped he would. With Ayrion's luck, the wizard wouldn't show and would leave him eating his words.

Ozlin and Hanani eventually nodded, and everyone went back to their food. After the meal had been consumed, the group retired to the common room to chat by the fire. Ozlin pulled out his pipe and joined Tameel and Bek for a smoke, stuffing the bowl with tobac from a pouch he carried in the pocket of his shirt. It didn't smell quite as sweet as what Tameel and Bek used, but it was laced with the scent of cloves.

Ayrion sat in his usual spot in front of the bay windows where he could look out over the front lawn while contemplating his next move on the batmyth board. Bek walked over and joined him, the bowl of his pipe still glowing. He chewed on the stem for a while before finally moving one of his pieces.

"I feel as you," Bek said, keeping his voice lowered so the others by the fire wouldn't hear. "Not sure if this is the safest place to relocate their people. Still, they need help."

Ayrion leaned forward in his seat to study the board. "I just don't want to be responsible for their safety, not when I don't know how much longer I will be here. Even if we brought their people to live in the dorms, there's just no way to regulate their movements. Curiosity alone will drive them to see what is beyond the walls, and in a place like this, curiosity could get more than just themselves killed. Open the wrong door around here, and we all might die."

Bek chuckled. "You're being a little dramatic, aren't you?"

"Perhaps, but better safe than sorry." Ayrion rolled his dice and reached for one of his pieces to move it up three places to block Bek's perceived attack, but as his fingers wrapped around the wood, the short hairs on the back of his neck stood. He was being watched. He glanced over at the fire, but no one was looking in their direction. He twisted in his seat, but other than Taylis and Marissa tossing a small cotton-filled sack behind him, there was no reason for the strange feeling.

"Are you alright?" Bek asked.

"I don't know. I get the feeling . . ." He glanced out the window and saw Nyalis standing in the middle of the yard with his staff in hand. The wizard was looking directly at him.

Bek turned and shuddered. "The man gives me the shakes. How long do you think he's been standing out there?"

"Long enough to get my attention, I guess," Ayrion said. "Tell the others I just went for a walk. No telling when I'll be back."

"Don't forget to mention the people at Wellhollow," Bek said as Ayrion stood.

"First thing," Ayrion promised, leaving the others to the warmth of the fire and slipping out the front door. The rest were too caught up in their conversations to even notice. Only the guards saw him leave, and they didn't seem to care one way or the other. Ayrion buttoned his coat and pulled on his gloves before starting down the steps and across the snow to where the old wizard waited beside the fountain. The torches lining the buildings and walkways provided more than enough light to see by, even without his Upakan sight.

"Aren't you cold?" Ayrion asked, noticing Nyalis wasn't wearing much more than his usual robe. His hood was up, holding the snow from his hair, but Ayrion doubted it did much to fight against the frosty wind sweeping across the front of the buildings.

"I haven't been here long," Nyalis said, which was going to be Ayrion's next question.

Ayrion joined him in front of the fountain. "You could have simply come inside."

Nyalis smiled. "How are our guests settling in?"

"Well enough. It seems the people of Upper Wellhollow are running out of food. The snow is blocking the passes, and Ozlin doesn't believe their people will survive much longer. They came looking for help." Ayrion was a little worried about mentioning Zynora's suggestion, not really sure how the wizard would respond. "It was suggested . . . well, a proposal was submitted that they bring their people here for the winter."

"Good," Nyalis said before Ayrion could even suggest why it wasn't the best idea.

"Good? Don't you want to take some time to think about it? This place is proving more dangerous by the day. I think it hardly safe for an entire community of mountain folk who wouldn't know a spell from a child's ditty if you sang it to them. Come to think of it, neither would the rest of us, and many among us are wielders."

Nyalis laughed. "The people of the mountains have ever been the caretakers of Aero'set. It's in their blood . . . their heritage."

Ayrion gawked. That was one of the last things he'd expected to hear. "I don't understand."

"Did you think that this place ran solely on its own?"

"Well, from what we've seen so far . . ."

"What you've seen so far doesn't hold a thimble to the true manpower required to keep this place running. I'm doing my best, but I am but one person. When Aero'set was sent from this realm, those in service here decided to remain close by in case they were ever needed once more. They, of course, didn't realize how long that wait would be, and over the centuries, they have slowly forgotten who they once were, relegated to simply guarding the passageway inside." He took a step back. "So, yes, Aero'set has returned, which means its caretakers should as well. It is amazing how much knowledge is lost when generations forget, or refuse, to pass on what they have learned to those coming behind." Nyalis gave Ayrion a poignant look. "As you will soon discover."

"What does that mean?"

Nyalis studied Ayrion a moment, then turned and started for the south exit. "Come. I have something to show you."

Chapter 11 | Ayrion

THEY LEFT THE DORMITORY compound and headed south over the bridge, their way guided by streetlamps that seemed to light themselves. They passed the circular pavilion with its ornate sculpted animals and then continued south past the arena, which sat atop a smaller rise on the left. Ayrion had yet to take a closer look at the place, and it sounded like the half-faerie and his companions had beaten him to it.

He stared up at the building on the rise above the arena, with its long glass ceiling. According to Ty's description, that was the library where they had fought off the pygmies. Ayrion could see the tower they had described attached to the back; however, the moon wasn't bright enough to tell whether it was missing its dome.

Nyalis clicked his tongue as if guessing Ayrion's thoughts. "Not looking forward to building a new one."

Once they hit the crossroads, Nyalis took them west and out through Aero'set's main gate and crossed the bridge, which led into the woods that separated the river from the valley on the other side. There were no streetlamps here, but the sky had begun to clear, revealing a bright moon for the darkened road ahead. Pale rays cast strange shadows down through the bare branches above, like long emaciated fingers reaching out to grab the unsuspecting traveler.

The wizard didn't seem to need a torch, not missing a step. Ayrion had heard Ty and his brother discuss a type of magic they had come across that allowed them to see at night, much like an Upakan. Was Nyalis using something similar? He wondered what other kinds of magic were out there that could lend aid in time of battle.

Ayrion didn't ask where the wizard was taking him, since the road they were on went to only one location: the garrison. Soon enough, the trees opened, and they started through the graveyard of dry-docked ships. The drive split off the road to the right, curving around in front of a two-story warehouse that butted up against a narrow port in the river.

There were no ships in the water, all having somehow been moved onto land and propped up with braces that ran down each side. The gold trim around the dark wood on each ship glistened in the moonlight. Some of the vessels were large enough that it would have required the main bridge leading into Aero'set to raise in order for them to pass fully beneath.

Ayrion finally stopped alongside one of the tallest ships and tilted his head. He had never seen black ships before. If the wood had been painted, it was the finest job he'd ever seen, considering there was no flaking or chipping, even where the waterline should have been. "What were all these used for?"

Nyalis turned and looked up at the vessel. "Aero'set's fleet was considered one of the largest in all the Five Kingdoms."

"Fleet? The school did that much trade with the other kingdoms?"

"Trade? Sure, but these," he said, pointing at the underbelly of the black hull, "these were not used for trade. These are warships."

Ayrion's head shot up. "Warships?" He turned and looked down one of the rows on the right, back toward the water. "Was the river much wider back then? I have a hard time believing that a single pier was enough to harbor all of these. For that matter, how in the name of Aldor did they manage to move them from the river over here?"

Nyalis gave him a strange look. "These ships were not made to sail the river."

Ayrion stared at the wizard a moment, then up at the enormous vessel. What was he missing? "I don't understand."

Nyalis smiled. "They were made to sail the skies."

Ayrion almost laughed. Sail the *skies*? Was this another one of Nyalis's attempts at humor? If it was, the man was terrible at it. The thought of something this monstrous floating through the air was preposterous.

Then a memory surfaced of one of the cave paintings inside Harok Laos back at Wellhollow. Ships with tall sails had been depicted surrounded by billowing white clouds. Ayrion studied the wizard. He had thought perhaps the clouds were representative of a thick fog, such as the kind that rolled in from the Bay of Mist between the Sidaran mainland and the Isle of Tallos, but if it was because these ships had actually sailed through the air . . .

"How is that possible?"

The wizard chuckled. "Magic, of course. What did you think? Granted, a little more complex a weave than normal, but effective once used correctly."

Ayrion's mind raced. The possibilities alone were staggering. "Anyone who possessed ships such as these could conquer all of Aldor. Could you imagine being able to transport entire armies from one kingdom to the next without any forewarning? City walls would be nearly useless. You could lower your troops into a city without a month-long siege. You could set up archery stations that fired from above." His mind soared with ideas. "The possibilities would be endless."

Nyalis cleared his throat. "Yes, well, that is true if you are the only one to possess such transport. However, during the Wizard Wars, every kingdom had their own fleets, and both sides were equally matched." Nyalis cocked a brow. "And there were more than ships that rode the skies during that time. The dragon riders proved equally effective in taking down battleships such as these." He pursed his lips and stroked his long white beard. "Deadly and beautiful."

Ayrion stood in silence, hardly able to take it in. Ships that flew through the air, battles that took place in the skies, dragons and dragon riders. The Second Age must have been an incredible time to be alive. And frightening.

"But," Nyalis pointed out, "the sole purpose of airships was not warfare. Though, coming from a military background such as yourself, I can see why that would be your first inclination. Imagine how unified Aldor could become with travel times being cut from weeks to days, or from days to mere hours? The wizards were the peacekeepers across the land, emissaries that kept rival factions to a minimum. We were feared but respected. Firm but fair. Our purpose was in the service of Aldor, to the betterment of all its people, which is a wizard's highest calling."

"If that was the case, then why the fleets of battleships?" From what he could see, he counted at least two to three dozen ships of varying sizes, and with a full complement, they could hold anywhere from five to eight hundred soldiers.

Nyalis sighed as he looked up at the enormous vessel once more. "Those didn't come until later. It wasn't until Aerodyne's betrayal and the rise of the White Tower that such things were needed." He shook his head." Those were dark years indeed. It doesn't take faeries to enslave humanity. They tend to do a great job of that all on their own."

"Do they still fly?" Ayrion asked, suddenly considering how much time it would save him in reaching Aramoor.

"I'm afraid not. It takes more than just a single spell to operate. The basic magic is simple, much like rowing a boat is simple, but it requires a lot more skill to navigate over great distances. Attempting it would be as foolish as trying to cross the Rhunarin in a trading vessel and only knowing how to row. You attempt to take one of these up and lose control, and that's the end." Nyalis stared up at the ship a moment longer, then turned and headed back to the road. "Come. I didn't bring you out here to discuss ancient airships."

Ayrion followed the wizard through the rest of the shipyard to the garrison ahead, staring at those he passed, imagining what it must have been like to fight from the deck of a ship hundreds of feet in the air. Nyalis waved a hand at the garrison gate, and the great doors opened just far enough for the two of them to walk through. Torches along the battlement and all through the inside yard burst to life as if it knew they were there and wanted to make sure they were properly welcomed.

"I don't think I'll ever get used to that," Ayrion said, glancing around the open yard.

"What?" Nyalis turned, and seeing the torches, smiled.

The garrison was rectangular, with an opening in the far northwest corner that led to the training yards in back. The practice fields were laid out so the mountain formed a natural barrier on at least two sides. A second gate to the right led across the river and into the northern part of Aero'set, which was a wise precaution in case the main bridge to the south was to ever come under siege.

The garrison construction wasn't all that much different from the one in Aramoor, though like many of the buildings in Aero'set, the stone was white, while Aramoor's was grey. Barracks lined most of the surrounding walls, while what appeared to be the main office complex was straight ahead.

Nyalis started them toward the main building. Ayrion could see the stables on the left, which he passed daily on his way to the practice fields. They were partially built into the side of the mountain, and he wondered if that helped keep the horses cooled during the hot summer months—if Aero'set had hot summer months.

As they neared the main building, Ayrion realized that it, too, had been built into the interior of the mountain. That was interesting.

The wizard lifted his hand once again as they approached the front, and the doors opened, torches inside bursting to life as soon as they crossed the threshold. Ayrion had never been inside any of the garrison buildings before and was surprised to find the floors were made of marble—white with dark veins that gave the interior a refined feel rather than the utilitarian air of a military compound.

He stepped into the open lobby and found that it was much larger than it had looked on the outside. The walls were ornately carved with depictions of great battles, and true to Nyalis's earlier descriptions, many of them took place aboard the warships with full sail and their colors streaming, lined with armed soldiers ready to fight. It was breathtaking.

Nyalis waited at the center of the room, watching Ayrion as he studied the scene. Behind the wizard, standing at the center of the large chamber and rising all the way to the second-floor ceiling, were three enormous sentinels, chiseled from the same pale stone as the buildings. The warriors stood with their backs to each other, one hand resting on top of a shield, the other holding a blade. They stood at attention, not as though about to fight, but in the stance of a soldier ready to spring into action if needed. It was quite the striking pose.

"Do you see anything you recognize?" Nyalis asked with the hint of a smile, which Ayrion took to mean that whatever the wizard had brought him here to see was in this room.

Ayrion stared up at the three statuesque warriors, studying each more closely. Their faces didn't look familiar, staunch as they were—jaws set, eyes sharp, gazes strong. They were in uniform, but it was hard to tell what sort without the colors to go with it. Their shields bore a crest, similar to the symbol carved, painted, or cast into most of the architecture and décor throughout Aero'set: a rising sun with three stars overtop, a sword piercing the sun.

"I don't recognize the crest," he admitted. "I have seen the sun and stars before, but not with the sword."

"It's the crest of the guardians of Aero'set, the protectors of the Wizard Order. They were the fiercest warriors in all the kingdoms. Their motto is inscribed around the base of the platform behind me. Speak Only Truth. Live With Honor. Fight For Justice. Or another way to put it would be: Truth In All. Honor Above All. Justice For All. The three stars of the crest stand for each. *Truth. Honor. Justice.* Those words kept peace in Aldor for centuries."

Ayrion moved to get a better look at the engraving around the base and nearly choked. The three words of their motto reached out and grabbed him by the scruff of the neck and squeezed so hard he couldn't breathe. The words weren't scripted in Aldoran, but he recognized them nonetheless. All three had been engraved into his very soul since he was a child.

RAJU. KOVAA. ORPA.

They were the three clans of the Upaka.

Ayrion looked up. "What games are you playing at here, wizard?"

Nyalis smirked. "Recognize them, do you?"

"You know I do. Every Upakan knows what these words mean. Raju stands for *Swift*. Orpa stands for *Strength*. Kovaa stands for *the Hidden*."

"Bah!" Nyalis said, waving a hand flippantly through the air. "They mean no such thing. Usurped to meet your own ends." He turned to the statue and pointed to the base with the butt of his staff. "I wanted you to see this for yourself. I wanted you to see your heritage, and how far from it your people have fallen. Have you never asked yourself why it seems that wherever you go, you find yourself as a protector of others?"

Ayrion's mind raced all the way back to his time on the streets with the tribes, and his nickname: *Protector.*

"What is it they call you in Aramoor? The Guardian Protector?"

Ayrion balled his fists. He wasn't the Guardian of anything anymore. He'd failed his mission. Failed his king.

"Did you think that was just coincidence?" Nyalis asked. "It is literally built into the fabric of your being. The Tanveer . . . or Upaka, as you now refer to yourselves, were created as the paladins of the wizards." He spun in a circle. "This is your home, my young friend. These very halls have been stained with the blood of your people going back centuries. Their sacrifice was the thread that kept the peace alive, that eventually enabled the Wizard Order to defeat Aerodyne and his followers. Even after so many years, the Tanveer still hallowed their training, though it disgusts me to see it put to such use as mercenaries, mere killers for hire. Your forefathers would turn over in their graves if they could see what their progeny have become."

"Why did we leave?"

"Ah. A good question, but one with a sad answer, I'm afraid. There was a matter of contention between the Tanveer and the wizards. After Aerodyne's defeat, signaling the end of the Wizard Wars, what remained of the wizard council decided to go into hiding. Most of those with magic had been lost during that horrific battle, and the devastation that had been brought on Aldor had caused the people to turn against magic altogether. We could see the writing on the wall and decided to remove Aero'set from the reach of any who would wish to use it for their own means."

"I don't understand," Ayrion said. "What was the contention?"

"The problem was that the Tanveer didn't wish to leave. After all those years of fighting, and the losses suffered, they believed our decision to hide Aero'set from the world was the coward's choice, so they left in anger, vowing never to return. And it wasn't that we didn't understand or sympathize, but the time of the jun'ri had already been foretold." He stopped and stared at Ayrion a moment, then smiled. "Well, what do you think of your newfound heritage?"

Ayrion was too dumbfounded to know what to say. Paladins of wizards? Guardians of Aero'set? He'd be lying if he said he wasn't completely shaken to learn that his ancestry had bled and died to keep the Five Kingdoms at peace. It was about the last thing he could have expected to hear, considering how they were viewed now. His people, who were known and hated throughout Aldor, were once its protectors? The Tanveer.

"It's a lot to take in," was about all Ayrion could manage.

"True," Nyalis said, still smiling. "You don't know how wonderful it is to see you standing here in this hallowed hall. The first of the Tanveer to return." He wiped one of his eyes. "I have been waiting such a long time for this day."

Ayrion was so astonished by the wizard's reaction he almost didn't catch what he'd said. "What do you mean, the first?"

Nyalis's smile disappeared. "I mean, it is time the Tanveer came home. And I can think of no one better to facilitate that return than the Guardian Protector himself."

Ayrion's stomach knotted, and he flinched once more at the mention of that name.

"You were meant for much more than the protection of kings. You are the guardian of an ideal that held the Five Kingdoms together for almost a millennium. The world needs people like that to look up to once more, to believe in. They need hope. Heroes that can light the way."

"I am the farthest thing from a hero. And I'm certainly not a guardian. I failed my duty and don't have the right to such a title."

Nyalis looked at him a moment before speaking. "Heroes are not born by great deeds, but by their willingness to stand for what is right no matter the cost."

Ayrion turned back to the three warriors and stared at the words around the base. "What is it you are asking me to do?"

"I want you to bring the Tanveer back to Aero'set. Their place is here, not hiding away in some underground husk of a long-dead city. They need to reclaim their heritage, re-earn the respect of the kingdoms."

Ayrion wanted to laugh. The thought of anyone respecting the Upaka was ridiculous. The only respect Aldorans had for the Upaka was born out of fear at the edge of a sword. Perhaps that was how it had been during Nyalis's time as well. Regardless, Ayrion couldn't drop everything and go traipsing across Aldor in hopes of somehow talking his people out of their holes. "I have more pressing concerns—"

"And those concerns can wait. Your vengeance against Dakaran will have to be put aside—for now."

Ayrion looked at the wizard, surprised.

"What? Did you think I was unaware of what took place at Belbridge? You think I don't know of Dakaran and Valtor's treachery? I know much more than that, but now is not the time for it. Trust me when I tell you: Your time will come. But right now, your people need you. And sooner than they realize."

What did he mean by that? Turning, he looked up at the faces of the three warriors, and for the first time, he noticed the eyes. They weren't the eyes of an Aldoran, but the eyes of an Upakan. Even with the light-colored stone used to sculpt the three, Ayrion could see the eyes were missing the natural shading around the middle, nothing more than a single dark circle surrounded by white.

It was true. Aero'set was indeed his home.

The thought of returning to the Lost City after such a long time, the chance to see his family once again, had his heart pounding. If there was one thing that could have possibly stopped him from returning to Aramoor and seeking vengeance, it would be this—returning to the Lost City to reclaim his people's heritage.

But how?

"There's no way my people would ever be willing to leave the Lost City, especially to come to a place filled with magic. Besides, I'm the last person they would listen to. I'm the outcast. The Upakan who was banished."

"You are the Upakan who has lived his life amongst the people of Aldor. You are the Upakan who tamed the street tribes of Aramoor. You are the Upakan who rose through the ranks to become the king's champion. The Guardian Protector. I have a feeling that your people hold more respect for you than you know."

Ayrion doubted his people held him in any higher regard than when he was a child. The wizard clearly didn't know the length of an Upakan's memory.

"How would I even get them to listen to me, let alone convince them of a heritage they know nothing about? One where they are the protectors of *wizards*, no less."

"They will be more willing to listen than you think," Nyalis said.

Ayrion's jaw tightened. "Why? What do you know?"

Nyalis turned and headed back across the marble tiles for the front entry. "Let's just say your return will be the least of their concerns. In fact, they might even welcome it."

Welcome it? Ayrion left the statue of the Tanveer behind and started after the wizard, the doors shutting behind him as soon as he stepped through and onto the outside steps.

"Why do you think they will welcome it?" Ayrion was suddenly picturing an army of Black Watch troops and bulradoer marching across Keldor for the Lost City. Were his people about to come under attack? If so, Ayrion felt sorry for the Tower. No one knew those tunnels like the Upaka. Even with the aid of magic, the Tower's soldiers wouldn't stand a chance.

Nyalis started across the yard for the front gate. "The Upaka have delved a little too deeply inside those tunnels over the years."

"What do you mean . . . too deep?" Ayrion asked, rushing to catch up.

"It means they are coming dangerously close to releasing something that should have remained buried, something that will need to be stopped before it finds its way to the surface."

Ayrion shivered as Angioma's face suddenly appeared, and he remembered the vision the elderly oracle had seen while inside Harok Laos. She had told him that she had seen an underground city in need of saving, something dark and ancient lurking just beneath the surface. At the time, he had no idea what she was referring to, but now that his memories had been returned . . . had she been referring to the Lost City? It had to be.

"I was going to ask you to continue working with Ty and the others a while longer," Nyalis said, "but under the circumstances, it seems you are needed elsewhere, so I suggest you start packing. You leave tomorrow." The wizard waved his arm back toward the gate as they passed through, and the great doors shut behind them, all the torches inside suddenly going dark.

"Tomorrow?" How was he going to be able to pack for a journey like that in a single day? Ayrion still didn't know what it was he was supposed to be helping his people contain. He drew a deep breath, realizing that none of that mattered if his family truly was in danger. He looked up at the airships as they passed through the middle of the yard. "You're a wizard. Surely, you could make one of these fly."

"Making it fly and flying it are two very different things entirely. No, I'm afraid you will have to travel the old-fashioned way: on horseback."

"What is it you believe they might unleash?"

"A very old enemy."

Ayrion exhaled in frustration. "And does this enemy have a name?"

Nyalis stopped and turned. "Khuls."

Chapter 12 | Ayrion

KHULS? ARE YOU SURE that's what he said?" Zynora asked, her face growing pale as she sat rather still on the couch beside her husband. The others had waited up in hopes of speaking with the wizard, all except Nel, apparently, who had taken Taylis and Marissa up to bed and hadn't returned.

Ayrion shifted uncomfortably in his seat beside the grand fireplace in the north wing common room. "Yes, he said khuls."

Everyone had heard the stories of the khul hordes from back during the time of the Wizard Wars, tales of an army of half-human monsters that were said to have been created and controlled by Aerodyne.

"Why would there be khuls living under the Lost City?" Tameel mused as he puffed away on his pipe. Ayrion didn't think he expected an answer.

Bek had his own pipe in hand. "You don't think it's true, do you?"

Ayrion shrugged. "I couldn't say."

"Nyalis doesn't lie," Ty said from the sofa, sandwiched between Breen and Narendi. The draakar was sprawled on the rug directly in front of the fire, close enough that anyone else would have been unable to stand the heat.

"He does have a tendency to bend the truth, however," Breen added, "or at least not give you all of it."

"Did he say anything else?" Zynora asked.

"Only that urgency is required."

"And he said you couldn't take one of those flying ships?" Ty asked.

"Nyalis made it very clear. We aren't to use the ships."

"Hang the khuls and hang those flaming ships!" Ozlin spat, having remained uncharacteristically quiet through most of the discussion. The room had apparently warmed enough for him to remove his bearskin coat. "What I want to know is what Nyalis said about helping Wellhollow."

Hanani nodded silently on his left, and their three guards stood quietly against the back wall, though they were clearly listening eagerly to the conversation.

Ayrion had intended to speak more on the Lost City but realized he hadn't once spoken of what Nyalis had said concerning the mountain folk. He'd been so caught up in his own unexpected discovery that he had completely left out what he had learned of Wellhollow. "That's right. I completely forgot—"

"You forgot?" Ozlin bellowed. "You didn't even mention it to the wizard?"

"Yes, of course I mentioned it," Ayrion said, cutting the magistrate off before his face reddened any further. "It was the first thing we discussed. Though, I'm not so sure how thrilled you'll be by what he had to say."

Ozlin and Hanani shared a concerned look. "So, he said no, then," Hanani said.

Ayrion shifted again. The leather of his seat closest to the fire had grown warm. "Quite the opposite, actually."

Ozlin's face brightened. "So, he's willing to help?"

"He's willing to let us winter here until the passes open?" Hanani asked.

"Yes, and yes, and still more."

Ozlin furrowed his brow as he leaned forward. "More?"

Ayrion took a deep breath, almost nervous about how they would respond. "The wizard has indeed opened the doors of Aero'set to your people, but . . ."

"But?" Hanani leaned forward to match her husband.

"But not for just the winter. He wants your people to move to Aero'set permanently. Apparently, your people and mine share a linked past."

Neither Ozlin or Hanani said anything, and neither did anyone else, all waiting with bated breath for Ayrion to continue.

"While the Upakans, or Tanveer as Nyalis called them, were the guardians of Aero'set, it seems the mountain folk of Wellhollow were its caretakers." He paused, waiting for what he had said to sink in.

After a while, Hanani finally spoke. "I don't understand. What do you mean by *caretakers*?"

"Nyalis said that back when this place was still in operation, your people were its caretakers. You kept the school running." He shook his head. "Don't expect me to explain what all that entails. I have no idea. But apparently, like the Upaka, Aero'set was, and still is, your home. The wizard said that that knowledge of our pasts had not been passed down properly and was forgotten over time. But at least your people decided to remain close by and continue watching over the place, even though you didn't exactly know what it was you were guarding. My people decided to crawl into a hole on the opposite side of Aldor and hide from the world. I would have to say your people were certainly the more honorable."

Ozlin and Hanani were left speechless as they stared at Ayrion. The three guards at the back exchanged curious glances.

"I told the wizard I wasn't sure that was such a good idea," Ayrion said, the continued silence growing uncomfortable. "This place is a mystery, full of magic and dangers. Open the wrong door and who knows what could be unleashed."

Hanani, once again, was the first to speak. "We could at least stay within the walls of this dormitory, correct? It is safe here, is it not?"

"As far as we can tell," Zynora said. "But how long could you keep your people contained to these four walls?"

"That was my concern as well," Ayrion said. "But if Nyalis wants your people to resume whatever duties they were performing prior to Aero'set's disappearance, then they will have to venture out at some point. I only hope the wizard will be here to help."

"And perhaps with more people around to help," Ty said anxiously, "he will have more time available to spend with us?"

Ayrion knew what that meant. The half-faerie had been moping around the school for weeks, hoping the wizard would begin instructing him in magic.

"I don't know if my people will be willing to leave their mountain," Ozlin said.

"They would hardly be leaving their mountain," Bek added. "It's right there across the valley. You can practically see it from every window."

Hanani laid her hand on her husband's arm. "I have a feeling that once they hear of their heritage, most will want to. At this point, they don't have much choice, not until the passes clear at least. And maybe by then, they will have made this place home. One meal up at these tables, and I can't see anyone wanting to leave."

"I wish I could be around to help with the transition," Ayrion said.

"So, you're going, then?" Ozlin asked.

"It's my family. I don't have a choice."

Zynora lowered her cup of tea. "Say no more. Tameel and I will begin packing tonight."

"Packing? Where do you think you're going?"

"With you, of course. You didn't think we'd let you go wandering all over Aldor without us, did you? We've been with you from the beginning. You aren't about to run off and leave us behind now. Besides, you'd be lost without us. Probably end up halfway to the Razor Spine before you realized you'd gone the wrong way."

Ayrion almost chuckled. If anyone were to get lost, it would be Tameel. Half the time, he let the horses guide their way while he slept in the driver's seat.

Tameel pulled his pipe from his mouth and grinned sheepishly. "You know better than to argue with her. In the end, she always gets her way."

Zynora nudged her husband playfully in response, but then turned and shot Ayrion a look he had come to learn meant she was not going to budge. He raised his hands in defeat.

"Fine, Creator help me if I were to ever try to tell you no." Truth be told, he had been hoping for their company. He just didn't want to be the one to ask.

"And what about us?" Bek said. "Am I supposed to sit around here in comfort while the three of you go off to battle some age-old enemy? Not on your life."

Ty, Breen, and Narendi all shared a hesitant look. "I guess we can come as well," Ty said, his offer not quite so emphatic as the others.

Ayrion shook his head. "Nyalis wants the three of you here in training." There was a snort from the direction of the hearth, and Ayrion turned. "My apologies. The *four* of you." The draakar lowered her head back to the floor.

"But we can help," Breen said, a little keener than his brother, but not by much.

"And you could use my spear," Narendi added, the only one of the three who actually sounded interested by the prospect of going off to fight a bunch of khuls.

"You can continue our training on the way," Ty added. "Besides, we survived a pygmy invasion. I'd say our skills are growing."

"They're improving, yes," Ayrion said, "but you are a far cry from being battle ready."

Ty's eyes tightened, though he tried to keep a neutral face to appear unaffected by Ayrion's comment. "I've survived a Tallosian incursion, an arachnobe army, a dark witch's possession, a maze monster, a water monster, an orm feeding ground, Riverland slavers, and a battle with the Tower's guards and over a dozen bulradoer. I think I can hold my own."

Ayrion smiled. It was easy to forget how much the young faerie had been through already. "If it were up to me, I'd be more than happy to take your help, but Nyalis believes you can do more good here, and as you pointed out, the wizard doesn't lie."

Ty pursed his lips. "Using my own words against me. Well played." He stared at Ayrion a moment. "We really would be willing to come."

"I know. Just not this time, I'm afraid."

"The wizard didn't say anything about *us* not coming, did he?" Bek asked.

Ayrion shook his head. "But this is hardly the place for children. The Lost City is dangerous enough without the added weight of a possible khul invasion." It felt strange even saying the word *khul*. Nightmares out of a child's bedtime stories. Myths so long removed, they hardly seemed real.

Bek sighed. "I will talk with Nel tonight and see—"

"There's no need," Nel said as she stepped out of the corridor behind them.

Ayrion wondered how long she'd been there listening. She walked over, and Bek quickly stood and offered her his seat. "The children and I will remain here."

"Are you sure?" Bek asked, resting a hand on her shoulder. Nel slowly ran her fingers over her short hair. It had been over a month since Zynora had excised Argon from his possession of Nel, but it was clear in more ways than just the slow regrowth of her hair, which was little more than fuzz at this point, that she had yet to recover from the ordeal.

Nel took her husband's hand and smiled. "I'm sure that I do not wish to be in the middle of another battle. The children and I would be more of a hindrance than a help, anyway. We will remain here, and I will continue with their schooling."

"And I would be glad of your help," Hanani said. "When we begin bringing our people down, it will be nice to have someone here who knows the place to help get them settled."

"I don't know how much use I'll be. We haven't explored much farther than the walls of the dorm."

Hanani nodded. "Which is all we should as well, from what it sounds like, at least until this wizard you speak of can show us what he would like us to do."

"We will be here to help as well," Ty said. "Breen, Narendi, and I are probably the most familiar with the school." There was a low growl by the fire, and the half-faerie turned and looked at the draakar. "Sorry, Kraea as well."

Hanani and Ozlin both glanced over at the red-scaled creature lolling in front of the hearth and pasted stiff smiles on their faces. They had been very thankful for the draakar's help during the battle and its aid during the fight with Mangora and her arachnobe, but Ayrion didn't blame them for still being wary of getting too close.

Nel smiled and looked up at Bek. "You see? There will be plenty around here to keep us busy until your return." She squeezed his hand. "You better return, and in one piece, you hear me?"

Bek leaned over and kissed her on the forehead. "I promise."

"I hope no one's expecting *us* to be going as well," Ozlin harumphed. "I've got enough on my plate worrying about keeping my people fed and sheltered.

I don't need to go looking for more trouble."

Ayrion sighed. "No. You are needed here. Besides, you're going to have plenty of trouble of your own if you are to take over the care of this place."

Ozlin frowned but didn't respond.

"Then it's settled," Zynora said, placing her cup of tea on the table in front of their sofa. "Tameel, Bek, and I will accompany you tomorrow, which means we should start packing."

Tameel grabbed his wife's hand and stopped her before she made it up. "We can wait for that until morning. Right now, we need to get a good night's sleep while we still can. Might be the last in quite a while."

As badly as Ayrion was wanting to get a move on, Tameel had a point. Glancing around the room, he noticed that he wasn't the only one with red eyes or who was fighting the urge to yawn.

Zynora looked at the others as well and sighed. "I suppose you're right. Besides, your snoring kept me up last night."

Tameel shook his head as he stood, then helped Zynora to her feet before turning to the others. "We bid you all a restful evening . . . what's left of it." The two headed for the stairs but stopped before making it to the hallway, and Tameel turned back around. "Wait just a minute. How are we going to go anywhere? Ol' Lerra is in Wellhollow, and the passes are blocked."

Ayrion turned in his seat. He hadn't even stopped to consider that. All the talk of Wellhollow being blocked off by the snow, and he had forgotten that their wagons were still there. In fact, other than the pass leading down to Lower Wellhollow, he had no idea if there was another way out of this valley other than perhaps the river. But the river wasn't going to prove all that useful since they didn't have a boat and it ran in the opposite direction of where they needed to go.

"He's right," Bek said, looking at Ayrion as if Ayrion was going to magically have the answer.

"I can confirm that the passes are indeed closed," Ozlin said, pulling on his bearskin coat. "After those black wielders were driven out, we sent men down to see where they might have gone, wondering if perhaps they had cleared the passes themselves. But if they had, they must have resealed them after they went through because the snow was still there, and there was no sign of them.

"Ask Nyalis," Ty said. "I'm sure if anyone can clear a pass it'd be him."

"But if he clears the passes," Ozlin pointed out, "that might make it more difficult to talk my people down off the mountain."

Zynora waved Ozlin's comment aside. "I think if they see this place for themselves and what it has to offer, they will come of their own accord."

Ozlin thought a moment, then nodded. "Perhaps you're right."

Ayrion leaned forward and rested his elbows on his knees. "I'll try to find Nyalis tomorrow and speak with him about the pass. I'm sure he'll have a solution."

Bek and Nel were the next to leave, followed by Ozlin and Hanani. Ozlin's earlier sparkle of excitement at getting to show his wife their magical bedchamber seemed to have waned over the course of the evening's discussions. In fact, Ayrion didn't think the man looked at all happy as they followed the others to the stairs, his guards close on his heels. Ty, Breen, Narendi, and the draakar were the last to leave. Ayrion remained in his seat, but he could hear them talking in the hall behind him. A moment later, Ty returned.

The faeling walked over and joined Ayrion in front of the fire, taking a seat directly across from him, his white hair turning a deep amber on the side facing the hearth as it reflected the fire's light. Ty looked a little wrong-footed, which wasn't anything new. It was the way he usually looked whenever Ayrion was around. Ayrion waited for the young man to say what was on his mind, but he seemed hesitant, or perhaps unsure. Ayrion was about to say something himself when Ty finally cleared his throat.

"I wanted to say that I'm sorry about the apple incident. I really didn't think it would hit you. The way you move . . ." He paused and stared at Ayrion as if waiting for Ayrion to validate in some way what he was thinking.

Ayrion tried not to smile. He could have answered him, but Ty had hit him in the back of the head with an apple. It hadn't been very honorable.

Ty continued to stare, then finally mumbled, "Anyway, I just wanted to say I was sorry."

Ayrion chuckled. "I did see the apple coming."

Ty's head lifted. "I thought so. Then why didn't you move?"

"Because I don't care to reveal things like that about myself if I don't have to." He grinned. "And I rather enjoyed watching you squirm."

Ty stiffened in his seat. "So you do have magic?"

"I do. But what you call my *abilities* are not all magic. I have spent my entire life training my body to fight. There is no magic that can replace hard work. I might be able to anticipate an opponent's moves, but that doesn't mean I can stop them, not without the skill and practice necessary to make that happen. You never want to make the mistake of relying solely on your gifts, even when, as in your case, they may be great. Magic is no match for training and common sense. Trust me on that."

"How are we to continue our training without you here?"

Ayrion had thought about that on his walk back from the garrison, and there seemed to be only one solution. "For now, Narendi can take over where I have left off. She is very skilled with the blade, and it wouldn't hurt you to learn the spear as well, if for no other reason than to understand that not all weapons are used the same. In the hands of a skilled armsman, each can be just as deadly. She can help you progress until I can resume teaching upon my return. Who knows, perhaps we will have some actual Upakan instructors here for you to learn from when I do."

Ty didn't look enthusiastic about that particular possibility.

"Get some sleep," Ayrion said. "The four of you have had quite a grueling day."

Ty stood. "Good night, then." He looked a little less uncomfortable than when he had first sat down.

"Oh . . ." Ayrion stopped Ty before he reached the corridor. "And please keep what we've discussed to yourself."

Ty nodded and then disappeared into the hall.

Ayrion leaned back in his seat and let the warmth of the flames cover him. He closed his eyes for a moment and took a deep breath, slowly releasing the tension in his shoulders. Tomorrow was going to be a long day, and he needed the rest. He stood and headed for the stairs. As tired as he was, after everything that had been revealed, he doubted he'd be able to sleep much tonight, perhaps not for several nights to come.

Chapter 13 | Ayrion

MORNING ARRIVED TO FIND Ayrion already up and waiting. As predicted, his sleep was short and restless. He'd spent half of the night agonizing over what all he would need to pack for a journey to the Lost City—though in the end it was nothing more than his normal fare: clothing, weapons, food—and the other half worrying about the kind of welcome he was sure to receive.

He stared at a map he had found in one of the rooms downstairs. It bore a complete diagram of the Five Kingdoms, noting areas as far as the Isle of Tallos to the east, the Wengoby Desert to the west, the Caldera to the north, and the Copper Islands to the south. If Nyalis was able to clear the passes for them, it seemed the fastest route would be to go cross country, just north of the Grasslands of Tekoa.

He certainly didn't want to travel south to Minotha and take the road from there west across Sidara. Such a route would require extra travel time, and Ayrion didn't think another trip through Lord Talmanes's territory would prove the wisest choice, not after he burnt down the lord's home on his last visit.

Finding westward trails across the grasslands might prove even more challenging, since they were bound to be covered in snow this time of year. Of course, none of that would matter if they couldn't make it out of the mountains in the first place.

Ayrion rubbed his tired eyes, then grabbed his swords and coat and headed down to the common room to stretch his legs. He found Tameel in front of the fire, chewing on his pipe and sipping on a tankard of something that had a strong smell of cloves.

"Up early, I see," Ayrion said as he joined the old tinker in front of the fire.

"Never made it to bed," Tameel grumbled. "Crazy woman got to thinking about what all would need to be packed and then spent the rest of the night making lists. And by making lists, I mean dictating what she wanted for me to write down." Tameel's eyes had dark circles, even darker than before he'd gone to bed. He studied Ayrion for a moment as he slowly released a long trail of smoke that snaked all the way to the ceiling. "You don't look all that rested yourself."

Ayrion smiled. "Afraid not. Too many things plaguing my mind."

"Yes, that was quite the revelation last night. What do you think about it all?"

Ayrion chuckled. "Which part? The fact that my people were once the revered paladins of the wizards, or the fact that they might be coming under attack by an enemy that no one has seen in over a thousand years?"

Tameel pulled his pipe from his mouth and pointed the stem at Ayrion. "Yes, that one." He laughed. "The world seems to have gone right mad, doesn't it? Or perhaps it's us. Sometimes it's hard to tell the difference. All we can do is put one foot in front of the other and hope we don't trip over them."

"Sage advice," Ayrion said. Tameel was good at simplifying problems. The tinker had a way of not getting bogged down in the details, of focusing on the overall goal. Zynora, however, was a sharp contrast to Tameel. She, like Ayrion, took every detail into account, no matter how small, which more often than not only resulted in mountainous levels of stress. But as Zynora was quick to point out, if no one paid attention to the small details, nothing would ever get done.

The two sat quietly for some time, lulled into complacent silence by the cracking and popping of the fire and the mesmerizing way the flames danced across the wood. A fretful voice whispered in the back of Ayrion's mind that it didn't matter how tired he was or how much he wanted to just keep sitting there—time was running out. There were still things that needed to be done before they could begin their long journey across Aldor.

He shook his head, trying to clear the thoughts before they began the same litany that had kept him up most of the night, and stood. Leaving Tameel to the comfort of his pipe, Ayrion walked out onto the front porch for some fresh air.

It was another cold morning, the grey dawn just bright enough to see his breath rising in front of his face. All around the yard, Ayrion watched as one by one the torches extinguished, the morning light creeping over the tops of the buildings. It wouldn't be long before the others made their way down for breakfast, and then the real work would begin. He had hoped to find the old wizard to ask him what they should do about the passes, but as usual, the man was nowhere to be found.

He walked down the steps and started around the outer walkway that surrounded the open yard. Most mornings, Ayrion and Bek would rise early enough to get a jog in before starting the day, but today Ayrion didn't want to work up a sweat before breakfast, especially considering he wouldn't be spending the day in training. In fact, he wasn't really sure why he was out here at all. He should be inside getting ready, but for some reason he just couldn't bring himself to finish packing.

He kept his stroll to a fast pace to fight against the brisk winter air, which was beginning to sting his face and burn the tops of his ears. After one trip around the dormitory square, Ayrion felt that his mind was sufficiently clear and returned to the front porch of the north wing and stared out at the open yard, hoping to spot Nyalis standing there by the fountain, waiting.

No such luck.

There wasn't much sense in standing out in the cold for no reason—though he did appreciate the way it had helped clear his mind—so, taking one last look toward the southern gate and finding it empty, he headed back inside.

The warmth of the common room had him quickly removing his swords and long coat, leaving his dark shirt underneath to dry at the back where he had begun to sweat through. The room had filled since he'd started his walk. Bek and Nel were talking with Tameel, Zynora, Ozlin, and Hanani, and Ayrion could hear Taylis's and Marissa's hurried steps coming down the stairs, who were no doubt anxious to eat. The magistrate's guards were back in their place against the wall, keeping an eye on the others, and most importantly on Ayrion. All three had reached for their weapons when he had first entered, clearly not expecting someone to come walking in.

"You look how I feel," Bek said from across the room with a smile. He walked over to join Ayrion by the door. "You should have let me know you were going for a run this morning. I would have joined you."

Ayrion smiled. "I didn't. Just clearing my head."

"Did it work?" Bek leaned in. "I barely slept a wink. The wife had me up half the night talking. Ever since Argon and his plague of shadows, she hasn't wanted to leave my side for more than a few hours." He frowned. "To put it mildly, she's not too happy with the idea of me being gone for so long, especially considering where it is we're heading."

"Then perhaps you should stay," Ayrion said, though it pained him to suggest it. When it came to a fight, there were few Ayrion felt safer having at his side than Bek.

Bek shook his head. "She knows I need to go. If I stayed here and something were to happen to all of you, I don't think I could live with myself. Besides, having the folks from Wellhollow here will help." The big trapper glanced over his shoulder to where Nel was quietly chatting with the magistrate's wife near the hearth. "I believe Hanani has formed an attachment with Nel and the kids, which will give Nel someone to lean on while I'm away."

Ayrion nodded. "As long as you're sure. You know I want you with me, but I also know what Nel's been through, so I'll leave that up to the two of you."

He turned at the sound of more footsteps coming from the central hall. The faeling and his companions stepped out of the corridor and looked around the room. They, at least, appeared to have gotten some sleep, unlike the rest of them. Ayrion hated stopping their training, as they were just finally getting into the swing of things. He hoped Narendi would be able to keep them going. If Ty would commit himself, and the four of them didn't find some new way of getting themselves killed, then perhaps Ayrion would return to find his students greatly progressed.

A bell rang, and everyone started across the room, funneling down the right corridor and back to the dining area. Ayrion and Bek were near the front of the group, as they were closest to the hall, but it was Taylis and Marissa who made it inside first, accomplished by shoving their way past the others, Taylis nearly tripping Bek as he ran between his legs. Ayrion chuckled inwardly. He was going to miss them.

Stepping inside, he was surprised to find Nyalis waiting for them at one end of the table.

"I'm glad you're here," Ayrion said on his way to the opposite end. "We have a few things that need to be discussed." He left his coat and swords hooked on the back of his chair and waited for Nyalis.

Nyalis nodded but didn't say anything.

"Ah," Ozlin barked as he stepped into the room and spotted the wizard, "just the man we needed to see." He introduced Nyalis to his wife.

Ty and his companions were the last in, the draakar bringing up the rear as she made her way behind the wizard's chair and over to the corner where her tray of meat was usually waiting.

"It seems we have a bit of a problem," Ozlin started right in, but Nyalis held up his hand to stop him.

"Later," was all the answer Nyalis gave, leaving Ozlin with nothing to do but take his seat and wait with the others, though his face said he wasn't happy about it.

Nyalis sat quietly until everyone had found their place. Last to sit were Ozlin and Hanani's three guards, taking chairs directly across from the magistrate. This time they behaved in a more civilized manner as they waited for the food to appear. Ayrion wondered how they had enjoyed their rooms, and if Hanani had been sufficiently impressed after the buildup from her husband.

Before Taylis and Marissa got the chance to begin their ritualistic arguing over who got to call the food, Nyalis clapped his hands three times, and the table burst to life with smells that had Ayrion's mouth watering. Their goblets filled as well, each to their own personal preferences. Ayrion's had a strongly spiced hot cider that warmed his insides on the way down.

Some of those at the table were already reaching for the ladles, but a poignant clearing of the throat by the wizard stopped everyone. As soon as he had their attention, Nyalis offered a quick thanks to the Creator for their bounty and then nodded for them to continue.

Ayrion joined the others in filling his plate from the platters and bowls closest to his seat. He waited to see if Nyalis was going to speak before digging into his food, but at the moment it seemed the wizard was just as preoccupied with filling his plate as the rest, so Ayrion proceeded to eat.

Breakfast conversations consisted mostly of discussing everyone's bedchambers. It started with Zynora asking the magistrate's wife what she thought of their accommodations. After a very long-winded but enthused description of the new room—it came as no surprise to anyone that it had been another type of mountain dwelling, though one much larger and fancier than the one they shared now—the others jumped in and began to describe the rooms they had created as well. There was no doubt they could have spent the rest of the day talking about how wondrous it was to have rooms that changed to their every whim, but they had more important things that needed discussing.

Nyalis finished eating, took one final sip from his goblet, and wiped his mouth. He then turned to Magistrate Ozlin. "So, what was this problem you wished to discuss? I hope it has nothing to do with your people's willingness to return."

Ozlin cleared his throat. "No, not exactly, though that is something we need to discuss further before I try convincing my people to up and leave the only home they've ever known. But no, the problem is the passes leading out the mountains. They were completely blocked during the battle with those sons of faeries, the Tower's wielders."

"Our wagons are up there," Tameel said. "Me and the wife and Bek are planning on accompanying Ayrion to the Lost City, but we can't get down the mountain with all the snow."

Ozlin looked at Tameel, then back at Nyalis. "What he said."

Ayrion took an even more direct approach. "Would you be able to clear the passes for us to get down the mountain? We don't know if you have any wizard's tricks up your sleeve that would help get through the snow."

"Wizard tricks, huh?" Nyalis leaned back in his seat and stroked his beard. "I might have a *trick* or two available. How soon are you wanting to leave?"

"The sooner the better," Ayrion said. "If my people are in trouble, then I want to be heading down the mountain before dark, if that's possible." He turned to Tameel and Zynora. "How much do you have left to pack?"

"The hardest part won't be gathering our belongings," Zynora said, "so much as toting them across the valley and up the mountain to Wellhollow. Most of our stuff is still up with the wagons. Food is the biggest issue at this point."

"I can take care of that," Nyalis said. "I can provide you with gold enough to purchase what you need."

Ayrion figured they could make their first stop in Lower Wellhollow to get supplies to last at least until the next town they came across.

"And you're sure we can't take one of those fancy flying boats out there?" Tameel asked hesitantly.

"If we had a captain and crew to operate one, I would be more than willing to let you try, but unfortunately, we don't, nor do we have the time to learn. As I told Ayrion, it takes more than magic to fly an airship."

Tameel sighed. "Couldn't hurt to ask." His head lifted. "Of course, if you had some special magic for making our wagons fly, I could certainly handle that."

Everyone laughed at the suggestion, which seemed to be offered in humor. Even Nyalis chuckled. "Afraid the magic doesn't work like that," he said.

Ozlin, on the other side of the table, pursed his lips and stroked the braid of his beard.

"Yes, Magistrate?" Nyalis asked.

Ozlin cleared his throat. "What is all this caretaker stuff about? We don't know anything about magic, so what is it exactly that you would be expecting us to do?"

"Magic is certainly not a requirement for the role of caretaker," Nyalis said, leaning forward to rest his arms on the table. "There is much about Aero'set that is not operated on magic—grass still needs cutting, trees need trimming, bushes and flower beds still need tending; the buildings themselves need maintaining. If we were to squander our magic on such things, it would leave less for more important matters."

"I thought they cleaned themselves," Breen interrupted, which for him was rare. Like Ayrion, Breen wasn't the most talkative of people, something Ayrion appreciated. "The school has been left unattended for a thousand years, and there's hardly a trace of dust."

Nyalis smiled. "That will change soon enough. When we shifted Aero'set out of this realm, it was placed in a sort of . . . hidden bubble that wasn't affected by time in the way we think of it. For us it has been a thousand years, but for it . . ." He shrugged. "There's no telling. It could have been a few moments. So things like dust and everyday wear were temporarily suspended." Nyalis turned to Ozlin. "The point is that the school needs to be maintained, which requires caretakers."

"Even if we brought all of our people down," Ozlin said, "I don't see how they would be enough to keep up with a place this size."

Nyalis cocked one of his bushy white brows. "When I said *your people*, I wasn't just referring to those living on top of the mountain."

Ozlin stiffened. "You aren't suggesting we bring those traitors up from Lower Wellhollow, are you?"

"They are your kinfolk, are they not? Part of the original settlement that left Aero'set? As such, they hold just as much stake in this place as you, and as you say, you can't do it on your own."

"But . . . but you don't know them the way we do. Marak would sooner stick his axe in my back than work with us. We haven't spoken in almost ten years."

"Then it sounds like you are due for a meeting," Nyalis said with a hint of a grin. "Besides, you might be surprised. I have a feeling that the Tower's bulradoer didn't leave Lower Wellhollow completely unscathed. This might be the perfect chance to extend the arm of friendship, because one way or another, it is time all of your people returned home, and I do mean *all*."

"Would we be living here, in this place?" Hanani asked.

Nyalis nodded. "At least for now. The caretakers have always resided in the lower city on the southern edge of Aero'set. You will have your own community, privacy away from the goings-on inside of Aero'set, yet close enough to be there when needed. I haven't yet had time to check on the buildings there, but when I do, we can eventually look at setting up a residence for you. The dormitory here was for apprentices of magic. Those coming to learn, as well as those here to teach. Obviously it could be some time before we see any sort of semblance to those days, but I hope that eventually . . ."

"You want to open the school back up for wielders?" Ty asked, beating others to the question.

Ayrion hadn't yet heard what Nyalis's ultimate goal was for the school, only that they would need Aero'set if they were to survive whatever was coming.

"Of course." The wizard leaned back in his seat, scanning the faces of those gathered. "It is a school for magic, is it not? Which stands to reason that it will at some point need students."

"But there are no other wizards around to teach magic," Ty said. "For that matter, how would you find wielders willing to come and learn? Most are doing their best to keep their magic hidden. It's not like we can send out a proclamation that we have just opened a school of magic and are seeking wielders."

Nyalis didn't give any hint as to what he was feeling. "No, I suppose we can't. If it became openly known that the school had been rediscovered and put back into use, the White Tower would no doubt build a permanent fortification around Wellhollow just to keep any from entering. But as it stands, Mangora's attempt at opening Harok Laos resulted in the destruction of her bloodstone. She left the mountain believing the key useless. Hopefully, it will be some time before they learn of your success."

"But that won't last," Ayrion said. "They will send more troops, or spies, or even their corax."

"The corax are unable to fly here," Nyalis said. "The school has protection spells against their intrusion. But as you say, the Tower will not sit idly by, which is why the Tanveer's return is of such importance. Aero'set needs its guardians here as a deterrent. It is not a coincidence that the Tower has always kept their distance from the Lost City. They do not wish to start a conflict with the Tanveer, at least not yet."

Ayrion didn't like the way that sounded. But he had always been curious as to why the Upaka had never had a visit from the Black Watch. He wasn't sure how his people would have reacted if they had. They didn't know their own heritage. Ayrion stared down at his father's black onyx ring and the white crest at its center. Knowing Brim, the head of Ayrion's former Upakan clan, he would have turned any wielders over to the Tower just to keep them from causing him any undue trouble. His mind shifted back to the reason they were there, and he scooted his seat back from the table. Most had already finished their meals.

"The sooner we can get to the wagons, the better chance of us making it down the mountain before dark."

"Aye," Tameel said, wiping some gravy drippings from his beard. "We should be ready to leave within the hour."

Ayrion looked at Bek, who in turn looked at his wife, and she nodded.

"I should be ready by then as well," Bek added.

"We want to go, too," Taylis said, Marissa agreeing with a firm nod.

"The only place you two are going is up to clean your room," Nel said as she, too, stood. The children groaned all the way out the door.

Ayrion smiled and stood as well, joined by the rest. He turned to see if Nyalis needed him to stay but found the wizard's seat empty. The man was sneakier than an Upakan. Ayrion left the dining room and followed the caravan down the hall, across the common room, and around to the stairs leading up to their rooms. Reaching the second landing, he started down the corridor, passing Tameel and Zynora just as they were stepping into their chambers.

He opened his room to find it the same as he had left it. There was a new change of clothes, however, folded and waiting on the end of his bed. He wondered what would happen if he took them along, if they would vanish as soon as he left Aero'set or the wards around the surrounding valley. It would be rather embarrassing to have the clothes he was wearing disappear while walking into Wellhollow.

Still, he brought them along just in case, simply deciding to save them for another day—provided they were still around.

His bags were already packed, including the rolled map he'd been studying the previous night. He wasn't sure how accurate it was, but given it came from a place like Aero'set, he figured it was probably more accurate than not, especially considering some of the townships depicted couldn't have possibly been around a thousand years ago. Whoever had created the map either had done so with some sort of foreknowledge as to how the world would look in a thousand years, or the map had somehow adjusted itself. Either way, it was a good tool to have around.

Ayrion waited for the others down in the common room, each with a satchel or carry bag on their shoulder. Ayrion took Zynora's, freeing up her hands to help Tameel if needed. Bek was clothed head to foot in his hunting furs, chatting with Ozlin about the making of his zabatas. The magistrate was clearly intrigued.

"Anyone seen the wizard?" Zynora asked.

Ayrion shook his head, then looked over at Ty, who was lingering in front of one of the windows overlooking the yard. "Do you see anything?"

Ty shook his head.

"Should we wait?" Bek asked.

Ayrion shrugged. They needed Nyalis to clear the passageways, but the wizard knew they were planning on leaving within the hour. The longer they waited, the more difficult it would be to get down the mountainside. "I say we start for Wellhollow. Who knows? He might have already gone before us to start clearing the pass."

The others agreed, and they all headed out the door, even those who were being left behind. Bek kissed Nel and the kids, and Ayrion waited for them to finish before offering his own goodbyes. For Marissa, he had a warm hug and a kiss on the cheek. For Taylis, a firm handshake, but only after Taylis had put his crawly-killer back in his pocket. "Make sure you keep them safe," Ayrion said to the little boy, rubbing the top of his head. Taylis nodded confidently.

Ayrion turned to his pupils. "Make sure to keep up with your training."

"I will keep them trained," Narendi said, and knowing her, she would.

"And please, for the love of Aldor, try not to get yourselves into any more trouble."

Ty smiled a little too eagerly. "We'll do our best."

Chapter 14 | Ayrion

YRION LED THE SMALL BAND across the yard and through the southern entrance. Ozlin and Hanani had decided to accompany them back, eager to bring their people down from the mountain before their situation got any worse. Hanani stuck to Zynora's side, the two chatting and laughing as the group walked through the southern half of the city toward the main gate. Ozlin, however, was a different story.

One look at the magistrate and Ayrion could tell something was weighing heavily on him, as the man quietly stared at the ground in front of his feet. Ayrion thought it likely was Nyalis's words about reaching out to Lower Wellhollow. He didn't know what exactly had caused the rift between the two peoples, but it had certainly left its mark. From what Ayrion had pieced together, it had something to do with the guarding of Harok Laos, but he didn't think it a good time to bring the subject up, especially since Ayrion wasn't exactly Ozlin's favorite person.

The trip across the valley took the rest of the morning, and the sun had already passed its zenith by the time they finished a quick lunch and started up the stone steps for Harok Laos. Ayrion had to stop several times on the way to let the others—mainly Tameel and Zynora—catch their breath, and by the time they managed to reach the top, they were all good and winded, their legs shaking from more than the icy gusts pummeling down from the peaks above.

The stone doors leading into Angioma's cavern stood ajar, as they had since Ty first opened them. They were too massive to be moved by hand. Inside, the cavern was lit by troughs of oil that lined the left and right sides, their light illuminating the ancient stone carvings that filled every inch of the walls. On the right, Ayrion spotted the image he'd seen of ships floating through the clouds. He wondered what else he might find if he took the time to look. There were so many carvings, it would take days to really see them all.

Leaving Harok Laos, they passed several sets of guards on their way through the tunnels, stopping only briefly inside Angioma's former living chamber. Her bed, rocker, and table were right where she had left them; even the rugs the blind oracle had used as guides to navigate her home remained untouched.

Ayrion's chest tightened as he looked around the lonely room. Images of the old seer's last moments haunted him. The way she had stared up at him, having known since she was a child that his face would be one of the last things her hands would feel before she died. He missed the old woman, her straightforwardness being one of the things he admired most about her. She was not one to shy away from telling you what she thought. She had gifted them each with a foreseeing. Part of his was already coming true—an underground city that needed saving. She had also given him other visions: *A black horse riding at the front of an enumerable host, its rider carrying a set of twin blades.* To be honest, that could have been a vision of the battle that took place at Belbridge, depending on what she considered an enumerable host. She had also told him that she had seen those long passed returning—whatever that meant—and a queen with a broken heart.

Sadly, none of her visions were very uplifting. No happy reunions, or enemies defeated, or vengeance taken on deserving usurpers. It sounded like Ayrion's future was going to be fraught with great battles and possibly greater sadness. He had a feeling that Angioma's final prophecy dealing with the broken-hearted queen was that of Queen Ellise after finding out that her husband had been killed in battle.

Once again, his mind wandered back to Aramoor and those he had left behind. He would be back one day. Just as soon as he could make sure his family was safe, he would settle things with Dakaran.

They left Angioma's chamber and started into the tunnel on the other side. It was a long walk, but they did eventually exit the mountain and were once again out on the open plateau that was Upper Wellhollow. Ayrion was surprised to find how much of the damage had already been cleared. He turned and looked up at the upper levels where the archers had originally been set and where most of the bulradoers' blasts had been levied. The narrow walkway in front of the buildings was almost completely wiped away, making it nearly impossible to reach, and the fronts of many of the homes had collapsed altogether.

There were scorch marks coating most of the stone, as though an angry artist had decided to destroy his canvas by splattering it with fistfuls of thrown paint, except the only color he used was charcoal.

The most surprising find after the battle was how little damage had been done to the two wagons, which had been parked just to the right of the pass entrance. Tameel and Zynora grinned as they unlocked the back of Ol' Lerra and started up the steps. Tameel stopped only long enough to rub a couple of the boards where the green and gold paint had faded and to speak a gentle greeting to her. Ayrion couldn't quite make out everything he said, but it had something to do with wondering if Ol' Lerra had missed him.

Ayrion left the wagons and walked over to the entrance of the pass, which led down to where he and Bek had first met the Black Watch troops and brought them up. The floor of the pass was covered in snow instead of bodies, unlike the last time he'd seen it. After talking with one of the watchmen, they had learned that the fallen warriors from Wellhollow had received a parting ceremony and a respectful burial. Those from the Tower had simply been tossed over the side of the cliff to be dashed apart on the rocks below, their blood and flesh calling out to the carrion birds to come and feast.

Looking around, it was hard to believe there had been a battle at all. The newly fallen snow had all but covered the atrocities that had taken place just a few weeks back.

The memories, however, were not so easily wiped away.

A familiar whinny behind him caught Ayrion off guard, and he quickly turned to find Shade trotting across the plateau toward him. The black warhorse had been stabled with the other horses in one of the buildings on the lower level. Ayrion could sense Shade's delight at seeing him.

"Hello, my old friend," Ayrion said as he rubbed the horse's snout. Shade nuzzled him in return. "I wish I had a way to bring you to Aero'set with me, but those steps are just a little too steep for a horse to climb." Ayrion had hated leaving him behind. It was the first time they had truly been parted since their first meeting on the Rymiran Plains all those years ago.

Shade shook his head, then raised his upper lip and stuck out his tongue as if to say he wasn't too happy about the situation either.

"Good news is," Ayrion said, rubbing behind the horse's ears, "we are going on a very long journey, all the way across Aldor. I have a feeling that by the time we get there, you'll be good and tired of my company."

Shade shook his long black mane, and Ayrion smiled. "Yeah, me neither."

"Any sign of the wizard?" Bek asked, walking over from his inspection of the rover wagon next to Ol' Lerra.

Ayrion turned. "I haven't seen him, but perhaps they have." He pointed at Ozlin and Hanani, who were standing outside their own home over near the face of the cliff, speaking with their tall butler, Kuwa.

"Only one way to find out," Bek said, and they started across the plateau.

Ayrion had never seen Kuwa without his formal serving coat on, but today it had been replaced with a dark fur coat. Ayrion wondered if the other had been damaged during the fight.

"Have you seen the wizard?" Ozlin asked when he saw them coming.

Ayrion shook his head. "We were coming to ask you the same."

Ozlin frowned. "Kuwa says he's seen no one, but he's also been helping with the work crews all morning, so he doesn't know for sure."

The tall butler smiled as he curled the ends of his thick mustache. "I can keep my eyes open for you," he said.

Ayrion nodded. "That will be helpful, thank you." Though he didn't know how helpful, if the man was busy clearing out the inside of caved-in homes.

"In the meantime," Ozlin said to Kuwa, "I want you to gather the townsfolk for a meeting. We'll hold it over by the entrance to the tunnel." He glanced at Ayrion and Bek. "If you're still around, I'd appreciate you being there to speak with the people about the need to relocate."

Ayrion was surprised Ozlin was asking him for help. He must be desperate. Ayrion wasn't exactly sure how he could help encourage the people of Wellhollow to vacate their homes, but he figured it would be good practice for when he reached the Lost City. "We'll do our best."

Ozlin gave his belt a tug. "Can't ask for more than that."

"Let us know if you spot Nyalis," Ayrion said, and then he and Bek left the magistrate to his work and headed back to the wagons.

"Don't envy him," Bek said. "He's got his work cut out for him. I remember how difficult it was for me and Nel to leave Belvin. It's going to be quite the task to relocate an entire community." He chuckled. "It makes me wonder how Abiah has been managing. Nothing like being promoted from town taverner to town magistrate overnight, especially when half the surrounding communities were lost to a plague. Nope." He shook his head. "I don't envy either of them."

Ayrion agreed. It was quite the burden being placed on all their shoulders. They reached the wagons about the same time that Tameel and Zynora were stepping out the back.

"Any word on Nyalis?" Zynora asked.

"Afraid not," Ayrion said. "Though, it sounds like Ozlin would like us to stick around to help him break the news to his people. I believe they are going to be holding a meeting over by the tunnel entrance shortly."

Zynora turned to look. "We were wondering why they were gathering."

Tameel rubbed the top of his head. "Perhaps Nyalis will make an appearance before the end."

Zynora hmphed. "Be nice if he could show sooner and answer what I'm sure will be a host of questions."

Ayrion doubted the wizard had the time, or desire, to sit around and convince a group of mountain folk they needed to leave their mountain. And as much sympathy as he had for the people of Wellhollow, Ayrion didn't want to stand around either, not when his family could be in danger.

The gathering was growing quickly at the northeast corner, to the point that even standing on the back steps of the wagon wasn't enough to still see

Ozlin's head at the front of the crowd. He was able to see Kuwa's, though. The man was at least half a head taller than anyone else in Wellhollow.

Ozlin's voice suddenly boomed over the crowd, echoing off the surrounding rock as he tried to quiet the people down.

"Guess that's our cue," Ayrion said and started for the gathering. The sooner they were able to put the townsfolk at ease, the sooner they could look at moving on.

"Aye," Bek added, moving alongside, "let's get this over with."

Tameel and Zynora moved in behind them.

When those standing in back saw them coming, they began to move aside, tapping those ahead to do the same, so that by the time Ayrion and the others reached the assembly, they had cleared a path straight down the middle and all the way to the front. The people seemed excited to see them, the younger ones pointing as they walked by, while the older ones tipped their heads and offered warm smiles. Ayrion hoped they could use that in their favor.

The human corridor ended at Ozlin and Hanani, who were doing their best to persuade the townsfolk to vacate Wellhollow. It didn't seem to be going all that well.

". . . leave Wellhollow?" an older man on the left asked. "We just fought and died to protect it."

Ozlin raised his hands once again in a vain attempt at quieting the crowd. "The wizard says that our place is down in Aero'set."

"Since when do we go listening to wizards?" a woman in the crowd shouted back, which was quickly followed by echoes of the same sentiment. "I never thought I'd see the day when Ozlin Beartooth stooped to anyone, let alone a wielder."

Ozlin's cheeks grew as red as his beard. "I bow to no man! But I also have the common sense not to butt heads with a wizard! He says that our people were the caretakers of Aero'set. Well, we've been sitting here guarding this lump of rock for centuries, not knowing why we were even doing it. Now we do!"

"More importantly," Hanani cut in, "there is food there, all you can eat, shelter from the cold, rooms that shape themselves to your very wish."

"It's all magic!" someone shouted from the back. "We'll have no part in that evil. Look what it did to our town!"

Ayrion sighed. This was going to be more difficult than he'd thought. Perhaps it would have been best for Hanani not to have mentioned the shifting bedchambers.

"Magic isn't evil," Ayrion said, quieting the crowd. "It's just different."

"Don't tell us it isn't evil," the older man in front who'd spoken earlier said, as he pointed over at what was left of their homes. "Look what it's done to us."

"I didn't say it wasn't powerful," Ayrion amended. "I said it wasn't evil." He walked over and grabbed one of the torches off the wall in front of the tunnel and carried it back. He held it up for everyone to see, those near the front scooting back, no doubt afraid he was about to perform some magic and burn them all. "Is this evil?"

Whispers filtered through the crowd, but no one came out and openly answered the question.

Ayrion looked at the older man who seemed to be speaking for the rest. "Would you call this torch evil?"

The old man rubbed his white beard nervously, casting about at those around him.

"Well?" Ayrion asked.

"Suppose not," the man said. "But what's your point?"

"My point is that the flames from this torch, or from your hearths at home, or the candles beside your beds that you read with at night, are no different from that of a wielder's fire. The only difference is that a wielder can produce more of it. We use fire to keep us warm, to cook our food, to light our homes, but if left unattended, it can burn entire towns and forests to the ground. Would we call the fire evil? No. The bulradoer are evil. But it's not their magic that makes them that way, it's how they choose to use it." A thought hit Ayrion, and he drove the point home further. "Would you say that the oracle was evil?"

Ozlin stepped forward and raised his finger toward the crowd, eyes flaring. "Careful how you answer that."

The old man near the front gulped and quickly shook his head, others in the crowd doing the same. Angioma had been revered by the people of Wellhollow, all the oracles had, but they had also feared her.

"Angioma was not evil, though she was a wielder. She used her gift of foresight to help the people of this community. Even as she lay dying, she was using it to help others." There was a tightening in Ayrion's chest that had him fighting to keep his composure.

The crowd waited in silence for him to continue.

"The point is—"

"The point is, you silly nincompoops," Zynora cut in, "that if you stay here, you're going to either starve to death or freeze, probably both."

Ayrion was completely caught off guard and tried to think of a way to tie in what she'd said back to his original thoughts, but before he could, people at the back suddenly started shouting and drawing their weapons.

Surely Zynora hadn't upset them enough to come to blows?

On closer inspection, the people seemed to be turning in the other direction, looking back toward the entrance to the pass. What were they doing? Ayrion drew one of his swords as shouts that they were under attack rose from those on the other side. Ayrion grabbed Zynora and Tameel and pulled them out of the way and over toward the side of the rockface to keep them from getting trampled.

"Move!" Ozlin shouted, pushing his way through the crowd.

Ayrion raced to catch up with the magistrate, Bek right beside him. The three men cleared a path through the anxious bodies, everyone pressing tightly together as they moved toward the tunnel and away from the pass. Ayrion was the first to break through to the other side.

Armed men and women, wearing much the same as the townsfolk of Wellhollow, poured out of the pass and up onto the plateau. The entire front entrance was filled with fur-lined bodies. Ayrion drew his second blade as he stared at the growing number of people coming up. Had the snow been cleared already?

Ozlin got one look at the large man leading the pack and snarled. "It's Marak!"

Ayrion turned and looked at Marak, the magistrate of Lower Wellhollow, and Ozlin's sworn enemy. *Well, this couldn't have come at a worse time.*

Chapter 15 | Ayrion

OZLIN HELD HIS BATTLE-AXE at the ready. "Marak. That flaming son of a faerie thinks to attack while we are at our weakest. He's come to claim what's ours."

"Marak?" Bek looked at Ayrion. "Isn't that the leader of Lower Wellhollow?"

Ozlin spat, then shouted so Marak could hear him, "He's the leader of nothing. A pack of rabid dogs."

Ayrion tensed, hoping for all their sakes that Ozlin wasn't correct. They certainly couldn't afford another conflict this soon after their battle with the White Tower. Half the people in Upper Wellhollow weren't even armed, most still carrying shovels and buckets from where they had been clearing debris from collapsed homes. The women and children were quickly being ushered toward the back. At least this time they had a way to escape through the tunnels.

"I'll be hanged if I let you take one inch of this mountain!" Ozlin shouted across the plateau. The men of Upper Wellhollow gathered around Ozlin, Ayrion, and Bek, waiting for the signal.

Ayrion couldn't believe this was happening all over again. He watched the fighters on the other side and wondered how he was going to tell them apart from the men he was standing with. They all looked the same, apart from the fact that those he was with were holding hammers and chisels instead of swords.

"Enough!" a voice boomed across the plateau, shaking the very rock under their feet.

Everyone froze, including Ayrion, as the throng coming up from Lower Wellhollow parted and Nyalis walked out to the front.

"What's that wizard doing with them?" Ozlin groused.

Nyalis and a small company from Lower Wellhollow started toward them.

Ayrion released a heavy sigh of relief and walked forward to meet them, Bek on one side, Ozlin on the other. With Nyalis there, hopefully this meeting wouldn't turn into a conflict. They joined Nyalis, Marak, and a couple of Marak's men in the middle. Marak, who bore some very stark similarities to Ozlin: red hair, strong cheekbones, and a tendency to wear the full hide of an animal with its head still attached for a cloak—his being that of a grey wolf. He looked Ayrion and Bek over, pausing momentarily on Ayrion when he caught his eyes. The leader of Lower Wellhollow grunted, then turned to Ozlin but remained surprisingly quiet with his sword gripped tightly in his hands.

"What is this, wizard?" Ozlin asked. "You bring our enemies here to drive us out? Did you not believe me capable of talking my people out peacefully?"

Nyalis slammed his staff down on the stone, and the rock under their feet shook, causing those standing nearby to take a cautious step back. "Your brethren are not your enemies," Nyalis said, his voice sharp, "and they are here for the same reason you are: to return to Aero'set."

Ozlin sneered in Marak's direction. "I thought you didn't believe in all the tales of what lay beyond Harok Laos. Why would you leave your home for a place you've never even seen?"

"What home?" Marak growled back. "They burned it all. We have nothing."

Ozlin looked confused and for once had nothing to say.

"The Tower's wielders don't take defeat well," Nyalis said. "When they reached the bottom of the pass, they took out their anger on Lower Wellhollow."

Ayrion looked beyond Marak to the crowd of people gathered at the mouth of the pass, most carrying nothing more than the clothes on their backs. He hadn't even considered the possibility that the bulradoer would turn around and attack the other community simply out of spite. He figured they'd be doing everything they could to get back to their precious Tower.

Ozlin's sneer disappeared, his grip loosening on his axe. "We hadn't heard."

"How could you?" Marak said through clenched teeth. "No one's been able to get through the passes since they left. Without food and shelter, my people won't survive. We're digging new graves every day."

Ozlin lowered his axe altogether, looking ashamed for his earlier words.

"I don't beg," Marak said, "but when the wizard came this morning and told us of a place where there was food and warmth for my people and, more importantly, that we were its rightful stewards, I pleaded for him to show us the way. We don't want no handouts. We work for what we get."

Ayrion was rather taken aback. This couldn't have turned out better had they planned it. He passed a sideways look at Nyalis, then shook his head. No. There's no way the wizard could have known.

A thought struck him. "How did you get down the mountain so quickly? It took us the rest of the morning and part of the afternoon just to make it here."

"I used a mirror," Nyalis said, but nothing more.

Ayrion remembered Ty talking about the mirror he and his companions had traveled through from the Riverlands, and how it had brought him out somewhere in the lower mountains behind Wellhollow. "Can something like that be used to return to Aero'set?"

"Yes, if used properly."

Ayrion glanced over his shoulder at Shade and smiled. He now had a way to bring the big warhorse with him.

The wizard stared a moment longer, then turned to the two magistrates. "Do you think the two of you can work together long enough to bring these people down the mountain safely, without it turning into a civil war?"

Marak sheathed his sword, prompting Ozlin to do the same with his battle-axe. They both looked at each other, then nodded at the wizard.

"Good, because if I have to get involved, it will not be pleasant for either of you."

Ayrion had no idea what that meant and was sure neither of the men wanted to find out. He was glad to see Hanani making her way over. She would be a good mediator to keep the two in check.

Nyalis left the magistrates to stare each other down and started for the wagons. "Walk with me," he said to Ayrion and Bek as he passed.

They followed him over, Tameel and Zynora already there with the back door of Ol' Lerra open. If Ayrion were to look inside, he had no doubt he'd find all their weapons lying ready to grab. He turned to Nyalis as they slowed. "So, I take it the passes were clear?"

"They are now," Nyalis said as he turned and looked up to see where the sun was in the sky. The afternoon was quickly waning. "You'll need to hurry if you plan on reaching the base of the mountain before dark. Here," he said, pulling out a hefty coin purse and handing it to Bek. "This should be enough to cover your journey. Though, admittedly, I had thought you would be able to restock supplies in Lower Wellhollow before you left. Perhaps Ozlin and his people can at least find you some tinder before you leave. Where they are going, it will hardly be needed."

Bek thanked him and started to stuff the coin pouch in his pocket but was stopped by Tameel.

"We'll take that," he said, snatching the purse from Bek. "Safer to keep it in the wagon." Tameel handed the pouch to Zynora, who then climbed inside the back of Ol' Lerra to place it in one of the wagon's many hidden compartments.

Bek looked at Ayrion and shrugged. Ayrion chuckled. Ever since Ayrion had known Tameel, he had always insisted on handling the coin.

Nyalis then pulled Ayrion aside. "This is for you," Nyalis said, pulling out a chain with a crystal attached at the end. It was bigger than most transferals he'd seen.

Ayrion smiled and waved it off. "I don't need one of those." He was surprised at the wizard offering it to him. He thought Nyalis knew that his magic was innate.

"This isn't a transferal. It's a lume crystal."

"A what?"

"It will make sure that you are never without light." Nyalis placed the crystal in the palm of his hand and cupped his other hand overtop and whispered, "*Luminate.*" As soon as he did, rays of light burst through his fingers. He waited a moment, then whispered into his hands once more, "*Luminor.*" He opened his hand, and the crystal's light faded back inside. He handed the crystal to Ayrion. "Even a Tanveer's eyes require at least some light."

Ayrion hung the chain around his neck and tucked the crystal underneath his shirt before the two rejoined the others. "It seems you have things well in hand here," Ayrion said to Nyalis, glancing back over at the two magistrates, who appeared to be holding a civil conversation without the use of weapons. He turned to the others. "Best we start down the mountain while we can."

Zynora pulled her colorful cloak tighter around her shoulders, the charms from her headdress jingling in the wind. "While you men are getting the horses hitched, I'll have a talk with Ozlin and Hanani about finding us some provisions."

"Don't forget to have his men bring the ropes," Tameel added as she was walking away. "We won't get down the pass without them."

She waved her hand over her head to acknowledge she'd heard.

Ayrion watched as Zynora met with Ozlin and Hanani over at the side. Whatever she had said, it must have lit a fire under Ozlin, for it wasn't an hour later when the wagons were packed and stocked with what little provisions Wellhollow had left to offer, and their men had the pulleys set up and were helping lower the wagons down the pass. Both Upper and Lower Wellhollow townsfolk pitched in. In fact, Ozlin and Marak both stood at the front of the line, side by side, holding on to the thick ropes as they slowly lowered the two wagons down into the pass.

At the bottom, Bek released the final hook from the back of the wagons and shook the rope to let those at the top know they could pull them back up.

Nyalis remained up top with the people, apparently intending to escort them all to Aero'set himself.

Ayrion stayed with Shade, riding ahead of the wagons to watch for anything that might prove a hindrance. The mountain pass continued to drop small slides of snow, like miniature waterfalls that fell from the upper rock and down the sides of the pass. Ayrion ran his hand under one such fall as they passed near the edge. He had to admit, they were quite beautiful.

He'd barely made it around the second bend when he pulled back on the reins, spotting where the avalanche of snow had been sent by the bulradoer. It was an incredible sight; snow packed as high as thirty feet filled both sides of the cliff face, with a perfectly cut tunnel straight through, just high enough and wide enough to fit one of their wagons.

Tameel and Bek slowed the horses behind him when they saw the mountain of snow ahead.

"Now that is a sight to behold," Tameel said softly, not wanting to risk speaking too loudly and burying them in another slide.

Ayrion started for the entrance to the passageway, Shade's hooves walking along the already-packed snow from those that had just traveled up from Lower Wellhollow. The snow inside looked different, almost translucent. He climbed down off Shade and walked over to get a closer look. Sure enough, the inside of the tunnel seemed to have been hardened into ice, as though the snow had been melted and then immediately frozen to form the opening. Ayrion wondered how Nyalis had managed it. He was about to turn and wave them forward when he caught something in the corner of his eye and stopped. "Is that . . ."

He walked over to the left side of the passageway and leaned in, his breath sending a layer of fog across the icy wall. Using the sleeve of his coat to wipe away what his breath had hidden, he startled and took a step back. There was a face in the ice, twisted and contorted into a permanent scream. The man wore the white uniform of the Black Watch. He must have been one of those caught in the path of the avalanche.

Taking another step back, Ayrion noticed there were more. His eyes widened as he stared down the frozen passageway to discover there were bodies everywhere, some even coming through the ice—desperate arms and legs and heads poking out of the frozen tunnel, begging for help that would never come.

"Now that is a somber sight."

Ayrion jumped at Zynora's voice just over his right shoulder. He'd been too engrossed by the icy tomb to hear the others walking up behind him.

"Eerie, if you ask me," Bek said.

Tameel pulled off his hat reverently. "Well, the sooner we get through, the sooner we can put it behind us."

"I don't know if I'll ever be able to put something like this behind me," Bek said, staring at all the mangled corpses lining the passageway ahead.

Tameel scratched the top of his head, then placed his cap back on, pulling it down over his ears. "I can try."

Not wanting to remain any longer than he had to, Ayrion headed back to Shade and the wagons. Once everyone was aboard, Tameel gave him a nod, and they started in. Shade's hooves echoed down the tunnel of ice, the cracking under his feet sending chills up Ayrion's back, as though at any time the ice could break and drown them in snow and dead soldiers.

Behind him, the wagons rose nearly to the top of the tunnel, forcing Tameel and Bek to scrunch down in their seats to keep from hitting their heads on some of the dead limbs sticking through the ice.

The pace was slow, as the horses' hooves and the oak wheels tended to slide a bit on the ice. As thankful as Ayrion was for the passageway, he wished it hadn't been necessary. There was nothing like walking through a catacomb of ice and flesh to put one on edge. They hadn't even left Wellhollow and already this trip was leaving a pit in his stomach.

Ayrion wasn't sure how long they traveled. It felt like hours, but they finally rounded another corner, and he spotted the end of the ice ahead. The corridor of rock beyond was a welcome sight. Shade carefully made his way to the end and stepped out of the mouth of the tunnel and back onto the snow. He immediately shook his mane with a whinny. Ayrion could feel the horse's relief through their link.

The sun had long since fallen beyond what was needed to enjoy the warmth of its rays, and the clouds overhead were changing colors, which meant they didn't have long before the way ahead would be shrouded in darkness. Wanting to get ahead of it, both Tameel and Bek stopped to light the lanterns hanging from the sides of the wagon in order to help guide the horses.

Ayrion didn't recognize most of the terrain, though there was a fork that led off to the right that he thought he remembered on their trip up. A marker had been chiseled into the rock to point to the correct route, and Ayrion took it. By the time they reached the end of the pass, the stars were just blinking into existence.

"Best if we make camp here," Tameel suggested. "Don't know how much damage the town might have suffered or how much debris might be lying about. Don't want to take the horses through there without more light."

It was a good idea, and Ayrion swung down from Shade to help Tameel unhook the horses. They set up a tarp overhang on the sides of the wagons for the horses to shelter out of the weather and filled each with some of the dried bedding they had used in Upper Wellhollow. After seeing to their feed and water, they headed into the back of Ol' Lerra for some supper of their own. It was a little tight, but manageable.

Zynora had some biscuits cooking with a few slices of salted meat and cheese to stuff them. It wasn't the type of spread they had grown accustomed to over the last few weeks in Aero'set, but at this point Ayrion was feeling grateful to have gotten even this much, considering the losses that both mountain communities had suffered from the White Tower's attack.

After helping Zynora clean up after the meal, Ayrion joined Tameel and Bek outside as the two smoked their evening pipes before heading off to bed. The conversation was minimal, mostly discussing whether Nyalis would be able to settle both Lower and Upper Wellhollow into the magic school without another conflict. The consensus was that considering the state both towns were in and the losses they had each suffered, neither was probably wanting to add to it. In fact, it might encourage them to find a way to work together for healing. Either way, it was a problem left for others. They were sure to have plenty of their own without taking on any more for themselves.

Ayrion slept in the rover wagon with Bek, finding it easier to sleep with only one person's snores than two. He woke to hints of light streaming through the cracks around the door. Rolling over, he found Bek's bed empty. How long had he been gone? He quickly pulled on his boots and coat and grabbed his swords on the way out. The soft grey of the pre-dawn filled the lower mountainside trail. Smoke rose from the stack at the top of the green tinker wagon, signaling the others were up and breakfast was underway.

Not bothering to strap on his swords, he carried them around to the back of Ol' Lerra, greeting Shade on the way by. "How did you sleep?" Shade blew out his lips and nodded. "That's good. Me too." Ayrion left the warhorse to his grain and headed in to find everyone sitting around the table. "Why didn't you wake me?"

Bek smiled. "Because you needed the sleep. Not going to do us much good to have you dropping from your saddle."

Ayrion took a seat on the edge of one of the cots. "I have to admit, I do feel better." The pressure he'd been feeling in his head that had left him a little lightheaded the day before seemed to have passed. He couldn't remember the last time he'd woken to find the stars already gone. Accepting a glass of hot tea, he sipped slowly, enjoying the warmth as it went down.

"What are your plans?" Tameel asked as Zynora handed out their breakfast, which consisted of biscuits from the previous night's meal and a bowl of porridge sweetened with honey and softened with cream.

"I'm hoping to find an open trail from here to Aldwick, stay north of the grasslands if possible. It's the most direct route across this part of Sidara." Ayrion wasn't very familiar with this part of the world, having only traveled it once as they had come up from Woodvale.

Tameel pursed his lips. "Not many roads lead across country like that. On horseback, it would be less of a problem, but with the deeper snow, these wagons won't be able to plow through without getting stuck."

That was what Ayrion was afraid of. "What do you suggest?"

"We take the road out of Minotha. It stretches as far as Aldwick."

Everyone frowned at the mention of Minotha. The last time they'd traveled through Minotha, Ayrion had been captured by a young lordling and his mercenaries, only to escape and set fire to the man's entire estate.

"That's what I was afraid you were going to say," Ayrion said. He thought a moment. "Doesn't seem we are left with much of a choice. I would certainly prefer a more direct route that doesn't have us coming within a horse's gallop of Lord Talmanes's district, but I'd hate to try crossing the grasslands and get stuck halfway through and be forced to turn around and take the alternate route anyway."

No one said anything as they thought about their options.

Ayrion frowned. "We'll wait until dark to enter Minotha. That way, perhaps we can ride through without anyone the wiser."

Bek sighed. "As good a plan as any, I reckon."

The others seemed to agree—at least no one argued the point—and the rest of the meal was eaten in silence as they contemplated the journey ahead and what might await them when they reached Minotha.

As luck would have it, they found Tofflin's ferryboat still in one piece, with its rope attached and waiting to be drawn. Ayrion had worried that the bulradoer might have burned it on the way out. Perhaps they had kept it around in case they were inclined to return. Regardless, he was thankful to find it still intact. He wasn't sure how they would have gotten the wagons across Virn Run without it.

The snow continued to fall the first two days out but then stopped on the third as the skies cleared. The sun was bright enough off the snow that Ayrion was forced to pull out his shaders. He felt self-conscious wearing them, at least until Bek asked if he had a spare set that he could wear.

"Wow, where did you get these?" Bek asked. "I've never seen their like." He raised his pair back and forth in front of his eyes several times before finally putting them on. "They really work."

Ayrion smiled as he rode alongside the wagon. "I had them made in Aramoor. My people use them whenever they come aboveground."

Bek nodded. "I like them. I'll have to get a pair commissioned for myself."

The next several days came and went as they kept a slow but steady pace, stopping occasionally when they reached a deeper pocket of snow that had to be dug down to allow the wagons to pass. It didn't seem as though there had been much traffic, as most of the road showed little in the way of tracks. Ayrion was beginning to wonder if word had spread back to some of the smaller communities that Wellhollow had been destroyed. Either way, the road was rather void of travelers.

They stopped a few miles north of Minotha inside a thicket in order to hide the wagons from any passersby. The sun was still high enough in the sky to warm the face but low enough that they knew it wouldn't last long.

"I'll take one of the horses," Bek said, "and ride into town to see if there's anything we should be concerned with." He looked at Ayrion, Tameel, and Zynora. "I have a feeling all three of you would be too easily recognized."

He had a point. Ayrion would have liked to have ridden in, but Bek was the safest choice. "Watch for any sign of Talmanes's mercenaries. And see if they have any checkpoints set up at the entrances to town."

Bek nodded, then swung up onto Shade, the only horse not hitched to one of the wagons.

Shade whinnied, and Ayrion patted the horse's neck. "Now, you take good care of him."

"I plan to," Bek said.

Ayrion looked up. "I was talking to the horse."

Bek shook his head. "Any final thoughts?"

"Don't get caught," Tameel said.

"And see what their food supply is like," Zynora added. "We're nearly out of everything."

Bek nodded, and with a gentle nudge of his boot, he guided Shade back to the road. Ayrion watched as the two disappeared beyond the trees. He didn't like being the one staying behind, and especially didn't like someone else taking his horse, but there was little he could do about it now. He could only hope the two managed to stay out of trouble.

Chapter 16 | Ayrion

THE SUN HAD ALREADY SET by the time Ayrion heard horse's hooves coming up the road. He left the wagons and headed through the trees to see who it was, his black coat blending with the surrounding darkness. As soon as he spotted Bek coming over the rise on Shade, he stepped out to greet him. "Any trouble?"

"Yes and no," Bek said as he swung down out of the saddle.

"What does that mean?" Ayrion took the reins from Bek and rubbed Shade's neck. The warhorse nickered his approval.

"I'll tell you back at camp," Bek said as he left the road and started down the narrow opening between the trees.

Ayrion looked at Shade and Shade looked back, then shook his head.

"I agree completely," Ayrion said, and they both headed into the woods after Bek.

"I see you made it back in one piece," Tameel said, his pipe clenched between his teeth as small puffs of smoke rose from the bowl. "I hope things went well?"

Ayrion slowed as he and Shade entered camp. "Was anybody watching the roads in and out of Minotha?" He tried directing Shade over to the wagons, but the horse kept dragging his feet, clearly upset that Ayrion had stopped rubbing his ears. Ayrion finally pulled a carrot from his pocket, and Shade nearly knocked him over trying to get at it.

"The good news is that I didn't see anyone guarding the roads," Bek said. "However, the bad news is that it's because they have more important things to worry about than watching the roads."

Tameel pulled the pipe from his mouth. "Why? What did you see?"

"It looks like Endric Talmanes might have enacted some sort of revenge against the town. A number of the buildings looked to have been burned."

"Burned?" Zynora shared a troubled look with Tameel. "What about Aylin and Misha? They would have been the first home Endric would have gone after."

"Who?" Bek asked, looking at Ayrion for clarification. Bek and Nel hadn't arrived in Minotha until after the incident with Endric, so they weren't aware of the two Sil'Rhivanni.

"They run the chandlery in town," Zynora said. "Did you happen to see if it was one of the buildings that was burned?"

Again, Bek shook his head. "Afraid I don't know. It looked like most of the damage took place toward the center of town."

Zynora and Tameel shared another concerned look. The chandlery wasn't that far from the town square. "We need to check on them, Tameel," Zynora said.

Ayrion groaned inwardly. As much as he didn't want to waste more time that could be spent getting them closer to the Lost City, he also couldn't just turn his back on people who had been hurt because of him. If the three of them hadn't stopped in Minotha on their way to Wellhollow, none of this might have happened.

Zynora looked at Ayrion, as if guessing his thoughts. "They are two of our oldest friends."

Ayrion knew there was no point in arguing. She wasn't about to leave without making sure her friends were safe, and he wasn't about to leave without her. Apart from her Dar' Rhivanni gifts of healing—which had saved his life on more than one occasion—there was the issue of Zynora's magic. She had demonstrated the power of her discharges in several battles already, each one turning the tide in their favor. The two tinkers might have been slowing his progress, but in the end, what they brought with them was worth waiting for.

"We'll wait till dark and go in on horseback," he said, looking up through the trees. They wouldn't have to wait long. The brightest of the stars were already blinking into existence, and the shale grey of the sky was melting into deep charcoal.

He looked at Tameel and Zynora. "You two will need something to cover those outfits. We can't risk drawing attention."

The couple looked down at their colorful tinker garb and climbed inside to change, or at least hide their Rhivanni colors with plain hooded cloaks.

"You as well," Bek added, looking at Ayrion's black clothing and blades.

Ayrion looked down at his coat. "Guess you're right."

He left Shade with Bek and climbed into the back of the red rover wagon. He removed his coat and swords, replacing them with a dark-green cloak and a single sword from their stockpile of weapons. He didn't like the way it bounced at his side, but better that than someone recognizing him.

By the time Ayrion and Bek had unhitched the horses and saddled them for use, Tameel and Zynora were out and ready to go. Tameel wore a short sword at his waist. Zynora, however, carried no noticeable weaponry, though Ayrion wouldn't have put it past her to have a knife or two stuck in her bodice.

Ayrion was the last to mount, helping Zynora and Tameel up before swinging onto Shade. He twisted in his saddle. "If anything happens and we are forced to part ways, we'll meet back here by morning. Agreed?"

Everyone nodded.

"Who has the coin pouch?" Bek asked.

"I do," Tameel said, patting the side of his chest.

Ayrion turned and nudged Shade into a slow trot. A few moments later, they emerged from the trees and onto the snow-packed road for town.

They passed the split in the road that led north around Lake Wenigapu toward Lord Talmanes's estate and continued on into town. The streets were fairly quiet on the outskirts, and nothing much seemed changed, but then again, Bek had said the most significant damage had happened near the center of town. Still, Ayrion would have thought to have seen at least some small aftermath leading in.

The streetlamps had been lit, which proved helpful in guiding their way. There were a number of people on the road, which was a strange thing to see at this hour, leaving Ayrion to wonder if the troubles were ongoing.

The people they passed stared, and not in a friendly way. They were armed, but that wasn't too much different from the first time they had ridden through. However, the people seemed far more on edge now than what they had been the last time, jumping at the sound of their horses' hooves coming up behind them and quickly scurrying off the street when they saw them coming.

Up ahead, Ayrion could see the chandlery on the left. The square three-story building seemed untouched. Ayrion could just make out Misha's brightly colored curtains in the windows. He heard Zynora breathe a sigh of relief once she realized it had not been burned, although two of the buildings across the street bore signs of fire. One had lost its entire second floor.

"Strange that Endric would have burned that building and not the chandlery," Tameel said.

They pulled into the drive on the left side of the chandlery, which ended at the small barn where Aylin kept his horses. Ayrion had barely dismounted before Zynora leaped off her horse and ran for the side entrance leading into Aylin's workshop. Ayrion and the rest quickly tied their horses in front of the barn and hurried to catch up.

Ayrion could hear Zynora calling the older couple's names from another room as he, Bek, and Tameel stepped into the workshop. Ayrion was immediately met with the euphoric smells of Aylin's candles, too many wonderful smells to name, and all blending into some blissful menagerie of aromas that had him wanting to stay awhile and drink it in. A shout from Zynora had them all rushing into the sitting room where Misha would take her tea.

Loud footsteps came down the stairs on the left, and Ayrion reached for his sword just as Zynora burst into the room. Seeing them all standing there startled her, and she yelped.

"Well?" Tameel asked.

"They aren't here," she said worriedly. "I even checked the shop out front." She hesitated. "You don't think . . . You don't think Endric took them, do you?"

"Let's pray not," Tameel said, taking a quick look around the room.

Zynora walked over to the rug and kicked it back, revealing Aylin and Misha's hiding spot underneath. She pointed at the fingerhold in the floor, and Ayrion knelt down and opened it. Inside the cubby were a couple of coin pouches along with a polished wooden box. Ayrion recognized the box as the one Aylin kept his special ashim berry candles in.

"It's all still there," Tameel commented, peering inside the hole in the floor.

Ayrion lowered the boards back into place, and they covered it with the carpet.

"We should find out why the streets are packed with people," Bek said, looking through the sitting room, across the shop, and out the windows at the front. It was too dark to see faces, but the torchlight and lanterns were visible enough. "Might help us determine what happened to your friends."

Zynora nodded, and they left the chandlery the same way they had entered, out the side. After stabling the horses in the barn, they went the rest of the way on foot, attempting to blend in with the other townsfolk. Ayrion turned to Bek and pointed to a couple walking just in front of them. "Ask where everyone's going. I would, but I don't want to risk them seeing my eyes."

Bek nodded and hurried to catch up with the couple. "Pardon me," he said. The man and woman turned and then took an immediate step back when they saw the big fur-laden trapper staring down at them. "I'm new in town, and—"

The man drew his sword and pulled the woman behind him. "Stay back if you know what's good for you." Before Bek had a chance to say anything, the two were running up the street.

Bek turned and shrugged. "Not very friendly, are they?"

"Scared, more like it," Ayrion said. This was worse than when Endric had sent his collectors into town. "Let's keep going, but keep your distance." The crowds appeared to be heading in the same direction—the center of town, but when they got close enough to see the small fountain in the town square, they realized that the people were taking the road to the right instead, the one that ran east to west, dividing the north half of town from the south.

They followed the stragglers who were hurrying to catch up with the rest. Halfway up, they took another street to the left, one Ayrion and Tameel recognized, and they followed the others straight to the Red Fox Tavern, the same tavern where he and Tameel had stopped for a celebratory drink after selling most of their armament to the local merchants in town.

With their hoods up, they walked inside. The larger common room and the lobby in front were packed with bodies, and there was hardly room enough to move about, but they did manage to push their way over to the corner on the left side, where the entryway met the common room. Ayrion kept as close to the wall as possible and out of people's way, not wanting to draw any more attention.

He spotted Marzell, or Marz as she preferred to be called, behind her bar in the main room on the left, taking orders and filling drinks as fast as her short arms would allow. How she managed to keep her hands moving down the row of tankards without spilling was impressive, especially considering the patch over her left eye. The red-haired taverner shouted at those still coming in, inviting them to purchase a round as well.

Tameel started for the bar, but Zynora pulled him back with a hard look. Shaking her head, she turned and looked at the small platform on the other side of the room, where performers would usually entertain the patrons. Tonight, it was being used by what Ayrion had to guess were the town's leaders. He couldn't see much over the heads of the crowd, but he saw enough to pick out at least one man standing above the rest. He had his hands in the air, trying to gather the people's attention.

"Do your friends wear tinker colors as well?" Bek asked unexpectedly.

Tameel and Zynora turned. "Yes." Zynora looked up at Bek. "Why?"

"I think I see them. They're up on the platform."

"On the platform?" Zynora turned, but she was too short to see much of anything.

Ayrion tried standing on his tiptoes, but he couldn't quite get high enough. "I can't see what's going on," he said. "Too many people." The smoke filling the room didn't help; it muted colors and stung his eyes.

Bek finally leaned over and lifted Zynora off her feet. She shrieked in surprise, then caught herself and peered over the crowd.

"Yes, I see them," she said ecstatically, then slapped Bek's arm. "You can put me down."

He lowered her back to the floor, and she straightened her dress and cloak. "They're both up there," she said, passing a relieved look at Tameel, who smiled his delight at the news.

"What's happening?" Zynora asked a couple of ladies on the right, who were trying to see over the men in front.

"The scouts are back," one of them said.

"Scouts?" Ayrion asked, but the woman was already speaking once more to the lady next to her. He tried to make sense of the situation. Was the town sending people out to keep an eye on Endric, to warn them when his mercenaries were on their way to town? That didn't make sense. Why would they need to call a town meeting in the middle of the night if their scouts were only a few minutes' ride around the lake?

A loud banging drew everyone's attention over to the bar, where Marz was smacking one of her tankers down repeatedly on top of the wood, continuing to do so until she had everyone's attention.

"Quiet down!" she shouted. When the crowd did, she smiled at the lanky man on stage, whose arms were still outstretched. "Alright, Hinkle, let's get this meeting underway. I don't want to be here till midnight cleaning up."

The people all turned to the man on the short platform, and he lowered his arms with a nervous smile. "Thank you, Marz," he said. The glow from the chandelier over his head reflected off the bald patch above his horseshoe hairline. "As I'm sure most of you have already heard, the scouts have returned. And you'll be pleased to know that the wielders have left our neck of the woods."

Wielders? Ayrion looked at the others and frowned. "You don't think . . ."

"Where are they now?" someone shouted from over on the right, near the front.

"And who's keeping watch in case they decide to return?" another called out on the left.

Hinkle raised his hands once more to quiet the growing unrest. "We will keep men posted on the roads just in case, but I don't think they'll be back."

"But you don't know that," a woman in the middle said.

"No. No, I don't. But there's only so much we can do. And to answer your first question, they are heading south on the main road."

"Back to the Tower, no doubt!" a man on the right shouted. "And when did the White Tower start employing wielders to do their bidding? Has the whole world gone mad?"

Ayrion hmphed. The world was going mad, and those out here on the outskirts of society were only just now feeling the repercussions. "I guess Endric wasn't to blame after all," he said, keeping his voice low.

"No," Zynora sighed. "We are."

"You think they attacked Minotha just out of spite?" Bek asked.

"Ask what's left of Lower Wellhollow if they're capable of such pettiness."

"I believe they will return," Hinkle said from the platform, drawing their attention back to the stage. "Word has it that they were coming from Wellhollow."

"Those mountain folk can't be trusted," a woman on the right called out. "They probably told them we had ven'ae down here just to save their own skins."

"Then you'd be a fool," Zynora countered loudly, causing everyone nearby to turn, including Ayrion, who quickly pulled his hood a little higher up on his head. He groaned. Zynora was about to drop them right in the middle of this thing.

"We just came from Wellhollow," Zynora continued. "There's nothing left."

"Who said that?" Hinkle asked, and the crowd split down the middle from the stage all the way to where their small group was standing on the left.

"Zynora? Is that you?" a familiar voice called out from the front, just before Aylin and Misha walked out to join Hinkle at the edge of the platform. Zynora pulled her hood back, and as soon as Misha saw her, she hopped off the stage and ran to the back, nearly knocking Zynora off her feet as she wrapped her arms around her.

Ayrion pressed even further against the wall as everyone turned to watch.

"We thought you were dead. We hadn't heard a word since the night of the fire."

"We thought it best not to linger after that," Zynora said, having to unwrap herself from Misha's arms. "We only just arrived, and when we saw the damage, we were worried Endric had sent his men after the town for revenge."

"Endric hasn't left his home since the fire," Misha said with a grunt. "So much has happened since then."

"Misha," Hinkle called from the platform, "who are our visitors? Do they have knowledge of what the Tower is doing up here?"

Zynora looked at Ayrion, but there wasn't much for it now. She'd already called them out in front of the entire town, so he nodded, and they started through the very nervous-looking townsfolk toward the stage.

Ayrion made it onto the platform and took a moment to greet Aylin and Misha.

"Whatever happened to your horse?" Aylin asked.

Ayrion smiled. "I found him. He's doing just fine."

"I'm guessing your finding him had something to do with the loud explosion that shook half of Minotha, and half of Lord Talmanes's estate going up in flames?"

"Wait," Hinkle said, moving around Aylin. "You had something to do with the fire?"

Ayrion sighed. He wished people would learn to keep their mouths shut.

"These are the people responsible for it," Misha said before Ayrion could stop her.

Ayrion turned. "I don't think this is the time or place to be mentioning something like that. Are you trying to get us—"

"Folks!" Hinkle shouted, quieting down the mounting restlessness that was spreading across the common room as the people waited to find out who the newcomers were and what they knew, "I have just learned from Aylin and Misha that our visitors were directly responsible for the fire at Lord Talmanes's property."

Ayrion's hand dropped to his sword as he looked around the stage for some place to hide Zynora and Tameel if they got rushed. Beside him, Bek's hands were resting on the head of his hatchets as he stared out across the faces of the Minothans.

Surprisingly, no one drew their weapons. In fact, no one really moved at all. Had they not heard what Hinkle had said? Suddenly, from somewhere in the back, someone started to clap their hands, then another, and another. Pretty soon, the entire room erupted in applause.

Hinkle turned and shook each of their hands. "We want to thank you for your service to the town."

Ayrion was the last to shake his hand. "I don't understand."

Hinkle looked confused.

Aylin smiled. "After you attacked Endric and burned down half his father's estate, his men split. Once they realized they weren't getting paid, they left him to the mercy of the town. Needless to say, we haven't heard a peep out of him since."

"Well, that's a blessing," Tameel said.

Ayrion wondered what happened to the two Upakans Paran and Siranu. Most likely left with the rest when they realized their contracts were no good. Now that he had his memories, he knew that he hadn't recognized either of their faces, which meant they must have belonged to one of the other two tribes. He wondered if he'd run across them again, and if so, would they recognize him?

"Please," Hinkle said, motioning for their group to join him at the front of the stage. "Tell us what you know of these wielders and why the Tower has openly attacked us without provocation. You say they did the same to Wellhollow?"

The people pressed toward the front to hear what they had to say. Normally, Ayrion would have been the one to address them, but because of his eyes, he figured it best to let someone like Zynora or Tameel relay what had taken place. Him being spotted as Upakan would only instill more fear and distrust, especially considering Endric's choice in hired protection.

Zynora and Tameel took the next hour to describe what had taken place at Wellhollow, both Upper and Lower, wisely leaving out the bit about Harok Laos and Aero'set and wizard's magic. They did convey that the White Tower had been training dark wielders for some time, and that they believed the bulradoer had not attacked due to any specific orders by the Tower, but out of their own hatred at having been defeated by a rugged group of mountain men and women.

This news did seem to set the town a little more at ease, though it didn't negate the damage and loss of life that had taken place because of it. Even with the earlier comments of distrust in the mountain folk, the town genuinely seemed disheartened to hear that Wellhollow had been demolished. They even went so far as to ask whether there was something that Minotha could do to help, but Zynora assured them that the time to help was long past and that they should expect an influx of people seeking goods from those communities farther north. Many depended on Wellhollow for their food and living and were now going to have to rely on Minotha, as it was the largest of the townships in that part of Sidara.

After Tameel and Zynora had finished taking questions, Hinkle, Aylin, and Misha spent the rest of the meeting discussing with the people the work schedule for the week, as there were many homes and businesses in need of repair. Once the people had been dismissed, Hinkle waited around, presumably to see if there was anything more he needed to know.

"We'll make sure you have provisions enough to reach Aldwick," he said. "If that's where you're heading. Least we can do for your help with Endric Talmanes."

"Aye," Marz said as she walked over to top off their drinks. Tameel was the first to thrust his out for a refill. She smiled at Ayrion on her way by. "My offer still stands, handsome. If you still want to know about my eye, I've got a lovely room in back where we can discuss it."

Tameel chuckled, and Bek outright laughed. Ayrion simply shook his head. "Tempting, but I think I'll have to pass."

She rolled her shoulders. "Your loss."

Ayrion turned and thanked Hinkle for the promised provisions, then motioned to the others that it was time to leave. Waiting on the supplies was going to set them back, but without them, they'd never be able to reach Aldwick. Most important was the extra feed for the horses. They could have foraged for themselves, but that wouldn't have been enough for the horses, and it would have wasted a lot of time, time they didn't have. Waiting an extra half day for supplies was a more than reasonable trade-off.

After leaving the Red Fox, Ayrion, Tameel, and Bek rode out to collect the wagons. They drove them into Minotha and parked outside the chandlery, but instead of forcing Aylin and Misha to set up rooms for everyone, the four slept in the wagons. They woke the next morning to a large breakfast that Aylin and Misha had risen early to prepare, one that required Ayrion to loosen his belt as he ate a third helping of griddlecakes.

Shortly after they had finished, a wagon pulled around the side, laden with supplies that had been provided by some of the local merchants. Ayrion and Bek loaded everything into the wagons, and after saying their goodbyes, the group left the chandlery and made their way west through town.

Before long, the city of Minotha, Lake Wenigapu, and Endric Talmanes were behind them, and ahead was nothing but one long open sea of snow-filled plains—the Grasslands of Tekoa.

Chapter 17 | Ayrion

AYRION ADJUSTED HIS SHADERS, glancing back over his shoulder at Bek on the second wagon and smiling to see the big man wearing Ayrion's spare set. Hunkered down in his furs, Bek looked like an enormous badger sitting on the front of the wagon wearing a pair of spectacles. He smiled when he caught Ayrion looking and waved as he worked to keep his horses in line, following the deeper ruts being left by Ol' Lerra's wheels.

The road leading across the plains had well-packed snow in some places and deep powder in others, as storms had washed across the grasslands at varying times, blanketing entire swaths in snow and leaving others relatively untouched. The road itself was well kept, wide enough for at least a single wagon—in some parts two—and level enough that they didn't have to worry about tipping, unlike the foothills farther north.

The constant glare coming off the snow around them gave Ayrion a slight headache, but he found he could live with the discomfort in exchange for being able to see anyone coming from a safe distance. There were more travelers than he would have expected for this time of year. There wasn't a day that went by that they didn't wish at least half a dozen others a good journey. Much like their trip north from Woodvale to Wellhollow, they passed several smaller communities that had sprouted along the roadway, nothing compared to the size of Belvin or Minotha, or even Woodvale for that matter, but large enough to have a shop or two. One even had a smithy, which they stopped at to reshoe one of Bek's horses.

By the end of the sixth day, they had reached the outskirts of Aldwick. Ayrion couldn't believe how quickly they had crossed from the center of Sidara to its western boundary. It had taken them nearly the same time to make it from Wellhollow down to Minotha, but that stretch of road had been across more rugged terrain.

"There she is," Tameel called out from the front. The window behind his seat opened, and Zynora stuck out her head to take a look. "How long has it been, Mother, since we passed this way?"

Zynora pursed her lips. "At least five or six years, I reckon."

"Perhaps we could make a sale or two while we're here," Tameel said, his eyes brightening.

Ayrion pulled Shade a little closer to the wagon. "The only thing we are going to do is look for a flatboat large enough to ferry us across. Either of you remember if they have a running ferry here?"

"Can't say as we've ever crossed here before," Tameel said. "We usually take the ferry down at Hedgemont on the southern side of Praxil Lake. It's the closest crossing over the Taloos River after leaving Elondria."

Zynora smiled. "I'm sure a city this size will have a ferry, especially with it being the only one between Praxil Lake and Lake Baeron. If not, there is always Storyl, which is a lake town south of here. They have a full shipyard, but they mainly work off the lake, so I'm not sure if they'll have a way to ferry larger cargo like wagons."

"Sounds like we need to take a look," Bek said from the wagon behind as he stood from his seat to see the others. "What are their views on tinkers?"

Ayrion looked at Tameel and Zynora, who shrugged in return. "It's been several years," Tameel said. "People's views tend to change like the shifting of the wind."

Ayrion looked at Bek. "Perhaps you and I should go in and have a look first."

Bek nodded. "We can park the wagons in those trees over there."

Ayrion looked at the copse of trees on the left and then at Tameel and Zynora. "Are you fine with staying here while we look around?"

"As long as you bring me back a couple of fresh tarts," Tameel said with a hungry smile. "None of that day-old stuff they try passing off as freshly baked, either. Make sure the bottoms aren't soggy."

Ayrion chuckled. The thought of tarts took him back to his youth and Master Endle's bakery, which he and his wife, Storella, had run on South Avis. Best cheese tarts in Aramoor.

"I'm sure I can manage to find a tart or two," Ayrion said, then turned and directed the two wagons off the road and into the hardwood on the left. It was decent enough cover to keep the sun out of their eyes and the snow off their heads should the weather change, which Ayrion had learned could happen rather quickly out on the plains.

Leaving Tameel and Zynora to watch the wagons, Ayrion and Bek rode into town. They were quite the pair as they headed through the main gates of Aldwick, one decked from head to toe in brown fur, the other in black leather. Ayrion wasn't all that concerned with whether people stopped to stare or moved out of the way when they saw them coming. Hopefully their appearance would deter any cutpurses from believing them an easy mark and intimidate the ferry owner into offering a fair price.

The city was about the size of Minotha, though perhaps not as clean. As they neared the river, the smell of fish permeated many of the streets. "Have you ever been here in your travels?" Ayrion asked Bek as they slowly made their way down the main thoroughfare.

Bek shook his head, keeping an eye on the passing shops as well as the townsfolk milling about the streets. "The edge of the grasslands is as far west as I've been. Most of my trappings were up north."

They continued side by side, stopping every so often to keep from trampling someone who was not paying attention to where they were. It seemed the good citizens of Aldwick believed that those on foot had the right of way, a far cry from the beliefs held in Aramoor. He remembered nearly getting trampled by Lord Gerrick's carriage while trying to save a small boy who'd wandered into the streets chasing a frog.

A little farther in, Ayrion thought he spotted a bakery down one of the streets just after the town square. He'd have to make sure to stop there on the way back. Most fruits weren't in season, but he was sure to find some sweet cheese tarts, which were his favorite anyway.

"I think I see the river ahead," Bek said, all but standing in his stirrups.

The road they were traveling didn't quite end at the river like he had thought, but it diverted around a long row of buildings and warehouses. They pulled to a stop at the end of the road and looked both ways. "Let's try down here," Ayrion said, motioning to the left. "I think I see some docks."

Sure enough, there was a small port with several piers attached, each long enough to handle at least one ship with a sail or a couple of the smaller oared boats.

"I don't see a ferry," Bek said. "And I don't think any of these ships are going to be wide enough to fit a wagon."

Ayrion shook his head. "No. These won't work. Most are fishing schooners, no doubt running between . . ." Ayrion froze. "It can't be." His heart sped up as he stared at the sleek dark wood and black sail of the ship on the very end.

"What can't be?" Bek asked. He leaned forward in his saddle. "What are you looking at?"

Ayrion could hardly believe it. He hadn't seen that ship in nearly fifteen years. "That's the—"

Bek jerked with a pained shout and pulled back on his horse's reins, causing his horse to rear and throw him into the street. Ayrion turned to see an arrow protruding from the big man's back.

"Get out of the way!" someone behind them yelled, and Ayrion spun Shade just as another arrow zipped past and out over the water.

Ayrion leaped out of the saddle and yelled for Shade to run. He couldn't risk the big warhorse taking an arrow as well. As soon as Shade started up the road, Ayrion felt the sharp pain of an arrow tear through his chest. A breath later, another impaled his left leg. He staggered backward and drew one of his swords as he looked down at the damage.

Pain made his head swim. He reached for the arrow in his chest . . . and everything around him spun. Suddenly, the vision died, and he was back in his saddle once more.

Not sparing the time to even breathe a sigh of relief, he leaped off Shade and shouted for the horse to run, quickly stepping to the right as he did. The two arrows that were meant for him flew by and ricocheted off the cobbled street behind him.

"Move!"

Ayrion drew his swords and turned as a man came barreling out of the alley and charged at him. He had shoulder-length red hair and a face that said he meant business. Behind him were at least a dozen men in white uniforms.

Black Watch.

Chapter 18 | Ferrin

ARE YOU CRAZY?" Ferrin shouted at the man in black leather standing at the edge of the alley. "Those are the Tower's guards. Run!"

Ferrin moved out of the alley's mouth to keep from getting struck by an arrow and turned to look at the docks on the other side of the street. He'd never make it back to the *Wind Binder* without being spotted by the guards, and he didn't want to risk leading them back to Captain Treygan and his crew. Treygan and Ismara had done enough for him already.

He tightened his grip on his swords. Where was Lenara when he needed her?

Right, he'd ordered her to stay with his sister and the others outside the city while he and Myron went to purchase horses. That was a stupid mistake.

As soon as they had seen the Black Watch, he and Myron had split up. Myron had taken one road, Ferrin another, hoping to divide the guards. Unfortunately, Ferrin had drawn the group with the bowmen.

Not seeing another choice, he turned to take up a position on the side of the alley and found the man in black doing the same. "Didn't you hear me?

Those are Black Watch! Get out of here!"

"Yeah, I heard you."

Apparently, the man had no intention of leaving. There was something familiar about him, but Ferrin couldn't quite place him. Behind them, another man—at least he looked like a man; it was hard to tell with all the fur—climbed to his feet with an arrow sticking from his back.

"Don't worry about me," the fur-clad man said derisively, then snatched two massive hatchets from their sleeves and stumbled over to the other side of the alley to take up a position next to the man in black.

Were these fools trying to get themselves killed?

Well, it would be their funerals, though he wasn't about to turn down a few extra blades. Maybe they could distract the guards long enough for Ferrin to . . . Ferrin's breath caught in his throat when he saw the man's swords. "Where did you get—"

He didn't get the words out before the Tower's guards poured out of the alley and he was fighting for his life. Any townsfolk still on the street ran, disappearing down other side streets, blind alleys, and into the closest residence that would open their doors to let them in. These soldiers were part of the same group that had been hunting him in Rhowynn, and they had somehow managed to find them here. It had to be those flaming corax creatures.

Ferrin spun left, using his longer sword to defend and his shorter one to attack. As soon as the guards' blades touched his, his magic dove into them, twisting them into unusable pieces of metal. He loved watching the look of shock on their faces just before he plunged his sword into their chest, gut, or neck. Within a matter of seconds, he had three down.

On the other side of the alley, the man in black moved like no one Ferrin had ever seen before. Nothing even came close to touching him. The way he danced through their swings and thrusts had Ferrin watching in awe. It seemed most of the guards had suddenly decided to set their sights on the other two, leaving him with an unexpected opening. But he couldn't seem to pull himself away. The large half-animal man was a force to be reckoned with as well. Even with the arrow sticking from his back, he was still carving up the Black Watch like a butcher working on a rack of ribs.

Ferrin turned to take advantage of the chaos and run but stopped.

Sometimes he really hated having a conscience. After all, this was his mess. He slammed into two men on the right who were trying to flank the man in fur, throwing both to the ground. He stabbed each and swung for a third guard. As soon as the man's blade struck Ferrin's, it immediately contorted on itself. The man's eyes bulged, and he threw the twisted metal down and ran for the alley. Out of nowhere, a small knife flew through the air and buried itself in the escaping man's back. Ferrin was shocked to realize it had come from the black swordsman. How had he managed to throw a knife while holding two swords?

Ferrin turned for the next guard, but there weren't any. Dead men in white uniforms covered the street around them.

Shouts came from the docks, and all three spun to find Captain Treygan and his men charging across the street, weapons in hand. The man in black and the one in fur raised their weapons, expecting another attack.

"Don't be alarmed," Ferrin said, motioning for the two to lower their swords. "They're with me."

Treygan and his men slowed when they saw the fight was over, but not Ismara. She kept running straight for them. What was she doing? Ferrin moved out of the way as she ran past him and leaped on the man in black.

"Ayrion!" She kissed him hard on the mouth.

Ferrin's jaw dropped as he and everyone else stood there watching in shock; even the half-animal man beside him looked taken aback. Ismara finally released the swordsman and took a step back to get a good look at him, but before she could say anything, Treygan himself shoved his way through and wrapped his arms around the man, nearly knocking him over.

Ferrin's mind reeled. What was going on? Who was this man?

The man in black laughed. "I can't tell you how good it is to see the two of you!"

"How long's it been?" Treygan asked.

Before the man could answer, the rest of the crew started pushing their way through, Bones and Bray, or Needle as most called him, were first in line, then Whitey, who actually lifted the swordsman off the ground when he hugged him, knocking his own wide-brimmed hat off in the process. Even grumpy old Kettle was there to shake the man's hand. Ferrin caught the hint of a smile under Kettle's long mustache, something Ferrin hadn't seen in all the time he'd known him.

Ferrin and the man in fur just moved to the side to let the crew get their turn.

"I'm Bek," the man beside him said, as calm as if he didn't have an arrow sticking from his back.

"Ferrin," he replied with a nod. "Might want to get that looked at."

Bek attempted to look behind him, then gave up. "Seen worse."

Ferrin didn't want to ask. He didn't want to keep standing in the open either. "We might want to get off the street." He seemed to be the only one who realized how ridiculous it was for all of them to be standing there surrounded by a pile of dead bodies, especially Black Watch. "There's more where they came from." He glanced back up the alleyway.

Treygan turned and ordered his men to start grabbing bodies. It took two trips, but they managed to drag the dead into the alley and cover them with whatever they could find—old barrels, broken crates, stacks of brick and wood. Somehow, they managed to hide all eleven before Treygan sent the crew back to the ship.

The man in black, who the others were calling Ayrion, was the last to leave the alley. He carried one of the Black Watch's swords, one that Ferrin had twisted in on itself. "Someone want to explain this to me?" the man said. "I found several more just like it."

Treygan turned and looked at Ferrin.

Ferrin shrugged. It wasn't like he could exactly hide it. "What can I say? It's a gift."

The man cocked his brow. "That's quite the gift." He tossed the ruined sword back into the alley.

Ferrin turned at the sound of heavy hoofbeats coming down the street behind him. It was a lone horse, one of the biggest Ferrin had seen, and absolutely regal. It held its head high as it trotted along, as if expecting those around it to bow when it passed. Whoever he belonged to was sure to be in a state of panic, losing a valuable animal like that. Then the enormous stallion walked up to the man in black and whinnied. Ferrin shook his head. *Of course.*

"I thought you'd left the city already," Treygan said to Ferrin as they both watched the swordsman pull a carrot from his long black coat and feed the horse.

Ferrin stared up the street. "We were looking for horses. The others are just outside the gates."

"*We?*"

"Myron's here as well. We split up when the Watch started chasing us." He glanced up the road. "We said we'd meet here at the docks if we lost them. I took the longer route, so he should have already made it back."

Treygan pursed his lips, his hand resting on the bone-handled dagger at his waist as he, too, glanced up the street. "I'll send some of the men out to look. We'll find him."

"I can help," the man in black said as he and Bek walked over.

"I guess you two need to be properly introduced," Treygan said. "Ferrin, this is Ayrion, the one I'd told you about who'd sailed the Shemoa with us all those years ago."

Ferrin vaguely remembered a discussion they'd had concerning a young boy Treygan had met who was skilled with the blade. Ayrion pulled back the hood of his coat, and Ferrin understood why. He was Upakan.

"Ayrion, this is Ferrin. A new acquaintance, and the only man to ever escape the White Tower. The two of you have quite a lot in common, I think."

Ayrion held out his hand, and Ferrin took it. "Nice to meet you," Ferrin said. "I appreciate the help back there."

Ayrion nodded. "Only too happy to give it. Killing Black Watch seems to have become something of a hobby of late."

"More like a way of life, if you ask me," Bek said.

Treygan turned and smiled. "And who's this rugged-looking scrapper who doesn't seem to realize he has an arrow sticking from his back? Just the kind of man I'd like to have on my crew."

"This is Bek," Ayrion said. "One of the few men I'm proud to call friend."

Treygan shook Bek's hand. "With friends like that, I feel sorry for your enemies. The man fights like a bear."

Bek tried not to wince as he turned to Ferrin. "I can help you look for your comrade."

Ferrin stared at him a moment. Was he touched in the head? How much blood had he lost? "And how do you plan on running all over the city with that sticking out of your back?"

Captain Treygan looked at Ferrin, and Ferrin could see he was waiting for him to say something about Rae being able to heal him, but Ferrin had no intention of giving that information out to a couple of strangers, even if they were close to Treygan. When Ferrin didn't respond, the captain pointed toward the *Wind Binder*. "I can have Needle take a look. As you recall, he's quite proficient with a stitch."

Ayrion shook his head. "We have a Rhivanni healer with us who can deal with it." He turned to Bek. "Let Tameel and Zynora know what's happening, and that I'll be a little late getting back."

Bek nodded and walked over to collect his horse, which was lapping up water from a split barrel down by the pier.

Ayrion joined him. "Don't move." He grabbed the arrow sticking from Bek's back and snapped the shaft as close to his back as he could. Bek growled and bit down against the pain. Ayrion then adjusted the furs to hide what was still visible. "About as good as I can get it." He helped the man up in his saddle. "Good luck."

"You as well." With that, the man in fur guided his horse up the street, disappearing as he turned right on the main road, which ran straight for the city's gate.

Ayrion looked at Ferrin. "Any idea where your friend might be?"

Ferrin shook his head. "We just arrived this afternoon. It's our first time to Aldwick, so I have no idea where he might have gone." He was really regretting the decision to split up.

"What does your friend look like? Any noticeable way to spot him, color or cut of his clothing?"

Ferrin almost laughed.

Treygan actually did.

"What did I say?" Ayrion looked confused.

"You can't miss him," Treygan said. "Just look for the man with the nose."

"What does that mean?"

Ferrin smiled. "Trust me. You'll know it when you see it." He looked at Treygan. "We'll head south. Can you send your men north?"

"Consider it done."

Ferrin looked at the swordsman. "You ready?"

Ayrion nodded, but before they started up the street, he turned. "Do either of you know if Aldwick has a ferry? I have a couple of wagons that need to get across the river."

"You'll want to see Trunken," Treygan said, and pointed north up the road they were on. "Follow this road past the main stretch and keep going till you spot the ferry on the left. Can't miss it."

Ayrion nodded. "Appreciate it."

"My pleasure."

"Do you think you can watch my horse while we look?"

Treygan looked up at the large animal. "I can try. And don't go leaving town without coming to see me. We have a lot to catch up on."

Ayrion nodded, but there was a bit of hesitancy behind it. He then turned and motioned to Ferrin, and they took off down the street, heading in the opposite direction of where Treygan said the ferry was located.

"When we split ways," Ferrin said, "Myron went south, so I figure this will be the best place to start looking."

The swordsman didn't say anything, just nodded as they kept a steady pace down the road, their boots thumping the cobble. They passed several streets before seeing anyone. Most of the people around the docks were still in hiding after the short battle, but those farther away appeared unaware there had been any conflict.

The swordsman caught Ferrin looking at the two weapons riding on his back and shot him an inquiring look. "What is it?"

"I was just curious as to how you came by blades such as those." Ferrin had been commissioned by the former king to create them. How had this man come into their possession? Was he there when Rhydan had been killed, or was he a scavenger who had found the weapons after the battle?

One look at the man and that notion seemed ridiculous. Ferrin didn't get the impression the swordsman had ever been a scavenger of anything. Still, he had to wonder how the man had ended up with a set of swords that he had made for the king.

Could have been gifted to him, or might this man have had something to do with Rhydan's death? That thought stood the hairs on his arms on end. Who was he running beside? How well did Treygan really know Ayrion? He couldn't have known him that well. He said he hadn't seen Ayrion in fifteen years. A man could change quite a lot in that time.

The swordsman didn't respond, and Ferrin wondered if he'd stuck himself in the middle of something he shouldn't have.

"They were a gift," the man finally said.

The hint of remorse in the way he said it was curious. Then it hit him, and he almost tripped on his feet. Why hadn't he put two and two together sooner? "You're the . . ." He stopped without finishing. It was almost too absurd to believe. Besides, he'd heard that the Guardian Protector had died with the king. Hadn't he? Perhaps he had something to do with Rhydan's death after all. Ferrin's blood ran cold.

They started past a set of three-story homes on the left, and he jerked the swordsman into the alley between and threw him against the wall. Before he could even get his knife out of its sheath, Ayrion was behind him, having spun out of his hold, and was now pressing him against the wall with a knife to Ferrin's own throat.

"What do you think you're doing?" Ayrion asked, his Upakan eyes boring into Ferrin's, but Ferrin refused to back down. He'd managed to slip his short dagger out and press it to the man's midsection.

"I want to know where you were when the king was killed."

The swordsman's face fell slack. He stared at Ferrin a moment, as if unsure how to answer.

"I know who you are," Ferrin said. "And I know where you got those blades."

"And what is it exactly that you think you know?"

"I know they were a gift from the king"—at least that was his best guess—"and I can't think of anyone he'd be willing to give them to except perhaps his Guardian." Ferrin held the Upakan's gaze, not letting those pale grey eyes intimidate him. The man's blade at his throat was doing a good enough job.

"Did you have something to do with his death?" Ferrin kept his own blade pressed against the swordsman's gut, angled upward. If the Upakan were to slit his throat, he'd be sure his final act would be to take him with him.

Ayrion's eyes were heated. "I had nothing to do with Rhydan's death, and for your own well-being, I suggest you never say that again." He continued to hold Ferrin's gaze. "How are you privy to such knowledge? I've never seen you at court. By the cut of your clothes and your speech, you hardly seem like one of the aristocracy. A tradesman would be my guess, the size of your arms says one that's not afraid of hard labor. A cooper, perhaps, or a smith."

"I'm a swordsmith by trade," Ferrin said. "The one who created those blades in the first place."

Ayrion released his knife and took a step back, this time shock on his face as he looked at Ferrin as though having only seen *him* for the first time. "Now it makes sense. Those guards' swords back in the alley." He looked down at the dagger in Ferrin's hand and smiled. "I see you've crafted other such weapons."

Ferrin looked down at the long knife and its similar black blade and smiled. "Nothing like the two you carry. These I made on the run." He held the dagger up a little higher, and Ayrion examined the blade.

"Not a scratch. That is quite the gift."

Ferrin slid the blade back into its sheath. "So how does the king's Guardian, who was supposed to have died with him in Belbridge, wind up out here in the middle of nowhere without a scratch?"

"I didn't walk away from that battle either."

Ferrin cocked his head, not exactly sure what to make of a statement like that.

"A bit of a long story, I'm afraid."

"One I'd be interested in hearing as soon as we find my friend."

"And I'll be interested to hear how someone escapes from an inescapable prison." Ayrion looked down at the dagger still resting in Ferrin's hand. "I don't believe you'll be needing that."

Ferrin looked at the blade and frowned, then sheathed it behind his back. "Well, now that introductions have been properly given, how about we find my friend?"

They left the narrow opening between homes and started back down the street, taking the last road to the left before it reached the outer wall. This street looked like it followed the city's fortification, which rose behind the homes on their immediate right. The road circled around, and Ferrin guessed it would eventually lead back to the main gate. So far, there had been no sign of Myron or the Black Watch. The people they passed didn't seem in a hurry; no one looked like they'd just come across a group of the Tower's guards running down the street.

"I get the feeling your friend didn't come through here," Ayrion said.

"I'm getting that same feeling." Ahead, Ferrin could see the watchtowers rising above the buildings, signaling that they were nearing Aldwick's main gate. "Perhaps we should try one of these less-trafficked streets. Knowing Myron, he's not likely to keep to the main thoroughfares."

Ayrion nodded, and they started down a road on their left that looked to run behind the city's merchant district.

"Ferrin. Ayrion."

Both men turned to find Bones jogging down the narrow street behind them.

"Captain Ismara says they found your friend." The tall dark-skinned man stopped, a little out of breath. Ferrin didn't know if he'd ever get used to the skeletal white paint that decorated his face. "The Black Watch have him."

"What?" Ferrin ground his teeth. He knew what that meant. This particular group had been after them for at least two weeks, and they were hardly going to be sympathetic, knowing what they had done to Sylas and his regiment in Rhowynn.

"We can go after him," Ayrion said. "They won't have gotten far."

"If he's still alive when we catch them," Ferrin added. "He's one of theirs, or at least used to be. He's one of the reasons I was able to escape the Tower in the first place. They aren't going to be gentle with him once they make camp. And they don't travel alone. They'll have two or three of those bulradoer with them."

"You know of the bulradoer?" Ayrion asked, then waved it off. "Right, you said you were a prisoner of the Tower. We can still catch them."

"We can't on foot," Ferrin said. "Remember, we were here to find horses, and we never got the chance."

"Then you can ride with me," Ayrion said. "Let's get back to the docks. The rest of the crew can follow us as soon as they purchase more."

The swordsman was clearly someone who liked being in charge, but at the moment, Ferrin wasn't going to argue, especially considering he was correct.

"Fine," he said, and all three started running for the docks, using the backstreets as much as possible so as not to attract attention.

They ended up passing through the very alley where they'd left the dead guards. It didn't appear anyone had disturbed their resting place. Then again, if the Watch had already left the city, it was doubtful they had any intention of coming back to retrieve the bodies.

"My guess is that they will make camp somewhere outside the city," Ferrin said as they crossed the street for the docks, "probably just south of the wall, and wait for the rest of their men."

The swordsman's face darkened.

Ferrin stopped on the other side of the street. "What's wrong?"

"I left my traveling companions in those very woods."

Ferrin frowned. "I hope they know how to hide. Those I'm traveling with are there as well, but they're used to keeping themselves hidden."

"Kind of hard to hide a couple of tinker wagons."

"You're traveling with tinkers? Now I'm really curious."

Bones ran down the boardwalk for the *Wind Binder*, no doubt to relay the message. Ferrin turned to say something to the swordsman and found him already swinging up into his horse's saddle. The enormous animal hadn't been there a moment ago. Had he come from the *Wind Binder* on his own?

Ayrion trotted the horse over and leaned down, offering an arm. "Get on."

Ferrin grabbed the man's arm and swung up behind him. This was going to be an uncomfortable ride, not to mention embarrassing. He wrapped his arms around the man, feeling extremely self-conscious in doing so, and they started up the street. They turned right on the main road leading out of Aldwick, and Ayrion nudged the stallion a little faster, taking care to keep from trampling the pedestrians on the way. Several of Aldwick's finest were forced to jump out of the way to keep from getting hit, shouting obscenities as they did.

They reached the main gate and had no trouble getting through. The guards seemed to only be checking those coming in, and not very diligently as Ferrin remembered. He had come and gone without being stopped once after escorting the wagons out of the city, then going back in for supplies.

The cold wind whipped across his face as the stallion picked up speed on the open road, kicking up snow and mud with each heavy thump of his powerful hooves.

Ferrin could see the tree line ahead on their right, and he pointed northwest to a specific spot he thought he recognized as where the rest of his traveling companions had set up camp, but Ayrion turned them a little farther south instead.

He was about to ask where they were going, but then he saw splashes of red and green through the trees, which could only be the backs of a couple of brightly painted tinker wagons. The man wasn't kidding. There was no hiding them.

"We don't exactly have time to stop," Ferrin said, impatient to get back to his own campsite and see if the others were still there.

"We do if you want my help," Ayrion said as he pulled to a quick stop behind the wagons.

Ferrin gritted his teeth. The man certainly knew how to win an argument. He only hoped it didn't result in the death of his friend.

Chapter 19 | Ferrin

HE BACK DOOR OF THE green wagon opened, and an old man and woman—clearly tinkers by their colorful baggy clothing—came rushing out. "Oh, we were so worried," the woman said, wiping blood from her hands on a purple cloth. "When Bek returned with this"—she held up the remnant of the arrow she had dug out of Bek's back and threw it into the woods—"and told us what happened, we feared the worst."

"How is he?" Ayrion asked.

"A little of Isha's cream and some Rhivanni magic and he'll be—"

"I'll survive," Bek said, stepping out of the wagon behind them. This time, he wasn't covered in fur. His shirt was off, and his shoulder and back had been neatly bandaged. He was a big man, not quite as thick in the chest and arms as Ferrin, but still muscular. "Let me change, and I'll be right with you."

Before the old woman could stop him, Bek hopped down and headed for the back of the red wagon. He was moving surprisingly well for a man who'd just pulled an arrow from his back. Ferrin wondered if the old woman had a gift similar to Rae's. Then again, if she had, Bek wouldn't have needed all the bandaging.

"And who is this?" the old man asked, looking at Ferrin.

"He's the reason for the Tower's guards," Ayrion said.

Ferrin cleared his throat. "You didn't have to put it like that."

"Is it not the truth?"

Ferrin ground his teeth. It seemed just about every time the man opened his mouth, Ferrin wanted to shut it for him. He turned to the older couple to explain. "A friend of mine was taken by the Black Watch. We had a run-in with them in town."

"Yes, we saw them riding by from the trees," the woman said. "Had us worried."

"You did? How long ago was that?"

"Not long. They were heading away from town." She pointed south down the road.

"Did you notice if they kept to the road, or if they veered off toward the woods to make camp?"

"Sorry, son," the man cut in. "Afraid that when we spotted them, we rushed inside and locked the doors. Didn't see much after that."

Ferrin groaned and looked at Ayrion. "We need to go."

"We need to think before we act," Ayrion countered, then turned to the older couple. "Zynora, are you fit to ride? We might need you."

She nodded.

"She doesn't go anywhere without me," the old man said, and they both headed back inside the green wagon.

"What are you doing?" Ferrin asked. "We don't have time to wait for a couple of elderly tinkers."

"You'll be glad we did."

Ferrin wanted to strangle the man. The longer they waited, the greater the chance his sister, Rae, and Suri could be in trouble. He hoped they had seen the Watch and remained hidden. Although, if they had seen Myron with them, Ferrin was afraid Lenara might do something foolish like go after them herself. He wouldn't put anything past that crazy woman.

Ayrion climbed down. "Help me with the horses."

Ferrin hopped off the massive stallion, and they saddled two more horses. By the time they finished, Bek and the older couple were out and ready to ride—which left Ferrin once again riding double.

"This is Ferrin," Ayrion said to the tinkers as he helped Ferrin up behind him. "His friend's name is . . ." He glanced over his shoulder at Ferrin.

"Myron," Ferrin said.

"And apparently," Ayrion said, "we will recognize him by his nose."

The others shared a confused look, and Ferrin rolled his eyes.

Ayrion nodded toward the tinkers. "This is Tameel and his wife Zynora. They are members of the Dar'Rhivanni."

Ferrin offered a half smile. "Pleasure." It would have been more of a pleasure if they weren't sitting there exchanging introductions instead of riding after the Black Watch.

"Nice to meet you, young man," Tameel said.

Ayrion twisted in the saddle. "Where did your friends make camp?"

Ferrin pointed farther south. "Maybe half a mile."

Ayrion nudged the large horse, and they started out of the trees, the other three directly behind. Ferrin still couldn't figure out why Ayrion would want to put the old couple in the middle of a possible battle. Did he not realize what the bulradoer were capable of?

They headed back to the road and started south at a decent gallop. The older couple were surprisingly good riders, having no trouble keeping up with Ayrion's enormous stallion. Ferrin spotted a break in the tree line ahead and directed them straight for it. Smoke rose from a lone fire, pointing the way. The trees cut inward around a formation of rock that rose a few feet over their heads. "This is the place," he said, now almost certain.

Ferrin hopped off the back of Ayrion's horse as they passed the large pile of rock and ran for the tree line, following the trail of hoofprints in the snow. Behind him, Ayrion, Bek, and the tinkers rode up to the trees, then dismounted. Bek, who had a bow and quiver hung over his good shoulder, grabbed the bow and nocked his first arrow. Ferrin drew his sword, not sure what to expect as he neared the small clearing where they had set up camp.

There was wood still burning on top, but no one within eyeshot. They couldn't have been gone that long. He hoped they hadn't all decided to go after Myron, or worse, had been spotted by the Watch and taken as well. No, he reasoned, if the watch had been here, there would have been a pile of bodies.

Lenara would have seen to that. He heard the others coming up behind him and started to turn.

"Ferrin?"

Ferrin spun back around and spotted a head peeking out from behind one of the larger trees on the other side of camp. "Elson?"

Elson breathed a heavy sigh of relief as he stepped out from behind the tree, sword in one hand, flask in the other. "You gave us quite the scare."

Ferrin's twin sister, Myriah, stepped out behind Elson as Rae and Suri poked out from another tree beside them, all four rushing to meet him by the fire.

Rae had her arms around him first, ending with a passionate kiss, followed by Myriah, who gave him a firm hug of her own. "We were worried when we saw the Black Watch ride into Aldwick." His sister released him and stepped back beside Elson. "They have Myron."

"I know. We're here to rescue him."

"Who's we?" Elson asked, taking a quick swig of his drink to steady his nerves as he looked beyond Ferrin to the four just now entering the campsite. "Who's your friends?" He nodded toward Ayrion and Bek. "Those two look like they can handle themselves in a fight."

"No time for introductions," Ferrin said. "Do you know which way they went?" Ferrin searched the trees behind them. "Where's Lenara?"

"She went after Myron," Rae said, holding Suri close as she studied the four newcomers with a careful eye. Suri stared at the others as well, clutching Tippi protectively against her chest. The large pinecone was missing a few of its scales but was otherwise in surprisingly good shape.

Ferrin groaned. "Of course she did."

Elson shook his head. "I tried to stop her, fool woman, but she ain't about to listen to anything I say." Ever since Lenara and Elson had decided to join Ferrin's small band of misfits, they had been at each other's throats, bickering about anything and everything, especially Elson's continuous drunken state.

An explosion shook the forest, raining snow down on them from the surrounding trees. Ferrin spun as Ayrion snatched the swords from his back and turned in the direction of the blast. "What was that?"

"Sounds like Lenara found the Watch's camp," Ferrin said. He ran over and untied Elson's horse, which was thankfully still saddled, and swung up. "Protect the women!" he called back to Elson as he spun the horse around and rode straight for the opening in the trees. He heard Rae shouting behind him that she didn't need protection. The swordsman was also shouting at him to wait, but he had to get to Lenara before she got herself and Myron killed.

Everything Lenara did was impulsive. She never thought anything through—not that what he was doing at the moment was any better, but it seemed she had left him with little choice. It would have been a whole lot smarter to have waited till nightfall, but then again, who knew what kind of torture they could inflict on Myron in the meantime.

Glancing over his shoulder, Ferrin could see Ayrion and Bek just breaking through the tree line behind him, with the tinker couple not much farther back. There was no reason for stealth at this point. Every moment they waited, the chances of his friends being killed grew.

Another explosion sounded as several balls of fire flew into the air ahead on the right, inside the tree line. Some of the hardwoods had flames engulfing their upper branches. Ferrin drew his sword and directed his horse off the road and straight for the trees.

A stray blast of wind shot from the trees, snapping several of the smaller ones in half as it came for him. He tried turning his horse, but it was too late. *This is going to hurt.*

The blast hit him and the horse. He flew out of the saddle and cartwheeled through the air, landing in a pile of snow about fifteen feet back. He pushed himself up to a sitting position and waited for the world to stop spinning. His horse wasn't thrown quite as far and was just getting back to its feet when Ayrion and the others rode up and hopped out of their saddles.

"We go on foot," the swordsman said, helping Ferrin to his feet. He was surprised to find he hadn't lost his sword in the fall. "Riding in on horseback will make us even larger targets," Ayrion added. Before Ferrin could get a word in, Ayrion and Bek were running straight for the trees and the balls of fire between.

Ferrin looked at the older couple behind him, and they simply smiled and shrugged. He turned and ran after the swordsman and his fur-laden friend, drawing his dagger in the process. He was taller than Ayrion, his legs longer, allowing him to catch up before they hit the tree line.

The woods were alive with magic: orange fireballs, flaming green and blue bulradoer weapons—ter'aks, Lenara had called them—and of course, at the heart of it all, two blazing red whips streaming through the darkness like fiery serpents, striking at anything within reach. Ferrin and the others hadn't even reached the first of the trees when the Black Watch ran out to meet them. Ferrin felt an arrow whiz by his head, then another straight for Ayrion, but the swordsman batted it away with one of Ferrin's dragon blades like it was an afterthought.

Bek stopped long enough to get a couple of shots off himself, both hitting their marks and dropping two men in white face first in the snow.

Ferrin sprinted ahead of the others and was the first to reach the Tower's guards. He plowed into the wave, his swords swiping aside their attempts to skewer him as he latched onto their blades with his magic. He could feel the heat building inside him as he sent it through the raw metal, twisting and bending it to his will. The magic seemed to come easier, even more so than with those in the alley. The smallest connection of their swords with his and he had the steel curling around their arms. His blood was pulsing in his ears, only heightened by the thunderous cracks from Lenara's whips and the heavy booms coming from the trees.

The archers ceased firing to keep from hitting their own and joined the battle. Beside him, Ayrion and Bek ripped through the Tower's ranks. There weren't nearly as many as there had been in Rhowynn with Sylas. Cheeks had brought at least three companies with him. This time there looked to be only one, though there did seem to be at least three bulradoer in the fight ahead. One wore the typical black robes and the other two wore grey. Ferrin wasn't sure what the difference was, as they were all fighting together to bring Lenara down.

Ferrin cut his way through the heart of the Watch's ranks, twisting metal and plunging his short sword into one warm body after another, until he was thoroughly covered in their remains. He wanted this to be over. He wanted them dead. They'd been chasing him since he'd left the Tower, and he wanted it to stop. If he could just kill these, then perhaps they could find a way to escape, and this time remain hidden.

Ferrin spun and deflected a blade meant for his head, then thrust his short sword through the man's neck. The guard coughed up a mouthful of blood, his face as contorted as his blade. Ferrin yanked his sword back out and the man dropped face first into the red-stained snow.

"Watch out!"

Something hit him from the side, and he was thrown to the ground. He looked as an orange ball of fire struck the tree behind him, instantly melting the bark and several layers of the tree's flesh. He rolled over to find Ayrion on top of him. The swordsman spun and was on his feet before Ferrin managed to even recover his sword.

Ferrin hopped to his feet, and the three men turned to look at the magical battle ahead, but before they got the chance to catch their breath, another wave of uniforms came charging in from the trees on the left.

Where had they been hiding?

Ferrin raised his swords and readied for impact when an unexpected torrent of power tore through the trees, toppling many and sending the entire squad of Black Watch flying like ragdolls. Ferrin watched, slack-jawed, as most were flung against thick trees farther in and left broken and bleeding in the snow. Others simply vanished from sight.

"What in the name of Aldor was that?" Ferrin asked. He turned to find the old tinker woman standing a couple dozen feet behind them. Her arms were raised in the direction of where the Tower's guards had been. Behind her, her husband was trying his best to keep her upright. "Did she just do that?"

Ayrion nodded. "I told you we would want them here."

"That's an understatement." Movement on his right caught their attention, and all three men turned to find a lone guard about twenty feet away. He held Myron bound and gagged in front of him with a dagger to Myron's side.

"I see what you mean by the nose," Bek said offhandedly.

Really? Ferrin wanted to slap the man in the back of the head.

"Don't come any closer," the scared guard shouted as he slowly backed farther into the woods, away from his fallen compatriots.

"You don't want to do that," Ferrin said calmly as he took a step closer. "Just let him go and leave. We won't stop you." Ferrin considered briefly that he might have even meant it.

"I said stay back!" the guard shouted, continuing to pull Myron farther in and away from the wielder battle. The man was undoubtedly terrified, and frightened people could do very stupid things. The guard moved up against a row of thick underbrush.

Ferrin had to stop him before he pulled the two of them inside. Once out of sight, he'd no doubt kill Myron and make a run for it. "Please, just let him go. You have my word, nothing will—"

The guard took another step back and was yanked off his feet and into the brush, leaving Myron to drop into the snow. The guard's screams were horrific and seemed to last for quite some time before everything finally went silent.

"What in the Pits was that?" Bek asked, his eyes wide as saucers. Neither he nor Ayrion took another step closer to the undergrowth, their weapons up.

Ferrin ran over to pick up Myron off the ground, cutting his ties and loosening the gag.

"What took you so long?" Myron griped as he rubbed at his raw wrists.

"Don't move."

Ferrin looked up to find Ayrion and Bek staring right at them, eyes bulging.

"What?" Ferrin asked.

Ayrion raised his sword and pointed in their direction. "Behind you," he whispered. "Don't move."

Ferrin slowly glanced over his shoulder and saw Nola's white face sticking through the brush, blood dripping from her fangs. "There you are." He smiled and reached up and rubbed behind the frostwolf's left ear, one of her favorite places to be scratched. "She's with us."

Ayrion and Bek looked at each other, no doubt wanting to know more, but another loud boom shook the forest, and they all turned. Nola disappeared back into the brush, no doubt to finish her meal and to keep as far from the wielders as possible. She was probably the only smart one of the lot.

"I appreciate the help, whoever you are," Myron said as he and Ferrin walked over to join the other two. Myron grabbed a sword from one of the fallen guards on their way.

Ferrin looked at Myron and frowned. His face bore several dark bruises, and the cuts on his clothing were stained with blood. "You look like they worked you over pretty good," Ferrin said.

"Not enough to stop me from giving these Tower whelps a taste of their own metal." He held up the dead guard's blade to emphasize his point.

Bek smiled. "A man after my own heart."

Ayrion looked over at the tinkers, then back at Myron. "Do you think you could keep them safe?"

"Keep who safe?" Myron turned and looked at the old couple, who were just now leaving the tree line. "If that's what you need."

"She's Rhivanni," Ayrion said. "Have her look at your wounds while you do."

"Where's Rae?" Myron asked.

"She's back at camp," Ferrin said, willing Myron to not say more about her abilities. "Just let them see to your wounds for now."

Myron nodded and headed back to where the tinkers were waiting at the edge of the forest, and they took up a position behind a couple of fallen trees.

Another ball of fire flew past, and the three men dove to the right. Quickly, they scrambled back to their feet and rushed toward the battle ahead, doing their best to keep behind larger trees until they were within a stone's throw of the four wielders.

"I've never seen bulradoer fight each other," Bek said as they stared in awe over the trunk of a fallen tree. "And you say you know her?"

"Yes," Ferrin said as he watched Lenara fight off the other three's attacks, swinging her whips wildly and yet somehow still managing to maintain one of her invisible shields. "I just don't know how we can help her." The other three bulradoer wielded ter'aks of their own—two green swords and one blue. "I've defended against one of those fire weapons before." He looked at the dragon blades in Ayrion's hands. "I'm guessing those will do the same."

"They do," Ayrion said matter-of-factly as he studied the battle ahead.

Ferrin began to cough. Half the trees surrounding the small glen were on fire now, their smoke filling the whole area with a thick haze that left Ferrin's eyes watering and his lungs burning. His swords might withstand their ter'aks, but they certainly wouldn't stop a ball of fire or one of their blasts of wind. Before he managed to find a workable idea, Bek was out from behind the tree, his bowstring pulled to his chin.

He released the arrow, and it buried itself in the back of the closest bulradoer, which happened to be one with grey robes. The wielder's green sword vanished as he fell.

"I can't believe that worked!" Ferrin said, clapping Bek on the back excitedly, but before the man could nock a second arrow, the black-robed bulradoer turned and unleashed a ball of fire straight at them. They dove behind the tree, and the flames split around them, but the damage had been done, and the large pine began to snap.

Ferrin looked up to see which way it was falling and leaped in the opposite direction. The tree shook the ground when it hit. He quickly rolled to his feet, looking for another place to hide.

"Look out!" was all the warning he got from Ayrion before he was lifted off his feet by a burst of wind that flung him backward, and he slammed into the side of a nearby oak.

Chapter 20 | Ferrin

ERRIN HEARD HIS BONES snap and screamed as he dropped helplessly onto the snow.

He couldn't move.

The pain was excruciating. It felt as though he'd been stabbed by a dozen blades. He tried to open his eyes, but they were watering so hard he couldn't see. Air wheezed in and out of his lungs in clumpy, wet gasps, threatening to stop at any moment. He whimpered almost uncontrollably as he fought against the searing pain coursing through his body.

He tried looking down to see the damage, but he couldn't move his head. All he could do was to keep blinking his eyes and forcing the next inhale. He'd seen the aftermath of the old tinker woman's blast and the broken heaps of bodies she'd sent into the trees. He was probably just as broken. An image of bones jutting through his skin and his limbs twisted into unnatural positions had his heart racing even faster.

Why wasn't he dead? He wanted to die, yet still he fought to stay conscious, the pain pulling him in and out as he watched the battle raging through tear-filled eyes.

Ayrion left his hiding place behind one of the trees and started for the bulradoer. Why wasn't Bek going with him? The forest suddenly began to darken. What time was it? Was the sun setting?

Then, unexpectedly, everything came back into focus, and he was yanked back to consciousness. When he awoke, he realized Bek was kneeling beside him.

The hiss of fire and steel had Bek spinning back around. Ferrin caught brief glimpses of colored light from the battle ahead, but it meant little through the crushing pain. Taking a deep agonizing breath, Ferrin tried to speak. "How bad is it?" His words were barely audible.

Bek stared at him, the horror in his eyes saying enough. "Just hold on."

Ferrin didn't know if he could. He could feel his life slipping away.

Another hiss of fire and Bek turned, moving far enough to the side this time that Ferrin was able to catch a clear view of the battle as he dipped in and out of consciousness.

In the clearing ahead, Ayrion had engaged the second grey-robed wielder while Lenara fought against the one in black. Even through his blurred vision, the brightly colored weapons helped distinguish who was who. It appeared this black-robed bulradoer was a little more competent than the ones Lenara had fought outside of Rhowynn, which meant she hadn't cut him in half yet and he was still holding his own, even managing to steal some ground. Red and blue sparks filled the haze as the two weapons interacted.

Ferrin coughed, and blood splattered in the snow in front of him, drawing Bek's attention. The man stared down at him a moment, pity in his eyes, then turned back to the fight. Ferrin started to drift once more, but he fought against it, focusing on the battle.

Ayrion was holding his own as well. He didn't have an invisible shield like Lenara, but the man didn't seem to need one. Every time the grey wielder tried to conjure a ball of fire or send a fist of air against him, he somehow always managed to get out of the way just in time. Ferrin's dragon blades were beautiful to watch in the swordsman's hands. Green sparks flew from the bulradoer's ter'ak with each strike against them.

The grey bulradoer was clearly growing impatient, lashing out wildly as he fought to cut the swordsman down. Ferrin didn't know what kind of training the Upakans were given, but it was beyond impressive. The man moved like something otherworldly, his swords seeking an opening against the bulradoer's invisible shield.

The forest around him dimmed once more, and Ferrin fought with everything he had to remain conscious. Another crack from Lenara's whips brought him back.

The black-robed bulradoer shouted and called down a stream of lightning similar to what Ferrin had seen Lenara do back in Rhowynn that had killed all the remaining Black Watch, including Lord Harlin.

Lenara raised her shield, and the bolt of lightning ricocheted up into the trees. The resulting thunderclap was deafening as the force of it expounded outward, leaving Ferrin to feel as though his body had been set on fire from the unexpected jolt. His stomach roiled at the pain, nausea washing over him, but he managed not to vomit. It seemed it was the only part of him he could still control.

"How bad is it?" a voice asked, coming up behind him. It sounded like the tinker woman.

Ferrin couldn't turn to find out.

"It's bad," Ferrin heard Bek say, trying not to look at Ferrin when he did. "I'll see what I can do."

Ferrin hoped they didn't try moving him. He was barely managing consciousness as it was. If they turned him over, he'd black out for sure. Though, at this point, that might have been a kindness, except he somehow knew that if he did black out, he wouldn't have the strength to keep himself alive.

Another crack of lightning, this one green, was called down by Lenara, but the other bulradoer managed to get his shield up in time, though the force of the attack sent him stumbling backward.

The concussive force of the attack shook the trees and rocked Ferrin. He could feel the darkness closing in, and his mind flooded with thoughts of the future. More importantly, a future without him in it. He wondered what would happen to Rae and Suri if he died, where they would go. Would Myron watch after them? Would his sister?

"Ferrin!"

Ferrin's eyes opened. He knew that voice, and he tried to call to her, but nothing came out.

"Move," he heard another familiar voice say, and Treygan suddenly appeared beside him with Rae moving around to drop into the snow in front of Ferrin. Tears swelled in her eyes when she looked down at him, but he continued to focus on his breathing. He had a feeling if he stopped, so would the air. She closed her eyes and reached out to place her hands on him.

"Wait," Zynora said. "What are you doing?"

"I'm healing him," she said. "Now keep quiet." She closed her eyes again and placed one hand on his forehead, and the other she slid inside his coat, up under his shirt.

Ferrin jerked slightly at the cold touch of her hands on his chest, and immediately bit down on his tongue to keep from crying out as she sent her magic down into him, reminding him of his time on the inquisitor's rack all over again. He remembered the first time he'd seen her, the way she hadn't been willing to look him in the eyes. She never managed it even after a dozen healings. He remembered how she had tried using him for information to spend more time with her daughter. Unfortunately, it was that information that had sent Sylas to Rhowynn in the first place. A lot had happened since their time in the Tower, and what had started as a friendship of convenience had blossomed into something much more.

Her magic was slow at first, and he could feel the familiar chill of its tendrils as it worked deeper inside him. He cried out as the bones began to move back into place. He could actually feel them moving, reminding him of when Cheeks had snapped his fingers one by one.

As soon as the last bone had pulled back within the skin, the soothing balm of her magic started to work its way through his body, sucking out the pain. His ragged breaths grew stronger, and for the first time since he'd fallen, he was able to move his head enough to look down and see that the rest of him was slowly coming back to life. His fingers and toes were first, then his arms and legs. Soon he was able to push himself up into a sitting position, noticing several holes in the front of his shirt where his ribs must have poked through, each covered in congealed blood and snow.

As soon as he was able to move, the others helped them both around to the other side of the tree and out of direct line of fire from the wielders. They'd barely propped him against the rough bark when Rae's eyes rolled up in the back of her head, and she collapsed into his lap.

"Someone help her."

"Give her to me," Zynora said. "I know what she needs." The old tinker looked hardly able to stand herself, let alone able to help Rae, but she turned and nodded at Bek, who then lifted Rae into his arms and carried her out of the trees. Ferrin was half tempted to leave as well, to make sure Rae was alright, but the hissing of steel and flame from the other side of the tree stopped him.

He took a few quick glimpses through the smoke-filled trees of Bek with the tinkers. He also thought he saw his sister's fiery hair and possibly Elson. Turning, he noticed he was surrounded by the crew of the *Wind Binder*, each taking up a defensible position within the cover of the surrounding trees. They crouched, looking ready, swords in hand as they waited for a signal to charge.

"You didn't leave us much of a fight," Treygan said behind him, noting all the dead guards across the way. He peeked out from behind the tree. "And it looks like Ayrion and Lenara are giving those two a run for their gold." He looked at Ferrin. "What should we do?"

Ferrin shook his head. "Afraid there's not much we can do."

"Ayrion told me not to engage the wielders," Bek said, joining them behind the tree.

"Where's Rae?" Ferrin asked and turned, but the smoke was too thick to see anything.

"She's in good hands," Bek said. "Several of Treygan's crew are watching over them."

Ismara crouched beside her father, her long auburn hair rippling in the breeze under her captain's hat, looking ready to charge in herself and defend the man in black at a moment's notice. In truth, they all looked ready. The Upakan must have made quite the impression while aboard the *Wind Binder*.

"I guess we watch, then," Treygan said as he spun his bone-handle knife around in his fingers.

Ferrin knelt beside the tree he'd been smashed against, the snow in front of it drenched with his blood. Looking at the size of that stain, he couldn't believe he was still alive.

In the clearing ahead, Ayrion and Lenara continued their battle with the two bulradoer. Bek drew another arrow and let it fly at the remaining grey-robed wielder, but the arrow was deflected by the bulradoer's shield and nearly struck Ayrion. They all gasped as the swordsman spun to the side and batted the shaft away before it hit him. As soon as he did, the bulradoer turned and released another ball of flame in their direction.

Ferrin was the first to leap out of the way, not planning on getting caught unawares this time. He scrambled back to his feet and behind another tree already occupied by Bones. The white paint around the dark-skinned man's face made him look skeletal, which always put Ferrin on edge, but he guessed that was the point. Bones had both his kamas in hand and looked ready to fight.

"What are we waiting for?" Bones asked in his usual deep voice.

"We're waiting for one of them," he said, pointing toward Lenara or Ayrion, "to give us a signal that they need our help. Right now, we'd just get in the way."

Bones released a deep-throated growl. He clearly didn't like the idea of standing there doing nothing any more than Ferrin.

The two watched in silence as Ayrion continued to work his way around the grey bulradoer, drawing him farther away from the one fighting Lenara. He couldn't seem to penetrate the wielder's shield, but the wielder in turn couldn't seem to land a strike. Ayrion had neatly sidestepped or ducked or batted away every attempt. Sooner or later, one of them was bound to slip up. As soon as the thought crossed Ferrin's mind, Ayrion tripped on something and went down.

Ferrin's breath caught in his throat, and he and Bones quickly stepped out from the protection of the tree to make a run for the bulradoer.

They were too late.

The grey wielder raised his sword to cut Ayrion in half, but Ayrion swung first. His black blade drove underneath the invisible shield and severed the bulradoer's foot while his sword was still in the air, and Ferrin was left to wonder whether Ayrion had tripped at all.

The bulradoer screamed, and with only one foot, leapt on top of Ayrion, clearly hoping to drive his fiery green blade straight through Ayrion's chest. He hit nothing but snow as Ayrion rolled out of the way just in time to keep from getting skewered.

Ayrion spun, and with a single fluid motion drove one of his swords through the man's unprotected back. The bulradoer jerked twice and then went still, the blade of his ter'ak vanishing, leaving nothing but the hilt.

As soon as Ayrion had made it to his feet, the ground around the black wielder erupted, and Ayrion dove back as dozens of roots shot out of the snow and up under the bulradoer's shield, where they latched onto the Tower's wielder. The man's sword was yanked from his hands, its blade immediately blinking out of existence as the vines curled around his arms and legs, pinning him in place, forcing him upright.

Ferrin stared in wonder as the bulradoer struggled to break free of the roots' grip, shouting and cursing at the top of his lungs. Bones searched the ground around the trees where they were standing, clearly worried they might come alive as well. Ferrin couldn't help but look himself. It was a rather unnerving sight. Just when he thought Lenara couldn't have surprised him more, she calls the trees to her service.

With the bulradoer disarmed and roots now encasing his body like a wooden cocoon, Ferrin and the rest of those in hiding dared leave the trees to venture a little closer. They had to use their cloaks to breathe, the smoke had grown so strong.

Ayrion looked at the bulradoer, then at Lenara, and with a polite nod, he left the two and walked over to where Ferrin and the others were gathered.

"The Tower will hear about this, Lenara!" the bulradoer spat, his shoulders and head all that remained visible. "This is treason!"

She lowered her whips, the flaming red brands hissing in the snow as she walked over to stand in front of the man. "It's not treason when I am the one who has been attacked."

Ferrin couldn't see the bulradoer's face with his hood up, but he could definitely hear fear in the man's voice.

"What Sylas did to you was not condoned by the Tower," the bulradoer said, his tone notably softening. "You must know that."

Lenara sneered. "The fact that you even know what happened to me says otherwise. Sylas received his orders directly from Valtor."

There was a momentary silence. "Come back to the fold. I'm sure all will be forgiven. The Tower is not without mercy."

"We both know that isn't true." Lenara smiled, and Ferrin shuddered. He'd seen that smile before, and it had never ended well for those she had offered it to. She took a step back and raised her hand, and the roots began to move. Before the man could say another word, they pulled him straight into the ground. His screams lasted only long enough for the ground to swallow him whole.

Ferrin gulped as he watched the two red brands vanish. Lenara promptly collected the bulradoers' ter'aks and then turned and walked back through those gathered, like nothing had happened. The rest stood there a moment, staring at where the bulradoer had been and the upturned soil that was all that was left of him.

"Well, I've seen enough," Kettle said, looking a little pale as he turned and followed her out.

Ferrin was the next to leave, stiffly making his way through the smoke-filled trees to find Rae and Suri. He hoped she had managed to recover enough to ride back to camp. He took a moment outside the trees to wipe the tears from his eyes and fill his lungs with a couple of deep breaths before making his way over to the road, where he found Rae being cared for by the tinkers.

Suri, Myriah, and Elson were there as well, gathered to watch over Rae. Myron also, but he was sitting next to Zynora. He had some sort of white cream covering the deep bruises on his face. The crewmen from the *Wind Binder* Treygan had sent with Rae saw Ferrin coming and left to join the rest of their crew at the edge of the forest.

"How is she?" Ferrin asked. Her eyes were still closed, which had him worried.

"She is resting," Zynora said. "I've given her a sleeping tonic and infused some of my own healing into her. Healers are incapable of healing themselves, you know."

Ferrin nodded. Rae had told him as much before they left the Tower.

"Like any wielder," Tameel said, "their bodies are only capable of so much. Once spent, they have little choice but to rest and eat." He patted Suri on the head comfortingly as she attempted to introduce him to Tippi.

"Or drink," Elson added as he held up his leather flask with a wink.

"Don't worry," Myriah said. "I'm sure Rae will be fine by morning."

Ferrin looked at Myron. "How are you?"

"Been better, but I'll survive." He touched his face where the cream was covering. "Whatever this is, it seems to be helping."

"It is a healing balm all the way from the Wengoby Desert, created by the Imbatoo people."

Myron turned. "You've been to the other side of the Khezrian Wall?"

She smiled. "No. Afraid we haven't had that pleasure yet, though we did recently meet one of their princesses."

"An actual princess?" Myriah asked.

The old woman nodded.

Myron smiled. "That sounds like a story worth hearing."

"And perhaps one day you shall."

Ferrin knelt and ran the back of his fingers over Rae's cheek. "She's freezing. We need to get her warm."

"We can take her back to our camp," Zynora said. "Keep her out of the weather. She can sleep in one of the wagons."

Tameel looked up at the falling snow, which had begun to thicken. "At the very least, this should help keep the fire contained."

Ferrin looked at the burning trees behind him, then stood. He hadn't thought about the fire spreading. But Tameel was right, the snow should help to quell it before it did any further damage. At least he hoped it would.

"I'll get the horses." Ferrin trudged back through the shin-deep snow to where most of the others had gathered.

He wondered how much more of this they could take. It seemed no matter where they went, the Tower was there waiting on them. Ever since their escape, it had been one battle after another. Was there anywhere they could go that the Tower wouldn't find them?

"How is she?" Ismara asked as Ferrin approached. The others turned.

"The tinker woman gave her a sleeping tonic to help her rest."

"And how about your friend?" Bek asked, wiping his hatchets clean of blood on the snow before meticulously drying them.

"She's seen to his wounds as well." Ferrin turned to Elson, who had followed him over. "We should move our camp over to theirs."

"Aye, it'll be dark soon," Treygan said. He looked at Bones. "Best get the men ready. We'll make camp with them tonight." He then looked at Ayrion. "That is, if you don't mind an old riverboat captain sharing your fire."

Ayrion smiled and clapped Treygan on his shoulder. "Couldn't think of anyone I'd rather share it with more."

With that, Ferrin grabbed their horses, and he and Elson started back for the road.

Chapter 21 | Ferrin

ERRIN WALKED HIS HORSE out to where Zynora and the others sat waiting. He handed the reins to Elson to give Zynora and Tameel a hand with their horses. The older couple slowly trotted off in the direction of their camp. He waited long enough for them to ride out of earshot before turning to Elson.

"Why did you bring Rae here and not stay back at camp like I told you?"

"I didn't," he said with a slight slur as he took another swig from his flask. "She brought me. I had to chase after her just to catch up. And clearly it was a good thing we did, 'cause look at you. You wouldn't still be here if we hadn't."

"I'm grateful she was here, but next time keep her in camp. She walked right into the middle of a battle."

"Excuse me for asking, but how's that any different than what happened in Rhowynn?"

Ferrin ground his teeth. "I don't want her in the middle of any fight. I don't care if you have to tie her to a tree, don't let her go running off."

Elson gave him a look that said he'd like to see anyone try tying her to a tree.

Truth was, seeing her lying there unconscious, especially because of him, had Ferrin rattled. He knew how dangerous an overuse of magic could be for a wielder, especially a healer. The thought that she could have died because of him was unsettling. He probably shouldn't have taken it out on Elson, but he didn't have anyone else.

Behind them, Lenara headed back into the burning forest and disappeared inside the smoke. Ferrin wondered if she was going in to put out the fire.

Bek lifted Rae onto the front of Ferrin's horse, then took Suri with him.

"See if you can pack up the camp," Ferrin said to Elson, who was standing beside a brown mare, looking like he wasn't sure how to get on her. How much had he been drinking? "We are moving to the tinkers' campsite. It's about a half mile north of ours in the trees on the left." He waited for Elson to nod that he understood before starting back toward the tinkers' campsite. He hurried his pace to catch up with Bek and Suri. He didn't want to let the little girl out of his sight.

By the time they arrived, the snow had thickened even further, and what little light the late evening sun had provided was now gone. With a little help from Myron and Myriah, Ferrin dismounted and carried Rae over to the back of the green wagon where Zynora and Tameel stood waiting. Suri ran alongside him.

The inside of the wagon was surprisingly warm. A small stove in the corner had the place feeling cozy and inviting. He laid Rae on one of the cots, and Zynora pulled up a stool beside it. The older woman placed her hand over Rae's forehead and mumbled something under her breath before turning to look up at him.

"Best to let her rest. If she wakes, I'll be sure to let you know." It seemed her polite way of telling him to leave.

Ferrin waited a moment longer, watching the steady rise and fall of Rae's chest, before stepping back outside. Most of the *Wind Binder* crew was hard at work, setting up temporary shelters beneath large tarps and canvas oilcloths. Several of the crew had already begun to scavenge for extra wood, while others, under Kettle's direct supervision, tended to the evening meal.

Taking a moment to look through the camp, Ferrin realized Elson was nowhere to be seen. He wondered if he should go see if his friend needed help packing up their gear from the other site. It looked like Lenara hadn't returned, either. If Nola was back, she was staying hidden for the moment, which wasn't unusual. She usually kept to herself except when she was in the mood to get her head scratched, or when she was bringing them fresh game she'd caught.

He headed over to where the horses were being penned and started to untie one when the crunch of snow near the entrance had him turning. Both Elson and Lenara rode in, each with several carry bags and blankets strapped to their horses.

"Over here," Ferrin said, waving them over to the makeshift corral. Once dismounted, they began to unsaddle the horses and carry the gear over to a couple of empty spots on the right side of the fire, where the others had apparently set them a place. Myron and Myriah were there and helped them unload the bedding and supplies. Myron was already looking more stable on his feet. Whatever was in the tinker's balm seemed to be working.

A single sheet of canvas draped between some long wooden stakes provided just enough room for the five of them to set up their bedding. Suri had opted to remain with her mother in the wagon. The thick overhanging limbs from the surrounding trees helped slow the falling snow, giving their bivouac a fighting chance. Better the snow than a hard rain, he figured. Ferrin remembered some of the shelters they'd survived inside on their trek down through the lower Razor Spine Mountains. It was a wonder they hadn't frozen to death. And now their company had grown by three. They would have been hard-pressed to find shelter to fit all of them on that journey.

Elson handed Ferrin one of the satchels he'd carried over and then plopped down beside him. Ferrin had been surprised at Elson's declaration of leaving Rhowynn. Admittedly, the man had few friends there, apart from those on the wielder council he could stand talking with, which Ferrin could have counted on one hand with two missing fingers. Other than that, there wasn't much tying him to the city. So Elson had sold his home and worldly goods, claiming he had decided to see the world, or at least the part of it that Ferrin was planning on traveling through, and then followed them out.

Ferrin wasn't quite sure how he felt about his friend giving up his home and life to follow him around Aldor. The responsibility weighed on him. More than that, each new tagalong diluted their once-intimate group.

Lenara also had been an unexpected new addition. Apparently, the Tower was the only home she had really known. Ferrin had thought, now that she was free of her obligation to the bulradoer, she might have tried returning to Cylmar, but it seemed she didn't quite relish the idea of going home just yet, or at all. He hadn't pressed the issue. Clearly, having another wielder around— especially one as powerful as she was—was a good decision, and it had already paid off in abundance.

"How do you think they found us?" Elson asked.

"We probably spent too long in Rhowynn after the battle," Ferrin said. "Should have left sooner."

"That's my fault," Myriah said. "I didn't realize how long it would take to get Harlin's things in order." There had been a lot more involved in closing her former husband's affairs than they had at first believed, what with him being a member of the upper classes. His estate had to be valued and then sold at auction. "I'm just grateful we were able to find buyers who wanted the entire lot as is, and on short notice. Certainly better that than having to sell it piecemeal. That would have taken forever."

Ferrin's sister had walked away from Rhowynn a very wealthy woman, making the bag of gold Ferrin had procured from the Tower look downright miserly. He stared at his sister a moment as she examined Myron's injuries. Even with the Tower still chasing him, Ferrin counted himself lucky to have her back in his life. And if he were being honest with himself, he was grateful to have all of them.

Ferrin looked at Elson, and Elson smiled when he caught Ferrin staring at his flask, holding it out to offer him a nip. Ferrin waved it off. "No thanks. Last time I indulged you, my head thumped for a day. I prefer to get my warmth from the fire."

Elson shrugged. "Suit yourself." He offered it to Lenara next.

She harumphed. "Keep your brew to yourself, you drunkard."

Elson sighed, then took a quick swig and corked the end. He stared at the bulradoer. "One of these days I'm going to get you to have a drink with me." She growled, and he turned back around. "I'm telling you, Ferrin. I'm wearing her down."

Ferrin placed his hand on Elson's shoulder. "I wouldn't hold my breath."

Ferrin sat at the edge of their makeshift coverlet and let the fire warm him. Myriah finished with Myron and walked over to sit next to Lenara. On Ferrin's right, Elson and Myron scooted to the edge of the canvas's protection to be closer to the warmth of the flames.

The rest of the *Wind Binder* crew, along with Ayrion and Bek, chatted quietly as everyone waited for whatever Kettle was briskly stirring in the large pot. The smell of it had Ferrin's mouth watering, though knowing Kettle, it was sure to be overly peppered.

Ferrin leaned forward to catch Lenara's attention. The hood of her robe was back, allowing her frizzy auburn hair to hang loose behind her. The gold flecks in her raspberry-colored eyes shone bright against the firelight. "Do you have the ter'aks?"

She didn't reply at first, but she did eventually offer him a quick nod as she scanned the faces around the fire. She stopped on Ayrion and Bek, and her eyes narrowed slightly as she studied the two new additions.

"Can I see one of them?" Ferrin asked.

Lenara's jaw tightened momentarily, but she removed one of the bladeless hilts from her robe and handed it to him, drawing the others' attention. He'd held other ter'aks before, those collected from dead bulradoer they'd already faced, but he still found them fascinating. The hilt was much like what you'd expect to find on a sword crafted for those who had the gold. The workmanship was exquisite, silver wrought with decorative gold leaf runes.

"Is that one of those fire weapons?" Treygan asked. "You mind if I take a look?"

Ferrin passed the hilt to his right, and it made its way around the fire, everyone taking a look as it went past, until it reached the riverboat captain. Treygan studied it a moment, handling it carefully. "How does it work? It won't ignite and kill me, will it?"

Ferrin looked at Lenara.

"No, it won't ignite," she said. "Unless you call its name, and even then, only a wielder can do that."

Treygan handed the ter'ak to Ayrion, who took a moment to examine it as well.

"Very similar to others we've collected," he said.

Lenara looked surprised. "You've handled a ter'ak before?"

"A few, but they were dormant."

"So any wielder can use it?" Bek asked, taking the weapon from Ayrion and spinning it in his hand.

"Hey, watch where you're aiming that thing!" Needle said as he quickly leaned back when Bek swung the weapon in his direction.

"Yes," Lenara said. "Any wielder who knows the ter'ak's name can call it forth."

Bek tried passing the ter'ak on to Needle, but Needle took one look at it and shook his head, so Bek handed it to Whitey, who then passed it down to a couple more crewman before it made its way back around to Lenara.

"What's its name?" Ismara asked.

Lenara held the weapon out toward the fire. "Seravis." Blue flames shot from the crossguard and out to form a long deadly blade. Those sitting closest quickly scooted back and out of reach.

Ferrin could feel the heat coming from the weapon even though there were two others between Lenara and himself. Lenara held the blade for a moment, then released the magic, and the blue fire vanished.

Treygan shook his head. "The White Tower employing wielders and using magical weapons from another age. I don't even recognize this world anymore. How are we to defend against things like that?"

"The same way they did in the Wizard Wars," Ayrion said, "and the Faerie Wars before that. With wielders of our own."

Many of those around the fire turned and looked at Lenara.

She seemed oblivious as she tucked the ter'ak back beneath her robes.

Treygan cleared his throat. "That was . . . that was quite some trick with those roots, Ms. Lenara. I can honestly say I've never seen anything like that before."

"And hopefully never will again," Kettle mumbled as he continued stirring.

She smirked. "I borrowed that from a wizard I had dealings with quite a few years back."

Ayrion stopped cleaning his blade and looked up. "You know Nyalis?"

Lenara turned, her face tightening. "Do you?"

Ferrin was confused. Who was this Nyalis?

"We were with him not more than two weeks back," Ayrion said. "How do you know him?"

Lenara frowned. "I had a slight run-in with him about sixteen years ago. And by run-in, I mean he tried to kill me."

Ferrin gaped. Lenara had fought a *real* wizard?

She straightened her robes. "Of course, in all fairness, I was trying to kill him as well."

Ferrin continue to gape.

"And you're still alive?" Bek asked, astounded. He looked at Ayrion and chuckled. "Nyalis must have been in a hurry or something."

"I won't lie," she said. "He's a tough old bird. Took down several bulradoer, a couple of sniffers, and nearly an entire praad of corax before making his escape. Never knew what happened to him after that. Spent the last sixteen years looking."

"Who is this Nyalis?" Ferrin cut in.

"Aye," Ismara added. "How about filling the rest of us in." The crew of the *Wind Binder* sat with eager eyes and ears, waiting for an explanation.

Lenara turned. "Nyalis is the last remaining wizard from the original council established by . . . you know who."

"That's not possible," Treygan said. "That would mean he would be . . ."

"A thousand years old," Lenara finished. "Yes, clearly he's found a way to sustain his life." She looked at Ayrion. "Where did you find him?"

"It's more like he found us," Ayrion said, seemingly cautious in his answer. His head cocked slightly to the side. "So you were one of those the Tower sent to hunt down the faerie?"

Ferrin's eyes bulged, the breath nearly catching in his throat. "The what?"

The entire campsite went eerily silent. Even Kettle's ladle sat motionless in the pot as he, too, stared in awe at the man in black.

Treygan turned. "Did you just say . . . *faerie*?"

Bek gave Ayrion a strange look, as though perhaps wondering if Ayrion had said too much.

"I trust Treygan with my life," Ayrion said to Bek, then looked across the fire at Ferrin. "And Treygan trusts them. Anyone who can survive the Tower and live to talk about it has my respect. And if the Tower is hunting them down, I would say they're on the right side of things."

"And if they're caught, who's to say they won't talk?" Bek pointed out.

"Who's to say we wouldn't either? Nyalis was very specific when talking with me that he wanted to restore . . . it, which means he will need to begin bringing others in."

Ferrin stared at the two men across the fire. What were they referring to? Bring who in? And what was all this about faeries?

"What in the hallowed Pits is everyone talking about?" Elson asked with a somewhat noticeable slur.

"Restore what?" Lenara asked Ayrion hungrily. She scooted to the edge of their shelter, looking as excited as Ferrin had ever seen her.

"Again," Ferrin asked, more forcefully, "what are you talking about?"

And once again he was ignored as Ayrion held Lenara's gaze. "Where do your allegiances lie, bulradoer?"

"With myself," she said without even a moment's hesitation.

Ayrion smiled. "An honest bulradoer. What's the world coming to, indeed." He then turned to Ferrin. "You were asking about the faerie."

Among other things, Ferrin wanted to say.

Ayrion looked at Lenara. "Should I tell him, or would you?"

Lenara sighed. "There has long been a prophecy of a coming Marked One. Not much has ever been written about them, not even when or if they existed or would ever exist. But the Tower has ways of tracking magical disturbances, places where great magic has been used. There was one such disturbance, larger than any we had seen before, and I was sent to find the source. Turns out, it was a baby."

"I remember when that happened," Myron said. "The whole Tower was up in arms."

Lenara paused. "I forgot you were there."

"Hadn't been there too long. A few months, perhaps."

"Rae would have been there as well," Ferrin added, pausing to look over at the green wagon. "She was born and raised inside the Tower."

Lenara waited to see if Ferrin would say more before finally continuing. "As I was saying, a team was sent to find this disturbance, and what we found was the wizard and a newborn child. What we hadn't expected to find was that the child was a faeling." She looked directly at Ayrion when she said it, no doubt to judge his reaction, but his face never changed.

"What's a faeling?" Myriah asked Lenara.

"Someone who is half human and half faerie."

"Is that even possible?" Ferrin asked.

"It is extremely rare." Lenara turned to Ayrion once more. "You don't seem all that surprised by this revelation. You know who it is, don't you?" Her eyes narrowed. "You've seen him. Is the faeling with Nyalis?"

Ayrion leaned forward, and Ferrin thought he spotted perhaps a modicum of concern. "You seem intent on learning his whereabouts."

"So you do know of whom I speak."

"Perhaps."

She smiled. "What is he like? Has he shown you his power? What can he do? Does he look more Fae or human?"

Ferrin stared at Lenara, growing a little concerned himself. She seemed downright obsessed.

She paused a moment after noticing the strange looks being cast her way. "I've spent the better part of my adult life looking for this child. Of course I'm interested." She thought a moment. "I wonder if Mangora has managed to find him yet?"

Ayrion's face hardened.

"Do you know this name?" Lenara asked.

"We might have had a run-in with her."

"That's putting it mildly," Bek said under his breath.

"What do you mean by that?" Lenara asked, her fists clutching the thick material of her robe's sleeves. "When I was sent to hunt down the metallurgist," she said with a quick nod in Ferrin's direction, "the Tower was sending another group to go after the faeling, but that was months ago. I believe Mangora was to lead it, and judging by your expression, I take it she found him."

"In a manner of speaking," Ayrion said.

"And I take it that since the faeling is with Nyalis, she was unsuccessful in her attempt?"

"Not for a lack of trying," Bek growled.

Lenara smiled. "That's her third try." She chuckled, something that seemed almost out of place for her. "Valtor isn't going to be happy to hear about this."

"Who is this Mangora everyone is talking about?" Ferrin asked, once again feeling completely lost within the conversation.

"Not everyone is talking about her," Ismara said, sounding just as frustrated. "This seems to be a very one-sided conversation."

Lenara took a deep breath. Ferrin could hear her rolling her eyes in the forced exhale. "Mangora is one of the Ahvari witches. She has been with the White Tower for longer than I've been alive, perhaps even longer than Valtor. In fact, she was the first to locate the faeling after we lost him to the wizard. Found him living in Easthaven of all places."

Ferrin stiffened. "Easthaven? That's where we are headed now. Are you saying we could be riding into another conflict with the Tower?"

"Doubtful," she said. "Mangora tried to capture him there but failed. The wielder council in Easthaven was stronger than the Tower realized. And the attempt drew the eye of Sidara's overlord, so it is highly doubtful the Tower will try again so soon, or in such a brash manner." She harumphed as she looked at the fire. "They should have sent me. Instead, I got assigned to you."

Ferrin smiled. "Glad to see the Tower cares so much. Wish they cared a little less."

"Wish they cared a *lot* less," Myron said, touching the white spots on his face where Zynora had plastered the cream.

Ferrin grimaced. "True." He looked at Lenara. "Why haven't you mentioned any of this before?" A spark ignited in the back of his mind, the answer suddenly becoming very clear. "Wait, is that why you wanted to accompany us, because you knew we were heading for Easthaven?"

She stared at him a moment, her deep raspberry eyes boring holes into him. "Perhaps."

"Then what? You plan on using him as leverage to get yourself back in good standing with the Tower?"

Her eyes sparked. "If I return to the Tower, it won't be of my own volition. And they better pray I never do."

The fireside grew quiet as Ferrin stared her down. Lenara's expression said she meant it. "Then why go?"

"Like I said, I've spent my entire adult life searching for him. I don't want it to be for nothing."

"If that is why you travel to Easthaven," Bek said, "then you're wasting your trip. The faeling isn't there."

Lenara turned. "What? Then where is he?"

"Somewhere safe from the Tower's reach," Ayrion said.

She stared at the two men for an uncomfortable length of time, confused at first, but then something changed, and her face brightened. "You found the Wizards Keep." She gripped the folds of her robe. "You've seen Aero'set. Where is it? What is it like? I can't believe the school has been found after all these centuries."

Ferrin groaned as he leaned forward and wiped his face with his hand. "And because we don't like being left completely in the dark once again, what are you three talking about now? What is a wizards keep? And what's this about a school?"

"Aye," Treygan said, "a little more information would be helpful."

Lenara finally pulled her attention away from the other side of the fire long enough to address Ferrin. "Aero'set is an ancient school for wizards, built by the Fae nearly two thousand years ago after their arrival in our realm. After the Faerie Wars, it became the seat of power for the Wizard Council. It was used to train wielders in the arts of magic, but after the Wizard Wars, it was rumored to have been sealed away, hidden from all. Valtor has been searching for it for as long as I've been in the Tower."

Ferrin felt like a child just learning that there was more to the world than what lay just beyond his backyard—half faeries, magical weapons, Ahvari witches, wizard schools, not to mention he was sharing a fire with the Guardian Protector himself. And the Guardian Protector, Lenara, and the White Tower somehow were all tied together? What was happening? Despair crept over him. It seemed the world was closing around him, and he was beginning to feel like no matter where they ran, there was no place they could hide.

Lenara stared at Ayrion and Bek from across the fire. "So, will you answer me or not? Have you seen Aero'set?"

"We have," Ayrion said, and Lenara began to quiver. It was the most emotion Ferrin had seen from her since her explosive rage back at Sylas's camp.

"Can you tell me of your meeting with Mangora?" she asked. "And start with how an Upakan and a couple of tinkers managed to end up in the middle of all this."

"Not by choice," Ayrion was quick to point out. "I was traveling with Tameel and Zynora north to Wellhollow when we first came across Bek outside of Belvin. They were having some difficulty with a strange outbreak that turned out to be some form of dark magic created by an ancient wielder named Argon."

Lenara nearly choked. "Who did you say?"

"He said his name was Argon. A former general of the Dark One."

Ferrin could feel his blood pressure rising. He wondered if it was too late to take Elson up on his offer for a pull from his flask.

Lenara shook her head in disbelief. "So the Tower managed to release him after all." She sounded impressed.

"You knew about this?" Bek demanded angrily.

Once again, Ferrin had no idea who or what they were talking about, so he sat back and listened, hoping someone would explain.

Lenara stared at the fire a moment before answering. "I knew Valtor had been messing with some of the ancient artifacts we had discovered in one of the Tower's lower vaults. They found one of the Dark Wizard's grimoires." She stared at the fire a moment, then turned back to Ayrion and Bek. "But you actually saw him, talked with him?"

Bek hmphed. "We didn't just talk with him, we fought him. He was turning my people into creatures called—"

"Vulraak." Lenara nodded. "Yes. It was written that he had the ability to bend people to his will."

"More than bending," Ayrion said. "He turned them into monsters."

"How have we not heard of this sooner?" she asked. "Belvin isn't that far away."

"Because Ayrion stopped him," Bek said.

Lenara stared at the man in black with an incredulous look on her face. "You. You faced Argon and won?"

"Not without help."

Clearly the king chose his protector well, Ferrin thought. *The man's been hunting down and killing ancient wielders out of legend.* Something struck him, and he turned and looked at Myron. "I bet that's what the lunatics in Woodvale were going on about."

Myron's head lifted. "You could be right." He looked at Ayrion and Bek. "They kept going on about some kind of plague turning people into cannibals up north and ran us out of town, afraid we would spread it. A group of them even tried hunting us down after we left. If it wasn't for Nola, we might not have survived."

Hearing her name, the enormous frostwolf padded into the camp and took a look around, but when no one acknowledged her presence or walked over to give her some attention, she turned and disappeared back into the snow-covered forest.

"Every time I see that thing, I shiver," Bek said.

"Aye," Treygan added. "Imagine traveling with it aboard your ship."

Bek nodded. "Got to admit, she is a beautiful creature, whatever she is."

"A frostwolf," Lenara said, briefly explaining where her kind were located beyond the Shroud, which led to explaining how the ancient protective barrier had been raised around the frozen northlands.

They spent the rest of the evening and well into the night swapping battle stories of what they'd been through over the last several months. Ferrin told them of his time spent in the Tower, the torture he'd endured. He told them of Rae, who had it worst of all, being born and raised inside the place, being forced to watch men and women tortured on a daily basis, even being forced to bear a child in hopes of raising up more healers they could use.

He told them of his escape and the help he had received from not only Rae and Myron, but also by his cellmate, Azriel, which was the reason he was heading to Easthaven in the first place. He told them of their narrow escape from Iraseth by throwing themselves into Virn Run, and then barely making it out of the mountains. Nola and how she had brought them food, though at the time they didn't know who, or what, it was that was supplying it, then described how she had saved them outside of Woodvale. With some reluctance, he told them of Suri's connection with the giant wolf, then of being chased by Sylas across Aldor for months only to come to a final head outside of Rhowynn.

Captain Treygan and Ismara jumped in when Ferrin's story reached Storyl and told of their narrow escape from the lake town aboard the *Wind Binder*, ending with their run-in with the white cloaks that morning in Aldwick.

Ayrion and Bek told of their journey after the battle with Argon to Upper Wellhollow, mentioning some run-in they had with a lord's son in Minotha and the burning of his estate. Apparently when they arrived in Wellhollow, they found the Tower already there and searching for the faeling.

Ayrion went on to tell them how Mangora had captured the faeling and of the battle that had taken place in Upper Wellhollow, the number of Black Watch and bulradoer they had defeated, of the faeling and his friends breaking free in time to help them. Lenara was an eager listener. From the questions she asked, Ferrin could tell she was particularly interested in the faeling's abilities.

"Why would Mangora have searched for him in Wellhollow?" Lenara asked. "Seems quite a distance from Easthaven."

"Apparently," Ayrion said, "the Tower knew that the faeling was searching for an ancient key that would lead them to Aero'set. Mangora said she didn't know where the pieces of the key were to be found, but that the Tower did know roughly where the missing school was located, so they sent her there to find both."

He finished the tale with their battle inside the mountain, something about a key that didn't work, a giant spider creature called an arachnobe, something called a draakar, and finally the witch's narrow defeat and escape.

"That is quite the tale," Treygan said. Most of those around the fire stared in wide-eyed wonder.

Kettle finally began dishing out the stew, but most had lost their appetites, too excited by the incredible stories of adventure and magic and death to care much for food. Ferrin accepted his with a smile but ate slowly, not even noticing whether it had been overly seasoned or not.

Once everyone had their food, Ayrion described his time in Aero'set and told them that the wizard had now sent him to the Lost City to bring his people back to what was their rightful duty as the protectors of the school. He also said that this wizard believed the Upaka could be in danger.

"In danger of what?" Treygan asked. "I don't think even the Tower would risk a full-on assault on the Upaka."

"The wizard mentioned something about khuls."

"Khuls?" Lenara's eyes widened. "They were said to have been exterminated after the Dark Wizard was imprisoned. Are you sure that's what Nyalis said?"

"Are you saying they're real?"

"Of course they're real. Haven't you read the histories?"

"Apparently not the right ones. Nyalis said that my people have tunneled too deeply under the mountains, and that what was once buried is at risk of being released . . . or something like that." He stared at Ferrin's group from across the fire. "We could really use your help in vacating my people from the Lost City. Like Bek said, if you're heading to Easthaven in hopes of seeing the faeling, you'll be disappointed, but if you were to help me with the Upaka, you could return with us to Aero'set."

Lenara turned and looked at Ferrin, the eagerness in her eyes giving away what her vote would be. Ferrin looked at Ayrion. "I travel to Easthaven to fulfill a promise I made to Azriel. I don't care one way or another about meeting some half-faerie person. I just want to find some quiet place away from the eyes of the Tower to live out my life, not go risking it by running headlong into yet another dangerous situation."

"If safety is what you're after," Ayrion said, "then Aero'set is the only place in Aldor you are going to find it. It's the one place the Tower has no admittance. Keeping a promise is important, but no more so than helping me save my family from destruction, and Aldor from a possible invasion."

Myron leaned over. "It does seem they need the help."

Ferrin looked at Myriah, and she smiled. "You did put your promise on hold to come save me, perhaps doing so again isn't too uncalled for."

Ferrin turned to Elson, the one person he could always count on to protect his own hide. Elson raised his flask in salute. "I did say I wanted to travel."

Ferrin sighed, not liking the direction this was going. "I will need to talk with Rae first before any decisions are made."

Ayrion nodded. "Fair enough."

"I wish I could go," Treygan said, "but I'm afraid my place is on the water. I have a ship and crew to think about, and where you're planning to travel is one place we can't reach. The most I could offer is passage outside of Oswell, but it would take you farther out of your way, and I wouldn't be able to haul the wagons."

Ayrion patted the riverboat captain's shoulder. "I understand."

Ferrin wished *he* understood, but he seemed to be swimming in a haze. The last thing he wanted was to go traipsing off to the Lost City—the one place in Aldor no one dared venture—with the intent of telling a society of mercenaries that they needed to leave their home. Let alone the possible risk of finding their city infested with khuls, whatever those were.

He stood and left the others to the fire and walked over to the green wagon and knocked. Tameel opened the door, and Ferrin looked inside. "How is she?"

"Ferrin?" Rae's voice was weak but clear.

Tameel moved aside, and Ferrin climbed in the back, shutting the door behind him. Rae was sitting up in the cot, eating some of Kettle's stew. She looked frail, and the fact that Zynora had to hold the bowl as Rae spooned it into her mouth didn't help. Suri sat on the edge of the bed, playing with Tippi. She smiled when Ferrin walked in.

"You are looking better," Ferrin said to Rae as he stood over her cot.

Rae smiled. "So are you. It was bad."

Ferrin sat on one of the empty stools. "I know. I could feel it. If you hadn't been there, I probably wouldn't be here now. But don't think I'm not still mad at you for leaving the camp to come find me. 'Cause I am. You could have been killed."

"And so could you. You act like you are the only one that should take any risks."

He wasn't sure how best to argue the point, so he let the matter drop.

Tameel walked over and sat in a chair next to the small table at the back. "It sounds like they've been having quite a lively debate out there."

"That's one way to put it," Ferrin said, then gave them a brief overview of what all had been discussed. He finished with Ayrion's request for them to help bring the Upaka back to Aero'set.

The tinkers sounded overjoyed at the idea. Ferrin, on the other hand was anything but. He just wanted to find someplace in Aldor to go and hide, but after hearing Ayrion's story of wanting to do the same after the madness of Belvin and ending up in a battle in Wellhollow, Ferrin was wondering if there was anywhere left in the Five Kingdoms to run to.

"They have risked their lives to help us," Rae said. "Should we not do the same?"

She was right. The swordsman and his team had risked their lives to help save them, leaving Ferrin owing a rather large debt.

"Tippi wants to help," Suri said, raising her pinecone.

Ferrin looked at Rae, and she laid her hand on his. "I go with you. Whatever you decide."

He patted the top of her hand gently, then stood, and Zynora moved back in to continue helping her eat. Rae was right. If it hadn't been for these people risking their own lives to help them, Myron would probably be dead right now. Chances were good they all might have been. He walked back outside and over to the fire, everyone turning to see what he would say.

"It appears we will be joining you."

Chapter 22 | Adarra

ADARRA'S HANDS WERE TREMBLING as she closed the book and sat cross-legged in front of Jonas's cell, staring quietly at the enormous Tallosian through the bars. Her hands didn't tremble from the cold, even though cold was seeping up from the stones through the layers of her dress and thick stockings, but because she knew her time was running out. Things had happened fast since Lord Barl had given his consent for her to join the ambassadorial team to the Northman's homeland. Their ship was set to sail at the end of the week, and she felt completely unprepared, even though she had already finished her checklist two weeks prior and had spent that time double-checking, triple-checking, and re-examining it over again.

Nothing could bring about failure more than unpreparedness. Well, that and bad luck.

She kept her dress tucked under her legs. "You've been quiet today." She wondered if he was sensing her own anxieties.

"Thinking," he said.

"Oh? What about?"

"Seeing the sky."

Jonas had been told of their upcoming journey and was pleased with the thought of leaving his cell. The remnants of the face paint he had worn during their battle had finally washed off, revealing even more of the long scar of melted flesh that ran up the side of his face and partway into his scalp. He had yet to tell her how he'd gotten it.

She had insisted the jailer give Jonas some blankets, partly to keep him from catching his death of a cold, and partly because she had hoped it would encourage him to put away his hideously obscene cloak of human hair.

No such luck.

Most days, the Northman was uncouth and irritable, but after all the time she spent in the cells, and the more time they interacted, she sensed there was something different about him. She couldn't quite put her finger on it. He wasn't as wild as he had been months earlier when they had first brought him in, and there were times when she would catch a look in his eye that gave her pause. There was a gentleness to him, but she had no doubt if the man ever managed to break free, he'd leave a pile of bodies in his wake.

They stared at each other through the bars. She still couldn't understand why he had chosen her of all people to communicate with. Of anyone, she would have thought he would have been more inclined to speak with her father or Lord Barl.

"Are you happy to be returning home?" she asked. "Only five days until we leave." She reinforced her words by raising one hand up in an arc fashion to signify the rising of the sun and then lowering the other hand to signify its setting, followed with five raised fingers to indicate how many risings and settings.

Communication with Jonas had grown easier of late, with Adarra having spent more days in the dungeon talking with him than not. The constant back and forth proved much more reliable and useful than poring through dusty old books like Aelbert's *Guide to Understanding Languages*. She had already been through four different texts on deciphering the Tallosian dialect. However, it was Braunche's *Breaking the Code: A Guide to Navigating Northman Speech* that gave the clearest translation, which meant it seemed to have been written by someone who had actually seen a Tallosian before.

She had been rather surprised by the speed at which Jonas had picked up the Aldoran common tongue. He clearly had an aptitude for learning.

Besides getting familiar with his language, she did her best to learn Jonas's customs, hoping to find some common ground. It proved more difficult than she had anticipated, considering his people were governed by a completely different system than those living in the Five Kingdoms. She had thoroughly studied Roland's *History of the Isle of Tallos*, but there was no substitute for first-hand knowledge.

The Northmen were tribal, living under the rule of the Dogar, which consisted of the five Tallosian houses, similar to the Provincial Authority that ruled Aldor. The people of Tallos were aggressive, living off a warrior's code that respect had to be taken, not earned. The strongest would lead, the weaker forced into subservience. It was almost animalistic. And if you ever stepped out of place, judgment was as swift as it was deadly.

Then again, was it really that much different from most societies? Exchange strength and prowess for wealth, and you would have something very similar to Aldor. In both circumstances, all one could hope for was that those at the top were decent and honorable.

"Do you have family waiting for you back on Tallos?" she asked. She'd never attempted asking anything as personal before, but the more time they spent together, the easier it felt to ask such questions. "Do you have a wife or children?"

Jonas shook his head. He seemed to be deep in thought as he stared at the bars between them.

"You've told me of the Five Houses, but you haven't mentioned which is yours." She was hoping to draw him out.

He shook his head once more. "Not important." He finally looked up, shifting his scalp cloak tighter around his shoulders. "I believe we will not arrive early."

It took her a moment to catch what he was saying. "You mean, you think that we will arrive too late?"

"Was that not the correct way to speak it?"

She smiled. "Close enough." Her smile faded. "I hope you are wrong, though. The last thing we want is war. Our magic is very powerful and would not be kind to your people if they were to attack." She knew how much his people feared magic, which was strange considering they had aligned themselves with Mangora. But desperate people rarely acted rationally. "I would much rather we use our magic to help rid your people of this black death you speak of. Find a way to make peace."

According to Jonas, they had experienced an infestation that had wiped out all crops, leaving his people without food. Jonas had been a part of a search party sent to barter for provisions. Unfortunately, it was Mangora who had found them first, and she had promised them food in exchange for their help with capturing Ty. When the spiders arrived, those of the Tallosians still alive had fled, leaving Jonas behind.

If those warriors made it back to Tallos, there was no telling what sort of stories had been passed along to the Five Houses. Hopefully enough to give them pause in deciding whether to attack outright. Then again, the Northmen weren't known for their passive attitudes when it came to fighting. Jonas was probably correct. It might already be too late.

Adarra slid the book from her lap and placed it inside her satchel, then buckled the top before standing. Her legs ached, and not just from sitting on them for so long.

"Are you injured?" Jonas asked.

She looked up from rubbing her thighs and shook her head. "No. Just sore."

"Why?"

"I've been training."

"Training?"

She felt foolish admitting it. "I've been learning how to . . . how to fight."

Jonas pursed his lips and then nodded sharply. "Good."

It didn't *feel* very good. Lyessa and Darryk had worked her and Fraya uncommonly hard the previous day. She had requested Fraya use her gift of healing on them, but Lyessa said it would be cheating. She had, however, allowed Fraya to heal a dislocated finger Adarra had acquired during one of their grappling sessions.

There were times Adarra wanted to wallop Lyessa over the head when she wasn't looking. Still, no matter how frustrated she got at her friend, Adarra knew how advantageous the lessons would be, especially considering where she was about to set sail for.

"How long?"

"How long what?"

"How long you've trained."

She took a deep breath, once again embarrassed by the answer. "Only a few months." She'd started just after Ty and Breen had taken off on their quest to find the key. "But we've been practicing almost every day. I'm definitely getting better."

Jonas pursed his lips once more. She couldn't tell what he was thinking. He was probably laughing on the inside.

Before now, the closest Adarra had ever come to wielding a staff was the handle of a broom as she swept the floors of their home. And she had certainly never brandished anything longer than a butcher knife before. Now she could wield a staff, a sword, or even use her own hands and feet to defend herself. The one weapon she had been given at least some training with before now was the bow. She would never be able to claim the kind of marksmanship that her father and older brother could bring to bear, but she could at least shoot straight enough to bring home meat, as long as the animal wasn't too far away. And standing completely still.

"When will you return?" Jonas asked, remaining seated as Adarra lifted her satchel and slung it over her shoulder.

"Same time tomorrow," she said, pointing her fingers straight up to signify noonday.

He grunted, which she took to mean he would miss her, or at least their conversations. Not knowing what else to say, she smiled and then turned and headed back through the cells toward the front. She knocked on the door leading out. A moment later, the peephole opened, and Sergeant Finnly's face appeared.

"Are you ready to leave, milady?"

"I believe so," she said, and waited quietly as the sergeant grabbed his keys and unlocked the door, opening it wide for her to walk through.

"Will you be back again today?" Finnly asked. "Perhaps later this evening?" The sergeant was a portly man with rosy cheeks and a strangely cheery disposition for a jailer. He always seemed to have a bright smile for her when she came to visit Jonas. She couldn't tell if he was simply like this with everyone or if he was purposefully paying her special attention. He wasn't exactly what you would call attractive, and he was closer to her father's age than her own, but he seemed kind, and she always stopped to chat with him before going in. She doubted he got much in the way of conversation down in the cells.

"I don't believe I'll be back today," she said with a smile, "but you never know."

He tipped his hat. "I hope you don't mind me saying, but I don't like the thought of you having to travel to Tallos, milady. Not a place for a genteel woman such as yourself. Could be dangerous."

"Thank you, Sergeant, but there's no need for worry. Commander Tiernan is sending a company of Sidara's finest along to ensure our safety."

Finnly straightened. "I wish I could accompany you as well. I would be sure to keep you out of danger. No harm would come to you with me there, I assure you."

She smiled. "I have no doubt. Well, I better be going. Lots to get done before then."

"Of course," Finnly said, tipping his hat once more with a formal bow. "I look forward to seeing you on your next return."

Not wanting to give him the wrong impression, she simply smiled and then turned and headed up the stairs and out through the main lobby. She stopped at the front doors and looked out. The garrison yard was busy as always, especially with everything that had happened over the last several months, from the White Tower's intrusion to the arrival of the overlords and a failed attempt on their lives, to a possible coming attack by the Tallosians. It seemed their quiet city had become quite the center of attention of late, and not in a good way.

The sun had hidden behind the clouds, leaving a harsh bite to the air, and she pulled her fur-lined cloak tight around her shoulders as she walked down to where she had left Thistle tied to the rail in front. Placing her satchel inside one of the bags, she climbed up into the saddle. The stiff leather was cold, even through her dress and the stockings, sending a shiver up her legs. She was starting to wish she had accepted Lyessa's offer and worn one of her extra riding outfits. But as much as Adarra had wanted to see what a pair of trousers felt like while riding, she just couldn't bring herself to put them on, especially not in public. Something about wearing pants felt strange. It had been awkward enough when she had begun wearing them during their training.

Lyessa could get away with wearing trousers wherever she wanted because she was Lyessa. No one was going to question the overlord's daughter. It also didn't hurt that Lyessa looked stunning in anything she wore. Adarra, on the other hand, was short, with plain brown hair and freckles, and apart from the very womanly curves she'd been endowed with by her mother, there wasn't much about her to recommend . . . except perhaps her close relationship to the overlord's daughter. She still couldn't understand why it was that Aiden had set his eyes on her. The man was beautiful, too beautiful for his own good. She figured that one of these days he would wake up and realize he had made a grave mistake and leave.

Her teeth began to chatter, and she quickly grabbed the reins, turning Thistle around and nudging her toward the eastern gate. She took Lynden Street back through town, which eventually crossed River Street just below the East Inn. The flavorful aroma wafting from the inn's chimneys had her stomach growling. The hitching rails were already filled in front, so she directed her horse to the corral in back. Apparently, she hadn't arrived early enough. The common room inside was sure to be full of hungry soldiers wanting something other than garrison fare now that the Sidaran Assembly had recalled the troops.

She left Thistle to wander around the open pen with the other horses and headed for the back door. With a quick tap of her shoes on the edge of the step, she shook off what mud and slush she could before going in. Shutting the door behind her, she took a moment to straighten her dress while letting her eyes adjust to the dim interior light.

As usual, the corridor on the left leading into the common room was filled with lancers, most mingling about with a tankard in their hands and light conversation on their lips. Bue and Noreen Aboloff, the proprietors of the inn, had begun setting up small tables and chairs in the long hall for those not looking to eat a full meal. On the right, a hallway led back to the guests' lodging.

She headed left.

Pipe smoke filled the corridor, thickening the closer she got to the main room. Several of the soldiers turned and stared as she passed, which was a little jarring, but she pretended not to notice as she kept to the center of the hall. Clearly, these men had been away from civilization for too long if they thought she was worth ogling at. The sound of a hundred different conversations filled the air as she stepped into the lobby. It was just as she had feared. The common room was packed to the brim.

She stood at the corner, keeping out of the way of those making their way into the hall from the bar on the left. *This is going to take a while*, she thought as she slowly scanned each table, looking for her father.

"Good noonday to you, Miss Adarra," a voice called out on her right, and she turned. Bue Aboloff was standing near the front doors, greeting customers as they entered.

Adarra smiled and waved. "Good noonday to you as well. Business is looking good."

"Business is *very* good," he said with a pleased smile.

She was surprised to see Bue manning the doors, as he was the inn's head cook. It was well known that Bue's wife, Noreen, had little to no talent in the kitchen, but when it came to organization and management, she was a stickler, and she handled their books very well, leaving her husband with the responsibility of making sure the people were fed. Adarra figured they must have hired more help in the kitchen to keep up with the unexpected numbers in town. And it wasn't all just from the lancer recall.

There seemed to be more and more Sidarans moving from the outer districts of the kingdom to be closer to Easthaven. There had even been several caravans of people who had traveled over from the region surrounding Belvin, just on the other side of Reed Marsh. Tales of some plague, which Lyessa's father had sent riders to investigate, had the citizens of Easthaven worried about further outbreak. Worried enough that they had demanded the caravans not be allowed entrance into the city for at least two or three weeks to make sure they carried none of the plague with them. Tensions were also growing hot near the Sidaran–Briston border, as the two overlords seemed to be in greater conflict. It appeared the whole world was beginning to come apart.

"Kellen is upstairs, if you're looking," Bue said, pointing to the stairway behind her.

"Thank you." She turned and headed up the stairs leading to the balcony. Reaching the top landing, she found it just as full as the main floor below.

A hand went up in the back and waved, and she started for it. It wasn't until she was halfway across the balcony that she spotted her father's face. He was sitting at the end of two tables in the corner that had been pulled together to seat what appeared to be most of the wielder council. Interestingly enough, even with the packed crowd, all the tables directly across from theirs were empty. A few patrons at the tables near the back stared at her when they realized where she was heading. She smiled and kept going.

When her father had mentioned getting lunch that morning before they left for town, she hadn't expected everyone else to be joining. She had been hoping for some quiet time with her father. They hadn't seen much of each other of late; both were always on the go, their paths rarely crossing until late in the evening, and usually by that time one or both were off to bed. Her father was spending most of his time with Overlord Barl and Commander Tiernan as they worked to strengthen the Sidaran defenses, while Adarra was spending most of her time with Jonas, or Lyessa and Fraya, or holed up in the overlord's library, hunting down pertinent information for her upcoming venture.

"I was starting to wonder if you were coming," her father said as he rose from his place on the end to let her by. Everyone seemed to be present except Gilly, who hated large crowds.

"I ran a little long with Jonas this morning," she said as she took her seat, which happened to be directly across the table from Sheeva. The nightwalker was never far from Adarra's father. Her golden eyes reflected the light from the candelabra at the center of the table, giving her an almost feline appearance. The woman rarely spoke, and if she did, it was usually in response to her father. He was the only member of the council she seemed willing to open up to. All Adarra had managed to learn was that it had something to do with her father's moonstone necklace.

Adarra took a sip from the tankard her father must have ordered for her—warm apricot tea, her favorite. She cooed softly as it went down.

She couldn't help but notice the heads that kept turning in their direction from those sitting nearby.

"Pay them no mind," her father said.

"Hard not to," Feoldor grumbled from three seats down. "Ever since our standoff against the Tower at the garrison, and then again at the Assembly building, word has spread. It didn't help when Barl declared Sidara a safe haven for wielders. Can't hardly show my face around town anymore. A few lancers here, some Assembly members there, pretty soon word spread like wildfire. Before the end of the week, everyone knew who we were. Well, at least most of us." He leaned forward and looked at Adarra. "You've managed to keep off the watch list for now, though sitting with us is bound to raise some eyebrows."

She smiled. "It helps when your magic isn't visible."

"Just be glad you're abrasive enough that people tend to stay away from you," Orlyn said to Feoldor. "I can't get a moment's rest to get my work done. Many of those coming into the shop aren't there to purchase. They're just hoping to see me make some flowers grow." He pressed his thumbs to the side of his head. "The bell over the door doesn't stop ringing. Half the children in Easthaven have dragged their mommas and pappas in to see some magic."

"And you love every minute of it," Reloria said with a smirk.

Orlyn lowered his arms with a grunt, but a smile crept around the corners of his mouth.

"Regardless of the inconvenience," her father said, "Barl has taken a great risk in opening his kingdom. Probably the first to do so since the Great Purge."

"There have been a couple of others who have tried over the centuries," Adarra said, having read some of the histories from Overlord Barl's collection, "but never with any success. They were usually forced to back down by the Provincial Authority. And if that didn't work, the overlord would usually suffer an unfortunate accident, or the other kingdoms would declare war. No kingdom has been able to maintain a safe place for wielders. So Father is correct—this is a dangerous move for the overlord."

"I'd say we're already at war, or on the brink," Orlyn said.

"Aye," Feoldor agreed. "The Tower seeks our deaths, and that puppet king seeks everything else."

The council was right, things had grown more difficult for the wielders since Barl's announcement, even in their quiet community. Not all of Easthaven's citizens were happy about the decision. Some had made it known.

Thankfully, most of those were too afraid of magic to want to take it any further than sending angry looks in their direction.

"It's going to take time," Veldon said from the end of the two tables. "Hopefully, things will calm down soon enough, and we can get back to the business of our lives. I can't say business has changed all that much for me since people have learned of my magic, but then again," he said with a smug look, "I'm the only way they can transport goods, so they don't have much choice in the matter."

Orlyn shifted in his seat, causing his rune-covered staff to roll slightly from its resting place against the back of his chair. "You mentioned running late at the cells. How is our Tallosian guest doing these days?" He clearly wanted to change the subject.

Adarra placed her tankard back on the table. "To say he's anxious to be let out would be an understatement."

Orlyn smiled. "I'm sure." He took a sip from his own mug and wiped the grey whiskers around his mouth with the sleeve of his robe.

Feoldor hmphed. "Mistake if you ask me. Can't be trusted. None of them can. Brutish monsters running around with human cloaks. Ain't right."

Orlyn's face paled, and he slowly set his drink down.

"Well, no one asked you," Reloria said, staring uncomfortably at the stew on her plate. "Quit trying to scare the girl."

Feoldor sighed. "I was just saying. No need to get huffy."

Reloria leaned over and tickled his side whiskers. "You'll know it when I get huffy."

"Stop it." He brushed her hand away, looking embarrassed by her flirtation.

"Feoldor is right about one thing," Veldon said from the other end of the table. "Meeting with the Northmen will most likely prove dangerous. In all my years running the Easthaven docks, can't say as I could count on one hand the number of boats that have set sail for Tallos. And most of those didn't return. They don't call it the Bay of Mist for nothing. Fog as thick as Bue's stew. Not to mention there's reefs out there that can rip the hull of a ship wide open with a single pass. Many a vessel has been lost to that stretch of water."

Adarra's father cleared his throat. "I thought we were here to cheer her up, not frighten her to death."

The table grew quiet a moment, then those who had spoken quickly offered their apologies. Even Feoldor served up a half-hearted assurance that the journey wouldn't be as bad as he'd thought. Unfortunately, Adarra knew it would almost certainly be worse. Getting to the Isle of Tallos would be the easy part, if the stories from the books she had read were even partly true. The way Jonas described it, they would never reach the mountains without his help. She wasn't sure how much of that was him speaking the truth and how much might have been him making sure he wasn't left behind.

Jonas had already told her of the dangers that awaited them on Tallos. He spoke of the moross that made their home along the coastline where the fog tended to settle. He'd never actually seen one, so he wasn't sure what they looked like, and any who had had never returned to tell their tale. He told of wild jinga that hunted the grasslands between the coast and the forest surrounding the mountains. He spoke of pits of sand that could swallow an entire razorback whole. There were wolf packs that hunted the forests and lower foothills, and rumors of talarin that made their nests in the upper cliffs.

It was not a place one would choose to visit.

"I'm just glad Jonas will be there to help translate," she said. *And to help guide us through what sounds like a death trap*, she thought. "I honestly believe he wants what's best for his people, and I don't think that's war."

"I hope not," her father said. "We don't wish to see a war either, not with Rhydan's son on the throne and the White Tower threatening incursion. We have enough to deal with here without having to worry about the Tallosians invading. Sidara hasn't seen a real battle in hundreds of years."

"There's been a few dustups with Briston over the years," Veldon corrected, playing with the piece of flint hanging around his neck.

"Sure," her father said, "but nothing more than territorial disputes, and nothing to the extent of recalling the Sidaran Lancers. Most of those ended in civil negotiations."

"Jonas's people are starving and desperate," Adarra said. "I think they will be willing to listen, especially with the amount of food we will be bringing with us."

"Still," Fraya said beside her as she tried to adjust the yellow bow in her hair, "I wish you weren't the one having to go. You've taught Jonas enough of the Aldoran tongue now that he can manage on his own, can't he? I don't see why you feel that you need to be there as well. He's not your responsibility."

Looking around the table, Adarra could see that Fraya wasn't the only one holding such sentiments.

"It's more than just teaching Jonas how to communicate," Adarra explained for what felt like the hundredth time. "It's having someone there that he trusts to communicate with. Besides, Commander Tiernan is sending an entire company of lancers with us. And I was told yesterday that a Captain Holverd will be there to lead them."

There was a grunt beside her, and she turned to look at her father. "Is something wrong?"

He looked up from where he'd been studying the rim of his tankard. "No. Holverd is capable enough, at least from what I can tell from my meetings with him."

She stared at him a moment. "What aren't you telling me?"

"I'm just surprised that he is Tiernan's pick. From what I've seen of the man, he has a bit of a chip on his shoulder when it comes to the Northman. I believe part of his regiment were on protection duty the day we faced Mangora. They were the ones guarding Overlord Barl and Lyessa when the attack took place."

"Are you saying that he won't be very objective when it comes to the Tallosians?" she asked.

Her father shrugged. "That I can't say, but I do know that if anything were to go wrong, he would be one of the men I would want there watching your backside."

"If he could derail our negotiations, then we need a replacement. Should I talk with the overlord about it?"

Her father shook his head. "No. Let me. I have a meeting with him and Ambassador Lanmiere later this afternoon. I can mention it then."

"Are you sure?" she asked. "Fraya and I will be over there later for our training. I can talk with him then."

Fraya groaned at the mention of training. "Don't remind me."

"I'm sure," her father said, then offered a sympathetic smile to Fraya.

"With everything that has happened, I'm very grateful to Lyessa for taking you two under her wing. Learning to defend yourselves will prove valuable, and having someone as skilled as Darryk there to train you is an opportunity you don't want to squander."

Adarra nodded. Of course, he was right. Who else could claim they had been given personal instruction by the head of the overlord's guard? Still, she wished the training came as easily to her as her books. She'd spent countless hours poring over martial defense manuals, but there was a world of difference between retaining text on a page and applying it. Unlike her ability as a memoriae to instantly memorize and store everything that came into her field of view, using that knowledge was one gift she had certainly not yet acquired.

"Excuse me," someone said, and the council turned in their seats. A young man stood nervously behind Orlyn with his hat in his hand. A little boy stood beside him with wide eyes.

"Can we help you?" Veldon asked.

The young man cleared his throat. "I'm sure you get this all the time, but my son has not stopped pestering me since we sat down. He's . . . he's never seen magic before," he said, lowering his voice when he did. "Would you mind showing him something? We'd be much obliged. Of course," he said with a gulp, "we don't want to put you out, though."

Veldon smiled and looked down at the boy. "I'm sure we can manage something." The dockmaster motioned them over, and the father moved his son around toward the end. Veldon pointed to the candelabra on the table, and two of the flickering flames rose off their wicks.

The little boy gasped and grabbed his father's arm. "Look, Papa."

"Yes, I see it."

The two tongues of flame swirled around each other and then flew across the table and landed in Veldon's palm. He held them out for the young boy to see. The boy dared to move a few steps closer, at least until his father grabbed his shoulder. They both watched as the flame danced about in his hand. A moment later, Veldon released them, and they flew back to the candles they had occupied.

The little boy clapped with glee.

"Thank you," the father said, and walked his son back to their table.

"And that's what it's like at my shop most days," Orlyn said. He turned and looked at Adarra. "Which reminds me. If you have some time this evening, I would like it if you could come by the shop. I have something . . . Well, I believe it will be of importance to you."

Adarra nodded, curious by what the apothecary might have. "I can try to come by after my practice later this afternoon."

Orlyn nodded. "Good." A smile crept across his face. "I will see you then."

Chapter 23 | Adarra

HE REST OF THE MEAL was eaten without any further comment on Adarra's upcoming trip, though there was plenty of discussion on the council's role in the defense of Easthaven and the possible need to begin some training of their own.

Each of the members were endowed with their own unique gifts, but until they had been forced into a confrontation with the Tower's wielders, none of them had ever used their abilities to defend themselves and others before.

By the end of the meal, they figured it might be prudent to begin learning how to better use their magic in their defense and even set up a formal meeting to discuss it later in the week, giving the members time to mull over their ideas and have them ready to present at the meeting.

After leaving the East Inn, Adarra stopped by BookBees to see if Master Townsend had acquired any new reading material from the previous week. She knew his typical shipments didn't come until the first of the month, but she could always hope. To her disappointment, no new shipments had arrived, so she spent the rest of the afternoon in the overlord's library, reading through more of his collection while waiting for the next grueling round of training to begin.

The sound of practice swords clacking in the yard caught Adarra's attention, and she looked up from her book. It was too early for training. Fraya hadn't arrived yet. And as far as she knew, Lyessa was still busy working with her father in his study. Curiosity getting the best of her, she decided to put her book down and see who was out there. She peered out one of the windows that looked across the back courtyard and beyond to the training field. Inside the snow-packed ring at the center of the cordoned-off area, Aiden was busy trading blows with Darryk.

Her cheeks flushed. Anxious to watch, she left her books where they were and pulled on her jacket before going outside to get a closer look. She had already changed into her training clothes upon first arriving, which was nothing more than one of Lyessa's old riding outfits, one she didn't mind getting dirty and ripped. It consisted of a pale blue tunic that was very snug around her chest, a dark jacket that hung to her knees, a pair of trousers that were too long, and some boots that fit surprisingly well.

Quickly, she made her way across the courtyard and took a seat on one of the benches that fronted the practice area. Aiden's shoulder-length brown hair was pulled back with a leather cord in similar fashion to the way Darryk had cinched his own to keep it out of his face. The biggest difference was Darryk's had more than its fair share of grey streaked throughout.

She enjoyed watching Aiden fight. He was so graceful, having come a long way from where he had been months earlier during the battle with the Tallosians. He was a quick study. She envied that about him. Why couldn't she pick it up as easily? She watched as Aiden circled Darryk, his sword moving in harmony with the older instructor's as they performed a kind of dance of blocking and striking. Aiden's green shirt was darkening at the center of his chest as his hard work began to bleed through. Overtop his shirt, he wore an unbuttoned leather jacket that matched his bright hazel eyes.

He was beautiful.

Aiden noticed her watching and stopped to smile and wave. As soon as he did, Darryk swatted the back of his legs with his practice sword, and Aiden hopped around the ring, yelping like an injured pup. Adarra covered her mouth with her hand to keep from laughing.

"Keep your eyes on your opponent," Darryk scolded.

Aiden bared his teeth as he turned and raised his sword. He lunged and struck, spinning as soon as Darryk threw his obvious attempt aside and came back around with three quick strikes: low, high, low. Then he shifted stances for another round: high, high, mid. Darryk deflected each, but it was taking him longer to do so.

Aiden's focus was singular. She could see anger in his eyes as he swung his wooden sword, coming at their instructor from all sides. His speed was impressive, though his technique was loosening, coming unraveled at the seams. His hands were unsteady, his sword barely reaching, but he clearly wasn't about to give up, determined to gain that point. Whether it was in the hopes of impressing her or in simple retaliation for being humbled, it wasn't clear, but if he wasn't careful, he was about to—

Aiden overextended, leaving his arm open for Darryk to grab, and Darryk yanked him forward and kicked his legs out from under him, sending Aiden face first into the slush. Before Aiden could spit snow and roll over, Darryk was kneeling on top of him, his practice sword pressed against the back of Aiden's neck, holding him down.

"What did I tell you about those emotions? You have got to get them under control, or they are going to get you killed." Darryk climbed off him and shook his head with a sigh.

Aiden's face was red, at least the part not covered in snow and muck. He slowly climbed back to his feet, and to his credit, didn't try to retaliate. He also didn't look in Adarra's direction.

"I need a break," Darryk said as he carried his sword out of the ring. "And you need time to cool off." He stopped at a bench two down from the one Adarra was occupying and picked up his coat, then headed for the house. "Come back after I finish with the girls, and we can see how you're faring then."

Aiden didn't say anything, just snatched his fallen sword out of the snow and walked over and plopped down beside Adarra. He pulled a handkerchief out of an inner pocket and tried wiping the sweat and sludge from his face. "Sometimes, I want to wring his neck."

Adarra chuckled. "Can't say I haven't felt the same a time or two."

Aiden looked at her, and they both started laughing.

"Sorry, for distracting you," she said.

He looked down and smiled. "It was worth it."

She blushed.

He stared at her a moment, then reached over and tucked a fallen strand of hair back behind her ear. She swallowed, suddenly feeling warm enough to unbutton her jacket.

"You're very graceful out there," she said. "I wish I could pick this up as quickly as you. I'm afraid I'm not very coordinated. A bit of a clumsy oaf, actually."

"Hardly," he said. "I've seen you practice. You're probably better than most of the girls in Easthaven."

"Oh, so I'm good for a *girl*, huh?"

"No. I, uh . . . that's not what I meant. I . . ."

She smiled and rested her hand briefly on his leg. "I'm just giving you a hard time."

He relaxed and looked out at the ring a moment, then suddenly turned. "I could give you some pointers if you like?"

Finally, she thought. She was wondering if she was going to have to make the suggestion herself. Men were so clueless sometimes. Well, most of the time. She smiled. "Yes, I would like that. If you don't mind."

He hopped up and offered her his hand. "Not at all."

She took his hand, and he helped her to her feet. From there, he walked over and collected one of the other practice swords from the weapons rack and motioned for her to follow him out into the ring.

She met him in the middle, where he offered her the second sword, and they moved into their respective stances. He was much taller than she was, even taller than Darryk, which made it all the more intimidating, but that also meant there was more target to strike at. She quickly ran over in her mind all the possible maneuvers and counters, visualizing not only what Darryk and Lyessa had demonstrated during previous training, but illustrations she had seen in some of the military training manuals she had studied.

There were numerous counters and blocks and stepping positions, depending on what move he made first. If he advanced, should she retreat or sidestep, should she block or deflect, should she counter, and if so, where and how? The information was coming so quickly she couldn't keep up with it, and before she could determine what she wanted to do first, Aiden made his move.

She blocked quickly, barely getting her weapon up as images and text on how far to raise her sword and at what angle popped into her mind, along with demonstrations by Darryk and Lyessa of how to move into a counter and strike back. She grasped at one and swiftly pivoted, bringing her sword around for a strike to the midsection. But when she came close to landing the hit, Aiden was no longer there. His sword easily swatted hers to the side as he moved in for the kill.

Before she could call up how to parry or block or move out of the way, his sword was at her throat. She lowered her weapon with a frustrated huff.

"You're thinking too hard," he said.

"What?"

"I can see you running through moves in your head before you ever raise your sword. You need to quit thinking about it and let your body do the work. Repetition builds muscle memory."

"You don't think I know this?"

"I'm sure you do, but sometimes it doesn't hurt to be reminded." He released her and stepped around in front. "I did the same thing when I first started out. Always overthinking everything, not wanting to make a mistake." She wanted to smack him over the head. He had started at the same time as her. "Thinking too much made my reactions slow," he said. "But the more I practiced, the less I needed to think about it."

She wanted to roll her eyes. He was acting like she was a complete novice. Of course she knew all of this. Unfortunately, as much as she hated to admit it, he was right. She wasn't letting her body do the work, trying to rely on her memoriae gifts, magic that clearly didn't work when it came to *applying* what she had put to memory.

Forcing down her initial irritation, she took a deep breath. "I do tend to overthink things. Habit, I guess."

He smiled. "Too smart for your own good, aye?"

She smiled. "You know, I don't think I'm moving just right when I counter, though. Can you show me what I'm doing wrong?"

"Sure," he said, and moved back into place and held up his sword, waiting for her to take her place in front, which she did. "I'll swing low, and you block and pivot."

She nodded and waited for him to make the advance. She didn't have to wait long. As soon as she moved into her stance, he lunged, and just like he promised, he swung low and to the left. She quickly pivoted and countered with a swing of her own to block but made sure not to twist far enough. The swords struck with a loud clack just before reaching her leg, and she raised her sword to get in a hit of her own, but Aiden stopped her and took a step back.

"Wait. You need to move your hips more when you pivot for the block. Don't rely on just your arms." He walked around behind her and placed his hands on either side of her waist, causing chill bumps to run up her back. "Now, go ahead and perform a low block once more."

As soon as she swung her sword down to deflect the imaginary attack, he pivoted her to the right, twisting her hips around with his hands to make sure her entire body moved with the sword.

His breath was warm on the side of her neck as he scooted closer to angle her body in the right direction, his hands still firmly on her sides. She could feel his chest rise and fall with each new breath, and she matched it. If all her lessons were this exciting, she would probably be much further along in her training by now.

"I think I've got it," she said, and turned. His face was only inches from hers as she stared up into his eyes. Before she knew it, his hand was behind her neck, and she was being pulled in for a kiss. She spun the rest of the way around just as their lips met, and she threw her arms around him to keep from pitching over as her legs nearly gave out and the world began to spin. He tasted of spiced wine, and his clothes smelled of lavender and sweat, which on him was an intoxicating combination.

By the time he released her, she was completely out of breath, as though having just run three hard laps around the yard. He waited a moment, his strong arms holding her tight to him, before finally letting her go and taking a step back. Her heart was thumping hard enough to hear, so she took a deep breath to slow it. As soon as she was sure she wouldn't trip over her own feet and land face first in the snow, she made her way back to the center of the ring and retook her place.

Aiden was grinning like a fool. Then again, so was she. She forced herself to think of anything but the way his lips had felt against hers. Clearing her mind, she raised her sword and waited for his attack. This time when it came, she met his sword with a full pivot, allowing for a more forceful strike as she eagerly threw his attempt aside.

"Good," he said with an encouraging smile, then frowned and shook his hand. "Maybe don't swing quite so hard next time."

They continued sparring for the next half hour as she waited for Fraya and Lyessa to arrive. She did her best to try keeping her mind clear of the images wanting to take over and instead let her body take control as much as possible. More times than not, they had to stop for him to reposition her. More times than not, she moved out of position just so he would. Either way, one thing was certain, the speed of her reactions had definitely increased, allowing her to actually land a hit every now and then.

By the end, both their shirts were soaked and their foreheads dripping. She grabbed a couple of the sweat cloths next to the weapons rack and joined Aiden on the bench. She tossed him one of the cloths, as his handkerchief was hardly large enough, or thick enough, to do any real drying, and he wiped his face.

"When do you leave?" he asked, placing his practice sword beside him on the bench.

"The end of the week." They had had this discussion before, on more than one occasion, and just like Fraya and Lyessa, Aiden never let up on his determination to talk her out of going.

"How's the Tallosian's lessons coming along? Can he understand what you are saying yet?"

She knew where Aiden was going with this, the same place those on the council had tried taking her over lunch a few hours ago. "Jonas's instruction is going well, and yes, he seems to be able to understand most of what I say, and before you say it . . . no, learning our tongue isn't enough. I need to be there to help facilitate this first meeting."

Aiden's fingers tightened around his sweat cloth. "Tallos is not a safe place, especially for someone like . . ."

She turned, her face hardening. "Like what?"

"Like . . . nothing."

"No. What were you going to say?"

"I was going to say it's not safe for someone as kind and decent as you."

She kept her glare a moment longer, knowing that was most certainly not what he was going to say.

"The Northmen are savages. You can barely keep up with me in the ring, and I'm not very good. How are you supposed to defend yourself?"

"First of all, I would hope that it doesn't come to that. We are planning on lending aid, not going into battle. But if it does, Overlord Barl is sending a full company of lancers to escort us. And Jonas will be there to help."

Aiden frowned, twisting his rag even tighter. "Yes. Jonas. You seem to be spending a lot of time with him. Just don't forget, it was only a couple of months ago when he was trying to kill us. You can't trust him. You can't trust any of them." His face suddenly brightened. "That's why I've decided to go with you."

Adarra stiffened. "What?"

"You heard me. I'm going with you. No one will be more determined to keep you safe than me. Besides, my parents aren't expecting me back for another few weeks. Plenty of time for us to go to Tallos and back."

"You can't go," she said, probably more forcefully than she should have, judging by the stunned look on Aiden's face.

"Why not?"

"Because . . ." She couldn't say because it was too dangerous, since that was his excuse for why she shouldn't be going. Regrettably, she found herself without any excuse at all. Why had her mind gone blank? "Because the overlord would kill us both if something were to happen to you while under his care."

"Something already did happen to me," he said. "And right inside your family's cottage. I was sliced open and nearly died, remember?"

She frowned. "How can I forget?" She placed her hand on his. "I wouldn't forgive myself if something happened to you because of me. I have to be there, you don't."

"If you're crazy enough to go on this expedition, then I'm crazy enough to follow you."

As much as she wanted to rebuff him and call him an idiot, there was this overwhelming sense of relief at the thought of him being there. She needed to tell him no and put her foot down, but instead she asked, "Are you sure?"

"I'm sure I want to keep you safe." He leaned over and kissed her cheek, but before he could straighten, she grabbed his neck and jerked him forward, kissing him full on the mouth.

"Should I clear my throat or something?"

Adarra jerked back and turned to find Lyessa and Fraya standing a few feet behind their bench, both with wide grins on their faces.

"That was quite the kiss," Fraya said. "I feel like I need to rub some snow on my neck after watching."

Adarra's face heated. "You should have said something."

Aiden just sat there with a quirky grin on his face. The stupid oaf was enjoying this way too much.

Behind them, Adarra could see Darryk making his way across the courtyard. Perfect, now she just needed to spend the next couple of hours being humiliated even further, and with Aiden there to watch, too. She gritted her teeth and grabbed her practice sword from the bench and started out into the ring. She was angry enough to fight all three of them at once.

Thankfully, she didn't have to. In fact, the training went unexpectedly well that day, even earning her several compliments from Darryk and Lyessa on her noted improvement. She didn't know if it was solely because of a hardened determination not to look the fool in front of Aiden or because she was doing her best not to let her magic get in the way. Regardless, she did seem more comfortable with their sparring than any time prior. Not that she was suddenly a weapons master, but at the very least, she wasn't ending up on her back in the snow quite as often.

After training with various weapons—archery being the last—and spending a good half hour practicing their open-handed combat, Adarra, Fraya, and Lyessa decided to go inside for their ritual baths as Aiden remained behind to continue working with Darryk. This time, Adarra didn't stay to watch, feeling too awkward to even look in his direction as she followed the others back to the house. She did manage a quick peek over her shoulder and found him watching. She blushed and quickly picked up her pace.

Gina had the water nice and hot by the time they'd stripped and climbed in. Adarra and Fraya were over there so frequently, Lyessa had decided to leave the two extra tubs in her bathing chamber to keep the staff from having to constantly haul them in and out. Lyessa's nanny collected their clothes, then went from tub to tub, washing the grit and sweat from their hair. Adarra was sure hers was the worst, considering she had spent the most time on her back in the snow. Gina's islander hands moved through Adarra's hair with long soothing strokes as she lathered in the soap, doing her best to straighten the mess she had made during practice. As soon as Gina had finished rinsing the soap from her hair, Adarra rinsed the rest of her body and stood.

"Where are you going?" Lyessa asked. "You kiss Aiden like that and now you're going to run out without us getting a chance to talk about it?"

Adarra grinned sheepishly. "I promised Master Orlyn that I would stop by his shop on my way home." Which wasn't exactly a lie. She was going to stop by. She also wasn't ready to talk about what had happened with Aiden yet. Especially with Lyessa. It wasn't all that long ago that Aiden had been her betrothed.

"I forgot about that," Fraya said. "Any idea what he wants to show you?"

"None," she said as she finished drying off with the towel Gina had laid out for her. She went into the next room to dress, then sat on a stool for a few minutes to let Gina comb out her hair. Not waiting until it was dry, she said her goodbyes and rushed down the stairs and out to her horse, which the groom had waiting for her.

With a boost, she climbed into the saddle and started down the road, her teeth chattering against the gusts snaking through the trees. She was starting to wish she had stayed a little longer. At least long enough to dry her hair completely. But she was anxious to find out what Orlyn had for her. It was the first time he had ever invited her to come to his shop.

Chapter 24 | Adarra

SHE TOOK RIVER STREET south through town, passing the Sidaran Assembly Hall on the right and the East Inn on the left. It was even busier than before, now that the day was winding down and people were leaving work. The sky was awash with color as the sun set below the rooftops.

Pulling to a stop on the left side of the street, a couple of shops down from the East Inn, she sat in front of a three-story building with a sign above the door that read APOTHECARY in gold lettering. Below the letters was a drawing of a mixing bowl with a smattering of valerian sprouts.

She tied Thistle out front and walked inside, the bell over the door jingling as she entered. She was immediately greeted with a dozen different aromas, all blending together to form a cacophony of goodness that left her feeling remarkably relaxed. Green ivy with small white flowers crept up the walls and across the ceiling via wooden beams overhead. There were even a few sprouts growing up from some of the cracks in the floorboards, opening into blossoms that should not have been able to grow during the cold winter months. Orlyn certainly had a way with plants.

There were still several customers inside, some perusing Orlyn's well-stocked supply, others talking with him at his worktable. Most of those had small children with them, and it was clear by the eager way the children stared up at the tall apothecary that they were hoping to see some magic. Orlyn stopped his measuring and pointed to one of several potted plants he had placed along the side of his worktable. As soon as he pointed, several flowers budded, then burst into bloom on the plant.

The kids clapped and laughed and asked him to do it again. Adarra chuckled and shook her head. Master Orlyn was right. He was having a difficult time getting anything done as he moved from one patron to the next, helping them gather what they needed, taking the time to suss out exactly what each customer was there for and the particular remedy for it, all while doing his best to keep the little ones happy. It was quite the juggling act.

Adarra turned and studied the display at the front as she waited for Orlyn to finish, then slowly worked her way down the left aisle, examining each jar as she went. The shelves were draped in ivy as well. They wound their way around the numerous glass containers of seeds, powders, buds, leaves and a host of other plant parts that were used to cure anything from upset stomachs to sudden bouts of anger, or at least that was what one of the jars claimed. That jar contained what looked like pieces of tellareen mushrooms, something Orlyn bragged about taking in small doses with his evening tea to help him sleep.

Adarra made it halfway around the left side of the shop and had just started up the second aisle when the bell over the door rang once more, and she looked up to find that all of the customers had gone. How long had she been staring at the plants? She saw through the window it was near dusk, and the building across the way was barely visible, at least until a lamplighter paused long enough to light the streetlamp in front of the vintner's.

"It was busier than usual," Orlyn said, peeking around the aisle. "I didn't even see you come in. Have you been waiting long?"

"Not really," she lied. "Just admiring the variety."

"Yes, you won't find another apothecary for a hundred miles that can boast a winter stock like this."

"Do you ever get questioned about it? You know, from those who have a less-than-equitable affinity for magic."

He smiled and shook out the baggy sleeves of his faded green robe. "I just tell them that I keep a special crop in the cellar."

She looked up and cocked her head. "Do you?"

He laughed. "Of course."

She'd never seen his cellar before. To be honest, she never even stopped to consider where he got all of his plants and herbs from. For some reason, she'd always just pictured the tall floratide wandering about the forest collecting things as he went, which, if she had stopped to really think about it, didn't make much sense, since many of the plants and herbs he sold weren't native to the Sidaran Forest.

"Would you care to see?" he asked.

"Yes, please."

Orlyn's eyes brightened. "Let me close up, and I'll take you down. What I have to show you is in the cellar anyway." He bustled about, drawing the curtains on the windows and locking the front door before snuffing out all but the lantern sitting on his work desk.

He grabbed that lantern and led her into the back of the shop. Adarra had never been any farther than that table, which Orlyn used to measure out his products for purchase. She was curious to see what an apothecary's workroom looked like.

"This way," he said, and opened the door.

She followed him in. The work room was about half the size of the main shop and filled with built-in shelves along the walls, lined with bottles, jars, and urns of various sizes, colors, and shapes, no doubt holding an assortment of vegetation. There were even plants hanging from the ceiling to dry, and canvas bags full of seeds and grain lying open in the corner. There was a mixing table with instruments for cutting and grinding, as well as rows of stoppered bottles containing an assortment of colored liquids. No doubt this space was where Orlyn crafted his herbs and tonics. There were several shelves of books, which quickly drew her attention, a few lying open on one of the tables, and one large tome in particular that rested on a podium in front of a table with several jars and a stone mixing bowl.

A welcoming fire in the hearth to the right kept the room comfortable, but the aroma was much more potent than in the shop out front—dizzying, even.

Orlyn smiled when he saw her reach for the table to steady herself. "Yes, it can have that effect sometimes. I've been working with it long enough that it doesn't bother me quite so much. However, there has been a time or two that I woke in the morning to find myself down here on the floor instead of in my bed." He chuckled. "The mushrooms are the worst, you know. Come." He grabbed his rune-covered staff from where it rested against one of the tables and led her to a door on the left. He glanced over his shoulder as he reached for the handle. "There are very few who have ever seen what you are about to." With that, he opened the door and disappeared inside.

Behind the door was a set of stairs leading down into the shop's cellar. From the top of the landing, it didn't appear to be anything out of the ordinary, nothing more than an average stairwell that one would expect to find in any sizable building, except of course for the thick growth of flowering ivy that clung to the walls and ceiling and even bunched around the sides of the steps. It left barely enough room at the center to place her feet.

She followed the lamp light down to the bottom of the stairwell and the open doorway, which Orlyn had already walked through. It was cooler down there than it had been upstairs, but not cold. She stepped out of the stairwell and gasped.

The floor and walls and ceiling disappeared, and she felt as though she had stepped through some magical portal into one of the most beautiful, lush forests she had ever seen. The ground was covered in soft grass with budding flora. There were even trees, though dwarfed, with ivy growing up the trunks. There were bushes and vines and beds of flowers with fragrant blossoms she'd never seen or smelled before. There were plants of all shapes and sizes, of which the most eye-catching were the mushrooms. The heads of each stood as tall as Orlyn, all sporting patches and lines of various colors. The sight nearly stole her breath.

"Watch this," Orlyn said as he lifted the lantern and blew out the wick. The amber light vanished and was suddenly replaced by a pale blue ambience that filled everything with a soft moonlit glow. It seemed to be coming from the small blooms on the ivy, which appeared to be wrapped around everything. In addition, the trees produced their own radiance, as balls of orange light filled their limbs. She had never seen anything like it before, never even dreamed of anything like it.

"What do you think?" the apothecary asked, his face beaming.

"I don't think I have words to describe it," she said, still turning to take it all in. "How did you . . ." The words simply faded on her lips as she drank in the incredible fragrance, which had her nearly as lightheaded as the workshop above.

"Magic," he said as he walked over to a troop of tall mushrooms and rubbed his hand along the fibrous gills. "I've been working on these for years, if you can believe it. Most are my own creations. I take a trait from this plant and add it to another, and the next thing you know, I have something wondrous. Though I must admit, it is hit and miss. It's taken me years to find the right combinations."

"It's the most incredible thing I've ever seen," she said as she walked over to a bouquet of large rose-like flowers with bright-green-and-purple buds. The petals were as big as her hand, and the flower stems stood as high as her shoulders. She took a whiff, and her legs nearly buckled.

"Careful with those," Orlyn said, walking over. "They are my newest design. Afraid the scent is still a bit strong."

"How do you keep them growing without sunlight?"

"Ah, now that was the tricky part. It took me a year to figure out that I needed to mix in some attributes from low-light plants like Bristonian evergreens and certain species of snake plants in order to allow them to grow in minimal light. I do have a couple of small windows at the back that look out on a blind alley. They let in indirect light through the day, but with these added traits, the plants have managed to thrive."

"Aren't you worried about people looking in?"

Orlyn shook his head. He placed the unlit lantern down in the grass and motioned for her to follow. They walked through the small garden forest, passing one never-seen-before species after another, until they reached the back where there were several large willow-type trees with long hair-like branches that draped all the way to the ground. However, instead of green branches, these were a soft lavender.

"The branches are thick enough to keep people from seeing in, but thin enough to allow some of the light to filter through." He placed his staff on the ground, and the runes began to glow.

Suddenly, the snakelike branches parted all the way to the back wall, revealing the hidden windows behind. Adarra gawked as the branches then returned to their normal state, all but a couple of strands that reached out and gently stroked her cheek. She giggled softly as chill bumps ran up and down her arms. She couldn't stop smiling, even after the branches had returned to their dormant state.

"If I had a place like this, I'd never leave."

Orlyn beamed, then finally turned. "Come. I have something I want to show you."

"You mean there's more?"

She followed him to the other side of the cellar and found an empty spot where the grass had not grown. In fact, the cordoned-off area was filled with sand, and yet inside, several stalks of diverse plant life were poking through, plants that wouldn't have normally grown under such conditions. There was a strange pungent smell as well, no longer the sweet fragrance of the blossoms from the other side, but something much stronger. It wasn't bad, just different. It had the lingering aroma of lemon and basil. There was even a trace of mint.

"I've developed these to grow with little to no water, and yet produce a yield that could feed an entire family. Imagine what we could do if we created plants that could thrive in these conditions? Plants that could grow with barely any water or very little light and still yield their fruit."

Adarra realized where he was going with this. "Are you saying these plants could help the Tallosians?"

"I would imagine so, but just being able to survive in harsh conditions isn't enough for the kind of blight the Northmen are dealing with. Their problem is plant killers."

"You've created edible plants that are impervious to insects?"

"In a manner of speaking. For example, did you know that plants such as lemongrass, basil, rosemary, marigold, and even mint are known for repelling certain insects? There is something about their fragrance that repulses them."

Now she knew where the smell was coming from.

"Also," Orlyn said, "petunias, though very sweet-smelling, have strong sticky hairs that catch insects and allow their roots to feed off the nutrients from the insects' bodies."

Adarra shivered. "I'll never look at a petunia the same way again."

Orlyn chuckled. "I took some of those same attributes, along with a few others of my own design, and built them into these crop plants here."

"What kind of crops are you growing?"

"Quite a few, actually. I have one variation of a gold potato, a red core carrot, some Keldoran sweet corn, barley, lentils, and even wheat. I've stuck with some of the most basic staples, since merging these characteristics is very difficult and time consuming. Took me half a year to figure out how to work this potato," he said and grabbed one of the closest bushy stems that had some dark purple flowers sprouting from the top, and pulled the plant up by the roots, revealing several large tubers growing underneath.

"Amazing." Adarra walked over to get a closer look. She pulled one of the potatoes loose and wiped off the sand.

"Go ahead," Orlyn said eagerly. "Take a bite."

She lifted it up and bit off a small chunk on one end. It was a little bitter and quite starchy, much like every other potato she'd ever cooked. She smiled. "It tastes like a potato." She looked down at where the plant had been displaced, and the sand had already filled the hole. She still couldn't quite get her head around the idea of bug-resistant, low-water, low-light plants. "How fast can they grow?"

"Ah. Now you're thinking like a horticulturalist." Orlyn knelt and placed the plant back down where he had pulled it from and stuck his staff in the sand next to it. The runes began to glow once more, and the plant suddenly started to move. The roots and tubers sank back down into the dry soil. Once the plant had been restored to its place inside the short row of potatoes, Orlyn stood. "Sadly, unless a floratide like myself is there to spur the crop's growth, I'm afraid their life cycle is much like your typical plant. Nature doesn't wish to be rushed. All life grows at its own pace; this is no exception."

"So it's not something that can be immediately beneficial to the Tallosians?"

Orlyn shook his head. "Not if you are hoping to use the seeds from these plants to feed them now. Those mountains are probably capped a good portion of the year, which means they would need to wait until even later in the year to start planting, unless, of course, they grow their crops somewhere down in the lower foothills."

Adarra sighed. She had been hoping for something more immediate, not that what Orlyn had created wasn't extremely valuable. But she needed something to pacify Jonas's people now, to keep them from invading. It wasn't like they could simply carry enough food over to feed an entire nation, even if that nation was roughly the size of Easthaven. Still, it was a great start, one she was excited to share with Jonas to see how he thought his people might react. "Do you have seeds for these plants?"

Orlyn stroked his beard a moment. "I don't have enough in stock to feed an entire people, but I should have enough to get them started. The seeds harvested from their first crop could be enough to see a substantial growth by the second and third." There was a moment's pause. "I know it's not exactly going to fix everything right now, but they will make a big difference later."

Adarra looked up and smiled. "I'm sorry. I don't want you to think that this isn't somehow helpful. It's miraculous, and it will go a long way in providing stability for the people of Tallos. I just hope that we can find something to use to deter them from invading now."

Orlyn's bushy brows lowered over his eyes. "It's ironic if you think about it. A swarm of beetles invade their land and devour their food. So what do the Tallosians plan to do? Invade Sidara for the same purpose."

The irony wasn't lost on her. However, she needed to figure out how they were going to keep the invasion from happening in the first place. "I hope these plants will be enough to hold the Tallosians off. At least, long enough to establish some form of dialogue between our peoples."

The problem was if she just showed up with bags of seeds, how was that going to prove anything to the Northmen? All they would have is her word that they were special and could do what she claimed. She would almost need Orlyn to go with her, but there was no way she could bring someone his age along on a mission this dangerous. If something were to happen to him, it would be on her head.

"I'll stop you right there," he said. "I can already see those gears turning. I have no intention of traipsing off to Tallos to try talking a bunch of Northmen into not attacking us. I'm too old for that. I would only get in the way."

"Unfortunately, without someone there to prove that these seeds work, they will be of little use." She looked up at him a moment as he stared down at his plants. "But you're right. It will be dangerous, and I wouldn't force anyone to go who didn't want to." She turned and looked back toward the stairs. "I best be getting home. Father will be getting worried."

Orlyn looked up from his preoccupied gaze at his new creations. "Yes, yes, of course." He walked her back to the stairs, where he retrieved his lantern. Adarra paused a moment before stepping back inside the stairwell, just to take it all in one last time. Depending on how the upcoming mission went, this could be her one and only time to see it. It really was beautiful. With a sad smile, she turned and headed up the stairs.

She left the shop and started south through town. The sky was clear and the moon and stars bright, making it easy to guide Thistle home. As she had expected, her father was sitting beside the fire with pipe in hand, awaiting her arrival.

"Had me worried, girl," he said, standing to help her with her satchel of books. "Do I need to stable Thistle?"

Adarra walked over and plopped down in the rocking chair. "No, I already did. Someone had already put water in her bucket and feed in her bag."

Her father smiled as he placed her books down on the sofa. "Are you hungry? There's some stew in the kitchen. Won't be too warm, but it's there if you want it."

Adarra hadn't eaten since lunch, and after the workout she'd had at Lyessa's, her stomach should have been complaining rather loudly, but eating was the last thing on her mind. Still, she knew she needed to try, or she'd be waking in the night with stomach pangs. "I guess I could eat a little."

She stood and headed into the kitchen, dishing up a bowl of her father's stew. She carried it back to the table, where her father met her as he took his usual seat on the end. She sat down next to him and then looked at the three empty seats at the table.

"I miss them too," her father said, and she turned and smiled, feeling the weight of her absent family. She hoped that wherever they were, they were safe. Looking down at her food, she stared at the chunks of meat, carrot, and potato, her mind racing back to Orlyn's cellar and his insect-repellent plants. How was she ever going to convince the Northmen, who were fearful of magic in the first place, that she had magic seeds that would grow crops that would be impervious to plant-killing insects?

She finally lifted her spoon and took her first bite. "How did your meeting go with the overlord and Commander Tiernan?" she asked. "Did you talk with him about your reservations with Captain Holverd leading the expedition?"

"I did. But Tiernan assures me that Holverd is the best man for the job. More importantly, the commander doesn't want to risk the mission by suddenly pulling the one leading it mere days before they take off, and then dropping that responsibility on someone else, which I can understand. Holverd has had ample time to prepare. It wouldn't make sense to make that large of a change this close to send-off."

Adarra gritted her teeth, but her father might be right. Dropping that responsibility in someone's lap now would probably prove just as dangerous, if not more so. Still, she didn't relish the idea of a man with a possible vendetta being the one to lead a mission of this importance.

"How was your training today?" her father asked, giving her a quick looking over. "Was Fraya forced to use any healing?"

"No. No healing today," she said, then lifted her head. "I did find that my magic has been hindering my ability to learn, though."

"Oh? How so?"

She went on to explain how the images from her memory were clouding her mind and keeping her body from being able to respond naturally. In short, she was spending too much time thinking and not enough time acting.

"Makes sense." He smiled and placed one of his big hands gently over hers where it rested on the table. "As long as you are improving, that's all I'm concerned with."

She spent the rest of the meal telling him about Orlyn's secret forest under his shop, and the bug-resistant plants he had created, and how she would take the seeds from those plants and use them to barter for peace with the Tallosians. She hoped it was fine that she had told her father about Orlyn's creations. Orlyn hadn't forbidden her, but he also hadn't given her any indication that he had wanted that news spread about.

After cleaning her dishes, they said their goodnights and headed for bed.

Adarra's night was a restless one, as she constantly found herself waking to thoughts of plants growing about her room, covering her like a cocoon. She also dreamed of meeting the Tallosians, and of offering her seeds, but they refused, and the expedition ended in a bloody battle that had her waking in a cold sweat.

She was more than elated to see the first rays of light peeking through her shutters the next morning. Her father must have been up early, because he was gone by the time she poked her head out of her room. After looking out the front window, she could see that the barn door was unbarred, which meant her father was either inside saddling Your Highness or had already left.

She ate a quick breakfast of oats and honey with some thick slices of bacon, extra crispy, just the way she liked it, and washed it all down with some fresh cream her father had purchased the day prior. She cleaned up after her meal, dressed, and then decided to head into town to meet with Jonas. She was anxious to tell him about the seeds and see what he thought about using them to open negotiations between their peoples.

In the barn, she saddled Thistle, taking a few minutes to give Waddle and Acorn some much-needed attention. With her brothers gone and her and her father spending so much time in town, the two horses were sadly being neglected.

She started to tear up at the thought of Breen and Ty and said a quick prayer for her brothers' safety as she finished filling Waddle's feed bucket. They had expected them back much sooner, and with each passing week they didn't show, it left her with the sinking feeling they never would. She walked Thistle out of the barn, shut the door, and mounted. She pulled on her gloves and raised her hood, then nudged her horse into a slow trot.

It was a cold and windy ride through the streets of Easthaven. The sun had once again disappeared behind another onslaught of darkening grey skies, which meant more snow. The days between falls were thankfully increasing, allowing for more of it to melt, which meant they were nearing the back end of winter. Hopefully spring would be there before long.

The Easthaven garrison was busy and crowded as usual, with men in green and gold and brown uniforms scurrying about like worker ants. The distinct ringing of steel on steel filled the yard as soldiers ran through their routines.

Adarra rode Thistle over to the garrison stable and left her there. She didn't know how long she might be inside and didn't want her horse standing out in the snow, which, from the look of things, was sure to begin falling at any moment. She carried her satchel of books over her shoulder and made her way across the yard and into the main building.

"Good morning to you, Miss Adarra," Orlis said. The elderly watchman at the door tipped his hat as she entered.

"Good morning," she offered back, along with a warm smile, before making her way across the open lobby for the stairs on the right, leading down to the cells.

"Mistress Adarra, it's so nice to see you this morning," Sergeant Finnly greeted, rising quickly from his seat and walking around his desk to meet her. "I didn't expect you so early." He took her hand and kissed it as he offered a formal bow. She tried to hold back a chuckle. The man was certainly laying it on strong this morning.

"How is our guest?" she asked.

"Quiet as usual." The short man fidgeted back and forth, grinning from ear to ear. He clearly had something he wished to say.

"What is it, Sergeant?"

"I've spoken with Captain Holverd, and he says that he is granting me permission to join your expedition to Tallos. What do you think of that?"

Adarra was utterly dumbfounded.

Finnly's beaming countenance slowly sank the longer she stood there in silence. "You are not pleased by this news?"

"I . . . I'm just surprised. What about your duties here?"

"There are plenty who can be assigned to them until I return."

She had no idea how to respond. What could she say to make him understand how dangerous this was going to be? "Sergeant, I don't believe you've thought this through. There's a great likelihood that we might come under attack. The Tallosians are a very violent people."

"Which is why I need to go. To keep you safe."

"I will have an entire company of lancers there to keep me safe."

Finnly's smile vanished altogether. "Are you saying that you do not wish me to come along?"

She groaned inwardly. How did she end up in this situation? She should have agreed to let Aiden join her in the cells when he had asked. Perhaps if he knew that her affections lay elsewhere, the sergeant wouldn't have been so eager to go. "I just don't want to see something happen to you, that's all."

He stepped forward and took her hand once more, cupping it between his own. "There is no need to fear for me, milady. I promise I can take care of myself."

She forced a smile and thanked him for his kindness, then quickly requested to be let into the cells. Finnly unlocked the door and allowed her to pass, then stepped inside to lead her back, but she told him that she could find it on her own. After a reluctant moment, he nodded and shut the door behind her.

She stood there a while, staring at the stone walls ahead. This expedition was getting more complicated by the day. First, she was being saddled with an expedition leader who was quite possibly carrying a rather hostile chip on his shoulder when it came to Northmen, then the one person who really needed to go in order to make the seeds work wasn't, and now a sergeant she didn't want to see go, was. She shook her head and started back through the cells, trying to push the other thoughts aside and focus on what she was going to say to Jonas.

She wasn't halfway through when she heard a raised voice ahead. She stopped at first, unsure what to do. Who else would be down here? Finnly hadn't mentioned letting anyone else in the cells. Had Jonas broken free? She crept forward, hoping to hear what the voice was saying as she circumnavigated her way through the passages toward the back. She didn't recognize who was speaking, but whoever they were, they were clearly angry. She stopped at the end of the next row of cells and peeked around the corner. A large bald man in a Sidaran uniform stood in front of Jonas's cell, about four down from where she was. There were three other uniformed lancers with him.

"You hear me, Northman? One wrong move and I'll slit your throat and leave you to the scavengers. You understand me? Too many lives are at stake. The only reason you're being allowed to accompany us is that the overlord believes you will be of use." He took a step closer to the cell, his hand resting on the hilt of his sword. "I don't share his confidence."

The man looked about her father's age, not quite as tall, but just as big in the chest and arms. His head was completely shaved, but he wore a thick goatee that hung a few inches below his chin. For a split second, she wondered if he had shaved his head specifically for this mission as a deterrent to the Tallosians. She guessed it was one way to keep from getting scalped.

This was worse than she thought. The man turned and started back down the row of cells in her direction, the other three following just behind. She didn't have anywhere to hide, so she stayed where she was against the wall as he marched around the corner.

He startled when he saw her and stopped. She could see the wheels in his head spinning, as he was no doubt wondering how much of what he had said she had been privy to. He removed his hat. "I take it you are the interpreter?"

"My name is Adarra, and yes, I've been working to learn the prisoner's tongue and teach him our own."

"My name is Captain Holverd. I will be the expedition leader."

Her heart sank. This was exactly what she'd feared. The man leading the mission had a deep-seated grudge against the very people they were looking to communicate with.

"I will leave you to it, then." He nodded and continued on, his men following.

She waited until she could no longer hear their steps before heading down the passageway to meet Jonas. She found him standing at the back of his cell. It took him a moment to realize she was there. When he did, he quickly met her at the front, where the light from the torch illuminated his face. He didn't appear hurt in any way. It didn't look like the captain and his men had done anything more than threaten him.

"What did they say to you?" she asked, dropping her satchel of books on the floor beside her.

"They do not trust."

She stared up at him a moment, then nodded. "I'm sorry about that." She wasn't exactly sure what to say to make the situation better.

"I hold no anger. I would do same."

At least he hadn't taken it personally, not that it quelled the overall problem their expedition leader's attitude presented. She worried how that would affect her efforts. Not only could it derail any talks, but if he were to act on his sentiments, it could put them all in harm's way.

Adarra stared at the cell a moment, then finally lowered herself down into a sitting position and pulled out her books to get started on their next lesson. She suddenly felt overwhelmed, and worse, alone. She wished her brothers were there to help her, and paused to say another quick prayer for their safe return before opening the first book and delving in.

Chapter 25 | Ty

I DON'T CARE WHAT NYALIS SAID," Ty whispered to the others as they sat quietly in front of the hearth in the common room. "I want to go home. It's been over two weeks since the others left for the Lost City, and other than our daily practices, nothing much is getting done here. We're just sitting around the dorm most of the day, staring at the walls."

"A nice change of pace if you ask me," Breen said from the other sofa as he raised his arms behind his head in a relaxed pose. "Besides, we aren't just staring at the walls. Nel has us watching Taylis and Marissa, remember?" He offered Ty a wry grin.

Ty groaned. "Don't remind me." It was another aspect of being left behind that he was finding less and less agreeable. It wasn't that the two rover children were bad. It was that Ty would have rather been spending his time learning new magics. He was chomping at the bit to do something. Anything.

His time at Aero'set so far hadn't quite lived up to what he had envisioned when he had first started out on his quest to find the shorlock. The school was impressive enough, at least the small portions of it they had been allowed to see, but he knew there was so much more to discover, depths of magic that they hadn't even yet scratched the surface of. And yet, for all their time spent inside of Aero'set, Ty wasn't any closer to learning about his gifts than when he had first arrived.

"I guarantee that if we were to leave," he said, "no one but Nel would even know we were gone. Clearly Nyalis doesn't seem to care. When was the last time any of us even saw him?"

"He can't be blamed," Narendi said, her legs tucked under her as she sat on the other end of the sofa from Ty. "He has full hands."

Ty sighed. "You mean his hands are full."

"That's what I said."

"His hands are more than full if you ask me," Breen said. "Quite the task to relocate an entire people into a magical place where no one has set foot in nearly a thousand years, and then teach them how to run it, or at least how to keep it up. That can't be easy."

"No, I'm sure it's not," Ty said. "Maybe he could let us tag along. Blazes, I'd be happy to learn more about how Aero'set operates as well. Better than just sitting around here." He turned and stared at the fire. "Which is why this would be the perfect time to go. With all of Nyalis's attention focused on settling the people of Wellhollow, we could be halfway home before anyone noticed we were gone. Besides, the only thing Nyalis seems worried about is us skipping our training, but we'll have Narendi there to keep us to it."

"You don't have to convince me," Breen said. "I want to go as well, but we're kind of in the middle of nowhere. Even if we somehow managed to scrounge up some horses, it would still take us weeks to make it out of the mountains and across the Sidaran Forest."

"Too bad we don't have Gilly here to take us by water," Ty said. "We could cut across Crystal Lake and down the East River."

Breen leaned forward, resting his elbows on his knees. "I bet you could do something similar. You do have a slightly better understanding of your voda gifts now."

Ty shook his head. "And how exactly am I supposed to do that without a boat?"

Breen frowned. "Didn't think of that."

"I think we should stay and train," Narendi interjected.

Ty turned. "I thought you said you wanted to see our home?"

"I do. But I don't wish to upset Nyalis."

"He's not going to be upset. We won't be gone long. But we need to let our father and sister know that we're alive."

"And what about me?" Kraea asked as she raised her head from her favorite spot in front of the hearth.

Ty looked at the draakar, her red scales glistening in the warm firelight. "I hadn't thought about that."

"Thought about what?" Breen asked.

"What do we do with Kraea? She would kind of stick out in Easthaven, don't you think?" Ty chuckled. "Can you imagine us walking into one of the wielder council meetings with her in tow?"

Breen laughed. "Feoldor would lose his bladder for sure."

Ty laughed. In fact, he laughed so hard he nearly lost *his* bladder. But after a couple of deep breaths, he settled down long enough to wipe his eyes before he and Breen turned and looked at Kraea.

Kraea cocked her horned head. *"Don't even think about leaving me behind."*

Ty smiled. "Wouldn't dream of it." He turned to Breen. "We could leave her at the cottage when we go into town. She can't get in much trouble there."

"Hey. You'd be amazed at how much trouble I can find."

"Are you trying to talk me out of taking you?"

"What did she say?" Breen asked.

"She said that she is very capable of finding trouble."

Breen looked at Ty and shook his head. "Just another reason why the two of you are perfect for each other."

Kraea snorted and laid her head back on the soft fur rug in front of the fire.

"It seems I have no choice in staying if everyone is determined to go," Narendi said. "But how are we to arrive at your home? We have no horse, and I do not believe Kraea will want us to ride her."

Kraea's head shot up. *"No one is climbing on my back like I am some brainless animal. I'll bite the first person that tries."*

Ty hmphed. "I have no intention of getting on your back, you overgrown cave lizard. Quit griping. Besides, I have a better way to get home."

The others turned.

"Well?" Breen asked. "Are you going to make us guess?"

Ty smiled. "We'll take the mirror."

"What mirror? You don't mean the one in the library with all the dead pygmies?"

"I wish. That would make it a lot easier. But no. I don't know the name of that mirror, and I doubt Nyalis is going to give it to us."

Breen shook his head. "Then where are you—"

"The mirror outside Lower Wellhollow," Ty said with a grin. "The one we came through from Tulgava Rashuvi."

Kraea released a throaty growl. Any mention of the great tree or the Live Market tended to set her off.

Both Breen and Narendi looked dumbfounded. "And where exactly are we supposed to be taking the mirror?" Breen asked. "There's no mirror in Easthaven."

"No, but there is one close by."

Breen stared at him a moment, then his eyes widened. "You don't mean . . ."

Ty nodded. "Yep."

"Yes, what?" Narendi asked. "Where are we going?"

Ty smiled. "We are going to visit an old friend."

"And when do you suggest we make this great escape?" Breen asked.

Ty stood, growing suddenly excited at the prospect of going home. "We leave tonight."

"Tonight?" Narendi shot up, as did Breen, both looking concerned.

"What better time? The sooner we leave, the farther we get from Aero'set before anyone realizes. Nel will probably just think we skipped breakfast for an early practice, and who knows when Nyalis will ever check in. We'll probably be in Easthaven by that time."

"What about food?" Breen asked. "There's no one in Wellhollow to get supplies from."

"We can grab some from the dining room before we go. I'm sure we can pack enough in our bags to get us down the mountain."

"This is crazy," Breen said, though there was a hint of a smile at the corners of his mouth. "Are we really doing this?"

"Unless you can give me a reason why not."

The others stood in silence. Even Kraea was without argument as she stared up at them.

"Fine," Ty said. We'll meet back here as soon as we finish packing."

With that, they all headed up the stairs for their quarters. Kraea followed Ty into his, since she had taken up permanent residence with him. She sauntered over to her spot in front of the fire while he scurried about the room, grabbing anything and everything he thought he might need, starting with his travel clothes.

It didn't take him long to strip. He even took a few minutes to warm his clothes in front of the fire before putting them back on. Kraea chuckled, as she usually did whenever he changed in front of her. It was her way of trying to make him feel uneasy. But after weeks of living together and sharing each other's every thought, being naked in front of her no longer bothered him.

His undergarments were nice and warm when he put them on, leaving him anxious to get underway. Quickly, he gathered his weapons and a spare change of clothes. Not wanting to forget his flute, he wrapped it snuggly inside his spare tunic to keep it better protected. He had spent more time playing it over the last couple of weeks than he had over the last several months. With so much downtime, he had found it one of the only activities that kept his mind calm.

After taking a couple of minutes to look over the room in case he had missed something, Ty hefted his bag over his shoulder and started for the door. "You coming?" he called back to Kraea, who was still huddled beside the fire.

She groaned. *"I hate the cold."*

Ty opened the door and turned. "I know. But I can promise you warm fires once we arrive in Easthaven." Ty wondered what his father would think of having to share his fire with a draakar. He knew Adarra would love it. She'd no doubt spend every waking moment demanding Ty interpret for her as she grilled Kraea in the ways of the draakar, demanding to learn everything she could about them and putting it to paper for her memory.

Kraea reluctantly stood and stretched, then trotted across the room and out so Ty could shut the door behind them. He turned and looked at Breen's and Narendi's rooms, listening to see if he could hear them inside, but there was nothing. Perhaps they had already finished and were downstairs waiting on him. He made his way down the hall to the small reading area at the top of the staircase and then started down.

He reached the bottom and found Breen waiting on one of the sofas, his pack resting on the cushion beside him. Like Ty, he had his sword and dagger strapped to his waist, but he also had his dark Sol Ghati bow and quiver of black arrows leaning against the armrest.

"Did you bring a change of clothes?" Breen asked.

Ty nodded. "Did you grab your water bladder?"

Breen also nodded. About that time, Narendi walked in with her bag in one hand and spear in the other. She was wearing her winter travel clothes, opting for the green cloak this time instead of the deeper red that she typically wore. She even carried a knit cap for her head but hadn't yet put it on. She stopped in front of the fire and looked the two of them over.

"Are we going?"

Ty nodded. "As soon as we see what food we can get from the dining room." He carried his pack down the hall on the right and into the dormitory's eating chamber. The long table was empty save for the candelabras and greenery that ran down the center. The others came in behind him. He placed his pack down at his feet and took a moment to picture in his mind what they might need for food, hoping the table's magic would act in the same way their bedchambers did. Generally, the table chose their meals for them. He clapped three times, and three places appeared in front of them, along with several trays of cold meat, biscuits, cheese, fruit, and nuts.

"I'm really going to miss this place," Breen said, taking a bite from one of the pieces of cheese.

"Won't argue with you there," Ty said as he went about gathering up some of the food and wrapping it in the large napkins the table had provided with the meal.

Breen and Narendi did the same, while Kraea walked around to the other side of the table where she found her dish waiting with a sizable piece of fresh meat. She didn't bother with worrying about saving it for later, and instead guzzled it down. By the time she had finished and licked clean what was left around her mouth, Ty and the others had gathered up the remaining food.

They saved only enough for a quick snack themselves before heading back for the common room and out the front door.

The wind had died down considerably, but the night air was crisp, their breath misting in front of their faces as they stared at the snow-covered yard between the torch-lit dormitories.

"Are we really about to do this?" Breen asked.

Ty smiled as he fought back a slight shiver. "Just think, by the end of the week, we could be sitting in front of the hearth watching Father puff away on his pipe while Adarra scribbles in one of her journals.

Breen smiled. "Can't think of anything better."

"Staying out of this flaming cold would be better," Kraea grumbled.

"I very much want to meet your family," Narendi said. Though, the way she said it had the hair on the back of Ty's neck standing on end. It was the same eagerness she had demonstrated when parading Ty through the Imbatoo village to introduce him to her father.

Ty did his best to ignore the comment as he hefted his pack higher on his shoulders and pulled his own knit cap on and down far enough to cover the tops of his ears. "Here we go." With that, he headed down the stairs to the snow-packed walkway and across the yard, past the large fountain at the center, and out through the southern gate.

Streetlamps lit the way as they headed south through Aero'set. No one spoke as they passed the arena on the left, eventually reaching the crossroads that led west toward the city's entrance. Taking a moment to make sure no one was around to see them, they headed right, keeping their eyes open for any of the mountain folk that might be wandering about the place. Ty was starting to miss the days when they were the only ones living in the school.

Soon enough, the gates rose out of the darkness ahead, two monoliths guarding the passage to this side of the river. Voices ahead had Ty and the others quickly moving to the side of the road, where they stopped to see where the voices were coming from. Breen pointed toward the gate tower on the right. There were lights coming from one of the lower windows.

"You don't think Nyalis already has them setting a watch, do you?" Breen asked.

"That would be just our luck," Ty said. "Though, I'm not sure why."

"Why what?" Breen asked. "Why it would be our luck?"

"No, why Nyalis would post a sentry. There's no one here. You couldn't find this place if you wanted to."

"How do we cross?" Narendi asked.

Ty paused a moment. "Ru'kasha Kor." The surrounding night brightened. "That's better."

Breen followed suit. "Forget about that sometimes," he said with a smile.

Behind them, Narendi huffed.

Ty stared at the gateway ahead and the towers on either side. "I don't see anyone. I think they're inside."

"Apparently, they're the smart ones," Kraea said. *"Only fools would be out in this cold."*

"If we are quiet," Ty said, "I think we can sneak past."

Breen grabbed Ty's arm before he could start. "Why don't you try putting one of those shields across the door to hold it shut, at least until we pass."

Ty's face brightened. "That's a good idea." He started toward the opening in the gate wall. There was a single passageway leading through the center, wide enough for a couple of wagons or a company of soldiers. He stopped before he reached the wall, just as soon as the door came into view. It was located inside the passageway on the right.

The windows on the outside were coated in ice, making it impossible to see in, but also impossible to see out, which was great for them. He quickly thought about what he wanted to do and started drawing the air to him as quickly as possible, hoping that no one decided to open the door right at that moment.

"Are you done?" Narendi whispered behind him, not helping his concentration in the least.

He hardened the air and started to form it in front of the door when a sudden outburst of laughter from inside broke his concentration, and the shield unraveled. He bit down and tried again, gathering the wind and hardening it. This time the door opened, and he nearly shrieked as he dove into the ditch, along with Breen, Narendi, and Kraea. Someone from inside stepped out and looked around.

"There's nothing here," the man said. "It was just the wind." The door shut once more, and Ty chanced raising his head long enough to realize whoever it was had gone back inside.

Frustrated, he climbed out of the ditch, wiped off the snow and quickly gathered the wind once more. He hardened it over the doorway and then sealed it with his magic glue. "That should do it," he said and motioned for the others to follow.

Quietly, they reached the gate, pausing only for a moment when they passed by the door, just long enough to try hearing what was going on inside before quickly making their way through the stone wall and across the bridge. Once they reached the other side, Ty released the magic, and the shield vanished. He nodded at the others, and they disappeared into the woods on the other side of the river. Breen lit a torch he'd packed and used it to help light the way for Narendi.

No one said a word until the road wound out of the woods and ended at the edge of the mountain valley standing between them and Harok Laos. "I figure we won't reach Wellhollow till morning, or close to it," Ty said, staring ahead at the wide-open expanse in front of them. It was too dark to see the silhouette of the mountains in the distance, even with the aid of magic, so he couldn't be sure.

"Let's get on with it, then," Kraea complained as she pressed her clawed feet down into the snow. *"The sooner we get up to those caves, the better."*

Ty nodded, and they started across.

Chapter 26 | Ty

THEY REACHED THE MOUNTAIN stairs sometime in the wee hours of the morning, after spending the majority of the night crossing the Valley of Needrin. By the time they had made it up to Harok Laos, the first signs of dawn were creeping over the peaks to the east, behind Aero'set. They paused on the landing briefly and stared out across the open valley to the mountains on the other side. Ty could just make out some of the white stone of Aero'set as the first of the sun's rays burst through.

"Still can't believe we found this place," Breen said softly as he, too, stared at the magical school.

"It does all seem like a dream sometimes," Ty admitted. "There are days I wake up and wonder if it's real. Then I hear Kraea snoring and wish it wasn't."

Kraea growled, then turned and left the others on the ledge, heading through the stone doorway behind them into the mountainside. The doors leading into Harok Laos were still open, as they were no doubt too large and too heavy to shut.

With a reluctant sigh, Ty turned and started for the open doorway, Breen and Narendi right behind him. The inside was dark, since the troughs on either side had been extinguished before the people of Wellhollow had passed through. Breen held up his torch, and the shadows danced across the pictorial images etched into the walls, giving them an almost lifelike appearance, as though the carvings were alive and moving on their own. The room was filled with them; there was hardly a blank space to be found on the walls.

Unfortunately, they didn't have time to study the unfolding history, so Ty headed for the tunnel on the other side that led back to Upper Wellhollow. They reached the next cavern where the old oracle had made her abode. Ty was struck by how simple her living space had been. There was a bed on the right with a rocking chair beside and a pile of books stacked against the wall, which seemed odd, since Ty had heard the old woman had been blind. Apart from a few small odds and ends and an empty table with two chairs, there was nothing more to be found save for the well-worn rugs spread across the floor, fashioning a makeshift walkway of sorts.

They kept going. Breen took the lead since he had the torch, and Kraea brought up the rear. Kraea didn't seem to have much problem seeing in the dark. Ty noted her eyes glowed a deep gold whenever the firelight hit them just right.

It took a while, but they finally managed to traverse the tunnel's passage back to the mountain village.

"Who goes there?" a voice called out just beyond the tunnel's opening as they neared.

Ty drew his magic. Who could possibly be up here?

"Horgith, is that you? You're early."

Breen turned and looked at Ty, and Ty shrugged. "It's not Horgith," Ty called out as they continued slowly forward. "It's Ty from . . ." He almost said Aero'set, then thought better of it. Whoever it was might not be familiar with the school. ". . . from Easthaven."

They reached the opening and found three bearded men standing guard at the entrance. "I remember you," the one who'd called out said. "You were with the man in black."

Ty didn't bother correcting him as he and the others stepped out of the tunnel. "Why are you here?" Ty asked. "The rest of your people have already left."

The three men sheathed their weapons. "We're here to guard the entrance to Harok Laos. We rotate every three days, but our replacements don't usually arrive until the evening." He looked at the four of them and cocked a brow. "You must have walked all night. Are you here to relieve us?"

"Afraid not," Ty said. "We have our own duties to attend to, which unfortunately requires us to travel back down the mountain."

One of the men shook his head. "Don't envy you that journey. We had to make it on the way up from Lower Wellhollow. Gave me nightmares for days."

Ty looked at Breen, then back at the three men. "What are you talking about?"

The man looked stunned. "You haven't heard about the ice tunnel?"

Ty shook his head. "What ice tunnel?"

The three men shared a concerned look. "No way to describe it, really. But you'll know it when you see it. Just try not to look too deep."

"Too deep at what?" Breen asked.

"The face of death." The men took a step back and waved them on through. "Good luck to you."

Ty grimaced as he passed the guards and started for the open passage on the other side of the plateau. The town of Upper Wellhollow was about as quiet as a tomb, a far cry from their initial arrival and the battle that had ensued. He could still picture his fight with the bulradoer as he stopped briefly to stare at a pile of singed boulders near the edge of the mountain pass.

"What did he mean, face of death?" Narendi asked, clutching her spear tightly as she cast about the empty town cautiously.

Ty shrugged. "No idea. But whatever it is, he said we won't miss it." He glanced over the side at the snow-covered incline leading down into the ravine. "Keep your eyes open." With that, he started down.

"Do you think Nyalis managed to clear the snow from the avalanche?" Breen asked as they made their way quietly along the narrow canyon, with its stone walls towering far above. His voice echoed softly into the distance, causing him to lower it even further.

"I would imagine so. I didn't see the tinker wagons up top."

"Good point."

Every so often, they passed a thin stream of falling snow piled near the edge of the canyon. Icicles hung from protruding rocks, some as tall as Breen. Ty did his best to stay as far from the edges as possible. If one of those icicles were to land on his head, it would make for a very messy end. The thought had Ty so unnerved that he raised a shield to hold over their heads each time they passed another cluster.

They'd barely made it around the fourth bend when they reached the remains of Zynora's avalanche. Ty could still remember what it had been like seeing all that snow cascading down through the canyon above them, knowing they were about to be crushed underneath it, only to have it suddenly funnel back down the tunnel on an invisible slide.

"Guess that's the ice tunnel they were talking about?" Breen said as they stared ahead. "They were right. You can't miss that. Not sure what they meant by not staring too deeply, though."

Ty shrugged, and they started for the circular entrance. The sky overhead was beginning to brighten as the sun cleared the peaks farther east. However, it was still dark enough within the canyon for Breen to keep the torch. It also helped when they periodically needed to warm their hands and faces.

Ty reached the edge of the tunnel and stopped. "Impressive," he said, staring into the long burrow of ice.

Breen moved up beside him. "I wonder how Nyalis managed it?"

"With magic," Narendi said, shaking her head as though Ty and Breen were two of the dumbest individuals she'd ever encountered.

Ty chuckled.

Kraea walked over and placed her foot on the floor of the tunnel. It slid until she dug down into the ice with her claws for a better grip. *I don't like this place. Let's get through it quickly.*

Ty took a step inside ahead of the others, careful to keep his balance on the ice, though there was enough snow and slush near the entrance to keep him from slipping. He walked farther in while the others waited at the edge. There was a spot that had been wiped clean on the side, so he started for it. Suddenly, he yelped and hopped back, but instead of landing on his feet, he slipped and landed on his backside, clawing at the ice to get away from the wall.

"What is it?" Breen shouted, already leaping into the tunnel and rushing over to help Ty back to his feet. Narendi and Kraea followed him in.

Ty gulped as his brother yanked him off the ground. "It startled me is all."

"What did?"

Ty took a moment to wipe the wet snow from the back of his trousers as he tried to determine if what he had seen was real or just his mind playing tricks on him. He cautiously made his way over to the wall to find out. "Now I know what they meant by looking too deep."

The other three followed him over.

"Flaming Pits," Breen uttered softly as soon as he spotted the faces staring back at him through the ice.

The dead soldiers' eyes were open, their faces twisted in horror. Ty turned and stared down the long passageway of death in front of them. Somehow, the tunnel of ice felt even colder, and a deep-seated chill ran down his back.

Ty pointed ahead. "Look." There were parts of bodies sticking out from the ice: arms, legs, heads. Some had half their torso reaching through, as though still trying to pull themselves free. It was one of the most terrifying sights he'd ever seen. Even more so than the dead pygmies. Something about these people being frozen in place, staring at them as they passed, was enough to keep him from wanting to go any farther.

The ice itself sounded as though it were alive. It creaked and groaned, sending haunting echoes down through the frozen corridor, as though beckoning them inside to join the countless others in their final resting place.

"I don't like this place," Narendi said.

"That makes two of us," Breen agreed.

Ty's stomach suddenly knotted, and he turned. "What do you think you're doing?"

The others turned as well to find Kraea on the other side of the tunnel with part of an arm hanging from her mouth. She stared at them a moment, then spit the limb out. *"I was hungry."*

"You were hungry?" Ty's face twisted. "That's disgusting."

Kraea grinned. *"For once, I agree. It tastes terrible when frozen."* She then sauntered off down the tunnel, leaving them to watch in disbelief. *"Come on. I don't like it here."*

"What did she say?" Breen asked, sounding like he wasn't sure he wanted to know.

"She said it didn't taste so good frozen."

Breen shook his head. "Let's just get through this place as quickly as possible."

"Sounds good to me," Ty said, and they immediately started after Kraea.

The constant creaking and groaning of the ice around them rubbed on Ty's nerves as he imagined the ice over their heads cracking and burying them alive under a mountain of snow. Something grabbed his arm, and he spun around, igniting his fire.

"Whoa, it's just me," Breen said, staring at the blue flames that were now aimed in his direction. "You might want to put that out."

"Sorry." Ty released his magic and dropped his hand. "This place has me on edge." He scooted to his right to circumvent a pair of legs protruding from the wall, but just as soon as he was about to clear them, one of the legs twitched. Ty yelled and stumbled back against his brother, nearly tipping them both over.

"What happened?" Breen asked, scanning the tunnel.

Narendi turned as well, bringing her spear to bear. "What did you see?"

Ty pointed at the dead soldier's leg. "It moved."

Everyone came to take a look. Even Kraea, though reluctantly since she was pushing them to hurry.

They stared at the leg for several minutes, but nothing happened. Finally, Kraea walked over and took a bite of the dead guard's calf. *"Nope. Frozen like the rest."*

"I promise you, the leg moved."

"Let's just keep going," Breen said nervously, and they started back down the tunnel once again.

Ty was beginning to wonder if his imagination was getting the better of him. He could have sworn he'd seen the leg move. Maybe it was just the man's trousers moving. They did have the occasional gust that slipped through. Regardless, he did his best to push the thought away and keep going, trying his best not to look at the surrounding dead. Unfortunately, the more he tried not to look, the more he ended up doing so.

"How long do you think this tunnel goes for?" Breen asked.

"Hopefully not long," he said as he raised his hands and blew on them, then motioned for Breen to hold the torch a little closer.

They made it around several more bends, the tunnel slowly angling downward, letting them know they were at least heading in the right direction. The creaks in the ice seemed to be getting louder and were coming at faster intervals, which had Ty picking up his pace. He had no idea how long they'd been walking through the ice, but it felt like an eternity.

"Whoa!"

Ty stopped and turned to see what had happened. Breen was a few paces behind him with the torch held up in the air as he stared at a couple more soldiers hanging from the ice above. "What is it?" Ty asked, walking back.

"I think that man's arm moved."

Ty felt another chill run down his back and swallowed as he forced himself to look up.

"What is happening?" Narendi asked, stopping once more to walk back and see what the two were doing.

"Breen said he thought he saw that arm move."

Narendi huffed and lowered her spear. "Not again."

Suddenly the soldier's hand jerked, and they all yelped.

"I told you I wasn't seeing things," Ty said.

A loud creak shot through the ice, and the arm moved again.

Ty started backing away, pulling the others with him. "I think we need to keep—"

The ice groaned once more, causing the rest of the body parts hanging from the ceiling to move as well. Suddenly everything went still, and before Ty could take another step, the bodies broke through the ice. Breen and Narendi dove backward to keep from getting hit as a loud crack shot through the tunnel.

"Run!" Ty shouted as he pulled Narendi to her feet, his brother already scrambling up to his.

The hole where the bodies had dropped through opened, and snow poured in like a waterfall, filling the tunnel behind them as they ran. The ice continued to groan, cracks forming all along the side and top. Kraea was farther up the tunnel, but as soon as she saw what was happening, she scrambled forward, her claws digging into the ice as Ty and the others raced to catch up.

Ty spared a passing glance back over his shoulder and wished he hadn't.

The snow tore through the tunnel behind them like a tidal wave, the ice around them shattering like glass as they ran with everything they had to stay ahead of it. One look at the coming torrent and Ty knew they couldn't.

"Keep going!" he shouted and turned around to face the wave. He gathered the wind to him, all that he could, and shaped it around the tunnel like a cork, sealing it with his magical glue as he fought to hold the ice in place. The wall of snow hit the invisible barrier like a battering ram, and the ice he had fastened his shield to gave way, shattering to pieces. All Ty could do was watch as the wave slammed into him.

But instead of Ty being crushed by the snow, his shield held. The force of the snow piling up behind his shield shoved Ty forward until he was being hurtled through the tunnel at an incredible speed. He couldn't move. His back was pressed against the shield as he rode the wave through the tunnel. Ahead, Breen, Narendi, and Kraea ran as hard as they could.

"Watch out!" he shouted, just before Breen and Narendi were scooped up and carried down the passage with him. Kraea scrambled across the ice in front of them, her claws digging in hard as she raced to keep ahead of the wave, but even she wasn't fast enough, and the invisible wall slammed into her back and pressed her up alongside the rest.

All of Ty's focus went to keeping the shield in place, the terror of what could happen if he lost that focus forcing him to fight through the fear threatening to swallow him as the deafening sounds of ice and snow drowned everything else out. They rounded another bend in the ice, and suddenly there was light ahead: the end of the tunnel. They broke through the entrance as the snow poured out into the canyon beyond.

Soon enough, the force of the snow began to lessen, and the shield slowly began to lower until the last of the wave puttered out. Eventually, they came to a stop up against the right side of the ravine.

Breen was the first on his feet, still clutching his torch, though it had been doused by the snow before they exited the tunnel. "I can't believe we're still alive," he said as he helped Narendi up, then Ty.

Ty released his magic, and they all sank ankle deep into the snow as the hardened air dissipated underneath them.

"I hate this place!" Kraea said, shaking the white powder off her red scales

as she searched for better footing.

"That was very enjoyable," Narendi said, surprising Ty with a wild grin as she started after Kraea.

Ty looked at Breen, and they both shrugged. They turned and looked at the canyon passage behind them and the snow that now filled it. They clearly wouldn't be coming back this same way when they returned. Breen was right. It was a miracle they had survived.

"I wonder if you could have stopped the snow itself," Breen said. "It's frozen water after all."

"I didn't have time to think about it. I just grabbed the first thing that popped into my head."

"Good thing Nyalis had you practicing those shields."

"I know. I doubt I would have been able to hold one that large for so long if he hadn't."

Turning back around, they left the ice and snow and bodies behind, hurrying to catch up with the other two. As they did, Ty reached out with his magic and sent it into the snow at his feet to test his brother's theory. Breen was right; he could connect with it, though it didn't feel quite the same as water. It seemed lighter, but he didn't think that was the correct word. He attempted to grab hold of it with his magic and fling it at Breen.

A six-foot swath of snow lifted off the ground and slammed into his brother from the side. Ty stared, wide-eyed. Breen was covered from head to toe in powder. It even clung to his beard, brows, and lashes.

"Breen, I'm sorry. I didn't mean to throw that much." He tried his best to keep from laughing, but one look at his brother's face, and he couldn't help it.

Breen turned, wearing a blank expression that Ty had learned long ago meant he was in trouble. Ty tried to back away, but Breen leaped on top of him. Ty went down shouting, his face buried under the snow as his brother held him down. After a moment, Breen climbed off, and Ty pushed his way up to his hands and knees, spitting snow. Breen looked down at him and started laughing. Ty couldn't help but laugh as well as he slowly crawled back to his feet.

"What are you two fools doing?" Narendi asked, walking back to see what had happened. "Why are you covered in snow?"

Ty and Breen looked at her, then at each other, and started laughing all over again. It felt good to laugh, especially after what they'd just been through. Narendi, however, didn't find it all that humorous and walked off in a huff.

The rest of the morning and most of the afternoon was spent making their way down the mountain passage and back out to the foothills below. They reached what was left of Lower Wellhollow just a couple hours before sunset.

"Wow, they weren't lying," Breen said. "The bulradoer did a number on this place." There were very few buildings still standing, most charred from fire; many looked like they'd been hit by a rockslide.

"I wonder if they've returned to the Tower," Ty said. He hoped the bulradoer weren't lingering nearby. He sent out some feelers through the surrounding mountainside and forest below, but he couldn't feel any of the dark stain left by the Tower's wielders. "I think we're fine."

After taking another quick break to rest their legs and eat, he led them through the rubble that was Wellhollow. They didn't dally, quickly making their way out through the back of town and around to where Mangora had set up the White Tower's encampment. The snow was still packed from where they had set up their tents, and the pits for their cook fires were all in place. The ground was littered with the remains of empty crates, worn clothes, old food, and empty barrels—things discarded haphazardly by a large troop on the move.

They reached the spot where their prison transports had sat and stopped. The snow was dug out where the wheels had been. "Seems a long time since we were here last," Ty said, "and yet it also seems like yesterday."

"I know what you mean," Breen added. "Surreal."

"Surreal?" Ty looked at his brother. "You're starting to sound like Adarra."

Breen chuckled. "Don't think I'll ever be that smart."

"I can still smell the arachnobe," Kraea said as she sniffed at the snow around the wagons.

"You think it's still here?" Ty asked, his hand igniting in flame as he spun in a circle.

Breen stopped his inspection of the rocks on the other side of where the wagons had been and hustled over. "What's still here?"

"Kraea says she can still smell the spider."

Breen started to unhook his bow.

"*No,*" Kraea growled. "*It's not here. I'm just saying its stench still is.*"

"Oh." Ty lowered his hand, extinguishing the flames. "Never mind. She said that it's not here, just its stench."

The others weren't as quick to lower their weapons, taking a few minutes to look around, but after a while they did eventually decide to press on. Ty led them back through the narrow passage in the rock toward the mirror they had come through from the Live Market.

They held their breath as they passed by what remained of the two corpses that Mangora's spider had killed and partially eaten. Ty wished he had been able to kill her back inside Harok Laos. The thought that she and her spider were still alive bothered him more than anything. He had a promise to keep, a debt owed for the life of his mother. Yet somehow, whenever the chance arrived, he was never able to make good on it.

By the time they reached the left branch in the rock, Breen was forced to light their torch once more, as the sun had set far enough to keep the passageway shrouded in darkness. The deep ravine ended at a small opening with the mirror built into the rock on the other side. They quickly crossed over to it.

"Took you long enough," someone called out behind them.

Ty jumped, as did Narendi, and they all drew their weapons and spun. Ty's hand was in the air, covered in flame, the blue fire lighting the wall on the other side, where Nyalis sat quietly on one of the rocks, his long staff resting in his lap.

"How did you know where we were going?" Ty asked as soon as he managed to catch his breath long enough to speak.

The wizard smiled as he climbed down and walked over to join them in front of the mirror. "It wasn't difficult. You've been threatening to leave for the last two weeks, and when I realized you were no longer in Aero'set, I had a feeling this is where you'd come. I almost tried the mirror in the library, but I was pretty sure I had never said its name aloud, and unless you have somehow picked up the skill of reading ancient Fae, I doubted you'd go there. Which left me with two options. Either you'd try to make your way on foot, which seemed highly unlikely, or you'd make for the mirror here."

Ty gritted his teeth. "I hate that you know me that well."

Nyalis smiled.

"So, are you going to send us back?" Breen asked.

Nyalis looked at them a moment, and then sighed. "No."

Ty was shocked. "Really?"

"The caretakers are taking up a lot of my time at the moment, and with Ayrion gone, I guess this would be a good time for you to return home. But . . ." He pointed his finger at them. "Only if you promise to return before the next full moon."

Ty tried picturing in his mind what the moon had looked like the last time he'd seen it. From what he could remember, it wasn't half full, which meant they had a little over two weeks to spend in Easthaven before returning. He brightened at that thought. "Agreed."

"Here," Nyalis said, pulling a book from his robes. "I want you to give this to your sister and invite her to return with you."

"Adarra?" Ty took the book and looked at the cover. *Academic Guide to Conjuring for Novices.*

"Yes. I greatly wish to speak with her."

"You want her to come here?"

Nyalis cocked his brow. "I believe that is what I just said."

Ty looked at Breen, but his brother appeared just as surprised, so he finally nodded and stuffed the book in the top of his pack.

Nyalis smiled. "Good." He then turned to Narendi. "I've been meaning to give you this for some time but never seem able to remember." He sighed. "Don't ever get old, my dear." He proceeded to pull a gold bracelet out from his robe, very similar in design to those she had worn before she left the Imbatoo, and placed it on her wrist. It was created from two thin pieces of gold that had been beautifully woven together. The one big difference between this one and her others was the crystal set into the center.

Ty looked at the setting. "Is that . . ."

"Yes. It's about time she was able to do more than simply feel her magic."

Narendi held up the new jewelry. "I feel . . . different. What is it?"

"That is your magic coming alive for probably the first time," Nyalis said. "Go ahead, touch the snow."

She started to lean over.

"No, no, no. I mean with your magic. Feel the water inside it."

She hooked her spear back over her shoulder to free up her hands and then stretched them out toward the snow on the ground. "I do not know what to do."

"Touch it," Nyalis said, "with your mind."

Narendi raised her hands, and suddenly the entire top layer of snow inside the gorge shot into the air, raining back down on top of them all.

Kraea roared as she, and everyone else, was completely covered.

"And I thought Ty was bad," Breen said, shaking the snow from his hair and out of his beard. Ty wiped off what had collected on top of his knit hat and coat.

Nyalis chuckled, then looked at Ty. "Now that you have a rudimentary sense of your own voda gifts, perhaps you can help her with hers."

"I don't know how helpful I can be, but I guess I can try." Ty's knowledge was nothing more than instinct. He had no idea how he was supposed to help Narendi.

Nyalis took a step back and looked the three over. "Be careful to watch out for each other. Things are progressing quickly in Aldor, tensions rising, kingdoms on the verge of war, as we've seen already with the fall of Cylmar. I'm not a seer, but I don't need to be to see that things are not getting better. Just another reason why Aero'set's return is of such importance. The sooner we can begin to draw wielders to our side, the better our chance of standing against the Tower will be."

With that, Nyalis walked over to the mirror. "You might want to remember this for later," he said back to them. "Solnari Cushlora. Abienan Lavoris." The runes around the mirror's frame burst to life as the glass within began to spin, until it formed the image of a large darkened room with bodies scattered throughout. There was no need to guess where the mirror had opened. Ty could see the shelves of books on the other side.

Nyalis struck his staff on the ground, and the crystal at the top brightened into an almost blinding light as he stepped through the mirror, filling the library tower with its brilliance and revealing what remained of the pygmy war party. He turned and smiled as the mirror began to spin once more. Before Ty knew it, the wizard was gone, and they were once again staring at their own reflections.

"Did you remember the mirror's name?" Breen asked.

Ty nodded. "Abienan Lavoris." He repeated it to himself several more times, driving it into his memory. Breen, on the other hand, pulled out a small booklet and writing utensil and jotted it down. "At least now we have a way back, what with the snow now blocking the passage up to Harok Laos." He looked at Ty. "Do you know the name of the mirror we are going to?"

Ty nodded. "It was the first mirror I ever went through, and it took me quite a while to figure it out. So by the time I did, its name was burned into my memory." Ty walked over to stand in front of the mirror and reached for his magic, letting it permeate the surrounding frame. "Solnari Cushlora. Ra'hanisra Tulgarin."

The runes around the glass began to glow once more, and the glass itself liquified and spun, eventually forming a small hollowed-out wooden room with unique designs carved into the floor. Taking a deep breath, he looked at the others and smiled, then stepped inside.

Chapter 27 | Ty

TY STEPPED OUT OF THE MIRROR. It was like walking through water but without the need to dry his clothes afterward. The sensation always left his skin tingling. The room on the other side was warm compared to the frozen gusts that had been beating down on them from the upper peaks of the Angoran Mountains, and it smelled strongly of newly cut wood with a slight hint of a spice he didn't recognize.

He quickly took a look around to see if anyone was there, and then motioned for the others to come through. There was a single lantern hanging from the wall behind him, providing enough light to see. It hung at the bottom of a winding circular staircase, which led to a single landing farther up.

Kraea was the last through the glass, and by the time she made it in, the small chamber was feeling rather cramped. The glass on the mirror spun once more, and the image of the snowy ravine vanished, replaced with a reflection of themselves and the tiny room they now occupied.

"Where are we?" Narendi asked, her spear in hand.

"You won't need that here," Ty said, pointing to her weapon.

She held on to it anyway as she studied the staircase all the way to the door at the top. Ty was the first up the stairs, followed by Breen, then Narendi, and lastly Kraea.

"You didn't get the chance to meet her last time, did you?" Ty called down to Breen.

Breen shook his head. "Too busy chasing after you."

Ty reached the top of the stairs, but before he could open the door, the entire place began to shake, and everyone grabbed the railing.

"What was that?" Narendi asked, looking out over the rail and up into the darkness of the enormous trunk above them.

Ty chuckled. "That was Abinayu greeting my return."

"Who is Abinayu?" Narendi asked.

"You're standing in him."

"What?"

"Something about this place feels familiar," Kraea said.

Ty turned. "Abinayu is a living tree." The staircase shook once more as the inner trunk twisted slightly. "Sorry," Ty called out, hopefully loud enough for Abinayu to hear. "I mean he is the guardian of the marsh. He was also at one time a member of the Fae." Ty remembered what the former faerie had told him on their last visit and shuddered. He had revealed that there were those on both sides—human and faerie—that would see Ty destroyed because he was an anathema, a product of an unholy union, especially to the Fae. Abinayu had told him that the offspring of those unions were dangerous and quickly exterminated.

"How did he become this?" Breen asked, reaching out to carefully touch the inside flesh of the tree. "I can feel something pulsing below its skin."

Ty opened his mouth, then stopped. "You know, I never asked him."

"We are standing inside one of those magic people you told me of?" Narendi asked, looking a little queasy at the thought.

Ty nodded. The Imbatoo had no real knowledge of the Fae and their coming—at least none that the Wazeri had recorded and shared with Narendi's people. Ty reached out with his hand and pressed it against the wood. It was warm to the touch, the faerie's life pulsing just below the surface. He opened himself up to his magic and connected with the tree as a way of greeting, assuring the ancient faerie that he was there in a friendly capacity. As soon as he did, the door in front of him opened.

Ty had barely got his foot out of the trunk when he had to duck the head of a broom that came straight for his face. It missed him and hit Breen, who was stepping out just behind him. Ty grabbed the handle before it could be swung again. "It's just me, Douina. Ty." He peeked out to find the old witch standing there with one hand firmly grasping the broom's arm and the other holding a ball of fire.

As soon as she saw him, her eyes narrowed. "So, you've returned, have you? I take it your quest was unsuccessful, then? That's a shame."

"Actually, quite the opposite," Ty said, releasing the broom, which she then lowered beside her, but she kept the flames up to better see.

"And who's in there with you? I can hear them breathing." She tried peering beyond him and into the open doorway. "Come out so I can get a look at you."

"It's just my brother, Breen," Ty said as he stepped the rest of the way out of the tree and then partway down the steps to give the others room to exit.

"Your brother, you say?"

"You aren't going to hit me again, are you?" Breen called out from the inside.

"Depends on if I care for the smell of you."

Breen slowly stepped through the doorway, his hands up to show he held no weapons. As soon as his eyes landed on Douina, his mouth dropped.

Her brows lowered. "What are you staring at?"

Breen looked at Ty. "You were right. She looks just like her. Scary."

Douina sneered. "So, I take it you've had the unfortunate pleasure of meeting my sister as well?"

"Yes, ma'am," Breen said as he moved aside to give the other two room to leave the tree.

Douina held up her ball of flame and cast a gaze back at the door. "There's more of you?"

Narendi stepped out next, her spear up as she stopped to look the old woman over. "She is the exact image."

"That's an interesting accent you have there," Douina said. "Wengoby, if I were to guess."

Narendi's head lifted. "I am Imbatoo. You know of my people?"

Douina smiled. "A long time back, but yes. Honest folk. Very pleasant to commune with, as I remember." She turned back to the tree. "There is someone else still inside. Come out before I have Abinayu shut you in."

A sudden clawing noise broke from the trunk as Kraea scrambled up the steps. Douina took a step back at the sound of it and raised her broom as Kraea tore out of the tree, not wanting to get locked inside. Douina shrieked as the draakar dove through the entrance and out into the yard.

"Don't worry, she's with me," Ty said. "She won't harm you."

Kraea growled. *"Speak for yourself!"*

Douina took a step forward. "I'm hardly concerned with her harming me." The old woman quickly scurried down the steps and over to where Kraea stood several feet from the trunk. Kraea bared her teeth and growled as she approached. "It has been years since I've seen a draakar, and not one as beautiful as she."

Kraea's lips closed, and she seemed to relax slightly, the bowed muscles in her shoulders lowering as Douina began to circle her.

"Beautiful scale work, good set of horns, nice upright posture. Yes," Douina said. "A very lovely draakar."

"I like her," Kraea said. *"Perhaps I won't eat her after all."*

Douina chuckled and lowered her flame. "You'll find I'm too tough to chew anyway."

Both Kraea and Ty turned. "You can hear her?" Ty asked.

Douina waved the question off, then finished her examination and took a step back to look them all over. After a long moment, she finally nodded. "Come. I have a pot of tea on the fire. You can tell me of your adventures." She turned and started back toward the cottage.

Ty nodded to the others, and they followed. He was the first inside after Douina, stopping to remove his dirty boots at the door before directing the others to do the same. Kraea tapped her feet on the frame before entering, and Douina closed the door after her with a swipe of her arm from across the room.

The inside of the cottage was the same as Ty remembered. Flowering vines, which Ty now knew to be Abinayu's roots, climbed the walls, working their way across the ceiling and down the railing at the back, where a tight circular staircase provided access to a second-floor loft. Her sitting room and kitchen were as cluttered as ever, perhaps more so around the fire, as there were several additional crates of dried herbs stacked beside the hearth.

"Feel free to grab yourselves a chair," Douina said, pointing to the table behind them as she lowered herself into her rocking chair in front of the fire.

Kraea walked over and curled up in front of the blaze at the old woman's feet. She made a sound that reminded Ty of a cat's purring. Clearly, she was thankful to be out of the snow and ice and back in front of a warm fire.

After unloading their gear and weapons by the door, Ty walked over and took the rocking chair opposite of Douina. Breen grabbed two seats from the table and carried them over for him and Narendi.

"That is a Sol Ghati bow, if I'm not mistaken," Douina said, staring at the dark bow and arrows resting against the wall by the door. She lit her pipe and took a couple of quick puffs, sending smoke curling up into the rafters. The tobac had a strong smell, and yet at the same time a hint of sweetness. "Haven't seen one of those in many a year. In fact, the last time I saw one was with Valtor when he came looking for the shorlock all those years back." She took a long slow puff from her pipe and leaned back in her chair as she stared across the way at Breen. "Where did you get yours?"

Breen looked at Ty, who could tell his brother wasn't sure if he should say or not, so Ty nodded that it would be alright.

"I found it in your sister's shop."

Douina choked halfway through her puff, the embers glowing from the pipe's bowl, casting deep shadows across her face that made her eyes seem even more sunken. "Mangora owned a shop?" she asked, the smoke trailing up overhead. She suddenly burst out laughing. "My sister was about as organized as I am. I can't imagine her keeping books and selling trinkets."

Ty grimaced, remembering his first experience inside Mangora's den. "I wouldn't exactly say she sold trinkets . . . or anything for that matter."

"It was located in Easthaven," Breen said, "where we are from."

"It was how she first came to discover who I was," Ty said, then spent the next few minutes telling Douina of his first visit to her sister's shop.

"Hiding in plain sight." Douina chuckled. "Sounds like Mangora."

Ty and Breen then went on to expound, in greater detail, all of their dealings with Mangora while in Easthaven, from the hiring of the Tallosians to capture Ty, the call of her arachnobe army, even how she had used a numori to take control of Ty and try to use him to kill the overlords.

Douina frowned. "It seems my sister has been quite busy over the years. Valtor has twisted her into something I wouldn't even recognize."

"It gets worse," Ty said. "That wasn't our last encounter with Mangora. She was waiting for us near the entrance to Aero'set."

Breen cleared his throat, and Ty turned. "Is it wise to say too much?" he whispered, passing a cautious glance over at Douina.

Douina chuckled. "There are no secrets here, boy. As soon as you stepped out of Abinayu, I knew everything you had ever done. I'm a mind reader. Your thoughts are mine."

Breen's jaw went slack. So did Ty's, and they both gulped. "You can read my thoughts?" Breen asked, looking a little horrified.

Douina leaned back and released a loud, throaty cackle. "No, I can't read your thoughts, you giant oaf. There's no such thing as a mind-reading wielder. What has Nyalis been teaching you?" She laughed some more, which was followed by a few minutes of strong coughing that had her out of her chair and pouring a cup of tea from the pot over the fire. She took a sip to moisten her throat before sitting back down. She stared at the three of them and shook her head. "So, you've had a more recent encounter with Mangora. I'd be interested to hear it."

Ty started from the beginning. He had told her of his quest at their last encounter, so he proceeded to spend the rest of the evening filling her in on every facet of how that journey had taken place, starting with his near drowning after stepping through the mirror inside Abinayu, to his and Breen's meeting with Tirana and the Karpaathians and their curse to guard the maze.

He told her of their journey through the maze and his trial of fire. He then did his best to describe the underground lake and the lake monster and how they had gotten the piece of the key from the hidden passage under the water.

From there he described barely escaping the creature's tentacles to finding themselves inside the Wengoby Desert. Narendi added how she had found them both lying half dead, buried under one of the dunes, and how she and her people had brought them back, only to discover they had found the Mazota

Wanjenga. She described her care of Ty and Breen and her nursing them back to life.

Ty then expounded on their confrontation with the Wazeri and their trek through the orm-infested desert lands in search of Zwaneri a Wakale, an ancient temple's ruins guarded by the Wengoby Priests.

After Ty told of their collection of the third piece of the shorlock, he described their journey into the Riverlands and their discovery of the Live Market and their freeing of Kraea. Kraea added the bravery of her mother as she fought the evil traders, killing the head of the market, Dalibor, in the process, which allowed them to flee through the mirror at the top of Tulgava Rashuvi.

"And that's when we had our final run-in with Mangora," Ty said.

Douina scooted forward in her seat, her eyes locked on Ty.

"She was waiting for us just outside the mirror when we came through. I was knocked unconscious as soon as I stepped through the glass, and when I woke, I found myself in the back of a prison transport with a durma around my neck."

Douina grimaced and raised her hand to her own neck. "Those durmas are nasty business. Gives me chills just thinking of them." She took another sip of tea and waited for Ty to continue, so he described the horrific ritual he had borne witness to. Douina's hands were shaking as she leaned forward in her seat.

"Are you telling me that my sister performed the Sola de Blanava?"

"Yes. It was terrible."

Douina lowered her head. "I can't believe she is so far gone. Bloodstone creation in such a way was established by Aerodyne and his followers. Very, very dark magic that feeds on death instead of life." She shuddered. "What has my sister gotten herself into?"

She sat in silence a moment, then asked Ty to continue. He told her of their journey up the mountain and the battle that had ensued with the bulradoer and the Black Watch troops Mangora had brought with her, beginning with the avalanche. He described the battle as best he could, at least the parts he had fought, including having to face off against several bulradoer and their ter'aks. He told her of being saved by an Upakan, though he left out

Ayrion's name, or that he was the Guardian Protector. He then told her of their final confrontation with Mangora and her giant arachnobe inside Harok Laos.

Douina demanded every little detail, so Ty gave it, even how they had used Kraea's blood mixed with his own to create a true bloodstone. Kraea's head shot up during that part, long enough to make sure Ty gave a true depiction of her bravery and how she had been gravely wounded while trying to protect an old seer. Ty finished with the opening of the doors of light and his own near-death experience trying to return the Keep of Aero'set back into their realm.

"And we have spent the last several weeks there in training," he said, then frowned. "Well, weapons training. Apparently, Nyalis is too busy to teach us any real magic. About two weeks ago, Nyalis sent most of our party off to the Lost City to bring back the Upakans. Apparently, at one time, they were the guardians of the school." He shrugged. "Who knew? Anyway, we thought it would be a good time to return home and let our family know that we are alive." He looked at Douina and smiled. "And here we are."

Douina sat back in her seat, placing her cup on the table next to her and picking up her pipe, which she lit by whispering something into the bowl. "It sounds as though you have had quite the adventure, my young friends."

Ty stood and poured himself another cup of the tea, then refilled Narendi's and Breen's before retaking his seat. The tea was dark and a little bitter, with just a touch of honey to cut the strong flavor, but it was deliciously warm, and he found it soothing on his throat, especially after so much talking. "Nyalis wants us to return to Aero'set by the next full moon, so we might be coming through here again."

She smiled. "You are always welcome." She leaned forward and mumbled something under her breath. She then raised her hand toward the hearth and moved it slowly in a circle as if stirring an invisible pot. As soon as she did, the ladle hanging near the fire lifted and lowered into the pot and began to stir the tea.

Ty and the others watched in awe. "How are you . . ."

"A simple binding spell," she said. "It allows me to join my hand to the spoon. Nothing any apprenticing mage couldn't do. The most difficult bindings, though, are with animate objects. Those take years to master, and even then, most wielders never make it beyond a rudimentary understanding."

"Could you teach me?"

She chuckled. "You would need more formal training first. Not something I have time for this evening."

"Where did you learn your magic?" Ty asked. "You seem knowledgeable. Are you similar to a wizard?"

Douina laughed. "Hardly. The teaching required for that has long since passed, I'm afraid, apart from Nyalis, of course. My magic was taught to me from birth. When my family learned of my and my sister's gifts, we were sent to a secret coven of Ahvari witches, which was founded millennia ago by Pinnella Ahvari." Douina frowned. "Though a lineage like that isn't exactly something to be all that proud of, considering Pinnella was one of Aerodyne's wielders." She took another puff and let the pale smoke snake upward into the rafters. "To be honest, most of that sort of magic was lost after the Great Purge. Simple spells are all we have left."

"Doesn't seem all that simple to me," Breen said.

Ty had a thought. "You ought to come back to Aero'set with us. Nyalis said that we would need instructors, and you seem to be one of the few who still has any sort of knowledge when it comes to magic. He says there is a war brewing, and we need as many wielders with us as possible."

"Does he now," Douina said, continuing her rocking as the embers from her pipe's bowl lit her drawn face. "Afraid my days of teaching are over." She exhaled another trail of smoke over her head. "No, no, I prefer to spend the rest of what time I have left with my plants and with Abinayu. He would get awfully lonely with me gone."

"But you could visit anytime," Ty said desperately. "Every day, in fact. With Abinayu's mirror, you could come and go at will."

She chewed on the stem of her pipe a little longer as she stared at the dimming fire in the hearth.

"At least consider it," he said.

"Considering it is about all I can promise," she said as she stood from her seat with a yawn. She left the room and returned with some blankets for them to spread out in front of the fire.

Ty didn't know what time it was, but he had a feeling dawn would be there soon, and he quickly closed his eyes. Before he knew it, he'd drifted off.

Chapter 28 | Ty

Y WOKE TO A HAND on his shoulder. Turning over, he found Breen kneeling beside him, yawning, which of course drew a sympathetic yawn from Ty. "What is it?" Ty asked grumpily, not appreciating having been woken while resting so comfortably. He'd been happily dreaming he was back inside the heart of Aero'set, down in the Meeisredon, swimming around in the warm pools below the crystal falls that made up the Pentarium. It was a piece of his home, after all, and he found himself strangely drawn to it.

"I think we might have overslept," Breen said, and moved out of the way so Ty could see out the front window behind him. The sun was casting a short shadow across the sill, barely reaching inside the cottage, which meant it was nearly overhead.

"Not again." Ty quickly sat up and looked around.

"She's not here," Breen said, "but there is food waiting on the table."

Ty glanced over at the table and then took a moment to stretch. "How long have you been up?"

"Only just." He pointed, and Ty turned to find Narendi still asleep, whimpering softly. Kraea, on the other hand, snored like a lumber saw, her short gangly wings curled around her like a blanket.

He wondered how quickly draakar grew to full height. Rather quickly, he imagined. She wasn't as big as her mother, but she was very clearly gaining ground.

"Time to wake up," he called out to her through their link. He wasn't about to walk over there and try shaking her awake. The last time he'd tried that, she'd almost stabbed him with her horns.

One of Kraea's legs jerked, but then went still.

"Kraea, it's time to get up."

She growled and stretched her legs, her eyelids parting slowly as she looked around the room. She glanced over at the window and yawned, then slowly crawled to her feet and shook herself like a dog after a swim in the river. Sniffing the air, she turned toward the table and pranced over to see what Douina had left, while Ty rolled over and gently ran his hand down Narendi's arm.

Narendi clutched Ty's hand and rolled over, pulling him down beside her.

"Hey, wake up," he said, jerking his arm free while trying to scoot away.

She turned over and stretched, then looked up at him and smiled. "Good morning. I dreamed of you."

Ty stood. "I didn't need to know that." He grabbed her hand and helped her up, and she immediately sniffed the air.

"Something smells good." She turned and headed for the table, where Kraea was already chomping on a piece of uncooked meat that Douina had laid out on a platter for her on the floor.

Ty took a moment to look outside and see if he could spot their host, but there was no sign of Douina anywhere around the front of the cottage, so he joined the others at the table. Surprisingly, the food was still warm in their covered bowls, and they quickly dished it out. There was some porridge with cinnamon and honey, biscuits, eggs, and even some sausage links. It was quite the feast, and not at all what Ty would have expected in the middle of Reed Marsh. He ate it gratefully, and by the time he had finished two full helpings, he was feeling ready to take on the wetlands.

The front door opened as they were clearing the table, and Douina walked in wearing a wide-brimmed hat, a mud-stained apron over her dress, and a pair of gloves. "Ah, I see you've finally decided to grace the day with your presence. Thought you were going to sleep it away like the last time.

"The last time you drugged me," Ty said.

She smiled and took off the hat. "True." She closed the door and proceeded to untie her apron and hang it on one of the hooks behind the door. She stuffed her gloves in one of the apron's pockets, then headed for the table. "I see you finished your meal, good. I hope it was satisfactory. I don't get much in the way of guests out here," she said with a chuckle. "The only entertaining I do is Abinayu, and he doesn't exactly eat . . . or talk, for that matter. In fact, he can be a very unpleasant houseguest when he wants to be." A couple of the root vines on the wall shook, and the flowers swayed slightly.

She ignored them.

"We need to get a move on," Ty said, "if we plan on getting through the marsh before dark. I don't want to get stuck out there overnight."

"Why not? It's rather beautiful out there at night."

Ty grimaced. "Our idea of beauty is quite different."

She smiled. "You can find beauty in every living thing if you look hard enough."

Ty tried to imagine what kind of beauty he could possibly find in the razorback that had tried to kill him on his last trek through the marsh, or the swamp monster that had eaten it. The only thing he could think of when it came to the bog was the smell of death and the constant fear of dying. Deciding it best not to argue the point, he walked over and began folding his blanket by the hearth.

"Don't worry about those," Douina said. "I'll get them later."

Ty went ahead and finished and then placed the blanket down on the rocker he'd sat on the previous night, but he did leave Breen's and Narendi's blankets. Breen and Narendi were too busy getting their travel packs ready to notice. Once finished, they strapped on their weapons and finished by pulling on their cloaks.

Douina joined them at the front. "Do you mind?" She held out her hand to see Breen's bow, and he handed it over. She studied it a moment, holding it up to get a better look at the grip, or rather, the runes and decorative markings around it. "Hmmm." She handed it back but didn't say more, which had Ty curious.

"Is there something wrong with it?"

"No. Just wanted to see about something."

"About what?"

"About whether or not it was the same bow."

Ty waited, but she remained oddly quiet. "Well, is it?"

"It appears that it is."

Ty looked at Breen's bow. "You're saying his bow used to belong to Valtor?" He looked at Breen. "Wouldn't that be something?"

"Yes," she said. "But, of course, it used to belong to someone else before that. A Westland ranger, I would assume. They were the ones gifted with the weapons, after all."

Ty nodded. "Nyalis mentioned as much, though he didn't tell us anything about them." He looked at his brother and smiled. "I still can't believe we've actually been to the Westlands."

Breen smiled as well. "It is incredible to think about. We've seen things and been to places that no other Aldoran has in over a thousand years."

Ty nodded, though he could have been just as happy not having visited those places. Ty put on his coat and hat, then strapped on his sword and dagger before lifting his pack and hooking it over his shoulders.

Douina opened the door, and they all walked out into the warm sun. Ty knew he better enjoy it while it lasted. As soon as they broke through the heavy veil of hanging vines protecting Douina's little paradise from the rest of the swamp, it would soon be gone.

"I appreciate you letting us stay," Ty said to Douina as she walked them down to the edge of the enclosure, where a moss-covered path led up to the edge of the long hanging greenery.

"The pleasure was mine," she said. "It isn't often that I get to enjoy a fire with company." She stood in front of the wall of green and raised her hands. The vines started to move, half parting to the left, the other right, leaving an open doorway between for them to pass through.

The marsh ahead was dim, the sunlight choked by the thick branches and vines and a low-hanging fog that settled across the water. It was a night-and-day difference from Douina's small sun-filled glen. Ty wasn't looking forward to navigating the swamp all over again and was starting to wonder if he'd made the right choice taking them that way. Perhaps they should have taken the longer route around Crystal Lake and through the Sidaran Forest. Unfortunately, if they had, it would have probably taken the full two weeks to get there.

Taking a deep breath, he looked at the others. "No sense in staring at it."

"I don't like this place," Narendi said.

"I'm with her," Kraea added.

Breen just stood there quietly waiting on Ty. He knew what awaited them. He'd been through it before.

Ty turned to Douina. "I meant what I said. I hope you'll consider coming back with us to Aero'set."

Douina smiled. "I said I would think on it, and I will. Best you get a move on, though, while you can. Do you know your way?"

"Nyalis told me to stick to the path."

She pursed her lips a moment, then nodded. "I'm sure I don't need to tell you, but stay out of the water."

Ty offered a half-hearted grin. That was one thing she certainly didn't need to remind him of. Ty turned to the swamp, and after taking a deep breath to steel his nerves, started in. As soon as they had cleared the thickest of the vines, the green wall behind them dropped back into place with a swish, and Douina vanished behind it.

The sounds of the marsh took over, as did its stench, enough to make Ty wish he hadn't eaten that second helping of breakfast.

"This place smells very bad," Narendi whispered, casting about at every snap of a twig or splash of water.

"You get used to it," Ty said.

"Really?"

"No," Breen added.

Ty took them forward. "Keep to the center of the path and we should be fine."

Cautiously, they headed into the swamp. It didn't take them long before the wall of green guarding Douina's home disappeared as they were swallowed completely by the massive wetlands and surrounding fog. It seemed the farther in they went, the darker it became. The sun was unable to pierce the pervasive mist that covered the marsh, bringing with it a wet chill. It wasn't as cold as the mountain pass they had traveled through the previous day, but the dampness made it much more miserable to bear.

Narendi slipped on some of the wet clay and went down, catching herself with her spear before she hit the ground. "Can you teach me those words to see better?"

Ty stopped. "That's a good idea." He looked down at the bracelet Nyalis had given her, noticing she was once again wearing her bonding bracelet on her upper arm. He tried to ignore it. "Reach for your magic and repeat after me. Ru'kasha Kor."

"How do I reach for my magic?" she asked.

Ty scratched the top of his knit cap. He'd never been asked that before. How could he explain what just came naturally to him? What was it that he did? "You need to . . . It's like . . ."

"It's like looking inside yourself," Breen said. "If something doesn't feel right, you think about what it is that feels off. You determine where the discomfort is, so you know what you need to do to fix it. You can feel magic as well. It warms your insides, somewhere here," he said, rubbing at a spot between his gut and chest.

"And the more you use it," Ty said, "the easier it becomes. Pretty soon you won't even think about it—the magic will just be there when you need it."

Narendi nodded, taking in what they were saying. She paused a moment, her expression hardening as her brows lowered in concentration. After a long moment, she finally looked down at the same spot Breen had pointed and shook her head. "I do not think it works."

Ty hmphed. "How do you feel the water? When you touched the snow yesterday, what did you do then?"

"I imagined what it would feel like to reach down and stick my hands in it."

"Okay. Then do the same now." He looked around. "Can you think about the water at the edge there?" he asked, pointing at some reeds growing beside the pathway. "Imagine sticking just one finger in and swirling it." He didn't want her thinking about sticking her whole hand in like she had with the snow.

Last thing they needed was for her to—

All of the water along the entire front of the pathway for at least ten paces in either direction suddenly burst into the air, drenching them all in sludge. Ty gagged as he fought to wipe the horrid-smelling slime and muck from his face, feeling rather thankful he had kept his mouth closed.

"Ah, yuck! This stuff stinks worse than you in the privy after a bowl of black beans," Kraea said.

Ty ignored her and shook as much of the bog from his clothes as possible, then turned and stared out across the water, hoping that her attempt at reaching her magic hadn't caught the attention of one of the marsh monsters. After a minute with no further movement in the water, Ty breathed a small sigh of relief and turned. "I think perhaps giving you that crystal might have been a bit premature on Nyalis's part." He tried once more to wipe the sludge from his face. The smell had his stomach turning. "Maybe we should forgo teaching you how to see at night. You try calling up night sight and you might end up blinding yourself."

"Or us," Breen said, trying his best to clean the swamp water from his bow.

She wiped her face. "Sorry. I do not know why my magic does this."

Ty walked over to the edge of the pathway, where the reeds had been growing before Narendi blew them all over the place, and knelt down to scoop up a handful of water to clean some of the mire from his face. He'd barely gotten his face wet when he spotted ripples in the water farther out, moving in his direction. He stopped and looked up, staring out at the deeper part of the swamp. The water was stirring.

He raised his hand. "Shhh."

The others joined him at the edge.

"What is it?" Narendi whispered.

The ripples began to grow in number and size. Ty felt the hairs on his arms rising. "We've got to get out of here."

Chapter 29 | Ty

DARK TENTACLES BURST from the water just offshore and sent Ty and the others stumbling backward, grabbing for their weapons. In a way, the long snakelike arms reminded Ty of the ones they'd fought in the Aero'set arboretum, except these were attached to a giant eel-like creature large enough to take down a razorback.

"Run!" Ty had barely gotten the word out when the creature's tentacles smashed down across the narrow path in front of them, blocking their escape. He unleashed a torrent of fire into the closest, melting two of the slimy arms in half. A loud screeching hiss broke from the water deeper out, where the mist and fog were keeping everything concealed. Breen nocked an arrow and took aim before Ty had a chance to even turn. Beside him, Narendi and Kraea held themselves at the ready. Ty felt a bit of anxious excitement from Kraea.

Another arm broke from the water, swiping both Breen and Narendi aside. Kraea was immediately on top of the arm, ripping it apart with her fangs and claws while striking at it with the short horns on her tail. The tentacle flung her to the side and recoiled back into the water. Kraea hit the mud and nearly slid into the dark water on the other side of the path, but she managed to dig in with her claws to keep from going completely over.

Ty conjured one of his shields and threw it around his brother just as another arm smashed into Breen from the side. The force was enough to knock both Ty and Breen off their feet.

"I lost the shield!" Ty said.

Breen immediately turned, still on his knees, and nocked the next non-magic arrow, burying it into the creature's arm.

Narendi stabbed the tentacle with her spear, giving Ty and Breen a chance to get back to their feet. Ty sent another torrent of flame into it, shearing it off near the edge of the water just before it had wrapped around her. The long slimy tentacle landed on her and began to flop around. She threw it off and scrambled back to her feet as a dozen more tentacles broke from the water.

Ty's heart dropped, and he looked at Breen. There was no way they could fight them all off. He could see the same thought in his brother's eyes.

Ty unleashed several volleys at once, shearing off two or three of its arms, but it wasn't going to be enough. Panicking, he turned his magic to the water and sent up several tentacles of his own, similar to the ones he had created in the underground lake, except these water tentacles had hands on the ends. The hands grabbed at the marsh monster's arms and fought to hold them back, but there were too many for Ty to stop them all. He didn't have the ability to conjure that many arms. Where was Gilly when he needed him? The little dwarf could have probably sucked the creature back under or pushed it deeper into the swamp.

Kraea shrieked somewhere on Ty's right, and his concentration faltered. One of the larger arms had wrapped around her, and she was being lifted into the air.

"Get this thing off me!"

"Hold on! I'm coming!" Ty released his hold on the water, and his hands ignited in blue flame. He lashed out, sending a salvo at the creature's arm. It hit, but the tentacle was much bigger than the others, and his fire didn't burn all the way through. The arm pulled Kraea away from them and out over the water before Ty could release another volley.

Ty screamed at the creature and gathered the wind, slamming it down into the water, trying to spear the tentacle. The burst of air hit the fog and scattered it off the surface, leaving the marsh ahead freely visible. Ty shuddered as the top of the eel-like creature's head rose above the surface.

"What is that?" Breen shouted and released another arrow. It buried itself to the fletching in the top of the monster's head but did little to slow it.

Ty delved into his magic once more and wished once again that he knew more about it. He grabbed hold of the water and conjured a giant hand to grab the creature. He conjured another one and began to beat on the monster's side, but it wasn't causing enough damage to hold it back. Kraea screamed for Ty to do something as she bit down and clawed at the slimy tentacle, fighting to break free before she reached the creature's opening mouth.

"I can't stop it!" Ty shouted.

Beside him, Narendi threw down her spear and rushed to the edge of the water and drove both fists deep inside. The entire swamp exploded, water shooting twenty feet in the air, trees coming up by their roots. The marsh monster wailed as it was sent flying into the air with everything else, its tentacles flailing. It was even uglier than Ty had imagined, with just as many tentacles under the water as above. The arm holding Kraea loosened, and she was thrown free, landing in a pile of bog off the path.

She scrambled for safety. Ty gathered the wind and hardened it over the sludge where she was, giving her something sturdy to run across instead of sinking into the mire.

The swamp creature landed back in the water and immediately disappeared beneath the surface as limbs and vines and parts of trees came raining down on top of them. Ty raised a second shield over their heads, and Kraea barely made it underneath before the worst of it hit.

They waited for some time before Ty finally got up the nerve to lower the shield and come out. By the time he did, the marsh had been completely upended, at least the part they could see. The path was blocked on all sides by trees and fallen limbs and tangled vines. What had been merely an annoying smell before was now an unbearable stench as everything, including themselves, was covered in freshly churned stagnation.

"What just happened?" Breen asked, wiping black sludge from his face.

Narendi looked down at her hands. "You told me to feel the water."

Ty stared out at what remained of that part of the swamp and shook his head. "First of all, thank you for saving our lives. I'm not exactly sure how you did it, but I'm glad you did."

"Aye," Breen said, gawking at the destruction.

"Second, I think it might be time to take that bracelet off."

He didn't have to tell her twice. Narendi's hands were still shaking from the aftermath as she quickly pulled the crystal-encased jewelry off her arm and shoved it into her pack. She gave him a sharp look. "You are the one who told me to do it."

Ty nodded. "Well, I think we can all agree that I'm not exactly the most qualified teacher. I don't know what Nyalis was thinking. I'm terrible at this."

"Tell Narendi I said thank you," Kraea said as she checked herself for injuries.

Ty turned to Narendi. "Oh, and Kraea says to say thank you for saving her life."

Narendi smiled. "You are most welcome." She started to stand but then faltered, and Ty quickly grabbed her with the wind. "That takes a lot out of you, doesn't it?"

Ty smiled. "I think that's why Nyalis has been so insistent on our training. He wants to get us strong enough to handle it."

Breen gathered up his sword and bow and then helped Narendi pull her spear out from under one of the large mushroom-covered limbs blocking the path behind them. "We need to keep going. We've still got a long way to go, and to be honest, at this rate, I don't see us getting through before dark."

Ty looked up on instinct to see the placement of the sun but quickly realized it was a wasted effort, as the fog and copious overhang blocked all sight of the sky. Breen was right, though. At the speed they were going, they probably wouldn't get through until the next morning.

After taking a moment to check his own pack, Ty took one final look around the damage and then started climbing over the piles of trees blocking their way. His clothes were soaked, which had his hands shivering as he climbed through the debris left from Narendi's untrained magic. He still couldn't believe the amount of power she had unleashed without even meaning to do so. Now, if she could only learn to control it. He wondered if Gilly could help with that.

Once they reached a safe distance, Ty decided to attempt Nyalis's trick to dry their clothes. He lit Breen's torch with his blue flames and then gathered a small breeze and used it to move the heat around them. He even set up a shield overtop to keep the heat in while it circulated. It took a while, but the fire did its job, and pretty soon they were warm enough to keep going.

Ty kept them to a manageable pace as they worked to get as far from the marsh monster as possible, at least as manageable a pace as the fog would allow. He kept a slow stream of magic moving in front of him, using the wind to keep the haze pushed aside. He had no idea how far they had gone since the attack, but it felt like several hours. The haze ahead was thickening, and by the time they reached it, more fog had rolled in behind them, cutting them completely off from the rest of the marsh.

"I'm really getting tired of this stuff." Ty raised his hands once more, but before he could gather enough wind to force the fog off the trail, Breen touched his shoulder. Ty turned. His brother had his finger to his lips and was pointing back down the trail behind them, which was now completely covered in haze.

Ty cocked his head, listening for whatever it was that had Breen on edge. He looked at Kraea, who was standing closest to the fog. *"Do you hear or smell anything?"*

"There's something . . ."

A loud hiss broke through the fog, and Ty's hands immediately ignited in flame. Kraea backed away. Ty knew that sound all too well. Razorback. He'd faced this creature more than once. Another shrill broke through the fog, and everyone bunched together, bow and spear and flame at the ready. Kraea stood next to Ty, teeth bared.

"These things are strong and won't go down easy," Ty said. "Get ready to jump out of the way if it charges. And watch out for its tail." Ty snuffed out the flame in one hand and reached for the wind, hoping to use it as a battering ram to knock the razorback into the swamp if it came at them.

Another cry sounded, this one closer. It must have picked up their scent. The ground began to shake, but all they could do was stare helplessly at the wall of mist in front of them.

"Where is it?" Breen asked.

Ty started to use some of the wind to move the haze, but just as soon as he did, the giant razorback tore through the veil, and he gasped. It was even bigger than the one the marsh monster had eaten.

"What is that?" Kraea shrilled.

Ty sent a spear of blue flames straight for the creature's chest. Beside him, Breen's bow buzzed, and an arrow flew past. Both fire and arrow ricocheted to the left, missing the creature entirely, as the razorback came to an abrupt halt about ten feet in front of them.

"Stop trying to kill my ride!" a familiar voice shouted, and Douina peered around the giant lizard's head. She clicked her tongue, and the creature turned sideways, far enough for her to see them. She was sitting in a saddle attached to the razorback's lower neck, between two protruding spikes.

Ty was speechless. Apparently so were the others, as no one said a word, merely staring at the bizarre sight. The razorback's long, forked tongue shot out, and it turned its head to look down at Kraea. Kraea quickly shuffled behind Ty and as far from the muscular creature as possible.

Douina reached her hand into the air, and several thick vines lowered from the surrounding trees. They gently wrapped around her and lifted her off the razorback and into the air, and she was carefully lowered down onto the path in front of them. It was a familiar sight. The first time Ty had come across Douina, she had taken him on a ride through the trees as well. Of course, it hadn't been as pleasant an experience, since those same vines had held him out over one of the marsh monster's open jaws.

Ty stared at the elder witch. "Why are you here?"

"Whenever there is a disturbance in the marsh, Abinayu sends me to investigate. And from what I saw back there, it was more than just a disturbance. Swamp looks like the Creator scooped out a piece with his hand and flung it in the air."

Ty, Breen, and even Kraea, turned and looked at Narendi.

She shrunk back. "Sorry. It was an accident."

Douina looked at Narendi as well. "That is quite the accident. If I'd known you were prone to accidents like that, I would have had you sleeping outside last night." She crossed her arms. "Someone want to explain why you four look like you stopped to take a dip in one of the bog holes?"

Ty told her of their encounter with the marsh monster and Narendi's unexpected use of magic to save them.

Douina shook her head with a sigh. "Gather your things. Nobis and I will take you the rest of the way, if for no other reason than to make sure you don't destroy the rest of the marsh on your way out."

Ty looked around. "Who's Nobis?"

Douina reached back and patted one of the razorback's thick, scaly legs. "This is Nobis." As though on cue, the razorback leaned its head back and released an ear-piercing shrill that had them all raising their weapons.

Ty watched the creature, especially its spiked tail. "You named him Nobis?"

"It means *fog* in the old tongue," she said, "or more accurately *thick fog*. I thought it appropriate." Douina raised her hand once more, and the vines reached down and lifted her back up into the saddle. "Let's be on our way, shall we?" With that, she clicked her tongue, and the razorback turned, waiting on the four of them to start moving.

Ty remained in front, using his magic to keep the way ahead clear as they pressed forward. Kraea walked alongside him, not wanting to linger near the back where she had been, since that was where Nobis was. In fact, Narendi and Breen were pressed quite close as well, none of them wanting to get within striking distance of the giant lizard.

It was rather nerve-racking having the razorback stalking behind them, each step shaking the ground, knowing that at any minute it could snatch one of them up in its powerful jaws. Ty hoped Douina had full control over the creature. The rest of their trip was made in silence, and they stopped only to rest their feet or test the ground to make sure the way ahead was stable. Ty had twisted his leg on his first trip by stepping in a bog hole. He didn't wish to repeat the experience.

They ate a quick meal of dried meat. Unfortunately, their packs had been thoroughly drenched during their encounter with the marsh monster, leaving their biscuits rather on the pasty side, so they were forced to discard them altogether and leave it for the scavengers.

Thankfully, Ty's pack had proven the driest of the lot, which he was grateful for, considering he was the one carrying the book Nyalis had given him for Adarra. During their meal, he took the book out to inspect it. The leather binding was a little damp, but the pages seemed crisp and the ink unsmeared.

The marsh continued to darken as the day wore on, and night crept up on them like an owl on a field mouse. Before they knew it, Ty was resorting to his night sight to keep his footing.

"Aha!"

Ty startled and turned to find Douina pointing straight ahead. "It appears we have found our exit."

Sure enough, just ahead, the pathway widened, and the dark waters of Reed Marsh fell behind. Ty recognized the spot where Nyalis had parted ways with him months earlier. It almost seemed a lifetime ago. So much had happened since then. He remembered how scared he had been when Nyalis had told him that he was to enter the marsh alone.

Seeing the place had him all the more excited. Besides leaving the marsh behind, it also meant they were that much closer to home. He had half a mind to keep going, just for the thought of being able to hug his father and sister once more, not to mention being able to lie in his own bed. His quarters in Aero'set were far grander than the small bedroom he and his brother shared, but there was something about their little cottage that lent itself to a peaceful night's rest, no doubt due to the familiarity.

"Where will I sleep?" Kraea asked, reading his thoughts.

Ty pursed his lips. *"In the barn with the rest of the animals, I imagine."*

Kraea growled at him, and he laughed. She knew he was joking, but it didn't stop him from having a poke at her. It certainly never stopped her.

"I will say my goodbyes, then," Douina said. "I gather you can find your way home from here?"

"We can," Ty said, staring up at the monstrous razorback. "Thank you for the escort."

She smiled down at him. "It was our pleasure." She patted Nobis's neck. "I hope that your next visit will be less . . ." She looked at Narendi. ". . . eventful."

Narendi shied away with an embarrassed smile.

"We will do our best to leave the marsh as intact as we can," Ty said.

Douina nodded. "I will see you on your return, then. The next full moon, is it?"

Ty nodded.

"Very well, I will be sure to have a kettle of tea on for when you arrive." She gave them each a quick looking-over, then clicked her tongue, and Nobis spun about. His spiked tail swung wide, forcing Ty and the others to hop back or risk getting hit. She clicked her tongue again. "Forward." Nobis lumbered down the narrow path leading back into the marsh, and the two disappeared within the surrounding mist.

"Well, that was . . ." Breen trailed off as he stared at the shroud of fog behind them. "Not looking forward to going back through there in a couple of weeks."

Ty exhaled slowly. "Me either."

"We probably should set up camp here," Breen said, studying the small patch of open ground between the taller reeds. "I don't really remember much in the way of places to sleep along the northeast side of the marsh. Do you?"

Ty shook his head. "There's a spot me and Nyalis stopped at with some larger rocks, but nothing open enough to sleep on." He looked around and shrugged. "I guess here is as good a place as any. We'll just need to rotate a watch tonight."

The others agreed, and Breen volunteered to go first.

They ate another quick meal of more dried meat and fruit, just enough to squelch any hunger pains, while Kraea headed into the reeds and didn't return until she had caught a couple of small conies. She swallowed them down fairly quickly, since neither had much meat on their bones, leaving her stomach to growl most of the night.

The morning arrived with the speed of one of Breen's arrows, and by the time Ty had nodded off from his turn at watch, he found himself waking to the feeling of something touching his cheek. He opened his eyes, thinking it was Kraea licking his face like she did when she wanted him up sooner, and found Narendi. He ignored the kiss and sat up to find Kraea and Breen kneeling at the edge of the clearing, studying the path east toward home.

"Come," Narendi said. "It is time we go."

Ty gathered his things, and after a quick breakfast of the remaining dried fruit and nuts, they started down the trail. The sun was up, but the trees were still too dense to see it, leaving them to judge time by their own intuition and the growling of their stomachs. They passed the pile of rocks Ty and Nyalis had rested on during his first visit but continued on without stopping, hoping to make the rest of the journey in a single day. If Nyalis could do it at whatever ancient age he was, then the four of them should have no problem.

It was nearing the end of the afternoon when they finally left the last of the swamp behind. The farther east they went, the less gnarled the trees became, melding to natural hardwoods. The ground stiffened, no longer squishing under their feet, as the snow became more visible in the trees and across the ground. It was strange how the farther they moved from the marsh, the colder it got, especially when the limbs overhead spread until they could see the sun's rays. The smell of mire and death was replaced so slowly that it took a while for Ty to even realize he was no longer having to breathe from his mouth.

Birds once again chirped and sang as tree rats raced up and down the bark. The forest was alive with life, and it was a welcome sight. By late afternoon, they reached the trailhead leading south to the East River. The northern path led to what had been Dorbin's cabin and the arachnobes' feeding ground.

"You're thinking about Dorbin, aren't you?"

Ty looked at his brother and nodded. "I was wondering if anyone gave him a proper burial."

Breen rubbed his beard. "Reckon there isn't much left to bury. Scavengers would have fed on the remains."

"Probably so." Pushing the thought aside, Ty turned his attention back toward home and started south down the trail, their pace increasing the closer they got to the river. It wasn't an hour later before Ty caught the first sounds of water ahead. His heart pounding as he and Breen sprinted through the brush to reach it, leaving Narendi and Kraea to catch up.

Ty skidded to a stop at the edge of the river, grinning from ear to ear as he stared out across the bluish-green water that rippled as it churned over the large submerged rocks at the bottom. He knew it all too well, having spent his childhood swimming in this very spot. The water looked to be up and was sure to be ice cold, making any notion of swimming across out of the question. In fact, there was still some ice along the outer edges, up against the bank where the current was weakest.

"How do we get across?" Narendi asked as she and Kraea joined them at the water's edge.

Ty looked across the water to the other side. "That's a good question."

Chapter 30 | Ty

THERE'S OUR BOAT," Ty said, pointing to a snow-covered lump in the brush on the far side of the river.

"And how are we going to get the boat over here?" Breen asked.

Narendi took a step toward the water. "I could—"

"No!" both brothers shouted at the same time.

Kraea laughed.

Ty smiled. "I think perhaps it would be best if I did it."

"What are you going to do?" Breen asked.

Ty thought back to what Nyalis had done, but there was no way he could repeat it. The wizard had caused thousands of sprouts to poke up out of the ground and carry the boat down to the water. Ty remembered how mesmerized he'd been watching it. He stared at the far shore. If he could get the boat down to the river, he believed he could get it across, using the water as a guide, but how was he going to get—

"Why not make a bridge?"

Ty looked at Kraea. "What do you mean?"

"You can harden the air to make a shield. Why not use it to make a bridge the

same way you did to help me out of the bog?"

"Yeah, but that was something simple, just steps over the mud. This would be across the entire river."

"What are you two talking about?" Breen asked. Narendi stared at the two of them curiously.

"Kraea is suggesting I make a bridge of hardened air and lay it across the water for us to use to get to the other side."

"You mean like the way the bulradoer diverted the avalanche?" Breen asked.

Ty pursed his lips. "I'd forgotten about that. But yes, I guess it would be something similar."

"Can you?" Breen looked at the river. "It took half a dozen of their wielders to create the one at Wellhollow."

Ty shrugged. "I don't know. I fashioned a smaller one to help Kraea out of the marsh, but nothing as big as this."

"Why not do what Gilly does and simply turn the water to ice for us to walk across?"

Ty shook his head. "I don't know how. And judging by the speed of that current, it might be safer for me to try the bridge. Except I don't think I could secure something that big and keep it from shifting or tipping."

Breen's face brightened. "What about something smaller? Something you could use your magic glue with." He thought a moment. "Like a hook. You could harden the air to make a thin pole hook, then attach it to the boat with some of your magic glue, and we could pull it down to the water that way."

Ty's head lifted. That was actually a good idea. He looked at the snow-covered lump on the other embankment. "That could work." He hadn't considered something as simple as lassoing the boat. He'd never tried to create a specific shape like that before with hardened air, only flat surfaces for shielding or fists of air for attacking. It definitely had to be safer than building an entire bridge for them to walk on or turning part of the East River to ice.

Reaching out with his magic, he pictured a long pole in his mind as he gathered the wind to him, imagining as he did the air hardening around the pole. He could feel it in his hands as it began to take shape, and he tightened his fingers around the end, excited by the fact that it seemed to be working.

His mind drifted momentarily as he thought of all the other ways this type of magic could be useful—like prodding at a hornet's nest in a tree from a safe distance—but as soon as his thoughts shifted, the pole dissolved in his hands, and he was forced to start again.

This time, with his focus under control, he shaped the air, grabbing hold of the end. Much like his shields, the pole didn't have any weight to it, and he found that he could stretch it across the entire river without it overpowering him. Carefully, he lifted the pole slightly up as he worked to extend the end over the side of the boat. It was hard to see, but not as hard as a typical shield. It wasn't the same as looking through a flat piece of glass, more like the neck end of a bottle.

"Almost there," his brother said, trying to be encouraging as everyone watched anxiously from the waterline.

"More to the left," Narendi said.

"No, right," Kraea countered.

Ty ground his teeth. "Stop helping." He fought to keep control of the very long pole and slowly lowered it down on top of the snow-packed mound.

"You got it," Breen said, clapping Ty on the back excitedly, nearly causing Ty to lose his grip. "Now just use your magic glue stuff and pull it down to the water."

Ty wanted to roll his eyes, but he was too busy concentrating on sealing the pole to the boat. Once he had the pole glued to the front, he tested it by giving it a firm tug. It seemed to be holding. Now for the easy part—dragging it down to the water. He set his feet and pulled. It didn't budge. He tried again. This time the boat rocked, sending some of the snow falling to the side, but still, it was no closer to the water than when he'd started. "I think I'm going to need some help."

Breen and Narendi moved behind him, and Ty extended the rod far enough for each of them to grab hold. When he gave the signal, they all pulled. This time the boat did more than shift; it slid forward through the snow. Their father must have secured the tarp covering it to the ground, because the boat slid out from under it as they moved it toward the water.

Ty smiled. It was working. Using the wind, he pressed it against the sides of the boat like two invisible bookends to keep it upright as they maneuvered it down into the water. "I think I can get it from here," he said, and released his hold on the pole and let the hardened air dissipate in his hands.

This time he reached out to the river, and the water rose on either side of the boat, forming two hands to guide it forward. It took a bit of time for Ty to maintain his grip on the magic while working to keep the boat from tipping.

"How am I supposed to fit in there?" Kraea asked.

"We'll have to make two trips, I guess," Ty said. He looked at Breen and Narendi. "Kraea was wondering how she was going to fit in the boat."

Breen nodded. "Hadn't thought of that. We can go across first, and then you can send the boat back for Kraea."

Kraea grumbled, clearly not liking the thought of going across alone, but there was no other way to fit her in the boat with the rest of them. She seemed to be getting bigger by the week. Her head now reached as high as Ty's shoulders.

"It'll be fine," Ty said to her. "I won't let anything happen."

She huffed. *"You'll regret it if you do."*

Ty tossed his pack in the boat along with the others and climbed in, waiting for Kraea to help push them offshore. Breen used the boat's one paddle to steer, while Ty used the water to propel them forward. Ty gripped the sides of the boat as he concentrated his magic toward the back, forcing the boat to continue moving in the right direction. Only once did the boat veer, but Breen was able to right it quickly enough. Pretty soon they were stepping out on the other side, and Ty was sending the boat back across for Kraea, who was waiting nervously on the north embankment.

Keeping the hardened bookends in place on the sides of the boat and using the water to push it forward, Ty managed to maneuver it next to the shoreline, looking for a spot that would keep it as level as possible to give Kraea an easier way to get in. She crawled in carefully. The boat shifted side to side momentarily from her weight as she stepped over the two seats. Ty managed to keep it upright, using the water's pressure on either side. Kraea sprawled across the seats, her tail hanging over the side but out of the water. Her nose touched the front of the boat as she peeked up over the sides to look at Ty.

"Don't you tip me," she said. *"You drop me in the water and I'll . . . I'll keep you up every night for a week. You know I can."*

"I'm not going to drop you," Ty said as he reached into the water with his magic. He reformed the two hands he'd used before, one on either side. It was a little easier than trying to juggle both voda and vanti magic. Though, he had to admit, he was getting better at both.

Kraea yelped as the boat suddenly jerked forward. *"I'm warning you!"*

"I heard you the first time."

Ty could feel Kraea's unease as he slowly moved the boat away from the calm water near the embankment and out into the river itself.

"You're doing fine," Narendi shouted to Kraea, trying to calm her nerves.

"I'll be doing a whole lot better when I get out of this boat."

Ty smiled. "Oh, you want out of the boat? I can help with that." The watery hand on the right jostled the side of the boat, and Kraea roared.

"I'll eat you!"

Ty chuckled.

"You think that wise?" Breen asked.

"Probably not. But it's awfully funny." Ty refocused his efforts on the boat, which was now about halfway across. "Quit your complaining. I told you I won't let you—"

"What's that?" Narendi asked, and Ty turned to see the front end of a small ship rounding the bend just west of them. It was heading directly for them.

"Drat!"

"What's going on? Why have we stopped?" Kraea poked her head up over the side and growled when she saw the ship heading straight for her. *"Get me out of here!"*

The riverboat was still far enough away that they probably couldn't see Kraea, but by the time he could manage to get her to shore, they would be able to. And if he pushed the boat faster, he risked losing control and tipping her into the river. If that happened, there'd be no way of hiding her then. Not to mention, she'd promised to eat him if he did.

Ty turned, looking for something to use to hide her instead, and spotted the canvas. He hardened some wind around it and yanked it into the air. Thankfully, the snow fell off, and along with it, the added weight. He quickly floated it out over the river, keeping it as close to the water as possible in hopes that the riverboat was still far enough away to notice. He then raised it up over the side.

"What are you doing?" Kraea asked.

"Quiet. I'm trying to hide you from those on board." He draped the canvas over the top. *"Pull your tail in."*

Kraea's tail disappeared underneath the coverlet, and Ty lowered the watery hands below the sides of the boat so they wouldn't be as noticeable. He glanced over his shoulder at Breen and Narendi. "Pretend like you are pulling the boat across with a rope."

"But there is no rope," Narendi said.

"That's why I said *pretend*! Hopefully, the soldiers won't notice."

Both Breen and Narendi moved behind Ty and began to draw in their imaginary rope. Ty raised his hands as well, more to concentrate on the magic than for the looks of holding something. He kept the boat moving as fast as he dared without taking the chance of tipping. He couldn't force it to move too quickly, or it would look suspicious.

The small ship was moving upstream at a very fast pace, as the men worked their oars in perfect synchronization. Several had already spotted them and had moved to the side of the ship to take a look.

"Don't move, Kraea." Her boat was only twenty feet offshore, but the riverboat was close enough now that they had to stop pulling their pretend rope and simply let the current do the rest.

Ty kept Kraea's boat moving. It was nearly there, but so was the ship and the men staring over the side at them. Ty struggled to think of something he could do to divert their attention. Frantically, he sent a fist of water careening into the back of the ship. The riverboat shook so hard that a couple of the men nearly fell over the rail as others scrambled to see what they'd hit.

"Did you see that?" Breen asked.

Ty looked up. "What?"

"I think those men were wearing uniforms under their coats."

Ty stared at the men on board as they scrambled to the other side of the ship. "I don't see anything."

"I only saw it when those two nearly went over."

"What kind of uniforms were they wearing?" Ty asked.

"Bristonian, I think. I saw blue and white."

"Why would Bristonian soldiers be heading up the East River here?"

"Maybe Overlord Meyrose is holding another meeting with Overlord Barl."

Ty stared at the ship as it began to pass. Most of the men had their hoods pulled up, so he couldn't really see their faces. However, the man on the top deck shouting out orders had his hood down, which was surprising since his head was bald. He was average height and wore a patch over his left eye.

"Quit looking at that ship and get me out of here!"

"Hurry," Ty said to the others, moving down to the edge of the water. "Help me get the boat up on land."

Breen and Narendi ran down to help pull the boat up as far as they could, which wasn't very far considering how heavy Kraea was. They did manage to get the nose out of the water and far enough to ensure it didn't get sucked back in. *"Don't move, Kraea,"* Ty said as he worked to keep the canvas over the boat. *"I'll let you know when you can come out."*

Ty and the others watched from the shore as the riverboat passed by. He didn't see any blue-and-white uniforms, but that didn't mean they weren't there under the men's thick coats. Everyone aboard had left off their inspection of the three of them and had now firmly set their attention on the water around their boat as they scoured for perceived rocks. One of the men on the upper deck was shouting out orders, and the rest scrambled to obey. Soon enough, the ship had moved beyond them and was swiftly making its way upriver toward Easthaven.

"That was a close one," Breen said. "Strange to see a ship of Bristonian soldiers this close to Easthaven."

"Can I come out now?" Kraea asked.

"Yes, you can come out now." Ty pulled back the canvas, and Kraea nearly knocked him over trying to get out of the boat and back on land.

"I hate water!" Kraea said. *"And I hate this cold!"* She looked at Ty. *"And I'm starting to hate you."*

"So, just another typical day then, huh?" He smiled, and she stalked off up the trail as Ty and the other two pulled the boat back up to its typical resting place and covered it with the canvas. Ty hefted his pack over his shoulder and then paused long enough to grin at Breen.

"What?"

"We're close enough to almost smell the fire from the chimney."

Breen smiled. "Let's go."

The sun had already set in the sky, and the once-colorful clouds were beginning to darken as they broke from the woods behind their homestead. Ty and Breen stopped just shy of the small bridge behind the house. Ty's hands were shaking as he caught his first glimpse of their family's cottage. Turning, he spotted his mother's resting place beside the large oak just behind the iced-over creek, and tears flooded his eyes.

Breen wrapped his arm around Ty's shoulder. "We did it."

"This is your dwelling?" Narendi asked, looking at the snow-covered roof of the cottage across the way. "It is very nice."

"Not much to look at," Kraea said with a snort.

"It might not be Aero'set," Ty said, "but it's home."

They crossed the bridge and started around the side of the house. The doors to the barn were shut.

"I don't see a fire in the hearth," Breen said with a hint of concern as he stared up at the main chimney. "A bit strange for this late in the day."

Ty pulled up short before heading down the walk to the front door. His brother was right. "There are no lights on inside. I figured Adarra would be in the middle of preparing supper by now." He drew his sword and looked at Breen. His brother was already nocking an arrow as Narendi unhooked her spear.

"What's going on?" Kraea asked. *"Are you trying to surprise your family or scare them to death?"*

"I'm being cautious," Ty said as he started for the front door. He didn't call on his flames in case there was someone around who shouldn't see. Now that they were back home, he was going to have to go back to being careful of his use of magic, back to keeping it hidden.

They reached the front door, and Ty turned the handle. "Ru'kasha Kor." His brother called up his night sight as well, and Ty pushed the door open with his foot. Breen rushed in first, his bow swinging right, then left around the front room. Ty followed him in.

The front room and kitchen were bright enough to see with the aid of their night sight, and Ty sent one of his magical webs through the rest of the house. He tapped his brother on the shoulder. "There's no one here. I would feel it if there were."

"Should have done that from outside," Breen said.

"Sorry, didn't think about it."

They lowered their weapons, Narendi being the last to do so, and Ty and Breen did a quick visual search of the rest of the house. Sure enough, there was no one there.

"Where is everyone?" Ty asked, finally returning to the front room, where Narendi and Kraea stood waiting. Kraea walked over to the hearth and looked inside.

"Embers are cold. Hasn't been used in some time."

Ty joined her and looked inside. "She's right. There hasn't been a fire here in at least a day or two."

"And Adarra's room is a mess," Breen added.

Ty hmphed. "How's that strange?"

"It's messier than normal. Looks like half her stuff is missing, including her books." Breen headed for the front door.

"Where are you going?" Ty asked.

"To check the barn."

Ty headed out with him. Narendi and Kraea did as well, and they all trekked across the snow-packed trail to the front of the barn. The footprints clearly said that someone had been there since the last snowfall. They reached the front doors, and Breen pulled back the bracer and opened the left one.

A loud whinny came from the back stall when Ty walked in. "Waddle!" Ty rushed to the back and opened the stall to get to his horse. Waddle nuzzled him when he did. "I missed you too."

"I don't ever see you doing that for me," Kraea grumbled.

"I also don't sit on your back."

"Looks like Thistle and Your Highness are missing," Breen said. "Adarra and Father must still be in town."

Ty turned. "Should we wait on them?"

"Let's go back to the house and make a fire and wait for them there," Kraea

suggested.

"But it doesn't look like anyone has been here in a day or two," Breen said. "Acorn's trough is nearly empty. Perhaps we should ride into town and see if we can find them."

"But what about my fire idea?" Kraea asked.

Ty chuckled. "I guess you'll have to wait on the fire."

Kraea blew out her lips. *"But I thought you said I couldn't go into town? And don't get any ideas of telling me to wait in this freezing, smelly place. I'm not a horse."*

"Fine," Ty said. "I'll start a fire in the house, and you can sleep in there until we get back."

Breen frowned. "That might not be the best idea. What happens if we don't find Father in town, and he or Adarra arrives home before we do and finds a draakar sleeping in the front room?"

Ty frowned as well. "Good point."

"Unlike you," Breen said, "they can't hear her. One growl and Father will kill her."

Kraea puffed out her chest. *"I'd like to see him try."*

Ty shook his head. "No, you wouldn't. Where do you think Breen got his gift of aim from?"

"Fine," Kraea grouched. *"I'll stay in the barn."* She looked up. *"The loft should be safe enough, yes?"*

Ty looked up at the second-floor overhang where they stored the hay. "Should be fine. I don't see why anyone would be searching up there this late in the evening."

"So," Breen said from Acorn's stall as he rubbed his horse's ears, "we are decided, then?"

Ty looked at Narendi, and she nodded. "I guess so. Unless you have a better idea."

Kraea cleared her throat.

"No," Ty said. "Building a fire and sleeping in the front room is not a better idea."

Kraea stuck her long tongue out at him.

Breen glanced around the empty barn. "Perhaps they are staying with the overlord for a few days. Might be a reason for the way Adarra's room looks, or why most of her books seem to be missing. Not sure why she feels she would need to carry them with her, though. They're all in her head."

Ty chuckled. "You know how she is with her books. Treats them like they're her own children." Ty shuddered. "Can't imagine Adarra with children."

"I think she'd make a good mother," Breen argued, then pointed to his head. "She'll certainly have the know-how."

Ty couldn't argue there. His sister had more information swimming around in her skull than most scholars who'd dedicated their lives to the pursuit of knowledge.

Ty led Waddle out of his stall and began saddling him. By the time they finished and had the horses outside and ready to go, the first of the stars were beginning to shine through.

"I forgot something," Ty said and ran back to the house. He found his carry bag on the sofa and grabbed Nyalis's book. What better way to greet his sister than with something new to read? Especially when it came from a wizard. He left the house and joined the others at the barn. Climbing up onto Waddle, he reached down and helped Narendi up behind him, and they turned and started down the drive for the road.

They kept the pace slow, not wanting to risk injuring the horses in the dark or them getting sick from a hard ride through freezing night air. Narendi clung to Ty as they bounced along. Thankfully the earlier afternoon wind had dissipated. What little of the moon was visible reflected off the fallen snow, brightening the road ahead.

They skirted the East Hill Orchard with its sad-looking fruit trees—a copse of gangly, leafless branches with nothing but snow to cover their nakedness. Though Ty thought they didn't look much better in the spring and summer either. From there, they continued north until cresting a final rise and spotting the lights of the city in the distance. Ty's heart began to pound as they made their way down to the East Bridge. The city had never looked so good, or so small.

Stopping at the foot of the bridge, Ty was surprised by how trivial it seemed. It had always been so impressive growing up, all that stonework spanning the entire length of the East River. But after having traveled across the entire known world and beyond and having borne witness to such architectural wonders as Aero'set, poor little Easthaven just didn't seem to compare.

"Looks smaller somehow, doesn't it?" Breen said, as if reading Ty's mind.

Ty nodded. "Yet I wouldn't trade it for a dozen Aero'sets." He looked over at Breen. "Well, maybe a dozen."

Breen nodded with a smile.

"This is your people?" Narendi asked, staring over the bridge at all the homes fronting the waterway and beyond.

"This is our people," Ty echoed. "The city where we grew up. What do you think?"

"I think I would like to see more."

Apart from Aero'set, the town of Wellhollow was the first real city Narendi had seen. Ty couldn't wait to show it to her during the daytime, to take her to all the best places. And he knew right where he wanted to start. First thing in the morning, he'd take her to Reloria's Sweet Shop for one of her chocolate-glazed sweet rolls. Peyla would always send over fresh bread from her bakery around the corner, and Reloria would top each with various types of glazes, each morning with something new, depending on her mood.

Ty's excitement faltered, however, when he pictured him and Narendi sitting there stuffing their faces and Lyessa walking in. Suddenly his heart was beating for a different reason. The Sweet Shop would have to wait. He couldn't risk showing Narendi around until after he'd had a chance to explain to Lyessa why she was there, and he still wasn't sure how he was going to do that.

"Where do you think we should check first?" Ty asked.

Breen looked across the river. "The East Inn will be the only thing open this late."

"Good a place as any, I suppose." Ty licked his lips. "Besides, I wouldn't mind a pint of Bue's hot cider while we're at it."

Breen licked his lips as well. "What are we waiting on?" He nudged Acorn, and they started over the bridge.

Ty tightened his grip on the reins, and Narendi tightened her grip around Ty. He'd been dreaming of this moment for months, of once more riding down River Street. He still couldn't quite believe they had finally returned. With a deep breath, he nudged Waddle with the heel of his boot, and the three of them started over the East Bridge.

Chapter 31 | Ty

STREETLAMPS LIT THE snow-packed cobbles as they made their way up River Street toward the heart of Easthaven. Ty kept Waddle to an unhurried walk. He wanted to take it all in, every familiar building, every alley and side street, all the places where he had played as a boy. After the glistening white stone buildings of Aero'set, the city looked run down, but there was something about it that felt right, something that the towers of the ancient magical school just didn't have, and that was the feeling of home.

They slowed as they came to the city square where River Street met Wood Lane. The streets were mostly empty as people were home finishing their suppers and getting ready for bed. Ty stopped at the fountain and pointed east, down Wood Lane, which ran all the way to the docks.

"You see that street there?" Ty said, pointing to the first street on the right. Narendi nodded.

"Mangora's shop is down there."

She shivered. "Then let's not go there."

"We aren't. The East Inn is up there," he said, pointing north.

"Good."

Ty clicked his tongue, and Waddle started back up again. "That's Reloria's Sweet Shop," he said, pointing to the corner building on the right. Its windows were dark and porch empty, as the shoppers had already headed home for the evening. He glanced around the square, but other than a patrol of lancers crossing on their way to the barracks, no one else seemed to be wandering about the city. Even still, he leaned in a little closer. "She's a telasero."

"What is a telasero?"

"She can make things taste like anything she wants. I'll take you tomorrow." They continued on, passing one shop after the next. "And that is Orlyn's apothecary," he said, pointing to the sign above a door on the right. "Remember, he's the one I told you about who can control plants, a floratide."

They passed the vintner's shop on the left, which sat at the corner of River Street and Lynden. The inn sat at the opposite corner, and Ty and Breen directed their horses to a couple of empty spots on the hitching rail in front.

"And here we are," Ty said enthusiastically. "The East Inn."

Narendi slid down off the back of Waddle and walked around to the front. "It's bigger than I imagined."

"You probably don't need to take that inside," Ty said, pointing to her spear as he swung out of the saddle.

She looked at Breen. "He carries his bow."

Ty could see he wasn't going to win the argument, so he dropped it and turned to Breen. "Stay here. I want to have a quick look inside first."

"Why?" Narendi asked.

"Because I want to make sure that certain people aren't there before we go in."

"Like who?"

Again, another argument he couldn't win. Breen was trying not to chuckle. "I want to make sure the girl I told you about isn't in there."

Her eyes narrowed, so he knew she understood who he was talking about.

"Last thing we need is a fight on our first day back."

She crossed her arms. "I still don't see why we can't wait inside," she said. "It's cold out here."

"I'll make it quick." He left them on the walkway and headed up the steps to the front. Surprisingly, there was no one there to greet him when he entered.

The lobby only had a couple of people inside, and they were too preoccupied with their conversation to pay him any mind. No one seemed to be waiting for a seat, which meant the evening crowd had already made it in.

Beyond the lobby, the common room was filled with a thick haze, with many of the patrons enjoying their evening pipes. It was also quite loud with conversation and laughter, nearly covering the evening's entertainment, which happened to be Master Ethen with his five-string vielle and bow. The lanky carpenter sat on a stool on stage, keeping spirits high with a rather amusing rendition of "The King's Son." It painted the king's son in a very unflattering light.

Ty kept his hood up as he made his way around the left side of the lobby. He stopped just under the staircase, close enough to see the common room while keeping to the shadows as much as possible. Most of the tables were filled, those sitting at them sipping on their drinks while engaging in light conversations. Many of those closest to the bar wore Sidaran uniforms. There were even tables lining the corridor on the left leading back to the guest quarters. Most of those sitting there were soldiers as well, which was odd for this time of year.

There had been an increasing number of lancers in Easthaven, even before he had left on his quest, but now they seemed to be everywhere. They had even spotted several patrols moving through the streets as they made their way from the East Bridge to the inn. He wondered if something had happened while they were gone. Had the Tower tried attacking again? He hoped not. He stared out across the tables, looking for anyone he recognized, namely a beautiful young woman with flaming red hair. He didn't see her anywhere, nor did he see his father or sister, but he still had one place left to look.

Taking the stairs, he headed up to the balcony, a spot that was sure to be engrained in his memory for the rest of his life. It was where he and Lyessa had shared their first kiss.

"Can I help you with anything, sir?" one of the servers asked just as Ty reached the top landing. The man was on his way back down the steps.

Ty shook his head. "Just looking for someone."

The young man nodded and carried his empty tray back down to the main floor. Ty did a quick sweep of the balcony tables, but not seeing his father or sister or anyone else he recognized, he turned and made his way back down. He exited through the front door and waved the other two up.

"Did you see them?" Breen asked.

"I didn't see anyone, which is kind of strange." He pursed his lips. "Were you still wanting to get a tankard?"

Breen looked at the front door, then shook his head. "Nah. I'd rather keep looking."

"Me too." Ty headed back down the steps for the horses, leaving Narendi still standing on the porch, confused.

"We aren't going to get a drink?" she asked.

Ty turned. "We'll get something after we figure out where my father and sister are. Come on."

Narendi huffed as she marched back down the walkway and over to the hitching rails. "What was the purpose of going in there, then?"

Ty swung up into the saddle and reached down to help her up. "To see if Father and Adarra were in there. And they weren't. So we look somewhere else."

Narendi mumbled something under her breath as she held up her arm for Ty to pull her up. She then wrapped her arms around Ty and squeezed, and not in a friendly or affectionate way.

Ty looked at Breen. "Want to try the Harbor House?"

"That was going to be my next suggestion." Breen turned his horse around and started west down Lynden. They took the second side street on the left, which ran directly in front of the Harbor House, then proceeded to a side alley which led around back. This time, Ty and Narendi remained on their horse while Breen dismounted and walked up to the door and knocked. After a while, Ty could hear chains behind loosened and the door cracked. As soon as the light spilled across Breen's face, the door was flung wide, and Master Eliab stepped outside, his mouth gaping as he cradled his double crossbow in his arms.

"Mathter Breen." He looked over and spotted Ty, and his eyes widened further. "Mathter Ty. I can't believe ith you."

The former Sidaran captain was a sight for sore eyes. Ty barely gave Narendi time to slide down before he was hopping out of the saddle. He quickly tied Waddle off to a nearby barrel, grabbed Nyalis's book for Adarra, and headed up the back steps to greet the old gatekeeper. "It's very good to see you, Master Eliab. Have you seen our father or Adarra anywhere?"

Master Eliab gave them a funny look. "How long have you been back?"

"We just arrived this evening."

"Tho you haven't heard."

"Heard what?" Breen asked, tying Acorn off and heading back up the steps behind Ty.

Eliab gave Narendi and her spear a careful looking-over, his finger edging slightly closer to the crossbow's trigger. "Who ith thith?"

"This is Narendi," Ty said. "She's with us. Another wielder in search of safe harbor."

Eliab lowered his bow and stepped back inside. "Very good."

Breen walked in behind him. "What haven't we heard? Are Father and Adarra well?"

"They are well. At leatht, I believe tho. Betht to let the councthil tell you," Eliab said, moving further out of the doorway. "They are meeting downthtairth."

"They're here right now?" Ty asked as he and Narendi stepped through the door and into the back of the kitchen. His heart started to pound. This was perfect. He looked over at Breen and grinned. "We can surprise them."

"It will definitely be a thuprithe," Eliab said as he moved around behind them to shut the door. He got it halfway closed when something slammed into it from the other side and threw him into Breen.

Ty spun and conjured his flames just as Kraea barreled through the door and knocked him into the table.

Eliab shrieked at the sight of the draakar and raised his bow, but Ty managed to get a shield up just as the trigger snapped and two bolts flew across the room. They hit the invisible barrier and ricocheted into one of the cabinets on the left, shattering a couple of dishes on the shelf.

"What in the flaming Pith ith that?" Eliab shouted, his back pressed against Breen.

Ty raised his hands. "She's with us, Master Eliab."

Breen grabbed Eliab's hand, which was already reaching for his sword. "No need for that. She won't harm you. I promise."

Ty spun on Kraea. "What do you think you're doing? You were supposed to wait for us at home."

"Who ith he talking to?" Eliab asked.

"I did, for a while," Kraea barked back. *"But it was cold and smelly, and the entire place stank of arachnobes."*

Ty bit down on his tongue. "How did you find us?"

"I followed you," she said.

"Did anyone see you?"

"I don't think so."

"You don't think so, or you know so?"

"I know so. I can remain hidden when I want."

Ty wondered how something her size with red scales was able to remain unseen moving through the city streets.

"Have you looked out there? The streets are practically vacant."

"Yes, we just rode through. And fine, you have a point."

"What are you two going on about?" Breen asked. "You're frightening poor Master Eliab here."

Ty turned and looked at Eliab, who was clutching his bow to his chest. "Sorry. Where are my manners—"

"You've got to have manners to lose them," Kraea remarked.

Ty growled at her, then turned to Eliab. "Master Eliab, this is Kraea. She is a draakar we rescued in the Riverlands. Kind of a long story, which I'm sure can be saved for later. And before you ask, no, I have not lost my senses and started speaking to myself. I have the unfortunate luck of being able to hear her thoughts."

"You're not the only unfortunate one," Kraea said.

"It thpeakth to you?"

"She does."

"It ith intelligent?"

"Well, that's debatable."

Kraea swung her tail around and hit Ty in the leg, and he hopped up and down for a minute. He was half tempted to hit her with a fist of air, except he might topple what was left of Eliab's dishes.

Eliab didn't say anything, just stared with a funny look on his face. "I have never theen a draakar before." He took a step closer. "Will it bite?"

Kraea growled, and Eliab immediately stepped back.

Breen left Eliab and walked over and shut the back door. "Best to keep out prying eyes."

Eliab placed his crossbow down on the table long enough to throw the bracer and chains back across the door. He then took a moment to nock two more bolts before starting into the next room. "Come, I will take you down."

Ty looked at the three of them, stopping on Kraea, and grinned. "This is going to be interesting."

Breen looked at Kraea as well. "To say the least."

They followed Eliab into the next room, where the door leading down to the cellar was. Ty's heart was pounding so hard he was finding it difficult to breathe. He was about to be reunited with his family. He couldn't wait to tell them everything that had happened to him, the places they'd been, the things they'd seen. There was so much to tell, he had no idea where to start. He couldn't wait to see the looks on their faces when he and Breen walked through the door, even more so when Kraea did. He almost laughed thinking about it.

"If the old man is any indication how the rest will act, you might not be laughing long."

Ty's smile dropped. She was probably right.

They reached the bottom of the stone steps and started through the simple accommodations the council had provided for wielders on the run. He looked inside one of the rooms at the side whose door was opened and saw stacks of crates. It appeared the makeshift rooms were being used more for storage now than anything. Which made some sense now that Overlord Barl had made Sidara a safe haven for wielders.

Ahead, Ty could see a golden outline around the meeting room door, signaling it was in use. His hands were shaking by the time they made it across the cellar. He could hear muffled voices coming from the other side. He'd pictured this moment so many times in his head, and in so many different ways. Still, catching the entire council at once had to be one of the best. He looked at Breen, who was nervously rubbing his hands together. "This is it."

Breen smiled.

Eliab stood in front of the door, waiting for them to give him the nod to open. Ty glanced over his shoulder at Narendi, who was busy fiddling with her spear, trying to adjust it low enough so that it didn't catch the top of the door on the way in. Beside her, Kraea was busy sniffing at a barrel of dried dates. Maybe it *was* best to have Kraea here after all. It would certainly be easier to introduce her to everyone at once.

With a deep breath to steel his nerves, he tucked Nyalis's book for Adarra under his arm and turned to Eliab. "Don't tell them who it is, just that there's a couple of wielders outside looking for lodging."

Eliab nodded, and Ty stepped to the side and out of the doorway so he wouldn't be seen when Eliab opened it. The old gatekeeper knocked.

"Come," Veldon's booming voice called out from the other side, sending chill bumps up Ty's arms. Ty shuffled his feet as he waited. He couldn't believe how excited he was, and how nervous. He wasn't sure why he was so uneasy.

"You're nervous because you fear me growing hungry and eating someone."

Ty turned and Kraea gave him her most dashing smile, which would have horrified just about anyone else.

"Mathter Veldon," Eliab said from just inside the door. "There are a couple of wielderth outthide who theek shelter."

There was a moment's pause, which for Ty felt like hours, before Veldon finally replied.

"Did they mention how they found us?"

"Uh, no thir, jutht that they needed shelter."

"Very well, tell them to wait in the kitchen. As soon as we finish here, I'll be up to greet them."

Ty could hear Eliab clear his throat. "I . . . I believe they wish to introduth themthelveth."

"You brought them down here?" Veldon didn't sound pleased, and Ty could hear several chairs scooting back from the table.

"I, uh . . ."

"Very well, let them in."

Master Eliab hustled out, looking a little flummoxed. Ty patted the older man on the shoulder to reassure him and then looked at Breen. Breen nodded, and they both headed for the door.

"We are just a couple of travel-worn wielders looking for a place to stay," Ty said with a beaming smile as they stepped into the room.

The entire chamber leapt to their feet.

"Ty, Breen!" their father's voice boomed.

Ty barely had time to pull off his cap before their father had pushed his way around the side of the table and snatched them both in his arms. Ty wrapped his arms around his father and breathed him in. He smelled of trees and soil and the great outdoors.

As soon as they parted, his father looked at him. "You seem bigger," he said, squeezing Ty's shoulders.

Ty smiled. It had been several months, so he might have grown a little, not to mention everything they had been through. "I've been training," he said, but before he could finish, a flash of red swept across the top of the table and leapt on top of him.

"Ty!"

By the time Ty realized who it was, Lyessa's lips had found his. She wrapped her arms around his neck and nearly squeezed the life out of him. He'd pictured this moment a thousand times, but whenever he'd imagined it, they weren't standing in the middle of the wielder council chambers with everyone watching. But at that moment, he didn't care as he wrapped his arms around her and held her tight.

An angry yet familiar cry behind him was all the warning he had before Narendi flew into the room and slammed into Lyessa, throwing them both backward onto the table.

Lyessa's arms were ripped from Ty's neck, sending him stumbling forward.

No one else moved as the two women rolled across the top of the table—Narendi shouting that she'd kill the woman who'd dared put her lips on Ty, and Lyessa shouting for someone to get the lunatic off her.

A sudden flash back to Ty at the Imbatoo encampment had him remembering the way Bolo—Narendi's former betrothed and captain of the Mzwati—had attacked Ty when he had seen him wearing Narendi's bracelet. Ty suddenly wondered if such violence was a cultural thing.

Everyone else stood there with mouths gaping.

Lyessa managed to get her feet under Narendi, and she kicked her backward off the table. Narendi scrambled to her feet as Breen tried to grab her and pull her away from the table and Lyessa.

"Unhand me!" she shouted and spun around him before he could get a firm grip on her arm. She yanked her spear from her shoulder, looking for Lyessa. "I challenge you to the death!"

Ty's father tried helping Lyessa down from the table, but as soon as her feet hit the floor, her sword was out of its sheath and in her hand.

"Challenge me to the death?" Lyessa wiped a stream of blood from her lip. "Who is this crazy woman?"

Wondering if he was insane, Ty stepped between the two.

"Move!" Narendi shouted at Ty. "And I will show her the end of my spear."

"I'd like to see you try," Lyessa said, raising her sword.

Ty stayed between them but quickly conjured a shield just in case. "I'm not moving. Just, please, let me explain."

"I'd say an explanation is more than deserved," Lyessa said, her face as red as her hair. "Now someone tell me who this fool woman is!"

"I am Narendi Unsala, princess of the Imbatoo, daughter of King Diawandy Unsala . . . and wife of Ty."

Lyessa's mouth dropped open, and she turned and looked at Ty.

In fact, everyone turned and looked at Ty.

For a moment, Ty thought Lyessa was going to plunge her sword into him. His right eye started to twitch as the air wheezed from his chest. This was not the way he had pictured this happening at all. Why was Lyessa even here? This was the wielder council meeting room, and she wasn't a wielder. Of all the times for her to decide to get involved, why did it have to be tonight?

"I can explain," he said. If looks could kill, Lyessa would have burned him alive right then and there.

Lyessa's jaw tightened. "Why is this woman claiming that you are her husband? Are you . . . are you bonded?"

"Yes," Narendi said with a sharp grin.

"No!" Ty countered. "We are not bonded!" He turned and shot Narendi a harsh glare.

Narendi rubbed the top of her shaved head. "I have performed the rite of union with my father, and he agreed I am to be yours."

Ty ground his teeth. They had already discussed in great detail why he was not her husband. Why was she bringing this up again? "That might work for the Imbatoo, but here in Sidara, the man gets a say as well." Ty held her gaze, his magic resting at the edge of his fingertips in case he needed a way to hold her back.

"I think someone better explain what is happening," Ty's father finally said, moving up beside Lyessa. The rest of the council remained where they were, not sure what to do.

Ty looked at Breen. "Keep her from killing anyone, will you?"

Breen looked at Narendi and nodded as Ty turned to face the rest of the council.

"As you have heard, this is Narendi Unsala. And yes, she is princess of the Imbatoo people. She saved me and Breen in the Wengoby Desert a couple of months back. If not for her and her people, we wouldn't be here today."

"Did you say the Wengoby Desert?" Orlyn asked. He held his rune-covered staff protectively in front of him as his eyes danced between Lyessa and Narendi.

"I did. Breen and I have been from one side of Aldor to the other over the last several months, and even to places beyond." But that was a story that would clearly have to wait now that these two had ruined his triumphant return home. He gritted his teeth as he turned and pointed at Narendi. "Narendi and her people helped us find one of the missing pieces of the shorlock. And somewhere along the way," he said with an annoyed look in her direction, "she decided she was to be my first wife."

"Yeah, well, I've got something to say about that," Lyessa shot back defiantly, raising her sword once more.

"Did you say *first* wife?" Feoldor asked, his eyes brightening as he fluffed his side whiskers.

Reloria elbowed him in the side. "Don't get any ideas."

Ty nodded. "Yes, the Imbatoo take multiple wives. Narendi's father has . . ." He turned and looked at Narendi, and she set her jaw.

"Three."

"Your father has three wives?" Veldon asked from the far side of the table as he nervously mopped the top of his head with his handkerchief.

Narendi nodded.

"That sounds rather unpleasant," Fraya said from the back of the room as she looked fondly at Breen. Others grumbled in agreement.

"It's not our place to judge," Ty's father said, then looked at Ty. "Go on."

"Anyway," Ty continued, "when we left the desert through one of the traveling mirrors, Narendi jumped through just before it shut off."

"A traveling mirror?" Orlyn asked. "What do you mean it shut off?"

Ty looked at Breen, and his brother shrugged. This was going to be harder than he thought, but he had to start somewhere. "The wizard council were the ones who divided the shorlock into four pieces to keep it safe. As you know, they hid them all over Aldor, and as we discovered, even to places beyond."

"Beyond what?" Veldon asked. "There is nothing beyond."

Ty held up his hand. "I can only answer one question at a time. If you'll give us a moment, we'll explain everything." He kept pausing to look at Lyessa and Narendi, trying to make sure they weren't about to charge one another. "As I was saying, those same wizards set up magical mirrors that can take people just about anywhere. As long as you know the name of the mirror that you are at and the one you want to exit, it's like stepping through a door."

Eyes brightened around the table, and Ty could see they had a thousand questions, much like he had when he had first heard about the mirrors, but he needed to get the situation with Lyessa and Narendi calmed down first, so he continued before they started in on him. "The problem was that after we made it through the mirror and out of the desert, I got so upset with Narendi for jumping through that I forgot the first mirror's name, which meant I had no way to send her back."

"She can't return home?" Reloria asked. "The poor dear." Reloria started to pull a piece of wrapped candy from her purse, but one look at Narendi's hardened face, and she dropped it back in.

"So," Ty continued, "she has been with us ever since. Saved our lives on more than one occasion. She was trained to fight by the Mzwati, who are Imbatoo warriors known as the dune runners of the desert, and without her, we might not have survived to find the missing pieces."

Narendi's anger seemed to soften a little, the more Ty built her up to those standing around the table, so he proceeded. He just hoped Lyessa didn't take all the praise he was giving Narendi the wrong way. "She has been a great ally in our endeavor to bring back the keep of Aero'set." His smile vanished. "Now, if only I could make her understand that there is more to being married than simply claiming you are."

Narendi sneered.

"She does speak Aldoran, though, correct?" Veldon asked.

"She does," Ty said.

"Though it's not her people's native tongue," Breen added. "How many of us can say that we could learn a second language?"

Ty looked at Narendi. "You can put the spear down now. It wouldn't do you much good in here anyway. You're standing in a room full of—" Before Ty could finish, the space behind Narendi folded in on itself, and suddenly Sheeva was there with a knife to Narendi's neck.

Narendi squeaked and stiffened as the white-haired nightwalker pressed against her.

Ty's breath caught in his throat. What was Sheeva doing? Didn't she realize he had it under control? He quickly raised his hand. "Sheeva, you don't have to—"

A roar sounded from just outside the room, and a red flash of scales and claws barreled through the door and landed on top of Sheeva.

Chapter 32 | Ty

SHEEVA SHRIEKED WHEN THE draakar hit her and immediately vanished as the two went down and skidded across the room. Ty was beyond relieved that Sheeva had not cut Narendi's throat before she went down.

The council chambers turned to chaos as shouts and screams echoed off the walls. Fire ignited in Veldon's hands as gusts of wind encircled the room. Even Ty's father had a couple of his knives out and at the ready.

"Kraea! Stop!" Ty hit her with a fist of air that sent her careening into the back wall before she could latch on to Sheeva's neck or before Sheeva buried her dagger in her side. He ran and jumped in front of the draakar, hoping he didn't step on Sheeva in the process. "Wait! Stop! She's with us."

All thoughts of the earlier conflict between Lyessa and Narendi quickly vanished as the rest of the council retreated to the other side of the room. Sheeva was nowhere to be seen, which had him worried. He looked at his father. "Please ask Sheeva to back off."

His father called to the former assassin, and she reappeared in front of him, daggers in hand, prepared to attack anything that came near him. Ty breathed a small sigh of relief and slowly scooted backward until he bumped into Kraea. Ty could see the concern in his father's eyes at seeing him that close to the draakar, so he reached back and hugged Kraea's neck to show that she wouldn't harm them.

She purred. Well, she released one of her low, softer growls, which Ty had relegated to her purring. *"You can let go of my neck now,"* she said. *"Unless you're planning on wooing me."*

Ty released her neck. He wanted to kick her in the leg.

Well, this was proving quite a disaster.

"This is Kraea," he finally said, gathering everyone's attention, even Lyessa's, who was standing at the back with the rest of the members. "She is a draakar that we rescued from a live auction in the Riverlands just after leaving the desert."

"Tell them about Mother."

"I will," he whispered. "Give me a chance."

"You will what?" Ty's father asked.

"She wants me to tell you about her mother."

The council members looked confused, murmuring amongst themselves. All but Lyessa, who was back to staring Narendi down.

"What do you mean she wants you to tell us?" his father asked.

Ty motioned to the open door where Eliab was crouched. "As I was telling Master Eliab earlier, I have a particular bond with Kraea. We can hear each other's thoughts, which allows us to speak to each other without actually talking."

"She can hear everything you're thinking?" Orlyn asked. "How very unpleasant."

"We don't exactly hear everything, not unless I use our link to talk specifically, but we can read what the other is thinking emotionally. I admit, it was strange at first," he said, passing a quick glance behind him, "but we've grown accustomed to it, I think."

"Speak for yourself."

"Oh, shut it."

"Are you talking to her now?" Fraya asked, standing next to Gilly, holding the very nervous dwarf's hand.

"Yes."

"Tell them about Mother."

"I will, give me a chance." He smiled at the council members. "Kraea's mother was being auctioned at the market as well, and she gave her life to save ours. She fought off a dozen or more slavers to give us a chance to escape." Ty took a step forward and raised his hands. "You can lower your weapons. I promise she won't hurt anyone. She's very protective of us. We've been through a lot together, including a very ugly battle with the White Tower."

"The White Tower?" Veldon lowered his hands, and the fire in them snuffed out.

"Now that sounds like a story worth hearing," Feoldor said, lowering his hands as well, and the wind whipping around the room slowly died.

Ty's father slid his knives back inside his coat and nodded for Ty to continue.

Ty looked around the room. The only two people still armed were Narendi and Lyessa, and neither looked willing to give up their weapons.

"Narendi, you don't need the spear," he said, then looked at Lyessa. "Please."

Lyessa eyed Narendi a moment longer, then finally sheathed her sword, though her hand didn't stray far from the hilt. Seeing Lyessa sheath her blade, Narendi finally lowered her spear and hooked it over her shoulder. As soon as she did, the room seemed to relax, tension easing as some of those at the back moved forward to find their seats.

Veldon, Gilly, and Sheeva remained where they were, not wanting to retake their place at the front near Kraea and Narendi. Instead, they found a couple of empty chairs against the back wall and pulled them up to the table.

Ty noticed Narendi kept a close eye on Lyessa as Lyessa retook her seat between Ty's father and Fraya. "You two actually have quite a lot in common," he said, earning him a tongue click from Narendi. "No, really. Both of your fathers are rulers of your people, both of you were trained in combat since you were young, and you're both very protective of those you care about."

And you're both extremely strong willed, he added, but not out loud, though Kraea chuckled.

"Clearly it's not the only thing we have in common," Lyessa said, giving him a sharp look.

He turned and motioned for Breen and Narendi to take their seats. Kraea made her way over to Ty's chair—which used to be Veldon's—and sat down, holding her head high enough to see over the table. Ty was the last to sit.

He took a minute to study the faces of those sitting with them. As he scanned the table, he suddenly realized there was one very important face missing, and he reached under his arm. The book was gone. He turned and spotted it on the floor by the door. He must have dropped it during the scuffle between Narendi and Lyessa. Standing, he walked over and retrieved it, motioning for Eliab to join them, since the man was still waiting just outside the room with his crossbow firmly in hand.

Eliab waved him off. "It be wielder bithneth. I will get back to my potht."

"It's fine, Eliab," Veldon called out from the back of the room. "I'm sure you'll want to hear this as well."

Eliab stuck his head in the door. "Thank you, Mathter Veldon." He shut the door behind him and walked over and took a seat in the corner.

Ty returned to his chair at the head of the table and sat down, then looked at his father. "Where's Adarra? Nyalis asked that I give her this book when we arrived. He also requested that she accompany us on our return."

His father's head lifted. "Return?" He didn't look happy hearing that.

Lyessa scooted forward in her seat. "You're not staying?"

This was the part Ty had not been looking forward to revealing. He took a deep breath. "Nyalis gave us until the next full moon before we need to return to Aero'set and continue our training."

"So you managed to complete your quest, did you?" Orlyn asked, looking anxious to know where Ty and Breen had been for the last few months.

"We did, and we'll tell you all about it in just a moment, but . . ." Ty once again looked at his father. "Where's Adarra? Wait, let me guess. She's sitting in the overlord's library researching some new origin of plant life."

Ty's father frowned, and the rest of the council members suddenly looked like they'd rather be anywhere else at that moment, several even lowering their heads or turning away so as not to meet his eyes.

"What's going on?" Breen asked, leaning forward to rest his big arms on the table.

"I'm afraid Adarra won't be returning with you," their father said.

Ty's heart skipped a beat when he looked at the downtrodden faces of those gathered. Had something happened to his sister? If she'd been injured, Fraya would have healed her, but she wasn't there, and the troubled looks being passed around the members could only mean one thing. "Is she . . . She's not—"

"No," Ty's father said. "She is alive and well." He pursed his lips. "Well, I guess that depends on how you look at it."

Breen stiffened in his seat. "How you look at what? Where is she? What's going on?"

"Your sister is currently aboard a ship heading for the Isle of Tallos. Set sail this evening, in fact."

Ty smiled. "Is that a joke?"

His father, however, didn't smile. "Anything but, I assure you."

Ty's smile slid from his face. They were serious.

"Why in the name of Aldor would she want to go to Tallos?" Breen asked.

"And why would you let her?" Ty added.

Ty's father cleared his throat. "She discovered through her time spent with Jonas that—"

"Jonas?" Ty thought a moment. "You mean the Northman we have locked in the cells?"

"He's not there anymore," his father said. "She took him with her."

Ty leaned back in his seat, utterly dumbfounded. "Has she completely lost her mind? Why would she go to Tallos of all places, and with him? Did anyone else go with her?" Ty looked around the table, but all the members were clearly there and accounted for.

Ty's father held up his hand. "If you two will give me a moment to explain, I might be able to answer your questions."

Ty and Breen shared a worried look, then finally nodded.

"As I was saying, during Adarra's discussions with Jonas, your sister discovered that the Tallosians who had attacked us were only a scouting party—"

Ty's head shot up. "They mean to attack?"

His father's jaw tightened, and Ty sighed. "Sorry, please continue."

"Apparently, the Tallosians have lost all their crops to something they are calling the Black Death. From what your sister could make out, the crops were eaten by some sort of insect swarm. Because of this, their people are starving, and in desperation, they sent out scouting parties to the mainland to search for food. Unfortunately, Jonas's party happened across Mangora, and she promised them provisions in exchange for their help in capturing you. Since their efforts failed miserably and they fled without any of the promised food, we can only assume more will be coming."

"How many more?" Breen asked before Ty got the chance.

"According to Jonas, all of them. We could be looking at an invasion."

"Desperate people will do anything to stay alive," Orlyn said.

Ty remembered how difficult it had been standing up to those they had fought outside his home. If that was nothing more than a small scouting party, he couldn't imagine what it would mean for Easthaven to suddenly find themselves facing off against an entire army of scalp-wearing savages.

Ty's father continued. "Jonas said that his people are ruled by the Dogar, which consists of the heads of the five houses of Tallos. No idea how many actual Tallosians there are or how large a force we could be dealing with, but the scouting party was from just one house."

"Why didn't you go with her?" Breen asked, a question Ty had been wondering as well but was too embarrassed to ask.

"Oh, I wanted to, but Overlord Barl insisted that he needed me here to help him with preparations in case Easthaven found themselves under attack."

Doesn't Barl have military commanders for that? Ty wondered. The overlord seemed to rely heavily on Ty's father, which was strange. Not because his father was incapable, quite the opposite, but he was the overlord's game keeper, not a soldier. Ever since the battle with Mangora, Lord Barl had all but taken Ty's father into his personal confidence. Sometimes it seemed he shared more with him than with Lyessa.

"My father sent an entire company of Sidaran Lancers with her," Lyessa said, earning a sneer from Narendi. "He also sent Ambassador Lanmiere to help negotiate."

"Don't forget Aiden," Fraya chimed in.

"Aiden?" Ty's mouth dropped. "You can't be serious."

Lyessa sighed. "We couldn't persuade him otherwise. Not even Adarra. He said he wasn't about to let her go traipsing off to Tallos with Jonas alone. That someone needed to be there to keep an eye on him."

Ty laughed. "And he thinks he's the man to do it?" He looked around the room. "I can't believe no one from the council went with her."

"That was more Adarra's decision than ours," Fraya said.

Ty's father nodded. "She believes having a group of wielders show up on the Tallosians' doorstep might not be the best way to open discussions. You know how paranoid they are about magic."

"I'd be more paranoid about their choice of clothing."

"Jonas seems to believe that they will be able to come to some sort of arrangement. Orlyn provided seeds."

"Not just any seeds," Orlyn clarified, straightening his robes with a proud smile. "They were specially created by myself over a period of several years."

"Probably end up poisoning the lot of them," Feoldor mumbled, then smiled. "Fix our problem, though."

Orlyn glared at him from across the table. "My plants are not poisonous. They are, however, swift growing and capable of surviving in minimal light, not to mention impervious to most bugs."

"That's all well and good," Breen said, taking a little of the wind out of Orlyn's sail, "and not to disparage your work, but seeds aren't exactly going to feed an entire people in the next few weeks, are they?"

Orlyn shook his head. "Sadly, no. But we think they will serve as a bargaining chip for us to open negotiations."

"My father sent as much food as the city could put together on short notice," Lyessa said. "It won't be enough to get the Northmen through the rest of the winter, but it will be a small start to opening a more permanent trade between our peoples."

Ty smiled. She was already sounding like a ruler. His mind wandered for a moment, and he tried picturing Lyessa addressing the Sidaran Assembly. She definitely had the bearing. One day, her father's title would be passed to her, as his was from his father, and she would find herself the overlord of Sidara. Narendi, too, was destined to rule, but she would one day have to return to her people for that to happen. Ty passed a sideways glance at the Imbatoo princess, and his smile dropped when he noticed the glare he was receiving in return.

He looked away, shaking his head as he did. "I still can't believe Adarra is on her way to Tallos. Of all the people to ask, why her?"

"Again," his father said, "it was more her choice than anyone's. She is the only person who can come close to speaking their language. She's been working with Jonas for months, trying to teach him ours."

"Was she able to?"

"In a manner of speaking. He seems quite skilled at retaining knowledge. I doubt I would be able to do the same in such a short time."

Ty was confused. "If he can interpret, then why did she need to go?"

"Because he refused to go without her."

"What?"

Their father shrugged. "He's formed some sort of . . . attachment to her."

Breen's fists balled. "What sort of attachment?"

"Not like that," their father said, then paused. "At least, I hope not."

"Actually," Fraya cut in, "that might be a good thing."

Everyone around the table turned, and she shrunk back in her seat. "If he has an emotional attachment, he's going to be more willing to keep her safe, isn't he?"

Ty hated to admit it, but she had a point, not that it was a good one. The thought of his sister being led by that savage up into the mountains of Tallos had him wanting to hop on the next ship across the Bay of Mist. The Tallosians couldn't be trusted. He would no doubt lead them into an ambush, then sew her scalp onto his cloak . . . unless he wanted her alive for other reasons. Ty shivered at the thought and did his best to get the image out of his head.

"I believe he will keep her safe," Ty's father said. "From the little I saw of him while the lancers took him aboard the ship, he seems unyielding without her presence."

"Unyielding?" Feoldor hmphed. "That's putting it mildly. It took half a dozen men to get him to the wagon from the barracks, and that was only after Adarra showed up."

Reloria placed her hand on Feoldor's arm. "But did you see the way he calmed when he saw her? There's no doubt she's had an effect on him, and if they do run into trouble, I can't think of anyone in that convoy I'd want protecting me more than that monster of a man."

Feoldor stared at her a moment and frowned. "Wipe that grin off your face."

She noticed the others staring and straightened her bonnet. "I'm just saying."

Ty's father leaned back in his seat. "Regardless, there's not much we can do about your sister at this point other than to ask the Creator to keep her safe." He shifted in his seat. "Now, I want to hear all about this journey of yours. You say you've been to places outside of Aldor? What was that like? I'm anxious to hear everything."

Ty took a deep breath and slowly released it, letting the tension ease slightly from his shoulders. He'd been sitting rather stiffly as they discussed the concern over his sister's rather ludicrous decision. His father was correct, though. Worrying about Adarra would serve no purpose at this point, so Ty attempted to pull his thoughts away from her and refocused on why they were there in the first place. He reminded himself this was the moment he had been dreaming about for months. It might have had a disastrous beginning, but surely he could salvage it with the tale of all that had befallen him and Breen since they had left Easthaven. Leaning forward in his seat, he rested his forearms on the table like his brother and folded his hands.

"I'm not even sure where to begin."

Chapter 33 | Ty

I'LL TELL YOU WHERE you can begin," Lyessa said. "You can start with that wretched wizard spelling me and my men and leaving us drooling on ourselves at your house while he whisked you away before we even got the chance to say a proper goodbye."

Ty cleared his throat. "But we . . . we said our goodbyes at . . . uh, the East Inn."

Lyessa blushed.

"Why did Nyalis let you go?" Fraya asked Breen. "I thought Ty was supposed to go alone."

"Exactly," Lyessa echoed. "Why did he let you go when he wouldn't let me?"

Breen fumbled over himself a bit before admitting he hadn't exactly been given permission to go either but had followed Ty anyway.

Lyessa ground her teeth. "If he hadn't spelled me, I would have gone as well."

Ty's father raised his hands. "Apparently, whatever was meant to happen, did. Let's be thankful we are all here and safe."

Most of those around the table agreed. Lyessa, however, passed a quick but angry glance at Narendi, and Ty realized why she was so upset with Nyalis. If she had gone with them, Lyessa figured Narendi might not have laid claim to Ty.

Not wanting to linger on the sore subject any longer, Ty quickly shifted the conversation back to the retelling of their adventures, starting first with his journey through Reed Marsh. He described everything about it—from the smells to the sounds. Eventually he got around to his encounter with the razorback and the marsh monster. He ended with his first meeting of Douina.

The room grew silent when he told them of his initial fight with someone he had thought to be Mangora. Many around the table wondered aloud if that was where she had gone to hide after her battle with Ty's family, but Ty quickly allayed their fears by revealing that "Mangora" turned out to be Douina, her twin sister.

The room buzzed with conversations as Ty fielded questions about this woman who apparently had made the marsh her home. He told them of the small garden-like paradise she had set up inside the marsh, which was only made possible by the presence of Abinayu, the mirror's rightful guardian. The council members were stunned into silence after hearing that Ty had not only communicated with the great tree, but that the tree had turned out to be a long-lost member of the Fae.

From there he told them of finding the first mirror inside Abinayu and what it had felt like stepping through. He also told them how he had ended up at the bottom of a river with his pack snagged on a fallen tree, and of Breen showing up just in time to save him.

The two told of their meeting with Tirana and the cursed people of Karpaath. Oddly enough, it wasn't the fact that the Karpaathians had been trapped there for over a thousand years that spurred the council's interest, it was learning that the village they were in was not part of Aldor but most likely located inside the Westlands.

Leaving Karpaath, Ty took them through the mountain and out across the Maze. "Stone walls twenty feet high," he said, "dead bodies littering every inch, rat-sized insects that were attracted to flame, black pits that transported you from one part of the maze to another, tunnels filled with water that sucked you under, walls that moved and reformed, a living fog of dead spirits, and on top of all that a maze monster."

The council was speechless.

After Breen described the giant lizard-like creature that was three or four times the size of a razorback, Ty told them of his face-off with the wall of fire.

"So you just walked through the flames?" Fraya asked.

Ty nodded.

"You're an idiot," Lyessa said. "Why would you do something so . . . idiotic?"

"Because the entire thing was a test of my *faith*."

"Sounds more like it was testing your stupidity, and you failed miserably," Lyessa shot back.

Ty gritted his teeth but continued by describing the first piece of the missing key, and then telling how they had made it through the next mirror to find themselves in a place of complete darkness.

He could still remember vividly how frightening it had been. He described what they had first seen when he used his blue flames to light the surrounding cavern. The fact that they were stuck on a small island in the middle of an underground lake, with the mirror they'd just arrived through on one side and another, similar mirror on the other side.

"I like it," a voice from the back called out, and Ty looked up to see Gilly sitting there with a big smile on his face. He had a cup of water resting in his hands. The water inside was swirling just above the rim, forming various shapes each time it rose.

Narendi watched him with interest. Ty wondered if she could sense how he was using his magic, since they shared the same gift.

"I wish you had been there," Ty said. "We could have really used your help."

Ty went on to describe their adventures under the water and the awakening of the giant lake monster. He and Breen both told of their battle with the creature and its tentacles and their narrow escape up the well to the small cavern where the three identical pieces of key lay waiting.

They described how they had accidentally discovered which piece was the correct one using the piece they already had and, in so doing, had brought the ceiling down on them. Ty told of using an air shield to deflect some of the rocks as they raced for the well.

"Wait, you created a shield of air?" Feoldor asked.

Ty nodded. "In fact, I got the idea from you."

"From me?" Feoldor straightened in his seat.

"I remembered the shield you created during the council's fight with Mangora in the Sidaran Assembly."

Feoldor fluffed his side whiskers. "That's right. I forgot about that."

Ty smiled. "I can't tell you how many times those shields have kept us alive."

Feoldor glanced around the room to see who was looking, stopping on Orlyn in particular, even going so far as to smirk in the apothecary's direction. "You hear that, you old geezer? I helped keep them alive."

Orlyn rolled his eyes. "What I heard was that Ty's shield kept them alive. You had nothing to do with it. In fact, if you'd been there, you would have probably suffocated them."

Feoldor sneered, and Ty continued. He expounded on their final battle with the lake creature as they fought to get to the second mirror. He told of the creature capturing Breen and of using the water to create tentacles to save him.

Gilly bounced up and down in his seat with excitement, grinning from ear to ear as Ty described using the water to fight off the monster. Gilly even created a similar tentacle from the liquid in his glass.

"As soon as I got Breen back to the island, we grabbed our gear and dove through the mirror."

"One of the tentacles came in after us," Breen said, "but the mirror sheared it off when it reformed."

Ty's father sat back in his seat and exhaled. He then pulled out his pipe and began to stuff it. Orlyn did the same, and they both took a few quick puffs as the others attempted to gather their thoughts. "That is quite the tale," Ty's father said. "All I can say is I hope this wizards' school is worth all of this."

Ty shared a smile with Breen and Narendi. "Believe me, it is. But we'll get to that."

"Tell them how I saved you," Narendi said.

Ty turned. "It's coming. Give me a minute."

"*And when are you going to tell them of the live market?*" Kraea asked, which was the first time she had spoken since they had begun his retelling of the accounts.

He looked at the draakar, who sat quietly, eyeing everyone, especially Sheeva.

"*I don't like the way she looks at me,*" Kraea said. "*I don't like her eyes or her smell. She smells familiar.*"

Ty wondered what she was talking about, though he did happen to notice that Sheeva's eyes did bear a remarkable semblance to Kraea's. It wasn't so much that they were both amber in color, but that they both shared the same catlike slits for pupils. It was eerily strange.

"I'll get to that after I tell them about the third test."

Kraea growled softly, and not in a friendly manner, more annoyed than anything as Ty finally turned to the council. He took one final pull from a tankard Breen had been so good as to fill from the pitchers on the table, and then proceeded with the story.

"The mirror took us to a small chamber inside the Khezrian Wall," Ty said. "Of course, we didn't know it was the Khezrian Wall at the time, only that we were once again surrounded by rock. We followed the passageway until it led us through the mountainside and out onto a blinding horizon filled with nothing but sand. Dunes as far as your eyes can see."

Narendi smiled.

"From there we followed the compass straight into the desert, where we quickly discovered that traveling during the day was not a good idea and were forced to travel only by night. I don't know how long we walked those dunes, but by the time we had run out of water, we were barely able to put one foot in front of the other. Which, of course, was when we ran into the mother of all sand storms. The entire sky behind us was black, and it was coming straight for us."

"What did you do?" Reloria asked, chewing rather vigorously on a soft piece of taffy as she listened.

"We stumbled down into one of the clefts between the dunes and dug in, covering ourselves with our blankets just before it hit us. After digging ourselves out, we were too weak to move. Our tongues were swollen, our skin burnt. We basically lay there, not expecting to get back up."

"And that is when I saved them," Narendi blurted out. "White-skins know nothing of the desert. Do not respect its ways." She shook her head and then told the council how her people had found them, dug them out, and brought them back to their village. She told how she had spent several days nursing them back to health.

"They were very badly burned," she said, "and it took most of Isha's cream to heal their skin."

Orlyn cleared his throat. "What is this Isha cream you speak of? Sounds interesting."

Ty perked up. "That's right. I almost forgot. We brought back a few of the plants used in creating the cream. I knew you would like to get your hands on them. The Imbatoo call them wamini. They grow along the rocks behind her village, and I can definitely speak to its effectiveness. I've never seen skin regrow so quickly." He looked at Fraya. "Without magic, of course."

Fraya smiled.

"Do you have some with you?" Orlyn asked, anxiously rubbing his hands.

"Afraid not. We left them in our packs back at the house. But I will bring you some tomorrow when we come into town."

Orlyn smiled. "Yes, I would like to see this plant very much."

"Are you finished?" Narendi asked, looking annoyed with Ty for interrupting her story.

"Sorry. Go ahead."

Narendi went on to describe the blistering on their faces, hands, and necks. "It took a long time to get them clean," she said, offhandedly mentioning something about bathing them.

Ty spared a quick glance at Lyessa and noted her face was red. He was going to need to get her alone afterward and try to explain. He took over the story by describing the Imbatoo, starting with their village of tents. He told them of his first experience meeting the Mzwati, the Imbatoo's dune warriors, and the unfortunate standoff with their captain.

Narendi added in additional details about her people whenever she thought it called for. She described not only the Mzwati, but also the Wazeri, and between the three of them, they recalled the battle that took place inside the Wazeri school, and the attempted killing of the Mazota Wanjenga. They told of the prophecies about Ty and his eventual returning to the Imbatoo as a possible savior, or if the dead Wazeri were to be believed, their destroyer. Ty's father didn't seem to care for what he was hearing, and neither did Lyessa, especially about the part of him returning to the Imbatoo.

"And after we had healed enough to continue our travels," Ty said, "Narendi's father, King Diawandy, escorted us to Zwaneri a Wakale, which is an ancient temple located out in the middle of the desert. Unfortunately, we had to cross through the feeding grounds in order to get there."

"I'm sorry," Fraya said. "The what grounds?"

Breen looked at Ty, and Ty nodded for him to take it from there.

"Have you ever heard the stories about the orms?" Breen asked. "The giant wormlike creatures that swim under the sand and can swallow a man whole?"

A couple of those around the table nodded.

"Well, they aren't just stories." Breen went on to describe in rather graphic detail their encounter with the monstrous creatures. So detailed, in fact, that he had several people turning pale after describing what had happened to a few of their party during the battle. Even Ty was feeling a little nauseated reliving what had happened.

Ty took over at the part where he decided to draw the giant creatures away from the others. He then told of finding his way to the temple ruins and being taken inside to find the temple was anything but in ruins. He talked of the grandeur, as well as the great tree standing at the center of the main hall. He told them of their encounter with the priests and their use of glamour magic. He described their rooms that evening and how they could be made to change into whatever the person sleeping there wished.

Excited chatter filled the room as the council members discussed the many interesting ways they would have shaped their rooms had they been there.

He told them of the test of the two doors; how one had led to the fabled treasure of Tmoksuween, and the other to a dais with the next piece of the key.

"I wonder what happens to the priests now that the key is gone?" Orlyn asked. "Will they simply go back to wherever they came from?"

"From what they told us," Ty said, "the temple protects more than just the key."

"Like what?" Feoldor asked rather quickly, no doubt hoping for more treasure.

Ty shrugged. "They didn't seem all that interested in letting us know. They did, however, take us to the next mirror, which led us to the Riverlands."

Ty's father smiled and pulled the pipe from his mouth. "Are the trees as big there as they say?"

"Bigger," Breen said.

Ty went on to describe the trees themselves, including the circular walkways and the swinging bridges, and even the insides like the Beetle Bark Inn where they had stayed. From there, he and Breen talked about their time in the Riverlands: of going shopping with Narendi, of stopping to watch flat boats filled with caged animals float upriver to be sold at the Live Market. They even mentioned their first experience with tellareen mushroom gravy, which Orlyn found rather humorous. Ty also talked about hearing strange voices.

"I thought it was the mushrooms at first," he said, "but then I kept hearing them."

"That was Mother," Kraea said. *"She felt your magic."*

"Yes, I know, but at the time I thought I was going crazy. I don't exactly walk around hearing voices."

"Could have fooled us," Feoldor said, giving Ty a strange look, which was shared by a few others.

"Sorry," Ty apologized. "I often forget that I'm the only one who can hear her."

Orlyn cleared his throat. "The very definition of going crazy."

"Well, I promise you, I'm not. Kraea can hear and understand everything that is being said. She just doesn't have the ability to speak."

Some of those gathered looked skeptical.

"Go ahead," Ty said. "Ask her anything."

"How would we know that it is really her speaking in return," Lyessa asked, "and not just you making something up? Like if I asked her how old she is, you could just give us some random age and we'd never know if it was true or not."

She had a point, though he didn't care much for the way she was making it, as if she believed he would simply just lie to them. "Fine, then ask her to do something."

"Okay," Lyessa said with a wicked grin as she turned and pointed at Narendi. "Go chew on her neck."

Narendi was halfway out of her seat before Ty grabbed her and pulled her back down. He shot Lyessa a hard glare, but she just sat back in her chair, looking quite pleased with herself.

"Anyone else?" Ty asked.

Ty's father pointed the stem of his pipe at Kraea. "If you can hear and understand what we are saying, then I'll ask you to walk over to Breen and touch his left shoulder."

Ty looked at Kraea and nodded, so she slunk behind their chairs until she was in back of Breen, then she stood on her haunches, and with one long black claw, she tapped Breen carefully on the shoulder. Most everyone in the room watched in awe as the draakar then turned and made her way back beside Ty's seat and sat down.

"She is quite an incredible creature," Ty's father said, then corrected himself. "I guess I shouldn't say creature. I suppose draakar would be more appropriate?"

Kraea snorted, and several of the members clapped, Gilly the loudest, as he banged his mug on the table excitedly. A couple of the members even tried to make a request of their own, as though she were the hired entertainment for the evening, but Ty cut them off so he could continue with the story.

From there, Ty proceeded to share their journey up the river to the Live Market, and in doing so, of finding Tulgava Rashuvi, the great tree used by an ancient sect of wizards, possibly the wizard council itself.

With Breen's, Narendi's, and Kraea's help, he recalled the events that had taken place at the market: of his first meeting with Kraea and her mother, of Kraea's mother's bravery as she took on Dalibor and his men, and of her giving her life to save them. He told them of finding the red stone for the key and then giving it up in exchange for Kraea. He told them of their narrow escape through the mirror only to find Mangora and the Tower waiting on them when they arrived.

"I was conked on the head from behind," Ty said, "and when I woke, I found myself in the back of a prison wagon with one of those durma collars around my neck."

He told them of being forced to watch Mangora perform the Sola de Blanava ritual. The retelling took longer than he wanted, and by the time he finished, the room had grown deathly silent.

"Once she had her missing piece of the key," Ty said, "we were carted up the mountain by way of several passes that led to Upper Wellhollow. That's when things really got dangerous." He went on to expound on the avalanche and how it had been diverted over their heads by the bulradoer. He then told of their escape from the prison wagons and their eventual joining of the battle in Upper Wellhollow.

For the next half hour, Ty, Breen, and Narendi all chipped in as they laid out the sequence of events that had taken place during the battle.

Ty told them of being saved by the incredible swordsman who'd been traveling with the tinkers, and of the final retreat of the Tower as one of the tinker women used some sort of magic to blast the remaining bulradoer down the incline and back into the pass.

The council barely had time to catch their breath before Ty immediately started in on the most frightening events of all—how they had rushed into the mountainside through a winding passageway and found Mangora and her spider attempting to use the shorlock to open the great stone doors of Harok Laos.

Breen told of how he had been captured by Mangora and used as bait to force Ty to use the key and open the doors. Kraea made sure that Ty told of how she had risked her own life to help him get in the chamber and being gravely wounded in the process.

Ty told of how he had resorted to using glamour magic to shock and confuse Mangora with images of her twin sister, giving Narendi time to rush in and get one of the durma collars around her neck.

"Unfortunately," Ty said angrily, "Mangora's arachnobe managed to save her at the last moment, and they escaped back through the tunnel before we could stop her."

Ty's father balled his fists where they were resting on the table. Ty knew his father wanted justice for Ty's mother as much as he did.

Ty went on to explain how they had used the crystal from the old seer's pendant to fix the key, and how it had taken both his and Kraea's blood to get it to activate.

"Once it did," he said, "the shorlock burst to life, and the doors opened."

"So what did Aero'set look like?" Lyessa asked anxiously.

Everyone sat in silence, eyes wide, waiting to find out. Ty couldn't resist milking the excitement as long as possible, but as soon as Feoldor's eye began to twitch, he continued.

"It wasn't there."

"What?" the entire room called out at the same time.

"It had all been destroyed?" Orlyn asked. "You did all of that for nothing?"

"Not quite." Ty went on to explain his use of the key to bring back the Wizard's Keep, and how close to death he had come doing so.

He painted them an incredible picture of the buildings and bulwarks and towers as they were ripped from wherever they had been and brought back into the realm of man. "And just before I felt the last drop of life leave my body, the key released me."

"That's when Nyalis showed up," Breen said.

Ty nodded. "He was waiting on us, like he'd been expecting us the whole time. I have no idea where he came from or how he knew we would be there, but after introductions had been given, he took us into Aero'set."

Ty, Breen, Narendi, and Kraea ended their story by giving the council a long and very detailed overview of Aero'set itself, recounting all the places they had seen inside the school, including even the Meeisredon and the seats of power, not forgetting the Pentarium, a piece of Ty's own homeland. Ty was careful not to go into too much detail about where it was located, just that Nyalis had taken them to see it. It wasn't that he didn't trust the council members, but as he could attest, one never knew when they might find themselves the Tower's prisoners. It was best to keep something like that limited to as few people as possible.

The council got the most excited when they were told of the magical rooms that Ty and the others had been living in, and the meals that would appear at all hours of the day with just a clap of the hands. Ty's father was specifically interested in the flying battleships that lay dormant outside the garrison. They also didn't leave out having nearly been killed on more than one occasion during their explorations, which left some feeling hesitant about visiting, even more so when they were told that the only way to do so would be through Reed Marsh.

By the time they finished their tale with their trip back through the marsh and their battle with the marsh monster and Narendi's surprising use of voda magic—which had Gilly very excited—the morning light was seeping through the narrow window slits at the back of the room. They had spent the entire night talking. Strangely enough, Ty wasn't the least bit tired, even after their restless sleep outside the marsh the previous night.

"Oh," Breen said. "We forgot to mention the Bristonian soldiers."

Ty turned. "That's right. I forgot all about them."

"What Bristonian soldiers?" their father asked.

Breen told him of the ship they'd seen while trying to cross the East River, and spotting what looked like Bristonian uniforms under a couple of the men's coats.

"Which way were they heading?"

"Toward Easthaven," Breen said.

Veldon thumbed his chin. "There was a boat up from Briston, but I don't remember seeing any uniforms disembarking."

Ty's father pursed his lips, then promptly started chewing on the tip of his pipe. "Perhaps Meyrose is planning an unscheduled visit? I might stop by the overlord's estate as soon as we finish here, to find out."

Ty, Breen, and Narendi spent at least another hour fielding the council members' questions, with no end in sight. There was so much to talk about, so many smaller details that they had not shared during the retelling that everyone wanted to hear. However, during one of the longer pauses between answers, Orlyn finally scooted his chair back from the table. "As much as I would love to continue talking, I do have a shop that needs opening."

Reloria looked at him and yawned. "As do we all." She poked Feoldor in the side, and he turned and stretched. "How about walking me home?" she said.

He nodded, yawning himself as he pushed his chair back and then helped her up.

Ty stood along with the rest and watched as most of the council members slipped by and out the door. Fraya didn't wait until they were finished talking to grab Breen. He picked her up in his arms as they kissed. As soon as he put her down, they started for the door, clearly anxious to be out of there, but Ty stopped them.

"Take Narendi and Kraea with you, will you?" He turned to Narendi. "Please, go with Breen. I'll be home after a while." He felt awkward saying that, but it was the truth.

Narendi didn't move, at least not until Breen walked back inside. "Come on," he said, looking over at Lyessa, who was standing by herself near the back. "They need to talk alone."

Narendi eventually left, but she didn't look happy about it.

Ty walked over and shut the door. He turned, and they quietly stared at each other for what seemed like several minutes, neither speaking. Ty had no idea what to say. Of all the times he had pictured this moment happening, none of them had turned out like this.

"I'm sorry," he said, figuring that was probably the best place to start as he slowly made his way toward the back. "This isn't exactly how I wanted to see you again. It all just . . ." He reached out to place his hand on her arm.

She pulled away. "Things are . . . different now."

"Different? How? I'm still the same person you were kissing a few hours ago."

"Except now I find you've traded me in for a princess."

Ty balled his fists. "I haven't traded you in for anything. I already told you, I'm not married."

"She believes you are."

"Well, I'm not. I don't care how many times she shaves her head, I'm not her husband. We have not been bonded. I've already told her that you are the one I love."

Lyessa's head lifted, and Ty realized what he'd just said. He paused, suddenly recognizing how true it was. He'd nearly died more times than he could count, and one of the things he'd regretted most was never telling her how much he really cared. He took a deep breath. "I do love you."

She stared into his eyes a moment, then smiled. "I love you too." She took a step forward but stopped, her face growing more serious. "And she's not your wife?"

Ty sighed, wondering how many times he was going to have to assure her. "No. We are not wed."

Her smile returned as she stepped the rest of the way and wrapped her arms around him and kissed him. He started to wrap his arms around her, but she pulled back before he could. "Promise me you haven't bonded with her."

He huffed. "But I just told you—"

"I want to hear you say it."

Ty looked directly into her eyes. "I promise."

Lyessa stared back a moment longer, then smiled and kissed him once again, this time a deep lingering kiss. When she finally pulled away, Ty tried to inhale without sounding like he was gasping for air. He was thankful to be up against the wall, as his legs had begun to buckle.

Finally catching his breath, he directed her to a couple of chairs, and they spent the next few hours talking more about his journey, where he wisely added in the number of times he had missed her while he was away.

They finished their conversation with Lyessa telling him about her and Darryk's training of Fraya and Adarra, and how upset she and Fraya had been with his sister for taking off and leaving them behind. "Do you think she'll be alright?"

Ty sighed as he sat back in his seat and tried picturing his stubborn but quiet sister in his mind—short and curvy like their mother, with straight brown hair and freckles, and her nose always stuck in a book or three. "She's the smartest person I know. If she thinks she can do this, I have to believe she can."

Chapter 34 | Adarra

ADARRA LEANED OUT OVER the rail of the ship, hoping to get a better look at what lay ahead. She would have been able to see much better from the forward deck, but the last time she had attempted it, the wintery gusts had whipped across the deck and wrapped her hair around her face like a scarf. She'd rather avoid repeating that experience again anytime soon if she could.

The water was hard to see, save for the sliver that had the moon reflecting off the surface. Embarking at night was not her idea, but the captain wanted to reach the Ozrin Sea by early morning on the second day to give them as much daylight as possible to sail through the Bay of Mist. Had they waited to leave until morning, they wouldn't have reached the sea until late afternoon or early evening, which meant they would either have been forced to try crossing then and hope they made it before dark, or wait until the next morning and lose that much more time.

"How do they know where they're going?" Aiden asked, walking up behind her. He wore a thick woolen coat over one of the outfits he'd purchased just for the journey, as if the Tallosians would give an axe throw whether his shirt and vest had been worn prior to today. His sword was strapped low on his waist. Adarra's own sword only seemed to sit that low because she was so short.

"I have a feeling that Captain Mervall has sailed these waters a time or two," she said, turning back around to stare out across the river. Boat lanterns hung along the rail she was leaning against, making it difficult to see out, as the light from the nearest was shining back in her face. She finally gave up and turned around. "Besides, they've been throwing lead lines and taking soundings at nearly every bend in the river since we left the docks. I'm sure we'll be fine."

He smiled. "I'm sure you're right." He shivered and pulled his coat tighter around him as he stared nervously back out at the river. "Kind of nippy tonight." His breath misted in front of him. They hadn't seen snowfall in the last few days, but the sun still wasn't warm enough to melt what was already along the riverbanks.

They were only a couple hours out from Easthaven and weren't expected to reach Crystal Lake until morning. She half wished Gilly had come along. If he had been there to steer the ship, they would have probably made it all the way to the Ozrin Sea by the time the first of the sun's rays poked over the eastern horizon.

"How is your bunk?" she asked. The ship was only large enough for a single cabin, which was usually the captain's, but for this voyage, she and Aiden were sharing it with Ambassador Lanmiere. The captain had brought in a couple of spare cots in addition to his bed, which the ambassador had recommended Adarra take. However, Adarra declined, opting for a hammock instead, and left the captain's bed to the ambassador, whose aging bones needed it more than hers. Aiden took a cot. Other than dropping off their luggage, most of which consisted of Adarra's books, neither had spent much time inside.

"I'm sure it will be adequate," he said, trying to put on a brave face. She knew Aiden had never wanted for anything and was quite unused to roughing it. She doubted he'd sleep much on the trip over. "What about you?" he asked. "Have you ever slept in one of those contraptions before? It swings, doesn't it?"

She smiled. "I think that's why I'll like it. It'll move with the river, rocking me to sleep." She'd never been in one before, but it did look fun. From what she'd read, some described it like sleeping in a cocoon. Others that it felt like lying in a love's embrace. That sounded rather pleasant. "Have you seen the ambassador?"

Aiden pointed at the door on the back of the main deck, which led into the galley. Inside were the stairs leading down to the hull, where the crew slept, and where the food was being stored for the Tallosians. "The last I saw, he was heading down to talk with your savage."

"I wish you wouldn't call him that," she said. "He has a name, you know."

"Yeah . . . flaming savage. The man wears people's scalps for crying out loud."

"Jonas isn't the same man he was before. His people were desperate."

"Tell that to the permanent scar across my chest where he tried to gut me."

"There is no scar there and you know it. Fraya healed that months ago. Besides, that wasn't Jonas."

"Might as well have been."

She could see there was no changing his mind, and it wasn't like she could really blame him. No one, including her father, trusted Jonas. If she was honest with herself, she wasn't sure that she did either, not completely.

They had come a long way over the last several months, all the days she'd spent sitting cross-legged in front of his cell, teaching him about their ways while he did the same for her. It had been a difficult process trying to learn his language, and in turn teach him theirs. Surprisingly, he seemed to pick things up faster than she did, but that was probably because the Aldoran language was a bit easier to understand. The added hand gestures made the Tallosian language a bit more difficult. It had required a lot of patience on both their ends as they learned to work together, but in the end, she thought they had developed a mutual respect.

She turned and looked at the door leading into the galley. Now that Aiden had got her thinking about Jonas, she wanted to see how he was doing. Apart from when they had first brought him aboard, she hadn't been down to see him. Captain Holverd didn't seem to want anyone interacting with the prisoner while aboard, but she wasn't just anyone.

"Come on," she told Aiden and started across the deck.

"Where are you going?"

"Where do you think?"

"I think you need to stay away from him."

She ignored him and opened the galley door and stepped inside. The place smelled of uncooked meat, fish, and onions. It was too late to eat, but the galley staff were busy preparing for the next day's meals.

"My eyes are beginning to water," Aiden said, waving his hand in front of his face. "I hope they aren't planning on serving onions for breakfast."

Raised voices coming from the direction of the stairs drew Adarra's attention, and she headed straight for them. She followed the glow of the lanterns into the darkness below, the voices growing more pronounced, enough for her to make out who they belonged to. It seemed Ambassador Lanmiere was having a heated discussion with Captain Holverd.

Even apart from stumbling across Holverd in the cells threatening Jonas, the few times she had met the captain during their meetings at the overlord's house, she had found him to be a somewhat abrasive man, unpleasant even. But Lyessa's father had assured her that he was one of their best, and if things went sour, that they would want Holverd's sword on their side.

Adarra and Aiden made their way through the crew's quarters, which consisted mostly of rows of hammocks with unwashed bodies stuck inside. She was suddenly wishing for the onions. Some of the men were sound asleep, which she found rather astonishing, considering the boisterous argument taking place in the back. Their voices carried throughout the entire hull of the ship.

"Perhaps we should stay out of it," Aiden said, pulling Adarra to a stop as they passed the last of the hammocks to find a wall of barrels and crates blocking their view beyond. The containers of food were tied together with rope nets to keep from tipping and no doubt ran the length of the ship.

"No," she said. "Jonas is my responsibility. If this has something to do with him, then I should know." She pulled loose from his grip and started through the single opening and into the mounds of stacked provisions.

"How do you expect him to trust us with you constantly threatening to kill him?" Lanmiere shouted.

Adarra quickened her pace. What had they done to Jonas?

"I don't care if he trusts us or not," Captain Holverd countered. "I'm not here to be the animal's friend. I'm here to complete a mission, and I'll do whatever I think is necessary to see that mission through."

Adarra worked her way past the last of the barrels to a small open area near the back, where they had Jonas chained to one of the ship's main support beams. "Not if it means assaulting the one person we need to make that happen," she said, stepping out of the passageway and taking up a stance across from Holverd. Aiden shuffled in behind her, not looking happy about being there.

Adarra spotted the short whip in the captain's hands, then looked at Jonas, who was using the beam to shield himself from Holverd. There were bloodstained rips along the front of his shirt where the lash had ripped his cloak. She spun on the captain. "What do you think you're doing?" she shouted, shocking herself and Aiden, who literally jumped.

The captain's hand tightened on his whip, his other rubbing his shaved head. "This is none of your concern."

"I beg to differ. Overlord Barl put me in charge of the prisoner. I have every right to be here when he's being questioned."

"And the overlord put me in charge of you and everyone else aboard these ships. It's my duty to keep you safe, even if that means from the likes of him."

Adarra's face reddened. "He's not the one making me feel unsafe right now."

The captain snarled, then turned to one of the two soldiers standing behind him, a man Adarra knew all too well, as she was the reason he was even on this mission. "Sergeant Finnly, I want you to escort the ambassador and our young guests back to their cabin, and make sure they stay there."

Finnly looked at Adarra and frowned. The short, portly man with red cheeks looked very uncomfortable in his new position as he stared at her, unsure what to do. She wished he had stayed in Easthaven and kept to his former post as jailer of the garrison cells. Finnly looked at Holverd and noticed the captain was still staring at him and quickly saluted. "Uh, yes, sir."

Ambassador Lanmiere crossed his arms. "I'm a Sidaran ambassador. You have no authority over what I do."

"The overlord gave me command of this mission, and as long as you are under my protection, I do have that authority."

Lanmiere's eyes widened. "I will be having a word with the overlord as soon as we return."

Captain Holverd didn't seem to care. He simply marched back through the mound of food and disappeared somewhere inside the hammocks, leaving the ambassador to fume behind him. Lanmiere was a tall man with grey hair and an elderly disposition. He reminded Adarra of Orlyn at times, except right now, he looked ready to cross swords as he marched after Holverd to no doubt give the man a piece of his mind.

"Please, Mistress," Finnly said, wringing his hands. "I don't want to force the issue. He is my commanding officer."

Adarra's blood was boiling, but between Sergeant Finnly and Aiden's constant tugging on her arm, she finally nodded. She didn't want Finnly to get in trouble, and she still wanted to have words with the captain. She looked at Jonas. "Are you alright?"

He dabbed at the open wounds with his fingers and then sat down. "Yes."

She turned to Finnly. "I don't care what Holverd says. That man is my responsibility. Please see that he gets some food and water and a blanket." She waited for the sergeant to nod, then turned and marched back through the piled food and hammocks and up the stairs to the door leading out onto the main deck. Aiden and Finnly chased after her.

As soon as she made it through the door, she spotted Captain Holverd on the other side, climbing the stairs to the forward deck. She also saw Lanmiere, but he was presently engaged with the ship's crew, leaving her free to go after Holverd. "Captain! I wish to have a word."

Holverd glanced over his shoulder but then kept going.

She gritted her teeth. She was getting tired of him ignoring her and treating her like a child.

"Adarra, what are you doing?" Aiden asked, trying to pull her to a stop as he and Finnly stumbled out of the galley. "We are hardly in a position to argue with the man. I, for one, don't want him getting angry and chaining us down there with the Northman."

She straightened her dress, pulling her cloak tight around her neck as she did. "I'd like to see him try."

"You might want to listen to your . . . friend," Finnly said, giving Aiden a good looking-over, clearly not liking the way Aiden had his hand on Adarra's arm. "Captain Holverd is a good soldier, but he's also an angry one. He hasn't been the same after losing his men during that first Tallosian raid."

"The overlord put me in charge of Jonas's well-being," she said, "which includes making sure he cooperates with us to form a productive dialogue with his people. How likely do you think that's going to be with him being chained to a post and whipped like a rabid animal?" She could see in both Aiden's and Finnly's eyes that that was exactly how they saw Jonas, so she didn't bother debating her point. Instead, she started straight for the stairs.

"You're going to get us thrown off the ship," Aiden grumbled behind her, but he followed her across the deck anyway, Finnly right beside him.

Behind them, the ambassador looked to be finishing up his conversation when they reached the top of the stairs. Captain Holverd was standing near the bow on the left, watching the ship's captain, Captain Mervall, on the right, check the river's depth as one of his crew took another sounding. Mervall was a shorter man, certainly shorter than Holverd, but unlike Sergeant Finnly, he was rather thin and wore a thick mustache that curled slightly upward, giving the man the appearance of walking around with a constant smile on his face.

Mervall watched as the crewman pulled in the lead line and then called out the depth. The captain nodded and wrote something in a little black book he never seemed to be without, before finally turning and making his way back down to the main deck.

Adarra nodded at him as he passed, then headed straight for Holverd. His demeanor darkened when he saw her coming. "I wish to have a word with you, Captain."

Holverd turned and glared at Finnly. "I told you to take them to their cabin."

"I tried, sir, but they—"

"Don't blame him," Adarra fumed. "What I have to discuss needs to be heard."

Behind them, Ambassador Lanmiere was just reaching the top of the stairs and was starting in their direction. Adarra wasn't sure where this newfound will of hers was coming from, but she hoped it remained long enough for her to get out what she needed to say. "You might be in charge of this mission, but that doesn't make my charge any less important. The man down there is in my care. I am responsible for his well-being."

"His *well-being* is the least of my concerns," Holverd spat. "The animal and his people murdered an entire company of my men, and if he hadn't been stopped, he would probably be wearing their scalps right now. So excuse me if I don't give a flaming toss about his well-being."

Adarra bit down on her retort and forced herself to think before she flew off the handle and said something that did indeed get her kicked off the ship. The way Holverd was acting, she didn't doubt for a minute that he would. "As I understand it, you have a mission to complete, Captain, one given to you specifically by the overlord, and this mission could save numerous lives if successful. Overlord Barl isn't a stupid or rash man, so the fact that he gave a mission of this importance to you means that he trusts in your abilities."

Holverd's defensive posture relaxed slightly.

"What I'm saying is that my charge is there to see your mission complete, which is ultimately what we all want. That man you have chained in the hull might represent everything you hate about his people, and if I were in your shoes, I would probably bear that same resentment." She took a deep breath, steeling herself against the pain of her next words. "In fact, if you recall, my own mother was killed during that raid."

Captain Holverd nodded. "I remember."

"Then you can imagine the feelings I harbor for the Northmen as well. But I know how important it is to make sure this mission is successful. If we fail, it could mean war. I know I don't want something like that on my conscience. Jonas is our only tie to the Tallosians. I've spent nearly every day for the last several months working with a man who was partly responsible for the death of my own mother. If I'm willing to do that, surely you can curb your own anger long enough for us to see this through. Let me be clear: That man down there is our only hope of making this work. Feelings aside, how willing do you think he's going to be to help us if we treat him like an animal? How willing do you think the Tallosians are going to be to broker a peace when they see us dragging in one of their own, looking like he'd just spent the last two weeks beaten bloody in the stocks?"

"She speaks wisdom, Holverd," Lanmiere said, having listened in from the side. "I hope you aren't too stupid to listen."

Adarra tried not to roll her eyes. The ambassador was nicely undermining her attempt to make her point without injuring the captain's pride.

"We need the Tallosian on our side," Lanmiere continued. "I certainly wouldn't walk into the Northman's homeland, expecting him to not lead us into a trap after we've just spent the last couple of days beating him like a rabid dog. If this continues, I think I'll just remain aboard and let you fools go off and get yourselves killed."

Holverd stared at Lanmiere for a moment, then Adarra. "Fine. I'll leave him in your care, but make sure you keep him out from under my feet. You know how I stand on the matter. Don't make me regret this decision." With that, he turned and stormed off toward the stairs, ordering Finnly to follow on his way by.

Finnly gave a nervous smile toward Adarra, then scampered off after his captain. She hated having put Finnly in such a position. The man had been nothing but sweet to her, a little too sweet, unfortunately. She still couldn't believe he'd given up his post just to follow her to Tallos.

"You have quite the strong will, young lady," Lanmiere said with a warm, fatherly sort of smile as he laid his hand on her shoulder. "Just be careful how you use it."

She could see that he thought she had taken it too far when it came to Holverd, but seeing Jonas beaten like that had set something inside her off.

"I'll try to be more prudent in the future," she said.

"Good." The ambassador yawned. "What say we turn in for the night? Got a busy day ahead of us tomorrow if we plan on making the Ozrin by the following morning."

"I'll be in in a little while," she said. "I want to make sure they've given Jonas some food and water, and at the very least a blanket. We can't have our guest of honor dying on us before we get there."

Lanmiere's bushy eyebrows rose. "No, I guess not." He gave her a warning look. "Just be sure to stay out of Holverd's way. He doesn't strike me as someone who holds a short memory when it comes to those that hurt him. I suggest you do as he says and make sure Jonas and the good captain don't cross paths."

She nodded and started for the stairs.

"I'm coming with you," Aiden said, but Adarra shook her head.

"No, I'm going down alone. I think after everything that's happened, it's best I talk to him by myself."

"But I—"

She laid her hand on his arm. "I know you're just looking out for me, and I appreciate it. But I need to do this alone." Aiden finally nodded, and she stood on her tiptoes and kissed his cheek. "Thank you."

She left him there and headed to the main deck, and from there went down into the hull of the ship, but not before having one of the crew retrieve an extra blanket and a plate of food. She carried the blanket and food down and into the back of the ship, where she found Jonas still propped against the post he was chained to.

He stood when he saw her and looked past her toward the opening.

"No one is coming," she said, dragging over a loose crate to sit on. "I'm here alone."

It was the first time they were together without a set of bars between them. She found it a little unnerving. He was Tallosian, after all, and one of the biggest men she'd ever laid eyes on. He was every bit as big as her father and brother, and that scar running down the side of his face didn't help, not to mention his arms were thick enough that he could probably snap her in two with little trouble. The thought of that suddenly had her judging the distance of his chains and whether he could reach her from where she was seated.

She tossed him the blanket. "Here, I thought you might want this."

He slung it over his shoulders, blowing on his hands as he did. "Thank you." He looked at the plate of food, which wasn't much more than a couple of red apples and some dried meat. The galley hadn't had any fresh biscuits made. She would have to wait on those till morning.

She thought about placing the plate and cup on the floor and scooting them across the planks with her foot but then grew embarrassed by the thought and cautiously leaned forward and held them out instead. He took them, and their fingers touched for a brief moment, sending prickles up her arms; if they were close enough to touch, he was close enough to grab her.

It was probably a foolish thing to do on her part, but she'd wanted to give him at least the appearance of not fearing him. If he did manage to get his hands on her, he could probably use her to free himself. That alone had her scooting her crate back a little farther. Knowing Holverd, the captain might not be willing to trade her life for Jonas's. Besides his hatred for the Tallosian, if they were to free Jonas, their mission would fail, and she didn't see the good captain willing to return to Easthaven having given up their only viable means of dialogue with the mountain folk of Tallos.

"I've talked with Captain Holverd. He won't be back down here."

Jonas took a large bite out of the apple. "He has hatred in his heart. I know this look."

"Your people killed his men outside my home."

He nodded, then bit into a piece of the dried meat. "He wishes for a blood debt, then."

"Blood debt?"

"He wishes to fight me."

Adarra shook her head. "No. He doesn't wish to fight." In truth, if given the chance, Holverd would have gladly stuck a blade in Jonas and tossed him over the side. "But you are correct. He does hold anger in his heart, and it will be best if we keep you away from him."

"Do you think me unable to fight? Do you worry for me?"

Her palms began to sweat. She wasn't exactly sure how he had meant that. "I worry that something will happen to you, yes. Because, if something happens to you, then we won't be able to open a talk with your people. We need you."

He looked at her a moment, his eyes narrowing slightly. She couldn't tell what he was thinking, but he did eventually nod and take another bite of his apple, its juices running into his beard. "How long to reach the veil?"

"The veil?"

"Clouds over the water."

"Oh, you mean the Bay of Mist. We should reach the Ozrin Sea by the morning after next, depending on how the weather holds up." They stared at each other for a while in silence, long enough for Adarra to start feeling uncomfortable, so she stood, faking a yawn. "I'll make sure to have them send you a pail of water down tomorrow."

"Why?"

She pinched her nose. "Because you stink."

He belted out a hearty laugh, and she left him to his food as she headed back through the mound of provisions. She hoped she was doing the right thing by loosening Holverd's grip. There was a fondness there with Jonas that she had developed over the last several months. She didn't want to see him hurt, but he was still a Tallosian, and a very dangerous one at that. She couldn't let her guard down. There was too much at stake, too many lives depending on them to make this negotiation work, not just for Easthaven, but for Tallos as well. As long as she could keep Jonas away from Captain Holverd, hopefully the rest of the trip could be made without further confrontation. None of them could afford to have this mission derailed by sentiments best left unspoken.

One bout of uncontrolled anger could lead to war.

Chapter 35 | Adarra

ADARRA WOKE THE NEXT morning to a strong chill. The heated rocks she had stuffed in her bedding had long gone cold, leaving her shivering within her blankets. She hoped Jonas had survived with his blanket and cloak. She guessed it wasn't any less than what the rest of the crew had.

She turned over and looked down through the netting of her hammock to see that Aiden's cot below her was empty. A loud sucking inhale from the other side of the room said that Ambassador Lanmiere's bed wasn't. She quietly crawled out of the hammock and hopped down. Her back was a little stiff, more from the hammock than the cold. Once inside, she'd found it wasn't all that easy to turn over, so she had slept in the same position all night.

Sunlight splashed across her face from the cabin's windows, and she immediately started to sneeze. She didn't know why early-morning sunlight made her do that. It was just another topic she would have to research, not that she expected to find much information on the effects of sun-induced sneezing, but one never knew.

After tying back her hair and pulling on her boots, cloak, and gloves, she quietly opened the cabin door and slipped outside, doing her best not to wake Lanmiere. She liked the ambassador. He had always been very kind to her, one of the few on Overlord Barl's advisory team who she had always found very easy to talk with, not to mention always willing to listen. Others were not so agreeable, considering her too young, even though she was halfway through her nineteenth year.

She stood on the deck and watched the crew go about their chores, their movements almost like a song, each note with its own purpose, put together to form a wonderful sort of melody. She admired the organization. Yawning, she turned to see if Aiden was on the upper deck. She couldn't see him on the stern, but she did see Captain Holverd talking with Captain Mervall. They had a piece of parchment unrolled on the railing, and Mervall was pointing out something for Holverd.

From the gestures, Mervall appeared to be explaining to Holverd where they were, most likely letting him know when he thought they would reach the sea. Mervall had been the only captain willing to accept the overlord's mission, the only one crazy enough to risk taking a ship through the Bay of Mist. She wondered what that said about the man. No one else had been daring—or perhaps foolish—enough to sail to Tallos.

Mervall had made the journey only once, and that was years ago when he had taken a dare from another captain during a card game. Apparently, Mervall had been rather brash in his early years, and it seemed a streak of that daring still remained. Adarra was thankful for it, though she desperately hoped that his brazenness stemmed more from a strength of nerve than from simple recklessness.

She left the main deck and started up the steps on the port side, bracing herself for the cold she was about to face. Aiden was standing by himself at the bow, staring out over the water. Part of her was glad he had come—it gave her a familiar face to talk to—but part of her also wished he had remained in Easthaven where it was safer.

Aiden had been training with Darryk for the last several months, just like she and Fraya had been. Frustrating as it may have been that he was picking it up much quicker than either of them had, he was still a far cry from being ready for real combat. The memory of the way he had acted during the battle outside their home still reared its ugly head every so often, but there was no denying Aiden had changed. In fact, he had changed so much that despite all odds, they had formed an attachment.

It was the first romantic attachment Adarra had ever had, and it was wonderful. She had always been too shy or too awkward or too busy with her reading to really notice boys or get their notice in return. It was thrilling to have someone as beautiful as Aiden pay her the kind of attention he was, but his attention could be a bit smothering. She had found it exciting at first, to have him constantly there and doting on her, but the longer it lasted, the more difficult it became to get her work done, not to mention the number of arguments they seemed to have over Jonas.

Aiden didn't like all the attention she was giving the Tallosian, and she had to admit she wasn't sure how much of her time spent with Jonas was because of her desire to learn and teach or how much of it was simply wanting a break from Aiden's affection. Still, she would much rather have Aiden's attention than not at all.

"Good morning," she said as she walked up behind him.

He turned and smiled. "Good morning." He leaned over and kissed her, something she never grew tired of. She took a deep breath to steady herself as she looked up at him. "How long have you been up? Why didn't you wake me?"

"You were sleeping too soundly," he said, wrapping his arm around her shoulders. They stood at the railing's edge and stared out at the winding path of the river ahead. "Besides, you looked too cute to wake."

She elbowed him playfully. "The ambassador was sleeping rather soundly when I left."

Aiden chuckled. "I've heard millstones at the grind that weren't that loud."

Adarra laughed. She looked up at the side of Aiden's face, his medium-length brown hair blowing behind him in the breeze. "Apart from the snoring, how did you sleep?"

He squinted against the bright reflection of the low-hanging sun across the top of the water. "I slept as well as could be expected, under the circumstances." He looked down at her. "You?"

"Same."

He started to chuckle.

"What?"

"Did you know you coo when you sleep?"

She gaped at him. "I do not."

"You do." He then began to demonstrate what it sounded like.

She elbowed him again, and he laughed all the harder.

She thought about telling him he snored like a wild hog, but honestly, she hadn't noticed him snoring at all. It was the first time they'd shared a room together, and evidently, he even slept gracefully. The man was very nearly perfect—well, apart from the tendency to smother a person on occasion, and a lack of woodsmanship. Still, he was more or less perfect by noble standards, and he knew it.

"Where do you think we are?" Aiden asked.

Adarra stared out at the water, noticing the river had begun to widen. "I'd say we're getting close to Crystal Lake."

"Then you'd be correct," a voice behind them said, and they both turned to find Captain Mervall walking over. He carried his small black book in one hand, with a thick piece of rolled parchment tucked in the crook of his arm. "I was just tellin' Captain Holverd that we should reach the lake by breakfast. From there, we sail around the south shore, and if the winds allow, we should reach the eastern river by nightfall. We'll make better time crossin' the lake than movin' against the river's current. And if our luck holds, by tomorrow mornin' we'll be eatin' breakfast with an ocean view."

"Sounds like you have our route well mapped, Captain," she said.

"I should hope so. Been sailin' it since I was a boy." He pursed his lips. "Never made the trip haulin' this much weight before, though."

"What's the Bay of Mist like?" Aiden asked. "I hear you're one of the few who's actually made it across and back in one piece."

"I wouldn't exactly say it were one piece, but we did make it in and back out. Took quite a bit of damage over the reefs." He shook his head. "No reliable charts for them flamin' things. At least, none I've heard mention of. I ain't gonna lie to ya. It's an eerie place, the mist. It almost feels as though it's callin' to ya. I've heard of sailors going mad, attemptin' to sail through. Some swear they've seen shades movin' about the ship.

Aiden's eyes bulged. "You can't be serious."

Mervall shrugged. "Just tellin' ya what I've heard. Can't say I saw any shades myself, but I'd be lyin' if I said I didn't get the feelin' of being watched." The captain spat over the side of the ship with the wind, then turned and headed across the deck to talk with one of the crewmen. From there, he made his way back down to the main deck, barking out orders to those below.

Aiden turned and looked at Adarra. "You don't think he was telling the truth, do you?"

Adarra shrugged, not caring for the captain's inference any more than Aiden. "Probably just sailor superstitions getting the better of them."

"I hope so. I'd hate to think there was something actually in the mist."

She looked down the river once more, then turned. "Best we wake the ambassador. He'll not be happy with us if we let him sleep through breakfast."

They left the forward deck and headed down to the captain's cabin to find the ambassador already awake, though moving rather sluggishly. They waited on him to finish pulling on his boots before heading to the galley for breakfast. The tables inside were filled with crew and Sidaran soldiers, as everyone packed inside to get their food and find an empty spot around the limited number of tables.

When those in line spotted the ambassador, they moved aside, motioning for the three of them to cut to the front of the line, but Ambassador Lanmiere wouldn't hear of it, insisting they fill their plates first. Aiden looked disappointed, but Adarra smiled, approving the older man's refusal.

"These men are working hard every day to get us to our destination," Lanmiere said over his shoulder. "They need it more than we do."

They waited until everyone had been through the line before they went through themselves. There was hot porridge and honey, fresh biscuits, salted pork, and even some eggs. It was quite the fare for such a simple vessel. The men looked pleased, especially the sailors. Adarra followed Lanmiere over to the captain's table, as it was the only free one available, and took a seat, doing her best not to look at Holverd, who was seated to the captain's right.

"How'd ya find your accommodations, Ambassador?" Captain Mervall asked, seeming quite jovial.

"Quite conducive to a good night's rest," Lanmiere said. "My thanks for lending us your quarters, Captain. It is a fine ship you have here. You should be very proud."

"Quite proud, sir. And not just for the ship. I work with some of the finest sailors this side of Aldor," he said, the last part pitched loudly enough for the whole room to hear.

"Huzzah!" the sailors shouted in return, startling Adarra and Aiden and causing Lanmiere to fumble his spoon. Even Captain Holverd seemed surprised, though the only indication he gave was a raised eyebrow. As soon as he glanced in Adarra's direction, she quickly dropped her head and busied herself with her porridge.

Mervall wiped a line of froth from his mustache. "I reckon we'll reach the lake by the time you finish your meal, if we haven't already."

"We are making good time, then?" Lanmiere asked between bites of eggs that he washed down with some of his watered-down ale.

"The winds do seem to be favorin' us today. Let's pray they continue."

"How are your men, Captain Holverd?" Lanmiere asked, clearly wanting to put the previous night's unpleasantness behind them.

"Ready," Holverd stated.

Adarra wasn't sure if he was being snippy with the ambassador or if the man wasn't much of a conversationalist. Perhaps he just wasn't a morning person.

"How are they finding their accommodations?" Lanmiere asked.

"Cramped."

Lanmiere hmphed, passing an apologetic look at Mervall. "Yes, well, I'm sure it takes a while to get used to sleeping aboard a ship."

"I rather enjoyed my hammock last night," Adarra said, trying to lighten the mood.

Mervall smiled. "I find myself usin' it as much as the bed. There's somethin' quite soothing to bein' rocked to sleep."

"If you'll excuse me," Holverd said, gathering his plate and mug. "I believe I have duties that need attending to." He nodded at Captain Mervall and even at Lanmiere. "Captain. Ambassador."

The two men nodded in return, and Holverd left, carrying his dishes over to the wash bucket and dumping them in before making a swift exit out onto the main deck.

Lanmiere shook his head with a sigh. "Afraid this is going to be a long trip for either him or us."

Captain Mervall grunted in agreement.

After breakfast, Captain Mervall took the three of them up to the forward deck to get a good look at Crystal Lake, which she'd been told wasn't all that much different from being out at sea, just with smaller swells. Though, the captain had warned that even the lake could gather quite the storm-tossed waves when she wanted.

The entire horizon in front of them was nothing but water. Adarra had only been to the lake twice in her life, and that was with her father and brothers on one of their hunting expeditions. She'd never seen the ocean and was quite looking forward to the experience. She'd read all about it, from romantic sonnets that portrayed the beauty of a sunset glistening across the water to the more informative studies discussing the causes of tidal change.

It would probably be the last pleasant experience she had before they started into the Bay of Mist.

"What do ya think?" Mervall asked, pinching the ends of his mustache upward—not that they needed any help.

"I think that is a lot of water," Lanmiere said.

The captain laughed. "Couldn't have put it better myself."

Adarra spent the rest of the morning and afternoon trying to avoid Holverd, but there was only so much time she could stay in her cabin before she started feeling queasy and needed to come out for air. She also spent a good deal of time below with Jonas, in part because it was one of the only times she was able to talk Aiden into giving her some space.

Unfortunately, Aiden wasn't the only one who seemed to be overly concerned with her whereabouts. She was also having to contend with Sergeant Finnly. Sweet as the man was, he always seemed to be looming nearby, making sure she was safe, though she wasn't exactly sure what she needed protecting from with dozens of Sidaran Lancers aboard. Mostly, he seemed ill at ease with her tending to Jonas alone.

She finally insisted, rather forcefully, that he had nothing to worry about and that she needed to spend that time preparing Jonas for their upcoming meetings, and having others around watching would make him nervous, especially if they were wearing a lancer uniform. Finnly did finally agree to give her that time, but she still found herself scanning the decks for him before making a run from her cabin to the galley.

It took them the rest of the day to sail across the southeast half of Crystal Lake. The sun was out, and the prevailing winds from the southwest filled their sails, giving them that extra push Mervall was hoping for. By the time the sun began to set, filling the sky with a rich wash of gold and orange, the ship reached the eastern branch of the East River, and they headed into its mouth.

"With any luck," Captain Mervall said, walking over from having taken another sounding, "we should reach the Ozrin by mornin'."

According to the maps Adarra had squirreled away inside their cabin, the stretch of river running from the lake to the sea was fairly equivalent to what they had sailed between Easthaven and the lake. This part of the trek might be a little longer, but they were also getting an earlier start. They hadn't left Easthaven until after dark the previous night.

Adarra was rather excited about this leg of the journey, since according to her charts, the river would be passing through a small chain of mountains on its way to the sea. She'd never seen mountains before. The lake was the farthest she'd ever traveled, and that was with her father and brothers. Her thoughts turned to Breen and Ty. She wondered where they were, what places *they* had seen. More importantly, she wondered if they were still alive. She and her father had expected them back before now, and with each passing week, it became easier to worry.

Her father was doing his best to keep a positive attitude through it all, but whenever they spoke, she could see their absence weighed heavily on him. At least with her own mission, she found she didn't spend every waking moment worrying, at least not about them. Now she spent every waking moment—and some not awake—worrying about what would happen when they first met with Jonas's people: how they would be received, whether she would be able to convey the correct message, whether they would be willing to listen. Most importantly: Would she make it out with her scalp still attached?

It was that last question that tended to plague her dreams the most, many times waking her in the middle of the night.

"You coming?" Aiden asked, snapping her out of her musings as she watched the last of the lake fade into the distance. They had moved to the stern to get a better view of the second ship behind them as well as the lake, while doing their best to stay out of the navigator's way as he continued to take readings and call out orders to the sailor manning the helm.

She hadn't been on many ships, but those she had been on were smaller and guided by a manned tiller. She knew these larger vessels made use of a much easier system that funneled ropes from the helm's wheel on deck down into the hull below, where they were connected to a tiller by way of several pulleys. This mechanism allowed the ship to be steered by a single individual instead of requiring several men pushing and pulling the tiller on their own. It was just one of the many aspects to sailing she had studied in preparation for their trip. She had even taken the time once on board to explore below deck enough to follow the ropes as far as the bilge.

She sighed. "Yes, I'm coming." She pulled herself away from the beauty of the sunset glistening off the water behind them to the west and headed down to join Ambassador Lanmiere and Captain Mervall for supper. Captain Holverd had taken to eating his meals elsewhere. Perhaps it was their company, though Adarra preferred to think it was because he had a ship full of men to keep up with, which was no small task.

"Judgin' by the wind," Captain Mervall said, "I'd venture it were safe to say we will, in fact, make Ozrin before mornin'."

"That's good to hear," Lanmiere said, lifting a spoonful of stew. "Though I can't say I'm looking forward to crossing the bay."

"You and me both," Mervall added, not bothering to swallow his own mouthful first. "I'll be breathin' a whole lot easier once we reach Tallos." He wiped his mustache. "Then again, we might find the mist was the safer part."

Both Adarra and Aiden frowned when they looked at each other. The captain's lighthearted prediction didn't sit well with either of them. After the meal, which they had eaten quickly, as there were no pressing matters of discussion that required their immediate attention, Adarra and Aiden left the galley and made their way up onto the bow of the ship. The sun was nearly set, the sky halfway through its nightly transformation from slate grey to charcoal. The first of the stars were already beginning to show their faces.

Adarra blew on her hands as she stared out over the rail, her breath misting in front of her. "Just think, by this time tomorrow, we could be on Tallos."

Aiden groaned. "I'm trying not to."

She chuckled. "We could be one of the first Sidarans to set foot on the island in decades." Others had tried, but since none of their ships had ever returned, there was no way of knowing whether they had fallen prey to the treacherous waters of the bay or something else. She supposed Aiden was right. The thought of stepping foot on Tallosian soil didn't exactly fill her heart with glee either.

"What will we see when we get there?" he asked, and not for the first, or second, or even fifth time. Jonas was the only connection they had to the island, and what he had shared with her had sent chills up her spine. She didn't know why Aiden kept wanting to hear it. It wasn't like the news was going to get any better with each new telling.

Granting his request, she spent the next several minutes describing to him everything Jonas had told her, starting with the moross hunters that moved along the coastline, looking for shipwrecked survivors to wash ashore, and the jinga that stalked the tall grasslands between the coast and the forest. She mentioned the sandpits and the maze of reeds. She talked about the wolf packs that moved through the forested lands at the foothills of the mountains, and even the talarin that hunted along the cliff face. There were many other creatures on Tallos as well that Jonas hadn't been so forthcoming with, but he said that was because he hadn't seen them himself, only been told of their existence.

"But," she added at the end, "as long as we stick with Jonas, he says he can guide us around the worst of it."

"I wouldn't be surprised if we get there and find that there was nothing to worry about in the first place. I think Jonas is saying all of this just to make sure we bring him along. Awful convenient to have all of these horrific dangers that only *he* can take us through."

"You willing to take that risk?"

Aiden thought a moment, then frowned. "Guess not."

She blew on her hands. "I think I'll do a little reading before turning in."

"Good idea," he said. "My blankets are calling my name. I'll take your rocks down to the galley with mine to warm."

"Thank you."

They left the upper deck and headed back down to the cabin to find Lanmiere already inside and curled up under his blankets. His teeth were chattering.

"Can't say I've been this cold in some time," Lanmiere said in greeting as they shut the door behind them. "These old bones don't handle the weather like they used to." His blankets were pulled all the way to his chin, and he peeked at them over the top. "Think I'll turn in early. We've got a long, hard day tomorrow. I have a feeling I'm going to need all the strength I can muster."

"I share that feeling," Aiden said as he collected the bucket of bed stones, then took them to warm at the galley's fire.

"How are you doing, Miss Adarra?" Lanmiere asked, lowering his coverlet down far enough to see her.

Adarra gathered a couple of books from her satchels and climbed up into her hammock, which hung directly over Aiden's cot. "I'd be lying if I said I wasn't worried."

"You'd be a fool not to be. Captain Holverd might not acknowledge it, but much of the success of this mission rests on your shoulders. I hope our faith in your Tallosian isn't misplaced."

"At this point, do we really have much choice?"

The ambassador let out a long sigh. "I suppose not. The sad truth is that we are left with no good options."

The other sad truth was that the closer they got to Tallos, the more those same doubts had begun to plague her own mind. Was Jonas telling her the truth, or had he been using her to get back to Tallos all along? They would find out soon enough.

Aiden returned after a while, toting the freshly heated bucket of bed warmers, which he stuffed into all the beds. Adarra moaned softly as the warmth from the rocks seeped through her blankets. She spent the next hour poring over a couple of manuals dealing with Tallos—none of which brought to light any information she wasn't already privy to—before finally handing the volumes down for Aiden to place in her satchels.

Neither felt in the mood to chat, so they said their goodnights and pulled up their covers. It took Adarra a long while to finally doze off. Between thoughts of what lay ahead and the ambassador's steady snoring, sleep was slow in coming, and when it finally arrived, it was fraught with nightmares.

Chapter 36 | Ferrin

ON YOUR RIGHT. NO! Your other right!"

"Shut up, Elson!" Ferrin said as he swung back around in time to deflect Ayrion's blade. "You're not helping."

Elson held up his flask. "My mistake. You're doing just fine. No need to panic."

Ferrin gritted his teeth as he countered with several swift feints and strikes of his own, but no matter how close he came to landing a solid blow on the swordsman, it never seemed to connect. The man in black was always one step ahead. It was infuriating. Ferrin considered himself proficient with the blade— as a swordsmith he needed to be—but this Upakan was driving him crazy. The man was impossibly skilled.

He swung left, then feinted right, trying to get close enough to sweep Ayrion's leg, but as soon as he did, Ayrion spun and somehow ended up behind him. "Oh, for flames sake!" Ferrin said, throwing his hands in the air. "I give up! You hop around like a jackrabbit."

Ayrion laughed. "You've no small skill with the sword yourself. It's been a while since I've had a worthy opponent to lock blades with."

"Hey," Bek said.

Ayrion turned. "I said *blades*. You don't carry a blade."

Bek patted one of the hatchets at his side, mollified. "True."

Ayrion raised his sword and swiped it back down in a formal bow to Ferrin. "I mean it when I say you are very good."

"Are you kidding? You had me chasing my shadow like a headless hen. Don't think I landed a single clean strike the entire match."

"No, but you came closer than most."

Ferrin sneered. "Wipe that arrogant smile off your face, you black faerie. One of these days I'm going to land a hit, and you won't see it coming."

Ayrion chuckled as he collected their practice swords and handed them to Bek to place inside the red wagon. "How's your work coming?" Ayrion asked as they walked back to the fire where the others were seated.

Ayrion had asked him to add some of his special touches to the weapons the tinkers had stockpiled.

"They're coming along. Nearly halfway there." Thankfully, there had been enough room in the tinker wagons to store some of Ferrin's tools from his smithy, including his anvil, which had been aboard the *Wind Binder* until after their recent battle with the Tower. He'd kept the best of his gear and sold the rest with the shop before they left Rhowynn. However, he hadn't expected to be using them so soon. Each night, as the rest set up camp, he'd pull out his anvil and get to work. He'd drawn quite the crowd at first, as the others were curious about his magic, but there was only so much enjoyment one could get watching a hammer go up and down, and by the third night, most everyone left him to his work.

He'd been asked to start with Bek's hatchets. Ferrin had been surprised by how well-balanced they felt in his hands, even with their longer handles, thanks to the spikes on the back. He poured his magic into the steel, strengthening the handles and blades, as well as adding some decorative touches to each to give them some flair. He hated plain-looking weapons, so much so that he might have taken the changes a little too far.

Bek had been quite nervous at first, watching his hatchets get re-formed. Ferrin finally had to ask him to leave and trust that when he was done, they would feel even better in his hands than before.

With Bek no longer looking over his shoulder, Ferrin had felt a little more free to be creative. He started by taking what had been little more than a simple piece of wedged steel and gave it definition by lengthening the head. As he stretched the steel, he infused it with his magic, making it pliable to his wishes. He loved the way the magic felt as he worked, the control it gave him to shape the axe to his own vision with every stroke of the hammer.

He had serrated the beard, then thickened the spine and honed the cutting blade with a thinner grind than the steel had previously been able to support. He even went so far as to add holes between the blade and the handle, just for the look of it.

Once he had reshaped the spike into a curved claw, he etched a stylized badger's paw on either side of the axe head, since it seemed the trapper was continually covered from head to toe in badger skins. Ferrin had then finished by reshaping the handle, curving it to balance the newly shifted weight, and topped it with a small spike at the end, allowing him the option to fight with both ends.

All in all, he was quite pleased with the end result, and so was Bek. The man couldn't stop talking about them for three days afterward. There were times Ferrin would catch him sitting atop the red wagon, admiring the craftsmanship as he kept the horses moving. The one aspect that Bek had found the most intriguing was that the hatchets were lighter. Ferrin had told him that because of the strengthening process he used, he often didn't need to use as much steel, which enabled him to add the decorative elements like the holes, without worrying about the head snapping.

Having blades that wouldn't break or even scratch, and that could stand against wizard weapons such as the ones Lenara carried, would be a great benefit to them once they reached the Lost City. Ferrin didn't expect the khuls to be carrying ter'aks, but it wouldn't hurt to be prepared.

"I hear you are working on a special project of your own?" Ayrion said, jerking Ferrin back to the present. The Upakan stopped before they reached the camp's circle. "Want to share?"

"Not yet. Just a little something I've been working on in my own time. Might need your help with it once I get it finished, though."

"Oh? What sort of help?"

"I might need you to show me how to use it," he said, feeling awkward at the admission.

Ayrion lifted an eyebrow. "Now I am curious."

Ferrin smiled. "I promise you'll be the first to see it once I'm finished."

Ayrion nodded, and they joined the others.

Myron and Myriah were sitting in their usual spot in front of the fire, guessing how many miles they had traveled that day. It seemed they were making good time. The trip so far had been slowed by snow, but ever since crossing the Taloos River at Aldwick, the storms had lightened. The snow had even begun to melt in places, allowing their pace to increase as they trekked west toward Oswell. According to Ayrion, Oswell would be the last place they'd be able to stop and resupply before the long journey around the Northern Heights to his former home. Ayrion had been surprisingly forthcoming about the events that had led up to his banishment from the Lost City, doing his best to answer any pertinent questions the group might have to give them a better understanding of what they would be facing once they arrived.

Apparently, no outsiders had ever been allowed inside the city, not that Ferrin could see why they would want to visit. The closest any had come were the food wagons that arrived weekly from places like Chorazin, Pinnella, and Makeda, where farmers made a very profitable trade in growing and supplying goods to the Upakans. Apart from unloading the supplies at the outskirts of the ruins, no one other than Upakans had stepped foot below the surface.

Ferrin wondered how helpful they were going to be if they wouldn't be allowed past the entrance. Ayrion didn't seem too bothered by it, or at least not that he let on. The man could be quite reserved when he wanted to be, unless, of course, you had the unfortunate luck of facing him in the ring, then he grinned at you like a king's fool.

Ferrin looked around for Rae and found her and Suri behind the cooking table with Zynora. He hadn't been able to spend as much time with them as he would have liked since they had joined their new travel companions.

Ever since the two groups had merged in Aldwick, Rae and Suri had been spending a good deal of their time with the old tinker woman. Zynora had become an almost grandmotherly figure to Suri and had devoted quite a bit of time with Rae, instructing her in the ways of the Dar'Rhivanni, starting with the basics. She had said that every woman needed to know how to mend her own clothes. In fact, she'd even insisted on giving Ferrin and Elson a lesson or two in darning their socks.

"Can't expect us women to do it all," she said. Apparently, Myron and Bek were already versed in needle and thread, so they managed to wiggle out of her instruction, and Myriah was even more skilled than Zynora. Ferrin's sister had learned the art of needlework at a young age, supplying her, Ferrin, and Pinon with clothes enough to get them through their early years. Zynora and Tameel had been quite pleased to find that Ferrin and Myriah had been raised by a peddler. They felt it gave them a sort of kinship.

The only person Zynora hadn't been able to coax into her teaching was Lenara. One look from the bulradoer and Zynora decided it was a fight not worth having. Besides, Lenara seemed to have taken sick ever since leaving Aldwick and kept to herself. Ferrin wondered if she'd eaten some bad meat, but the sickness seemed to come and go at will. It was strange. He wouldn't have put it past Lenara to be using it to keep the others at arm's length.

A yelp from over near the wagons had everyone turning to find Tameel leaning against Ol' Lerra's back door, holding his chest.

"What is it?" Ayrion said, already out of his seat with one sword halfway drawn.

"That infernal she-wolf," Tameel griped as Nola came prancing around the back of the wagon. "I'm telling you. That beast derives pleasure out of frightening off what little life I have left. Whoever heard of a wolf big enough to saddle."

Nola lifted her lips and bared her fangs in what appeared to be a grin as she scooted past the old man and headed over to Ferrin's side of the fire. She snuggled up against the back of a log she had dug the snow out from and curled into a ball, staring up at Ferrin.

"Don't look at me," he said, glancing over his shoulder at her. "One of these days he's going to put an arrow in your backside, then we'll see how funny it is." He pointed at her paw. "You missed a spot."

She looked down and saw the blood staining the fur around one of her claws and began to lick it clean. Ferrin shook his head and turned around.

"I still can't get over how big she is," Bek said, joining Ayrion on the other side of the fire.

"Big as a hor'hound," Ayrion said.

Bek took his seat. "Not that I know what a hor'hound looks like, but I'll take your word for it. What was it the bulradoer called her? A frostwolf?"

Ferrin nodded, sparing another glance at Nola. Lenara had spun an interesting tale of the frostwolf's homeland, at least where she believed Nola had come from. It was said that no one had been inside the Frostlands since the creation of the Shroud. In fact, Lenara said the information had come from an obscure text she had come across in the White Tower. She had been as surprised as anyone to see the great wolf.

"How far to Oswell, you reckon?" Myron asked, watching Myriah, who had left him to help Zynora with the food. He turned back to the fire and anyone who might be listening. "I've heard it's close enough to the Slags to actually see razorbacks."

"If the roads hold out, we should reach the city by tomorrow," Tameel said, limping over to the fire from the wagon, all the while keeping a close eye on Nola. He plopped down on a stool beside Ayrion. As soon as he did, Suri ran over with a mug of hot tea and handed it to him. He thanked her with a gentle pat to the top of her head, then took a cautious sip.

"I've only been to Oswell once myself," Ayrion said, "and that was many years ago, back during my childhood. But I can attest to the razorbacks."

At their urging, he proceeded to tell the story of how he and his father had faced down two of the monstrous creatures and in the process set off a brush fire that had burned down most of the grasslands between the Slags and the Valley of Bones. By the time he finished, Zynora, Myriah, and Rae had finished their cooking and called everyone to dish up their plates.

Lenara wandered in from the woods behind them.

"Where've you been?" Elson asked as she met them at the cooking tables.

"Retching, if you must know."

"Still?"

"What, you don't believe me? Here, give me your bowl." She tried grabbing his bowl, and Elson snatched it from her and hugged it to his chest.

"Are you crazy?"

"Are you drunk?"

"No," he said, taking another quick pull from his flask. "I just need something to take the chill off."

"Then you must be really cold."

He sneered as she cut in front of him and handed Myriah her bowl. Ferrin's sister scooped out a helping from the pot and served it to her, and Elson grumbled something under his breath as Lenara left the others and headed over toward the wagons and away from the fire.

Lenara and Elson had been at each other's throats since Rhowynn, and it was starting to really grate on Ferrin's nerves. He had tried talking with both of them separately, and at one point, even together, but neither seemed willing to budge. Both continued to blame the other, promising that if the offending party would be willing to apologize, then things could go back to normal. Of course, neither was willing to do so.

For Lenara's part, she was pretty snippy with everyone of late, her mood changing on a whim. But who could blame her? Ever since the death of Sylas—or in her case, Joran—she had kept to herself more than usual. Ferrin didn't know what it was like to lose someone you cared about in that way, mainly because he'd never really cared about anyone like that until Rae. But just the thought of losing her or Suri . . . Well, he was willing to give Lenara as much space as she needed. Sooner or later, though, if things didn't change, he was going to have to talk with them again, for everyone's sake.

"Soup again?" Elson complained as Myriah scooped a ladleful and plopped it in his bowl. "We've been eating the same thing since Aldwick."

"And we'll continue to eat it until we purchase supplies in Oswell," she said.

Elson turned and looked at Ferrin, who was next in line, and Ferrin shrugged. There wasn't much he could do about it. Clearly, Elson wasn't used to roughing it the way the rest of them were. His family had always been able to provide him with the finer things in life. He wasn't anywhere near as wealthy as Lord Harlin had been, but he had never wanted for anything in his life and had spent most of his days carousing in the local taverns.

"Be thankful we have that," Ferrin said, looking at Elson's bowl. "There were days trekking down out of the Razor Spine Mountains that we had no food at all. In fact, if it hadn't been for Nola, we would have been foraging for grubs."

Elson shivered. "I wish you hadn't brought that image to mind." He looked down at his bowl and frowned. "Great, now I'm going to be imagining this stuff moving with each bite I take. Thanks for that."

Ferrin smiled and held his bowl up for Myriah. He thanked her and then grabbed a warm biscuit and a piece of dried fruit from the end of the table. It was meager fare, but one good thing about traveling with tinkers was they had plenty of seasoning to make the food more palatable. They also had honey, which made the biscuits quite enjoyable. Ferrin was determined to save his biscuits and honey for last, to end the meal on a positive note.

He took a seat beside Rae, who was helping Suri with her food. Suri, meanwhile, was in the process of feeding Tippi her soup. Eventually, she reluctantly placed the enormous pinecone down on the log and ate the food herself.

"How was your day?" Ferrin asked.

"Good," Rae said. "You?" She turned. "No, Suri. Use your spoon."

Ferrin chuckled as Suri attempted to dip the soup out with her spoon and raise it to her mouth without spilling, then finally gave up and drank it from the bowl.

"It's been rather slow," he admitted. There wasn't much for him to do but make sure his horse kept to the road, which wasn't difficult, considering the amount of snow on either side. "What have you and Suri been up to?"

"Our lessons," she said. They spent a considerable amount of time each day in the green wagon with Zynora.

"And what did you learn today?"

She pointed at him with her spoon. "You know I can't tell you that."

"Give it up, boy," Tameel said, taking a seat next to Ayrion. "The Dar'Rhivanni women are known for their secrecy. What they discuss behind closed doors will be one of the great mysteries of life. At least for ours." He chuckled. "It's also what makes them so alluring."

"And don't you forget it," Zynora said as she joined her husband.

Ferrin smiled at the older couple. They reminded him of the way his own parents used to rib each other, back before their passing. It was one of the few good memories he had of them.

A grumbling noise on his right had Ferrin turning to find Elson digging around in his bowl with his spoon. "I swear I saw something swimming in here."

Ferrin rolled his eyes. "As much as you've been drinking of late, I wouldn't doubt it. Time to lay off the bottle a bit, isn't it?"

Elson snorted. "I can stop anytime I want." Frustrated, he finally upturned what was left in his bowl in the snow and opted instead for another swig from his flask. He wiped his mouth and smiled. "I just don't want to." He turned and stared at the wagons where Lenara was sitting quietly by herself. "Rather unsociable tonight it seems," he said with a notable slur, and loud enough for the bulradoer to hear. "Thinks she's better than the rest of us with all her magic."

Ferrin turned and snatched the flask out of Elson's hands before he could drain its contents.

"Hey! What you think you're doing?"

"Saving you from any more embarrassment, and us from having to listen to it."

Elson tried grabbing the flask and almost tipped backward off the log he'd been using for his seat. "I need that. It's the only thing keeping me going."

"That's what worries me," Ferrin said, swatting at Elson's hands.

Elson's face was growing more heated by the moment. "I said, give me that flask!" He came out of his seat and all but leaped on Ferrin, who quickly wrangled him down into the snow.

"And you don't think you have a problem?" Ferrin asked. "You've been drinking nonstop since we left Rhowynn. If you are so miserable, then why did you come?"

Ferrin released him, and Elson climbed back to his feet and shook out the snow from his clothes. "Because!" He looked around at all the faces staring back, then turned and stumbled off toward the woods. "I've got nowhere else to go," he shouted back.

Ferrin looked at the others.

"That young man's got a problem," Zynora said.

"I've seen it before," Myron added, "during my time in the service. If you don't wean him off now, it's only going to get worse."

Tameel clicked his tongue. "It's not a pretty sight, those that are forced off it. He'll have some very rough days and nights ahead if that's what you intend. I've seen it take nearly a week to sober a man up, those that survived, that is."

"We can't let him remain like this," Ayrion said. "What good is he going to be to anyone, including himself? In his state, he'll put us all in danger. I won't take the chance of him putting my family's life at risk." He looked at Ferrin. "You said that he was on your Rhowynn wielder council. What exactly is he a wielder of?"

Ferrin looked at Myriah. He hadn't expected the question, and unfortunately didn't have an answer. Myriah shrugged, letting him know she didn't know any more about it than he did, so he turned and shook his head.

"I don't really know what Elson's wielding capabilities are. Elson was a member of the council long before Myriah and I joined, so we weren't around when he presented himself to the council."

"And in all of this time, you've never once asked him his gift?"

"I never felt I needed to. I figured if he wanted me to know, he'd tell me." Even as Ferrin spoke, he couldn't believe he'd never asked Elson about his gift.

"Has he always had trouble with the drink?" Zynora asked.

"Not like this."

"It grew worse after you left," Myriah said.

Rae cleared her throat. "I can heal him."

The others turned. Honestly, Ferrin hadn't even thought about that, but she probably could. That would make things a whole lot—

"No."

Ferrin turned, surprised to find Ayrion was the one advocating to let Elson continue as he was.

"What do you mean, no? Weren't you the one who just said that you didn't want him putting anyone at risk?"

"Exactly."

"Then excuse my confusion, but wouldn't healing him from his stupor bring that about?"

"No, it wouldn't. You don't help a drunkard by temporarily taking away their pain. That only enables him. Do you think he's going to drink more or less when he knows that all he needs to do is get some healing, then go right back at it again?"

Ferrin's fist tightened, but only because he hated to admit he was actually in the wrong this time.

Ayrion pointed toward the woods. "Your friend out there needs to feel the consequences of hitting the bottom of the barrel. He needs it to be as unpleasant as we know it will be. Consequences direct actions."

"I believe I can help him through it," Zynora said. "It won't be easy, but I should be able to get it out of him in a few days. But it will take constant monitoring."

"We can do that," Ferrin said, releasing a slow exhale. He was still irritated over what Ayrion had said. There was nothing more unpleasant than being talked down to in front of others, especially when they were your friends.

Myron turned. "Someone should probably go after him before he does something reckless."

And by *someone*, he meant Ferrin. Ferrin looked down at his half-eaten bowl of soup and sighed. He placed it on the seat next to him and stood. He'd known this day was coming, he just wasn't looking forward to it. In truth, he'd put it off longer than he should have, the others giving him leniency considering everything that had happened. But there was no hiding it anymore, and Ayrion was right: Elson needed to face that fact.

Ferrin left the others and headed into the woods, trudging through ankle-deep, and sometimes knee-deep, snow as he did, following Elson's tracks, which seemed to ramble all over the place. The trail stopped first against a tree where the discoloration in the snow below it said he had relieved himself, then they started back up. Ferrin was surprised how far Elson had managed to get when he finally found him face down, unconscious in the snow beside a pile of underbrush.

He quickly turned him over and found he was still breathing, but his face was covered in retch, which Ferrin wiped off with a handful of snow. He wasn't sure if his unconscious state would make getting Elson back to camp easier or more difficult. He bent over and lifted his friend's limp body up onto his shoulders. At least he wouldn't have to listen to him whine the whole way back.

Zynora stood when she saw him coming and motioned for him to follow her over to their wagon, where Lenara reluctantly moved off the step to let them pass. She stared at Elson as they did.

"Serves him right," she said with a noted smile, but it was quickly replaced with a sudden blanching as she grabbed her mouth and ran around the side of the wagon.

He shook his head and headed inside. "What's with my group these days?"

"Oh, don't worry about her," Zynora said. "She'll be fine. I've seen it more times than I can count."

"Seen what?" Ferrin asked as he dropped Elson down and helped Zynora undress him.

She stopped and looked up. "Are you saying you don't know?"

"Know what? Is it serious?"

"Of course it's serious." She looked at him like he'd lost his senses. "Having a child is always serious."

"Having a *what*?" Ferrin nearly choked on the words.

Lenara squealed from the top step just outside the open door.

Zynora looked up. "What? You didn't know either?"

Before Ferrin could say anything, Lenara stumbled down the steps like a drunkard herself and disappeared around the side of the wagon. Ferrin looked at Zynora, and she shrugged.

"I thought she knew. Best you go after her."

"Why me? I'm not the one who got her . . . whatever."

"No, but you're the only one she seems willing to talk to."

Ferrin looked down at Elson.

"Don't worry about him. He'll be fine." She paused. "At least, as long as he remains unconscious."

Ferrin could hear her cackling behind him as he rushed out the door and headed around the side of the wagon and into the woods. He wondered what the others were thinking, watching him chase after Lenara in the middle of the night.

How in the flaming pits of Aldor was Lenara, of all people, with child?

Chapter 37 | Ferrin

ERRIN RACED INTO THE WOODS, dodging low-hanging branches and skirting thick clusters of underbrush. He realized that he was half hoping he wouldn't actually catch Lenara. Dread weighed him down. He imagined it slowing his steps.

He had no idea what he was going to say even if he did catch her. He was still struggling to wrap his head around the very thought of Lenara being with child.

She was a bulradoer. She was, thanks to the Tower's loving guidance, probably the last person you'd ever want to be a mother. Hadn't she said she'd spent the majority of her life in the Tower?

The woods were dark. The light from their campfire was nowhere to be seen, and little moonlight filtered through the upper canopy, making it quite difficult to follow her footsteps.

What was he doing? This was crazy. The woman clearly didn't want to talk with anyone, and even if she did, that conversation would probably be best coming from another woman. What did he know of being a mother? He'd never married. His mother had died when he was just a child. Him being the one to talk with her was ridiculous.

The tracks in the snow were soon joined by smoke and glowing embers from scorch marks on trees. This last was enough to keep him going in the right direction but added a new wave of dread to push through. What was to keep her from turning her frustration on him?

He shuddered. His special steel blade wasn't going to stop her from setting him ablaze.

About the time he had talked himself out of going any farther, he heard what sounded like sobbing ahead, and he slowed. Lenara was the toughest person he'd ever met. She didn't cry. She made other people cry. He walked around a large oak, keeping a safe distance, and found her sitting in a pile of snow, her face buried in her knees as she hugged them to her chest. Several of the surrounding trees were still smoldering, giving him just enough light to see by.

He stopped. She had to know he was there. He had made as much noise as he could so as not to alarm her, though in her state, she might not have even noticed. What was he going to say to her? What could he say? Keeping back several feet, he knelt down.

"Are you alright?"

Lenara stopped crying but didn't raise her head.

"I can't imagine what you must be feeling." What man could? What woman could, given her circumstances? "Do you want to talk about it?"

He almost hoped she didn't. It was *Lenara* after all. A bulradoer. One he had seen kill en masse on more than one occasion. None of the others felt comfortable enough to spend any time in her company, not that she ever wanted any. The only one willing to go out of their way to engage her in conversation, besides himself, was Elson, and that was usually some form of sarcastic banter that ended in name-calling and threats.

Ferrin was the only one she had ever opened up with, and that was probably due to them being forced to spend days locked together in Lord Harlin's closet, not to mention fighting side by side against Sylas and the Tower's guards. He didn't exactly consider her a friend, but he also didn't go out of his way to keep his distance. Though, right now would have probably been a good time to start.

"Not to be overly curious, but, uh . . . how did . . ."

She finally lifted her head, her eyes red. "How did this happen?" she asked, placing a protective hand on her stomach.

"Well, yes."

Her face darkened. "Sylas."

It was Ferrin's turn to blanch. The thought of Sylas doing that to her had his stomach turning. But Rae had killed Sylas's original body, so did that mean . . . ?

"Wait, was it Sylas or was it Joren?"

She snarled, which he took to mean Sylas.

"But he knew," she said.

Ferrin shook his head, confused. "Who knew?"

"Joren knew. He could see everything that Sylas did."

Ferrin remembered her mentioning that to him during their time in Harlin's home. The whole mess was confusing and disturbing. How was he going to help her deal with something like this, something this significant? He thought a moment. Maybe he was looking at this all wrong. "So in a way it was also Joren who . . . you know."

"No!" Her eyes blazed and he flinched. "He never would have touched me."

Ferrin shook his head. "That's not what I meant. Of course he would never." He scrubbed his hand nervously across his face. "That came out wrong. What I meant to say was . . ." What did he mean to say? Staring at the tears running down her cheeks, he sighed. "You loved him, didn't you? Joren?"

She lowered her head, staring at the folds of her black robe. "Yes."

"Then maybe . . . maybe this is a good thing."

She looked up, desperation on her face.

"Sylas, for all his evil, thought to break you, to steal everything from you that he could to make that happen . . . even Joren. But"—Ferrin pointed to her stomach—"this is something that he will never be able to take, and Joren made sure of it. Sylas might have been inhabiting Joren's body, but he was nothing but a parasite. What you carry there is Joren's and Joren's alone. That is something Sylas will never be able to take from you. And Joren's last act in this world was to make sure of that. He might not have known he was to be a father, but his love for you was what kept his child safe. That is a legacy worth leaving, and it's something your child can carry with them proudly the rest of their days."

Lenara's expression softened, though tears still flowed freely. She turned and stared out at the falling snow. Suddenly a smile moved across her face, and she looked down at her stomach and placed her hands gently overtop.

He carefully helped her to her feet. "You do know that you're not alone, right? We will be here to help however you need."

She stepped forward and wrapped her arms around him.

He froze. It was such an uncharacteristic act for her that he didn't even get his arms up to hug her back before she let go.

"Thank you," she whispered, then turned and dashed back to the trees, where she proceeded to retch some more.

Ferrin waited for her to finish before they slowly made their way back to camp. The others stood when they heard them coming, but Lenara clearly didn't wish to discuss the issue and immediately went straight to a small tent, where she slept away from the others. Ferrin joined the rest around the fire, no one saying a word, which left the camp in a rather uncomfortable silence, apart from the occasional muffled shouts coming from the green wagon.

Elson must have woken, Ferrin thought, though it didn't seem important at the moment.

"So," Myron said, the first one to dare speaking. "Did we just hear what we thought we heard?"

"If you thought you heard that Lenara is pregnant, then yes."

Again, another round of silence swept over those seated around the fire, this time broken by Bek. "It is for certain?"

"Zynora seems to think so."

Rae stood, handing Ferrin her mug of tea.

"Where are you going?"

"I'm going to see if she needs anything."

Ferrin was going to ask if that was wise but decided against it. Instead, he smiled and watched her go. If there was anyone who could relate to what Lenara was going through, it was Rae. Not only had she been abused by those in the Tower for years, but a good majority of it had been done by the very same person.

Rae hadn't been around during the time of Ferrin's and Lenara's capture, so she hadn't heard Lenara's story. He doubted she knew anything about what Sylas had done. Now he wondered if he should have mentioned it to her before she saw Lenara, but he guessed she'd find out soon enough, especially if she told Lenara her own story. He only hoped it didn't cause a rift between the two women.

He looked around at the faces of those still gathered and could see the questions on each.

"I, for one, didn't know bulradoer had relationships," Bek said, scratching his beard. "Anyone know who the father might be?"

Ferrin caught the way Bek and Ayrion glanced across the fire at him and Myron. "It's not us," Ferrin said.

"Certainly not," Myron added, wanting to make it very clear that he hadn't been involved in any way.

"Best to let her tell you when she's up to it," Ferrin said.

Bek nodded, then shared a look with Ayrion that said he doubted either of them would ever learn who it was, since neither of them seemed all that anxious to ask.

Ayrion yawned, or at least gave a fair imitation of one, then walked over and dropped his bowl and mug inside the wash bucket, which was sitting near the fire to keep the water inside from freezing. "I think it's time we turned in. The sooner we get on the road in the morning, the sooner we reach Oswell."

Ferrin looked at Myriah and found Suri had crawled up in her lap and was half-asleep already, with Tippi cuddled snuggly between them.

"Guess I'm pretty tired as well," his sister said.

Myron offered to help her get Suri into her bedding, which Myriah gratefully accepted. He then crawled in his own bedroll on the other side of hers. "You need your sleep as well," Myron said to Ferrin, noticing Ferrin still sitting on his stool, staring off in the direction of Lenara's tent.

Ferrin wondered what she and Rae were discussing. He spared a quick glance at Myron as he stood. "In a minute. I think I'll check in on Elson first."

Ferrin passed Ayrion's bedding on the way to the wagon. Ayrion was just throwing his coverlet over himself, revealing his blades resting beside him.

Ferrin would have to be careful waking the man for his turn on watch. Bek's bedding was empty, as he had won the toss and had chosen to take the first watch.

With Ferrin's group adding an additional seven people and one giant wolf to the mix, the red wagon had become the lone storage for everyone's gear, leaving little in the way of room to sleep in as Ayrion and Bek had been doing.

There was light around the door of the green wagon, and Ferrin stopped to blow on his hands before knocking.

"Come in," Tameel's voice sounded from inside.

Ferrin opened it and stepped in, shutting the door behind him as he did. Tameel was sitting in a chair on the right while Zynora sat on a stool beside Elson's bed on the left. She was dabbing his head with a wet cloth, which she continued to dip in a bucket on the floor beside her. "How is he?"

About the time he asked, Elson released a mournful wail and began muttering incoherently.

"He will be better in the morning," she said, "but he still has a difficult road to travel over the next few days." She clicked her tongue. "The first two will be the hardest."

"For us and him," Tameel grumbled from his chair behind them. He shook his head as he stared at Elson. "Fool was going to drink himself to death."

Ferrin looked at his friend. Elson had always been a bit of a loner. He didn't really fit in at the wielder council meetings, which was probably one of the reasons why they got along so well. Ferrin remembered the first time he'd attended one of the gatherings. He'd spent most of it standing in the corner. His sister didn't seem to have any problem socializing with the others. She made friends rather easily. It was one of the few attributes they didn't share . . . well, that and the fact she had been born without a gift.

He remembered the first time Elson had spoken to him. He'd poured Ferrin a drink and spent the entire time making fun of the rest of those gathered. Ferrin found his sarcasm rather refreshing, and they had spent every meeting after playing hands of batmyth while the others gossiped.

Elson had always had a thing for the drink, but it had never been this bad before. Ferrin hoped they weren't too late. "Will he . . . ?"

"He'll live," she said, "though he'll wish he hadn't for a while. I've given him a tonic infused with some herbs that will aid in the drying-out process."

"Anything I can do?"

"Drive Ol' Lerra tomorrow," Tameel said. "It's pretty clear we won't be getting any sleep tonight."

"I guess that's the least I can do," he said, then looked at Zynora. "Is there anything else you need?"

She looked around. "Not at the moment, I reckon."

He nodded and opened the door, sparing a quick look back at his friend before returning to his bedding. He crawled inside and was about to turn over and go to sleep when he heard footsteps in the snow on the right and sat up.

As he hoped, it was Rae.

She stopped first to check on Suri, who was sleeping soundly with Myriah, before making her way over to where Ferrin sat waiting. She moved her bedding beside his, on the side closest to the fire, and crawled in.

"How is she?" Ferrin asked as they lay there quietly, staring at one another.

"She is . . ." She shook her head. "She is upset and happy and frightened and sick. She is with child."

Ferrin smiled. "I guess that's the best way to describe it." He kept his voice low. "Did she tell you how it happened?"

Rae didn't say anything, but she did nod. Ferrin couldn't tell what Rae was thinking, though she did look a little sad. "How are you? I know it couldn't be easy hearing about that, especially after what you've been through."

"I am fine. I have you."

Ferrin's smile turned into a grin.

Rae glanced over her shoulder toward Lenara's tent. "She doesn't have another you."

Ferrin wasn't sure if that was the best way to put that, but he got her meaning. Lenara was going to need someone to lean on. He and Rae were going to have to be there for her, as he doubted any of the others would be all that willing. Which wasn't exactly fair. They might be willing, but she would feel uncomfortable in the process. Of course, he was feeling rather uncomfortable himself.

"We'll be there for her," he said, and she leaned over and kissed him, then cuddled up against him and pulled her blanket up over her head.

Ferrin did the same. He didn't wake until it was his time for watch.

Chapter 38 | Ayrion

YRION PULLED SHADE TO a stop at the edge of the woods and stared ahead at the stone walls of Oswell. Just seeing them brought back memories. He had lowered Magistrate Sirias and his family over the side of those same walls on what had been his first and only contract as an Upakan. And strictly speaking, he and his father hadn't actually completed the contract as specified. The assignment had been to assassinate the magistrate, but instead they had chosen to make it look like they had by whisking the man and his family out of the city.

Although they had only stayed for little more than a couple of days, just long enough to prepare for and then complete the contract, he had surprisingly fond memories of the city.

Ayrion remained just inside the tree line to keep from being noticed. From what he could see, nothing had changed. There were very few travelers on the road, which was no doubt common for this time of year. Most appeared to be local farmers carting in winter crops to sell.

"Looks quiet enough to me. What do you think, boy? Should we risk it?" He rubbed Shade's neck, which earned him a whicker and nod in return.

"Couldn't agree more. And we could certainly use the supplies." He watched for several more minutes, especially keeping an eye on the gatehouse and those standing guard. It looked like a typical patrol. Most weren't bothering to check wagons, but that was probably because they knew everyone entering.

"Not much to see here," he said, then turned Shade, and they started back for the wagons. With no one to talk to but Shade, Ayrion found he had plenty of time to ponder over the latest additions to his band of traveling warriors.

One was recovering from constant intoxication and at the moment could hardly stand, another had just found she was with child and was retching even more than the drunkard. Still, even though he had no idea what use Elson was, Lenara had proven her worth several times over. She was quite literally one of the most powerful wielders he'd ever seen, including Ty, though from the way Nyalis talked, the faeling hadn't even begun to develop the level of magic he possessed.

The metallurgist was a rare find, and if the transformation he had worked on Bek's hatchets were any indication, Ferrin was worth his weight in gold. And as wonderful as it had been to have Zynora's knowledge of herbs and medicinal practices around during times of battle, having a true healer like Rae along outweighed both Ferrin's and Lenara's significant contributions.

And while there were weaker elements in the party, Myron seemed a good hand with a sword, and his time with the Black Watch in the Tower might prove useful down the road. But Ayrion didn't understand how Suri's magic worked. They said that she could communicate with animals, which was a talent he'd never really seen any other than Ty display. Then again, Kraea wasn't exactly an animal, and anyone who made the mistake of calling her one would deeply regret it. It was clear that Nola and Suri had a special bond; he only hoped it was enough to keep the enormous wolf under control.

Ultimately, Ayrion was happy to have gained their help, though it seemed a rocky transition so far. He knew Ferrin wasn't happy with Ayrion's recommendation to force his friend through the sobering process, but Ayrion wasn't about to risk everyone's lives on someone who seemed to want to throw his away.

Becoming a drunkard wasn't something that happened overnight or on a whim. From what he'd gathered from the others, Elson's drinking had been a problem for some time. It reminded Ayrion of Dakaran. The prince had always been known to have a taste for wine, but it wasn't until Ayrion had been named Guardian Protector that the drinking had really increased. He wondered what had spurred Elson down this same road.

Ayrion thought back to a time when he and Dakaran had been friends, especially the year Dakaran had been required to spend in the lancers with him. It was one of the longest stints the prince had gone without his vices. It was also one of the only times Dakaran had seen himself as just one of the guys, and not their future ruler, and that was mostly because he didn't have a choice. His father had stripped Dakaran of his title for that year of service and wouldn't restore it unless Dakaran completed the entire stint. In Ayrion's opinion, it was one of the best things that could have happened to him. It was also one of the last times they had been truly close.

It made him wonder if maybe he should assign Elson a task. It might not aid in his recovery, but it could be the boost he needed to stay sober.

As he neared the next bend in the road, he heard the distinct rattle of the tinker wagons just ahead, so he stopped Shade and waited. Bek and the red wagon were the first around the corner. Bek seemed to be holding the team back, keeping a slower pace, no doubt so Ol' Lerra behind him would be less likely to jostle those inside while they worked on Elson. Myron was the next in view, and he spurred his horse forward when he caught sight of Ayrion. He pulled alongside and waited for Ferrin, who was driving the green tinker wagon, to catch up.

As soon as the wagons came to a stop, the window behind the driver's seat opened, and Tameel stuck his head out between Ferrin and Rae. "Are we there?"

"We should reach Oswell before lunch," Ayrion said. "The city seems quiet enough from what I could gather. I didn't actually go inside. Best not to have a stranger ride in and then ride back out a few minutes later, only to return once more. How goes it with you?"

"He'll be fine. His fever's down, but he's still a bit delirious."

"A warm bed and proper meal will help," Bek said from the red wagon. "At least, it would me." He offered a cheeky grin.

Ayrion smiled. "I think I know just the place." He turned Shade around, and they started slowly back down the road toward Oswell. He wondered if the Golden Tassel was still around, and if Milly was still the proprietor. He also wondered if Hobb had ever made good on his threats to propose to the rambunctious innkeeper. He hoped he did get to see his old friend. The last he'd crossed paths with the ferryman was when Hobb had helped him acquire passage aboard the *Wind Binder* after his banishment from the Lost City.

Things had truly come full circle.

Ayrion kept the horses to a slow but steady pace, and he sent Myron ahead to watch the city's gate for anything suspicious, like white uniforms milling about. They reached the end of the forest and caught their first glimpse of the city's walls just before the sun reached its zenith. Ayrion's stomach had been growling for the last hour, which had him wanting to push ahead, but caution was their greatest ally, so he brought them to a halt just inside the tree line.

Dismounting, they all gathered near the back of Ol' Lerra. Tameel and Zynora took a break from tending to Elson.

"Why are we stopping?" Zynora asked. "Do you plan on eating lunch here? Not much but leftover soup, but we can warm it if we need to."

"Let's hope we don't need to," Myron said, bringing a few chuckles from some of the others.

"I think it best if we leave the wagons here," Ayrion said, "at least until we've taken a good look inside. We don't want to run into another incident like we did in Aldwick. Safest if we keep the wagons out where they can't get trapped behind the walls."

"Who stays with the wagons?" Ferrin asked.

"For right now, all of us, except perhaps Bek and Myron. They look the least suspicious."

Bek and Myron both looked at each other and shrugged.

"As soon as they return, we can see about getting a meal in town and restocking supplies. We'll need a couple of volunteers, though, to remain with the wagons."

"Tameel and I will stay," Zynora said. "We rather prefer our own beds anyway, and we have Elson to look after. Best if he weren't moved."

"Are you sure?" Ayrion asked.

Tameel nodded. "We're sure."

Their wagon was their home, and apart from their time in Aero'set, where they had shaped their room to resemble their wagon anyway, the two tinkers had spent hardly more than a night or two away from it that Ayrion knew.

"Just be sure to bring me some fresh pipe tobac," Tameel said with a wink.

"Better yet," Zynora said, "I'll make you a list."

"That would probably be wise." Ayrion turned to the others. "Any questions?" When no one spoke up, he looked at Bek and Myron. "Keep your eyes open for signs of the Tower's presence. If you can manage to ask the gate watchmen on your way in, I'm sure they could tell you if there are any white uniforms about. Just don't make it look too obvious."

The two men smiled. "I think we can manage it," Myron said. "If you ever want to know if there are Black Watch around, just find the closest brothel or most disreputable tavern."

Bek and Myron mounted and headed around the city wall toward the front gate, while the rest steered the wagons off the road and into the first clearing large enough to fit both. All the women except Zynora took shelter in the red wagon, while Ferrin joined Zynora and Tameel in the warmth of the green, leaving Ayrion the odd man out as he kept watch outside with Shade. With nothing better to do but stand there and shiver, Ayrion began to dig out a place for the fire, shoveling away snow and digging down far enough to reach the hard soil underneath.

Ferrin eventually joined him, and the two were able to gather enough wood for Zynora and Tameel to use that afternoon and evening, while the rest of the group hopefully found rooms at one of the inns. Ayrion knew they were growing tired of sleeping out in the cold and would appreciate a warm bed and bath, not to mention a hearty meal, which he knew Milly was capable of preparing if she was still around. He also knew this would be the last real stop they made before they reached whatever awaited them at the Lost City. Best to give them one day to rest. He had a feeling they were all going to need it.

"What do you plan on doing with your free time?" he asked Ferrin as they busied themselves setting up the fire to heat more water for Zynora.

"I'm going to see if I can find a smithy and finish this new project."

"I'm curious to see what it is. Is it for someone in particular?"

"Myself, actually. I've spent my entire life building for others, I've never once created anything just for me." Ferrin threw a log on the fire and watched the sparks scatter. "Just some ideas I've been fiddling with over the last couple of years. Never found the time to do anything about them before now."

Ayrion nodded. "I look forward to seeing it. Anyone who can design such weapons as these"—he patted the hilt of one of his dragon blades—"has my utmost respect. If you can create something like this for someone else, I can't imagine what you are fashioning for yourself."

Ferrin simply smiled, and the two stood a moment in silence, watching the flames dance across the wood.

Ayrion didn't understand why trying to have a conversation with the metallurgist always felt awkward and a little forced. He didn't have that problem with Bek—though he and Bek had spent a lot more time together, so perhaps that was the reason—or perhaps it was because Ferrin was the leader of his own pack, and merging the two was never going to happen without its own share of difficulties. He remembered what it had been like when Red had lost her tribe and had been forced to join with his own. It wasn't easy to become a follower once you were used to leading.

His stomach rumbled angrily at being forced to wait for Milly's cooking, so he was grateful it didn't take all that long before Bek and Myron returned from their trip into Oswell.

"We talked with the men at the gate," Bek said, "and it doesn't look like they've had any visits from the White Tower in some time. After a quick ride around the heart of town, I don't think they were lying. We even checked a few of the seedier taverns as Myron suggested, and it appears that Oswell is free of the Tower's eyes at the moment."

That is welcome news, Ayrion thought. "During your ride through, did either of you happen to see if an inn called the Golden Tassel is still there?"

"Aye. There were two good inns," Myron said. "One, the Golden Tassel, as you say, and the other the . . ."

"The Cockatrice?" Ayrion finished.

"That sounds about right."

Ayrion smiled. After all these years, the two inns were still in business, and no doubt still competing against each other, which wasn't difficult, seeing as how they faced each other on opposite sides of the street.

It didn't take their group long to unhitch the horses, mount, and make their way around the wall toward the city's gate. Zynora had drafted an extensive list of items needed, with the others adding anything they could think of, until the list had grown to fill both sides of a sheet of parchment. Thankfully, gold seemed to be no object. Between what Ferrin said he had absconded with during his escape from the White Tower and his sister's sudden onslaught of fortune from her deceased husband's estate, coin was certainly not in short supply. Even Tameel and Zynora were in good shape after the incredible amount of armament they'd managed to sell in Minotha. Ayrion, however, was starting to wish they hadn't sold as much as they had. Who knew if they might need it in the near future?

Before they headed around the wall for the front gate, Ayrion had them divide into smaller groups. Eight new faces riding in together might draw too much attention. Eight new faces riding in separately would as well, but perhaps not as much.

Bek led the first wave, which consisted of just him and Myriah. Best to give the appearance of couples, as they would hopefully be less conspicuous that way. Second was Ferrin and Lenara, who they managed to talk into wearing a long cloak over her robes. Ayrion doubted there would be many who'd recognize the black robes of a bulradoer, but he didn't want to take the chance. The last was Ayrion's group, which consisted of him, Myron—who the guards would hopefully recognize—and Rae and Suri.

Ayrion spaced the groups out as much as possible, which meant it would take longer to get inside, but when it came to safety, their stomachs would just have to wait. The watchtowers stood well above the city wall, which rose a good twenty to thirty feet, and the guards at the top held bows, but they stood relaxed, seemingly curious, or more likely bored, as they watched those coming and going.

Myron waved at one of the two men walking out to greet them.

"Back already?" the shorter guard on the left asked. He looked them over, Ayrion keeping his head lowered as much as possible without looking suspicious.

"Yes," Myron said with a friendly smile. "My wife and daughter didn't want to leave her brother." He pointed back at Ayrion. "He hasn't been feeling too well." Like Lenara, Ayrion had worn a cloak to hide his black coat and swords. "She sent me in earlier to gets herbs from the apothecary to help his upset stomach." Myron twisted in his saddle. "Appears they're working."

Ayrion rolled his eyes, still keeping his head lowered. The former Black Watch captain had a quick tongue, but if he spun any more of a yarn, they were going to be there till evening. "I don't think these fine gentlemen care to know about my queasiness." Ayrion put his hand to his mouth. "Sit here any longer, and I might be showing them what I had for supper last night."

The two guards grumbled, and the one doing the talking quickly waved them through.

Ayrion shifted in his saddle away from the guards on the left, but his eyes caught another guard on the right, who he hadn't heard approaching. Ayrion quickly averted his eyes, but he couldn't tell if he had averted them soon enough. Had the guard seen them? Blazes. He didn't dare turn to find out as they passed through the gates.

He looked at Myron. "Turn around and tell me what the guards are doing. I'm not sure if one of them spotted my eyes."

Myron turned and passed a quick look back toward the gate. "They're talking, but I don't think—"

"Are they looking this way?"

"I guess, sort of, but not any more than what I'd expect." Myron turned back around. "I can't keep looking or they really will grow suspicious. I'm sure you're fine. If they had seen something, they would have stopped us."

Ayrion held his breath, the tension easing the farther they got from the gate. Pretty soon the road angled to the right as it headed toward the center of town, cutting off the view of the guards behind them, save for the top of the watch towers above the buildings on their right. By the time they reached the merchant district, Ayrion was breathing much easier.

His eyes were a constant worry. He really missed being in Aramoor, where he didn't have to hide who he was. Out here, his eyes proved a constant reminder that he wasn't like everyone else, which was surprisingly something he had in common with the bulradoer.

Lenara's gold-flaked, raspberry-colored eyes were every bit as strange as his. He'd never heard of anyone with eyes like that, and apparently neither had she.

At least Ayrion had others who shared his strange attributes. He'd have to ask Nyalis when he returned to Aero'set whether the wizard knew of others with eyes like hers.

They caught up with the rest of their group just around the corner, and Ayrion led them through town toward the Golden Tassel. It had been over twenty years since he'd set foot in Oswell, but he remembered exactly where to go and directed them to the stable on the right alongside the inn. He stared up at the building, surprised by how much smaller it looked. The outside was more worn than he remembered, but Milly's yellow curtains still donned the windows.

They dismounted and walked their horses into the barn, where they found the stableman sleeping on a stool just inside the doors. Bek walked over to shake the old man awake, and Ayrion grabbed his arm. As soon as he realized who the sleeping man was, he motioned Bek back. Ayrion smiled. This would be even better than he'd imagined.

Chapter 39 | Ayrion

YRION SMILED AT THE sleeping man and held a finger to his lips, motioning for Bek to step back. The man's cheeks were heavier, the skin on his neck sagging a bit, and the beard held more white than grey, but there was no mistaking Hobb's rugged face.

Ayrion's heart pounded as he moved in behind the older man. He felt like a thirteen-year-old boy, about to play a fun prank on a close friend. Ayrion started to draw his dagger when Hobb snorted. He froze, waiting to see if Hobb was awake, but his eyes never opened. Carefully, Ayrion slid the flat end of the blade against Hobb's neck.

"Give us your money, old man!"

Hobb jumped with a start, then shouted when he saw the others standing over him. Ayrion caught him from behind to keep him from tipping backward off his seat. He pressed the blade a little tighter, and Hobb went stiff as a board.

"You can have it all. Take it!" Hobb fumbled around in his shirt for a small purse that hung around his neck and handed it back over his shoulder.

The others stared wide-eyed, wondering if Ayrion had lost his mind. Ayrion was doing his best not to laugh as he snatched the very light pouch from

Hobb and bounced it in his hand. "Is this all you've got?"

"It's everything. I promise."

"Pity. Then I guess I'll be the one buying drinks tonight." Ayrion lowered his blade and walked around in front of Hobb and knelt down so they were face-to-face.

Hobb froze as soon as he saw Ayrion's eyes. Then a hint of recognition set in, and Hobb's eyes widened. "Ayrion?"

Ayrion laughed. "Who else would be willing to buy you a drink?"

Hobb lunged at him, and Ayrion nearly toppled over as the ferryman's arms wrapped around his neck. "I can't believe it. After all these years."

"Twenty, to be precise," Ayrion said with a slight groan. The man was as strong as ever, which was no surprise after all that time pulling a ferry from one side of the Shemoa River to the other.

Hobb released him, and they stood. "Here, let me look at you," Hobb said, taking a step back as he took Ayrion in. "The years have certainly been kind to you. Unlike me."

Ayrion looked around the barn, then down at the rickety stool Hobb had been sleeping on. "What are you doing out here tending horses?"

Hobb frowned. "I'm out here cause that infernal woman inside won't let me near her kitchen."

"So you never married?"

"Of course we married. Love that woman. Just can't stand to be around her sometimes." He smiled like it was all a big joke, which to him it probably was. The two had been fighting with each other ever since Ayrion had known them; what was to stop them from keeping up with tradition?

Bek cleared his throat, and Ayrion turned. "My apologies. I guess introductions are in order." He put a hand on Hobb's shoulder. "Master Hobb was the ferryman I stayed with after my initial banishment from the Lost City. He introduced me to Captain Treygan and the *Wind Binder*."

Hobb scratched his head. "I don't think I want to take credit for pairing you with that scoundrel."

Ayrion laughed. "They are well acquainted with Treygan."

"Owe him our lives," Myron said.

Hobb looked quite astonished by that revelation.

"These are my traveling companions," Ayrion said and named them in turn, starting with Bek and ending with Suri, who made sure Hobb was properly introduced to Tippi the pinecone. "There are a couple more, but we left them with the wagons just outside the city walls."

Hobb pursed his lips. "That is quite the entourage. And where would you be heading with such a select group?"

"The Lost City."

Hobb's face tightened. "My, my, my. The banished finally returns. I have a feeling that will be quite the reunion." He frowned. "We've heard troubling rumors recently about those living in the ruins."

"What sort of rumors?"

"Word has it from those living in Chorazin and Makeda that the Upakans have vanished."

Ayrion's chest tightened. Were they too late? "What do you mean vanished?"

Hobb shook his head and leaned against the closest stall. "I don't know. Sounds like they've missed the last several caravans of food. Merchants from both cities, including Pinnella, have sent their usual wagons, but no one's been there to meet them."

The hairs on Ayrion's neck were beginning to rise. "Did they go in and look?"

"Doubtful. You know how your people are with outsiders. None of them would be foolish enough to risk climbing down into those tunnels, not even with the loss of revenue from their goods."

Ayrion looked at the others, concern mirrored on their faces as well. "I was sent to relocate the Upakans. There was some concern about them having delved too deeply under the ruins and releasing . . ."

Hobb's brows shot up. "Releasing what?"

"We aren't exactly sure, but from what we were told, it wasn't good." Ayrion didn't see the need to frighten everyone by announcing the possibility of a khul invasion, especially since most records barely went far enough back to even mention them. He still wasn't quite sure what they were.

"For all I know," Hobb said, "they simply packed up and moved on. Can't see how they managed to survive for so long in such a desolate place. All I can say is I hope that wherever they went, it is very far from here. No offense, but having a society of mercenaries and assassins living this close tends to make everyone nervous." He looked down the line at the row of horses waiting to be stalled. "How long will you be staying?"

"Tonight only," Ayrion said, "though after hearing this news, I'm half tempted to get right back on the road."

Grumbling behind him let him know how unpopular that decision would be.

"But I promised them a soft bed and a hot bath, so here we are." He hoped with a full day of rest, Elson would be healed enough for them to pick up the pace tomorrow with the wagons. To be honest, given the circumstances, he was considering letting Rae heal him after all. He'd just have to make sure that Zynora and Tameel kept a strict eye on the stronger drinks they had stored in the back of the wagon.

They unsaddled the horses, making sure they were fed and watered, before Hobb took the group in through the front to check in. Apparently, Hobb was also in charge of the desk. Ferrin paid the bill, and Ayrion handed Bek his gear to take up to his room while he followed Hobb through the common room toward the kitchen, where Hobb said Milly should be just finishing lunch. Ayrion hoped he could talk her into making a little extra for them.

He wondered if she would even remember him. He hadn't spent as much time with her as he had with Hobb, but most people didn't forget meeting a couple of Upakans and living to tell about it. Generally, if you saw one, it was the last thing you did. He followed Hobb over to the kitchen door, keeping to his shadow.

Hobb turned and put a finger to his lips. "Let me do the talking." He pushed open the door just wide enough to peek in, then motioned for Ayrion to follow as he slipped through the door. Milly had her back to them as she cleaned her oven, and they quietly tiptoed across the room. Hobb motioned for the other two attendants to remain quiet, which they did as soon as they saw Ayrion with his black coat and swords.

Hobb stopped behind his wife, then glanced over his shoulder to wink at Ayrion. Turning back around, he reached out and grabbed his wife's waist. She screeched and flung her wash rag straight in the air, and it landed directly on

Hobb's balding head. She grabbed the rag off his head and began to beat him with it. "What have I told you about sneaking up on me like that!"

Hobb wrestled the rag out of her hands. "We have guests, my dear."

She snatched the wet rag back and then looked up to see Ayrion standing behind her husband. She froze, mouth agape.

Hobb turned with a big smile. "Honey, you remember Ayrion, don't you?"

Her eyes opened even wider. "That's Ayrion?"

Before Ayrion could respond, she pushed Hobb out of the way and flung her arms around his neck, kissing both his cheeks. "Hobb tells me I have you to thank for his proposal," she said. "He said if it wasn't for your pushing, he would have never gotten up the courage to ask. In fact, if not for your prowess in the river, he wouldn't be here at all." She then took a step back and kissed her husband as though she hadn't just been beating him with her dishrag.

Ayrion smiled. They were quite the couple. "I'm just glad to see everything worked out. I was half afraid the old inn wouldn't still be here."

Milly flipped her wrist. "Oh, hon, this place will be here long after the two of us are rotting in the ground. So, what brings you to Oswell?"

"I'm actually on my way to the Lost City."

Milly clicked her tongue. "Best thing that could have ever happened to you was getting out of there. Why would you want to be going back?"

"Long story, I'm afraid. Suffice it to say, I have come to believe that my family could be in danger."

Milly looked at Hobb. "Yes, we've heard the rumors."

"I'm here with some friends. We just took lodging for the night, and we're hoping there might be some leftovers from lunch?"

She pursed her lips and looked around the room. "I guess I can scrounge some up. How many in your party?"

"Eleven."

Her eyes widened. "Eleven?"

"But three are still outside the walls."

"So, eight?" She took a deep breath and then nodded. "There might be enough left from lunch to reheat for you. Just give me a few minutes, and I'll see what I can do." She turned and immediately started barking out orders to the assistants, and Hobb quickly ushered Ayrion toward the door.

"Time for us to be going, lad, before we get a bowl or two lobbed in our direction."

"Wise man," Milly said behind them on their way out.

By the time they made it back to the common room, Ayrion found his group sitting around a couple of tables near the hearth. There were a few additional patrons there as well, most enjoying an afternoon pipe while keeping out of the cold.

"Any food left?" Bek asked, patting his gut.

"They're reheating it now. Should have something out shortly."

"Until then," Hobb said, "what can I get you to drink?"

The group made their orders, and Hobb headed over to the bar to start filling.

Ferrin stood. "I don't think I have time to wait. If we only have the day, I'm going to need all of it to finish my work, possibly the night as well."

"You can't stay and eat?" Myron asked.

Ferrin shook his head. He walked over to Rae. "I'll be back later to see how you're doing." He looked at Myron. "Keep an eye on them, would you?"

Myron waved him on. "Of course. No need to ask."

Ferrin then walked over to talk with Hobb about finding a local smith who might be willing to let him rent his shop for the day. Hobb gave him the location of two, noting which he thought was most likely to allow it.

Ayrion watched Ferrin leave. The man was certainly dedicated to his craft. Ayrion was anxious to see the finished product.

With Bek's help, Hobb returned with their tankards and several pitchers. Just about the time that the final mug was filled and placed, the door to the kitchen opened, and Milly and her crew swarmed out with several trays laden with bowls of rewarmed stew, some thick slices of cheese, and a couple of loaves that had probably been saved from the previous evening's meal. They weren't cold, but they weren't exactly warm either.

The bowls were distributed, and Ayrion picked up his spoon to take a bite, first blowing across the top at the rising steam. He'd been looking forward to this for some time, the smell forcing his mouth to water. Milly was known to be one of the best cooks in Oswell, and even though he hadn't said it aloud, he was growing weary of the vegetable broth they'd been eating for the last several days. As soon as he lifted his spoon to his mouth, the door behind him slammed open, and a group of Oswell guards poured into the lobby, swords drawn.

Ayrion drew his blades and was out of his chair before the first wave reached the sign-in desk. The rest at his table were up as well, as the armed men continued to pour in from the front.

Milly's assistants squealed and ran for the kitchen, only to be stopped as more men poured in from the back of the inn, surrounding the group.

Lenara started forward, her silver rods in her hands and looking hungry to wake their magic, but Ayrion stopped her. The last thing they needed was to unleash Lenara on the inn. By the time she was done, she'd probably bring the whole place down on their heads.

"What is the meaning of this?" Hobb demanded, looking around for whoever was in charge.

"What do you think you're doing in my kitchen?" Milly shouted at the guards still flooding in through the back. "You soil my floors and I'll have your hides!"

"That's the one there," someone said over near the front desk. A taller man, thicker in the chest than most, pushed his way through the group. Beside him was the watchman Ayrion thought might have seen his eyes.

Ayrion gritted his teeth. If they had noticed, why hadn't they tried stopping them back at the gate?

The larger man at the center, who Ayrion guessed to be the officer in charge, stopped several feet from where Ayrion and the others were standing, well out of weapon range. He took a moment to look them all over, but then stopped at Ayrion. "We will need you to come with us."

Ayrion quickly counted through the guards in the lobby, then glanced behind him at those filling the kitchen. Whatever they were up to, they had come prepared. "And what are the charges?"

"We are under strict orders. All Upakans are to be immediately escorted to the magistrate."

Ayrion couldn't help but wonder if this had anything to do with him and his father. They had been the ones commissioned to remove the previous magistrate. Obviously, whoever had taken his place had set a permanent watch for Ayrion's people. It was a wise precaution, and one that Ayrion didn't have time for.

"You are outnumbered, Upakan. Not even a fighter of your caliber can hope to escape here alive. Your companions can stay, but if they resist, we will have no choice but to deal with them as well."

Ayrion heard Lenara mumble something beside him, and about the time he turned, a ball of fire rose from the palm of her hand. He shook his head. This was not what they needed.

Gasps and curses spread around the room as the men nearest the front began pushing those behind them back.

"You take a single step in our direction," Lenara said, "and the innkeeper will be serving what's left of you for supper."

Ayrion raised his hand. "Not here. You risk burning down the inn."

"Don't you dare release that in here!" Milly bellowed from the other side of the room. "You set fire to my place, and *you'll* be the one I'm serving up."

Ayrion needed to calm the situation before it got any more out of hand. He looked at the others. "I'll go with them."

"The Pits you will!" Bek said. "Have you lost your mind? What if they decide to throw you in the dungeon, or simply execute you on the spot? If you go, we all go. I didn't just spend the last few months of my life fighting off ancient wizards, battling flesh-eating monsters, fending off the White Tower's guards and their wielders, not to mention black witches with giant arachnobes, just to have you rotting away in some prison cell in this puny, Creator-forsaken town."

By the time he finished, there wasn't a closed mouth in the lot. The Oswell guards looked half ready to throw down their weapons and run.

"Who are you people?" the officer asked nervously, his sword shaking in his hand.

"No one you want to know," Ayrion said and started toward them.

The entire company took a step back.

Ayrion pointed at the door with his sword. "Shall we?"

The men parted, no one wanting to get too close as Ayrion and his entire team made their way through the lobby and out into the road.

"And to think we were that close to getting that hot meal," Bek grumbled.

The guards escorted them through town, shooing curious citizens away until they reached the magistrate's estate. Ayrion remembered it well, having scouted it quite thoroughly with his father all those years ago. The mansion looked the same. The trees were taller and thicker, and they had dug up the bushes that used to grow along the western wall, but other than that, nothing much had changed.

The Oswell patrol ushered them in through the front gate, up the walk, and into the main vestibule. Ayrion had never seen this part of the house. Their visit had been relegated to the family's bedchambers. Half the guard waited just outside the door, while the other half filled the lobby to capacity.

Ayrion and his team stood in the middle, directly underneath a tiered chandelier that hung rather low from the ceiling. The men surrounding them kept their distance, no one daring to get too close, especially to Lenara, whose face was growing pale. Ayrion grimaced. This would be a really bad time for her to have one of her bouts of nausea.

"We have found another Upakan, Magistrate," a voice said from somewhere on the left, near the back of the staircase. The voice sounded like it belonged to the officer Ayrion had spoken with at the inn. "He was sitting pretty as you please at the Golden Tassel. Not caring who saw him. And he's not alone, sir."

The guards parted and the burly officer reemerged, along with an older man about average height, with grey streaks in his hair, and from the prominent dark circles Ayrion could clearly make out on what little he could see of the man's face, he didn't look like he had done much sleeping in the last few nights.

"This is him, Magistrate," the guard said, turning to point at Ayrion.

The magistrate turned to get a better look, and Ayrion's breath caught in his throat.

It can't be.

The magistrate stopped as well, then pushed a pair of spectacles higher up the bridge of his nose. "Ayrion? Is that you?"

Ayrion smiled. "Magistrate Sirias?"

Chapter 40 | Ayrion

"STAND DOWN, ALL OF YOU!" the magistrate said, then walked over and gave Ayrion a warm embrace and clapped him on the back.

Ayrion stood there, utterly stunned. This was turning into quite the reunion. "How are you . . . I thought you were . . . What are you doing back in Oswell?"

Sirias laughed. "That's a long story. And you. What's it been? Twenty years? I never thought to lay eyes on you again, let alone here in Oswell."

"Long story, as well."

"Then it seems we have much to discuss." Sirias turned to the officer. "You can dismiss your men, Captain." He paused, then looked cautiously over at Ayrion. "You didn't return to the Lost City, did you? You aren't on a contract?"

Ayrion smiled sheepishly. "Would I tell you if I was?"

Sirias stared at him a moment.

Ayrion laughed and clapped the older man on the back. "No, I haven't been back home since I rescued you from the Cylmaran slavers. But oddly enough, it is where we're heading."

Sirias glanced over Ayrion's shoulder as though realizing for the first time that he hadn't come alone. He took a moment to look the group over, then finally turned back to the captain. "I'll be fine, Captain. You can leave some men if it will put you at ease, but I trust this man with my life. He's saved it twice already."

The captain looked at Ayrion, seemingly confused, but finally turned and ordered most of his men out, leaving a handful behind.

Sirias turned to Ayrion. "Have you eaten?"

"No!" Myron said behind them. "We had just sat down when we were rudely interrupted."

Sirias called one of his butlers over and whispered something in the man's ear, and the man promptly departed by way of the right hallway and disappeared around the corner.

"Come," Sirias said. "I want to hear your story." He led Ayrion's group down a similar hall on the left and back to a large study with a roaring fire, which Rae, Suri, and Myriah were quick to maneuver in front of.

Sirias had another of his attendants run to get more seats. The magistrate waited until everyone was settled before he took his place by the fire. "I'm sure you are wondering how it is that I, of all people, would end up back inside the magistrate's office."

"That would have been my first question, yes," Ayrion said with a smile.

"Well, it's a bit of a funny story, really. Turns out that my rival, Ilban, who happened to be the head of the city council, was the one who had put a contract on my head. Lucky for me and my family that you and your father were the ones to take that contract."

Sirias turned at a knock on the door. The butler entered with several other staff members, carrying trays of drinks, along with several decanters filled with various colored liquids. There were also a couple of steaming cups of fresh tea, which the women were quick to snatch up, while the others chose between the ale, cider, and a selection of wine. Ayrion chose the cider, since the day had presented enough surprises already, and he wanted to keep a clear head.

He took a sip of his drink, which proved to be sweeter than he was used to, and relaxed in his chair, or as much that his swords would allow. "The last I saw of you, Magistrate, you and your family were heading down the coast toward Fayburn, I believe."

Sirias nodded. "Excellent memory. Though I'm afraid we only made it as far as Vinten. I managed to find work in the portmaster's office, keeping up with shipping ledgers. It wasn't hard work, but it was tedious. Vinten became our home for the next couple of years. To my surprise, though, one of the ships making port in Vinten was carrying passengers from Oswell. I can't begin to tell you how shocked I was to look up from my desk and find none other than my old friend Minkle standing there."

Before Sirias could continue, there was another knock, and the butler and his staff entered once more, this time with trays of sandwiches stuffed to the brim with meats and cheeses. A single whiff had Ayrion's mouth watering, and as interested as he was in the magistrate's story, the food certainly had his attention.

Sirias waited until everyone had their food and began eating before continuing. "As I was saying, Minkle was just as surprised to find me there as I was him, and we got to talking. I told them what had befallen my family, and how someone had put a contract out on us, and Minkle was quick to point out that it must have been Ilban. No one had any idea what had happened to me. Apparently, that was when Ilban made his move and got the council to vote him in as the new magistrate." Sirias shook his head. "Things went downhill from there."

Ayrion took another sip of his cider. "How so?"

"Come to find out, Ilban had lost favor with not only the council but the people themselves. He began exacting edicts for everything. He even raised taxes twice, most of it ending up in his family's personal coffers. Worse, people started disappearing, namely those who opposed what he was doing. The power went to his head. Eventually, he was tried and executed, and the rest of his family was run out of Oswell."

Ayrion leaned back in his seat and wiped the sauce from his mouth with a napkin. "That is quite the comeuppance," he said.

Sirias nodded. "Aye. Minkle begged us to return, as they had yet to fill the magistrate's seat, and since I was never officially voted out of office, the council thought it only reasonable that I should continue my sworn duties. So, here we are. I'm going on my fourteenth year back as magistrate, and couldn't be happier."

Ayrion washed down the last bite of his delicious sandwich with a swallow of cider, then promptly refilled his tankard. "That is quite the turn of events. I'm happy to hear things have worked out so well for you."

"The Creator has certainly blessed me and mine," Sirias agreed. "So, what have you been up to these last twenty years? Did you make it to Aramoor?"

"I did." Ayrion proceeded to give him a very condensed version of his life since they'd last met, taking care not to mention some of the larger events, such as his role as Guardian Protector, their discovery of Aero'set, or his work with faelings and wizards, or his battle with Argon and the vulraak. Much of what he skipped over had been some of the most interesting parts of his life, but it wasn't anything that the magistrate needed to know. He finished with the warning of what might be taking place with his people in the Lost City, without mentioning the khuls, and Sirias confirmed the rumors he'd heard as well, which wasn't anything more than what Hobb had already told them.

"It seems when it comes to interesting tales, you have me beat, sir," Sirias said to Ayrion. "And I have a feeling half of it wasn't told."

Ayrion smiled.

Sirias looked at the others, and for a moment Ayrion worried that the magistrate was going to start asking for all of their stories as well, but he didn't. Instead, he stood and ushered them to the door. "I can see you have business that needs attending to. I do apologize for the unexpected detainment, but after what happened the last time a couple Upakans paid a visit to my city, I can't be too careful." He offered Ayrion a curt smile.

"I can't say I wouldn't do the same," Ayrion said as he followed the magistrate out. Ayrion wasn't about to tell him that it wasn't the Upakans he spotted that Sirias needed to worry about. It was the ones he didn't.

Sirias stopped just shy of the front door and turned to shake Ayrion's hand. "I'd say I hope you will stop by on your way back, but if you do plan on relocating your people, perhaps that wouldn't be such a wise thing after all." He chuckled, but it was a nervous one that said he would probably be more than happy if the Upakans bypassed Oswell altogether.

"I thank you for your hospitality, Magistrate, and I do wish you and your family well. Be sure to give your wife and children my best. Who knows, perhaps our paths will cross again."

Sirias smiled. "Perhaps."

Ayrion and his team headed across the courtyard and back through the Oswell guards who had remained on the property after all. Sirias stood and watched from the porch, not turning to head back inside until Ayrion's group had passed through the gate at the front of the estate.

"That was quite the reunion," Bek said. "Should we prepare for any more unexpected visitors from your past?"

Ayrion chuckled. "Let's hope not."

Only a few of the Oswell patrol followed them back through town, splitting off at the main road, where they took the right branch back to the city's main gate.

The sun was still bright in the sky, but slowly dipping toward the west. "Probably best if we get our shopping out of the way before the shops close," Ayrion said, reaching into his coat to pull out Zynora's list. "Any volunteers?"

"I want a bath," Rae said.

Myriah quickly agreed, and added, "You men certainly need one as well."

"Why, whatever do you mean?" Myron asked with a wide grin, which she countered with a glare.

"I mean it. You reek something fierce."

Ayrion held up Zynora's list. "Then the faster we restock our supplies, the sooner we get those baths." Before he could say anything more, Myriah had snatched the paper from his hands, and the entire group was quickly making their way down the street toward the center of town. Lenara was the only one who lagged behind, her face pale.

"If you want to return to the inn, we can get the supplies," Ayrion said.

The bulradoer didn't argue and immediately turned and started walking briskly in the direction of the Golden Tassel. Ayrion didn't envy her. He just hoped it wouldn't last for too long. This was a bad time to have one of their strongest wielders out of commission.

It took the rest of the afternoon to find everything on the list, but they managed it, and by the time they had reached the inn with all their newly acquired goods, the sky was just beginning to color. They stored the bags of supplies in their rooms, and from there it was directly to the washing chamber.

"I suggest after supper that you get to bed early," Ayrion said. "We'll be leaving before the crack of dawn."

This time, no one complained, not when it meant getting some extra sleep, and in a real bed. The next two hours were spent taking turns in the washroom. There were only two tubs, and as dirty as they were, the water required emptying and refilling after each occupant.

Ayrion was one of the first in the tub after the women and found the warm water quite soothing. He washed and dressed and headed back down to the common room to find tables for the others. The room was beginning to fill, and he chose two tables against the right wall, which gave them a view of both the front door and the back. It also put them in a good position to see the stage and their entertainment, which was built across from them on the left side of the room.

By the time everyone had finished their bathing, the stars were out, and the staff was promptly arriving with their food.

"Perfect timing," Myron said, licking his lips as he took a seat next to Myriah.

Ayrion sat on the end, which kept his back to the kitchen but allowed him to see who was entering through the front. The inn drew quite the crowd that evening, and before long was filled to overflowing. Most kept their distance from the visiting travelers, casting furtive glances their way, but kindly left them to their food.

A flutist, who entertained the room with some languid melodies that had Ayrion's eyes feeling heavy, was eventually replaced by a hefty man toting a short-neck lute. His thick, stubby fingers were quite nimble on the strings, and by the second chorus, he had the crowd clapping and singing along to some rather witty verses of "Bart the Fool" Ayrion was unfamiliar with. Whoever this Bart was, he seemed to have been well traveled. There was hardly a place in Aldor Ayrion had been that didn't have a verse or two of their own.

A couple of the more well-plastered patrons decided to serenade the crowd with some lyrics of their own, each verse worse than the last, culminating in a rather vulgar tale that ended with Milly clobbering the two drunken men over the head with her dipping spoon. That was when Myron ushered Rae and Suri to the stairs to retire for the evening. The others weren't far behind.

Ayrion stayed until the only one left was Bek, who was simultaneously waiting on Ayrion. By the time they both realized that neither was wanting to be there, the lutist had finished, and the man playing the flute was making his way back to the stage.

Ayrion and Bek used the break between the entertainment to head for the lobby and the stairs up to their rooms. Ayrion glanced toward the front door, wondering if Ferrin was still out there working on his project, and if so, how much longer he had. He hoped the smith was able to finish it in time to get some sleep. At the top of the stairs, Ayrion bid Bek a good night and headed down the hall for his room.

The room was plain by Aramoor's standards, not to mention what they had been accustomed to in Aero'set, but the fireplace was well stocked and the bed didn't squeak too loudly. Most importantly, there were no rocks or roots underneath his blankets to keep him tossing and turning.

Ayrion removed his coat, and even his shirt, before crawling under the blankets. He closed his eyes and within minutes was fast asleep.

A knock on the door had him up and reaching for his weapons, which were leaning against the table next to his mattress. "Who is it?" he asked, still half asleep.

"It's Hobb."

Ayrion glanced over at the window, but it was still dark, though he thought he could see the faintest trace of grey creeping across the sky in the distance. "Just a minute." He sat up and took a moment to let his head clear before walking over and opening the door for the old ferryman.

"You asked to be woken early," Hobb said. "Don't sleep much myself, so I'm usually up before dawn to get the oven ready for Milly."

Ayrion yawned. "I must have slept hard. Don't remember even turning over last night." He thanked Hobb, who nodded and said he was heading back downstairs to start breakfast.

It took a while, but Ayrion finally managed to wake all the rooms and get them and their gear gathered below while they waited on breakfast to be served. Ayrion looked around. "Has anyone seen the smith?"

"He hasn't returned yet?" Myron said.

Some of the others looked at Rae, and she shook her head. "We haven't seen him."

Myriah sighed. "Knowing him, he's still banging away in his shop, probably has no idea what time it is. There were times I wouldn't see him for days once he got started on a project." She shook her head. "Someone might need to go—"

Before she could finish her thought, the front door of the inn opened, and Ferrin walked in carrying a long bundle under his arm and a wide grin on his face.

"That was spooky," Myron said.

Myriah crossed her arms. "Have you been out there all night?"

"I have, and it was worth it," he said as he shut the door and walked over to where the group was gathered just inside the common room.

"Did you even eat?" she asked.

He shrugged.

Ayrion eyed the wrapped bundle under Ferrin's arm, guessing it to be another sword by the shape. He pointed Ferrin over to one of the empty tables, as they were the only ones in the common room. It was still too early for patrons to be coming down for breakfast.

"Did you finish?" Ayrion asked, anxious to see what he'd been working on.

Ferrin nodded. "I did."

"You look happy with the outcome."

Ferrin's smile deepened. "I'll let you be the judge."

Everyone gathered around the table as Ferrin carefully set the package down and began to unwrap its contents. He removed the final piece of material and took a step back.

Ayrion could only stare in awe.

Up until now, Ayrion's dragon blades were the most exquisite pieces of weaponry he had laid his eyes on, but the blades Ferrin had crafted for himself were every bit their equal. There were two: one was the length of a full sword, maybe slightly longer, and the other was much shorter, about a third of the first blade's length, though bearing a very similar curved design. They weren't black like Ayrion's blades, but they had been treated so that the dark steel reflected the light.

"I've never seen anything like them," Myron said.

Myriah nodded. "You have outdone yourself this time, brother."

"It's the first chance I've had to create something for myself," Ferrin said, shifting nervously back and forth, like a boy who'd just given his mother a handful of flowers and impatiently waited on her praise. He looked once more at Ayrion. "What do you think?"

Ayrion shook his head. He wasn't even sure how to respond. "I think they are remarkable. I wouldn't have thought it possible to meld this many weapons together and still create something so beautiful. I can see the sword," Ayrion said, "but here where it widens, I can also see the battle-axe. It reminds me of a Bristonian ginesh, but more elaborate."

Ferrin handed the longer weapon to Ayrion.

It was lighter than he had expected, especially with the upper half of the blade being as wide as this one was. It was top heavy, which allowed for a more powerful swing and follow-through, but it didn't pull on the arm like a true battle-axe. Three barbs, each nearly double the previous barb's length, lined the back of the blade like jagged teeth waiting to rip open its enemy's flesh. The shorter blade also held barbs along its spine.

The sword seamlessly flowed into the axe, shapely curves that swept to angular points, like a stylized talon or fang. Unlike his own swords, both it and the shorter blade bore curved hilts that lacked protective guards and were fashioned into a pair of beautiful white wolves. Each head faced forward on the hilt so that the blades seemed to grow from their mouths. Instead of a pommel, the end of each hilt had been fashioned into a long flowing tail. The smith had also embellished the design with gold inlay markings along the center of the steel that looked mostly decorative, though they matched the wolves' deep yellow eyes.

Ayrion thought it a reasonable guess the smith had chosen to adopt the wolf motif in thanks to Nola. It seemed fitting.

Ayrion ran his fingers along the side of the blade. "Where did you get the . . ."

"The gold?" Ferrin smiled and pulled out a coin pouch from his pocket and bounced it a couple of times in his hand. "Put a little of the Tower's savings to good use."

Myron gave a sullen grunt.

They were indeed weapons of beauty, and Ayrion almost found himself jealous of them. At a nod from Ferrin, he picked up the shorter blade as well and walked into the lobby and away from the others, then proceeded to run through a couple of brief forms to test their balance. They felt natural in his hands. They didn't move as well as his own swords, but that might be because they were created for a man with a larger frame and arms. Satisfied, he returned the weapons to Ferrin.

"As I said, remarkable. I would be more than happy to help you develop a technique that suits them." He would have to think about the best way to train for such a unique set of weapons. It would need a blending of various styles.

"I would like that."

At that, the others gathered around to get their turn, each oohing and ahhing as they picked Ferrin's latest creations up and tested their weight and agility.

By the time the weapons had made it around the room, Milly and Hobb had their breakfast ready, which they ate quickly but thoroughly. Afterward, they brought down the rest of their gear and supplies and made their way out and around to the stables to saddle their horses. Ayrion was the last to mount as he stopped to say his goodbyes to Hobb and Milly.

He hugged them both. "Perhaps the fates will cross our paths once again."

Hobb released Ayrion's neck and stepped back. "Let's hope it doesn't wait another twenty years. Afraid I won't be around to see it."

"Send us a missive if you can," Milly said. "Let us know how it went for you in the Lost City."

"I'll do my best," Ayrion promised. "Perhaps we will stop through here on our way east."

Hobb smiled. "That would be nice."

The old couple waved as Ayrion mounted and the group headed down the road and back toward the city gate. It had been really good to see them, though he worried it could be the last time he would. His chest tightened at the thought, but he pushed it aside and focused his mind on what lay ahead. There was plenty there to keep it occupied.

Chapter 41 | Adarra

ADARRA STOOD AT THE BOW of the ship and stared at the wall of grey ahead. The Bay of Mist. It was even thicker than she had imagined. She'd seen mists before; none had ever looked like this. They should have named it the Bay of Impenetrable Fog.

An unexpected storm had blown in about the time they had reached the mouth of the river, and Captain Mervall had laid anchor to wait it out as he wasn't about to tempt crossing the bay in the middle of a storm. The storm hadn't been too severe, but it had lasted well into the afternoon, and instead of risking getting caught out on the open waters at night, the captain had decided to wait until the next morning to set sail. Even though it put them a day behind, it gave everyone, the crew especially, a chance to catch up on some much-needed rest.

Breakfast had been eaten quickly as everyone readied themselves for what lay ahead. The captain from the second ship had rowed over to coordinate strategies with Mervall and Holverd. It was decided that the boats would tie off to each other, using long bands of rope to keep from getting separated in the fog, and would use a bell to signal their locations to keep from accidently ramming each other.

"Nervous?" Aiden asked from where he stood on Adarra's left.

"Very," Ambassador Lanmiere said from Adarra's other side, not realizing the question had been meant for Adarra. Aiden smiled at the older man.

"I'll certainly be breathing easier once we reach the island," Adarra said, gripping the rail in front of them as the waves were a little rough heading out from the mainland after the storm. This was the first time she had seen the ocean. She'd read plenty about it. Most of the nautical texts she had found were from personal experiences penned by sailors who'd spent their lives on it, more poetic than educational. For Adarra's part, the ocean wasn't so different from Crystal Lake, in that all she could see was endless amounts of water stretching from one horizon to the other, but she didn't remember waves like this on the lake. And the spray that struck her face with each new wave tasted different.

The bow rose and fell, its continual cadence making her thankful she had kept her breakfast small that morning. Aiden, on the other hand, had already emptied his stomach twice. Adarra found that as long as she kept her focus on a single spot in front of her and maintained a constant flow of very deep breaths, she could manage not to repeat his performance.

It took nearly two hours to reach the fog. It had looked much closer due to its sheer size. Thankfully, the waves had abated by the time they reached it, and the two ships pulled alongside each other, waiting for a signal from Mervall to enter. The wall in front of them was enormous. As close as they were, Adarra couldn't see the end in either direction. She tilted her head, but she couldn't make out the top either. The motion made her dizzy, and she quickly looked back down.

Captain Mervall had one of his navigators at the back sound their bell, which hung from a stand at the helm. As soon as the last ring faded into the distant waters, the two ships started forward.

It was like sailing straight for the side of a cliff, and Adarra flinched as the tip of their ship went through. She lifted her arms and grabbed at the thick, low-hanging clouds, feeling the moisture in the air. It was every bit as thick as the early-morning fog that formed over the fields across from their home during the fall and winter months. Perhaps even more so.

"I don't like this," Aiden said as he turned to look at her.

He looked strange, as if he were a more faded version of himself. She swept a quick gaze around the ship. It was like everything had been drained of color. She could only see about half of the forward deck, and it startled her every time one of the crew appeared out of the fog. Sidaran Lancers lined the rails on both sides of the ship, all armed, all staring outward, which seemed a wasted effort, but one Adarra and the others were only too happy to indulge.

Captain Holverd had remained at the stern of the ship with Captain Mervall, a fact that played heavily in Adarra's decision to watch the fog from the bow. She wondered how Jonas was doing below, if the fog had permeated that part of the ship.

As they traveled farther in, she realized the fog had another effect she hadn't been prepared for, one which left her feeling even more unnerved than not being able to see. Silence wrapped the ship like an enormous snake, slowly enveloping them with its coils. All sounds seemed blunted and hollow, and Adarra strained to hear even a whisper from the following ship. The loss of the wind cut the chill, which she was grateful for, but she thought she would have preferred it to this eerie stillness.

"What just happened?" Aiden asked, tugging at his ears.

"Don't ask me," Lanmiere said, doing the same.

"I wasn't," Aiden countered, earning a grunt from Lanmiere.

Adarra stared out over the rail. "I have no idea what's going on." She snapped her fingers beside both ears, finding that even they had been subdued by a degree. She leaned over the side to see if the water was still there, since she couldn't hear it. It was, though the ebb and flow of the waves wafting against the wooden planks below made little to no sound. It was eerie, and chill bumps began to tickle her arms.

The ship's bell sounded in the distance. She had no idea if it had come from their ship or the other. "This is bad."

Aiden turned. "What do you mean?"

She could tell Aiden was the one talking since his lips were moving, but his voice sounded distant. It almost echoed back around from behind her. She reached out and ran her hand through the air. "There is something very wrong with this fog."

Both Lanmiere and Aiden turned, noticing the strangeness in the way their words sounded. "What's happening?" Aiden asked again, now raising his hands to snap his fingers as well. "Nothing sounds . . . right."

"That's what I mean." She turned toward the stern. "Listen for the bell." They waited in silence until its silvery call pierced the darkness. All three turned in different directions.

"I heard it," Aiden said, pointing portside.

"No," Lanmiere corrected, looking starboard. "I distinctly heard it over there."

They both turned and looked at Adarra, as if waiting for her to decide which of the two was correct. "I heard it as well," she said, then pointed straight off the front bow of the ship. "Out there."

They all shivered at the same time.

"I don't like this," Aiden said. "If we can't determine which way the bell is sounding from, how can the other ship?"

"The ropes," Adarra said, and they rushed across the deck for the portside stairs. One of the sailors appeared out of the fog, and Adarra yelped. Feeling embarrassed, she didn't turn to see if the man had stopped but kept going as all three headed down to the main deck. They worked their way down the side of the rail and found Captain Mervall and Captain Holverd arguing with several of the sailors and lancers standing around the anchor point.

"Who was watching it?" Holverd shouted, pulling off his fur-lined cap to rub his shaved head. His voice was angry, but his eyes showed a hint of fear.

The lancers pointed at the sailors, and the sailors pointed at the lancers.

"What's going on?" Adarra asked as they approached. A couple of the sailors startled as the three walked out of the fog, some drawing an X across their chest and spitting to the side.

"It's the rope," Mervall said.

"What about it?" Lanmiere asked, pushing his way to the rail to get a closer look. He gasped. "Where is it?"

Two of the sailors hefted what was left of the heavy cord that was still tied to the mast behind them.

"It's been cut," Holverd said. "I smell sabotage." He looked around. "Has anyone checked on the Tallosian?"

No one said anything, and Holverd reached for his sword.

"I'll go," Adarra said, and started across the deck before Holverd could stop her. Aiden chased after her, but Lanmiere stayed with the rest of the men, hopefully to calm the two captains down.

Adarra felt her way forward until she reached the galley door. She opened it and stepped inside, and Aiden shut it behind them.

"Hello, Miss Adarra," Sergeant Finnly called out, causing both her and Aiden to jump. The sergeant was standing just to the left of the stairs leading down into the hull. "What's happening out there? I thought I heard shouting. Captain Holverd has me standing watch at the entrance. I think he's worried that the Tallosian might try escaping."

"You haven't seen him, have you?" Adarra asked.

"Who? Holverd?"

"No. Jonas."

Finnly looked at her funny. "I saw him the other day."

"I mean recently."

He shook his head. "No. Why? Has something happened?" He reached for his sword.

"I don't believe so," she said reassuringly. "Captain Holverd wants me to check and make sure, though. The fog out there has everyone a bit on edge, I'm afraid."

"More than a bit," Aiden chimed in.

Adarra started for the stairs.

"You want me to accompany you, missus?" Finnly gave Aiden a distrustful look.

She smiled at him on the way by. "I'm sure I'll be fine." She headed down the stairs and through the crew's sleeping quarters to the maze of stacked crates on the other side. She hoped Jonas was still there. She hoped Holverd hadn't been right all along, and Jonas had simply been using her, biding his time until he could make his move. If he had gotten free, he could be anywhere. A chill crawled up her spine, and she quickly glanced at the top of the pile of crates.

Taking a deep breath, she pushed through the last of the crates and then released it with a huge sigh of relief. Jonas was still there, right where they'd left him, his hands still bound. He stood when he saw her and furrowed his brows when he saw the worried look on her face.

"What is the noise?" he asked, looking up at the ceiling.

"We have reached the fog."

Aiden remained behind her at the passage entrance, giving her plenty of room. He clearly didn't want to get any closer to the Northman than he had to.

Jonas shook his head with a grunt. "You must go backward."

"Backward? What do you mean? We can't sail backward."

"You must turn around. Go west."

"You mean east," she corrected. "Tallos lies northeast of Aldor."

Jonas shook his head. "No. You must turn west. Backward."

"That doesn't make any sense."

"Holverd was right," Aiden said. "He wants to run us across the reefs and sink us."

"He's not trying to sink us, you ninny. If we go down, so does he." She looked at Jonas. "Why west?"

He shrugged. "We went backward to get to you."

"That's preposterous," Aiden said.

"Everything about this fog is preposterous," she countered.

Jonas reached for her, but the chains on his arms clapped tight. "Hurry," he said, the tenor of his voice letting her know that if they didn't, things were about to get a lot worse.

She nodded and quickly ran back through the passageway. How was she ever going to convince the captain to do something as ridiculous as this? She raced through the sleeping quarters and up the stairs to the galley, startling Finnly enough that he yelped as she and Aiden tore out of the well behind him.

"What's happening?" he asked, his hand nervously clutching the hilt of his sword as he glanced back toward the open stairwell behind him. "Has your prisoner gotten loose?"

"No, but I don't have time to explain," she said back over her shoulder as she burst through the galley door and back onto the main deck. She could still hear raised voices, but they seemed to be coming from all around her. Focusing on what she knew and not what her ears were telling her, she quickly headed left across the deck toward the port side. "We need to change course," she called out as she saw the faint tracing of people ahead. Aiden was right beside her, close enough to feel his arm brushing against her own.

"What do ya mean change course?" Captain Mervall asked, his debate with Holverd momentarily put on hold.

"Was he down there?" Holverd demanded. "You didn't find him, did you?" He drew his sword before she could say anything and started for the galley door, but she grabbed his arm and stopped him.

"Yes, I saw him. He's right where you left him. He hasn't sabotaged anything. But he does say that if we don't change course immediately, we're all going to die." Jonas hadn't used those exact words, but they were clearly inferred.

"Change course to what?" Captain Mervall asked, looking down at the compass in his hand. "We're still headin' due east."

Ambassador Lanmiere glanced over the captain's arm to get a look at the compass for himself.

"That's the problem. We need to change our heading west."

Mervall looked at Holverd, and they both looked at Adarra. "That makes no flamin' sense," Mervall said. "That'll take us in the opposite direction."

"I know." She hoped her trust in Jonas hadn't been misplaced. She was risking all their lives. "He said that the only way through the fog is to travel . . . backwards."

"Backwards?" Holverd's face was reddening. "Have you lost your mind? What sort of spell does this man have on you?"

"We can't travel backwards!" Mervall said. "That's lunacy."

Adarra raised her hand. "Wait, not backward. The translation would be more like . . . opposite. We need to set an opposite heading from what we believe."

"That's insane," Holverd said, turning to look at Mervall, whose lips were now pursed. "You aren't actually listening to her, are you? You've been to the island before. Did you have to travel . . . backwards?"

Mervall bit down on his lower lip, and Adarra's heart sank. She could see it in his eyes. "You've never been to the island, have you?"

Holverd's mouth went slack as he stared at Mervall. He threw his hands in the air. "You've got to be joking! You lied about getting to the island?"

"I'm sorry. I needed the work, and no one else seemed willin' to take the job." He looked at Adarra. "Do you trust the prisoner's word?"

"You can't be serious!" Holverd shouted.

Mervall raised his hands. "Do you have any better ideas? The only man we know who's actually been to the island is tellin' us that we need to change course. I'd be a poor ship's captain if I didn't at least listen."

"You're a poor captain regardless. You lied to all of us."

"Lyin' about bein' to the island doesn't make me a poor captain, just proves I'm desperate. But when it comes to the water, there's no better hand at the sails than mine. And right now, we are stuck in a fog that has us hearin' bells from plum near every side of the deck, and a rope that has, for no apparent reason, simply split in two. I've got no idea where the other ship is and no way to find it. The only navigation bein' offered is from a man who's actually crossed these waters. So yes! I'm gonna take it seriously!" Captain Mervall pushed through the onlookers and headed straight for the stairs leading up to the ship's helm.

Adarra and the rest followed, those not assigned to stations below.

"Oriss! Turn us about!"

"Aye, aye, Captain!" The sailor at the helm grabbed the wheel and began to spin, and the ship tilted. The current was strong enough to keep them moving even without the wind in the sail. "What heading, Captain?"

"Due west," Mervall said, staring down at his compass. The ship continued to turn until Mervall raised his hand. "Hold her there, steady as you go."

The helmsman righted the wheel, then locked it off with some rope, and the ship slowly righted itself.

Mervall turned to the sailor standing at the bell. "Keep ringin' that flamin' thing! We've lost the other ship. Don't want it rammin' us by mistake."

The sailor grabbed the mallet and started whacking the bell as loudly as he could. Everyone was staring out all sides of the ship at the same time. They had no idea where the other ship and all its crew were, and at any moment it could come lumbering out of the fog on top of them. One thing was for sure, though, with the sudden change of course, the odds of finding their missing crewmen were proving less likely by the moment.

"What about the other ship, Captain?" Lanmiere asked, looking out across the starboard rail. "We can't just leave them out here."

Mervall twisted his thick mustache. "And how do ya suggest we help them? We don't know where they are. Blazes! We don't know where *we* are."

"That's half our food," Lanmiere said, shaking his head regretfully.

"What about the apothecary's special seeds?" Aiden asked.

Adarra panicked for a moment, but then she remembered they had stored them in the captain's cabin with them. "They're here with us."

"Well, at least there's that, then," Aiden said, as if that was all that mattered. That was the least of their worries.

"I'm thinking that this whole trip has been for nothing," Holverd said angrily. "Why are we worried about a Tallosian invasion when reaching Tallos is practically an impossibility? You think a bunch of savage Northmen are going to have the capabilities of relocating their entire people through this, when we can't get two ships through? We should turn around while we can."

"That call is mine to make, Holverd," Lanmiere said. "And even if I were to agree with you, which I don't, which way do you suggest we go? We are about as turned around as it gets."

Holverd looked out at the surrounding fog. "We're heading west. I say we keep going until we reach the Sidaran mainland."

"Wherever we're headin'. We ain't gettin' there fast." Mervall pointed up to what they could see of the sail. "No wind. The currents have us now."

Adarra stared out over the ship's rail along with everyone else, wondering where exactly the current was taking them. Captain Holverd was right: If they maintained their heading, they were going to run straight into the Sidaran mainland. She started wondering if perhaps she had misunderstood what Jonas had said, or maybe he had mistranslated. None of this made any sense.

"Did you hear that?" Aiden said, and everyone turned. He was standing at the starboard rail, looking out into the fog.

"Hear what?" Lanmiere asked, breaking away from the rest of the group to join him at the side.

"I thought I heard something out there."

Adarra and the others hustled over as well. She listened, but other than the faint sounds of the waves crashing against the ship and the occasional ringing of the bell behind them, Adarra didn't hear anything out of the ordinary.

Aiden shook his head. "I . . . I thought I heard— Wait, there! Did you hear it?"

"Hear what?" Holverd demanded. "All I hear is that infernal bell and you."

"It sounded like someone shouting."

Everyone pressed against the side and listened. Mervall even turned and hollered for the helmsman to stop ringing the bell. They all waited in silence. Adarra couldn't hear anything. It was a very eerie calm. She wondered if the pressure was getting to Aiden, causing him to hear things that weren't—

Wait. "Yes. I think I hear it, too."

"Aye," Captain Mervall agreed, pointing out toward the fog.

"Heard what?" Holverd asked. "I don't hear anything."

"It sounded like Captain Bismont calling out his position."

"I heard nothing."

Mervall turned to his helmsman. "Hard to starboard!"

"Wait," Adarra said. "We need to maintain a westward heading."

"Not if that's my ship out there."

The ship tilted once more as they began to turn about. Everyone remained quiet, listening for another sign that their fellow shipmates were within reach.

"I think I hear their bell," Holverd finally said, pointing even farther east.

Mervall directed the helmsman to give them more, and the helmsman spun the wheel even further. "Yes," Mervall said, growing excited. "I can hear it too. Dead ahead." He turned to the sailor beside the wheel. "Ring away. Let them know we're here." The sailor lifted his mallet and began striking the bell.

Where was the ship? Adarra strained to hear something, anything. How close were they? With each passing breath, the tension grew. Mervall and several of the others began calling out into the fog, shouting in hopes the other ship could hear, hoping to keep from ramming into her.

Adarra added her voice to the mix, but no matter how loud they shouted or how far they traveled into the fog, the sounds from the other boat never seemed to get any closer. Adarra finally turned to Mervall. "Captain, I think we need to turn around. I don't think anyone's out there."

"Then how do you explain—"

"Reef, Captain!" someone from the forward deck shouted back to them, and about the time they heard it, the entire ship lurched to the side with a loud crack, louder than anything they'd been able to hear so far.

A chill ran up Adarra's spine. They were about to be ripped apart on the rocks.

Chapter 42 | Adarra

"HARD TO PORT!" Mervall bellowed, and the helmsman hauled on the wheel, but it wouldn't budge. The crewman who had been manning the bell gripped the other side of the helm and heaved too, both men straining to turn the great wheel.

There was a strange scraping noise, and the ship suddenly jolted to the right. Adarra was knocked off her feet and rolled across the deck with several others, Lanmiere and Mervall among them. The others must have managed to grab the railing before the ship pitched, because she couldn't see Aiden or Holverd anywhere.

A heavy gust of wind came out of nowhere and hit the sails, pushing the ship farther into the shoals. Adarra and Lanmiere grabbed hold of each other and held on for dear life. Mervall, as spry as he was, jumped back to his feet and ran for the helm, shouting the entire way at the two men who were fighting to get it turned. The roar of the wind was anything but natural. It was deafening and sounded eerily like the wail of a thousand sailors sinking into the ocean's depths. Every hair on Adarra's arms stood on end.

"What is that?" Lanmiere tried asking over the wind.

"I don't know!" Adarra held on to the older man's arms as they fought to right themselves and keep from sliding any further across the deck.

Two more sailors reached the captain, and between the five of them, they managed to get the wheel turned. Adarra made it to her feet and helped Lanmiere to his. Her legs were shaking.

"Are you alright?" Aiden asked, rushing out of the fog.

Adarra jumped. "I'm fine." She tried to brush hair out of her face while still maintaining her grip on the ambassador.

Lanmiere took a moment to pat himself down. "Nothing broken, it seems." He turned and looked at the helm. "That sounded like we hit—"

"We're taking on water, Captain!" someone shouted, their voice punching through the wail of the wind.

Adarra turned.

Sergeant Finnly was standing at the top of the steps, waving his arms, his face white.

Her chest tightened, and she turned to Aiden. "Jonas is down there." She ran across the deck for Captain Mervall, who was holding up his compass, attempting to point out a heading to the helmsmen. "Captain!" She fought to be heard above the roar of the wind, "Jonas is still chained below. I need the key to release him."

"I don't have the key. Holverd does."

Her heart sank as she turned to find the lancer captain. He was heading down the stairs on the starboard side, so she raced down the port side to catch him. She could hear Mervall behind her shouting out orders for every available crewman to get below to help save the food.

Adarra flew down the steps, Sergeant Finnly and Aiden on her heels. "Captain." She rushed across the deck, bumping into crewmen and soldiers alike before finally reaching Holverd, who was shouting orders to his men over the gale. "I need a key to unlock Jonas. The hull is taking on water, and he's still down there."

Holverd turned. "Have you lost your mind? I'm not about to set him free on this ship."

"I didn't say you had to set him free. You can chain him to the wheel if it'll make you feel better, but we can't leave him down there to die. He's our only hope of making contact with the Tallosians. We need him alive!" She wanted to scream and tear her hair out in frustration. Every moment she wasted arguing with the captain, Jonas came that much closer to drowning. For all she knew, he might already be gone. "Send all the men with me you want, but we need to go now. Not to mention, we are losing our food."

She turned to see a line of sailors already making their way into the galley. She turned back to Holverd. "We need to bring the food up."

"Don't let your personal feelings cloud your judgment, Captain," Lanmiere said, making his way over from the stairs behind them. "We need the Northman, and we need those lancers down in the hull to help us save what food we have left. We've more than likely already lost one ship. Do you plan on losing this one too?"

Holverd ground his teeth but eventually nodded and headed for the door, ordering every lancer within sight to follow. Adarra raced into the galley and down the stairs, running into several sailors on their way up with their arms full of crates.

"How bad is it?" Holverd asked.

"Bad," one of the sailors said on the way by. "We need help down there."

Holverd turned to one of the lancers behind him. "Get more men loading crates." The lancer nodded and raced back up the stairs.

All of the men coming up from the hull were soaked from the waist down. That was not a good sign, Adarra mused as she started down the stairs after Holverd. She hit water before she reached the bottom and froze. It was ice cold. She panicked for a moment as the sensation rushed over her, but she pressed her lips together and willed herself to bear it, then continued down, tucking her dress between her legs as she went so it wouldn't float around her and get in the way. Her legs burned at first as the icy water rose above her waist. She was shorter than the men by a good bit, which meant more of her would be submerged. She stepped down off the last step and sank to her chest. It took her breath, and the room began to spin.

"This water is freezing!" she heard Aiden shout behind her, jolting her enough that she finally remembered to breathe.

Her teeth chattered, but she quickly pressed forward after Holverd, who was already halfway through the crew's sleeping quarters, dodging sailors and lancers alike as they rushed to save the food. She spared a quick glance behind her, seeing nothing but men making their way up and down the stairs. She was glad to see the ambassador had remained above.

She forced herself to keep moving through the water, doing her best to catch up with the captain. She needed to be there when he faced Jonas, but unfortunately her legs were much shorter than his, the soaked skirts of her dress weighed her down, and with the onslaught of men and crates pushing past, it was slow going—even with Aiden helping her forward. He all but lifted her out of the water at one point as he tried to keep her moving. There was a growing line of men behind them needing to get to the food.

The ship lurched once more, and Aiden grabbed her and pulled her back just as one of the sailors beside them lost balance and dropped a load of crates right where she'd been standing. Water splashed, and she squealed as the sudden spray of freezing water hit her face.

Stepping over the now-lost crates, they made it through the crew's quarters and on to the mounds of food. The crates were already being broken down, as sailors and lancers alike fought to save what they could, starting with the crates still above water. Hopefully, they had been wise enough with the stowing to have placed the more perishable goods, easily damaged by water, at the top.

Once they had passed through the first row of crates, the flow of men dropped off, leaving her and Aiden free to get through the rest of the passageway unhindered. Her legs were going numb, and her arms were tingling. She did her best to hold them out of the water, but they naturally wanted to press against her chest to protect against the cold. Her breathing was shallow now, each inhalation painful.

Thankfully, the fog wasn't as thick in the hull as it was above, which made it a little easier to see, though all she could see at the moment was her breath misting in front of her face. She tripped on something in the water and would have gone under if not for Aiden's quick hands grabbing her and pulling her back up. She stopped to catch her breath.

"How are you?" he asked.

All she could do was nod. She heard raised voices ahead and started forward, making her way through the last of the crates and into the small opening at the back.

Jonas was standing behind the support beam, or as much as his chains would allow, since they were fastened to hooks on the floor. Holverd's men moved to surround him. He growled at them, spinning left and right like a caged animal, as he watched them close in. The water was over his waist and rising. The lancers in front drew their swords but kept their distance as they tried working their way around the giant Tallosian.

"Wait, let me talk to him," she said, her voice faint and broken as it shook against the cold. She pushed past the guards to get between them and Jonas. Aiden surprisingly stayed with her instead of remaining in the passageway. She looked at Jonas. "We need to get you out of here." She held up her hands as though they were bound and then pointed at his chains. "We need to unlock those. Will you promise not to fight them when they do?"

Jonas looked at the encroaching soldiers and bared his teeth, but he did eventually nod and held out his hands. Adarra turned to Holverd. "Give me the key. I'll unlock him and—"

The ship canted hard to the left, causing everyone to plant their feet to keep from going under. A loud crack behind them, like boards being snapped in half, momentarily diverted all their attention as water suddenly poured in through a new hole on their right. Sailors rushed in to patch the tear with fresh wood but struggled to get a seal over the water now gushing in.

"Hurry!" Adarra shouted at Holverd, and he reluctantly handed over the key.

"Are you sure about this?" Aiden asked, staring up at Jonas nervously, his hand quivering on the hilt of his own blade.

She didn't bother answering. Instead, she took a deep breath and was about to dive under to where his chain was connected to the bottom of the beam, but Jonas grabbed her and shook his head.

Before she could say anything, he snatched the key from her hand and dove under the water himself. The soldiers all raised their weapons and quickly moved back as soon as he disappeared below the surface. Aiden grabbed Adarra by the shoulders and pulled her back as well. She watched the water around the beam, waiting for Jonas to break free, but he never did. She kept watching. It felt like minutes had passed. What was he doing? Was the lock stuck? Why was it taking so long?

She took a step forward, and the water broke, and Jonas came lumbering out of it. As soon as his head rose above the surface, the soldiers tackled him back against the crates, grabbing his chain.

She released a small sigh of relief that Jonas hadn't tried attacking.

"Give me the key!" Holverd shouted and raised his sword.

"Give him the key, Jonas, please," she pleaded.

Jonas looked at Holverd, then over at her, and finally raised his hand and tossed the key to the captain. She was surprised to see that his wrist shackles were still on. She had thought as long as he had been under the water that he might be unlocking them as well. The lancers probably thought the same, which was why they had leaped on him so quickly.

Holverd and his men escorted Jonas back through the maze of food, with Adarra and Aiden hot on their trail. She had to make sure not to let Holverd out of her sight. There was no telling what the man would do if he thought he could get away with it.

The cold was quickly catching up to her, and her teeth were chattering uncontrollably. She couldn't feel anything below her chest. They needed to get out of the water before they froze. They were just reaching the other end of the crates when another loud cracking sound erupted on their left and sent the entire ship reeling.

Ropes beside them snapped, and the left pile of crates and barrels shifted to the right, sending the entire mound down on top of them. Adarra went under first, a large barrel shoving her down within the passageway as it landed up against the crates on the other side, locking her in. A thousand pinpricks rushed across her face as the freezing water bit her skin. Her breath was ripped from her chest, the pressure of the barrel building as it crushed her against the floor of the ship.

She screamed and fought to move, but the barrel was jammed tight, the weight of it crushing her against the floor.

A hand wrapped around her arm, and suddenly she was being yanked out from under the overturned barrel and lifted out of the water. She sucked in a deep breath, coughing as she did, and wiped the hair and water from her eyes. She looked up to see Jonas's face and realized it was his arms wrapped around her. The top of her head barely reached the bottom of his enormous chest. She gasped for breath, only to discover that the man had clearly not followed her suggestion to bathe.

She pulled free and turned, seeing Aiden just ahead with his shoulder against a stack of barrels that were blocking their way out of the passage.

"Help!" he shouted to no one in particular.

Jonas lifted her halfway out of the water and carried her over to where Aiden was pressed against the side of one of the overturned barrels. "What's wrong?" she asked, and Aiden spun.

"It's Captain Holverd! He's stuck underneath, and I can't get him out. He's drowning."

Both Adarra and Aiden turned and looked up at Jonas. She could see in his eyes that he understood. She had no idea how she was going to convince him to save the captain's life.

Before she could even try, Jonas pushed Aiden out of the way and put his shoulder to the barrels and pushed. The pile started to shift. Aiden jumped in as well, and the uppermost barrels finally gave way, but there was still one wedged underneath.

Jonas took off his human-hair cloak and handed it to her, then dove under the water. It was the closest she'd come to the disturbing garment, and she was surprised, and revolted, to find that it was actually quite soft.

She stood beside Aiden and waited for what seemed an eternity for Jonas to return. It might have been too late. He'd been under for some time.

The water broke, and Jonas pulled Holverd out from underneath.

The captain's head was drooping to the side, and she realized they *were* too late.

Jonas dropped Holverd down on some of the fallen crates stacked above the surface, and as soon as he did, Holverd's chest convulsed. She started at first, then jumped forward and grabbed the captain's uniform. "Turn him over, quickly."

It took Jonas's help to get Holverd on his side, and as soon as he did, the captain spewed up the water he'd swallowed, coughing uncontrollably for several long minutes as he gasped for breath.

The captain opened his eyes, and it took him a moment to realize where he was. As soon as he saw Jonas's face standing overtop him, he reached for his sword, only to find it wasn't there. Holverd tried getting up and almost fell off the crates and back into the water. He was shivering uncontrollably. So was Adarra.

"Stop moving," she said as Aiden and Jonas held the man down. "You nearly drowned. Jonas just saved your life."

Holverd stopped trying to break free and stared up at the Tallosian in disbelief, a half snarl on his face. Behind them, the crates started to move, and the passageway opened as sailors and lancers filtered through.

"We thought we'd lost you for sure," Sergeant Finnly called out, the first one through the mound. He immediately rushed forward and gave Adarra a big hug and, seeing Captain Holverd lying there staring at him, immediately released her and saluted. "Sorry, sir. Didn't see you there. Do you need assistance?" Finnly didn't wait for an answer and ordered several of the men to come escort their captain out of the hull.

Surprisingly, Holverd said nothing to his men about securing the prisoner as they hauled the captain up the stairs and out. Adarra continued to shiver as the water in the hull continued rising, now almost above her chest. If they didn't get it stopped, the ship was going down, and all of them with it.

She was all but convulsing by the time she started to tell Jonas and Aiden they needed to leave, but before she could get a single word out, she was being lifted off her feet. She turned to find herself once again in Jonas's huge arms. He looked down at her, and she saw that his eyes were a deep green. How had she never noticed their color before? He carried her out of the crates, through the crew's hammocks, and up the stairs. Aiden was right behind. She didn't realize until they had reached the top of the stairs that she was still clutching the Northman's scalp cloak.

"You can put me down now," she said.

He did, and she handed the vile garment back to him, which he slung over his shoulders and tied off at the front. The long braid of his dirty-blond hair had started to come undone behind him, leaving strands plastered to the side of his face and neck. One thing was certain, his prolonged swim under the salt water had cut through the worst of his stench—or perhaps she was just growing used to it.

They left through the galley door and back out onto the main deck to find that the howling wind that had been so pervasive before had all but vanished, leaving the ship once more in a state of eerie silence and fog. Whatever was happening, it wasn't natural. Clearly, there was magic involved, and it wanted them dead, or at the very least, didn't want them reaching the island.

"We need to get you warm," Aiden said, starting her across the deck for the captain's cabin.

She looked at him. "You were down there too."

"Yes, but I didn't go all the way under like the rest of you."

A couple of lancers rushed by and into the cabin door before they got there. Each was carrying a pan of heated rocks from the galley. Adarra smiled. A couple minutes over some rocks and a dry change of clothes would do her wonders. She opened the door to find Holverd stripped down to his undergarments as the lancers were doing their best to warm him over the heated pails. Normally she would have blushed or at least turned around, but she was too cold to care, and apparently so was he, since he didn't even bother looking up to see who was there.

Not waiting for him to dress, she stumbled over to the side and started stripping herself, starting with her sword belt, something that no matter how often she wore, she felt uncomfortable with.

"What are you doing?" Aiden said, casting nervous glances at the lancers behind them.

"I'm trying to keep from freezing to death," she said, her teeth nearly clamped shut as she continued to unbutton her dress. She removed it, her bodice still protecting her decency, not that she cared too much about it at that moment. She knew she was going into shock, completely numb.

Jonas unhooked his cloak and held it up between her and the rest of the men on the other side of the room.

Aiden shook his head but didn't say anything, clearly not liking the huge Tallosian there watching her undress. With the cloak blocking her from the rest of the men, she stripped off the rest of her clothes and waited on Aiden to hand her a towel to start drying. Jonas switched places with Aiden and momentarily disappeared, leaving Aiden to hold the scalp-lined cloak up high enough to keep her naked body from being seen, though she thought it might have slipped a little at one point.

Moments later, Jonas reappeared with one of the buckets of heated rocks. He slid it under the cloak, and Adarra knelt down beside it, letting the warmth envelop her. They were too hot to pick up, but the heat wafting up from the pail was enough to get some feeling back in her extremities. It was strange, uncomfortable, and if she were honest, a little thrilling, to be sitting in such a vulnerable position with all these men standing around, but she didn't have time to think about it. She needed to get dried and warmed and back out on deck.

As soon as her arms and legs began to tingle, she pulled one of the riding outfits Lyessa had given her from out of her chest and began to dress. She didn't like wearing trousers in public, but under the circumstances, better those than a dress if she were to end up in the water once more, and as fast as the hull was filling, that was a likely scenario. She finished dressing by strapping her sword belt and dagger back around her waist. The belt was heavier with the added water and marked the waist of her pants when she fastened it on.

"I'm done," she said, and Jonas lowered his cloak.

"What about you?" she asked, looking up at the water dripping from the Tallosian's hair and face.

He untied his wet cloak and draped it over one of the chairs, then pulled his woolen shirt up over his head and began to wring it out. He couldn't take it completely off because of his shackles.

Both Adarra and Aiden stared in awe at the half-naked man's chest. He was even more muscular than she had imagined, not that she had spent that much time trying. Aiden was quite sculpted, and she enjoyed watching him practice with his shirt off, but Jonas was something entirely different. Her face flushed, but she couldn't seem to pull her eyes away, especially when she noticed the scars. Deep swells of resealed skin marked much of what she could see—stabs, cuts, burns, and some she didn't care to speculate how they had occurred. What had happened to him? Worse, what did that say about where they were going? What were they walking into?

Aiden shook his head, gaping every bit as much as she was. Jonas didn't seem to notice, or at least didn't let on that he did as he leaned over and grabbed the bucket of heated stones and lifted it to his face. He held it there a moment, then set it back down and grabbed a couple of the stones themselves and rubbed them on his chest, just over his heart. The heat didn't seem to bother him. Adarra reasoned that his hands were probably calloused enough that he didn't feel it.

Once finished, he dropped the stones back in the pail and carried the bucket over to the lancers surrounding Holverd. He handed it to them, then returned to pull on his wet shirt. She wished they had something dry for him to wear, but she doubted there was anyone on board who had something in his size. Jonas, however, didn't seem all that bothered by it and grabbed his cloak off the chair and slung it over his shoulders, then looked at her as though waiting for orders.

On the other side of the room, Captain Holverd argued with his men, slapping at them as they tried helping him get a dry uniform on. As soon as they finished, Holverd headed for the door, pulling his fur-lined cap back over his bald head. His stride was slow but determined. He stopped a few steps from the door and turned, staring at Jonas. He looked like he wanted to say something but simply couldn't force the words out. He finally reached into his pocket and tossed something at the Northman. Adarra looked down at Jonas's hand.

It was the key.

With that, Holverd turned and headed out the door, but not before ordering a couple of his men to stay behind, clearly not about to let Jonas out of their sight.

Jonas looked down at the key a moment, then fitted it into one of his wrist shackles, and with a simple turn, the latch released. He did the same for the other, and soon enough, his hands were no longer bound.

"What do you think this means?" Aiden asked.

"I think Holverd believes we're all about to drown anyway," she said, and started for the door.

Chapter 43 | Adarra

HE FOG WAS COLD and damp, and the unnatural silence still had Adarra's nerves strung tight as a lute, but at least the torrential wind that had driven them over the reef had ceased. Inside the galley, Adarra, Aiden, and Jonas joined Ambassador Lanmiere, Captain Mervall, and Captain Holverd to discuss their options and where to go from here.

Three lancers stood by the nearest bulkhead behind them, one of whom was Sergeant Finnly. He smiled each time Adarra happened to look in their direction. Holverd might have favored Jonas with freedom to move about the ship because he felt he somehow owed the Tallosian, but he wasn't about to let the man out of his sight.

"How are the repairs coming along?" Ambassador Lanmiere asked Captain Mervall.

"Slow, but our odds of survivin' are goin' up by the hour."

Lanmiere frowned. "I guess that's good."

The ship was still taking on water, but not to the extent it had been during Adarra's time in the hull. The ship's carpenter and carpenters' mates were working tirelessly to repair the breaches and seal cracks, but only after sailcloth had been spread over the damaged sections of the hull to temporarily keep more water from entering. She had read about the process, called "fothering," before but had hoped never to see it done in person.

"And the pumps?" Captain Holverd asked.

Mervall nodded. "Working as hard as they can. The pumps ain't my worry, though," he said, nervously pinching the ends of his mustache. "It's everything else. This never-ending fog that's got us hearin' things all over the ship. Gusts of wind that come out of nowhere. Deathly silence. It's unnatural." He shivered. "And if we weren't already headin' on a course away from this place, I'd tell us to turn back now. This ain't like nothin' I've ever seen before."

"That's because it's being aided by magic," Adarra said. She raised her head to find everyone looking in her direction. She nodded at Mervall. "You said it yourself. The fog isn't natural. You step out on deck, and nothing sounds like it should. The noises are muted, and what you can hear echoes off the fog in random places to make it sound like a conversation you're holding face-to-face is coming from behind you or beside you, or from nowhere at all. We all thought we heard the other ship, but we never found it. It was always just in front of us. And then there's the wind. You can't tell me that was natural. Was it just me, or was everything pulling us directly into the reef?"

"It wasn't just you," Aiden said, his hands wringing in his lap. "It's like it wanted us to drown."

"It wasn't until we set an opposite course, due west and away from the island, that it stopped," Mervall added. He shook his head. "None of this makes any sense." He looked up at Jonas, who was hovering over the back of Adarra's chair. "Did you run across wind like this, or the reef, or strange noises?"

Adarra looked up in time to see Jonas shaking his head. "We knew to row backward."

"How do you row backward?" Holverd asked, a tinge of angst in his voice.

"When we reach the fog, we turn our boat around and sail backward."

"I don't understand," Lanmiere said, then made a demonstration on the table with his hand being the boat. "Are you saying you rowed out to the fog, then turned your boat around . . ." He then spun his hand 180 degrees on the table. "Then continued out into the fog by rowing the ship backwards?"

Jonas shook his head and leaned forward between Adarra and Aiden to plant his own huge hand down on the table. "We row out to thickest fog, then turn and row backward," he said, demonstrating by turning his hand around like Lanmiere had, but this time instead of continuing in the same direction, he moved his hand like he was rowing directly back toward the island.

Adarra cut in. "So, you're saying that in order to leave the island, you had to row back *to* the island?"

Jonas nodded, and the others scratched their heads.

"I guess, in a way, it makes sense," Adarra said.

Lanmiere huffed. "I'm glad it does to one of us. Because I'm completely at a loss."

Adarra went on to explain. "If there is magic involved, then it seems clear that it doesn't want people reaching the island. And if Jonas is correct, it doesn't want people leaving it either. In fact, if what he says is true, then the only way to get to Tallos is by trying *not* to get there. It's actually quite ingenious if you think about it. Anyone who tries reaching the island will be lured onto the reefs, but it's those who purposely try *not* to get there that can."

"How did you know about this?" Captain Holverd asked Jonas skeptically.

"It is known to my people."

"Are you the one doing it?"

Jonas sneered.

"The Tallosians hate magic," Adarra said. "It's why they left Aldor in the first place. I doubt they'd be the ones using it now."

"It does seem unlikely," Lanmiere said.

Holverd slapped the table. "Someone is!"

"Well, it ain't no one aboard this ship," Mervall said. "If it were, then they'd be goin' down with us." He caught the concerned looks on everyone's faces. "That is, if we go down, which I ain't sayin' we are, just statin' a fact, is all."

"How long has the mist been around?" Adarra asked.

Lanmiere turned in his seat. "What do you mean?"

"I mean, what if it isn't one person in particular? What if the magic is coming from the mist itself?"

"The mist has always been here," Holverd said.

"Aye," Mervall agreed. "I ain't seen a map where it weren't. Why would you think it's the fog?"

Adarra shrugged. "Seems more likely to think that the magic is already here than to believe someone out there is calling it up, let alone someone on board one of our ships. If that were the case, then that same person would have had to have been on board the Tallosians' vessel as well."

"Exactly!" Holverd cut in, looking over at Jonas. "Which leaves only one person here."

"And if that were the case, Captain," she countered, "then why would he have warned us about it? In fact, we got caught on the reef when we veered away from the course he told us to keep to."

"She's got you there, Holverd," Lanmiere said. "Besides, like Captain Mervall has already stated, if he were trying to sink us, he was doing a right good job of getting himself sunk as well. Not to mention, he was chained below deck at the time."

Holverd apparently didn't care to get hit over the head with common sense, and frowned, but to his credit, he didn't argue. "I still don't like it."

"None of us do," the ambassador said. "But at this point it seems we have little choice. We've already lost one ship, so the prudent course is to keep going for as long as this vessel allows." He turned as another group of sailors rushed up from below, soaked from the waist down. "But I don't mind admitting that the thought of us sailing through magic-infused fog that wants us dead is not a promising start to this mission. I hate to think what awaits us once we get there."

The rest of the day seemed to drag like a watched pot. They couldn't tell where the sun was, couldn't even tell which direction the light was filtering in through. And even if they could, Adarra was convinced it would probably be a lie. All they could do was hold course to Captain Mervall's compass and pray that it, too, wasn't somehow being manipulated.

"Does it seem to be getting darker?" Aiden asked.

They were once again on the bow of the ship. Jonas, though silent, was a presence she could feel without looking. He stood just off to her left.

"It could be," she said, staring straight ahead into the fog, hoping to spot some sign that they were getting close to land. From the direction they had plotted, one would assume it would be the Sidaran mainland, but if what Jonas had told them was correct, they would eventually reach Tallos, unless, of course, they missed the island altogether and ended up sailing south below the mainland and out beyond the boundaries of what any maps showed. That would be her luck.

She let her mind wander, as it often did, contemplating where those uncharted waters led. Did they just keep going, or was there something else out there to be discovered? More than likely, she'd never know. But the eastern waters were only part of the secrets that teased at her imagination, places waiting to be discovered. She was also quite fascinated with what lay beyond the Westlands. The wizard had hinted of other cultures when recounting the origins of the magical bow Breen had found in Mangora's shop. Breen said he had mentioned something about rangers out of the Westlands, which had certainly piqued her interest.

She was also curious about what lay beyond the Gates of Bel'Taag to the north. She would love to be able to see those gates one day. She couldn't imagine something so large it spanned the gap between two mountain chains. It was said to be one of the great wonders of the Five Kingdoms, much like the walls of Aramoor, which was yet another landmark she would one day love to visit, though she knew she likely never would.

Aiden shivered. "Do you ever get the feeling we're being watched?"

Adarra looked up from where she'd been staring into the fog.

"Continually," Ambassador Lanmiere said as he walked over to join them at the rail. "But I don't know if it's from the fog or from the lancers Captain Holverd has following Jonas around." He chuckled as all four turned to glance over their shoulders at Sergeant Finnly and his accompanying guards.

Finnly and his men stood several feet back, not close enough to be included in their conversations, but not far enough that the fog caused them to lose sight of Jonas. She smiled at the sergeant, and he smiled back. She felt sorry for the man and once again wished he'd remained in Easthaven. He looked very uncomfortable being there.

Over on the port side, a sailor called out another sounding, one that had Captain Mervall glancing down at his black book and smiling.

"What is it, Captain?" Lanmiere asked.

"We seem to be reachin' shallower waters."

"What does that mean?" Aiden asked.

"Means we're gettin' closer to land. But which land that be, I got no way of tellin'."

Adarra stared ahead, as if somehow she could pierce the fog with her gaze. All of them did. Even the lancers standing guard moved up a step or two.

"How close do you reckon we are?" Lanmiere asked.

Captain Mervall waited for his crewman to call the next sounding. He jotted the figure down and looked up excitedly. "Very close," he said, and turned and hustled back to the stairs on the forward deck. "Cast anchor!" he shouted to those at the stern.

The clanging of an anchor being lowered echoed off the mist around them, and Adarra was pressed gently against the rail in front of her as the boat slowed. Below, the waves tapered off from where the ship had been cutting through them in the current.

"Has anyone thought about how strange this is?" Aiden asked. "In order for us to get to Tallos, we have to sail away from it, which only stands to reason that if we want to leave, as Jonas stated, we have to sail toward Tallos."

"We already know that," she stated.

"Yes, but here's the rub. If in sailing away from Tallos we are actually sailing toward it, then doesn't that also mean if we're sailing toward it, we're actually sailing away from it? How would we ever get there?"

Adarra tried thinking about the logic behind it and found that she couldn't. "I don't think there's a way to explain it. That's what makes magic, magic. Sometimes it doesn't play by the rules."

Lanmiere hmphed. "And sometimes I wonder if the Tallosians didn't have the right idea in trying to get away from it all in the first place."

Jonas grunted behind them. She still hadn't told him that she was a wielder. And since her magic wasn't all that overt, it wasn't something she had to worry much about, at least for now. She wondered if he would look at her differently if he knew. Perhaps not. But as superstitious as the Northmen were, it would be best not to test that theory.

"I think we've stopped," Aiden said, and everyone looked over the side of the ship. It did seem like they were moving more with the waves than against them, bobbing up and down like a buoy with the flow of the current.

"I think you're right." She turned to see if she could find the captain, but all she caught was a glimpse of what she thought was his hat as he descended the starboard steps. "Come on. Let's see what they want to do."

The four of them, along with their guard, headed across the forward deck and down the stairs to the main deck, where they found Captain Holverd organizing his men.

"What's going on, Captain?" Lanmiere asked.

Holverd turned, and seeing the ambassador, walked over. "Captain Mervall believes we are within boating distance, so I'm organizing a scouting party to see if we can't make shore."

"Might we want to wait until the morrow?" Lanmiere suggested. He glanced around the fog-lined deck. "I doubt it wise to send a ship out at the edge of nightfall."

Holverd turned and looked out across the deck as if noticing for the first time that it was getting darker, the ship's lanterns growing more prominent. He finally nodded. "We can wait for morning."

"Perhaps," Lanmiere added, "the fog will have dissipated by then."

Jonas shook his head. "It moves as it will. On shore. Off shore. It is alive."

Adarra didn't like the sound of that. By the looks on the others' faces, neither did they.

With the stress of leaving the ship having been postponed till morning, the crew had nothing better to do than take their evening meal. Adarra had no idea if it was indeed time for supper, what with the total lack of sun to indicate the time, but by the way her stomach was complaining, she guessed it was close. If so, then it was a wise decision to wait.

After their meal, Adarra, Aiden, Lanmiere, and Jonas headed for their cabin to turn in early. Jonas, who had been spending his nights chained to a post, was more than happy to take Adarra's spare cot, since she was using the hammock. But after just a few minutes inside the enclosed space, they all quickly agreed that Jonas needed to be bathed.

Thankfully, Adarra was able to talk Sergeant Finnly and a couple of the guards stationed outside their door to carry in a wash tub. Adarra tossed in one of the soap bars Lyessa had given her and stirred the water until she felt it was at least bearable.

"Uh, Adarra," Aiden said, "you might not want to turn around."

Adarra turned. "Why?" Her eyes bulged when she found herself standing in front of a very naked Northman, who apparently had no qualms about public bathing. She gasped and quickly spun around. "You could have warned me!"

"I *did*," Aiden said.

Lanmiere chuckled from over on the bed.

Adarra thought her face was about to burst into flame. She listened as Jonas stepped into the tub and sat down. "Is he in yet?"

"He's decent," Aiden said, and she cautiously turned back around.

Jonas didn't pay her any mind, apart from what she thought might have been a momentary smirk. Using the bar of soap, he began to scrub himself down.

"Don't forget his back," she said, pointing to Aiden and Lanmiere.

Aiden looked at Lanmiere, and they both shook their heads. "I'm not soaping his back," they both said.

Adarra gave a disgusted sigh. "Fine."

She walked over and took the bar from Jonas, who was trying to clean between his toes. Walking around behind him, she waited for him to pull his hair out of the way, then started to rub the bar across his back. He had nearly as many scars there as he did on his front. His skin was taut against his muscular frame, and she found herself slowing across the deeper wounds, even going so far as to trace a couple with her finger. What could have happened to him?

Lanmiere cleared his throat, and she suddenly realized she'd stopped scrubbing. Embarrassed, she kept going. "How did you get so many scars?"

Jonas leaned forward so she could scrub lower. "I get them during Ko Putaan."

"What is that?"

"We fight for better seats inside of house."

"You mean you fight each other for promotions?"

He thought a moment, then nodded. He started to stand, and she quickly grabbed his shoulders and pushed him back down. "What do you think you're doing?"

"I stand so you can clean back."

Her cheeks reddened again. "I'm not soaping your backside. You can do that yourself." She tossed the bar inside his tub, then walked over and grabbed his clothes, all but the scalp cloak. Holding her nose, she walked the smelly pile of laundry back over and dumped them all inside the bucket with him.

"What is this?" he said, rising halfway out of the tub once more before she could grab him and force him back down.

"Your clothes stink. They need to be cleaned." She turned and headed for the door, Lanmiere laughing as she did. "Come get me when he's dried and back in some clothes." She grabbed her overcoat on the way out.

The door shut, and she took a long, deep breath and let the air slowly release, watching it mist in front of her face. She kicked herself for getting so emotional. She should have stayed inside and just turned around, but instead she was standing on a cold, fog-ridden deck.

"Are you alright, Miss Adarra?"

Adarra turned to find Finnly standing to the left of the door. She smiled and walked over. "I will be once we finish this mission."

"I know what you mean. I wish we never came. This is not a good place. I miss Easthaven."

"Me too."

"Do you think we will see Tallos tomorrow?" he asked.

"It sounds possible. You aren't standing watch all night, are you? I hope you get at least a few hours in your bunk."

He smiled appreciatively. "I will be fine, missus, no need to worry. I told you I would keep you safe."

"Yes, but you can't very well do that if you are too tired to keep your eyes open." She patted his arm once more. "Promise me you'll get some sleep."

He sighed but eventually nodded. "I promise."

The door behind her opened, and Aiden stuck his head out. "He's dressed."

She nodded and then offered Finnly one final smile. "I'll bid you a good night, then, Sergeant."

"Sleep well, Miss Adarra."

She thanked him and headed back inside. Aiden had Finnly and the other guards retrieve the wash tub. Once they carried it out and shut the door behind them, she climbed up into her hammock and pulled up her covers.

"It's freezing in here," she said.

Aiden grabbed some stones from the bucket he'd retrieved from the galley and placed the heated rocks inside her bedding. He then kissed her goodnight, and for the first time, she felt a little uncomfortable doing so, but that was probably because Jonas was lying there just below, watching.

Aiden handed out the rest of the heated stones, finishing with his own bed before crawling in. He didn't look happy with being forced to sleep so close to Jonas and lay on his side so he could keep an eye on him.

Adarra wished them all a goodnight and then closed her eyes, but sleep was slow in arriving. When it did, it was plagued with dreams in which she was lost in one of the rowboats all alone out in the fog, as well as being left alone onboard with Jonas in random stages of dress or undress and trying to find a way to keep her distance.

Both instances left her feeling vulnerable.

She woke several times in the night only to return to more of the same. Needless to say, she was feeling only too happy to have one of the guards outside finally knock on their door to let them know morning had arrived and it was time for breakfast.

She rolled out of her hammock and nearly landed on Jonas, forgetting his bed was just below hers. She startled when she noticed him staring up at her.

"How did you sleep?" Aiden asked. He was already up and dressed by the time she had found the rest of her change of clothing.

"Not well. Unpleasant dreams." She glanced at Jonas and caught him looking and quickly turned away, focusing instead on getting her socks and boots on.

She hated having these feelings—whatever they were. Maybe she'd spent too much time with the Tallosian. His story had left her feeling empathetic, but there was something else there as well, and she didn't like it. It made her feel wrong somehow. She pushed the feelings aside and finished dressing.

Lanmiere, Aiden, and Jonas were all waiting for her at the door by the time she managed to get her sword belt and coat on. From there they all headed out on deck to see what everyone was doing. Adarra noticed Sergeant Finnly wasn't at his post, replaced by a tall lanky man with a very twitchy nose. "Sergeant Finnly didn't stand watch all night, did he?" she asked the taller guard.

He twitched his nose. "No, missus. But he did stay at least half."

She nodded and started across the deck. The fog didn't seem to be as thick today. Inside the galley, the tables were filled with soldiers and sailors alike, all waiting to find a seat, some taking their plates out onto the deck. Adarra waited in line with the others. Those standing closest moved aside when they saw Jonas. Once through, they found a seat at the captain's table, where Mervall was slowly nursing what smelled like a cup of hot tea and looking at least a little more rested than the day before. Captain Holverd was nowhere to be seen.

"Seems we will be sending a boat out in search of the mainland," Mervall said, sipping slowly while cupping his hands around the warm mug.

Lanmiere tugged softly on his grey beard, which hung only a few inches below his chin. "Am I the only one, or did it seem the fog wasn't quite as thick this morning?"

"You're not the only one," Mervall said, raising his mug in salute. "Let's hope it opens enough for our scouting party to see their way through."

Adarra hoped that was the case. Jonas seemed to believe the fog was alive and moved about at will. If magic was controlling it, was it being guided by set parameters? Was it simply running a course, or was it more involved? Magic was one element where her book knowledge did her little good, since there were no official books on the topic, at least none that she had ever been able to find.

They finished their meal quickly, wanting to get back out on deck to see the boat off. After turning in her empty plate and utensils, she, Aiden, and Jonas followed Mervall and Lanmiere back outside. There was a large gathering over on the port side of the ship where the crew, along with some enlisted help from the lancers, were lowering one of the rowboats down into the water.

Adarra, Aiden, and Jonas waited at the side as Captain Mervall and Captain Holverd chose the landing party. There were few volunteers from Mervall's crew. Holverd, on the other hand, didn't offer his men the opportunity and simply started calling out names. Long faces and sullen groans said those picked weren't happy about it. And why would they be? No one had any idea what was out there. For all they knew, they might be nowhere near land, and if they traveled too far from the ship, there was no telling if they'd be able to make it back.

Whoever went risked getting stuck out there.

"Perhaps we should tie off a line to the boat," Mervall said. "That way we don't lose them in the fog."

"A lot of good it did us the last time," Holverd said, but he eventually agreed, not that it was his decision to make. It was, after all, Captain Mervall's ship.

The crew went about gathering another long coil of rope and tied it off from the center mast down onto the back of the rowboat, where those who had been chosen were already climbing down.

"So, do they maintain a westward heading, then?" Mervall asked, looking at those standing nearby, stopping on Jonas.

Jonas shook his head again. "No. This close, you will go forward."

And by forward, Adarra took him to mean northeast—the direction they should have been traveling all along.

Holverd looked at Lanmiere, then at Adarra. She could see he wasn't quite sure he understood what Jonas was saying, so she explained that they needed to return to a normal northeast bearing. Holverd relayed that information down to the oarsmen, and they hooked their lanterns on the boat poles and pushed off from the side.

Adarra said a little prayer as she watched the boat and its crew slowly vanish into the fog.

Chapter 44 | Adarra

HOW LONG HAVE THEY been gone?" Aiden asked for the third or fourth time.

"Not long enough to reach the end of the rope," Adarra said, glancing over her shoulder at the large coil sitting beside the rail at the bottom of the steps on her left. Several sailors were feeding the rope up over the railing as the rowboat slowly made its way deeper into the fog. She kept waiting for the rope to magically split like it had when they were tied off to the other ship, but so far it seemed to be holding.

They stood on the forward deck, which was the highest point on the ship besides the mast, and stared out into the fog, listening for any sign that their landing party was still out there. Behind them, Sergeant Finnly and his accompanying guards waited quietly, keeping one eye on the water and the other on Jonas. She was glad to see that the dark circles around Finnly's eyes had lightened.

Looking over the side, more of the water was visible around the ship than before. In fact, she could now see completely across the forward deck, and if she looked toward the stern, she could just make out part of the helm. The fog was definitely clearing, though no one knew how far or for how long.

They waited in silence, no one wanting to move and risk missing anything. At one point, Adarra thought she heard what sounded like a shout, but she couldn't be sure, and since neither of the other two seemed to have noticed, she chalked it up to an overactive imagination.

The minutes dragged on into what felt like hours as those on the ship waited with bated breath for the rowboat's return. The coil of rope down on the main deck had stopped unwinding, and all the sailors and lancers alike were lined up and down the port side of the ship, watching and listening for any sign of their comrades. Holverd remained with his men on the main deck while Ambassador Lanmiere waited with Captain Mervall next to the helm.

"What's taking so long?" Aiden asked.

"Moross might have them," Jonas said in his broken Aldoran.

Adarra and Aiden turned.

He shrugged. "They hunt the shores."

Aiden's face paled. "Have you seen these moross?"

Jonas shook his head.

"Then how do you know they exist?"

"Others of my people have. They are very skilled."

"Your people or the moross?"

Jonas thought a moment. "Both."

Aiden leaned in to Adarra and whispered, "Don't worry. There's nothing out there."

His words might have been more convincing if his voice hadn't been shaking. And she might have been more inclined to believe him if not for the experiences they had suffered at the hands of the fog. There was more to this than Jonas wanting to manipulate the situation to his own end.

"I hear noise," Jonas said, and they all turned. Sergeant Finnly and his men took a couple steps closer to get a better look.

"Where?" Aiden asked.

"What do you hear?" Adarra added.

Jonas put his finger to his lips. "Shh."

Adarra strained to listen but didn't hear anything. Was it just the fog playing tricks on them again? Then she thought she caught something. A very faint splash.

"I think I heard it," Aiden said, and then the splash became more distinct.

Adarra turned and shouted toward the stern, where Mervall and Lanmiere were chatting quietly, "There's something coming!"

Everyone ran back to the side rail and listened. The splashes grew louder. They moved in a succinct pattern, a rhythm recognized by anyone who'd ever been out on the water. Sure enough, the rowboat loomed out of the fog ahead, the paddles beating the water at the same steady speed, drawing it closer with each new stroke. Adarra counted the heads of those inside the boat. They were all there.

Those aboard ship quickly began to haul the rope back up over the rail as they guided the boat over to the side. Adarra, Aiden, and Jonas anxiously made their way down the forward deck steps to await the boarding party's arrival, joining Lanmiere, Holverd, and Mervall, who were standing on the center deck. Most of those at the rail backed up to give those coming aboard plenty of room. A couple of the sailors remained to help them over.

A tall lancer with broad shoulders was the first over the rail. He immediately headed for Captain Holverd and came to attention with a salute.

Holverd clapped his fist to his chest in return. "Report."

"We found land, sir. The fog clears just before shore. The beachline is open for our boats if we want to begin transporting our people over."

"Was there any sign of Captain Bismont or the other ship?" Mervall cut in.

"No, sir. No sign that anyone had been there." The lancer turned back to Holverd. "I suggest we start with the lancers to set up a defensive before bringing over the civilians, sir."

"Did you see moross?" Jonas asked, and the soldier turned.

"Moross?" The lancer looked confused. "We didn't see anything but sand and snow. There is a rock line several hundred feet back from the water but not much else."

Aiden gave Adarra a curt look, but she ignored it.

"What about the food?" Lanmiere asked. "Should we begin transporting it over as well?"

"And how do you suppose we plan on getting it across the island?" Holverd asked, as he wiped the top of his forehead before readjusting his fur-lined cap. "Our overall mission is to make contact with these people, not haul a ship's worth of food across an island we know nothing about other than its supposed hostility. At present, it is safer aboard ship. If we do manage to reach the Tallosians and find them hospitable enough to enter negotiations with, I'd prefer not to have our main bargaining chip sitting there for them to take. Once we sign agreements, we can return with the Northmen, and they can arrange to transport the food back themselves."

"What food we have left," Captain Mervall grumbled.

Adarra might not have liked Holverd's pessimistic attitude about the perceived negotiations, but he made a good point. They didn't have enough manpower to carry all that cargo across the entire island, especially if Jonas was even half correct in his assessment of the dangers they could be facing. And it wouldn't be smart to bring the food and risk tempting the Tallosians to simply kill them for it.

"The longer we wait," Mervall said, nervously twisting his mustache, "the less daylight we have. If we're doin' this, then let's get on with it." The ship's captain started barking out orders to ready the other boat. Their ship only had two, which meant it was going to take several trips to get everyone offloaded and over to the island, not to mention all their gear.

Sure enough, it took the rest of the morning and most of the afternoon. The idea was to make camp there on the beach so they'd have plenty of daylight to begin their march across the island the next day. Jonas didn't like that idea because of the moross, but Holverd didn't want to risk losing daylight and getting stuck setting up camp in an even more precarious situation.

Adarra was one of the last to disembark. Captain Mervall helped her over the rail, and she adjusted her sword on her leg to keep it from snagging on the side of the ship as she slowly climbed down the rope ladder. Aiden and Jonas were already in the boat with their hands up to guide her down. Captain Holverd had been one of the first to leave the ship earlier that morning with his men, leaving Mervall to see to most of the final arrangements before coming over himself.

Adarra moved to the side of the front seat to give Mervall room to get down. He was the last to disembark. As soon as his feet reached the bottom of the boat, he untied the cord binding them to the ship and pushed off, looking up at the remaining crew still aboard. "She better still be here when I get back!"

"Aye, aye, Captain," one of the men at the rail shouted back down. A very sparse crew had been left to tend to the ship, and lots had been cast to see who those lucky few were. One thing was for sure, Adarra hadn't been one of them. Her sole reason for being there rested on the other side of the island. She had suggested trying to sail around to the other side, but apparently, according to some sketches Jonas had added to their map, there was no safe place to moor. There were nothing but sharp cliffs on the eastern face of Tallos, and with the way this magical fog seemed to work, it wasn't clear if getting there was even possible.

The safest thing they could do at this point was get ashore and go from there.

Adarra watched from over her shoulder as their ship vanished behind them, and they were once again encapsulated in fog. The boat was quiet, the sound of the oars dipping in and out of the water the only sign that they were still moving forward. Mervall glanced at his compass every so often to take another reading; it had become a nervous tic against the blindness of the surrounding haze.

Before they knew it, the fog thinned, and Adarra caught her first sight of the island ahead. It seemed much like she would have expected—a beach with waves and snow and sand. Just past the sand was a layer of rock, which led to a long row of tall plants of an odd yellowish-green color that ran for miles in either direction. The skinny poles that made up most of the plant were so tightly packed together that they gave the appearance of a solid wall. She couldn't see much beyond them, though she thought she caught a silhouette of the mountains off in the distance, but the closer their boat got to shore, the less noticeable they became.

The beach was filled with ship's crew as they awaited their captain. Ambassador Lanmiere waved at them from the front. He'd taken the boat just before theirs. Most of the lancers were busy setting up a makeshift camp about a hundred feet on shore and hopefully beyond any possible rising tide.

Adarra looked to her left and right. The fog wall stretched behind them down the waterway as far as the eye could see in both directions. She'd seen fog roll in before, but nothing like this. It stood as high as she could see and was just as dense up top as from below.

Jonas was one of the first off the boat, jumping into the surf to pull the boat the rest of the way on shore. Once out, they maneuvered the boat up onto the sand next to the other one to keep them from being sucked out by the tide. The long ropes attached at the backs were still there, ensuring that the boats could find their way back to the ship.

"What do you think?" Lanmiere asked as he walked over to greet them. "We could be the first mainlanders to step foot on Tallos in generations."

Captain Mervall looked around. "I think I'm ready to head back to my ship."

"What do they do?" Jonas asked, pointing at the lancers scurrying about up on shore.

Lanmiere turned to see what he was referring to. "Ah, they are setting up camp."

Jonas shook his head. "We should not stay here."

Lanmiere's brows lowered. "We haven't seen anything since we arrived."

Jonas continued staring down the beach where the fog seemed to be holding. "They will come."

"Who will come?" Holverd asked, walking down to meet them with several lancers at his side, one of which was Sergeant Finnly, who didn't look very pleased to be there as he stared nervously out at the surrounding fog.

"The moross," Jonas said.

Holverd shook his head. "Not this again. There is no moross. Look around. It's a completely empty beach."

Jonas turned and looked up at the sky, where the sun was beginning to lower to the west. "We shouldn't sleep here."

Holverd spared a passing glance toward the setting sun as well. "Where do you suggest we sleep?" He turned and pointed behind them. "On the rocks?"

Jonas shook his head. "Still too close."

"Do you even know where we are?" Holverd held up a rolled map he'd had tucked under one arm and opened it. "What part of the island did we land on?"

Jonas looked down at the illustrated depiction of Tallos and shrugged. "I do not know. My people travel along the water here," he said, pointing to the inlet on the south side of the island, where a river led from one side to the other.

"You didn't mention traveling the water before," Mervall said.

"Only here." He pointed to where the small bay on the south side narrowed to form the river. "Water not safe to travel."

"Why?" Holverd asked, still trying to determine where they might be in relation to the inlet.

Adarra shook her head. "If you would have been willing to meet with Jonas beforehand, you would have known that there are dangerous things in the water." Holverd's disdain for Tallosians had kept him from their scheduled meetings back in Easthaven.

Holverd looked at Jonas. "Have you seen these dangerous things?"

"No."

Holverd rolled the map and tucked it back under his arm, then glanced east down the beach. "I say we follow the waterline until we reach that inlet, and then follow it north to the mountains."

"No. You can't stay on beach. The moross hunt here."

Holverd's face tightened. "I'm not about to load up all our gear and go marching into an unknown terrain to set up camp in the middle of a jungle of reeds." He pointed to the wall of stalks. Adarra wondered if this was the reed maze Jonas had talked about as being part of the dangers they faced in order to reach his home. "At least out here," Holverd said, "we have the advantage of sight. If something were to come, we would see it. We try marching into that mess, and we won't see anything."

"You can stay and die," Jonas said, his face angry as he turned and grabbed Adarra's arm. "We go in the reeds."

"Wait," Adarra said, suddenly caught between the two and not knowing what to do except let Jonas drag her away from everyone else. "Jonas, stop." She tried pulling her arm away, but his hands were so strong.

"Get your hands off her!" Aiden shouted, rushing forward, but half a dozen of Holverd's men beat him to it and tackled Jonas to the ground, pulling Adarra down with them.

Holverd pointed at Sergeant Finnly, and Finnly placed the cuffs back on Jonas's wrists, shackling him.

"What do you think you're doing?" she demanded, trying to stop Finnly as Aiden pulled her back.

"What does it look like?" Holverd said. "You seem to forget he's a prisoner."

Adarra balled her fists. "But you allowed him his freedom aboard the ship?"

"Yes, and clearly that might have been a mistake. Were we to just sit here and let him carry you off into the night? Besides, what's to stop him from simply taking off and leaving us all here without any way of knowing how to reach his people? For all you know, that was his plan all along. Use your gullibility to bring him along, and then once we reach Tallos, he slits your throat in the night and takes off."

Lanmiere cleared his throat. "As much as I hate to admit it, the captain's right. We can't risk him running off without us, especially now that we're on Tallos." The ambassador looked her in the eyes. "Can you honestly say he wouldn't?"

She looked at Jonas, and as much as she wanted to believe he would stay to help, there was little reason keeping him there. If she were in his shoes, she would have probably made a run for it as well, especially after spending the last several months in a prison cell, then chained to a post in the belly of a ship, and nearly drowned in the process.

Jonas must have seen it in her eyes, and he immediately lowered his head. She felt guilty and embarrassed, but she couldn't bring herself to tell them he wouldn't run. Sergeant Finnly looked embarrassed as well by the situation, never once bringing himself to look in her direction.

"Well," Mervall cut in, no doubt trying to ease the tension, "I'm just glad I'm not havin' to go with the lot of ya. We'll stay to help ya get your camp up, but then I prefer to sleep in my own cabin tonight."

"At least stay for the evening meal," Holverd said. "We could use your cook. Give us at least one last good meal before we head inland.

Mervall looked around and, noticing all the hungry faces staring his way, finally conceded. "Fine. We'll stay for supper, but then we'll be off."

Captain Holverd looked pleased as Finnly escorted Jonas up the shoreline and back toward camp, and he set up a watch just in case.

"It's the right decision," Aiden said, moving alongside Adarra. "If I were

Jonas, I would have been gone as soon as my feet hit the shore."

"I know. But it still feels wrong."

Captain Mervall turned and looked down the western waterline, toward the fog in the distance. "Anyone else gettin' the strange feelin' like we shouldn't be here? What if this Jonas fellow's right?"

Aiden glanced down the beach as well. "Tell me again what these moross look like."

Adarra sighed. She was getting tired of describing them. "From what Jonas said, they're tall, very strong, and have hooks for hands, which they use to snatch people and kill them."

Aiden shivered. "I never feel any better after hearing that."

She grunted. "Then why do you keep asking?"

He shrugged. "Holverd's right about one thing, though. If something were to come, I'd rather fight it out here where we have room to move and see. I'd hate to think about being chased into that stuff back there," he said, pointing to the reeds.

Adarra looked at the forest of tall stalks and couldn't help but agree. Still, there was a strong nagging feeling that ignoring Jonas's warning might be worse. She was glad that Holverd set up the watch. "Here," she said, looking at Aiden, "help me with my bags, will you?"

Aiden and Lanmiere helped carry her satchels up the shore to where camp was being set. Small tents were being placed around several cookfires as teams made their way across the rocks to harvest stalks for burning.

The stalks grew ten to fifteen feet in length and were about as thick as Jonas's thumb. They also had small dark knuckles that formed at intervals along the outer shell. They were a yellowish color, but with hints of green that indicated they probably changed color during the warmer months. In and of themselves, they were a very thin, pliable plant, but when packed together as they were, they formed an almost impenetrable wall.

She stowed her satchels inside the small canvas shelter they had set for her beside the central firepit. Apparently, they wanted to keep her close to the middle of camp. Most of her bags were filled with books, but the bag she kept closest at hand contained the magic-wrought seeds Orlyn had given her to deliver to the Tallosians. She never let that one get too far from her sight.

The part of the sky she could see—what with the wall of fog still resting just offshore—had already changed colors by the time the evening meal was ready to be served. Adarra shared her fire with Ambassador Lanmiere, Aiden, and Captain Mervall. Jonas was being kept near the outskirts of the camp with a lancer guard.

The campsite had been fashioned in the form of three circles, each one smaller than the last, with the civilians' tents being at the center. Captain Mervall and his crew were next, forming a larger circle around them, and then Captain Holverd and the lancers took up the outer perimeter.

Adarra felt sorry for Jonas, as well as Sergeant Finnly, who apparently had been stationed on the outer edge, near Captain Holverd, and assigned to continue watching over Jonas.

The evening meal was consumed quietly, everyone too anxious to do much talking. Most were too busy staring out at the darkening beach, watching the water move in and out along the snow and sand as the last vestiges of light filtered from the sky. Adarra finished her plate and handed it back to one of the cooks, who stowed it with the rest for cleaning. She then readjusted her sword belt in order to stand and stretch.

Toting a weapon around all day was uncomfortable, especially with it bouncing against her leg, but she wasn't about to go anywhere without it. Her hand slid down to the dagger on her right, something she found herself doing more often of late, just as a way to remind herself it was still there. She was feeling very thankful for the weapons training she'd received over the last few months from Lyessa and Darryk. She only hoped she wasn't forced to use it.

As much as she enjoyed her memoriae magic, she really wished she had been gifted with something a little more useful, like Master Veldon's incindi magic or even Master Feoldor's control over the air; both of those would have been far more valuable right now than being able to recall everything she'd ever seen or read.

Mervall and his men finished their food quickly and were busy trying to clean and pack what gear they had in order to carry it back down to the awaiting boats. It was clear the ship's captain had no desire to stay the night on the island. She didn't blame him.

Adarra said her goodbyes, and Mervall wished her luck on her journey, stating that he'd keep the ship offshore and await their return. The captain planned on sending a boat in once a day to keep watch. The boat would row in at noon to check and see if they had made it back, and then return.

Leaving the sailors to their work, she headed down the beach to where Jonas was sitting on a piece of driftwood with a lancer guard surrounding him. She felt awkward going to see him after not standing up for him earlier, but she knew her conscience would make her feel even worse if she didn't check on him.

"Good evening, Miss Adarra," Sergeant Finnly said when he spotted her, though not quite as cheerfully as he normally would have.

"Good evening, Sergeant. Would you mind if I spoke with Jonas?"

"No, of course not. Go right ahead." He turned to his men. "Scoot back. You heard the woman. She would like to talk with the prisoner. She doesn't need you standing over her shoulder gawking."

Adarra smiled and thanked him, then sat down on the long piece of driftwood. She looked down at the metal cuffs on his wrists. "How are you doing?"

He stared due west down the darkening beachline. "I do not like these." He raised his hands and shook the chain between them. "I need free."

"Sorry. Afraid you make them nervous."

He turned and looked at her for a split moment before turning back to the beach. "You're afraid."

She lowered her eyes. "I'm not afraid. I . . . I just don't see any reason why you wouldn't grab a weapon and run. If I were you, I would have."

"I no leave, Spotted Warrior."

She blushed. It had been a while since she'd heard him call her that.

"But I need these free."

"I can try talking with Captain Holverd, but I don't think he's going to allow it."

"Then he wants I die?" He turned and looked her in the eyes, and she could see desperation. It startled her.

"Holverd doesn't want you dead. We need you."

"Then free me," he said, more forcefully this time, the shackles biting into his wrists as he pulled the chain taut between them. Was he trying to snap the links?

"What are you doing?" she asked, passing a nervous glance over her shoulder at the soldiers.

"Hurry," he said, turning back to the shoreline. "They come."

She turned. "What?"

Jonas stood from his seat, his back stiffening as he stared at the encroaching fog. "The moross. They're here."

Chapter 45 | Adarra

CHILL BUMPS RAN UP and down her arms as Adarra stared into the darkness ahead. She saw nothing but open beach and fog, but then she noticed something. The fog was much closer than it had been before. In fact, it seemed to be moving down the shoreline in their direction. Every hair on her body stood as she slowly rose to her feet, reaching for her sword. "Do you see them?"

Jonas shook his head. "I feel."

Adarra drew her blade and motioned Sergeant Finnly over. "You need to move your men back to camp. Jonas says the moross are here."

Finnly turned. "I don't see anything."

She pointed to the fog. "I think they're inside that."

Finnly drew his sword and waved his lancers over, and they backed toward the outer perimeter of the camp. Jonas tried forcing Adarra behind him, but she wanted to keep her eye on the fog, so she pushed his arm aside.

"What's going on?" Aiden called out behind them.

She waved him off.

Captain Holverd was the first out to meet them, no doubt noticing the drawn weapons. "What's going on, Sergeant?"

"Sir, the Tallosian believes those moross are here." Finnly pointed down the beach at the oncoming fog.

Holverd stared a moment, then shook his head. "I see nothing."

"In the fog," Jonas said.

"What is everyone looking at?" Aiden asked, causing Adarra to jump. She'd been so engrossed in the encroaching wall of mist that she hadn't realized Aiden had disregarded her wave-off and was now standing beside her.

"The moross are here."

"What? Where?"

She pointed straight ahead.

Captain Holverd drew his sword. The closer the fog came, the more nervous he got. He quickly ordered his men back, and the entire camp began to form ranks around the centermost fire pits.

Captain Mervall and his men were still loading supplies back and forth from the camp to their two boats when the lancers closed rank around those still inside the camp, including Mervall.

"What's happening?" Mervall asked, pushing his way to the front of the line where Adarra and the others were. Ambassador Lanmiere was right beside him. He stared at the oncoming fog. "Does that look like it's comin' right for us?"

"More than looks," Adarra said, her gut telling her that Jonas had been telling the truth all along. "Jonas believes the moross are here."

Mervall's eyes bulged. "I've got to get to my boats."

"Not enough time," Holverd said. The fog was now within a hundred feet, and part of it had shifted left, as though heading for the boats.

Mervall turned and shouted to those still loading things on board. "Shove off! Don't wait for us!" His men saw the coming wall and quickly pushed the boats out and jumped in, rowing as fast as they could. "Creator help us," Mervall whispered as he drew his blade. "This is just my flamin' luck."

"Free me," Jonas said, holding out his cuffs to Holverd. "I fight."

Holverd looked at him, then turned to Finnly. "Keep him back. In fact," he said, looking at Adarra, Aiden, and Lanmiere, "take all of them. They'll just get in the way here."

Finnly rushed over with several lancers. "Please, missus. I need to keep you safe."

She took one last look at the fog and nodded, for once agreeing with Holverd. Best to let the lancers do what they've been trained to do. They moved back through the ranks, which were taking up a fighting stance around the center fire pits. She could see Holverd's head above those at the front. The man was certainly no coward.

Captain Mervall moved back as well, but only as far as his men, who were standing directly behind the lancers. Adarra, Aiden, Lanmiere, and Jonas were escorted all the way to the center of the camp. Adarra left the others long enough to run to her tent and grab Orlyn's seeds and stuff them into one of the inner pockets of her coat. She couldn't take any chances of losing them. She looked at her satchels of books and felt a pang of regret, but there was little she could do about them now, so she ran to join the others.

She didn't know what was worse, standing at the front as the wall of fog closed in or standing in the middle and not being able to see what was happening.

Jonas turned to Finnly and held up his hands. "Free me."

Finnly looked at him, then at Adarra, and sadly shook his head. "I'm sorry. I can't disobey a direct order."

The fog was drawing closer, now less than a dozen feet from the front line, and still there was no sign of these moross. Adarra craned her head to see if she could hear anything, but other than the wind moving across the shoreline and through the reeds behind them, there was nothing that made her believe that they were in any immediate danger. And yet, like Jonas, she could *feel* it. There was something out there, something hidden within the fog.

She felt as though it was coming just for her. She didn't know why she felt like that, but every inch of her skin was now crawling. She couldn't help but believe that it was more than just her imagination.

Torches lined the camp but did little to help as the fog hit the front line, bringing with it a stillness that set Adarra's teeth to chattering. She watched as the wave of thick fog enveloped their campsite, just as thick as it had been aboard the ship.

She could barely see the lancers at the front as she turned in a complete circle. All sounds within the fog were once again muted and foreign, coming from all directions and putting everyone even further on edge.

Heads turned, bodies shifted, eyes darted about.

"What was that?" Aiden said, and everyone close enough to hear spun to the left, then right. One of the sailors nearly took her arm off as he swung a short sword at nothing. She barely stepped aside in time to avoid it.

The longer they waited, the more jittery everyone became. Adarra's nerves were on the cuff of her sleeve. If something didn't happen soon, she was afraid people might start attacking each other.

The entire camp was now surrounded by fog.

She stood at the center of those gathered, along with the ambassador. He had his sword drawn as well, though she wasn't sure how capable he was with it. No less than herself, she assumed. Aiden stood directly to her left, leaving Jonas to stand beside Lanmiere, with Finnly and his guards surrounding him. Jonas shifted positions, now searching the fog behind them, which had her suddenly looking as well.

They could be anywhere.

A scream echoed off the fog, and everyone jumped. Adarra spun to the left, thinking the scream had come from there, but there was nothing, so she turned to the front. Her heart was beating wildly, her knees trembling. Who had screamed? Was the fog simply playing tricks on them like it had aboard ship? Was there anything even out there?

A long thin pole with a sharp hook shot out of the fog ahead and plunged into the back of one of the lancers standing next to Holverd. The man shouted and was yanked away from the line and pulled inside the fog. Screaming billowed out from behind the shroud, human shrills that left her muscles trembling hard enough she was grateful she didn't have a full bladder. The screams soon turned to gurgled moans, and then everything went silent once more.

Aiden whimpered, his sword trembling in his hand.

The circle of lancers tightened as they moved to get away from whatever was out there, bringing them all the closer to the middle. Captain Mervall and his men moved back as well to stand just in front of Adarra. Another pole shot out, this one for Captain Holverd, but his sword was already up and waiting.

He deflected the hook before it could manage to bury itself in his back, then grabbed the pole.

"Help me!" he shouted. Two of his men grabbed the metal rod, and all three pulled as hard as they could, yanking whatever was attached to the other end out of the fog. The creature lumbered out of the darkness and into the light of their torches.

Men screamed. Adarra froze.

"What in the name of all that is holy is that?" Captain Mervall mumbled.

The creature was human in shape, with two legs and two arms, but it was the most disfigured human she'd ever seen. It was at least eight feet tall, with bone-thin elongated arms and hands. Its fingers were at least twice the length of a normal human's, with sharp talon-like claws. Leather skin wrapped around a skeletal frame. It had long wet strands of hair attached in patches on its head, like moss. But it wasn't those features that had her eyes bulging. It was its face. The creature had no nose, only two empty holes at the front where it should have been.

"Sniffers!" Captain Holverd shouted, and the entire company pressed even tighter, men calling out to the Creator, others cursing.

Adarra tried to move, but she was frozen in place as she watched Holverd lop off one of the creature's arms. It didn't even seem to notice and turned and swiped at Holverd with its other. Holverd ducked, and the claws tore into the man beside him, nearly severing the lancer's head from his body.

Adarra almost retched at the sight, her stomach shooting straight up into her throat. Beside her, Aiden bent over and hurled. Adarra's mind raced as she pulled up one image after another, every thought she'd ever written down, obscure texts, journals of memories she'd stored. Suddenly, one came to the front. She had heard the name "sniffer" before from Nyalis's story of rescuing Ty as a baby. She had no image to accompany the description, only the accounting, which she had recorded for future use.

"Can't be sniffers," Captain Mervall said, his voice teetering to the point of breaking. "I thought they was a myth."

"I've heard of such," Lanmiere said. "Used by the Tower for centuries to hunt down wielders." He turned and spared a quick glance at Adarra, and she quickly turned away, hoping no one else had seen him looking at her, especially

Jonas. "I've never actually seen one," the ambassador said. "Although, I've seen something very similar. It's how I got my injury during my hunting trip with King Rhydan last year. Though what we fought was much bigger and stronger and nearly took down an entire company of royal lancers. Probably would have if not for the Guardian Protector."

Ahead, Captain Holverd and the other lancers managed to run the creature through enough times that it finally went down for good. Lanmiere shrugged. "Apparently, this sniffer isn't quite as formidable."

Adarra breathed a small sigh of relief at that.

Suddenly half a dozen more hooks shot out of the fog, and men began to scream all around them. More poles shot out on Adarra's left from the direction of the waterline, and Aiden squealed as one just missed him and latched on to one of the sailors instead.

Mervall jumped at the pole and tried grabbing it before it snatched his man back into the fog. He pulled as hard as he could, shouting for others to help, but before they could get to him, the pole was yanked from his hands, and the sailor disappeared into the fog. Screams and shouts followed, and then one of the sailor's arms flew out of the fog and hit Aiden in the side. He screamed and retched all over again. This time Adarra joined him, unable to hold it back any longer.

As soon as she bent over, a hook flew out of the fog and swung over her head, just missing her by a handsbreadth. It was so close she could hear the swoosh of the metal as it flew past. She jerked back up and raised her sword. As soon as she did, one of the beasts came lumbering out of the mist for her.

Aiden swung, clipping the sniffer's side, but the creature smacked him in the chest and sent him flying sideways into Captain Mervall. They both went down. The sniffer stopped and raised its head. Even without nostrils, it reminded Adarra of a dog searching for its prey. It caught one whiff of her and released a loud, barking croak, similar to that of a bullfrog, and then rushed straight for her.

Adarra didn't have time to think. Her sword was up, and she managed to dodge the creature's first swing, plunging her blade into his gut. The sniffer shrilled, but Adarra sensed it wasn't a cry of pain; it was excitement at catching its prey. Talons dug into her arms, and she screamed as the searing pain shot through her. She lost her grip on her sword, feeling warm blood running down her arms from where they bit through the skin.

Lanmiere was the closest, but before he could get to her, Jonas leaped on top of the sniffer and wrapped his shackles around the creature's neck. The sniffer's grip was powerful, but not enough to stop Jonas. He yanked the monster backward onto the sand, pulling Adarra with it. Jonas heaved with all his might, and the sniffer thrashed about. It screeched loudly, then finally shuddered and went limp.

Adarra kicked herself free of it and crawled back to her feet, checking her arm. Blood seeped from two long gashes, and before she could grab a handful of snow to pack the wounds, Jonas was there, pulling her away from the creature and back from the fog. They had barely taken a few steps when two more came charging out of the mist on top of them.

"On me!" Sergeant Finnly shouted from behind, and he and his men rushed past, swords deflecting the hooks as the sniffers fought to breach the line. Beside him, Captain Mervall and his sailors fought with everything they had. They weren't trained in military tactics, but they stood their ground, swinging their swords like cleavers, overwhelming fear keeping them going.

Jonas pulled Adarra back farther from the fighting and shoved her at Aiden. Before she could stop him, he yanked the dagger out of her sheath and ran for the closest sniffer. He swatted one of the pole hooks away and slammed shoulder first into the creature's chest. It stumbled back, losing its balance. Jonas almost lost his as well when the creature grabbed hold of his manacles and nearly pulled him backward. He managed to keep his footing and shoved his new dagger straight up through the bottom of the creature's mouth, the tip bursting from the top of its skull.

The sniffer went down.

Jonas yanked the dagger back out and spun around about the time that Mervall and his men had cut the legs out from the second sniffer.

"Free me!" Jonas shouted at Finnly, who was moving back from the dead sniffer with what remained of his men. They were down two more, their bodies lying beside the dead creatures. Finnly's face was covered in blood, and he looked positively terrified. Finnly didn't bother looking at Adarra this time and immediately dug into his pocket for the spare key Holverd had given him.

Metal continued to clang all around them as the lancers did their best to hold off the attacks coming from all directions. Each new scream was another loss to their ranks, which were quickly being depleted. Jonas was right. They needed to get out of the open. They were sitting ducks.

"Got it!" Finnly shouted, pulling the key from his pocket. He turned to hand Jonas the key when one of the hooks swung out of the mist and planted itself in his shoulder. He turned and looked at Adarra. She saw the horror in his eyes as he was yanked backward. He didn't even have time to scream as he threw her the key and vanished into the fog.

"No!" Adarra screamed and ran straight for the mist. Jonas snatched her up before she could get through and barely managed to pull her back as Finnly's screams pierced the night. Her mind screamed with each new gut-wrenching wail from the poor jailer. Tears flooded her eyes as the huge Tallosian continued to pull her away from the wall of mist.

She fought against him, trying to break free, but Jonas was too strong, and he held her against him with a viselike grip. All she could do was stand there and listen. Like all the rest, Finnly's cries turned to garbled groans and then silence.

She shook from head to toe. She wanted to kill these monsters, she wanted to kill them all with her bare hands. Why couldn't she have powerful magic like her brother? Anger tore through her, followed swiftly by guilt at Finnly's fate, and she wished she could burn the sniffers to ash.

More croaking could be heard, and three more sniffers emerged, grabbing anything within reach with their long pole-hooks. The majority of the attacks were now coming from her side of the fog, and Captain Holverd moved his men over to compensate. "Get them out of here!" he shouted at Captain Mervall.

Jonas was still pulling her back as the lancers rushed in.

"We need to get off this beach!" Lanmiere shouted.

Holverd cut the head off of one of the sniffers his men were holding down, then shouted, "Retreat! Make for the reeds!"

Jonas unlocked his shackles and stuffed the key into his pocket. Adarra didn't even remember giving it to him. He released her, dropped the metal cuffs in the snow, and ran straight back, disappearing into the fog.

"Where's the fool going?" Aiden asked, his face pale, splatters of sniffer blood on his skin standing out in stark contrast.

Adarra tried to speak, but she was in too much shock to get the words out. "He's leaving us, isn't he?"

Before she could answer, Jonas reappeared holding a torch and one of the lancer's swords, no doubt retrieved from one of the fallen. He pushed his way back through the ranks and snatched her off the ground with one arm. Aiden and Lanmiere hurried to catch up, with Mervall and what was left of his sailors not far behind.

Holverd and the lancers disappeared from sight momentarily as Jonas started over the rocks toward the reeds. The fog wasn't quite as thick this far from the waterfront. Adarra hoped the lancers were able to hold the sniffers off, praying they wouldn't be overrun and could make it to the reeds themselves.

Jonas dropped her at the edge of the reed wall and placed her dagger back in its sheath at her side. She looked down, noticing for the first time that her sword was no longer in her hand. When had she lost it? Then she remembered the bite of the sniffer's claws on her arm. Her legs trembled, almost to the point of not being able to stand. Behind her, Aiden and Mervall were doing their best to steady Lanmiere as they ran to where Jonas had deposited her.

Adarra's heart pounded, and her mind swam. She focused on the flickering torchlight, willing herself to keep going.

What was left of the sailors huddled around Captain Mervall, waiting for orders, waiting for someone to tell them how they were going to get out of this mess.

A few of them looked at Adarra, but she certainly didn't have any answers. And all of these men were here because of her.

She started to cry. Poor Finnly. Tears poured down her cheeks.

"What do we do?" Lanmiere asked desperately, not looking at Mervall or even at Adarra, directing his question straight to Jonas.

Jonas turned. "We run. We hide."

"Run!" Captain Holverd shouted behind them as he and his men charged out of the fog straight for them.

All those still standing turned and ran into the reeds.

The long stalks were thick and tough to push through, many slapping her in the face and arms as they were displaced by those running in front of her. Sounds began to normalize the farther from the beach and the fog they got, the wind once again returning to whistle and howl through the taller shoots. Jonas's hulking frame was just in front of her, and Aiden raced to her right. Behind her, Mervall had one arm around Lanmiere as the two struggled to keep ahead of Holverd and the lancers.

Jonas led the way. No one had any idea where they were going except away from the beach. They ran for what felt like hours. Adarra could barely catch her breath, her chest heaving as she fought to force air in and out. Her legs burned, and her arms screamed in agony from the wounds the sniffer's claws had left behind. She stumbled several times, but the reeds kept her from going down all the way. Everything was spinning.

Her legs were about to give out when they finally broke from the reeds into an open pocket, and Jonas brought them to a halt. She dropped down onto the snow-covered rocks and fought to catch her breath.

"How are you?" Aiden asked, plopping down beside her. His breaths came in short, ragged bursts, almost as bad as hers.

She nodded but didn't have enough wind to speak.

They waited as Captain Mervall and his sailors, then Captain Holverd and his lancers, found their way into the opening and gathered near the center. It looked like they were down at least a third of their company. Half the men were bent over, gasping for air, while the other half collapsed on the ground like Adarra. Everyone was facing out toward the reeds, listening for signs of pursuit.

"Are they coming?" Aiden whispered, his eyes staring at the long stalks leading back in the direction of the beach.

Adarra didn't respond, still listening herself. She wasn't even sure who he was addressing his question to. She looked up at Jonas, who was standing just behind her, and whispered, "I can't keep going. I've got to rest."

Holverd looked at Jonas. "Will the sniffers follow us in here?"

Jonas shrugged. "They hunt beach."

"Then we'll stop here for tonight," Holverd said, walking over with one of the torches. His words were directed at her, but his gaze remained on the reeds behind them. "Unless, of course, you know of a safer place to be." He spared a quick glance at Jonas. If he noticed Jonas's cuffs were missing, he didn't show it.

"Safer to stay in reeds tonight," Jonas said as he stared off in the direction of the damaged stalks they'd just traveled through. "We set watch. If fog comes. We leave."

Holverd was covered in blood, and he seemed to be favoring his left leg. "We'll see to the wounded and get as much rest as we can." He left and gathered the lancers together on the other side of the small clearing. She couldn't hear what he was saying to them, but a few moments later the group dispersed, and the lancers began to take up positions around the entire opening, covering all sides.

"I have a feeling there won't be much sleeping going on this night," Ambassador Lanmiere said, then turned to Jonas. "Are you sure the sniffers— moross—won't come after us through the reeds?"

"Not been known before." Jonas didn't seem all that sure. Then again, he'd never actually run into these creatures himself. If these were the same sniffers that the Tower used, they could track Adarra all the way across the island if they wished. The way Nyalis had talked, they had tracked him for miles through the mountains, until he had finally dispatched them with magic. As she wasn't a wizard, she didn't have the kind of magic needed to fight sniffers, or anything else for that matter.

At this point, all they could do was keep watch for fog. She only hoped the sniffers didn't hunt without it. She didn't remember Nyalis mentioning anything about them using cover when he had dealt with them. Her skin began to crawl once more, and she scooted farther toward the center.

"I'm beginning to think we've made a huge mistake in coming here," she said, causing more than one head to turn in her direction. "I might have just sent us all to our graves."

"It wasn't your decision to come," Lanmiere said, easing himself down with Mervall's help. "And don't speak like that in front of the men. That's about the last thing they need to be hearing right now."

Mervall took a seat beside the ambassador. His face was splattered in blood and gore. It plastered one end of his mustache down, the other up. Lanmiere, however, seemed rather unscathed, having kept far enough back from the fray.

Adarra bristled but said softly, "I was the one to tell you of the possible Tallosian invasion."

"Which was your job," Lanmiere said, "but it was the overlord's responsibility to determine what to do with that information."

"Yes," she said, keeping her voice low, "but if I'd known what this place was like, I would have never suggested this envoy. We've already lost an entire ship and crew, and we barely made it ashore before we lost a third more. How are we to believe an entire people could make it across this cursed place and over to Sidara? This was insanity."

"Why are you saying these things?" Aiden asked.

She looked up, tears blurring her vision. "Why? Did you not see what just happened? Finnly's dead. *I* killed him."

"You didn't kill him." Aiden spared a quick nervous glance around at the other lancers, no doubt worried they might get the wrong impression.

Adarra didn't care. At that point, she didn't care about anything except getting out of there. She had read numerous accountings of what war was like, but none of those words on the page could have prepared her for this. There was no describing it. She didn't want to describe it. She didn't want to remember it, and yet, that was her curse. Magic that forced her to remember every detail. Every time she closed her eyes, she saw Finnly, the look of horror and pain and fear on his face as that hook sank into his shoulder.

She hobbled to her feet and stumbled off from the rest of the group to huddle by herself. She didn't care how close to the reeds she got. She couldn't face the others, not after what she'd done. She'd most likely sent them all to their deaths. Lanmiere was wrong. It was her fault. Why did she think she could do this? She knew why. Curse her brothers. Ty and Breen go off on a grand adventure to bring back the fabled Wizard's Keep, and somehow she thought she was capable of doing the same, of taking on her own adventure. If she ever made it off this island alive, she'd vow never to leave home again.

Aiden walked over and sat down beside her. "Lanmiere's right, you know. You didn't force any of these people to be here. You didn't force Finnly."

Her head shot up. "The only reason he was here was because of me. He came because he thought I needed protecting."

"He's a grown man. He was here because he believed it was the right thing to do. I still believe it is."

She wiped her nose with her sleeve. "Are you crazy? Coming here was a mistake."

"And if the Tallosians did invade, how would you feel then, knowing you could have done something about it? Seeing hundreds dead, maybe thousands."

"How could there be an invasion? We can't even land a single company on the beach without most of us dying."

"You heard Jonas. His people are more familiar with this place. They know where to go and when. We don't. If Jonas says his people are coming, I believe him. Are you saying you think he was lying?"

She dabbed at her eyes. She hated feeling like this, looking so pathetic and vulnerable, especially in front of Aiden. "No."

No, she believed Jonas was telling the truth. She believed it so much she had talked the overlord into setting up this mission in the first place. She just hadn't expected things to go like this. Then again, she didn't know what she had expected. Jonas had told her of the dangers, but that was then. Now they were real.

She leaned against Aiden, her hands shivering from the cold as much as from fear, and placed her head on his shoulder. She was glad he was there. She only hoped she didn't regret letting him come—that he didn't end up like Finnly.

"Close your eyes," he said. "Try getting some sleep."

She took a moment to look around the small clearing. Lancers lined most of it, and she saw that Jonas had followed Aiden and was sitting just in front of them. His presence, more than anything, gave her the assurance she needed to close her eyes. Though she feared what might be awaiting her in her dreams.

Chapter 46 | Ayrion

YRION PULLED THE SHADERS up over his eyes just as the early-morning sun began to rise over the peaks in the distance. His breath misted in front of him as he lifted a hand to signal those behind him to stop. He stared down into the valley of ruins below, ruins he hadn't seen in twenty years.

The Lost City was just as he remembered it. What buildings could be seen were half sunken into the ground. Broken towers and parapets rose from the dirt like emaciated fingers trying to claw their way out of a shallow grave. Though this grave was anything but shallow. Of the buildings that could be seen, some were deep below the surface—hundreds of feet in places—with tunnels connecting to them that stretched much deeper still. If Nyalis was to be believed, the Upakans' exploration into those tunnels had somehow released a long-held enemy of Aldor . . . or was about to.

Bek pulled the rover wagon to a halt at the top of the hill behind Ayrion. "Do you see anyone?"

Ayrion shook his head.

"Is that normal?" Ferrin asked as he and Myron brought their horses to a stop alongside Ayrion's.

"No, which has me worried."

The rest of their group disembarked from the wagons and gathered in front to gaze out at what was left of the once-great capital of Keldor.

"Welcome to the Lost City," Ayrion said. "A sad epitaph to a formerly proud community."

"Come look at this, Mother," Tameel called back to Zynora, who was the last out of the wagon as she helped Elson over to where the rest were standing. Elson was looking better than he had since leaving Oswell. His face was still pale, but he seemed more lucid, and his legs weren't shaking quite as much. Whatever she was doing to pull him off the drink was clearly working.

"Never thought to see it in my lifetime," Zynora said as she stared down in awe.

Bek stood to Ayrion's left and scratched at his beard. "You really used to live here? Not much to look at, is it?"

Ayrion didn't respond, but his friend was right. It wasn't much to look at. It was a wasteland of rubble and hidden pits, where one wrong step could see a person plummeting a hundred feet through what looked to be a normal piece of ground. The heart of the city was below the surface and still sinking at a measurable rate every year.

Ayrion's father had been the first to show him the markers, locations where others had the unfortunate luck to step in the wrong place and find there was nothing more than a thin layer of dirt and sand held in place by an even thinner layer of sediment. Much like an egg appeared solid on the outside, one ill placed foot, and the owner's weight would split the shell.

Bek rested his hands on his hatchets. "I can see why the Upakans chose it. One look and I already want to leave."

"You and me both," Myron said, rubbing at his nose, "but probably for different reasons." He scanned the closest of the dilapidated ruins. "I feel like we're about to walk into a nest of vipers. Dead before you even realize you've been bitten."

"They aren't that bad, are they?" Myriah asked Ayrion.

"Perhaps we should leave some of the group here," Ferrin suggested, "while the others go down for a closer look. Just to be safe."

Ayrion shook his head. "If they are here, then we've already been seen. Splitting the group now would only make us more vulnerable. We go together. Though," he said, glancing back over his shoulder toward the wagons, "we can only take *those* in so far. We can't risk moving that much weight over certain parts of the city without causing a cave-in."

Bek and Tameel both gulped at the same time, since they were the ones driving. "Perhaps we should leave the wagons up here," Tameel said, looking nervously down at the empty crags where buildings had once stood.

"It should be safe enough," Ayrion said, though in truth he didn't know for sure, since he hadn't set foot in the place in twenty years. He knew where the markers used to be; he'd just have to keep his eyes open in case there were new ones farther out.

"I don't like it," Rae said with one hand holding tight to Suri. "I don't like not knowing what we are walking on."

Nola appeared and sat down near Ferrin, her scouting apparently complete. The great frostwolf gazed down across the littered terrain. Ayrion wondered what she could see or smell. Her senses were surely much stronger than theirs. The wolf had remained unseen for most of the trip, but ever since they had rounded the southern corner of the Northern Heights and started across the now-barren lands surrounding Mount Ash, she had been spending more time with the group. There were no places for her to hide, no trees or tall grass, only snow-covered rock and sand, all mixed with a thick dose of ash.

"Whose idea was it to come here?" Everyone turned and looked at Elson, who was standing unsteadily next to Zynora. He shrugged. "What? You know you were all wondering the same thing. I'm just the only one drunk enough to say it." He pursed his lips. "Guess I can't use that excuse anymore, can I?"

Ayrion started to say something, but Elson continued.

"No, really. Whose idea was it to follow these crazy people into the heart of Upakan territory?" He looked at Ferrin. "I thought you had better sense than that. It sounds more like something she would do," he said, pointing to his right, where Lenara stood in her bulradoer robes, quietly studying the valley below.

She growled at him, and he quit pointing.

"We are here because it's the right thing to do," Zynora said, holding

Elson's belt to keep him from toppling over. "If what the wizard says is true, we might be the only thing standing between whatever's down there and the rest of Aldor."

Tameel gave his lengthening white beard a small tug. "Let's just hope we get there in time to stop these khuls from being released in the first place."

The others mumbled their agreement.

"No point in standing around," Zynora said, "when down there is where we need to be."

She turned Elson around and helped him back to Ol' Lerra, and the rest followed. Those on horses mounted. The others climbed either up on the wagons or inside. Soon enough, Ayrion's small company of fighters made their way down toward the first of the rubble. Ayrion was starting to get the feeling of Belvin all over again.

The valley below was quiet, eerily so. Normally, there would have been a class or two of trainees up top, or at the very least those working with the horses. But now, everything was bathed in the kind of silence that had the hairs on the back of his neck stiffening. They passed through the outer ruins, and Ayrion brought them to a stop before they started into the larger, more prominent remains heading toward the center of the city. So far, he'd seen no watchers, which caused the hairs on his arms to join those on his neck.

Something was wrong.

"We'll leave the wagons here," he said. "Too dangerous to take them further. Best we unpack what gear we think we'll need and load the horses."

Ayrion's hands shook slightly, and he rubbed them together. He'd been on numerous campaigns before, fought creatures born from the Pit, dark wielders and ancient wizards, but none of them had come close to putting him this on edge. The thought of setting foot once more within the Lost City had his heart racing. He felt like that same thirteen-year-old boy all over again. He took a deep breath and exhaled, then checked the swords on his back, reassuring himself they were still there. Their weight was a constant comfort.

Shade must have picked up on what he was feeling, because he pawed the ground with a powerful hoof, snorting uneasily. Ayrion rubbed his hand down the horse's mane. "It's alright, boy. We'll be fine." The words seemed almost silly. When was anything he did fine? In fact, if he was there, then things were generally anything but.

Once the horses had been laden with weapons, food, and whatever supplies they thought they might need, everyone gathered around Ayrion.

"We are going to form a single line," he said quietly. "Make sure you keep to it. Don't stray to either side. Remember, the ground here is unsafe. You could be standing on something solid, or you might be standing on a hundred-foot drop to your death."

Eyes widened as everyone looked down at their feet, or more accurately the ground under them.

"There are markers," he said, "so I'll do my best to keep us to the safest path. Just make sure to follow in my footprints." He looked over at Lenara. "How far do you think you can extend your shield?"

She gave him a curious look. "How did you know—"

"Your robes aren't moving in the breeze."

She frowned but then looked down the line. "I might be able to cover everyone if you don't stretch the line too far."

Ayrion nodded. "Good. We'll need it while traveling through the taller ruins." He didn't believe his people would open fire on them without warning, but at this point, he didn't want to take the chance. For all he knew, his people might have already vacated the Lost City, leaving the khuls to take over, which would leave them walking into an even more dangerous situation.

Moments later, Ayrion felt the wind that had been whipping around his face die, the ambient of sound around them muting as Lenara's shield encased the group. He was tempted to take his sword and stab outward to see if he could feel where the edge of the shield started, but he decided against it. He grabbed Shade's reins, and with one final glance back over his shoulder, started them in.

Bek was next in line, followed by Tameel, Zynora, and of course Elson, who was keeping as close as possible. Lenara rode close to the center of the group to make it easier to maintain her shield. After her came Myron, Rae, Suri, and Myriah, leaving Ferrin to bring up the rear. Nola walked beside Suri and Rae, her giant paws leaving tracks the wind rushed to cover.

"You better stay close," Suri told the enormous frostwolf. Nola appeared to understand and moved a little closer to Suri's side.

Ayrion kept his eyes open for markers. The wooden *X*s weren't as easy to spot as he remembered. They should have stuck out in the snow, but apparently, whoever was in charge of keeping them cleared off and visible had been slack in their duties. Several of them were partially covered, one barely sticking out far enough for Ayrion to notice. As soon as he spotted it, he stopped the caravan and used a long stick to reach over and wipe the snow from a small lump. As soon as the painted wood became visible, he altered course.

"You do know where you're going, right?" Bek whispered over Ayrion's shoulder.

"Vaguely. The last time I was here, I was only thirteen."

Bek frowned. "Wish you hadn't told me that."

Ayrion smiled. He always felt a little better with Bek around. Bek reminded him in a way of Barthol, never afraid to voice his opinion or call Ayrion out if he thought it was needed. Ayrion's mind drifted momentarily to his fellow brother in arms, hoping he had somehow survived the battle at Belbridge and made it back to Aramoor safely. He wondered, as well, what had become of Tolin and Asa. They had been down on the battlefield fighting the hor'hounds and hadn't witnessed Dakaran's and Valtor's treachery. He had no idea if they had survived. So many questions needed answering, so many wrongs needed to be made right.

Ayrion hadn't believed anything could have deterred him from returning to Aramoor, but the wizard had found the one thing that would: his family.

Like Tameel, he only hoped they weren't too late, but the farther into the ruins they went, the deeper his apprehension became.

"Shouldn't we have seen someone by now?" Bek asked softly.

"Yes," was all Ayrion replied.

A shout and whinny from behind had him and Bek both spinning. Myriah's horse had veered off the trail. The back legs of the horse were in a hole, with the front half clinging for dear life. The only thing holding it up was that one of its front hooves had been caught between two rocks. Myron held on to the horse's reins as Myriah shrilled for Ferrin.

Ayrion and Bek both sprinted back through the group as Ferrin rushed up from behind. Myron fought to hold on to the reins as he shouted at the horse to move.

"Get out of the saddle!" Ferrin shouted as he grabbed the reins just ahead of Ayrion and Bek.

"I can't," she cried out. "My foot's stuck!" The horse's weight had pressed the stirrup against the side of the hole, crushing her foot in the process.

The men tried to pull the horse up, but the more they struggled to keep the horse from going in, the more the ground gave way. The horse whinnied as it thrashed, causing it to slip even further.

"Stop moving, you stupid animal," Myron shouted, pulling with all his might.

Ayrion yelled at Lenara. "Put one of your shields under her and lift her up."

"I can't. It would collapse the ground around them and send them both to their deaths."

"Then give me the rope," he said, pointing to the coil on one of the spare horses.

She quickly untied it and ran it over.

By this time, Myriah was sobbing, whether from pain or fear, Ayrion didn't know. Both were valid reasons. "Hurry!" she pleaded. "Don't let me fall."

Ayrion unwound the rope and threw one end to Myriah. "Tie it off, quick!"

She caught the rope and began wrapping it around the saddle's horn.

"No!" Ferrin shouted. "Tie it to yourself, not the horse."

But Ayrion already had his end tied to Shade. He gave the reins to Tameel. "Walk him back, but keep to our footprints."

Tameel nodded and started the warhorse back until the rope went taut. Ayrion and the rest, even Elson, grabbed the rope. Ayrion hoped Myriah had tied a strong enough knot. He didn't know how they were going to get the horse out, even with the rope.

"Pull!" he shouted, and they all began to heave.

Shade pulled from behind, but with every inch Myriah's horse managed to gain, more ground gave way. The horse screamed in fear as it tried to heave itself up with just its front legs, but it didn't have the strength.

Ferrin shouted at Lenara, "Do something."

"What do you want me to do? I'm not a wizard. I've only been trained to use magic in combat." She released the rope and raised her hands, but before she could do anything, there was a snap, and the horse screamed as it and Myriah suddenly disappeared into the hole.

Ferrin roared and leapt for the edge.

Ayrion's heart sank. He quickly yelled to those in front of him to pull Ferrin back before they lost him as well.

"Wait!" Ferrin shouted, waving wildly. "She's still there. Hold on, Myriah!" Ferrin leapt back to his feet and grabbed the rope, bellowing for the others to pull.

Ayrion jumped back in line as well, calling to Tameel to ease Shade back. Slowly, they pulled on the rope, and soon Myriah's head popped up over the edge. Ferrin grabbed her arms, hauling her and the saddle the rest of the way up. They fell backward into the snow, and everyone huddled around the frightened woman.

"Why did you tie the rope to the flaming horse?" Ferrin said.

Myriah looked up, her face pale. "I didn't want it to die."

"Next time, don't worry about the horse."

Ayrion walked over to Bek, who was busy inspecting the saddle.

"Looks like the buckle snapped," Bek said, lifting a torn leather strap.

Ayrion nodded. "Lucky for her."

Bek stood and looked down at the hole. "Not so much for the horse. Do we know what was lost?"

"Mostly food, I think," Zynora said, walking over to get a look at the hole herself. "A few weapons." She clicked her tongue and shook her head. "Poor animal. Not a pleasant way to go." She leaned in. "I'm just glad it wasn't one of Ol' Lerra's. Tameel would be beside himself. Not that I'm pleased it happened to any of our animals, mind you."

Ayrion nodded, then retrieved Shade from Tameel, and they joined the others.

"I don't know what happened," he heard Ferrin's sister say. "The horse got spooked at something and moved off the trail for just a second." She looked up at Ayrion. "I'm sorry."

He offered an encouraging smile. "I'm just glad to see you're alive. You better have Zynora look at that foot, though."

"No need," Zynora said, nodding toward Rae, who was already kneeling beside Myriah.

Ayrion sometimes forgot they had a true healer with them. "While she sees to Myriah, I'm going to scout ahead and see if I can't find a safe route through." The others agreed, still too shaken to want to move anyway. Leaving them to it, he swung up onto Shade and headed deeper into the ruins.

Besides looking for safe passage, he also hoped to come across some sign that his people were still here. If the khuls had been released and his people were forced to retreat, he would have expected to see bodies. Unless, of course, the snow had somehow covered the evidence. Or they had been forced to retreat in another direction. One thing was for sure, he would know more the closer they got to the entrance.

They'd been going for at least a quarter of an hour when he finally stopped, spotting the top of a building he recognized, which meant they were getting close. He was surprised to find how little of it still stood aboveground. The last time he'd been inside, there were still a couple of floors visible. Now there was barely one. Had the city sunk that far in the last twenty years? He hoped the entrance hadn't sunk as well. If it had, there was no telling how they would get in.

Unfortunately, he didn't have time to look; the others were probably wondering where he was, so he turned Shade around and started back. The city was deathly quiet, his horse's hooves the only sound other than the wind whipping in and around the debris. It didn't take long for him to make it back to the others, where he found them mounted and waiting.

"We were getting worried," Bek said. "About to go look for you."

"Did you see anyone ahead?" Ferrin asked, his sister now riding double with him. She was still trembling from the ordeal.

Ayrion shook his head. "No one so far, but keep your eyes open."

He turned, and they followed him in, keeping very close to Shade's tracks as they ventured into the heart of what remained aboveground. The earlier sounds were once again muted as Lenara's shield encased them like glow flies in a glass jar. Blocks of stone were piled everywhere, remnants of buildings sunk long ago. A few towers and parapets still remained intact, plus upper portions of a couple of buildings that hadn't crumbled completely, their bottom sections possibly still whole as well but buried below the surface.

It didn't take them long to make it through the old city, since Ayrion had already found the best path, and soon enough he brought them to a halt across the street from what remained of the building he'd been looking for.

"This is it," he said. "The entrance to the underground, or at least the part of the city occupied by Clan Orpa."

He pulled off his glove to reveal his father's black onyx ring, bearing the white symbol of his family's clan. It was both a gentle reminder of who he was and a painful one of what had been taken from him. Mostly it connected him to his family.

"What are we waiting on?" Bek asked, staring at the building ahead.

"Do you see something?" Tameel asked.

Ayrion pulled his glove back on and shook his head. He saw no one.

The midmorning sun was just now rising over some of the taller buildings on their right as Ayrion started them toward the entrance. It used to stand high enough out of the ground for the front porch of the building to be seen; now it, too, had sunken, along with the bottom part of the doorway. It still looked tall enough to enter, but it might prove difficult for the horses, especially Shade. As soon as they reached the front, Ayrion dismounted, prompting the others to follow suit.

Those guarding the entrance should have already called out, but so far there was only silence. Ayrion signaled for the others to stay where they were and started for the doors. He wanted to call out to anyone who might be inside, but if his people were indeed gone from the place, he didn't want to risk alerting anything to their presence. Keeping his eyes on the windows above, he made his way through the snow and over to the two doors. Before opening them, he pulled off his shaders, not wanting to hinder his vision by stepping into a darkened room with them on.

The handle turned freely, and with a single push, the door swung open. Ayrion peered inside. The room was empty. He released a small sigh of relief. He'd half expected to find the floor littered with dead Upakans. If there had been a retreat, his people would have fought their way out. He was encouraged he hadn't seen signs of battle on their way in.

He turned and waved for the others to join him, and one by one they headed inside. He left Shade out front with the other horses, unstrapping the gear from his back. Nola made it in without too much difficulty, being able to crouch more easily than a horse. Once everyone had made it inside, Lenara released her shield, and the sounds around them returned, mainly the creaking of the building's timber and the wind whistling through the empty windows above.

"I was worried we might be walking into a tomb," Bek said, taking a quick look around.

Two of the three corridors leading off the main room had collapsed at some point and led nowhere. A third doorway stood at the back, but instead of taking them farther into the dilapidated construct, it opened into a tunnel of solid rock.

"I take it that's the entrance down?" Myron asked.

"It is," Ayrion said as he carried the first of the horse's packs in and placed them in the far corner away from the gaping hole in the back. "We'll unpack here. We won't have much use for the horses down below. Too easy to get their hooves caught in a crag and break their legs." He could feel Shade's disappointment at being left behind, but there wasn't much he could do about it. It was safer for him up top. "There are stables not far from here where we can leave the horses."

"No, Nola," Suri called out to the wolf as it sniffed its way over toward the opening at the back. "Don't go over there."

Nola snorted, then turned around and trotted back over to where Rae and Suri were huddled at the side with the rest of their group.

After unpacking the rest of their gear, Ayrion, with Bek and Myron's help, took the horses down the street to where the Upakans kept their stables. Thankfully, the building still stood, though parts of the roof and second floor had collapsed, but only at the back, which was unused at present.

There were quite a few horses inside, but no attendants. The horses didn't look to be starving, but for all he knew, his people might have left only a day or two ago. He walked Shade over to the closest empty stall and placed him inside.

Shade stuck his black nose out and nuzzled Ayrion's chest. Ayrion pulled a carrot out from one of his pockets. "Fine. But you better behave." Shade blew out his lips, and Ayrion gave him the carrot.

As soon as the rest of the horses were stabled, the three men headed back. They found Ferrin and Lenara standing protectively in front of the nervous cluster, everyone keeping a close eye on the tunnel entrance. Ferrin had his new weapons in hand, and Lenara kept her hands free, which were certainly weapons enough.

"Any problems?" Tameel asked.

"Not so far," Ayrion said. "Which I guess is a bit of a problem on its own." He looked at the pile of carry bags stacked haphazardly against the far wall. "I think it might be best if we leave as much as we can for now. I don't know what we're about to walk into, but it would probably be safer if we weren't laden down with supplies. We can come back up for them if the need arises."

"I was about to suggest the same," Ferrin said, turning his new blade over in his hand. "Then again, we could always strap them all to Nola and let her mule them down for us." He turned and smiled at the wolf, and she showed him her teeth.

Ayrion wasn't quite sure how much Nola understood. The little girl was capable of communicating with the frostwolf, but the giant animal also seemed to intuitively understand what the rest said as well, similar to how Shade understood him. The others began sifting through their gear, selecting what they thought necessary to take with them.

Apart from collecting their personal weapons, some food and scant supplies, they left the rest of their gear and gathered over near the tunnel's entrance. Ayrion stuffed his shaders into one of his coat's inner pockets. From here on in, his eyes were going to be one of their greatest assets.

It didn't take the group long to line up much like the one they had used to cross the ruins. Three torches were spaced down the line. Lenara didn't need a torch, but Ayrion had asked her to keep her magic hidden unless there was a definite threat. If his people were down there, Ayrion was already breaking the most fundamental of rules by bringing outsiders down, not to mention returning himself when he had been banished, so he didn't want to compound the issue by letting it be known there were wielders in his company.

An impatient growl rumbled from the center of the group, and Ayrion felt a smile play at the corners of his mouth. Clearly, Nola was tired of standing there and was ready to move, so he turned, took a deep breath, and started in.

Chapter 47 | Ayrion

YRION'S HEART RACED AS HE stepped into the stone passageway leading down to his former home. Memories of his earlier life flooded back, memories of his father walking him up this very tunnel on their way to Ayrion's first contract. He remembered how excited he had been. He had longed to one day wear the warrior's ring, determined to be the youngest in his clan to claim the title. And in a way, he had been.

He might not have been named an Upakan warrior, but he was the Guardian Protector, the highest military position in the Five Kingdoms. And yet, for all he'd accomplished, there was still a dark cloud of failure overshadowing him, one he had never dared hope to overcome until now. The wizard had given him a second chance, a chance to be the warrior he had always wanted his people to see. He knew how arrogant that sounded, but he didn't care. He supposed deep down he was still that thirteen-year-old trainee longing for his clan's approval.

That desperation for approval had cost him dearly.

First, it had cost him his family. His desire to beat Flon and not let the primary's son cheat his way to the top had ended in a fatal accident that had left Ayrion without family and home. The second, and just as painful, was losing Reevie and Sapphire and the rest of his young street friends. To fulfill his obligations to the crown, he had been forced to give up his role as Protector of the tribe to take on the much larger role of Protector to the king. One by one, his earlier friendships and ties had been replaced as new responsibilities and duties pulled him in the opposite direction.

His foot caught on a jut in the rock, and he stumbled, pulling him out of his musing and back to the present.

The tunnel wasn't dark. With the torches, there was more than enough light for his eyes to pierce the dim shadows ahead. He'd been in several caverns over the last year, the most recent of those being the one leading to Aero'set, but none of them had stirred him the way this one did. The rock and soil smelled familiar, even the way their footsteps echoed off the surrounding walls stirred something deep inside. He could feel it beckoning to him. He was finally coming home.

His thoughts shifted once more to his family. It had been years since he had seen them. The very thought urged his pace. He hadn't seen his mother and sister since the day he was banished. He'd run across his father and brother years later. He hoped they were all still alive, and that he wasn't too late. He didn't know what he would do if he'd lost his opportunity. Perhaps Nyalis had been wrong and there wasn't any danger. He might be a thousand-year-old wizard, but he wasn't all-knowing.

The passage leading down changed size as often as it changed direction. It widened in places, allowing the group to spread out, while narrowing in others, forcing them to tighten ranks and stretch the line in order to make it through. At one point, only two could fit between the encroaching walls and not get stuck, and it took quite a bit of coaxing on Suri's part to get Nola through. Eventually she did, with a little help from Lenara, who pushed her from behind with a shield of air, and they continued on.

So far, there'd been no sign of anyone, only the soft echo of their boots on the rock and the flicker of their torches as the occasional breeze whipped through the tunnel from below. The air coming up was warm, which wasn't generally the case during the winter months, unless you were exploring some of the deeper vents off of Triple Falls. Those were the areas Ayrion believed

Nyalis had been warning about. The fact that he could feel them had him worried.

It was believed, or at least rumored, that the lower shafts had at one time, centuries ago, been a very lucrative gold mine, which the original capital city of Rhowynn had been built on top of, its wealth securing it as one of the more prominent kingdoms in Aldor. Of course, after Mount Ash erupted all those centuries ago, destroying the city and forcing the inhabitants to evacuate, all thoughts of gold were long forgotten. He had the sinking feeling it might have found its way back to consciousness.

Ayrion thought he heard a rock skidding across the stone, as though having been kicked, and stopped. The others did the same. He listened for a moment, waiting to see if it came again.

After a moment, Bek finally leaned forward. "What is it?"

Ayrion shook his head. "Not sure. Maybe nothing." He started them going once more, but slower, his ears straining for any sound not linked to their passage.

Bek whispered once more. "Zynora wants to know how much farther."

"Not far," he said. Though, honestly, he wasn't quite sure. The original tunnel seemed to have changed partway down, and he kept waiting for something familiar to catch his eye, but after twenty years, he didn't recognize anything. For all he knew, this was a different tunnel altogether, or it might have been added on to. It wasn't unreasonable to assume the original passageway could have sunk as well.

Ayrion turned the next bend in the tunnel and brought them to a quick stop, scooting back so fast that Bek bumped into him.

"What is it?" Bek asked, reaching for his hatchet.

"We've reached the end." Ayrion peered around the side of the rock to find the opening into the main city not ten feet away. The shaft had been shored with wooden beams along the side and around the opening. The exit led out onto a blind alley with a narrow street leading off it. There were several residences set along the cobbled walkway, probably those in charge of guarding the tunnel's entrance. However, there were no lights in the windows. The stone structures were worn, the stone chipped and crumbling, the wood rotted through in places. Looking around, it seemed most of the buildings were about the same.

Most of the stone and wood were covered in algae from all the years spent underground. Ayrion remembered scrub duty, days where they would wash and scrape away the mold. Those were never good days. He remembered how much Jorn hated the cleaning.

In the distance, rising over the buildings ahead, Ayrion could just make out the top of the Justice Hall, a clear marker for the direction they needed to go.

"Are we there?" someone behind him asked.

"Can you see anything?" That time it sounded like Tameel.

Ayrion held out his hand to quiet everyone as he cautiously worked his way out from the side of the wall to get a better view. The city was eerily silent, no one on this street—at least the one just off the tunnel's entrance—no sound of trainees in practice, not even the occasional call from a stray animal running loose. The entire place seemed a tomb.

He motioned for everyone to go back down the way they'd come and away from the entrance. He kept them going until they reached the next bend, far enough away to not be heard. "The place looks deserted."

"I'm guessing that's not normal," Ferrin said.

Ayrion shook his head.

"You think they've already left?" Myron asked.

"And left the horses?" Ayrion shook his head. "I doubt it." He scanned the group. "Keep your eyes open. If you spot anything, let me know. And keep together. I don't want us spread out." Ayrion looked at Lenara. He didn't have to say anything. She nodded and raised her hands, mumbling something under her breath. The sounds around them disappeared as her shield once more dropped into place.

The shield made Ayrion uncomfortable. He didn't like walking around deaf to what was happening, but with a group this large, the benefits outweighed the risk. If it had just been him and a couple others, he would have preferred going without the protective barrier.

Back at the tunnel's exit, Ayrion took one last quick look outside before leading them through the mouth of the stone corridor and onto the awaiting street. During the city's initial collapse, entire sections had sunken together, cobbles and all, leaving many of the streets still intact, though looking rather worse for wear. The broken cobbles reminded him of the Warrens back in Aramoor, roadways that had been left unattended for decades. Still, they were passable, as long as you kept your eyes on the placement of your feet.

The Upakans were good at a great many things. Stone and woodwork weren't among them.

They left the tunnel and started into the city. Most of the streets were lined with homes similar to those just outside the entrance, though in better shape. However, the closer to the center of the city they traveled, the larger the homes became. Many had structural damage, with partially collapsed second and third floors.

"Look there," Bek whispered, tapping Ayrion on the right shoulder as they passed another street.

Ayrion turned to see a couple of the homes with smoke rising from their chimneys, and at least one had a noticeable glow coming from one of the windows at the front.

"Could be a good sign," Bek added.

"I hope. I would have expected to see a lot more, though." They continued down the street and onto the next, eyes darting in all directions as Ayrion led them through the back of the city toward the one place he figured they would find someone: the Justice Hall. Ayrion thought he caught movement down one of the side alleys, but when he turned, there was nothing there. He was starting to get the feeling of being watched.

Above them, single rays of sunlight shot across the rooftops from a few of the wider cracks in the cavern's ceiling. It allowed just enough light to make the inside visible, but not enough for those without Upakan eyes.

Ahead, the faint sound of what might have been voices filtered back through the streets, and Ayrion brought them to an immediate stop. The sounds were difficult to make out with Lenara's shield muting everything around them. In fact, Ayrion wasn't sure if what he was hearing wasn't just his own imagination, a desperate attempt on his part to keep his hopes alive.

"Am I the only one hearing voices?" Zynora asked. She clutched a long dagger in one hand and Elson's belt in the other. Elson didn't appear too unstable on his feet, but Zynora didn't seem to be taking any chances.

"I was wondering the same," Myriah said, huddled next to Rae and Suri, her ear pressed close to the side of Lenara's shield.

Ayrion scanned the surrounding buildings. Finding what he was looking for, he motioned everyone back to a shallow opening between two taller structures on the right and had them all squeeze inside. "Bek and I will scout ahead to see what we can find. Less chance of us being seen that way. We should be back shortly."

The others waited inside the small alleyway for the two to return.

Ayrion looked at Bek's torch. "Can you travel without that?"

Bek looked up the street, then nodded and handed his torch to Myriah.

Ayrion looked to the back of the group where Lenara was standing in the shadows. "You'll have to—" Before he could finish, the shield lowered, and the city's sounds came back. Now he could definitely hear voices ahead. He nodded at Bek, and they left the alleyway and started down the street. They reached the end and cut down the next, then took two more before finding one that had a direct line of sight to the center of the city square.

There was movement ahead, so Ayrion slowed their pace as both men moved to the side of the street and as close to the buildings as possible to keep from being seen. They were still too far away to see who or what was moving ahead, but Ayrion didn't get the impression that it was khuls, not that he knew what they were.

"Are those your people up there?" Bek whispered. He had both hatchets out at this point, especially now that he was no longer carrying a torch.

"I don't know. We need to get closer." Ayrion started them moving once more. It didn't take long for him to see that those in the square ahead were definitely human, and from the pale color of their skin and the similar dark hair, he was all but sure they were Upakan.

However, something about the square seemed wrong, and the closer they got, the more he realized it was the street itself.

It was the wrong color. Instead of the typical sand-colored stone used in the construction of most of the city, the cobbles were black, and not at all smooth across.

His fears grew as they continued, passing several more buildings, trying to get a better view. Suddenly he realized why the streets ahead looked odd, and he stopped, moving up against the side of the building.

His heart sank when he saw the bodies.

The entire square was filled with them, stretching from one side of the Justice Hall to the other. There had to be at least two hundred corpses strewn across the broken cobbles, nearly one third of the total number of his clan when he had left.

They were too late.

His family.

Panic set in, and Ayrion turned and ran back down the street. He didn't even wait to see if Bek was following. He had to get home. He had to see if his family was still alive. He cut back through the same streets they'd just traveled until finally reaching the cubby where the others were quietly waiting.

Bek stopped alongside, out of breath. "What's going on?"

"Follow me," he said to everyone, and without waiting around to answer questions, he took off once more. He slowed only long enough to allow the others time to keep up, or at the very least, so he wouldn't get too far ahead of them so they didn't miss which streets to take.

Memories flooded back as he worked his way through the east quarter, the part of the city he was most familiar with, as it was closest to his home. He had spent his childhood exploring those streets. They were the same streets he had taken every day on his way to class for training, or down to Triple Falls with his sister and brother to swim in the pools, or to the market with his mother. His feet moved with the assurance of someone who had never left.

It wasn't until he was only a couple of streets away that he began to wonder if his family even lived in the same house. For all he knew, they could have moved half a dozen times over in the last twenty years. It was unlikely, though, as most Upakans didn't have the luxury of moving.

What was left of the city was divided into three sections, one for each of the three Upakan clans. No one section was any grander than the next, each having suffered the same amount of damage in the quakes. Each of those sections was divided into quarters. Ayrion's family lived in the east quarter of the southwest section. It wasn't exactly the most up-and-coming part of the city, but it wasn't as bad as those living near the tunnels leading to the outside.

He reached the end of the lane and turned down the next, slowing when he spotted the lonely two-story stone building ahead on the left. Smoke billowing up from the chimney had him hoping like he had never dared to before, and he raced down the street for it. Behind him, he heard boots turning onto the lane, and he spared a quick glance over his shoulder. Bek was leading the others down the street in his direction, and by the time Ayrion reached the front of his home, the others were halfway to him.

Everyone slowed and then stopped as they gathered around him, staring at the front of the old home and the faint trace of light stemming from the pulled shutters around the front window.

"Well," Tameel asked, "what are you waiting for? Is this it or not?"

"It is," he said. After all these years, he was finally home, and yet for some reason he couldn't bring himself to take a single step toward it.

"What's going on?" Zynora asked.

"I want to go inside," Suri groaned.

For the first time in a long time, Ayrion was afraid. He'd faced down hor'hounds, vulraak, bulradoer, black witches, arachnobes, and even one of Aerodyne's generals, but at this moment, he couldn't find the courage to walk up to a simple door and knock. He was afraid of what he might find. After seeing the pile of bodies at the center of town, he was terrified of who would be inside to greet him, or more accurately, who would not.

He felt a large hand squeeze his shoulder. "I'm sure they are fine," Bek said. "You'll see."

Ayrion nodded. He sheathed his sword and started for the front door. His heart pounded with each step.

"Please be alive," he repeated to himself. He stopped at the door and glanced over his shoulder. The others waited in the street behind him, smiling, urging him on. If there were occupants living on this particular lane, he hoped they didn't pick right now to look out their windows.

Stopping in front of the door, he straightened his shoulders and knocked.

His heart was beating so fast he started to feel oddly lightheaded, so he took a deep breath. The sound of a lock being released was all the warning he had before the door swung open and a woman stood there to greet him. She was stunning, with long straight black hair, a strong face, and puffy red eyes that looked to have been recently wiped.

"Can I help you?" One look at Ayrion and she reached behind the door, no doubt to grab for a sword or bow from the rack on the wall.

Ayrion smiled. "Hello, Rianna."

His sister stopped, a look of shock on her face as she stared up at him, then her eyes widened. "Ayrion?" She rushed out the door and flung her arms around him.

Ayrion wrapped his arms around her, holding her tight as he buried his face in her neck. The door behind them creaked, and someone stepped through.

"Ayrion?"

Ayrion looked up, tears blurring his vision, but not enough that he couldn't recognize that voice and face. Twenty years he'd waited to see it again. Her hair might have greyed, and her face wrinkled, but it was still somehow the same. He released Rianna and stumbled forward. "Mother." He grabbed her and lifted her off the ground, laughing as he did. Rianna stood behind them with one hand still pressed against his back. He'd dreamed of this day for so long. He'd just never imagined it being like this.

Ayrion finally lowered his mother to her feet, and she took a step back, then reached up and felt along the sides of his face, cupping it in her hands. "My beautiful boy has finally come home." A moment later, her hands dropped to her sides, and her excitement was replaced with a look of concern. "I'm afraid there isn't much left to have come home for." Her eyes welled with tears.

Ayrion tried looking in through the doorway. "Where's Father and Jorn?"

His mother shared a concerned look with Rianna.

"I saw the bodies in the square," he said. "What happened?"

"I'm afraid we've brought this end on ourselves," his mother said, her words sharp and filled with anger. "Brim's lust for power has finally reaped its reward, and it's doomed us all."

What was she talking about? "I was warned that something might be coming," he said, "and we've come to help."

"We?" Both his mother and sister turned and noticed those standing in the street behind him. Rianna's eyes narrowed. "You've brought outsiders into our home?"

"They're more than just outsiders. Like I said, we're here to help. Now, where are Father and Jorn?"

His mother looked at him. "Jorn is down in the lower tunnels fighting with the others. Your father . . ." Her voice cracked, and Ayrion's heart skipped a beat as he found himself imagining his father's corpse lying in the middle of town square with all the others.

"He's not . . ."

His mother shook her head and then turned. "Come. He's inside, but I'm afraid I don't know for how much longer."

Ayrion quickly waved for his traveling companions to join them. He hoped they weren't too late.

Chapter 48 | Ayrion

I HAVE SOMEONE WHO CAN HELP," Ayrion said.

Rianna shook her head. "Our healer has already seen him. I'm afraid there's not much else to be done." She glared at those coming up the walk, starting at the sight of the giant frostwolf, and backed quickly into the house as Nola approached, taking their mother with her.

"No offense to your healers," Ayrion said, "but they aren't like the ones I have with me." He turned to see Zynora and Rae already making their way to the front of the group. Ayrion beckoned them in and followed his mother and sister into the house.

"Who are they, Mother?" a voice behind them asked.

Ayrion looked up to find a girl in her late teens stepping out from the back hall. She had to be Rianna's daughter. The last time he had seen his father and brother, all those years ago, they said she was pregnant with her second child, making Ayrion an uncle twice over. Judging by her age, she was the youngest. He wondered where his other niece or nephew was.

Rianna pulled the girl to her. "Ava, stay behind me."

"There's no need to worry," Ayrion said, offering a polite smile. "They might not look it, but they're actually here to help."

All three women stared at the rugged group of wayward travelers entering their home. Zynora and Tameel were the first through in their colorful tinker cloaks, followed by Rae and then Suri, who waved at Ayrion's sister on the way by. Next was Bek, and then Ferrin, who walked beside Elson in case the man decided to tilt too far to one side. They were followed by Myriah, Lenara, and Myron. Nola waited outside, sniffing around the front porch.

"Now, don't be afraid," Ayrion said, addressing his mother, sister, and the awe-struck girl standing behind them, "she will not harm you." He looked at Suri. "Call her in."

Suri turned to the door and waved. "Come on, Nola. It's warmer in here."

The giant frostwolf stuck her head through the door and sniffed, then slowly sauntered in, taking a moment to look around the room before making her way over to the far side, where she found a spot away from the heat of the fire and lay down.

"Her name is Nola," Ayrion said to the wide-eyed women. "She's a frostwolf from beyond the Gates of Bel'Taag. But that's a story for another time. Right now, I have two healers that need to have a look at Father."

Ayrion's mother shut the front door, keeping as far from the outsiders as possible. It occurred to him that it might have been the first time she had ever seen or talked with one. Keeping close to the wall, she moved behind Ayrion, Rianna, and Ava on her way to the back hall. Ayrion's company kept their distance and stood quietly on the other side of the room, not wanting to crowd the nervous women.

"Who are these people, Mother?" Ava whispered to Rianna. "And why did that man say he needed to look at *Father*? Who is he?"

Rianna placed her hand on her daughter's shoulder and smiled. "That man is my brother." She looked up at the others. "This way." She turned and headed down the hall.

"That's Uncle Ayrion?" Ava asked quietly as she followed alongside her mother down the dark corridor, casting furtive glances back over her shoulder. "That's the Banished?"

Ayrion cringed at the name.

"He's in here," Ayrion's mother said, and opened the master bedroom door.

Ayrion waited for his mother, sister, and niece to enter before stepping in himself. He took a quick look around the room. Not much had changed since the last time he'd been there. The bed and dresser were still in the same spots along the left and right walls, though the wood was more worn than he remembered.

He walked over to the side of the bed, and his breath caught in his throat. His father's face was disfigured on the right side as though it had been hit with a spiked mace. His breathing was raspy and shallow. Ayrion almost couldn't believe his eyes. His father had always been his hero, the man he had always strived to be, and looking at him now, in this state, he hardly recognized him.

Ayrion's mother grabbed Ayrion's hand and started to cry. "The healer says he's lasted longer than most. You know how strong your father is."

Ayrion squeezed her hand gently. "I'm counting on it." He gestured to Zynora.

"Alright," Zynora said, working her way to the other side of the bed, dragging Rae along with her. "Give us some room."

Rianna and Ava moved out of the way.

Rae studied what she could of his father's injuries, and then looked at Zynora. "Help me remove his wrapping."

Zynora drew her dagger, and Ayrion's mother's fingers dug into his arm. "What is she doing?"

Ayrion patted her hand. "Rae needs to place her hands directly on Father's skin."

"Why?" Rianna asked suspiciously.

"You'll see." He nodded for Zynora to continue, and the two began to cut away the thick bandaging around his father's chest.

Rianna's face hardened as she watched the two women. Her hand rested on the hilt of her dagger, which she had tucked into her belt.

"There's nothing to worry about," Ayrion said softly. "Just don't be alarmed."

"Alarmed about what?" Rianna looked even more worried and tried stepping in front of her daughter, who quickly shifted to the side so she could see what was happening.

Zynora finished getting most of the bandages cut away, enough to see how bad the injury truly was. The gaping wound down his front was leaking blood and had begun to turn black around the edges. Ayrion couldn't believe his father was still alive. Zynora sheathed her dagger and took a step back to give Rae plenty of room.

The short healer walked over and, ignoring the blood, placed one hand on Ayrion's father's chest and the other on his abdomen, directly over the wound. She stared at it a moment, her face building with determination. Ayrion knew that it took a lot out of a healer when using their magic on someone this close to death, but he had also seen how strong Rae was. From what Ferrin had said, she'd spent her entire life healing one broken body after another from inside the Tower.

Rae took a deep breath and closed her eyes.

"I don't understand," Ayrion's mother whispered.

"What is she doing?" Ava asked.

Before Rianna could say anything, Rae's hands began to glow a soft lavender, and his family gasped as the veins of her magic seeped down through the damaged flesh and spread throughout the body. Ayrion felt his mother tense as she clutched his arm. Rianna's and Ava's mouths gaped, and Rianna started forward to stop Rae, but Zynora quickly moved to block her. "Let her do her job, my dear. There is nothing here that will harm him, I assure you."

Something in Zynora's eyes stopped Ayrion's sister, and they both turned and watched as the open flesh began to knit itself together. Like a master seamstress, Rae wove the fabric of Ayrion's father's skin back together. Everyone watched in awe as his father's face began to reshape itself, the bones realigning and the sinew stretching overtop to once again form an image that Ayrion had seen repeatedly in his dreams for the last twenty years. His father's chest began to rise and fall in steady, fluid motions as his breathing deepened.

Soon enough, the purple veins of Rae's magic receded, slithering their way back into her hands and then disappearing altogether. Zynora stepped forward to steady her and helped Rae over to a chair in the corner, where the little healer gladly took a seat to catch her breath.

Rianna and Ava both watched as Zynora offered Rae a piece of dried fruit to chew on. She had their undivided attention—until Ayrion's father coughed.

He shifted slightly on the bed, his eyes flickering open.

"Narris!" His mother rushed forward, nearly climbing onto the bed to get to her husband. Rianna and Ava forgot all about Rae and raced for the bed as well, tears in their eyes.

"What happened?" Ayrion's father asked, lifting a hand to feel the side of his face. Not finding the damage he had expected, he looked confused as he slowly sat up with help from Ayrion's mother and sister. He leaned over to examine the wound on his stomach and chest, but there wasn't even a scar. "Have I died? Is this the afterlife?" He looked up and into the tear-filled eyes of the three women who were protectively huddled over him like hens hiding a single chick from an encroaching fox. They were clustered so tightly together that he didn't even notice Ayrion standing behind them at first, but as soon as his mind cleared enough to realize they weren't alone, he grabbed for his sword—which wasn't there—and tried getting to his feet.

"Stop, Narris," Ayrion's mother said, forcing him back down on the bed. "We are in no danger." She smiled. "Do you not recognize who this is?"

Ayrion's father stopped his struggling and looked up into Ayrion's face. Recognition set in, and his mouth opened in shock.

Ayrion smiled, tears staining his cheeks. "Hello, Father."

His father barely made it to his feet before Ayrion had his arms wrapped around him, practically lifting him off the bed himself. A funnel of emotions, all swirling at once like a whirlpool, threatened to suck him in. Dozens of memories flooded back from his childhood, exploding across his mind. How many nights had he lain awake dreaming of this moment, to be reunited with his family? If only it could have been under better circumstances.

"I can't believe it," his father said. "My son has returned." They held each other for a long moment, then his father finally released him and took a step back.

Ayrion wiped his eyes, the tears continuing to build as he stared long and hard at his family. He couldn't believe he was home.

"I see you are still wearing your coat," his father said, looking him over. His father and Jorn had been in Ecrin the day he'd purchased it.

Ayrion smiled, and he ran his hands down the front of the smooth leather. "It has served me well."

Rianna and Ava moved around to their side of the bed, taking turns hugging Ayrion's father. His father looked down at the red-stained wrapping hanging from his chest, then back at Ayrion. "I don't understand."

Ayrion pointed to the corner, where Zynora stood protectively beside Rae. "I brought a true healer."

His father turned. "You brought an outsider into the city?"

"Several, in fact," Rianna said, her voice tinged with disapproval.

"And you weren't stopped?" his father asked.

Ayrion almost laughed. "By who? You're practically the first Upakans we've seen since arriving."

His father pursed his lips, running his hand back along the side of his head, his fingers combing through grey-streaked hair. "Then things have gotten worse." He turned to Ayrion's mother. "How long have I been out?"

"Several days," she said.

He looked toward the open doorway. "Jorn? Davin?"

"They're still fighting," Rianna said, her hands quivering slightly.

Ayrion hadn't heard the name Davin before, but if that was Rianna's oldest child, that would make his nephew somewhere around fifteen or sixteen.

Ayrion's father turned, his smile slipping. "I'm afraid you've come at a bad time."

"Or perhaps the right time." Ayrion started for the door. If his brother and nephew were down there fighting, he needed to hurry. "Come. I'll introduce you to some friends of mine, and then you can tell me what's happening." He led his family back out to the front room, where the rest were all gathered. Tameel had found one of the rockers and was presently enjoying it, but when he saw everyone coming, he stood and smoothed his colorful cloak.

Ayrion's father, who had somehow found a sword between his bed and the hall, slowed when he saw his front room filled with some of the gruffest-looking individuals one could imagine, especially Bek, decked from head to toe in fur. The man looked like a bear. Ayrion's family stopped at the edge of the hall, not wishing to go further, and waited for Ayrion to make introductions as they scanned the faces of those gathered.

"What is that?" his father asked, pointing at Nola's hindquarters sticking out from behind the others. She was still curled against the wall on the other side of the room.

"That's Nola," Suri said, clutching Tippi to her chest. "She doesn't like it down here," she added.

Ayrion's mother smiled. "We aren't liking it much either at the moment."

Ayrion went around the room and offered introductions, ending with Rianna, who introduced him to his niece, who was finding the whole affair rather fascinating, and even went so far as to give her uncle Ayrion a hug.

She stared at him curiously as she moved back beside her mother. "Some of the instructors still tell stories about you during training."

Ayrion wasn't sure if that was a good thing or not. "Dorin isn't still teaching, is he?" Dorin had been the instructor who had always prided himself on his discipline, the main source of that discipline being that of his whips. Ayrion still bore the scars on his back.

"Dorin was banned from teaching not long after your leaving," his father said. "He passed a few years back. There wasn't but a handful of people who attended the ceremony. He had no family, and few that called him friend."

"Not surprising," Ayrion said.

Ayrion's father gestured for everyone to take a seat. With a little help from Bek and Myron, they brought in the chairs from the dining table, as well as any from the back rooms, giving them just enough for the entire group. Afterward, Ayrion's father removed what remained of the bandages from his chest and put on a shirt.

Once everyone had taken their seats, Ayrion looked at his father. "We saw the bodies in the square. What's happening?"

His father sneered. "What's happening is we have a power-hungry leader who's doomed us all for his own selfish gain."

"Mother said as much but didn't exactly explain what that meant."

"It started last year. One of the exploratory teams found a large vein of gold in one of the lower tunnels. It looked to be a rich one, so Brim immediately ordered excavation to begin. Those tunnels were already in poor shape, but the thought of gold had him pushing us to delve deeper still.

"At first, the people were excited by the possibility of a new source of wealth, one that would enable us to not rely on taking contracts to support our families. To be honest, I was in favor of that myself. You know how I feel about what we do." Ayrion nodded. "But after several months of digging, we came across something we hadn't expected: a small cavern not affiliated with the city itself."

"What do you mean by not affiliated?"

"There was writing on the walls, a language we've never seen before, pictures carved into the stone depicting a great battle. I don't know what battle. It was like nothing we had ever heard or seen before. There was something else: an enormous set of stone doors."

This all sounded rather familiar, and Ayrion shared a quick glance with Bek, Tameel, and Zynora.

"What is it?" his father asked.

"We have seen something similar. A cavern with inscribed images and a set of stone doors. The place was called Harok Laos."

"Here in the Northern Heights?"

"No. This was deep in the Angoran Mountains."

His father stopped rocking. "And did you open the doors?"

"We did, with help from a magical key that had been created by the last wizard council just after the Wizard Wars."

Ayrion's family looked stunned. Ayrion didn't blame them. Saying it out loud sounded ridiculous. His father leaned forward. "You found a magic key?"

"Well, we didn't find the key. We were only there when it was used." Ayrion waved his hand. "It is a very long story, which we can discuss at a later time."

"The reason I ask," his father said, "is because it might hold some bearing on what is happening here. We, too, opened our doors."

Ayrion's mother cleared her throat.

"Fine, we didn't exactly open them so much as burrowed through them."

"You cut through the doors?" Ayrion asked.

His father and mother both nodded.

"Then I'm not sure they were the same as the ones we opened. The doors in Harok Laos were spelled. There was no way through without the key."

"We didn't see any keyholes," his father said.

"It wasn't that kind of a key, more like a pendant, really. It was a talisman that unlocked a runic text around the doors' frame."

Ayrion's father suddenly leaned forward in his seat, excited. "There are symbols over our door as well, along with some pictorial references just above the frame that looked to be a warning of some sort." He frowned. "If only Brim had heeded it." His father reclined into his rocker once more and released a heavy sigh. "Whether we were supposed to have had a key or not, I couldn't say, but what I can tell you is that we were never supposed to open those doors."

"Why? What did you find?"

"Death."

Ayrion waited for his father to elaborate, but he didn't. Instead, his father stared out the front window in silence, a blank expression on his face.

"What do you mean *death*?" Tameel asked, an anxious look on his face shared by everyone else gathered in the room. "What did you find?"

"We found monsters. Creatures from the Pit." His father shrugged. "Honestly, I don't know where they're coming from, but as soon as we broke through, they were waiting. There were only dozens at first, but their numbers grew. They look very similar to some of the depictions on the walls of the cavern. Each one stands about eight feet. The back half of their bodies are covered in fur, the fronts have none, including even their arms and legs. They have tusks like a boar, and they are incredibly strong. Their fingers end in claws, which you've already seen can do quite a lot of damage." He patted his chest. "They also have very acute hearing. Their ears are three times the size of our own, much like your wolf's."

Nola lifted her head.

"Do they have any weaknesses?" Ferrin asked, already leaning forward in his seat.

His father frowned. "Not many. We've noticed that, like us, they tend to shy from light, which might be one reason why they only attack at night. But other than that, we haven't really found anything definitive."

"They don't attack during the day?" Ayrion asked, a very surprising and ultimately limiting tactic.

"Not so far."

This gave Ayrion a modicum of relief. At least he knew his brother and nephew weren't presently fighting for their lives at this moment while they sat and talked, provided the two were still alive.

"What type of weaponry do they carry?" Myron asked.

"Many rely on their claws and tusks, backed by brute strength, but there are some that carry crude metal cleavers and rock cudgels. We were able to hold them back at first, but as their numbers grew, that changed. We're not used to fighting pitched battles. We train for stealth and speed. Our greatest strength is no one knowing we're there. We simply weren't ready for this." He grew silent and stared thoughtfully out the window.

"We called on the other clans," Ayrion's mother said. "They were hesitant to help at first. I don't think they believed us, but one trip down to the front lines, and they had their fighters rushing in to help. But by then, Orpa Clan had suffered numerous losses."

"We've been fighting for two straight weeks," Rianna said. "Anyone trained with the blade has been ordered into the tunnels. Nearly a third of our people have died trying to hold them back." Her eyes welled with tears, and she broke down. Pretty soon, Ava was crying as well.

Ayrion looked at his mother.

"Rianna's husband and Ava's father, Lorn, was killed during the first week of fighting."

Ayrion had been so caught up in seeing his family and healing his father, he hadn't even thought to ask about Rianna's husband. He ached for her. "I'm so sorry for your loss." The words were inadequate, but he wasn't sure what else to say.

"We don't know where they're coming from," his mother continued, "or how many of them there are, but they don't seem to be letting up."

"We believe they are called khuls," Zynora said.

His father turned. "Khuls? What are they? How do you know of these creatures? In fact"—he turned sharply to Ayrion—"why are you even here?"

"I told you, we're here to help."

"How did you know we needed it?"

Ayrion started to answer but stopped. He wondered how they would take it. Then again, it was the reason Nyalis had sent him. They were going to have to find out eventually, so best to start with his family and judge how the rest might respond. "A wizard told us."

"A what?" his father asked.

His family looked about as stunned as they had when first seeing Nola. To most, wizards didn't exist anymore, to some they never did at all. If they were this stunned at hearing that there was a living, breathing wizard still wandering Aldor, how were they going to react when he told them that this same wizard wanted them to up and leave the Lost City to come live with him in some magical school that had been missing for over a thousand years? He smiled wryly at the thought.

"Well, I said I have a bit of a long story to tell, I guess now is as good a time as any."

So Ayrion began to tell them the story of his life, condensed as much as possible. He began with his time on the streets of Aramoor and the tribes, to his rise to Guardian Protector, skipping over a lot of what happened during that time to tell them of the Battle at Belbridge and the betrayal that led to the death of the king and Ayrion's own near demise.

From there, he told them of being rescued by Tameel and Zynora, his unfortunate loss of memories, and a few highlights of their adventures from Woodvale to Wellhollow, indicating which members of the group they met along the way. He also mentioned his run-in with a couple of Upakans during his capture by Endric Talmanes. Ayrion's father didn't seem to recognize either of their names, but that wasn't unusual, since they did belong to another clan.

When he told them of their arrival in Wellhollow and the battle that had taken place, Ayrion had to pause his story to explain the arrival of Ty and his friends and their mission to assemble the key, which led to both stories colliding inside Upper Wellhollow.

He told them of Ty's struggle with Mangora inside Harok Laos, and of Angioma, the town's oracle, giving Ayrion his memories back as a last act before passing. He told them of Ty using the oracle's stone to finish the key and open the doors.

It was here, more than anytime prior, that he sensed his family's eagerness to hear what happened next. They had been an attentive audience during the story, but with the similarities Ayrion had laid out between Harok Laos and what was taking place in the tunnels below them, he knew they hoped to find something to help their people. Ayrion tried to hurry. Now that his father had been returned to health, he wanted to get down there and see for himself what they were up against, but he needed to make sure his family understood what was happening. If he couldn't convince his own family, how was he going to convince those who had banished him?

"Where did the doors lead?" Rianna asked eagerly.

"They led to a hidden valley deep within the mountains, a place not seen in a thousand years."

He told them of Ty's final use of the key and the incredible return of the Wizard's Keep. With his companions' help, they described the ancient school of Aero'set and their time spent there, leading up to Nyalis revealing the Upakans' heritage to Ayrion.

"I don't understand," his father said. "Are you saying that our people used to live there?"

"More than live there. We were its guardians. Protectors of the wizard council. We were known as the Tanveer. Nyalis showed me a monument built inside the garrison. It bore all three of our clan's names." Ayrion told them of the true meaning of the words and the motto they represented. "Can you believe it? Our people were once respected throughout the Five Kingdoms."

"Wouldn't that be something if it were true." His father thumbed his chin. "Still, whether it's true or not, right now I'm not concerned with what we might have been." He stood, grabbing his sword from where it rested across the arms of his seat. "If we don't find a way to stop these creatures, there won't be a single Upakan, or Tanveer, left to guard anything."

Ayrion stood as well, the others joining him. Even Nola seemed to sense their intentions and stretched before getting to her feet. Ayrion's father turned and looked the group over, no doubt judging how useful they would be in a fight. He slowed when he came to Tameel and Zynora, and even Elson, who was still looking rather pale. His father's eyes narrowed, but he eventually moved on, stopping on Ayrion, or more to the point, the weapons resting on Ayrion's back.

Ayrion drew one of the blades. "I've been waiting for you to ask." He held out the sword to his father, who passed his own blade to Rianna and took it.

His father whistled as he eyed the craftsmanship. "It's exquisite. A king's weapon to be sure. I've never seen anything like it. What type of steel was it made from?" he asked, holding it up. "I don't see a single mark. No one could buff a blade this precisely, unless of course it has never seen use." He cocked a single brow in Ayrion's direction as if to say he doubted that was the case.

Ayrion chuckled, as did a couple of the others. "Oh, they've seen more than their fair share of use, trust me on that. However, if you'd like to know more about the swords, you can ask their maker." Ayrion turned to Ferrin. "This is the smith that was commissioned by King Rhydan to have them made for me as a gift."

Ayrion's father handed the sword back to Ayrion. "I still find it hard to believe that my son had the ear and respect of the high king." He turned and looked at Ferrin. "Your work is impressive, sir. I've never seen anything like it before. How is it accomplished?"

Ferrin smiled, then looked at Ayrion as if waiting to see if he should tell them they'd been created with magic. So far, Ayrion hadn't talked in much detail about how they had won their victories during his earlier exposition. He hadn't made mention of his companion's gifts, mostly speaking in generalities. Ayrion nodded, and Ferrin answered.

"They were created with magic."

"When I told you we were here to help," Ayrion said, "I didn't just mean a few extra swords." He turned and looked at his companions. "Most everyone assembled here is a wielder."

To his family's credit, they didn't draw their weapons, though they did scoot a little closer together.

"Ferrin is a metallurgist. I've seen him bend metal just by touching it. He can also manipulate metal ore in ways that can make them near indestructible. These blades of mine have even withstood weapons used by wizards."

Ayrion didn't say anything more about the others' abilities. He'd leave it up to them if they wanted to share or not, and right now it wasn't all that necessary. He turned to his father. "How do we get down to the lower levels? I want to take a look at what we are dealing with."

"I can take you," his father said, and then looked over at Suri and shook his head. "It is no place for children."

"Rianna and I can watch her," Ayrion's mother said. "She will be safe here with us. The creatures, *khuls* as you call them, have never made it as far as the main city."

Rae pulled Suri close and pressed them against Ferrin's side, her fingers clutching the little girl's cloak. Clearly, she had no intention of letting her daughter out of her sight.

"It will be fine," Ayrion said to her. "My mother and sister will take good care of Suri."

Rae looked up at Ferrin, and he nodded. "It will be safer for her here."

She looked at Suri, who was still clutching Tippi to her chest. "Do you want to stay here?"

Suri shook her head.

"I can stay with her as well," Myriah added. "I won't be of any use to you down in the tunnels."

"What is that?" Ava asked, pointing at Suri's large pinecone. In all likelihood, she had never seen a pinecone before. They didn't have trees inside the Lost City, or even on the surface above.

Suri turned to look at Ava and then down at her imaginary friend. She finally held the pinecone up. "This is Tippi."

"That's a pretty name. My name's Ava. What's yours?"

"Suri." She held her pinecone out. "Do you want to hold her?"

Ava smiled. "Can I?"

Suri took a step away from her mother and handed Tippi up to Ava, who took the pinecone and carefully examined it. "She is very unique," Ava said, and handed her back to Suri. "I have a friend too. He's a cave lizard. I named him Short Tail. You want to know why?"

Suri nodded.

"Because part of his tail is missing. One of the scalenbats tried to eat him, but they only got the tip. He's very friendly, though. You want to come see him?" Ava seemed to have a special way with the little girl that had Suri wanting to trust her.

Suri smiled and took another step forward, then stopped and looked back at her mother. Rae looked at Ava a moment, then finally nodded.

"Come," Ava said, starting toward the back. "He's in my room." The two girls left the others and headed down the hall. Ayrion could hear Suri trying to tell Ava about Nola.

Surprisingly, Nola didn't follow the little girl back but stayed with the others. It was almost as though she could sense something was about to happen, and she wanted to make sure she was a part of it. Shade was no different—which reminded him that he needed to see to the horses.

He looked at his mother. "We left our horses up in the stables. Can you make sure they are fed and watered?"

"We have someone who goes to the surface a few times a day to watch over the ones up there now," she said. "I'll make sure they do the same for yours."

Ayrion nodded his thanks and turned to his father. "Well, let's go see what we're dealing with."

Chapter 49 | Ayrion

HEY FOLLOWED AYRION'S FATHER back up the street. They had waited only long enough for his father to redress and arm himself, and for Ayrion's companions to drop off what gear they didn't need—mostly food—before heading for the tunnels.

Ayrion's father led them back toward the city square along a side street that looked little traveled and ran parallel to the main road, ending just across the square from the Justice Hall. The smell of the as-yet-unburied fallen rose to greet them. Ayrion slowed when they neared the end of the lane, staring out once more on how many had already given their lives. He looked up at the stone building that was the Justice Hall, and his back stiffened. He remembered his last day in the Lost City, standing before the Peltok, as his clan's primary read from the Shal'Noran, the set of rules that governed the Upaka, and pronounced sentence on Ayrion.

Ayrion stared at the whipping post that was still standing in front of the Justice Hall steps and shivered once more, his hands balling into fists. He remembered the feel of Instructor Dorin's whip across his back, at fighting to hold off the tears, of biting his tongue so hard it bled to keep from crying out.

He remembered the look in his family's eyes as they stood at the edge of the crowd, helpless, watching as Brim's unwarranted judgment was carried out.

"So many," his father said next to him, pulling Ayrion back to the present. "Each day the numbers grow."

Ayrion turned to see how the others were doing and noticed Elson being propped up by Ferrin. Elson seemed to be quite winded from their simple jaunt across town. In his condition, the man was going to be useless in a fight. He was surprised Elson hadn't demanded to stay behind with Suri and Myriah. He was either in too much pain to know what was happening or too weak to care. Or perhaps he still had enough pride to not let the others go without him. Either way, Ayrion figured the man had suffered enough and didn't want to risk bringing him down into the tunnels unless he knew Elson wouldn't be a liability.

Ayrion looked at Rae. "How are you feeling?"

She nodded. "I'm fine."

Zynora had made sure Rae had eaten while they talked to Ayrion's family. Both of their skills would more than likely be needed soon.

Ayrion's stomach was making him regret not having stopped long enough to grab a quick lunch himself before setting out. "See what you can do for Elson."

She looked at Elson, then cocked her brow.

"It's fine," Ayrion said. "We need him capable of standing on his own."

Myron shifted their one torch to give Rae some light as she walked over and placed her hands on the sides of Elson's head. She closed her eyes, and her hands began to glow.

Elson trembled as her magic seeped into him. "This feels very strange."

Ayrion's father watched. "Is that what she did to me?"

Ayrion nodded. "But more extensive."

It wasn't long before the soft purple glow of her magic faded, and Rae opened her eyes. She didn't seem drained like she had when healing his father, though Ferrin was ready to help if she needed him.

Rae took a step back, and Elson opened his eyes. He placed his hands against the sides of his head and rubbed. "It tingles." A moment later, he looked up, a shocked expression on his face. "The pain's gone." He smiled. "In

fact . . ." He took a moment to stretch as he checked his balance. "I feel great."
He looked at Rae. "Thank you."

She nodded, and everyone retook their places within the darker shadows
of the narrow lane. Ayrion moved back to the front, but before his father could
lead them out, Ayrion grabbed his arm and pointed to the left. The square was
beginning to fill with people, much more than what had been there earlier.

Most of the crowd was coming from a street on the left, a parade of
downtrodden folks, all armed, all covered in blood. Ayrion recognized the
scene, having seen it a hundred times before—fighters coming off the
battlefield at night, carrying the injured with them as they slowly made their
way back to camp for some food and sleep, only to get back up and do it all
over again. War was never pretty, certainly nothing like the valorous
undertaking the old bards sang about. There was very little glory to be had.

"Why are they returning?" Ayrion asked. It seemed a strange time to be
leaving the field of battle.

"To carry up the injured and the dead," his father said. "As I mentioned,
these creatures seem to be nocturnal, which leaves only a small window of
opportunity to regroup before it starts up all over again. We'll still get the
occasional clash, but they seem to relegate their main assaults for when the sun
goes down, which means we still have most of the day to talk the primaries into
accepting your help."

"And where are they?" Ayrion asked.

"Down with the others in the tunnels below."

Bck leaned forward. "We're underground. How do they know when the
sun is down?"

Narris shrugged.

Ayrion watched the fighters carry their dead and lay them near the others
before turning to help the wounded up the steps of the Justice Hall. "Have they
set up an infirmary inside the hall?" Ayrion asked.

His father nodded. "We had to move it there by the second day. There
were too many wounded for our physickers to keep up with. The other clans
have sent over their healers to help."

They watched as the fighters then made their way back toward the tunnels
on the other side of the cavern. "Let's follow them down. We can take the side

streets until we reach the other side."

Ayrion's father nodded and then ushered the group back down the lane and away from the square. They kept to the side of the stone buildings on the right in order to squeeze by Nola, who was quietly waiting behind the others with Lenara.

Whenever Suri wasn't around, the giant wolf always seemed to gravitate toward either Ferrin or Lenara. With Ferrin, it made sense, since he had been with her the longest, but from the way the others spoke, the bulradoer was the newest addition to their group, so Ayrion found it odd that the wolf would choose the most unsociable of the lot as a companion. Then again, maybe that was the reason. They were both outcasts in their own way. Of course, the same could be said of Ayrion and everyone else traveling with him.

The Justice Hall disappeared behind them as they took the second street to the right and started for the far side of the enormous cavern. The closer they got to the tunnels, the more derelict the buildings became. When the city had split and dropped below, the buildings nearest the edges had suffered the worst damage. By the time they had reached the far side, they were little more than piles of rubble.

"This way," his father said, and they followed him up a narrow street that bordered the cavern wall. They were forced to climb over heaps of rock and collapsed wood and stone as they made their way toward the first of several tunnel entrances that led away from the city and deeper underground. There, the similarities Ayrion saw with the Warrens Underground ended. These tunnels were not man made, so they weren't exactly uniform; neither were they lined with pavers to keep the place looking structurally sound.

Ayrion's father brought them to a halt outside the first, but Ayrion couldn't hear anything coming from it. "Third one down," his father said, pointing just ahead.

"Will it take us through those Triple Falls that you've told us about?" Tameel asked anxiously.

Ayrion shook his head. "Afraid not. Those tunnels are on the north side."

Tameel sighed, having mentioned on more than one occasion that it was a place he would like to see.

Ayrion had never been in these side tunnels before. They had always been roped off during his childhood. He was never sure why. He wondered how far down they went.

Taking a moment to make sure everyone was together, Ayrion's father motioned them forward. They left their spot behind some of the rubble and started across the main street. On the other side, a road had been dug out with pavers wide enough for hauling wagonloads of rock. They followed it past a second tunnel and onto the third.

Ayrion could hear the faint echo of boots before they even reached the mouth. He glanced inside, along with his father, but other than the odd torch bracketed into the wall, there was no sign of anyone coming or going. Ayrion nodded at his father, and they headed inside.

The tunnel was much like the one that led to the surface. It was wider in parts and narrower in others, but not so much that it was difficult to travel through. Even Nola didn't seem to have a problem traversing the winding corridors of rock.

"Do these tunnels narrow any further than this?" Ayrion asked when they came to one of the more tapered sections.

His father pursed his lips a moment, then shook his head. "I don't believe so. This is probably the extent of it. Why?"

"The narrower the passageway, the easier it will be for us to hold the creatures off. If we can compress their numbers, it might allow us to fight from a distance with archers. Create a killing field and use it to block their way forward."

"On that note," Ferrin said, "did you try resealing the doors?"

"No time," Ayrion's father said. "As soon as we cut through, they were waiting. They overwhelmed us so quickly that by the time we were able to muster a defensive, they had pushed us back. We haven't been able to reach the doors since. They tend to carry their dead back with them after the battles. Not sure why. They don't seem the type to respect any sort of burial rites—not that I know the first thing about these beasts or their culture, if they even have one." He waved Myron up. "Bring your torch over here."

Myron joined Narris at the left side of the cavern, and they all followed them over.

"This is what it's all about," his father said, pointing to a spot higher up on the wall.

Myron raised the torch, and the light caught a deep amber reflection off the rock.

"Gold," Ferrin said, reaching his hand up to run it across the rough surface. "I can feel it."

Ayrion turned. "You can?"

"Gold is a type of metal ore. I occasionally use it in some of my more elaborate creations."

"Can you tell how much there is?" Ayrion's father asked.

Ferrin took a step closer and placed both hands on the rock." He closed his eyes. A moment later, he opened them. "There's a large deposit here. It seems to stretch for quite some way into the mountain. No idea how far it goes."

Ayrion's father shook his head. "Ironic. Brim's desire for this gold led him to the one thing that is keeping him from it." He stepped back from the side of the tunnel. "Let's keep going. We still have a ways to go."

The tunnels led them through several open chambers, some smaller, some about the size of the foyer up top where they had left their gear. Ayrion frowned each time they reached another one of those chambers. These smaller caverns would make their fight much more difficult. If the khuls could push them back far enough to reach one of the openings, it would allow them to use their numbers to force the Upakans to retreat farther up the tunnel and closer to their home. Ayrion didn't know how far the tunnels stretched, but he hoped quite a distance.

They continued down the passageway, which seemed to narrow slightly the farther they went. The floor of the tunnel grew more littered with debris and loose rock, clearly indicating recent excavation. It reminded Ayrion of the mines at Belvin, and he glanced at Bek, who was walking just behind him.

"Seem familiar?"

Bek chuckled. "I was thinking the same thing, though these don't seem as unstable as the ones in Belvin. These don't need support beams." He shook his head. "How do we keep ending up surrounded by rock? First it's Belvin, then Wellhollow, and now the Lost City."

Ayrion shrugged. "Luck, I guess."

Bek hmphed. "We've got the worst luck I've ever seen."

After a while, Ayrion's father brought them to a halt some distance from the next bend in the tunnel. "We should be getting close."

Ayrion had noticed a faint noise coming from somewhere up ahead, but they weren't close enough to identify any specific sounds other than the occasional pounding of what he thought might be hammers.

"How do you want to do this?" Ayrion asked.

"I think it would be best if I go in and talk with the clan primaries alone first. Better to let them know I'm bringing some help down from above than to simply startle them by walking straight into camp."

"That sounds like a good idea," Myron said. "As jumpy as I'm sure your people are, we don't want them mistaking us for the enemy."

The others nodded.

"I'll be as quick as I can. If this was just Brim, he probably wouldn't even see me, but with the other primaries there as well, he won't have much choice." His father adjusted the bow on his back and then headed off down the passageway, disappearing around the bend.

Ayrion started back up the passageway they'd entered from.

"Where are you going?" Tameel asked.

"I suggest we move back behind the last corner. I don't want some stray Upakans rounding the bend, seeing us, and making a run back to the encampment before we can catch them." He stopped just around the next turn, and the others quickly followed, Lenara and Nola being the last to make it to the other side. This particular stretch was shorter than most, which meant they could post a watch on both ends.

"How open do you think they will be to our assistance?" Zynora asked.

"I don't know," Ayrion said, peeking out from behind the wall every so often.

"You would think very," Tameel said. "Help is help. I'd accept help from the Black Watch if the need were great enough." He hmphed. "Not that they would ever offer."

"Oh, they'd offer alright," Elson said, his first time to really speak since thanking Rae for the healing. "They'd offer to snap a durma right around your neck." He passed a glare in Lenara's direction, which she countered with a harsh look of her own.

"I've got a feeling they're desperate enough to accept anything at this point," Ayrion said. "I'd love to be a scalenbat on the wall to see their reactions when my father walks into camp. I'm sure most thought him dead. Anyone who'd seen the way he looked before Rae healed him will likely think him a spirit."

"I'm more curious what they'll think of you," Bek said. "If being banished is as big a deal as you say, and returning is punishable by death, we might be hopping out of the pan and directly into the fire."

Ayrion sighed. "You're not wrong, but we knew this was going to be an impossible task before we started."

Zynora grunted. "We tend to get our fair share of those, don't we?"

"And then some," Tameel added.

Ayrion watched as Ferrin and his friends sat quietly at the other end of the tunnel. They were a very tight-knit group. He hoped he wasn't about to lead them to their deaths. He'd done his best to convey just how high the stakes were, but he still felt responsible. It was bad enough having Zynora and Tameel along—Tameel especially, since he had no magic to use in his own defense—but asking total strangers to risk their lives for people they not only had no association with but also feared to some extent was difficult. Their agreeing to help said a lot about their character.

"What do you think of them?" he asked the others, keeping his voice down.

Bek, Tameel, and Zynora turned to look, but not all at once and not long enough to appear awkward. "I think they have their own problems," Bek was the first to say, "as we all do. But from what I've seen, and knowing what we're about to face, I'd much rather have them standing with us than not."

"If half of what your father said is true," Zynora added, "then we are going to need all the help we can get. The Great Father put them in our path for a reason. Who are we to refuse it?"

Tameel rubbed the top of his feathery white head. "Having an actual bulradoer fighting alongside us will be extremely advantageous. You saw what she did to those other bulradoer back at Aldwick. Just think what she could do here."

"And Nola," Bek added. "I doubt a full-grown mountain bear could stand up to something as big as her."

Ayrion agreed. "I believe Rae will be one of our greatest assets, so long as we can keep her out of harm's way, and she doesn't burn herself out with too much healing." He looked at Zynora. "I want you and Tameel to stay with her. She's going to need all the help she can get. Besides, I don't want either of you fighting on the front lines."

"But what if you need one of my blasts?" Zynora asked.

"We can make that determination when we see what we're up against, but for now, your knowledge of healing will be of far greater use helping Rae. The last thing we need is for you to use one of your blasts and lose your help for the next couple of days as you recover. It's going to be on you to help Rae through this. She's stronger than she knows, considering the amount of healing she's been forced to perform at the Tower, but she will need you there to make sure she doesn't overdo it. I'll probably keep Elson back with you as well. Any of you ever seen whether the man can even wield a sword or not?"

The others shook their heads.

"The only thing I've seen him wield is his flask," Zynora said jokingly.

"And his tongue," Bek added, causing the others to chuckle.

"I'll see if I can find out anything from Ferrin." Ayrion stood and started for the other side of the tunnel. He stopped halfway, and as soon as he caught Ferrin's eye, he motioned him over. "Do you know if Elson is capable with a sword? I don't want him stuck in the middle of a fight if he has no way of defending himself."

Ferrin glanced back over his shoulder at his friend. "Honestly, I'm not quite sure. He fought with us against the Tower's guards outside of Rhowynn, but I never really observed how skilled he was, other than to say he was one of the first down. Rae had to save him, but he then saved her from a wolf, so I don't really know. Why don't you ask him?"

Ayrion sighed. He wasn't exactly Elson's favorite person right now, having been the one to order his sobering, but Ferrin was right, there was only one way to find out. He waved Elson over.

Elson looked at the two curiously as he walked over to join them. "What is it?"

"Can you wield a weapon?" Ayrion asked. "I don't want you in the middle of a fight if you aren't capable. Besides getting yourself killed, you'll endanger the lives of those around you."

"I can use a sword."

Ayrion looked him in the eyes and held his gaze a moment, hoping to make him uncomfortable enough to perhaps recant if he truly was incapable of defending himself. But Elson didn't back down.

"Fine. Best we know now than when we find ourselves facing a khul rush."

Elson looked at the two of them, seemingly upset at having been questioned. "Is that all?"

Ayrion nodded, and Elson walked back and took a seat beside Myron.

"Keep an eye on him," Ayrion said.

"I always do," Ferrin said, "but speaking of those who shouldn't be on the front lines, what about those two?"

Ayrion turned to see he was looking at Tameel and Zynora. "They won't be. They're here to assist Rae. If the worst should happen and we're overrun, Zynora should be able to do enough damage to give them a chance to escape. As for Tameel, well, he won't let Zynora go anywhere without him."

Ferrin nodded, and they walked back to their respective sides of the tunnel.

"Well?" Bek asked. "Will our drunk friend be joining us?"

"Appears so. I only hope he can handle it."

They waited nearly a quarter of an hour before they heard the first signs of someone approaching. Drawing one of his swords, Ayrion had the others move behind him. He scooted to the edge of the corner and waited. He could hear the sound of a single pair of boots on the other side of the wall, the steps growing closer. Whoever it was, they didn't seem to be in a hurry. The steps stopped, and Ayrion raised his sword.

"Ayrion?"

Ayrion lowered his blade and dared a quick peek around the corner. His father stood a few feet back from the bend, so Ayrion stepped out and waved the others out as well.

His father walked over to join them. "All three primaries have agreed to meet."

Ayrion sheathed his sword. "And how did they take it when you told them who it was they were meeting?"

His father hmphed. "Needless to say, Brim wasn't very happy, but at this point they're desperate enough to accept help from anyone."

"And did you let them know that we were bringing wielders?"

His father offered a sheepish grin. "I figured it best not to place too much on them at once, not that they didn't have a lot of questions, especially since the last time they saw me, I was on my deathbed."

Ayrion sighed. "There was no way of hiding that. How did they take it?"

"I told them you had brought a healer, but I thought it best we let them talk to you first before telling them you brought much more than that."

Ayrion frowned, but his father was probably right. Best to wait to explain once they had an audience. The fact that their presence had not yet caused an uproar was monumental. His friends were probably the first outsiders to set foot inside the city of the Upaka, and he had never heard of a *banished* returning.

"I must warn you, though," Ayrion's father said, "getting the primaries to agree to your aid is just the beginning. Getting them to work together might prove far more challenging. This is not like the armies you are used to leading. These are three fractured clans forced to fight alongside one another out of sheer desperation."

Ayrion nodded. "One hurdle at a time."

Regrouping, they followed Ayrion's father down the tunnel toward the Upakan encampment. By the sounds of the hammering, Ayrion thought it just around the next corner, but instead they walked for at least another quarter mile before Ayrion's father brought them to a stop just shy of the next round in the tunnel.

"They have sentries posted just around the corner, and they will want to disarm you before we go in."

Ayrion shook his head. "That's not going to happen." Ayrion turned to Lenara. "Be ready with your shield." He noticed she was holding one of her ter'aks and shook his head. "Those are only for last resort." He turned and looked at his father. "Lead the way."

Chapter 50 | Ayrion

AYRION'S HANDS WERE TREMBLING, which he hid by checking his swords. He took a deep breath to steady his nerves as he passed one last glance at those behind him before following his father. The success of their entire mission balanced on how this meeting went. It would determine his people's future, possibly their very existence. His heart thumped as they rounded the bend. The tunnel ahead opened into another cavern, one large enough to hold the entire Upakan encampment.

He felt just as nervous now as he had been standing outside his family's door, wondering how many were still alive. He had been Banished, and now he was returning with an entire company of wielders.

The closer they got to the mouth of the tunnel, the more of the cavern he could see. There were several cookfires near the center of the cave, not enough to fill the cavern with smoke but sufficient to keep several hundred Upakan fighters fed. The cavern looked to have been separated into three individual segments with clear walkways between. Apparently, even in time of war, the three clans still refused to be joined.

Except for right now.

Clearly word had spread, as the entire camp had turned out for their arrival. Every man capable of wielding a blade stood to either side of the entrance in lines that stretched to the far end of the cavern, where a command tent sat. Three men in formal uniforms waited in front. Ayrion recognized the man on the left. Though much older and greyer, Brim was still massive—at least a head taller than the other two primaries—and his face was stretched in a silent snarl.

"Talk about a warm welcome," Bek quipped as they neared the entrance of the cavern. Just as Ayrion's father had said, the sentries at the front moved to stop Ayrion and his companions.

"You will not be allowed beyond this point with your weapons," the guard on the right said, taking a moment to look everyone over. His eyes widened when he spotted Nola.

"Then we will wait here until we are," Ayrion said.

The guards stared at him a moment as if unsure what to do, then turned and talked quietly amongst themselves. Soon after, one of the men took off running down the open aisle of fighters toward the command tent. A while later, he returned and whispered something to the man who'd addressed Ayrion in the first place. He turned, looking more than a little troubled.

"The primaries have agreed to you proceeding, but I warn you, one false move and you will be shown no mercy."

Ayrion didn't bother answering and motioned for his father to continue as the guards moved aside. Those closest to the tunnel's entrance quickly backed up when Ayrion and his companions stepped out of the stone corridor and into the cavern beyond. Many drew their weapons when they spotted Nola and took another step or two back. Ayrion kept his head high, his expression confident as they slowly made their way through the long procession.

The fighters looked beaten down, blood caking their uniforms as though not having been washed in weeks. Their eyes were sunken with lack of sleep. Many bore cuts and abrasions. Arms and legs were bandaged, some wearing slings. This was the look of an army already defeated, or on the verge of it.

Whispers filtered through the crowd as they got their first look at Ayrion, but so far, no one had made a move to stop them. He wondered how many even remembered him. He thought he recognized a couple of faces, one or two of his former teachers, even a couple of classmates, though after twenty years he couldn't be sure.

They were about two-thirds of the way through when he spotted a very familiar face on the left. *Jorn.* His brother was standing at the front, not bothering to carry a weapon. He was just as tall as Ayrion now, his face strong but his eyes tired. There was a spark of something else behind them as well. Resentment. Beside him, a teenage boy poked Jorn in the side and whispered. Jorn nodded. Ayrion wondered if that was Rianna's son, Davin. He had her eyes.

Ayrion didn't stop, but he did nod at his brother on the way by. Jorn's mouth tightened, and he shook his head. Ayrion tried not to let it get to him as he continued down the long row of armed men. Those on either side continued to scoot back as the group passed, no one wanting to get too close, especially not with a wolf the size of a horse bringing up the rear.

Ayrion's father slowed as they reached the end of the line and stopped about ten feet from the pavilion's entrance and the three men standing in front. He moved to the side to let Ayrion and his companions take their place in front of the primaries.

Ayrion stood at the center, letting those behind file out around him, and they took up a stance on either side. He did his best not to look at Brim, though he could feel the weight of the man's glare. Instead, he focused on the man in the middle. Whoever he was, he bore the crest of Clan Kovaa on the front of his uniform, which had Ayrion thinking once more of the statue inside the Aero'set garrison and the motto chiseled around its base. How was he going to convince these people that everything they believed about themselves was a lie?

Thankfully, at the moment, he didn't have to.

All he needed to do was persuade the primaries to let him and his companions join the fight. As soon as Nola and Lenara had found their place alongside the others, Ayrion's father bowed toward the primaries. "These are those I spoke of who have risked much to offer us aid."

Brim huffed, but Ayrion ignored it. The man in front wasn't as tall as Brim but was every bit as wide through the chest and arms. His face was hard, with several visible scars on the sides, hidden partially by his grey hair, which he wore long, most of which was tied behind his head with a cord.

He was the first to speak.

"My name is Sirak. I am the primary of Kovaa. And this is Zayden." He pointed to the man standing on his left. The third man was shorter than the other two and thinner. He kept his grey hair neatly trimmed, not long enough to cause a hinderance to his vision. "Zayden is primary of Clan Raju," Sirak said before turning to his left. "And you already know Brim, primary of Orpa."

Ayrion offered the first two a polite nod, not bothering with the same for Brim, as it would have been a wasted effort. "My name is Ayrion."

"Yes," Sirak said. "You are known to us, Guardian Protector of kings."

Ayrion was a little stunned by the acknowledgment of his title.

"I see you bear the Upakan ring," Sirak said, looking at Ayrion's hand.

"Illegally," Brim noted on Sirak's left.

"It was my father's. I wear it to remind me of who I am."

"What you are is Banished," Brim countered, drawing Ayrion's gaze for the first time, "and if it were up to me, I'd have you put to death right here."

Some of those traveling with Ayrion reached for their weapons but stopped at a motion from Ayrion. They were completely surrounded by Upakan warriors, most of whom held their weapons already drawn. Lenara, who was standing at the end on the right, had her hands loosely in front of her and her eyes on him, waiting for the signal to raise her shield. He kept from looking directly at her in case she got the wrong impression.

He didn't want them finding out that he had brought other wielders into their city until he had at least been given the opportunity to talk first. Ayrion turned and looked at Brim. "Then I guess it's a good thing that the decision was not up to just you."

Brim sneered.

"And it's a good thing for your people as well," Tameel added. "'Cause if it were, we'd leave you here to rot."

The unexpected outburst from Tameel caused Ayrion to lose track of what he'd been about to say. The old tinker was typically more restrained, and usually had better sense than to provoke an argument in such a precarious situation. Ayrion tried to think of how to counter Tameel's outburst, but before he could, the primary of Kovaa laughed.

"I can appreciate a man willing to speak his mind," Sirak said, nodding to

Tameel and Zynora. "We are familiar with the Rhivanni, though our paths do not often cross." He turned back to Ayrion. "We have agreed to hear you out, and we are true to our word, so long as you keep the peace. As you are aware, this is unprecedented for us, but these are unprecedented circumstances." He looked down the row at Ayrion's companions and pursed his lips. "We will allow three of you to enter. Choose who you will." With that, he and the other two primaries turned and walked into the command tent.

Ayrion took a moment to look at those behind him. They all looked anxious to be picked, but he could only choose two. He pointed at his father, since he was the only actual Upakan there who could stand for them. He also chose Ferrin, since he was the leader of his own group and deserved the right to represent them. The others waited quietly out front. Ayrion had left Lenara out on purpose. If something were to happen, she was the best chance they had for keeping the others safe, and hopefully she and Rae could keep Nola in check.

Ayrion waited for his father to enter, but this time his father deferred to him. Ferrin was next in, followed by Ayrion's father. The inside was very dimly lit, hopefully not too dim for Ferrin's eyes. If it was, the smith didn't let on. The tent had been arranged over one of the smoother sections of the cavern, level enough even for a table, though one leg had been shimmed to keep it from rocking.

Three chairs sat at the right side of the pavilion, but the three primaries remained in front, the formal position of judgment. Ayrion's father stood off to one side near the front, letting Ayrion and Ferrin take the lead spots as they faced the three men head on.

"We appreciate you granting us audience," Ayrion said, feeling as though he were back inside the palace, requesting a meeting with the king.

Zayden was the first to speak this time. Even though Ayrion had never met the Raju primary and he was far less intimidating in stature than the other two, the man had a reputation for speed and accuracy. There were few who could match his ability with the sword. "Normally we wouldn't have granted an audience, but when the messenger happens to be a man I watched get cut down days ago and proclaimed untreatable by our own healers . . . well, that tends to make one take notice, especially when that same man's sacrifice saved my own life." He looked at Ayrion's father, who was standing just to the right of the doorway. "And now he walks among us without so much as a single cut, claiming that his son has brought reinforcements to aid us in our time of need." He looked at Ayrion. "Banished or not, for my part, I am very interested in what you have to say."

"We already know where Brim stands," Sirak said, not even bothering to look in the Orpa's direction. "But like Zayden, I, too, am interested in how you plan on helping. I hope you have brought the Elondrian army with you, because I'm afraid it might take nothing less to put a stop to these creatures. We've been fighting for two straight weeks, and each day we lose more ground. We need reinforcements, fresh troops. Ours are on the verge of breaking, and our healers can't keep up with the injured."

Sirak, though a big man, looked completely overwhelmed. Ayrion could hear the desperation in his voice. He could see their uniforms were heavily worn and soiled with blood. Dark rings around all their eyes said that unlike their soldiers, the heads of the clans weren't taking the needed time off to rest. These men were on the verge of breaking themselves.

"I'm afraid I don't have the Elondrian army with me, or any army for that matter. But what I have to offer could be better." All three men looked past him and out the front flap to where Ayrion's companions were waiting just outside.

"I don't understand," Sirak said, brows lowering. "Apart from your giant wolf creature, you only have, what, nine people? And two of them are hoary-headed. What possible aid are you going to give that an army of Upakan warriors cannot?"

"First, we can provide aid in healing. As you've already seen, my father was near death when we found him not a couple hours ago. If you'll permit me a quick demonstration?" Ayrion pointed at Zayden's hand, which was wrapped from the thumb down across the wrist. He turned and called for Rae.

Brim reached for his sword. "We said only three."

"She will not harm you. She is a healer, nothing more."

"She's a wielder," Brim spat about the time Rae stepped inside the tent.

Rae let her eyes adjust a moment before spotting Ferrin and walking over to stand beside him.

"Yes, she's a wielder," Ayrion's father said, "and I'm alive today because of it."

Ayrion turned. "Zynora out there has a gift for healing as well, but that of Rhivanni, not of a true wielder. Both of these women will be of great use toward your effort in defending this city."

Zayden looked at Rae, then finally nodded. "Fine. I will allow it." He took a step forward and cautiously held out his hand.

"Have you lost your mind?" Brim hissed. "You can't let a wielder touch you."

Zayden kept his hand out.

"Go ahead," Ayrion said to Rae, and with a nod from Ferrin, she walked over and took Zayden's hand, just above the wrapping. She closed her eyes, and her hand started to glow.

Zayden quickly yanked his hand away and took a step back. "What was that? It felt like the fingers of death were crawling inside me."

Ayrion raised his hand. "That is just her magic taking hold. I'm sorry. I should have prepared you. It will feel cold at first, and then the pain will be taken away. It will not harm you."

Zayden hesitantly took a step forward and once again held out his hand. Rae clasped his fingers with hers and closed her eyes. Both of their hands began to glow a soft purple as the tiny veins of her magic worked their way down through Zayden's fingers and up under the wrapping. The inside of the tent brightened slightly, and the other two pressed forward to see what was happening for themselves. A moment later, the light faded away, returning the inside of the tent to its original, dimly lit state.

Rae took a step back, and they all watched as Zayden carefully removed the blood-soaked bandaging over his hand. He undid the final layer, and his eyes widened as he turned his hand over. There wasn't a mark on it, nothing but dried blood. Ayrion had no idea what type of injury he had endured, but by the surprised looks on their faces, it was clear the damage had been more extensive than a simple cut.

Rae didn't look like it had taken anything out of her to fix Zayden's hand. She moved back beside Ferrin.

"The pain is gone," Zayden said, holding his hand up as he moved his fingers around. He squeezed his fist into a ball and released. "Incredible. In fact, the pain in my arm is gone as well." He rolled his shoulder several times.

"I say it's evil," Brim said, his hand still gripping the hilt of his sword, "and we should be rid of it."

Ferrin moved Rae behind him and reached for his wolf blade, matching Brim's glare.

"I don't see how restoring my hand would be evil," Zayden said. "It seems to me that if it had been evil, it would have made things worse, not better. Darkness breeds death, not life."

"That's just what they want you to think, and then once your guard is down, that's when they strike."

"Nonsense," Ayrion's father said. "My guard couldn't have been down any further than it was. I was lying in bed with both feet on the other side, but she brought me back."

"Yes, and used you to get in front of us." Brim looked at the other two primaries, stunned that they weren't seeing what he was. "Kill us, and she could release those creatures on Aldor."

"Do you even hear how stupid you sound?" Ferrin said, his temper flaring. "For all we know, you're the one who is releasing them. You were the ones who let them out in the first place."

Before Ayrion could attempt to calm the situation, Brim drew his sword and swung at Ferrin. Thankfully, the weaponsmith's blade was already halfway out of its sheath, and their swords collided before it had taken off his head. As soon as Brim's blade touched Ferrin's, it bent backward and curled around Brim's arm. Brim shouted and stumbled toward the table, the other primaries doing the same as they reached for their weapons.

Ayrion didn't have time to think and yelled toward the open tent flap. "Lenara!"

Lenara lifted her hands, and his traveling companions ran for the opening just as the entire front line of the Upakan army charged. Lenara was the last in, and she quickly lowered her shield around the pavilion. The armsmen slammed into the front of the shield, the first couple rows smashing against the invisible barrier as those in back pressed to reach their leaders.

A vision struck, and Ayrion spun, drawing one of his blades as he did. He barely finished turning before he swatted away Sirak's well-aimed strike for his neck, dodging Zayden in the process.

"Move her back!" Ayrion shouted, and Ferrin grabbed Rae and pulled her toward the front of the tent. Ayrion's father held a blade on Brim to keep him out of the way as Ayrion tried to contain the other two.

The two primaries fought together, but not as one. They fought individually, the way they'd been trained, striking at random instead of simultaneously. Sirak relied on his size and strength while Zayden was far more swift and agile, but neither could manage to get the upper hand.

Ayrion swatted away their attacks, dancing between their blades. It had been a long time since he'd faced true swordsmen like this. He could have ended the fight at any time, but he wanted them to see the skill he brought to bear. If they didn't respect him as a fighter, they wouldn't respect what he had to say.

The world outside their tent seemed to vanish as the shouts and cries from the men in the cavern were diluted by Lenara's shield. Soon nothing could be heard but the deep resonating thrums of fists and steel beating against it.

"If we were here to kill you," Ayrion said, blocking another strike for his head from Sirak, while spinning to miss a thrust by Zayden, "we could have done so a hundred times over. We aren't here to harm you. We're here to help. And this isn't helping."

He ducked, and with a well-placed slice to the wrist, disarmed Sirak, then turned and kicked Zayden's legs out from under him. Ayrion was a little surprised by how poor of a showing they gave, but then again, they'd spent the last couple weeks fighting khuls. Once they were back on their feet, Ayrion marched them at sword point over to the three seats on the right side and told them to sit.

Both men plopped down in their respective chairs, a mix of fear and anger on their faces. Sirak cradled his arm to stop the bleeding.

Ayrion waved Rae forward. "See what you can do for them."

Ferrin followed Rae with blade in hand over to where the two Upakans were seated and waited for the two men to allow her to heal them. He left Brim on the other side of the tent with his sword's blade wrapped around his arm. Brim wasn't going to allow Ferrin or Rae to touch him anyway.

"Move," Ayrion's father said as he forcibly escorted Brim over to the empty seat on Sirak's left. Ayrion was surprised there wasn't smoke rising from Brim's head, his eyes were so aflame. One thing was certain: no matter the outcome with the khuls, Ayrion's family would have to leave the city. After this humiliation, Brim would be coming for them.

Ayrion sheathed his sword, then stood in front of the three men. He waited until Rae had finished healing the other two before addressing them. "This is exactly what I was hoping to avoid." His words sounded strange, almost muffled, and he turned to look at Lenara who was standing in the doorway, staring at the armed men outside the shield.

This wasn't quite how he had envisioned this meeting going, but it seemed fate had dealt the cards, and now he had to play his hand. So much was riding on this. He was going to have to make every word count.

Chapter 51 | Ayrion

YRION TURNED HIS FOCUS to the three primaries. The men's faces were hard, but their eyes were fearful as they stared at Ayrion and his surrounding company. This could work to his advantage, but they were running out of time.

"As you can see," he said, "Rae is not the only wielder among us. And if we were, as Brim put it, *evil*, with the intention of disrupting your efforts by killing off the leadership . . . well, we seem to be in the perfect position to do just that."

The three men sat in silence, waiting to see if that's what Ayrion had truly intended all along. Ayrion shook his head with a disappointed sigh. "But clearly, by the fact that you're still alive, that isn't our intention. In fact, apart from Brim's arm, you're in better shape now than when you first met us."

Both Sirak and Zayden looked down at their newly healed hands.

Ayrion looked at Brim. "And as soon as you're willing to get rid of some of that pent-up hatred you've been carrying around for the last twenty years, perhaps we can move forward. I'm sorry for what happened to Flon. I never got the chance to say that before. As bad as it was, it was an accident."

Brim mumbled something under his breath, though it wasn't loud enough for anyone to hear.

"I was only thirteen, and you banished me from my home. I think I've been punished enough, don't you?"

Brim's face hardened, but he kept his mouth shut, not voicing an opinion one way or the other.

Lenara left the front of the pavilion and walked over to stand beside Ayrion. She raised her hand, and all three men immediately scooted back in their seats. She conjured a ball of fire in her palm and waved it in front of them. "You better listen and listen good," she said, drawing their attention. "Regardless of what you think about Ayrion, you need to set it aside, because what you're facing out there doesn't care about your vendetta. They don't care about you or your families, or even this city. They have only one desire, and that is to kill."

Sirak's head lifted. "You know what these things are?"

"They are khuls."

"Khuls?" Zayden's brows rose. "There's no such thing. Khuls are a myth."

"Oh, I assure you, they are very real, as the bodies stacked in your city square can attest. They haven't been seen since the fall of the Dark Wizard, but from some of the books I've read, they match the descriptions of what you've been fighting here."

Lenara didn't say what books or where she had read them, thankfully. The last thing they needed at this point was for her to admit to being a former wielder for the White Tower. Ayrion wondered if that was indeed where she had found reference material for the khuls. He also wondered why she hadn't mentioned it before. There was still much about her he didn't know.

"No one really knew where the khuls went after the Dark Wizard's defeat," she said. "Many thought they'd been killed off. Others believed them to have been locked away in the Pits of Aran'gal with their master and his followers."

Ayrion pursed his lips. How had Nyalis known that the khuls would be here? Yet another puzzle the wizard hadn't seen the need to share.

"Regardless of whether you believe they are khuls or not," Ayrion jumped in, "the fact is, you're facing an enemy you can't possibly defeat on your own. You've already admitted as much. You were even willing to allow a group of outsiders to enter the Lost City and admitted to hoping I had brought the Elondrian army with me."

Brim glared at Sirak, but Sirak ignored him.

"Here's the truth," Ayrion said. "Our offer of assistance was not a ruse. Why would we risk coming down here, knowing what could be awaiting us if we did? From what I've seen, if our goal was to free these creatures and unleash them on Aldor, we could have just sat back and watched from a safe distance, because it's only a matter of time before they are free."

The three primaries looked at each other, then back at Ayrion. Ayrion could see their defiance begin to buckle. "But let's be clear," he continued, "if these creatures do breach these tunnels, there won't be any place in Aldor that will be safe." He motioned for Lenara to lower her hand and extinguish the fire. He then turned to Ferrin and nodded toward Brim.

Ferrin reluctantly walked over and touched the hilt of Brim's sword, and the blade uncurled from his arm. Brim sat particularly still while it happened. He didn't, however, allow Rae to heal any of the thin cuts where the steel had torn through his clothing.

Realizing the three primaries weren't going to move with them standing so close, Ayrion motioned everyone back toward the front of the command tent. Even then, it took a while for the three men to rise from their seats. Ayrion couldn't force them to comply out of fear. They needed to be persuaded on more equal footing if he was to gain their help.

Once all three were up, they walked over to stand in front of the table at the back. The table held stacks of papers surrounding a large unrolled piece of vellum. In the short time Ayrion had to peek at the parchment, it looked to have been a map of the tunnel system they were in.

The three men whispered quietly amongst themselves before Sirak finally turned to address them. "Even though we do not believe you are here to undermine our efforts, I'm not sure how easy it will be to move forward after what has just taken place."

Zayden pointed past them to the armed men banging against the shield outside the pavilion. "Those men out there are hardly going to trust you now." He huffed. "I hardly trust you myself."

Sirak tucked some of his grey hair back behind his left ear. "How do you suggest we proceed?"

Ayrion's father stepped forward. "It would help for them to hear from your own lips that you don't believe they pose any threat."

"A difficult task considering what they just witnessed," Zayden said. Brim remained uncharacteristically quiet. If he wasn't glaring at Ayrion, his contempt was being directed at Ayrion's father. Ayrion was going to have to keep his father as far away from the head of Orpa as possible after this.

"Trust has to be earned," Sirak said. "How do you propose to do that here?"

Ayrion turned to those standing behind him. "Move away from the opening and let them through." Bek and the others stepped aside and gave the three men a clear path out the front of the tent, where they stopped just on the other side of the shield. Sirak reached out and placed his hand on the invisible barrier, prompting Zayden to do the same. Even Brim dared a quick touch before Ayrion motioned for Lenara to drop it.

Lenara released the shield, and it felt as though Ayrion's ears had popped from a high climb in the mountains as the regular sounds from the cavern outside the pavilion suddenly rushed back in.

The armed soldiers started for the front, but Sirak raised his hands and stopped them, calling for their attention. The one upside to being in an underground cavern was that a single voice could be carried a great distance with little effort. "Sheathe your weapons," he said, his arms remaining in the air. "We are unharmed. In fact, they have even healed some of our injuries."

No one moved to obey, everyone staring past the three men to the group of outsiders standing just inside the tent's opening, so he repeated himself. "We are unharmed. You can put your weapons away." He waited until they complied before finally lowering his arms and continuing. "There was a misunderstanding," he said, "but it has been rectified."

Ayrion kept waiting for Sirak to elaborate on the fact that it was Brim who had instigated the incident and not them, but he never did.

"As I'm sure it is unnecessary to explain now," Sirak continued, "we have outsiders who have come to offer aid. And yes, as you've seen, there are wielders among them."

Hushed whispers filtered through the throng of armed men standing just a few feet from the tent. They looked ready to storm the pavilion at any moment and put an end to the perceived threat. Ayrion noticed Lenara's hands were partway up, clearly anticipating raising another shield if she needed to.

Sirak waited for the whispers to die down before continuing. "After speaking with them, we believe their offer of help to be sincere."

"Are you being coerced to say these things?" someone near the front asked.

Sirak growled. "I'm Upakan. No one pressures me to do anything." He looked out over the gathered crowd of fighters, waiting to see if anyone else would question him, and when none did, he continued. "As I was saying, we believe their offer of help is in earnest. And right now, we need all the help we can muster. They will be setting up an infirmary here to tend to our wounded, so if you have need of healing, you can make yourselves available."

Ayrion turned slightly. This was the first he was hearing about this.

Sirak nodded toward the head of Raju. "Zayden and I have seen firsthand the use of this gift," he said, holding up his hand, "and I assure you it's worth taking advantage of. But for now, go back to your duties. When our enemy reemerges from their holes, let's make sure we're there to greet them." He waited a moment, but when no one made a move to disperse, he shouted, "Dismissed!"

The soldiers slowly began to pull away from the command post, leaving only those standing guard. Ayrion was surprised there wasn't more of a backlash against the primaries' agreement to work with him and his team. He suspected that at any other time there would have been, but at this point, the fighters looked desperate to accept help from anyone.

Ayrion watched as the men returned to their designated sides within the cavern. Another problem he would need to address.

Along with guards stationed at the front of the command post, there were two other individuals who had stayed behind, a little farther back and to the right. Jorn, and beside him, the young man Ayrion was guessing was his nephew, Davin. Ayrion started for the open flap in the doorway to walk out and greet them but was stopped by Sirak and Zayden, who were on their way in. Brim didn't return with them, and instead disappeared into the encampment beyond.

"We can set up a tent over near the entrance for your healers," Zayden said, passing Ayrion as he followed Sirak across the tent. Ayrion turned as well, watching the two men take up a position around the table at the back.

"What about those up in the city?" Zynora asked.

Sirak turned. "How long will it take you to heal them? Because we will need you here to tend to those who are fighting, once it starts."

"How long do you believe until the khuls arrive?"

"We still have some hours left until nightfall, but with these creatures, you never know."

Zynora looked at Rae. "That should give us enough time to see to the most severe." She turned to Sirak. "But you must understand, healing isn't as simple as just touching someone. It takes a lot out of the wielder, which means she only has so much strength available before she can no longer heal. It can be extremely dangerous for healers to overuse their gifts. If they expend too much magic, it can kill them."

Both Sirak and Zayden looked at Rae, clearly troubled. "That is concerning," Sirak said.

Rae took a deep breath, scrunching a wad of her dress in her fist. "Which is why we should prioritize the wounded, from those at the point of death to those with minor cuts and bruises. I can keep those on the brink alive but will not be able to fully restore them, or I won't have the strength to heal for long."

Ayrion tried not to gape. Rae rarely spoke, mostly keeping to herself. From what Ayrion had heard from Ferrin and Myron, she'd come a long way since their escape from the Tower.

Sirak thumbed his chin but finally nodded. "I understand." He looked at Zayden. "See if you can set a guard outside the infirmary once it's up to make sure they are not overrun, and find some men you trust to put inside who can keep the flow of the injured moving in and out in an orderly fashion."

Zayden stiffened at the orders but eventually left the tent to see to the infirmary. Ayrion had thought Sirak was in charge since he seemed to be doing all the talking, but now he was beginning to wonder if they had a hierarchy at all. How were they going to be able to work together if there was no definitive command structure? Perhaps he had read the situation incorrectly.

"If we are to see to those in the city above before the khuls arrive, then we need to leave now," Zynora said, slowly backing toward the tent door.

"I can take them up," Ayrion's father volunteered. "My son and nephew are just outside. They can help."

Sirak waved for them to go, and Ayrion's father escorted Zynora and Tameel outside. Rae stayed behind to have a couple of words with Ferrin, who didn't appear to like the idea of sending her up into the city without him. Ayrion couldn't hear what they were saying, but after a moment, she hugged him and left.

Ayrion wanted to go talk to his brother and nephew, but Sirak clearly had other plans and motioned for him and those remaining of his group to join him at the table. The others gathered around, Bek and Myron on his left, Ferrin, Lenara, and Elson on the right. Nola curled in a ball in the back corner, looking asleep, but her ears stood perked.

"Why didn't you tell your people what it is they're facing?" Myron asked Sirak as they all stared down at the papers strewn across the top of the table.

"Because he's not stupid," Elson said. Ayrion still wasn't used to the man not slurring when he spoke. "Is knowing what these creatures are going to help them fight any better? Doubtful. Finding out that they're fighting against the Dark One's own army won't exactly strengthen their resolve."

The others stared at Elson a moment, even Ferrin. Like Ayrion, they seemed to be taken aback by the man's common-sense reasoning and the effortless way he presented it. Had the man kept the heart of a legislator—or at least a bard—hidden under the veneer of a drunk fool?

"Exactly," Sirak said. "In fact, I wish you hadn't told *me*."

"You're the one who asked," Lenara pointed out.

"Yes, definitely regretting that decision, unless of course you know of some way they can be defeated?"

The others all turned and looked at the bulradoer, but she simply shook her head. "Afraid not."

"The problem the Upaka are going to have," Ayrion said, looking up from studying the vellum map, "is that we have never trained to fight in this manner before. We're proficient in single, armed combat: speed, accuracy, and stealth. We've never had to fight as a unit, and never on this scale or with this many fighters. When was the last time all three clans were together in one place?"

A clash of steel erupted outside, and men began to shout. Ayrion turned and headed for the front of the tent, the others right behind him. The sounds came from somewhere toward the middle of the encampment. Sirak pushed past them and started into the throng of soldiers, Ayrion right behind him. He heard Ferrin telling Nola to stay put before rushing to catch up.

They broke through the crowd, soldiers quickly moving out of the way once they saw Sirak, moving even farther when they saw Ayrion and his companions. Ahead, a small group of men were battling each other; their uniforms marked them as from Orpa and Raju. This was exactly what Ayrion was worried about.

"Stop!" Sirak shouted, drawing his own sword as he headed for the fight. "Put down your weapons!"

Ayrion followed him, if for no other reason than to make sure he didn't catch a stray sword. On the other side of the gathering, Brim broke through and headed straight for the Orpa members who were still fighting. He didn't even bother drawing a sword, simply walking up behind the first man and nearly yanking him off his feet before throwing him into three others.

By then, Sirak and Ayrion had reached the Raju side, and the men finally pulled back. Sirak's eyes were bloodshot, the most color an Upakan's eyes could hope to have. "If we didn't need every flaming one of you, I'd have you before the Peltok this instant! We're here to fight monsters, not ourselves! Save it for them!"

Brim was next to throw in his two coppers' worth. "The next one of you I see bearing arms against each other is going into the tunnels to fight the creatures alone."

The men parted quickly, though they shot harsh glares at the opposing clansmen as they did.

Sirak nodded to Brim and then turned and headed back to the command tent. Ayrion took a moment longer to watch the crowd disperse before following.

"This doesn't bode well for our chances here," Ferrin said.

"We might find it safer to be standing against these creatures on our own," Bek added.

Myron nodded. "Inclined to agree with you there."

Elson and Lenara remained silent but kept a close eye on all the surrounding Upakans.

The small group headed back to the pavilion, finding Sirak already inside and standing behind the table once more.

Ayrion walked over. "You can't possibly hope to defeat these creatures with a divided force. If you want to survive this, you can't continue fighting like Upakans. I had to learn this the hard way myself. It wasn't until I joined the Elondrian Lancer Corps that I realized there was more than one way to fight. In one-on-one combat, we have no equals, but that type of training means nothing when it comes to a full military campaign. And if we hope to have any chance of defeating these creatures, we need to start working as a unit, which means getting rid of the idea that there are three different clans out there, and instead realizing that we are one single people."

Sirak stared out the front flap of the tent. "If only it were as simple as that."

"It's going to have to be."

"I'm open to suggestions."

"You can start by having them get rid of their uniforms," Myron said. "Or at least the patches and symbols that represent their respective clans."

Sirak stiffened. His hands tightened on the side of the table. "Those symbols, as you call them, are our identity. They make us who we are."

"They also keep you divided," Ayrion said. He wondered if this might be an opportune time to bring up the Tanveer but decided against it. They had already had so much dropped on them today. That revelation needed to wait for the right time, and this wasn't it. Instead, he directed the conversation to an equally important topic. "Who is officially leading this fight?"

"The primaries, of course." Sirak looked at Ayrion like he'd lost all sense of reason.

"And what happens when you can't agree? You can't have a functioning campaign without a clear chain of leadership. Those on the front lines need to know who to listen to. For example, who is in charge of drawing up battle tactics?"

Sirak looked a little confused as he stared down at his papers. Now that Ayrion was close enough, he could see that the large sheet of vellum in the middle was indeed a map of the tunnel system, most likely originally created in the excavation attempts to mine the gold. Sirak ran his hand back through his hair and looked up. "We don't really have any formal plans. When they come, we fight them for as long as we can until they finally pull back at dawn."

"How far do they retreat?" Bek asked, looking at the map as well. "Do they retreat all the way back to the doors?"

"At first they did, but the more ground they gain, the less they retreat. We haven't seen that chamber for nearly a week." Sirak looked down and pointed to a spot on the map that showed the end of a tunnel with a set of doors. "That's where we first encountered them." He moved his finger farther back, about halfway between the doors and the city above. "This is us here." It looked to be several tunnels back from the initial opening. Ayrion wasn't exactly sure what the map's scale was, but it seemed the khuls had pushed them back a concerning distance.

"And where is the khul encampment now?" Ayrion asked. "I'm guessing you have watchers set to keep an eye on them?"

"Yes." He pointed to a spot that was about a quarter of the distance between where they were and the chamber with the stone doors. "Their camp is here."

The flap at the front shook, and Zayden stepped inside. "We have a rudimentary infirmary set up near the tunnel entrance. When your healers return from the city, they'll be able to get to work." He walked over to join Sirak on the other side of the table and looked down at the map. "What were you discussing?"

"How to turn our divided forces into a single fighting unit."

Zayden hmphed. "Let me guess, as long as Kovaa leads the charge?" The contempt in his voice was barely veiled.

"We are the largest clan," Sirak countered, "so it would only make sense."

"Yes, if size was more important than skill."

Ayrion looked at the others and shook his head. How was he going to bring these divided people together? Nyalis had given him an impossible task.

The two primaries continued to argue until Ayrion finally butted in. "Like I said, unless the clans can learn to work together, there's no hope for any of us. Change like this has to start at the top." He held both their gazes, refusing to back down.

"And like I told you," Sirak said, "what you ask is no easy task."

Ayrion cocked a single brow. "Then I guess we've got till sundown to figure it out."

Chapter 52 | Adarra

A HAND GRABBED ADARRA by the shoulder, and she jumped, startling Aiden, who was standing just to her left. Relief flooded through her as she realized it was only Jonas. "Quit scaring me like that."

"Looks clear," Jonas said in his broken Aldoran as he stepped out of the wall of reeds and into the small clearing. "We can go."

Jonas had been scouting ahead for any signs of danger, keeping their rather tired and hungry group moving in the right direction. He was, after all, the only one who seemed to know where they were going, or at least did a fair job of impersonating someone who did.

They'd been traveling for two days through the tall reeds, and so far, there had been no sign of sniffer pursuit. Perhaps Jonas was right, and the Tower's trackers did indeed limit themselves to the shoreline. Adarra had feared they would continue to hunt her down once they had gotten a whiff of her magic. She couldn't imagine why there would be sniffers on Tallos, a place where no one came, and those that were here feared magic, so she doubted the sniffers had much to prey on.

The way forward had slowed to a crawl as they slogged through the reeds, which only seemed to grow thicker the farther in they traveled. Occasionally, they managed to find an opening, like the one they had slept in last night, large enough for everyone to fit. Sadly, they had left all of their supplies on the beach when they fled the sniffer raid, but an empty stomach was the last thing on Adarra's mind. Every time she closed her eyes, all she could see was Sergeant Finnly's face as he was pulled into the mist.

She awoke in a sweat several times throughout the night, her entire body shaking, Finnly's screams haunting her. The first night, no one had slept as they plunged through the reeds to get as far from the beach and the sniffers as possible.

The second night, their bodies were too tired to keep going, and they had stopped to get what little rest they could, but sleep was difficult to be had. They had forgone a fire in case it attracted unwanted attention, which forced them to sleep on top of each other just to keep warm.

Adarra left Jonas and walked over to where Captain Holverd and Captain Mervall were quietly conversing on the other side of the clearing. "Jonas is back. He says it's time to go."

They both looked up from the map and over at Jonas, who was standing quietly in the far corner. "We can't keep going like this," Mervall said to Holverd. "We have to find food and water. We won't make it another day without them."

There had been enough leftover snow on the ground to melt to keep at least a modicum of moisture in their bodies, but it wouldn't be enough. Mervall was right. They needed food.

Holverd turned, lifting his cap far enough to wipe the front of his bald head. "I'll get the men ready."

Adarra walked back across the clearing and over to where Ambassador Lanmiere and Aiden sat, waiting for the order to start up once again. Jonas stood just behind them, his back to the reeds.

"What did they say?" Lanmiere asked, holding out his hand for her to help him up.

"I told them Jonas was ready, so I'm guessing we'll be leaving shortly."

Lanmiere groaned, and not just from being forced back to his feet. "I could sleep for a week." He passed a quick glance over at the two captains. "Did they say anything else?"

"They were too busy discussing the food situation."

Aiden stood. "Yes, that's something I'd like an answer to as well. I feel like my gut is eating itself."

"Ironic, isn't it," Adarra said, placing her hand on her stomach. She, too, had been feeling the pangs of hunger creeping in. "We march across a deadly island to bring food to a starving people, and by the time we reach them, if we ever do, it will be the one thing we don't have to give."

The first day, they'd been too scared to even notice the hunger, but now that they had plenty of time to think about it, the ache was getting stronger. She was glad when Holverd finally motioned for Jonas to lead them out. She found that the discomfort lessened while they were on the move. It hurt more when they sat around with nothing to do but stare at each other.

Jonas turned and started into the thickest of the reeds, holding the dagger he'd picked up on the beach during their battle with the sniffers. They were supposed to be heading northeast as they made their way toward the mountains at the back of the island, but for all Adarra could tell, they were going in circles.

She had seen little of the sky since entering the forest of stalks, and what she had seen was covered in thick grey clouds, making it difficult to tell which direction they were going. She had to trust that Mervall, who kept a compass on him at all times, would make sure they were keeping true to their course.

Jonas led, with Holverd and half his remaining lancers just behind. Adarra, Aiden, and Lanmiere followed, sticking to the middle of the pack. Behind them were those of Mervall's crew who hadn't been lucky enough to get off the island when they had the chance, and then lastly, the other half of the lancers.

The pace was slow as the caravan snaked its way through the reeds in single file. Aiden walked just in front of Adarra, being careful not to slap her with the thick stalks as he pushed them aside. She did the same for Lanmiere, whose wobbly legs were taxed enough to keep him upright. No one talked as they focused on placing one foot in front of the other.

She wished they had a better idea of where they were. She had studied the map Jonas had drawn of the island for her back in Easthaven, since no one really had a good depiction of what it looked like. There was a river that split

Tallos nearly in two, running from the Bay of Mist, up across the island, and all the way to the mountains on the other side. Right now they were traveling under the assumption that they had landed somewhere on the western side.

However, if they had actually come ashore on the eastern side of the river, they were heading in the wrong direction completely. From what Jonas had said, it seemed he was trying to keep them on a northeasterly approach in hopes of finding the river. From there, at least, they would know where they were in relation to the mountains.

Adarra paused to blow on her hands. The mornings were always difficult. Her body was stiff from lack of sleep, not to mention the cold. She wished the sun would show itself at least once. She probably wouldn't be able to enjoy it all that much inside the reeds, but the thought was nice.

Aiden stopped in front of her, and she nearly bumped into him. "What is it?" She tried peering around him, but the reeds were too thick.

"I don't know. The person in front of me stopped."

"What's happening?" Lanmiere asked behind them, and Adarra turned and shrugged.

"Apparently they've stopped."

A swooshing of reeds on their left had them all turning. It came from somewhere deeper in. "What was that?" Aiden asked. "Did we lose someone?"

It happened again, this time on their right. It sounded like someone running through the stalks at an extremely fast pace. But there was no way anyone could move through the reeds that quickly. The hairs on Adarra's arms began to rise. Was it the sniffers? Had they found them?

A loud squawk pierced the silence, and behind them, someone screamed.

Everyone turned, grabbing their weapons, which were next to useless in growth this thick. The long knife in Adarra's hand shook as her eyes darted back and forth, trying to see what had happened, trying to catch a glimpse of something, anything. Another loud squawk sounded on their left, and everyone turned again. It was followed by another swooshing as the reeds were once again thrown aside. A moment later, there was another scream, this time just ahead of them.

"Jinga!" she heard Jonas shout from somewhere farther up, which was followed immediately by Captain Holverd.

"Run!"

Next thing Adarra knew, they were all running. Their line broke as men began to spread apart, trying to race ahead of the others and away from whatever was stalking them. More swishing filled the reeds around them. Adarra frantically tried to see what was out there as she ran, but there were only shadows, shadows moving through the reeds, shadows that were anything but human, shadows at least ten feet tall.

Her mind raced as she recalled everything Jonas had said about the jinga, but other than that they were some sort of animal that hunted the grasslands, she didn't really know much. From his description, they sounded almost birdlike.

Behind her, Lanmiere stumbled over his own feet and landed face first in a sludge of melting snow and dirt.

Adarra shouted for Aiden and turned to help the ambassador. Several of the lancers that were behind them ran by through the reeds on the side, not bothering to stop. Either they hadn't seen them or didn't care. She grabbed Lanmiere's arm and began to pull. A couple of the lancers that hadn't broken with the rest ran up and yanked the old man back to his feet.

"Hurry!" one of the men shouted just before something tore out of the reeds beside them and snatched the man up. The giant birdlike creature's beak pierced the lancer's chest as it lifted him in the air. The man screamed, but only for a moment, then he went limp. The creature dropped him back to the ground and began to feed.

It was like no bird she'd ever seen, and not just because of its size. It was an amalgamation of several different animals. The head rose nearly to the top of the stalks, and most of its ten feet of height consisted of a strangely long neck. The body, though shaped in part like a bird, was covered in a thick leathery hide, much like a reptile's, and the legs were those of a cat, covered in fur with exceptionally long claws.

The jinga leaned down and dug into the man's gut with its beak, ripping out a mouthful of entrails. Adarra's stomach leaped into her throat. The other lancers slowly began to back away, and Adarra, Lanmiere, and Aiden did the same, doing their best not to make any sudden movements. One of the crushed stalks snapped under Lanmiere's foot, and the jinga turned its head. As soon as it saw them, it opened its blood-soaked beak and released a shrilling squawk that had Adarra trembling.

Three more squawks somewhere in the reeds answered and then started in their direction.

"Run!" one of the lancers shouted, and they all turned and ran at the same time.

The reeds slapped Adarra's face and arms as she fled. She held her dagger in one hand, and with the other she tried to steady Lanmiere, who was fighting with everything he had to keep up. Aiden supported the ambassador from the other side. Behind them, the new jingas squawked in anticipation of their next meal.

The lancers began to pull away, and before Adarra could yell for them to wait, Lanmiere tripped once more and went down, this time taking both Aiden and Adarra with him. The lancers never stopped. They were too far ahead to even notice. Aiden started to jump back to his feet, but Adarra grabbed his arm and pulled him back down, pointing to the left. "Stay low." Quickly, they crawled into a small patch of thick reeds at the side of the path and lay as still as they could.

They'd barely pulled their legs inside when the first of the jingas tore past, its feet pounding the ground as it followed the sound of the lancers, who were still racing through the stalks ahead.

A second raced by as well, its catlike feet pawing at the sludge as it fought to catch up. A third squawk sounded just behind. This jinga slowed as it reached them and then started down the same path the other two had taken, but then it stopped. Its head rose, and it appeared to be sniffing the air.

Adarra's mind raced as it searched out every text she'd ever read on birds of prey. Most birds relied on their eyesight to find food, but some relied on their sense of smell. She'd read about a breed of vultures that could smell carrion from hundreds of feet away. Whatever these jinga were, they lived and hunted in a terrain where their eyesight would afford them little in the way of hunting. She had to imagine they relied on those other senses.

Quietly, she dropped her dagger and grabbed a handful of wet snow and mud and wiped it on her face and neck, using as little movement as possible. The other two must have realized what she was doing, because they started digging into the muck as well, covering as much of their skin as they could. The sludge was freezing, and several times she wanted to yelp as she layered it on, but she bit down, fighting to keep the discomfort inside.

The jinga released another loud squawk, and its head turned slowly in their direction.

All three froze. Adarra could feel her own heart thundering and lay as still as possible. *Please don't let it smell us*, she pleaded, repeating it over and over as though the more times it was said the greater the chance the Creator would hear her. The jinga sniffed the air again, and this time it turned completely around and started in their direction.

Adarra's heart sank as she watched it slowly stalk toward them, giant claws digging into the ground as its catlike feet headed straight for their hiding spot. She was the closest to the edge of the reeds and the first the jinga would grab if it found them. Slowly, she angled to the right to see if she could find her dagger. It was lying in the snow about a foot from her knee.

The creature stopped at the corner of the path the lancers and the other jingas had made and slowly stretched its neck out toward their clump of reeds. Adarra was on her stomach, so she couldn't see what was happening above her very well. With as little movement as possible, she slowly let her arm slide down her leg toward the dagger.

Above her, she could hear the creature's snorts as it tried to determine where they were. Apparently, its eyesight wasn't good, or it would have already spotted them. The reeds began to move beside her as the giant beak pushed its way through. She focused on her breathing, her mind racing as she desperately tried to think of what to do. Where was Jonas? He was supposed to be protecting her.

The jinga snorted again, this time close enough for her to feel its breath on her back.

The knife was close. She could feel it brushing her fingertips. Just a little more. She prayed Lanmiere and Aiden were able to fight back the urge to run.

She tried to look up without moving her head. Where was it? What was it doing? She was afraid to turn her head. Pushing through the fear, she slid her hand down, letting her fingers slip under the dagger's handle.

Not being able to see what the jinga was doing behind her had Adarra's imagination running wild, picturing the creature opening its mouth and getting ready to plunge its beak through her back. There was another snort that had her jumping in her own skin, and this time she was only barely able to fight back against the urge to jump up and flee. She couldn't take it any longer. She was about to break.

Suddenly, Aiden leapt up from where he was lying on the other side of Lanmiere, and Adarra panicked. She rolled over with her dagger in hand, half expecting to see Aiden's backside as he took off running through the reeds without them. Instead, he'd somehow managed to catch the jinga around its mouth with his arms and was fighting to keep it from opening its beak.

Adarra didn't hesitate. She jumped up and lunged at the creature, burying her dagger in its neck. Aiden was yanked off the ground, his arms still clinging to the beak. The creature stumbled forward, knocking Adarra backward as it fought to get Aiden off its head. Lanmiere cried out as one of the jinga's paws crushed his leg while he was trying to crawl out of its way.

"Hold on!" Adarra shouted, fumbling around for her knife. She fished it out of the mud and rushed the creature a second time.

The jinga swung its neck, and this time Aiden flew through the air, landing with a thud in a pile of reeds. The jinga turned, but before it could release another one of its squawks, Adarra buried her knife into its neck a second time and cut far enough to open its airway, keeping it from making any noise at all.

Blood sprayed from its neck and coated her front as the creature tumbled sideways, knocking her backward all over again. Its paws trembled for a moment, then went still.

Adarra crawled to her feet, but her legs were shaking so badly she didn't know if she'd be able to stay on them. She was covered in warm blood, which steamed in contrast to the patches of mud and snow she'd smeared on herself. The stench was nearly unbearable, and the taste in her mouth was even worse.

"Are you hurt?" Aiden asked beside her. When she didn't answer, he turned her around to face him.

She finally nodded. "I don't think so." She looked down and noticed she was still holding the dagger. That was strange. She couldn't feel it. Her hands were numb. "I'll be fine," she said. A groan behind them had them turning to find Lanmiere leaning against a pile of reeds behind them.

"It might be broken," he said through gritted teeth as he looked down at his right leg. He looked over at the creature. "Is it dead?"

They both turned and looked at the jinga. Its chest wasn't moving.

"It's dead," Adarra said, forcing herself to finally move, checking for injuries as she did. She used the snow to wipe her face clean and rinse the blood out of her mouth before kneeling beside the ambassador to examine his leg.

She prayed it wasn't broken. The last thing they needed was to be traveling through jinga-infested lands with someone who couldn't walk, let alone run. She felt along the bone, but she didn't notice any major deformations, and even though there were several places where his leg had reddened and was noticeably painful, there wasn't much swelling. Of course, lying in the snow could be helping to keep it down.

"I don't think it's broken, but we can't really know for sure. Best to keep as much weight off it as possible."

"And how do you suggest I do that? Lay here quietly and hope none of those things finds me?" He reached out. "Here, help me up."

Aiden took one arm and Adarra the other, and they pulled the ambassador back to his feet. He was unstable at first but soon found his bearings, testing the injured leg. He attempted putting some weight on it, and his face puckered.

"I think I can make it."

Adarra could see the pain in Lanmiere's eyes, but he wasn't about to take a chance at getting left behind. She looked at Aiden. "Cut four or five of the reeds. We'll tie them together as a support staff to walk with." She could have made a splint, but that would mean binding his leg to the point of it being immobile, and right now they needed him to move.

Aiden used his belt knife to cut several of the sturdier reeds, shortening them to an appropriate size for walking, then bound them together with the cord Aiden had been using to keep his hair tied back. While Aiden worked on the staff, Adarra cleaned as much of the blood off herself as she could. What she couldn't, she resorted to covering with wet dirt, then proceeded to rub the sludge into the rest of her clothing.

Aiden finished with the staff and turned, jerking with a start when he saw her. "What are you doing?"

"Making sure those things don't smell us again."

Aiden looked at Lanmiere, and Lanmiere simply shrugged. "Fine by me. Lather me good and thick. I certainly don't want those things smelling me."

They spent the next quarter of an hour coating themselves in mud. The snowy sludge was freezing, a fact she became especially aware of after smearing it through her hair. Aiden and Lanmiere looked like they'd been sharing a wallow with the hogs by the time they were finished, and she couldn't help but laugh. One look at her and each other, and they did the same. It felt strange to laugh after everything that had happened, but better that than the alternative.

"If we do find our people," Lanmiere said, "let's hope they don't mistake us for swamp creatures."

He took Aiden's staff and tested it by taking a couple of small steps around the opening where the jinga had fallen. Aiden had strapped enough of the reeds together that the staff didn't bend. A moment later, Lanmiere nodded, and they made their way out of the underbrush. The path through the reeds ahead had been cleared by their fleeing companions and the jinga who were chasing them.

"Which way?" Aiden asked, keeping his voice to a whisper as he looked up and down the narrow clearing.

She pointed in the direction the others had taken. "We'll keep heading northeast and hope we reach the river. My guess is, that's where our people have gone."

The other two nodded.

"Keep your ears and eyes open," she said, and they started through the reeds.

Chapter 53 | Adarra

ANMIERE'S INJURY KEPT THEIR progress slow, and the growling of their stomachs didn't help. Perhaps they could have carved up part of the jinga and cooked it, but that would have taken precious time they didn't have and would have required a fire they didn't dare start, and what if the bird then proved to be unsafe to eat?

A squawk broke the silence, and they froze. Reeds crackled to their left. Adarra held her breath as she waited for it to pass. She listened as the sound of the jinga's passing faded into the distance before exhaling as quietly as she dared. The mud they had caked to themselves seemed to be masking their scent from the creatures. More squawks arose ahead of them. These sounded eager to Adarra, rather than the searching cry of the jinga that had just passed. Most likely that meant they were engaged with what remained of the crew. A few steps closer brought the sounds of battle in range—men and jinga crying out, weapons slashing, while reeds whipped and crackled through it all.

Part of her wanted to rush ahead and join the fight, but the pragmatic side of her said that they should lay low and keep out of the way until it was over. Captain Holverd and his men were far more equipped to fight off the jinga than she, Aiden, and Lanmiere, who could barely stand on his own. Even Captain Mervall's deckhands would be more capable than the three of them.

Logic eventually won out, and they waited until it sounded like the fighting had begun to die down before moving on. Several times, they were forced to stop so the ambassador could rest his leg. He was hobbling as best he could with his crude staff. The leg was beginning to swell, but Adarra kept it packed with icy sludge to keep the swelling down enough for him to keep going. She still couldn't tell if it was broken or just badly sprained, but it was clear by the increasing number of rests that Lanmiere was forced to take that he wasn't going to last much longer. He needed sleep and food. They all did.

Aiden held up his hand, and they stopped. "Do you hear that?"

Adarra cocked her head. She didn't hear anything, at least at first, but then the faint swooshing sound of the reeds began to build. It was getting louder, and it sounded like it was coming right at them. She turned, trying to find the closest place to hide, spotting a small pile of rocks in the reeds on their right. It was only a few feet tall, but if they hurried . . .

She hooked Lanmiere's arm around her shoulder, and Aiden did the same, and they lifted the man off the ground as they rushed him away from the path of broken reeds they had been following. She could feel the pounding of the creature's feet on the ground behind them as they lowered Lanmiere down behind the rocks. Quickly, she and Aiden grabbed their weapons and dropped down beside him, huddling close together to keep from being seen.

They'd barely gotten their heads down when a jinga ran by. It didn't seem to notice they were there. They waited a few minutes before venturing out, but as soon as Adarra made it to her feet, another loud squawk broke through the reeds, and they dropped back to the ground. Terror washed through her as she realized this jinga wasn't approaching from the pathway. It was moving through the reeds behind them.

She stood and grabbed Lanmiere, Aiden joining her, and they tried lifting the ambassador to move him to the other side of the rocks, but as weak as Lanmiere was, it felt like they were pulling dead weight. They struggled to get him to his feet as the sound of the approaching jinga grew. They dropped him behind the rocks, and Aiden managed to make it down beside Lanmiere, but before Adarra could crouch down beside them, the bird lumbered out of the reeds, almost on top of them.

The jinga opened its beak and released a loud squawk.

It was too late.

The creature had seen her . . . but not the others.

Without stopping to think, she turned and ran. "Stay with Lanmiere!" she shouted back at Aiden, racing through the reeds for the path ahead.

What was she thinking? Her first impulse had been to protect the other two, but what about protecting herself? She broke through the last of the reeds and stumbled out onto the narrow trail. Behind her, she heard the reeds splitting as the jinga gave chase. She looked both ways, then took off running toward where she thought her shipmates might be. Perhaps she could outrun the giant bird.

As soon as the jinga lumbered out of the reeds and into the open corridor, it unleashed a bloodcurdling squawk and charged. One glance over her shoulder and she could see there was no way she would outrun it.

Adarra turned, keeping her eyes ahead, too frightened to look back. The reeds beat at her arms and face as she fought to keep her feet moving. Why hadn't she just stayed and fought? At least then there would have been someone to fight with. Still, the only reason they'd survived the last time was because the jinga hadn't known they were there, and Aiden had surprised it. Without that leverage, there was no way they could have lived through an actual battle with one of these creatures. The most they could have hoped for would have been for Lanmiere going down first and using that distraction to make a run for it.

The very notion made her sick, and she was embarrassed for even considering it. Perhaps her mind, knowing she was more than likely about to die, was willing to consider all kinds of horrible thoughts in an effort to stave off the end. Behind her, the jinga was catching up. She could hear it panting just over her shoulder, snorting as it came.

She pushed her short legs, racing as hard as she could. She had no idea how far away she was from the rest of their team, or if they were even still alive. Had they reached the river? Her breath came in panicked gasps, and her lungs screamed for air. She held her knife in her hand, gripping it so hard she lost feeling in her fingers. She rounded another bend in the path only to find another long stretch of broken reeds ahead.

Every hair on her body stood on end. It had her.

Without thinking, she dove to the left and into a thick patch of stalks. As soon as she did, the jinga tore past, stretching its neck out for her. It missed by a hairsbreadth and rolled into the reeds on the other side of the trail. She desperately fought her way deeper into the thickest of the growth. She spotted what looked like a burrow in between clumps of reeds and quickly crawled inside. The space was cramped, and she had to curl into a ball to fit, but she used her knife and hands to gather as much of the surrounding snow and muck to cover the opening, leaving just enough to peer out.

She could hear the jinga trying to crawl back to its feet from the other side of the path, squawking in anger as it thrashed about. She tried to slow her breathing, but there was just no stopping the heavy panting from her run and the terror of what was hunting her. She watched as the shadow of the jinga crouched at the edge of the reeds. Its head lifted into the air, and she heard it sniffing the wind.

It didn't know where she was.

The jinga's head cocked to the side. She didn't know if it was trying to listen or simply peer inside the reeds. What was it waiting on? About the time she wondered, the jinga's beak poked through the stalks a few feet away. Blood dripped from the tip.

She struggled to muffle her breathing, doing everything she could to slow her heart. She inhaled through her nose and out through her mouth. It wasn't working. She had no idea how good the creature's hearing was—hopefully no better than its eyesight.

The bird snaked a paw through the reeds, then another. Both stopped only a couple of feet from where she lay. She tightened her grip on her dagger. If she saw an opening, she was going to take it, but without others there to help, her chances of overpowering the beast were slim.

She got a good look at its massive claws. They were nearly as long as her dagger. A part of her brain prattled that all it would take with such weapons was one good swipe for her to bleed out in seconds.

The creature's head lifted once more as it tested the air, sniffing out any lasting trace of her. She prayed the coating of mire was enough to keep her hidden. *Please don't let it find me.* Her hands continued to quiver. The jinga cocked its head, birdlike, peering up and down at the same time. Slowly, it slid another paw forward, and Adarra tensed. If it moved the other foot, it was going to land right on top of her.

She didn't have any good options. The jinga's neck was too far away for her to reach, but she was out of options. She readied her knife and took a deep breath. *Please guide my aim.* The giant birdlike creature opened its beak once more and released another ear-piercing squawk.

It was now or never.

Adarra leaped up while the jinga's attention was momentarily diverted to its call and screamed as loud as she could, hoping to stun the creature long enough to get to its neck. The bird reared in response, and she ended up missing the neck and burying her dagger in the soft tissue just above its chest. The jinga backhanded her with its paw, clipping her in the chest as it attempted to leap back. The air was ripped from her lungs as she flew several feet to the right.

She landed on her back, gasping for air, thankful it had been the top of its paw and not the claws that had hit her. The reeds around her spun. Frantically, she crawled to her knees, suddenly aware she'd lost her knife. She fumbled around in the dirt before spotting it halfway between where she had landed and the jinga.

She looked up, and the jinga looked down. It opened its beak and lunged for her. She shrieked and dove straight ahead into the mud, wildly clawing her way forward to her blade. Her fingers wrapped around the handle, and she spun over on her back just in time to plunge the dagger in the bird's paw as it tried to pin her down.

The jinga leaped back, screaming in pain and fury as blood poured from the gaping wound. It turned. One look at her lying prostrate in the mud and the bird lunged. She yanked herself out of the mud's sucking grasp and rolled to the right, narrowly escaping the enormous beak before it plowed into the ground beside her. She tried to roll again but hit a thick stand of reeds. There was nowhere to go.

The jinga lifted its head and shook the mud from its beak as she fought her way back to her feet. She'd gone as far as she could. The jinga clearly knew it, as it leaned forward, beak spread. It lifted its paw, dagger-long claws ready for the kill. This was it. She gripped her dagger and screamed.

A deep roar exploded through the reeds on her left, and a figure dove out of the stalks and onto the jinga.

"Jonas!"

Her heart leaped as the Northman latched onto the jinga's neck and rode the creature like one would an unbroken stallion—but without the aid of a saddle or reins. He grabbed the bird's long neck with one hand and buried his sword into its side, striking it again and again until he'd nearly decapitated it. The jinga dropped with a sad gurgled squawk, and its head landed at Adarra's feet.

Jonas climbed off and walked over to where she stood with her back pressed against the reeds. He looked down at her, a grin forming across his face until he threw back his head and laughed.

She stared at him, speechless. Why was he laughing? She lowered her dagger and looked down at her mud-encrusted body. She did look quite the mess.

"I was worried for you, Spotted Warrior." He looked her over, checking for injuries, and then shook his head. "But I should have worried for the jinga." He laughed once more.

The sound of snapping reeds on the left had them both spinning as Aiden came rushing out of the stalks with his sword raised. He stopped when he saw the two of them and sighed. "Adarra. You're alive. Thank the Creator."

He had left Lanmiere hugging a stand of reeds near the opening and ran to wrap his arms around her. After holding her for a long moment, he finally let go and took a step back, his face furious. "Have you lost your flaming mind?" He grabbed his mouth when he realized how loud he'd spoken and nervously glanced around the narrow opening before turning and lowering his voice. "If you wanted to kill yourself, I'm sure there are plenty of easier ways to do it. Next time don't force me to participate." He looked down at the dead jinga, and his mouth twisted.

"Sorry," she said. "It was just instinct. I saved your backside, didn't I?"

"At what cost? If it's escaped your memory, you're the one who has to be there to meet with the Tallosians. You're the translator, for pity's sake. How do you think it would have made me feel to have volunteered to come on this mission to protect you, only to have you go running off and getting yourself killed for me." He shook his head. "It was stupid."

She knew he wasn't really angry at her so much as afraid of having nearly lost her, but she wasn't going to back down. She held his angry gaze a moment, then turned and looked at Jonas. "Where are the rest of our people?"

"The river."

"You found it?" Lanmiere asked, trying to hobble his way to where the others were standing. "Is it far?"

"Not far."

"We heard fighting ahead," Aiden said. "Was that them?"

Jonas nodded.

Adarra pointed back in the direction they'd come. "We ran into a little trouble of our own. We were cornered by one of the jinga, but we managed to kill it. Then we ran into more. This one," she said, kicking some slush over at the dead creature, "surprised us from behind. It saw me, so I took off running to draw it away."

"Smart to use mud," he said, looking the three of them over.

Adarra turned and glanced back toward the path. "How far to the river?"

Jonas started back through the reeds. "Come. I take you to the others."

They left the dead jinga and headed up the narrow pathway leading to the river. With Aiden's help, the ambassador limped his way along, one arm around Aiden's shoulders, the other clutching his crude reed staff. Jonas remained in front, his head on a constant swivel, as the sound of jinga moving through the reeds around them kept them on their toes.

Adarra moved up beside Jonas, glancing over her shoulder periodically to make sure Aiden and Lanmiere were still keeping up. Several times, she had to grab Jonas's arm to slow him down, as his longer legs tended to outpace the others. She caught him looking her way and turned. "What is it?"

"You look . . ."

I look what? she wondered. *Utterly ridiculous, most likely.*

"Fierce," he said, switching to Tallosian. There was a sparkle in his eyes. Was that pride?

Adarra shook her head. She must be seeing things. After the ordeal they had been through the past few days, it was no wonder.

They continued for at least another twenty minutes before Adarra heard the rush of water ahead. The reeds broke, and they found themselves at the edge of a soft embankment leading down to a river with a slow-moving current. It was wide enough that she couldn't have thrown a rock across, but it wasn't too wide to swim, not that she would want to, given the cold and how dark the water was.

To the left were several dead jinga, their blood saturating the ground from the reeds all the way to the embankment.

"They made it," someone called out on their right, and Adarra turned to find Captain Mervall walking over from what appeared to be the remainder of their diplomatic team. Bodies lay nearby, face down beside the embankment. They'd been composed in death as respectfully as possible, considering some were missing limbs. The image of the lancer they had watched being ripped opened by the jinga flashed across her mind, and her stomach turned. She looked away from the morbid scene, focusing instead on Mervall and his relieved smile as he walked over to greet them.

Captain Holverd joined him, and they both stopped when they got a better look at the state the three were in. Adarra thought numbly that they probably looked like a trio of corpses having just dug their way out of a shallow grave.

"What happened to you lot?" Mervall asked.

"Long story." She sighed. "We need to see to the ambassador's leg. It might be broken."

"I would have the lancer physicker look at him," Holverd said glumly, taking a moment to wipe his bald head before putting his cap back on, "but that's him over there." He pointed to one of the bodies lying on the embankment.

Lanmiere shook his head. "It appears things haven't gone so well here either."

"No," Holverd said. "We've lost another six, with three unaccounted for."

"There were three lancers with us," Aiden said. "One was . . ." He shook his head. "He didn't make it. The other two ran off through the reeds. We haven't seen anyone since. That is, until Jonas."

Adarra counted eleven lancers and four sailors still living, not including

Holverd and Mervall. It was a far cry from what they had started with. They had lost at least half of their original party somewhere in the Bay of Mist. So far, this mission had been a colossal failure, and Adarra found herself wondering once more why they had even come.

She turned and looked at the broken bodies stretched out on the dirt by the river and grimaced. How many of these men could have been spared? She had a newfound respect for those in positions of leadership, whether it was Holverd choosing the men to accompany them on this mission or Mervall volunteering his crew and ships to take them, or even Lord Barl assigning the task of going in the first place. A single decision from the top, and men lost their lives.

It was a position she would never wish to be placed in.

Jingas began to squawk in the distance, and everyone turned.

"Sounds like they're coming from where we just were," Aiden said. "I wonder if they found the dead jinga."

"I think they are regrouping," Holverd said, ordering his men to assemble. Once in place, he looked to Jonas. "How far do these reeds stretch?"

"Miles," Jonas said.

Holverd had Mervall bring over the map, and Jonas drew a circle with his finger around a large jut on the south side of the island that ran from the river in the middle to an inlet on the left side. The entire area was apparently the jingas' hunting ground.

"Which would put us somewhere over here on the northeastern side," Holverd said, staring intently at the drawing. "By the narrowing of the river here, I'd say we're nearing the upper end." He ran a finger south down the river where it widened the closer it got to the sea. "Still, there's no real way to tell, other than to follow the water north."

Jonas pointed to a spot on the coast near the river's mouth where it connected to the Ozrin Sea. "We travel this way to your land."

"This is the way your people came?" Holverd asked, sliding his finger down the edge of the darkened area marking the river's passage from the trees at the foot of the mountains to the sea.

"Yes. We don't go into reeds."

Holverd looked at Mervall. "We should have taken the ship farther east and anchored at the mouth of the river and come up from there."

Mervall curled his thick mustache. "Yes, well, that's easy to say in hindsight. But when you're floatin' around in magical fog that wants to kill ya, you set anchor wherever you can."

By the sound of the jingas' cries, their numbers were increasing. The lancers drew their swords and stood alongside Holverd in front of the path's opening, waiting for orders.

Mervall grimaced as he turned and looked at the reeds. "It sounds like we need to be on our way."

Adarra walked over to stand beside Lanmiere, who they had carried down closer to the water and away from the reeds and the sounds of the jingas. One of Mervall's crewmen sat beside him, packing his leg with snow before wrapping it with cloth they had salvaged from the dead and cut into strips. Aiden stood next to them.

"We should go," Adarra heard Jonas tell Holverd, and she motioned for the sailor to hurry. The man finished wrapping Lanmiere's leg, and he and Aiden helped the ambassador up. His legs were wobbly, and his forehead was soaked with sweat. She placed the back of her hand on his forehead. It was warm to the touch.

She moved back to where Holverd and Jonas were still looking at their map. "I don't know how much longer the ambassador is going to be able to continue. He's barely able to stand and is running a fever. At this rate, he may be delirious before long, which means we're going to have to carry him. He needs rest."

"We all need rest," Holverd said.

Jonas looked over at Lanmiere, then back at Holverd. "We need to keep going."

"Too late for that," Mervall cut in. He was standing over near the entrance to the narrow pathway leading into the reeds.

Adarra and the others turned.

"Hear that?" he said, his head angled toward the front line of stalks. "They're coming."

The squawking was indeed getting louder, as was the sound of the reeds crackling in the distance. They were out of time. She grabbed a sword from the small pile of weapons taken from the dead and ran to help Aiden carry Lanmiere back toward the rest of the group. Jonas helped them set the ambassador behind some rocks near the gently sloping embankment.

"Stay away from the water," Jonas said and then headed back to where the other men stood waiting.

Adarra stared out at the slow-moving current, then turned. "Will you be fine here?"

Lanmiere held his sword in his lap and smiled. "As long as you don't let those things get by you."

She tried to smile in return, but it was lopsided. "I'll do my best." With that, she looked at Aiden, and they both turned to face the reeds. The lancers were lined up between them and the coming jinga, but from the number of screeches and squawks barreling down on their position, there wasn't much hope for any of them.

Chapter 54 | Adarra

ADARRA'S SWORD QUIVERED in her hand, and her legs trembled as the sound of the approaching jingas built to the crescendo of an oncoming stampede. She waited for the tide to crash down upon them. Two of the lancers had fallen back from the rest, taking up a position to Adarra's left, closer to the water. They nocked arrows and held their bows ready.

Jonas peeked over his shoulder at her, and she attempted to appear calm, though every part of her wanted to throw down her weapons and run screaming. Her heart pounded in her ears, and she found herself morbidly wondering how much longer it would continue to beat. She looked at Aiden standing beside her, his hands shaking nearly as much as hers.

"I wish you hadn't come with me," she said.

He smirked. "Me too."

They both turned just as the first of the jingas broke through the reeds, releasing their bloodcurdling squawks. Adarra froze as the first jinga dove at the closest men in line. Holverd, who stood near the center, was one of them. He jumped to the side and swung, nearly severing the creature's head. Blood poured from the wound, and the jinga stumbled backward and into the next bird, who was just breaking from the path behind it.

The second jinga leaped over the first with its agile catlike paws and landed in the middle of the lancer formation. Men dove out of the way to keep from getting crushed under its claws. Mervall was thrown into the dirt as one of his men was snatched up by a jinga. The crewman screamed as the bird's powerful beak crushed him.

Adarra's gut turned over, and she dry heaved. The jinga was struck twice by arrows: the first in the chest, the second straight through its open maw. It squawked and went down.

Three more jingas tore out of the stalks, scattering men as they tried to leap out of the way. The lancers recovered and circled the creatures, hacking away while trying not to get snatched up or clawed. They managed to cut one bird's legs out from under it, and Jonas was there to finish it off with a quick thrust through the creature's eye.

Yet another was taken down by the archers, but the last managed to fight its way through the line and ran straight for the two bowmen. Both men threw down their bows and raced for the water.

"No!" Jonas shouted. "Don't get in water!"

The jinga stopped on the shoreline as the men dove in. It watched the two men, waiting for them to swim back to shore.

"Get out of water!" Jonas shouted once more, but he didn't have time to waste on them as another wave of jingas breached the wall of reeds.

Adarra and Aiden stayed where they were, protecting the ambassador, not that they could have done all that much. Behind them, the two men continued to paddle just offshore as the jinga waited patiently for them to return. They couldn't swim out there forever. Apparently, they realized that and started swimming farther down, but the jinga followed along the river's edge.

The two men made it a few dozen feet when one of them screamed and suddenly disappeared under the water. The second lancer shouted and immediately started swimming for shore. Behind him, the first lancer flew out of the water, his arms flailing and his face wracked in horror. Ragged stumps were all that remained where his legs should have been. He landed beside the second man and screamed for someone to help him just before he was yanked back under.

Adarra wanted to run down to help the second lancer, but the jinga was between her and the man in the water. "Stay here," she told Aiden and ran for the archer's bows, which were still lying on the embankment. Aiden shouted at her, but she ignored him.

She reached the two weapons and grabbed for the first, but the lower limb on the bow had been snapped, along with its arrows, all lying halfway inside the jinga's footprint. The second was still intact. She snatched it and an arrow from the quiver and spun. If there was one thing she'd learned from her father and brother, it was how to shoot. She nocked the arrow and pulled the string to her chin. It was a much stronger draw than she was used to, but fear gave her strength, and she took aim.

The lancer was just reaching the shore, and the jinga was anxiously bobbing up and down, ready to greet him, making her shot more difficult. She took a deep breath and exhaled half, just as her father had taught her. With the bird in her sights, she released. The string buzzed, and the arrow flew from the bow.

The arrow pierced the jinga's head. It squawked and went down just as the lancer climbed out of the water. He raced ashore, then turned to look at the black waters behind him, but there was no sign of the other man.

Something enormous broke the surface for a split moment, then disappeared back underneath. Whatever it was, it was covered in scales and appeared to have gills on the side along with what might have been legs and a tail. Like the jinga, it seemed *wrong*, a creature that had been spliced together from other creatures.

The lancer nodded his thanks, then drew his sword and ran to help the others. Adarra grabbed another arrow and turned as more jingas appeared. How many of these things were there? Three more of their party were down, two lancers and one of Mervall's sailors. They weren't going to survive this. One of the jingas broke off from the rest, having spotted Aiden and Lanmiere. Adarra immediately drew her bow. She released, and the arrow buried itself in the creature's chest.

It stumbled but didn't go down.

Lanmiere was up on wobbly feet beside Aiden as the two met it head on.

Adarra reached for another arrow, but the quiver was empty, so she threw the bow on the ground, drew her sword, and ran to help. She was barely halfway to them when the jinga slapped Lanmiere with its paw. He flew backward, landing against the pile of rocks he'd been sitting on. Thankfully, it had been a blow from the flat of the paw, not a rake of the claws, or he'd be dead. As it was, Adarra saw blood on his face from where his head had hit the rocks. He struggled to get back to his feet but was unable to stand on his own, and he slumped back down.

Aiden swung his sword and dagger as fast as he could, fighting to keep out of reach of the jinga's beak. He dove to the side as the bird raked at him with its claws. He rolled back to his feet and slashed at the creature's front right leg, forcing it back a step or two. Adarra ran in from the side, hoping Aiden could keep its attention long enough for her to drive her sword into its unprotected chest. Aiden dodged another strike from the jinga's beak and swung at its neck.

The bird hopped out of the way and right into Adarra, just as she lunged for its midsection. The jinga slammed into her, throwing her sideways. She hit the ground and rolled across the slush. The unexpected blow caught the creature's attention, and it squawked when it saw her, lunging for what it expected was an easy meal.

Adarra rolled to the right, and the jinga's powerful beak slammed into the ground beside her, covering her in a spray of mud and slush and blood. She barely had time to wipe her eyes before Aiden leaped on the creature and drove in his sword. The jinga reared and sent him cartwheeling to the side.

Her earlier arrow and Aiden's sword finally took their toll, and the birdlike creature dropped with one final desperate shriek. Adarra climbed to her feet and stumbled for Lanmiere, who was trying to turn over. Aiden clambered for his sword and quickly moved to cover them.

Adarra counted at least two more of their men down, and the rest were fighting just to keep to their feet. "Come on!" she said to Aiden as she started for the battle ahead. "They need our help." Better to fight as a group than wait for another jinga to break through and come for them.

"What about Lanmiere?"

"Don't wait for me," the ambassador said. "I'm useless. Go help the others."

Adarra ran for the closest group, which happened to be Captain Mervall and his remaining two crewmen. Captain Holverd and half his men were on the left, chopping down a particularly large jinga trying to break free from the reeds, while Jonas and the other half were in the middle fighting back two more.

As Adarra and Aiden neared the fight, Mervall tried to hack through one of the bird's legs. The jinga swatted him aside, and the ship captain flipped halfway in the air, nearly plowing into the ground headfirst in front of Adarra. She narrowly avoided tripping over him, then bellowed a high-pitched war cry as she dove for the bird's side. Her sword managed to cut through the thick leathery skin at the flank, but not deep enough to hit anything major.

Aiden buried his knife in the jinga's left leg just before getting swatted with it himself and tumbling back across the snow and rock. The jinga turned to finish him, but Adarra and the two remaining sailors jumped in front of it, diverting its attention long enough for Mervall and Aiden to get back to their feet.

One of the sailors on Adarra's right sprang to the side to keep from getting speared, but in doing so knocked Adarra backward. She landed in a pile of blood-soaked sludge. The jinga sidestepped Mervall's attack as he returned to the battle, nearly stepping on her in the process. She dove to the right to keep from getting clawed, but before she realized her mistake, she found herself underneath the jinga.

In a sudden panic, she drove her knife into the bird's underbelly. What came out stunk worse than anything she'd smelled before. She barely got her mouth closed before getting bathed in entrails. The jinga screeched and collapsed on top of her, crushing her under its weight. She couldn't breathe.

Pain shot through her chest. Her ribs felt like they were going to snap at any moment under the pressure. She tried to breathe, desperately pulling for air, but none was getting in. She could feel the darkness taking over, and her thoughts shifted to her family. Would they ever find out what had happened to her, or would they be forced to spend the rest of their lives wondering? For a brief moment, she welcomed the rest the darkness promised, but then air suddenly rushed back into her lungs as the jinga was rolled off her.

Mervall and Aiden grabbed her arms and pulled her out from under the creature's torso and helped her to her feet. She was astonished to find that none of her bones seemed to be broken. The snow must have cushioned her enough to absorb the force of the bird falling on her.

"Come on!" Mervall shouted. "No time to be lying around." He and his men turned as another two jingas broke from the reeds in front of them.

Adarra barely had time to catch her breath before the first attacked. She'd lost her knife. It was buried somewhere underneath the dead jinga, and she didn't have time to look for it. With arms barely able to move, she turned and raised her sword. Even Lanmiere, who was hardly able to keep upright, was there, swinging his sword wildly while holding himself up with his makeshift staff. What she could see of his face through the mud was pale.

"On your left!" Aiden shouted, and Adarra turned and swung at a jinga's head as it snapped for one of the sailors standing beside her. The sailor managed to dive out of the way but left an opening straight for her. The jinga's beak opened, and she angled her sword. If it swallowed her, she was going to slit its throat wide the whole way down.

The jinga started to lunge but stopped when a high-pitched whistle erupted from somewhere back near the river. All the jingas' heads shot up, their necks craning to find the source. The whistle grew louder, and the jingas slowly began to go back to the reeds.

What was happening? Adarra turned to see a man walking down the edge of the river, heading their way. He had a long grey beard, and his body was covered in thick grey fur. He didn't seem to be in a hurry, nor did he seem to be all that alarmed by the jingas, though they looked quite frightened of him.

The closer he got, the louder the whistle became, and the farther back the jingas went. By the time he neared their beleaguered group, the jingas had all but receded back into the reeds. None of Adarra's shipmates moved, too stunned by the birds' retreat. The elderly stranger continued to blow on a wooden pipe as he sauntered on through the middle of them and then walked right into the reeds after the jingas, taking the very path they'd entered from.

Adarra watched in awe as the fur-covered man disappeared into the forest of greenish-yellow stalks. She listened as the whistle faded into the distance and then vanished altogether.

"What in the sea's embrace was that?" Mervall asked, staring after the stranger who'd just saved their lives and didn't stop long enough to let them thank him.

"I don't know," Holverd said, his arm around one of his lancers, "but let's not waste it. Grab any extra weapons. We're leaving."

"What about them?" Lanmiere asked, pointing to their fallen comrades.

"Not much we can do for them now. If we stay, we will join them."

Adarra turned to find Jonas standing beside her, looking her over for possible injuries, not that she thought he could have done much if she had any. The ambassador dropped to his knees beside her, and she pursed her lips. "We need to make a litter."

Holverd turned, and she pointed to the ambassador. The captain frowned. "Fine, but be quick about it."

Adarra asked for Jonas to help, and they quickly cut down several thick reeds and bound them together with strips of cloth cut from the dead, similar to how Aiden had done for Lanmiere's walking staff. It didn't take long before they had a workable stretcher and placed Lanmiere on top. The ambassador barely had time to thank her before Holverd was waving them on. She spared a passing glance back over her shoulder at the men who'd fallen. She wondered if they, too, had families who would be waiting back home for their return.

"Best not to look."

She turned to find Jonas beside her again. She nodded, then turned her attention to what lay ahead, focusing on placing one foot in front of the other. She sheathed her sword. Her fingers were too cold and too numb to carry it anyway. With her luck, she'd probably drop it along the way and not realize. Her legs ached. Her back ached. Her empty stomach ached, despite the horror she'd seen. Every inch of her wanted to lie down and die.

Overhead, the sun had fallen below the reeds, and the evening colors were beginning to fade. It wouldn't be long before night was upon them.

"Who do you think that man was?" Aiden whispered to her as they trudged along beside Lanmiere's litter, which was being towed by a couple of lancers.

Adarra shook her head, then looked over at Jonas. "Do you know who he was?"

"He is Shayan."

"What's that?" Adarra asked. "One of the Tallosian houses?"

Jonas shook his head. "No. Cursed."

"I don't understand."

"He has bad stuff in him."

"I don't care what he has in him," Aiden said. "I want to know how he stopped those creatures."

"Dark powers," Jonas said, his lips curling into a sneer.

"You mean he's a wielder?" Adarra asked, finally realizing what Jonas was talking about. "He has magic?"

Jonas nodded.

"He must have if he was able to control the jingas like that," Aiden said.

Adarra was reminded of her brother's flute and how he used it to help him focus his magic. Was that man doing the same? She glanced back over her shoulder, half expecting to find this Shayan fellow following them, but every time she looked, there was nothing there but river and reeds.

They walked for at least another half hour before the tall forest of stalks on the left began to fall away, the first sign that they might be coming to the end of the jingas' territory. By this time the colors had completely faded from the sky, replaced by a drab grey that was darkening by the minute. Pretty soon the first of the stars would be making their nightly appearance.

Up ahead, Holverd brought them to a stop, once again giving those carrying Lanmiere a break and those with injuries a chance to catch their breath. They needed to find food, and fast, but out here, who knew where that would be, and it wasn't like they had been given time to forage while running for their lives.

Captain Mervall and a few of the other men lit torches. It was still bright enough to see without them, but Adarra had a feeling it was more to ward off other predators. Also, if they ran into something that wanted to eat them, it would be mighty hard to fight it off if they couldn't see it.

Both captains left the front and walked back to where Adarra and the others were sitting next to the stretcher. Mervall had his map in hand, and they clearly wanted to talk with Jonas about it. She tiredly pondered how easy it was for things to be turned on their head when your life was in peril. Not three days ago, Jonas was in shackles, now he was freed, armed, and the one they were going to for help.

"What lies ahead of here?" Holverd asked Jonas, pointing to a spot on the north side of where Jonas had circled earlier as being jinga territory. "Do the jingas ever leave the reeds?"

"I do not know that."

"Why not?"

"Because they hide in their mountains," a voice behind them said.

Everyone drew their weapons and turned. The same fur-clad man who had chased the jingas off earlier stood several feet away. He was clothed completely in animal skin. Even his feet were wrapped in some kind of skin shoes. His grey hair was matted and hung halfway down his back, his beard even further. What teeth he still had were yellowed. Several looked to have rotted. He looked half-mad.

At first glance, Adarra thought Nyalis looked younger than this man. And then she realized his accent was wrong.

"You don't sound Tallosian," she said, which, thinking about it, was a strange way to start a conversation with a man who'd just saved their lives. "Sorry, I should have thanked you for what you did back there. I don't know how you did it, but you saved us."

He smiled, revealing even more missing teeth. "Don't you worry about it, little missy. Those silly birds won't bother us as long as I have Matti here," he said, patting the short wooden pipe hanging from his neck. "They don't like it when she sings."

Before Adarra could ask him once more about his accent, the old man walked over and threw his arms around Aiden, who yelped at the unexpected embrace. The others raised their weapons.

Aiden stood there a moment, frozen, but then finally managed to pry the man's arms off him and push him back a step or two. "What's wrong with you?" he asked, pinching his nose.

Adarra, catching a whiff of the stranger, wanted to close hers as well, but refrained.

The man stepped over in front of Adarra and lifted a finger as though to poke her, but Jonas grabbed the man's arm before he could and shoved him back. The man stumbled but caught himself before going down, then looked up at Jonas and sneered. "Northman," he spat. He looked at the others. "Are you real?"

"What do you mean, are we real?" Holverd asked.

"You're Aldoran, like me?"

"You're not Tallosian?" Adarra asked.

The man spat off to the side. "Do I look like a rabid animal?"

No one dared answer.

Adarra took a step in the man's direction but kept out of arm's reach. "I don't understand. If you're Aldoran, how did you get here?"

He grinned and cocked his head, like Adarra had said something silly. "The same as you, I reckon. If you are who you say you are. If you're really there."

Aiden leaned forward and whispered, "What's wrong with him?"

"Quite a lot by the looks of it," Mervall whispered, then addressed the man himself. "How long have you been here?"

"Where's the boat?"

"What boat?" Mervall asked.

"Your boat, you oaf," the crazed man said. "Did you bring it with you?"

Mervall looked at the others. "The man's touched in the head."

The crazed man smiled. "Of course I am. And so are you. Why else would you come here?"

Adarra almost laughed. He had them there.

"We're here to negotiate with the Tallosians," Holverd said, not lowering his sword.

"Then you are all mad."

"What is your name?" Adarra asked. Lanmiere, being the Sidaran ambassador, probably should have been the one talking to the man, but he was too weak at that point to do much more than lift his head.

"You tell me yours and I'll tell you mine," he said with a childlike playfulness that reminded her of Gilly.

"Fine. My name is Adarra."

The man looked at her, then around at the others, clearly waiting for further introductions, which Adarra gave, at least of those she knew. Mervall and Holverd had to offer the names of those under them. When the last name was given, the fur-skinned man smiled. "I am Belakor, personal scholar to Overlord Saryn, and he will not look kindly on you if I were to be treated roughly."

Holverd hmphed. "He won't be looking kindly on anyone. Not that he ever did in the first place."

Belakor's head cocked once more, and he stared at Holverd, obviously having no idea what Holverd was referring to.

"Your master's dead," Holverd finally said, "and Cylmar is no more."

Belakor stared at him a moment longer, then produced a wide toothy grin. "Best news I've heard in years." His smile faltered. "Then you are not here to rescue me?"

"Rescue you?" Holverd laughed. "We didn't even know you existed until an hour ago."

Adarra offered Belakor a smile. "It seems as though we are the ones in need of rescuing." She looked around, no longer able to see the reeds with the torch's light now that the sky had darkened enough to see the stars. "Do you know of a place we can shelter for tonight? We need food."

"And I need to go home," Belakor said.

Adarra sighed. "Then I suggest a trade. If you will help us, we will take you to our ship."

Belakor's face brightened. "So you did bring one."

Adarra couldn't figure out how the man thought they would have gotten there otherwise. Then again, as Mervall said, he did seem touched in the head. "Yes. We have one. A big one. And we promise to take you with us back to Aldor in exchange for your help."

Belakor stared quietly at those gathered. He took a moment to slide his dirt-covered hand down his tangled beard, then promptly picked his nose and wiped the contents on the front of his coat. "I guess you have a deal," he said, holding out the hand he'd just picked his nose with to Adarra.

She flinched, but then she looked down at her own hand, which was covered in mud and dried jinga guts, and figured it wasn't much better. They shook hands, and Belakor walked over and looked down at Lanmiere.

"Looks bad. Might as well leave him for the jingas. Slow you down."

Adarra's jaw tightened. "We aren't leaving anyone."

Belakor shrugged. "Suit yourself." He marched to the front of the group and started forward.

"Wait," Holverd said, trying to catch up, directing his men to grab the ambassador. "Where are you taking us?"

Belakor didn't even bother turning. "Home."

Chapter 55 | Ayrion

ON YOUR LEFT!" Bek shouted. Another vision struck, and Ayrion spun to meet the khul as it dove for him. Its claws were bared and jaws open, and Ayrion could see hunger in its eyes. He leapt backward and sliced the creature open as it flew by, its black claws missing him by a handsbreadth. The khul hit the ground and rolled through half a dozen of Sirak's men to the right. Most saw it coming and jumped, but a couple had their feet taken out from under them and went down.

The khuls had proven to be a weird blend of half animal, half human. They could run on all fours just as easily as two, and when they stood, they were at least two heads taller than the tallest man there, who at the time was Bek. The front of their bodies were covered in a thick tanned hide, while the back was covered in coarse fur, some lighter, some darker. Like Nola, they had large fangs, but unlike hers, theirs grew from the bottom jaw up, like a wild boar.

"Move your men back!" Ayrion shouted at Sirak, about the time that another string of fire tore past and into the next wave of khuls. Ayrion lifted a hand to shield his face from the residual heat of the bulradoer's flames. Lenara had forgone her whips, as they were ill suited for fighting in such confined spaces. One overhead draw from those flaming weapons and she'd cut down half the fighters around her.

Part of the wave of khuls went down, nothing more than smoking husks of flesh that left a sickly sweet smell of cooked meat in the air. The smell lingered in the tunnels, permeating everything around them and turning Ayrion's stomach.

Ayrion cut down two as they tried to breach the line. The khuls' attack had been swift and deadly, and the Upakans hadn't been as prepared as they needed to be, especially with three different clans all vying for the same position at the front. Their ranks were falling apart, breaking as the three groups tried to separate themselves from each other. It was complete madness. If it wasn't for Ayrion's team, the khuls would have pushed them all the way back to the encampment. As it stood, they were only a few hundred feet away.

The injured were carried back through the tunnel to the infirmary, where Zynora and Rae, with Tameel's and Elson's help, were no doubt hard at work, trying to keep the men alive.

Ayrion didn't know how long they'd been fighting. Without the advantage of seeing the night sky, there was no way to tell, and as deep as they were under the city, there would be no light reaching them from the surface. Another wave struck, and Ayrion was there to meet them. His arms were beginning to tire from the constant motion, but he knew that if he or those with him pulled back, those behind would break for sure. Still, they couldn't keep going like this without proper rotation.

The khuls threw another volley of rocks toward the Upakan front lines, and Lenara's shield was there to deflect them, lowering just in time for the Upakan archers behind them to fire into the coming horde. Bek fought like a wild man on Ayrion's right, his hatchets chopping down one khul after the other. He'd been struck more than once, but so far his thick furs had helped protect him against the worst of it.

Beside Bek, Myron was doing everything he could to keep up. He was at least ten years Ayrion's senior, and his movements weren't as swift and precise as the others, but he fought with everything he had. Ayrion's father, brother, and nephew fought as a single unit on Ayrion's left, working to keep his flank protected as he focused on the khuls at the front.

Behind them, Nola crouched beside Lenara, leaping on any khuls that managed to break through. The enormous wolf was quick and deadly, burying its fangs into one khul after another, ripping open their necks before they could get their claws into her. Nola's face was covered in blood, with a few crimson runs along her pelt where the creatures' claws had raked her sides. Thankfully, her coat was also extremely thick, and she didn't seem to be seriously wounded.

Ferrin was the only member of their group capable of wielding a sword who wasn't on the front lines. Despite his protests, Ayrion had left him back at camp so he could add his special type of magic to as many of their weapons as he could manage. Even though Ferrin wanted to join the fight, Ayrion believed the smith's gifts would be put to better use working on their armory. He had an army of Upakan fighters to use, but only one metallurgist.

Now if only they would fight like an army.

Zayden and a group of his Raju fighters pushed past the Kovaa lines and were working their way up the side of the tunnel to the left of Ayrion's family. Unlike some of the tunnels they'd traveled through while coming down from the city above, these were much wider, forcing their fighters to spread out farther than Ayrion wished. Besides making it more difficult to protect their flanks, it was giving the three clans more opportunity for contention as they tried to separate themselves from each other.

Brim and Clan Orpa seemed to be the only one of the three not trying to push the others out of the way, content to remain behind and pick off the khuls that got through. Every now and then, Ayrion would glance over his shoulder to see where Brim was in relation to him or his father. He wouldn't put it past the Orpa primary to try causing an "accident" while everyone's focus was on the battle.

Ayrion spun between two hulking khuls, both carrying crude metal swords. He dodged right and sliced through the calf of the first, then deflected the second's blade and rammed his sword through the khul's gut. It released a deep throaty roar and bent just far enough for Ayrion to slide his second sword up through the bottom of the creature's jaw and into its head. It squealed and dropped. Ayrion yanked his blades free in time to stop the other khul's sword from being buried in his side. Using the dead khul for leverage, Ayrion jumped high enough to decapitate the first khul and then kicked its body into the ones behind it.

The Upakans were losing ground. No matter how hard Ayrion and the others fought, the khuls were pushing them back. Their numbers seemed endless, and if this fight had taken place anywhere other than in the restrictive confines of the city's underground, the khuls would have overrun them long ago.

"Davin!"

Ayrion turned just as his nephew disappeared under a group of khuls, along with several fighters from Clan Raju. Ayrion looked at Bek.

"Go!" Bek said. "I've got this." He and Myron shifted left to fill Ayrion's spot as others from Clan Kovaa shifted to fill theirs.

Ayrion ran behind his father and brother, cutting the legs out from under the khuls on one side while severing arms and heads of those on the other. He slammed into the pile of fur-clad flesh just beyond and started cutting them down, one by one.

Ayrion's heart raced, panic flooded his body. He couldn't let anything happen to his sister's child. She'd already lost her husband. He wouldn't allow her to lose her son as well.

With the creatures' focus on the Upakan fighters they'd managed to pin, they were hardly in a position to fend off Ayrion's blades as he drove them into the sides and back and neck of any khul that stood in his way. The swords slid in and out with hardly any resistance, until there wasn't a khul left moving. He sheathed one sword and reached into the pile to grab Davin's arm and pull him out.

His nephew was still holding his own sword in one hand, and a bloody dagger in the other that he'd buried in the khul who'd fallen on him. Ayrion didn't hesitate. He grabbed Davin and hugged him. After a brief moment, he released the young man and took a step back.

Davin looked a little stunned, but then he turned and looked at the pile of dead creatures around him. "How did you . . ."

"Are you hurt?" Ayrion asked.

Davin shook his head.

"Good." Ayrion patted his nephew's shoulder, then turned and ran back through the ranks for the front. Ayrion's father gave him a proud look as he passed, too busy to speak.

Ayrion reached the front just as it was collapsing around him. Myron had suffered another hit, thankfully not from the creatures' claws or blades, but enough to send him flying off his feet. Bek and Sirak were fighting to keep the middle and right sides held, but Sirak's men were already falling back.

"Hold the line!" Ayrion shouted as he delved further into his magic, letting it build, but not giving over full control. He spun between the khuls' blades and claws as they sought to dig into his flesh, ducking and weaving between every swing and thrust. He cut them down, severing arms and legs and necks, painting himself and everyone around him with the creatures' blood, and yet the khuls were not swayed.

The creatures seemed to have an endless supply of fresh troops. Where in the name of darkness were they all coming from? Ayrion's arms were beginning to slow, his hands long numb as his white knuckles clutched to his swords. His chest burned as he gasped for breath.

They weren't going to be able to hold. The sides were already giving.

It was time.

Ayrion yanked his sword out of the khul in front of him and shouted to Lenara, "Do it!" Then he cried to those fighting beside him, "Fall back!"

Ayrion ducked as Lenara sent another wave of flames into the coming horde, then raised her shield. The fire killed most of the creatures at the front, and the shield expanded to span the tunnel, holding back the tide of khuls flooding down the passage to join the fight. The Upakans quickly dispatched the remaining khuls that had the unfortunate luck of being on the wrong side of the invisible wall when it went up.

"How long do you think you can hold it?" Ayrion asked her.

Lenara's arms were up, palms extended toward the khuls. "How long do you need?"

She looked pale. Ayrion wondered if it was from the expended magic or motherhood. She'd been forced to use quite a bit of magic to keep the khuls from overrunning them. But she'd only done so in waves, doing as Ayrion had asked and holding enough in reserve to make sure she could maintain a shield as a last resort to give their forces time to retreat.

Ayrion turned and looked back toward the wall of fur and flesh beating against the barrier. "As long as you can give me."

"I might be able to hold for an hour, but no more. I need rest, and food."

"I'll have them run some food out to you. Can't help you with the rest, though." He turned and headed back down the tunnel toward their encampment. He needed to have a strong word with the primaries, and they weren't going to like what he had to say.

Several of the fighters remained behind with Lenara to keep an eye on the khuls in case they broke free. Most of them were from Clan Orpa, who had seen the least amount of action.

Nola remained as well, standing watch next to the bulradoer, guarding her as she struggled to keep the shield in place.

"We can't keep fighting each other and the khuls," Myron said as he and Bek joined Ayrion on his way back toward the camp. Myron was limping on his right leg, and there was blood on the side of his face. Bek, too, had some blood, but Ayrion couldn't tell if it was his or the khuls'.

"I know," Ayrion said. "And I plan on making sure the primaries do as well." Ayrion looked at Myron as they left the tunnel and headed into the Upakan camp. "Go see to your wounds. We'll be in the command pavilion."

Myron nodded and broke from the two, heading around to the other side of the cavern where the infirmary had been set up.

"Son? A word."

Ayrion and Bek stopped and turned as Ayrion's family hurried over. Before his father could say anything, Ayrion addressed Davin. "Do me a favor and see if you can get some food and drink out to Lenara."

His nephew's eyes widened slightly with a hint of concern. None of the Upakans wanted to get too close to Ayrion and his companions, especially the wielders, and of the wielders, Lenara was the one they seemed the most wary of. But his nephew eventually nodded and rushed off in the direction of one of the cookfires.

"What are you going to say to the primaries?" Ayrion's father asked.

"Something they aren't going to want to hear."

"I suggest restraint."

"Afraid the time for niceties is long past." Ayrion turned and marched for the main tent. He didn't have much time. Lenara gave him an hour. Hardly time enough to turn three groups of fighters into a single force. How could he bring them together? Whatever he did, it had to be symbolic. Noticeable. He stopped before reaching the main tent and pulled off his right glove.

He looked down at his father's ring and the single emblem blazoned in the middle. Once again, the statue of the three paladins inside the Aero'set garrison came to mind, all three emblems carefully carved along the base. An idea came to him, and he pulled off the ring and handed it to Bek. He whispered in Bek's ear, and Bek left them and started through the encampment.

"What was all that about?" Jorn asked.

"You'll see." At least, he hoped they would. Ayrion paused for a brief moment to listen to Ferrin's hammer as it filled the cavern with its melodic tune. Still trying to catch his breath, he continued his trek through the camp for the command tent.

Ayrion didn't bother waiting for the guards to give him admittance and walked straight past them and into the pavilion. One look at his face and the guards shut their mouths.

Ayrion found all three of the primaries waiting inside, each in their own chair, desperately trying to control their own breathing. They weren't as young as they used to be and certainly weren't used to fighting for such a prolonged period.

"I hope you realize," Ayrion said angrily, "that if it weren't for Lenara out there, the khuls would have overrun you already."

Brim sneered, but that was nothing new when it came to Ayrion and his family. The other two stiffened in their seats, but they at least appeared willing to listen.

Ayrion stared at the three men for a long moment, long enough to make them good and uncomfortable as he debated how best to deal with them. His father was right in that a direct assault might not produce the best results. Sure, he could humiliate them. Some leaders would have killed incompetent generals on the battlefield and replaced them, but Ayrion wasn't their leader. He wasn't a king or overlord or even a primary. He was the outsider. If he removed the primaries, he risked alienating all the men outside who had been trained their entire lives to derive their identity from their clan.

He needed another tactic.

Ayrion took a deep breath. "I haven't told you everything," he began. The three leaned in. "I haven't told you the real reason I'm here."

Ayrion's father cleared his throat over near the entrance. "Perhaps now isn't the best time."

"I believe it's the only time. If we are to have any hope of surviving this, they are going to need to learn to fight together." He looked at the three chairs and the men sitting on them. "In war, there can only be one commander, and right now we have three. Three separate forces that are spending just as much time fighting each other as they are the enemy marching on their gates. Unless you learn to fight as one, there's no point in going back out there, except to die."

The three primaries didn't say a word, though their expressions said enough. Brim looked like he would rather have his ears cut off than listen to Ayrion, while the other two bristled in their seats at being scolded for the way they were running their campaigns. But *that* was the problem. They were each running their own campaign instead of holding a united front.

"As long as those men out there view themselves as part of Kovaa, or Raju, or Orpa, they are never going to fight together. If you want to save your city, then you need to destroy it."

All three heads shot up at the same time.

"What do you mean destroy it?" Sirak asked, a look of shock on his face.

"Not the city itself, but destroy what it stands for, destroy the separation. This broken notion that there are three types of Upakans is nonsense. We are one people. Why in the name of Aldor did we ever change that? Why are there three clans? We all live in the same city. We should be working together."

"There have always been three clans," Zayden said.

"How do you know?"

Zayden spared a quick glance at the other two. "There just has."

"The founders set it that way when we first moved here," Sirak said. "Who are we to question why?"

Ayrion shook his head. Apparently, his people really were ignorant of their own heritage. He had wondered if perhaps those in leadership might have been more aware of the situation, but apparently they were as in the dark as the rest. "We are what's left. Are there no histories of where we come from, of who we are? Why we live on the outskirts of all society, hidden away underground like animals frightened of the world?"

Brim slapped the arm of his seat with his fist. "We fear no one. The world fears us."

The other two grunted in agreement.

"And why is that? Because we are skilled warriors? Because we have these strange-looking eyes? Would it surprise you to know that while you have been hiding away here in your holes, I have found where our people came from? I have found our true home."

All three men shifted in their seat, Zayden leaning forward the farthest.

"Would it surprise you to know that our people were not always looked on as they are today, and that at one time they were even revered among the kingdoms?"

Sirak laughed. "I would say that we have put our trust in a madman."

"And where is this place that you say we came from?" Zayden asked. "If it was indeed our home, then why did we leave it?"

Ayrion knew they weren't going to be ready to hear the truth, but he was out of options, and worse, he had no real proof of anything he was about to tell them other than it was too preposterous to even make up. "I recently uncovered a hidden city deep within the Angoran Mountains. A place, according to its histories, that our people were the protectors of. A powerful fortress that at one time maintained peace between the kingdoms."

He pointed at the rings on each of their hands. "Those emblems do not represent three individual clans. In fact, they don't represent any people. Each symbol signifies a single truth that when combined, forms the motto of the Tanveer. *Raju. Kovaa. Orpa.* When put together in the ancient tongue, it reads: Truth in all. Honor above all. Justice for all. We were the guardians of the Keep of Aero'set. We were the Tanveer."

There was still so much to tell, but Ayrion was running out of time.

"Even if what you say were true," Sirak said, the tenor of his voice saying that he didn't believe a word of it, "then why would we have left?"

"We left because it was removed."

"What was removed?" Zayden asked.

"The entire city was."

"It was destroyed?"

"No. It was hidden."

"How do you hide an entire city?" Brim asked.

"With magic."

Sirak looked at the others. "Are you saying we can do that here? That we can hide our city from these creatures?"

"No. That was done by magic more powerful than anything we have with us. That was performed by wizards."

"Why would wizards care about protecting an Upakan city?"

Ayrion sighed. Here came the difficult part. "Because the city didn't belong to the Tanveer. It was the head of the wizard council. It was a school built for wielders to come and learn their craft."

The men's faces hardened. "Why would we be anywhere near a school for wizards?" Sirak asked.

"Because we were the paladins of the wizards."

All three froze, the look on their faces bordering between shock and horror.

"We kept the order in Aldor," Ayrion said proudly. "We held the admiration and respect of every kingdom." He took a deep breath. "And I've been asked to bring you home."

"Asked?" Zayden, like the others, looked bewildered. "Asked by who?"

"By the one remaining wizard in Aldor. The Keep of Aero'set has been returned, and he wishes the Tanveer to take their rightful place as its guardians. To become the warriors we were sworn to be. Not this pathetic shell of a people we've become."

The flaps at the front of the tent moved, and Bek stepped in with Ferrin in tow. Ayrion could see his father's ring in Ferrin's hands, and he motioned Ferrin over.

"Were you able to do it?"

Ferrin handed Ayrion the ring. "Of course." He looked at the three primaries. "I can see by the dazed expression on their faces that you told them."

Ayrion didn't respond but kept his eyes on the three seats. "Whether you choose to believe me or not, none of this will matter if we don't survive here and now. Ironic as it may seem, the very creatures we are battling out there are the same ones we fought a millennia ago during the Wizard Wars. We stood at the forefront of that great battle as its victors, and now here we are again. Except this time, we fight as a people with a divided heart. And if we don't find some way to bring it back together, we aren't going to survive."

"And how do you suggest we fight in such a manner?" Zayden asked, the first willing to speak.

"We need to get rid of all semblances of what divides us." He turned and looked out the front of the tent. "Their uniforms have patches, do they not?"

Zayden nodded. "Of course."

"Then we need to get rid of them."

Sirak's fingers clenched the arms of his chair as he bristled.

"We need to separate the men into ranks, not clans. Archers with archers, spearman with spearmen. Those more skilled at close combat need to be together, no matter who they've pledged their loyalty to. I can't say this enough: Either we fight as one people, or we lose this war. I can't be the one to continue holding the front line. None of us can. We need to rotate our fighters. Give those at the front a chance to pull back and rest while those behind fill their place."

He watched the three men, hoping for some glimmer that what he was saying was getting through. Other than perhaps Zayden, the other two didn't look convinced. Ayrion gritted his teeth. He had to undo generations of division in less than an hour.

"Our people haven't fought like this for over a thousand years. And it shows. What I've seen so far looks more like a tavern brawl than an organized campaign, everyone rushing in to claim their piece of glory over the others . . . and our people are dying because of it. Go look at the bodies lying up in the city square. Who knows, perhaps they'll be carrying one of you up there this evening."

That thought seemed to get Zayden's and Sirak's attention, their eyes softening.

Ayrion held firm. "Unfortunately for all of us, we are out of time. We need to bring the clans together, but as long as they wear those patches, they'll never be willing to stand side by side. Take them off, and it's hard to tell one Upakan from another."

"They will with these," Zayden said, holding up his ring.

Ayrion smiled, holding up his own ring so the primaries could see, showing that it now bore all three symbols. "No longer a single emblem to represent one's clan, but three to represent our people, the motto of the Tanveer. Truth In All. Honor Above All. Justice For All. This is who we were, and it's who we need to be again."

A hand slammed down on the arm of the chair, and this time it wasn't Brim. Sirak looked Ayrion in the eyes. "I will not trade who I am for anything."

Ayrion held his gaze. "You're not willing to set your pride aside if it means saving your people?"

Sirak jumped to his feet, startling the other two, and then marched out of the tent. Brim looked at Zayden, then stood and followed Sirak out, smirking at Ayrion on the way by.

Zayden sighed. "You've persuaded me, but without the others, I'm afraid it won't be enough." With that, he stood and left the tent as well.

"That didn't go quite as I was hoping," Ayrion's father said.

Ayrion took a deep breath and exhaled. "Actually, it went better than I thought it would."

"Really?" Ferrin asked. "What part of that did you think went better? The part where they said shove off, or the part where they marched out and all but spat at you on the way?"

"I half expected them to leave as soon as I started talking about Aero'set and our Tanveer heritage. It's not like I have any proof apart from my word and those of a group of outsiders."

"Yeah, don't know how the wizard expected you to be able to manage that one."

Ayrion sighed. "We are a proud people, and a stubborn one. I didn't expect them to suddenly throw away everything they've held to be true and merge the clans just because I said so. It's going to take coming to the brink before they realize what I'm saying is true. I just hope they realize it before it's too late."

Chapter 56 | Ayrion

OW BAD IS IT?" Ayrion asked.

Lenara sat on a stool in the middle of the tunnel, holding back the horde of khuls beating on her shield. She was pale. Sweat beaded her forehead, and her arms were shaking.

"The food and drink helped, but I'm not going to be able to hold them much longer. Whatever you're planning, do it quickly."

"Do you have enough left for some fire?"

"Not if you want me conscious. As soon as I release this shield, I'm going to need to be taken back to camp. It will be up to you after that."

"Then save what you can. We might need another shield before this night is through."

"What you want and what I can do are two different things."

Ayrion beckoned at his nephew, who was standing off to the side of the tunnel with Ayrion's father and brother. "I need your help."

Davin rushed over.

"I need you to stay with Lenara. As soon as she lowers the shield, carry her out of the fight and back to camp. See that she gets anything that she needs. In fact, take her to the infirmary and have Rae look at her."

"No," Lenara said. "Rae needs to focus her magic on those who are actually injured. There's nothing she can do for me that some rest and food cannot."

Ayrion nodded, then looked at Davin. "Make sure you stay by her side. We can't afford to lose her."

"I'm touched," Lenara said sarcastically.

"Don't be. It's your magic I'm concerned about." He flashed her a sheepish grin, then headed back to the front as the first of the clans' fighters began to pour into the tunnel behind them. Sadly, what he said was true. If it hadn't been for Lenara's magic, the khuls would have probably pushed them all the way back to the encampment by now. No telling how many Upakans they would have lost in the process. He needed her abilities. He was really regretting not being able to bring Ty along. He could have used the faeling's gifts.

It didn't take long before all three clans were once again moving up to take their positions in front of the invisible barrier.

"Where do you want me?"

Ayrion turned, surprised to find Zayden and a couple of his men standing behind him. Even more so, to find that the Raju patch on their sleeves was missing. In fact, looking at the fighters standing behind them filling the left side of the tunnel, he noticed the patches on all their uniforms were missing.

Zayden smiled, though it looked strained. "I figure with your experience, we stand a better chance of surviving if we listen. So Raju is at your service, sir. What do you suggest?"

Ayrion turned. They didn't have time to adopt any formal maneuvers. He needed to keep it simple. "Move your archers to the side wall. They'll have higher ground and a better field of view. Also, bring your polemen up behind the first row of fighters. Hopefully they can slow the khuls' advance and give us time to meet them head on before they overpower us. And most importantly, organize the rest of your men into three groups and rotate them as often as you can."

Zayden nodded and started directing the men standing with him to see to it. Ayrion allowed himself a sigh of relief. He'd been wondering how best to force Sirak and Brim to see reason, and this could be it. Along with the benefit of turning one of the clan heads in his favor, if Zayden was able to get his troops in line, Sirak and Brim would have no choice but to see how advantageous it would be to follow Ayrion's advice. From what he had seen, Sirak's warriors were likely to break on the next run.

Ayrion watched as the Raju fighters got into position, waiting as long as he dared for them to find their place, but they didn't have the time needed to truly organize in proper fashion. One look at Lenara, and it was clear the wall was about to come down whether they were ready or not.

Ayrion stood at the front of the line, his hand in the air as he waited for Sirak to get his Kovaa fighters into place on the right. Unlike Raju, they proudly wore their clan's patches. The men in Kovaa were pressing against those in Raju, as the two clans were forced to bunch together inside the tunnel directly behind Ayrion and his team.

Brim and Clan Orpa were holding the rear.

Sirak had fire in his eyes when he looked at Ayrion, his anger still seething from their earlier meeting. It was going to take a lot more than Ayrion's words to convince him to give up his clan. Ayrion hoped it didn't take them getting wiped out.

Sirak was the one to convince. Zayden was apparently on his side for now. And Brim . . . Well, no matter what Ayrion said, Brim was never going to be on his side, so Sirak was the one Ayrion needed. Kovaa was the largest of the three clans, which would hold a lot of sway when it came to fighting a war.

Sirak finally managed to get his fighters into place as best he could, and Ayrion signaled for Lenara to release the shield. Lenara dropped the invisible wall that the khuls were still pounding and collapsed into Davin's arms. His nephew hefted the exhausted bulradoer up and promptly carried her back through the ranks toward camp.

Ayrion drew his second sword as he watched the mound of flesh and fur in front of them barrel down the tunnel like an unstoppable wave. To his left, Raju's poles bristled from the front lines, bracing for the attack. The Kovaa fighters on the right were bunched together so tightly Ayrion wondered how they were going to swing without killing each other.

A volley of arrows flew past from the Raju archers, carving a hole on the leftmost side of the front line as khuls fell. It took a while before the Kovaa archers got their first volley off, which was haphazard at best, and too slow to meet the front wave, striking at those behind. The Kovaa archers were too busy trying to stay out of the Kovaa fighters' way to be of any real assistance.

The khuls roared as they neared the Raju line, dropping as the polemen thrust, pulled, and thrust again, taking down one after another. With the help of the archers, the pile of dead and dying khuls on the left side began to grow, forcing the creatures to shift to the right and directly into Sirak and Kovaa's field of battle.

Sirak wasn't prepared to take on the full brunt of the khul force as they pounded against the Upakans' front line. Ayrion caught what he could from the middle as the khuls tried to push forward. Bodies and pieces of bodies began to stack at Ayrion's feet as his black swords moved with deadly speed and accuracy. He breathed through his nose as much as possible and tried to keep his mouth shut against the spray of blood as he continued to fight.

Bek was there as well, fighting to Ayrion's right. He stumbled as one of the khuls leaped over two others unexpectedly and slammed into him from the side. Ayrion spun and took the creature's head off before he could dig his fangs into Bek's shoulder.

"Thanks," Bek shouted and buried his hatchets into the head of a khul and the chest of another.

Myron was back on his feet, having been given a little healing from Rae during their earlier break. This time he was on Ayrion's left, fighting between Ayrion and the rest of Ayrion's family. He looked fit and rested, and proved it by cutting the arm from one khul and then burying his sword to the hilt in its chest.

Several khuls broke rank and charged their position. Ayrion took down the first two, but not before the others made it past. Myron fought them off as best he could, but rested or not, he was no match for three khuls and was forced back.

A roar from behind was all the warning they had before a blur of white fur leaped on the khuls. Nola sank her teeth into the neck of the first and flung it to the side, and then went claw to claw with the other two. One of the khuls attempted to climb on top of her while the other was being ripped apart, but Myron managed to cut its legs out from under it, and it went down. He buried his sword through its chest about the time Nola ripped open the second one's gut, then left it to die.

To Ayrion's right, Kovaa was breaking, never having recovered from taking the initial brunt of the khul charge. They were now going head-to-head with the creatures, which was a terrible idea when you were fighting something that much bigger and stronger. The Upakans were fast and deadly, dashing in and out as they struck like vipers, but the khuls were relentless and held vastly superior numbers.

By the time the Kovaa fighters had managed to start to shift the khuls' advance back toward the center, their clan was spending most of their time dragging their injured off the field. Their ranks were collapsing.

Ayrion danced between the creatures' claws, cleavers, and stone hammers. Using his visions, he cut them down in alarming numbers, but the more he killed, the more their attention seemed to focus on him. His legs burned, and his arms were growing heavy. Looking around, he realized none of those he'd been fighting with were still there. Not Bek, not Myron, not even his father or brother. They must have already swapped with those behind.

If he didn't do the same, he wouldn't be able to continue.

He wished he knew how much longer they had till morning. It felt like they'd been fighting for days. He spun and cut the legs out from another khul, kicked it back into the next, and used the small window to turn and call for those behind to take his place. But just as soon as he opened his mouth, the Kovaa front line broke. Sirak was one of the first to go down, and his men folded in to save him, which let even more khuls through.

The fools were about to open a full breach. Ayrion turned to shout for help from the Raju fighters, but they were already standing against the turning khul advance. He didn't have time to think. As fast as he could, he cut his way toward the right flank. Khuls were already making it past the right side of Kovaa, near the tunnel wall. If they didn't seal the breach, they were going to make it all the way through.

He cut, stabbed, and hacked through the creatures until he could barely keep going, forced to a standstill as he ran into a wall of khuls hammering to break through the right flank. His swords bit into anything with fur, but the creatures kept coming. His best just wasn't enough. He couldn't reach Sirak. For all he knew, the primary was already dead.

A horn sounded on his right, and a group of Orpa fighters suddenly broke through the line beside him, cutting their way to the front. Ayrion turned to find Brim standing directly on his right. He slashed down the khuls in front as fast as his sword and axe would allow. Brim turned, and for a brief moment, their eyes met, and the primary actually nodded, then jumped back into the fight, as though it was no strange thing to be fighting side by side with someone you had sworn to kill.

For a moment, Ayrion felt like he had never left Orpa. Pride swelled from within. His clan had finally recognized . . .

A cold dose of reality crashed over him, and he shook his head. Clan pride was killing the Upaka.

"We've got to reach Sirak!" Ayrion shouted, and Brim and his warriors followed him in, cutting their way forward. Like the tip of a spear, they pushed through the khuls and reformed the line in front of Kovaa, who were now fighting to drag their people back.

Ayrion caught a glimpse of Sirak as he was borne out. His front had been raked by claws. He looked much the way his father had when Ayrion had first seen him. His eyes were open, but who knew for how long.

The remaining Kovaa fighters, along with those of Orpa, quickly dealt with the khuls who'd managed to take advantage of the gap in their flank and dispatched them before they could make a break down the tunnel for their camp.

The Upakan line was holding, but they were losing ground by the minute. A quick glance over his shoulder, and Ayrion could see they weren't that far from the encampment. If they couldn't hold them here, everything would be lost.

"Didn't you take a break?"

Ayrion turned to find Bek and Myron on his left, cutting their way through two khuls to reach him. "No time. The line was collapsing."

"Well, it's not now," Bek said. "Get out of here before *you* collapse."

Ayrion knew they were right, and he pulled back, letting those behind move up. He pushed his way through the men still struggling to carry their fallen out.

He reached the end of the line and realized he was standing *in* the camp.

Panic washed over him. If they didn't do something to turn the tide, this fight was about to be over. If they breached the encampment, there would be no way to evacuate the wounded. He ran for the makeshift smithy on the other side of the cavern. He could hear Ferrin's hammer still ringing, but he was going to need the man's swords more than his magic right now.

Passing the command pavilion, Ayrion noticed that not even the guards were still standing in front. Every able body was either in the tunnel fighting or hauling the injured back to the infirmary. He stopped at the crude smithy, which wasn't much more than a small forge, an anvil, and some rough tools. "I need you."

Ferrin dropped his hammer and looked up. "Finally." He pulled off his leather apron, dunked his hands and head inside a barrel of water—which flattened his almost shoulder-length red hair to the back of his neck—then grabbed his belt and newly forged wolf blades and strapped them on.

Ayrion directed them toward the tunnel exit, which led back up to the city.

"Where are we going?" Ferrin asked.

"The infirmary. We need to get some help."

They jogged across the camp for the large tent near the exit. Men were lying in groups all around the outside, leaving only a single path to and from the infirmary's entrance, and Ayrion headed straight through the front flap.

The inside of the infirmary was even more packed than the outside, men with open wounds lying in cots and on the floor, waiting to be healed or left to die. Others were still carrying the worst in, and Ayrion moved aside to let them through.

Rae's face was pale, her eyes bloodshot as she went from one to the next, offering them just enough healing to keep them alive. Ferrin came in behind Ayrion, took one look at her, and started across the tent. "You need to stop."

Zynora met him as he was trying to lift her up and carry her out. "Leave her. She will be fine. I'm seeing to her." She stuffed a ball of something inside Rae's mouth, and Rae automatically began to chew.

Rae pushed Ferrin back. "I can manage."

"We will not let her go beyond what she is capable of," Tameel said, offering Rae a sip of something that held a hint of cloves.

"How goes the battle?" Elson asked, moving between the injured, cleaning wounds.

"The khuls are nearly on the camp," Ayrion said. "If we don't turn this around now, I'm afraid we might not survive the night." He looked at Zynora. "It's time."

"I've been wondering how much longer it would take before you came." She handed a jar of white cream to Tameel and started for the exit.

Ayrion turned to Ferrin. "I need your help."

Ferrin gave Rae a single kiss and then headed out the door behind Zynora. Ayrion looked at both Rae and Tameel. "I promise I'll bring them back to you." He turned and started for the front flap but was stopped as someone grabbed his arm. He turned to find Sirak lying on a cot beside the door.

The front of his uniform was covered in blood. "I wanted to say that I'm sorry . . ." He started to cough, spitting up blood as he did. "I should have listened."

Ayrion gripped Sirak's hand gently. "Save your strength. Your people need you." With that, he turned and walked out of the tent and met Ferrin and Zynora at the end of the narrow corridor of wounded and dying warriors. "Let's go. We don't have much time."

Chapter 57 | Ayrion

AYRION SKIRTED COOKFIRES and bedding as they crossed the camp to the tunnel on the other side. The rear of the Upakan force now spilled partway into the cavern.

"I didn't realize they were this close," Ferrin said, checking his new sword and dagger.

"Oh my, that does look bad," Zynora said, hurrying to match the men's longer strides.

They passed Lenara and Davin, who were both sitting at one of the cookfires while Lenara attacked a bowl of vegetable broth. She looked barely strong enough to lift it to her mouth.

"Still alive?" Ayrion asked, not slowing.

Lenara looked up and nodded but didn't say anything.

"Keep your eye on her," he called over his shoulder to Davin.

"I will, Uncle Ayrion."

Ayrion smiled. It was the first time his nephew had addressed him as family. He drew his swords as they reached the rearmost men. Most looked to be what was left of Kovaa's broken ranks. He wondered if Brim was still fighting at the front. Those on the left—he didn't see any patches, so he thought they were most likely Raju—looked to be in the worst shape, barely able to stand as they struggled to catch their breath. It seemed Zayden was keeping them rotated after all. *Good man.*

Ayrion turned to Zynora. "Whatever happens, stay between us." He grinned at Ferrin. "Time to break in those weapons."

"Not exactly how I was hoping to," Ferrin said as he fell in behind Zynora, following Ayrion as they pushed their way through the ranks.

"Move!" Ayrion shouted, forcing men out of his way. The ranks were so tight, he could hardly squeeze through. Ahead, he heard the clanging of steel and stone and the shouts of men and roars of khuls. It sounded like the Upakans were giving everything they had. Ayrion had tried to see if he could spot any of his friends or family near Raju as he fought through the ranks, but the tunnel was so completely packed he couldn't see much of anything beyond the men standing directly around him.

They were getting close. Ayrion could feel Zynora pressing against him from behind.

"Where've you been?" someone shouted, and Ayrion turned to find Zayden pushing through the fighters on the left to reach him. The front of his uniform was covered in blood, and he had a deep gash on the side of his face. "We can't hold them much longer. Where's that wielder lady of yours? We need her now."

"She's given all she had. It's up to us. How much longer till morning?"

"No idea."

"Have they ever not pulled back after daylight?"

"Not that I'm aware."

"Then let's hope we can hold until then."

Zayden looked behind Ayrion at Zynora and scowled. "This is no place for an old healer."

"Watch who you're calling old," Zynora shot back.

"Help us clear a path to the front," Ayrion said to Zayden. "Line your men to either side so we can get through."

Zayden began barking orders to the men directly in front of them, and within minutes, a very narrow corridor opened, just wide enough for Ayrion to push them through. The opening closed behind them, leaving them with nowhere to go. If this didn't work, Ayrion wasn't sure how he was going to be able to get Zynora back out.

Of course, if this didn't work, it might not matter.

The gap in the ranks ahead ended at the front, where Ayrion found his father and brother leading a force of Raju into the khuls on the left. They were magnificent. Even at his age, his father was keeping up with Jorn, swing for swing, methodical in their movements as they put every bit of Upakan training to the test. On the right, Ayrion could just make out Bek's head rising above the others. Myron was sure to be close by.

Ayrion turned to Ferrin. "I need you up here with me. We need to give her room to work. Make sure nothing gets by you."

Ferrin raised his wolf blades. "Nothing will."

Ayrion turned to Zayden. "Tell your men to pull back when I give you the signal."

"Why? What are you going to do?"

"Save our lives, hopefully." He didn't have time to explain more.

Ayrion's father cut down another khul on the right. "What do you need?" He got one look at Zynora and frowned but didn't say anything.

"We need to hold the line for as long as possible to give Raju a chance to pull back." The fewer people in Zynora's way, the better chance she had of making an impact. Ayrion had seen the aftermath of her magic firsthand, from Argon being blown through the front of Bek's cabin to her bringing an avalanche down on the Tower's guards and then blowing the remaining bulradoer out of Wellhollow.

"You heard the man," Ayrion's father shouted. "We hold the line!"

Ayrion looked at Zynora. "Do you have enough strength left?" He wanted to kick himself for not asking her that already. He hated to think he might have carried her into the thick of it only to find she was as spent as Lenara. He had no idea how much her own small healing took from her.

Zynora's mouth set into a thin line. "Move aside. I'm getting tired of everyone questioning my abilities."

Ayrion looked at Ferrin. "You heard her. Let's give her some—"

A pack of khuls broke through on the left between Bek and Jorn. The Raju fighters were thrown aside as the khuls barreled through their ranks. Ayrion barely had time to warn Ferrin before the first of the creatures were on top of them.

"Jorn! Protect Zynora!" Ayrion shouted as he hit the oncoming charge. He cut the legs out from the first two, tripping those behind and slowing the drive. He caught glimpses of Ferrin's white wolf handles from the corner of his eye as the smith began cutting and weaving through their ranks like a man possessed. If Ayrion didn't know any better, he would have thought him Upaka trained.

Ayrion's brother pulled back from the front and moved Zynora behind him, while Ayrion, Ferrin, and some men from Raju fought to hold back the oncoming horde. The creatures seemed to realize they were getting close to the Upakans' camp, and they pressed all the harder, forcing Ayrion to use every ounce of his magic to keep them from getting past.

He ducked under a long cleaver and jumped out of the way of a stone hammer; it slammed into the ground where he'd been standing. He cut the arm off the khul holding it, leaving the arm still gripping the handle as he plunged his second blade straight through its neck. He turned just in time to deflect a bludgeon as thick as a beam and opened the chest of the khul swinging it. Stepping over the dying beast, he leaped into the middle of three more, slicing and stabbing in quarters so close the creatures were incapable of moving.

He took a glancing blow to the side, turning his shoulder, but not far enough. The creature's claws ripped through part of his thick leather coat, slicing into his flesh. He winced at the sharp pain but kept his arm moving and stabbed the creature straight through its mouth just as it opened to roar its short-lived victory.

"Ayrion!"

He could hear his name being called, but he was too far in to turn. He dodged to the side as the next khul swept its claws for him, then darted back as another attempted to sink its teeth into his arm. Using his visions, he kept just ahead, but not by much. How far in was he? He dared a quick glance over his bleeding shoulder but saw only fur, fangs, and claws. He could hear his name being called, but he had no idea from where. All he knew was that he needed to keep his swords moving. If he stopped, he was done for.

His visions came so fast that he couldn't keep up with them. That hadn't happened since he had been swarmed by vulraak in Saeida, when his magic had completely consumed him to the point of taking over his body entirely. At some point, the visions became overwhelming to the point of him losing control. He ducked and cut the legs out from another khul, sending it to the ground in time for three more to take its place.

Something hit Ayrion across the back, knocking him into the khul in front of him, but he managed to point his swords as he fell, using his weight to drive them through its chest. He recovered and spun in time to duck a stone hammer, which slammed into the khul beside him, caving in the side of its face and sending teeth, fangs, and blood flying.

A roar sounded just behind him, and Ayrion spun to block the attack, but instead of finding another khul swinging for his head, Nola leapt onto the back of the pack and began tearing into the creatures, giving Ayrion just enough time to cut his way back out. The rush of the fight and fear of not making it back out had him trembling as he finally reached the Upakan line once more. He hadn't realized just how far he'd been drawn into the khuls' ranks.

Thankfully, they hadn't counted on a frostwolf.

Bek, Myron, and Ferrin rushed forward to meet the oncoming khuls as Nola pulled back from her assault and retreated behind the front line.

"Where did you think you were going?" Ferrin asked. "One minute you're there beside me, and the next you've disappeared altogether. Thought you were about to join the other side."

Ayrion glanced over his shoulder. "Zynora?"

"I'm here!" she called out from farther back. Jorn hovered in front of her.

"We need you!" Ayrion was hardly able to catch his breath. The Raju fighters behind him were holding the line for now. He looked for Zayden and found him just behind the front line on the left. "Order your men back!"

Zayden began shouting for his men to retreat. Just over his shoulder, Ayrion could see where the edge of the tunnel ended and the cavern began. Apparently, it wasn't that he had worked his way that deep into the khuls' ranks, but that the Upakan line had pulled back that far.

To his right, a mix of Kovaa and Orpa were still battling to keep the other side from breaching, but they were being driven back just as fast as the left side. If they were going to do this, they had to do it now. Once they broke from the tunnel, Zynora would lose a lot of the effectiveness of her magic. There was also the possibility the force might travel along the cavern wall and injure the Upakans as well.

He beckoned Zynora to him, and Jorn helped her forward, blocking those who were in retreat. On the right, Bek and Myron and a small company of Raju fighters were busy holding back the line. Ayrion's father, Zayden, and another company of fighters kept the creatures from breaking through on the other side. The archers had closed and were keeping a steady volley of arrows flowing into the leftmost khul ranks.

"Are you ready?"

Zynora nodded.

"I'm going to open the line and give you as clear a shot as possible. Don't worry about trying to hit those closest. We'll deal with them in the aftermath. Focus the blast straight down the middle of the tunnel and as far back as you can manage."

Ayrion could see that her hands were shaking, and a flash of uncertainty swept through him. Was she too drained but had refused to tell him?

Zynora took a deep breath. "I'm ready."

"Cut an opening!" he shouted, and those in front of him immediately began to split. As soon as they did, Ayrion saw another battering ram of khul fighters breaking away from the main force, heading their way. "Hurry!"

The khul charge was only feet away, their roars enough to shake the bravest to their core. Zynora lifted her arms, her hands still shaking. Ayrion tensed. The creatures were nearly on her. What was she waiting for?

He swept his blade, cutting down a khul that had come too close to his right, while trying his best to stay out of her line of fire. He stared down the oncoming charge, readying to spring into them, but still Zynora didn't fire.

The khuls were only steps away.

"Now!" he shouted, but nothing happened.

They were too close. Another couple of steps and they would have her. He couldn't wait any longer. With a cry, he rushed the horde. "Hold your ground!" he shouted at those behind him. He swung at the first khul and was suddenly thrown to the side. He thought he might have heard Zynora scream, but everything else was a blur as her magic struck a glancing blow and sent him, and those directly beside him, tumbling across the tunnel floor to the right.

The world around him spun as Zynora's magic swept a wave of khul and Upakan flesh away. He had been on the edge of the wave, so rather than being hurled down the tunnel, he was flung toward the other side, slamming into men from Kovaa and Orpa and the khuls they'd been holding at bay.

As soon as he stopped rolling, he tried to crawl to his feet, only to realize he was nowhere near the ground. He looked down to see he was on top of a pile of bodies, some of whom were just now beginning to move. He sheathed his swords and half crawled, half rolled down the pile of flesh. Stepping back onto solid rock, he drew his sword and turned, ready to take down the next in line, then blinked in confusion. The tunnel itself seemed to be spinning. Had he hit his head that hard during the blast? It didn't help that the force of the blast had snuffed out all the torches.

The light from the cavern behind them bled through just enough for Ayrion to make out that there was no one left to fight. Not a khul stood in the tunnel ahead, all the way to the corner. Dead khuls littered the ground. A large mound of bodies was piled near the back wall where the tunnel bent. Ayrion stared in awe. He had seen Zynora cut sizable swaths out of an enemy rank before, especially the vulraak, but he'd never seen her cause this much damage.

He focused on an odd sound at the edge of his hearing and blanched. The mountain itself was still groaning, and he suddenly realized he could feel a small tremor under his feet. He quickly looked up at the ceiling, worried they might have destabilized the tunnel and risked bringing it down on their heads. He stood there a moment in silence, but eventually, the shaking stopped.

A growl to his right caught his attention, and he turned to find a khul pulling itself up out of the pile he had just climbed down. Ayrion opened its neck with a flick of his wrist.

He turned and called for Zayden and his men to finish off the rest of them before they made it to their feet, and then went to look for Zynora and Jorn.

He spotted them and stumbled over to where Jorn knelt, cradling Zynora's head in his lap. Ayrion dropped down beside her to see how she was, but her eyes were closed.

His breath caught in his throat, and he immediately reached for her nose, but Jorn pushed his hand away. "She lives. But as soon as she did"—he looked up at the damage—"whatever she did, her eyes rolled up, and she passed out. I had to catch her to keep her from hitting her head."

Ayrion breathed a small sigh of relief as he placed his hand down over the old woman's. "Let's get her back to camp. I want Rae to look at her."

Jorn stood, and Ayrion placed Zynora in his brother's arms. Ayrion wasn't sure he trusted his own strength at that moment. Jorn bore cuts across his uniform, blood seeping through at least half of them. Ayrion needed Rae to look at him as well.

Jorn nodded toward the dead khuls. "What about them?"

Ayrion listened, but there was no sound of further pursuit. "We'll send out a scouting party to see the extent of the damage. If we're lucky, maybe it was bad enough they will crawl back in their hole until tomorrow."

"They haven't so far," Zayden said, limping over. He glanced at Zynora and then shook his head at the damage ahead. "Though they've also never been hit with something like that before either."

"I'll send some men to scout the tunnels and keep watch in case that wasn't enough discouragement for them today."

"You think they'll be back?" Myron asked, looking glum at the possibility.

Zayden stared out at the tunnel of corpses. "Your guess is as good as mine, but I'd rather err on the side of caution." He stood there a moment longer before finally limping off to find some volunteers.

"While we have the time," Ayrion said, "we need to see to our wounded." With that, he turned and helped Jorn carry Zynora back to the infirmary. He was thankful they had survived the night, but the damage had left their forces permanently crippled. Rae wasn't going to be enough to keep an entire army on their feet, which meant the rest was up to him.

He had so much to do and so little time to do it. And a voice at the back of his mind whispered that even if he managed the impossible and brought the clans together, it still wasn't going to be enough.

Chapter 58 | Ty

TY WATCHED WITH EAGER anticipation as Narendi bit down on the soft glazed roll Reloria had just brought to their table. It was still warm enough to see the steam rising from where the butter had melted into the icing.

"Well," he asked, "what do you think?"

Narendi took a moment to finish chewing, then licked the extra glaze from her fingers with a soft whimper and smiled. "I think it's wonderful."

Ty glanced over at Reloria, who was watching from behind the counter. He gave her a thumbs-up, and she smiled with a nod, causing her blue-and-yellow bonnet to tilt forward ever so slightly.

"I've never tasted something so wonderful," Narendi said. "Not even in Aero'set."

Ty cringed and leaned forward. "Best not to mention that here."

"Why? No one knows what it is."

"Best not to take that chance." He glanced around the room. There were quite a few people looking their way. Most would turn when he caught them looking, but it was starting to feel a little strange. He hadn't been gone that long, had he? He quickly felt the top of his head to make sure his cap was covering his white hair. It was. Perhaps it was Narendi they were looking at. She was the first Imbatoo to ever step foot in Easthaven, but it wasn't like she was wearing her typical Mzwati robes and spear.

Narendi didn't seem to be paying much attention to what was happening around her as she demolished the rest of the roll and started on the next. Ty tried not to pay attention and polished off a couple of rolls himself, washing each down with cream from his mug. He couldn't believe how much he'd missed Reloria's shop. She had quite the variety of treats, but these early-morning rolls were some of his favorites.

The longer they sat, the harder it was to ignore the stares and whispers, so instead of ordering another dish of rolls and chatting a while longer, he licked the leftover icing from his lips and stood. Narendi finished the rest of her drink and followed him up. They both waved at Reloria, who was helping another customer with their order but wasn't too busy to wave back and wish them a good day.

"Where do we go next?" Narendi asked as Ty directed her through the tables to the front.

"We'll go to Orlyn's next," he said and opened the door. They stepped out onto the covered porch, moving to the side to allow a family of four to pass. There were a couple of tables and chairs set up in front of the shop for those who wished to eat outside, but this early in the morning, the sun wasn't high enough to warrant it. "I promised him I'd stop by this morning and drop off those wamini plants. Then we'll head over to the East Inn for some lunch, or if we have time, maybe we can stop by Feoldor's and watch him create a beaker or two." Ty had only been to his shop once, but it had been fun to watch him heat and shape the glass.

"I want to come back here again," Narendi said, glancing back through the front window of the Sweet Shop. "I could spend half my gold in this place."

Ty smiled. "That's a lot of sweets." Not only did she have the gold and jewels her father had given her, but she had also managed to squirrel away a few of the gems from the Live Market.

A cold gust of wind had them pulling their jackets tighter. Ty took a moment to look around the city square and then up River Street, making sure to keep an eye out for anyone with fiery red hair. He had told Lyessa that he was going to be showing Narendi around Easthaven this morning to avoid any awkward confrontation, and that once he had finished, his time would then belong to her. Still, he wouldn't put it past Lyessa to show up anyway just to put them on edge. She had a talent for knowing exactly how to get under his skin, a skill she had been perfecting since their days in school.

So far, Narendi's tour had consisted of Josten's mill, the Easthaven docks, the garrison, and the front of the Sidaran Assembly building. They hadn't gone inside because it looked rather busy, and Ty hadn't wanted to suffer flashbacks of his time under Mangora's control.

He had also taken her to see the shops on Wood Lane, and even stopped long enough to show her where Mangora's place had been. The shield hiding her shop from those passing was still in place, but because Narendi was ven'ae, she was able to see past it. They hadn't dared to go inside.

The only places they hadn't stopped at so far were the East Inn and Orlyn's Apothecary.

After finishing a careful scan of the shops around the center of town and feeling confident that Lyessa wasn't lurking nearby, he stepped off the porch. "This way," he said, and they both started up River Street. The city felt so different now. Not that long ago, he would have considered it an adventure to ride into Easthaven. How grand it had felt. Now, it seemed almost ordinary. He was afraid Aero'set had spoiled him. Still, this was home.

The city was different in another way. Where it had always felt so inviting before—the people waving, stopping in the street to find out how each other were doing—it seemed almost cold now, and it wasn't the snow-packed streets. The people moved about the city with a more determined stride. Few lingered outdoors. Those who did remained near the walkways, since it seemed the streets themselves had been taken over by lancer patrols. You could almost feel the apprehension in the air.

Easthaven was like a calm waiting for the storm. No one seemed to know when it would hit, only that it would.

"What is this Apoth . . . curry—"

"Apothecary?" Ty smiled. "Orlyn is like Isha in a way. He uses herbs and other plants to make tonics and tinctures and basic remedies to help heal illnesses."

"Oh."

"You'll enjoy his shop. He has a lot of unique plants."

Of course, coming from the Wengoby Desert, every plant was unique to her.

They didn't have to go far before Ty was directing them off the street and over to the front of Orlyn's shop. Narendi stopped long enough to look up at the sign before following Ty inside.

The bell over the door announced their arrival, but Master Orlyn was busy with customers and not able to offer much more than a hearty "Welcome" and "I'll be right with you." He didn't even look up from his table at the back to see who it was he was greeting.

As soon as her eyes adjusted to the dimmer light inside, Narendi gawked at all the florae, specifically the ones growing up the walls, along the rafters, and up through the cracks in the floor. "Looks like Douina's," she said, "but even more."

Ty smiled. "Told you."

They moved through the aisles, slowly examining the broad selection of herbs as well as various plants filling each shelf, stopping every so often when Narendi wanted to inspect something more closely. She tended to stop and smell each new flower she saw.

They rounded the end of one aisle to find several children standing there, staring at them.

"Why are they looking at us?" Narendi whispered, trying to offer the kids a polite smile. "Everywhere we go, people are staring."

"You've noticed that too?"

"Of course. How could I not?"

"You hadn't said anything, so I thought it was just me." He started to ask what the kids wanted when a girl from the group finally spoke.

"Are you one of them?"

"Are we one of what?" Ty asked.

"One of those magic people."

Ty's eyes widened. He was suddenly at a loss for words. Was that why people were staring at them? Why would they think he had magic? "What magic people are you talking about?"

The girl turned and pointed at Orlyn.

Ty was even more stunned. How did people know that Orlyn had magic? He looked down at the girl. "Why do you think the apothecary has magic?"

She twisted her face like he was the most ignorant person she'd ever met. "Everyone knows." One of the mothers turned and, seeing him and Narendi, quickly pulled her child away, prompting the others to do the same.

What was happening in Easthaven?

"Is this strange?" Narendi asked as they moved to an aisle at the back where they couldn't be seen. "I didn't think they knew of magic here."

"It is strange. I've never had anyone ask me that before." He was reminded of his last encounter in the shop with a couple of magic-wary customers and how they had immediately informed the Black Watch of their suspicions that Orlyn was a wielder. It hadn't ended very well for either of them, as they had been taken into custody along with Master Orlyn. Ty wondered if the two had managed to escape during the battle with the wielder council in the Easthaven garrison or if they had been taken on to the Tower. As much as he hated what they had done, he didn't wish the Tower on anyone.

Narendi finished browsing the last of the shelves on that aisle and moved to the next, pulling Ty from his musings. He moved with her, and they continued to peruse some of the other shelves near the back. It took a while for Orlyn to finally notice them, and when he did, he waved. "Give me a minute to finish up here, and I'll be with you shortly."

Ty nodded. "No need to rush." For once, he didn't feel the pressure of needing to be anywhere specific. Normally, after waking, they were scarfing down their breakfast and rushing out to the Aero'set garrison for training with Ayrion. But this morning when he had opened his eyes, he'd closed them again and turned over to continue sleeping . . . until Narendi began pounding on his door, demanding breakfast before their practice.

Keeping her promise to Ayrion, she had both brothers out in the yard running through drills before their food even had time to digest. By the time they'd finished, all three were ready for a good scrubbing. They had spent the next hour or two refilling the tub, as they each took turns cleaning off what was left of Reed Marsh. The night before, they'd been too exhausted after their journey home to worry about bathing.

The bell over the door rang once more, and Ty looked up to see that Orlyn was no longer behind his table. Ty peered out from behind the shelf. The shop was empty. Orlyn locked the front door and started to pull the shade. "Closing early for lunch," he said to a couple of ladies peering in from outside, then pulled the shade the rest of the way and turned. "Good a time as any, I suspect." He motioned them over to his measuring table at the back.

"What is happening in Easthaven?" Ty asked.

Orlyn looked up. "What do you mean?"

"Didn't you hear those children? They asked me and Narendi if we were one of the magic people."

"Oh, that. Yes, well, I'm afraid that word of our deeds has spread through the city."

"What deeds?"

"After our battle with the Tower in the garrison, and more importantly, what took place inside the Assembly building, it looks like our secrecy has come to an end. When you find yourself fighting to save three members of the Provincial Authority, people tend to find out."

Ty gulped. "Do they know it *wasn't* me trying to kill them? That I was being controlled?" He began to panic. "Do the people think I'm here to hurt them?"

Orlyn shook his head. "The only ones who saw you have already been told, though if the overlords were to ever meet here again, it might be best to stay as far away from them as possible." He chuckled. Ty, however, didn't think it was all that funny. "Anyway," Orlyn continued, "there were plenty of lancer guards and Assembly members there who happened to witness our fight, and let's not forget Barl introducing us to the whole Assembly afterward. Something like that isn't going to stay hidden for long."

Ty nodded. "I remember. I can still see the looks on their faces when he brought that arachnobe in for them to see."

Orlyn grinned. "Yes, that was quite the shock, wasn't it?"

"To say the least."

"It wasn't long after that the news of who we were began to spread. The first few weeks after you left were the worst. Thankfully, people have been more curious than anything. Though there have been plenty who have been quite vocal about not wanting us here, or their disagreement with Barl's decision to open Sidara as a haven for wielders. He's taken a great risk. Your sister said that the histories have told of other overlords in the past who tried to be lenient to wielders. Apparently, it never ended well for them. Let's hope history doesn't repeat itself."

Ty nodded. "Which means we probably should be keeping a closer eye on Lord Barl."

"Aye," Orlyn said. "Your father is with him most days. No one I'd trust him with more. Other than yourself, of course." He stared at the pack on Ty's shoulder. "So, what brings you in today? Hopefully something for me?"

Ty placed the satchel on the table and opened it. "We brought those wamini plants for you to take a look at." He also pulled out a slip of paper and handed it to Orlyn. "I forgot that Isha wrote down her recipe for her healing cream."

Orlyn quickly scanned the list, pursing his lips as he did. "Hmm. It looks like one of the main ingredients is sherakin milk." He looked up. "Didn't happen to bring any of that along, did you?"

Ty chuckled. "Afraid not."

"I see. Well, at least I can take a look at these new plants of yours and see what properties they might have." He picked up one of the plants, which had long begun to wilt, and motioned them toward his workroom in back.

They followed him into the next room. Ty didn't remember ever seeing Orlyn's workshop before. It was bigger than he would have thought, and far more cluttered. There wasn't a shelf or desk or chair, or even a spot of the floor that wasn't occupied with a bag of this or a jar of that. Orlyn grabbed a pot from under one of the tables, filled it with some fresh soil from a nearby bag, and then placed it on top of a stack of books.

"What are you doing?" Narendi asked as she and Ty walked over to inspect Orlyn's work.

"Just wait," he said, then he stuck his finger in the dirt to make a small hole and placed the wilted stalk of the wamini inside. He then pressed the soil back around it and turned. "Hand me my staff, will you, please?"

Ty grabbed the long, rune-covered piece of wood and handed it to him. A moment later, the runes began to glow, and the plant started to move.

Narendi gasped, grabbing Ty's arm and pointing, then took a few steps closer and watched as the wamini went from brown and withered to green and vibrant, standing up on its own in the soil. "That is such a wondrous gift to have."

Orlyn smiled. "I won't argue with you there." He looked down at the plant and cocked his head. "I think I have the perfect spot for you." He picked up the pot and started for another door at the side. "Come. I think you will like this."

Ty followed him across the room and waited while Orlyn fished a key from his pocket. Unlocking the door, Orlyn gave them a quick smile, then headed down. As soon as the door opened, Ty was hit with a strong, pleasing odor that wafted up from the stairwell below. It reminded him of the forest, full of life. The smells were intoxicating. Some he had never experienced before. He wanted to shove Narendi aside and race down, but he fought the urge and waited for her to go in first.

The inside of the stairwell was filled with flowering vines, compact enough that Ty was having a difficult time not tripping on the ones growing around the steps. He heard Narendi gasp and rushed in after her.

He nearly tripped on his own feet, coming to a stop. "What in Aldor?"

It was incredible.

"It's like the glass house in Aero'set," Narendi mumbled, still in awe as she spun in a circle to take it all in.

She wasn't wrong. It was like stepping through a mirror and back into Y'tarra, the lush garden paradise Nyalis had taken him to. The In Between, as the wizard had called it. It was beautiful. There were plants he'd never seen before, some with colors so brilliant they made him want to squint, and the sizes were all wrong, but they were still perfect—mushrooms as tall as a man, fully grown trees that fit inside a house. It was extraordinary.

"What is this place?" Ty asked.

"It is home," Orlyn said.

"How long has it been here?"

"Oh, I've been working on these for many, many years. There have been others before them. As I run out of room, I tend to release those that have been here the longest in order to give room for the newer of my creations."

"It smells lovely," Narendi said, walking over to one of the large mushrooms to feel the gills along the bottom and stare at the colorful patches on top.

Orlyn moved to an empty spot of grass underneath a blue wisteria plant with streamers so long they trailed along the ground. He pulled a trowel out from one of the inner pockets of his baggy robe. He knelt and dug around in the dirt, just deep enough to place the wamini inside, firming the soil around the plant. Taking his rune staff, which was already glowing, he placed his hand on the soil, and the wamini began to grow. Once the stem thickened and the leaves retook their rich green color, the runes on Orlyn's staff faded, and he stood.

"I'll replant the others here beside this one." His stomach growled, and he patted his waistline. "But I guess I can wait until after lunch." He pointed back toward the door. "Shall we?"

Ty quickly spun once more, taking it all in. He could have spent the entire day examining the plants. But Orlyn was right. It was time to eat. Stopping at Reloria's for a midmorning snack had offset his hunger, but he was sure that by the time they reached the inn, his stomach would be growling with Orlyn's.

They headed back upstairs, and Ty walked back into the shop to collect his pack. He left the plants sitting on the table. "Looks like you have customers waiting." There was a group of ladies peeking through the front window.

"Yes, they won't give me a moment's peace," Orlyn griped.

"Does Mistress Sorna still come around?" Ty asked. "I seem to remember you telling us that she tended to hang around the shop more than most, but I didn't see her outside just now."

Orlyn blushed and cleared his throat. "I, uh . . . no, I haven't seen her today, though she does still come by. Lovely woman, though a bit forceful." He cleared his throat again. "Enough of this foolishness. Come, let's eat."

They followed the apothecary out through the back entrance and down the alley, which opened directly across from the side of the East Inn. From there, he poked his head out to make sure no one was watching, and they scurried from the alley, across the street, and around to the front, where they darted inside.

"This is fun," Narendi said.

"Greetings, Master Orlyn," Bue Aboloff said as they stepped into the half-filled lobby. "The chowder is piping hot."

Orlyn smiled as he patted his stomach. "Ah, just how I like it, thank you."

"And a very good day to you, Master Ty. Haven't seen you here since last year. I heard you were traveling to see family somewhere west of here. I hope you found them well." He glanced sideways at Narendi.

"I did," Ty said, quickly trying to think of what to add to it. "I had an uncle take sick, and my aunt needed help on the farm while he recovered."

"You're a good man, and your father too for being willing to let you go, especially so soon after . . ." He didn't finish.

Ty smiled. "Getting away for a while helped me deal with her passing."

Bue nodded. "I completely understand." His head suddenly lifted. "I hope you will be gracing us this evening with that famous flute of yours."

"What?"

"Don't tell me you forgot what day of the month it is. It's Performance Night tonight. And I can't think of a better way to draw a crowd than to say you will be performing. I know a certain overlord's daughter is scheduled to play," he said with a wink, then paused slightly as he noticed Narendi's face harden.

Ty blushed. Did everyone know about him and Lyessa? "I'll see what I can do."

"Wonderful." Bue then turned to Narendi. "Don't believe I've had the pleasure."

"Sorry," Ty said. "This is Narendi Unsala. She'll be visiting with us for a couple of weeks." Ty looked at Narendi. "This is Bue Aboloff, the proprietor of the East Inn."

Bue took off his hat and offered Narendi a flourishing bow. "Lovely to have you with us, young lady. I do hope your stay will be a pleasant one and that you will be sure to frequent the East Inn whenever you're in town."

Narendi smiled. "If the food is as good as it smells, I'm sure I will."

Bue bowed once more, then quickly turned to greet the next group coming in.

"Let's get a move on," Orlyn said, making his way to the side stairs leading up to the balcony. "Don't want the others eating all our food."

Ty and Narendi followed him up.

"What's this Performance Night?" Narendi asked.

"Twice a month, Bue and Noreen open the inn for a night of music and recitation. People come to eat and drink and listen to a wide range of performances, some good."

Orlyn cut in. "Some not so good."

"So are you good or not good?"

"Oh, he's very good," Orlyn said over his shoulder with a wink.

Ty shook his head. "I'm alright."

"And you will play that flute you made? I've heard you. You are good."

"Thanks. I'll play the one my father made."

"And Lyessa will be there?"

Ty could hear the tension in her voice.

"That's what Bue said. She usually performs with her harp."

"What's a harp?"

"I'm not sure how to explain it. It has a bunch of strings, and you pluck them to make music."

"Is she good?"

Ty was almost afraid to answer. "Yes."

Narendi frowned.

They reached the top of the stairs and found the balcony only half-occupied. The council's two tables at the back were already pushed together, and it looked as though two-thirds of the seats were already filled. Ty breathed a small sigh of relief when he realized Lyessa wasn't one of them. The last time Ty had visited the inn, apart from the quick look inside when they first got to town, was the day he had said his goodbyes to her. On their way across the balcony, he glanced over at the table near the edge where he and Lyessa had shared their first kiss. He suddenly couldn't think of anything else.

"Where all did you two go?" Breen asked, pulling Ty from his musings. His brother was seated at the back next to Fraya. It appeared they had saved Ty and Narendi seats next to theirs.

Ty held Narendi's chair out, then took his own. "I took her on a tour of the city."

"I'm guessing Reloria's was one of the first stops," Fraya said with a grin.

"It wasn't the first, but it was certainly one of them."

"Her rolls are delicious," Narendi said.

"Yes, they are," Fraya agreed.

Looking around the tables, it seemed Reloria and Feoldor were two of the council members who hadn't made it yet.

"Have you noticed the way people have been looking at us since we've been back?" Breen asked. "Fraya says that the city knows about the wielder council."

"I know," Ty said. "We had some children confront us about it in the apothecary. I couldn't believe it. People have been staring at us all over town." Ty glanced around the balcony and found more than one table with heads swiveling in their direction.

"Can't say I like it much," Breen said. "Easier when people didn't know who we were."

"Afraid that was always inevitable," their father said from the end of the table. "Especially with things moving in the direction they are. I'm just thankful the people have been mostly receptive."

"Aye," Orlyn agreed. "It could have certainly been worse. Making a few plants grow for my customers is a small price to pay. If this had happened in any other kingdom, who knows what might have been. As it stands, we find ourselves fortunate, indeed."

"Wonder if that means I can start taking my cap off?" Ty mused.

His father thumbed his chin. "It's one thing for people to recognize you. It's another to blatantly draw attention. If I were you, I'd hold off as long as possible, especially considering your short stay." The look on Ty's father's face said he still wasn't happy with his sons being whisked away from their home again.

Ty didn't like it much either, considering how much their father had already lost. Their mother was gone, Adarra was on some insane mission to the Isle of Tallos, and Ty and Breen were set to leave in a couple of weeks. When that happened, their father would be left with no one. It was kind of hard to run a homestead by yourself. Ty was going to need to talk with Breen about them hiring someone on to help their father while they were away. It wasn't like they didn't have the gold now to do it. The small bag of gold Nyalis had given them before leaving would hopefully be enough to help, as long as they didn't find need of it before then.

Feoldor and Reloria were the next to arrive, then eventually Veldon. By the time the dockmaster had taken his seat, the others had already finished at least one drink and were working on a second.

"About time," Feoldor grumbled. "I thought I was going to have to start chewing on Orlyn's arm. And we all know how tough and stringy that's sure to be."

Ty knew he was joking, but it brought back unpleasant memories of the pygmies inside the Aero'set library, and he cringed.

"Then I guess you arrived just in time," Orlyn said. "Last thing I want is to catch some wild disease from Feoldor's mouth." The two scowled at each other, at least until the waiter showed up, then all thoughts of cannibalism flew over the balcony rail as they quickly ordered their lunches.

The food was delicious as always. After hearing Bue going on about the chowder, Ty had decided to give it a try and was thankful he did. The meal continued mostly in silence as everyone focused on transporting the food from plate to mouth. Afterward, a couple of the men pulled out their pipes and had a quick smoke as they discussed the events of the day.

There wasn't much to discuss since their last meeting. Ty told them of his and Narendi's brief tour of the city.

"Sounds like you stopped by everyone's shop but mine," Feoldor said. "Ate at Reloria's, visited Veldon at the docks, even went to Orlyn's to drop off plants. Why is it no one wants to come by my place?"

"Cause it's hot as blazes in there," Orlyn said.

"Not all the time."

"Actually," Ty cut in, "I was planning on taking Narendi by later today if we have time before Performance Night."

Feoldor grinned. "Good. That will give me time to clean up a bit."

"If that's the case," Reloria said with a cheeky grin, "then you better get started now."

Feoldor scooted his chair back from the table. "You're probably right. I'll see you all this evening."

"Don't forget we have a council meeting tonight," Veldon said before he left. "I forgot it was Performance Night, but I guess we can meet briefly afterward, if it's not too late for everyone."

"Fine with me," Feoldor said, then scurried past.

Ty looked at Narendi. "You ready to see some more of the city?"

She smiled and they stood. "Can we stop back at the Sweet Shop?"

Ty nodded. "You don't have to ask me twice."

"You come by anytime you like," Reloria said. "Just make sure it's not when I'm on lunch."

Ty turned to Veldon, who was just rising from his own seat. "Are we meeting for anything in particular?"

"Yes, we mentioned at the last meeting that we needed to discuss arrangements for possible training. During our last two encounters with the Tower, luck more than anything kept us alive. We can't keep relying on its smiling face."

Ty knew how true that was. He wondered what ideas the group would have on how to train. The physical part would fall to Lyessa and Darryk, and no doubt Narendi, but those three were hardly equipped to deal with the magical side. Ty wondered if he'd be able to take some advantage of it and gain some side instruction on how to better use his gifts from those who'd had much more experience with them. Either way, he looked forward to the discussion.

Chapter 59 | Adarra

HE'S BACK," one of the guards near the entrance to the cave shouted. Adarra looked up from where she'd been perusing a stack of well-worn journals she'd found amongst Belakor's belongings. She probably shouldn't have been snooping, but she couldn't help herself, not when it came to the written word. From the notes and sketches, Belakor looked to have been studying the creatures on the island. She recognized the drawings of the sniffers and the jingas, and even possibly whatever had been in the water, but there were many other drawings of creatures she didn't know and fervently hoped she would never see.

"Where have you been?" Holverd demanded as soon as Belakor stepped into the main chamber, where the rest of their party was waiting. "You've been gone all morning. Thought you'd up and left us here to rot."

Belakor grunted and then shook himself like a dog, flinging half-melted snow from his beard and hair in all directions.

"So impatient." He turned and pointed at the tunnel that led to the outside. "I was hunting for breakfast."

Jonas shuffled in behind him, dragging a dead creature Adarra hadn't seen before. It looked similar to one of the drawings she'd seen in Belakor's journals—a hairless rat the size of a small hound, with the shell of a turtle on its back.

She smiled when she saw Jonas. The closer they got to the five peaks of Tallos and his home, the more she worried that she'd wake up and he'd be gone. So far, he'd kept his word, but surely the temptation was there. He had been their prisoner for several months. If the roles had been reversed, would she have chosen any different? Still, she was glad to see that so far she'd been mistaken.

Like Belakor, Jonas's hair and face were covered in snow, which had even formed icicles in his brows. Jonas dropped the carcass down next to the fire and then pulled out a knife and started to skin it. By the long slit down its front, it had clearly already been gutted, hopefully nowhere near their cave. They didn't want to attract predators.

"What is that?" Captain Mervall asked, walking over to get a closer look, nervously twisting his long mustache.

"Food," Belakor said.

Mervall grimaced.

Belakor rested his spear against the wall behind him, then took off his cloak and hung it on a peg that had been jammed into a small crevice in the rock.

Two of Mervall's remaining sailors stood with him as they watched Jonas work. The third was injured and lying on a blanket on the other side of the fire with a couple of Holverd's lancers and the ambassador.

Lanmiere's injuries were severe, especially his leg. He'd spent the entire night in a delirium, despite Adarra's attempts to bring down his fever. It helped that there was plenty of snow to pack around the wounds, but they were somewhat short on medicines. They had a few tonics and herbs that had managed to survive the sniffer attack and the trek through jinga hunting grounds, but not enough to treat everyone.

Belakor spotted Adarra holding one of his journals and walked over.

"I found these," he said, opening a satchel and showing her the contents. There were several species of plants inside, some Adarra didn't recognize. "These should help with swelling." He indicated a flower with white petals. "And these," he said, picking up a handful of purple roots, "will help with pain and sleep. I'll brew them in some tea." Before Adarra could ask what they were or how he was able to make tea, the older man closed his satchel and shuffled over to the table at the back, where he kept his cooking utensils.

"What did he say?" Holverd asked, suddenly appearing over Adarra's left shoulder.

"He found some herbs he thinks can help with our injured. He's going to boil them down."

"Did he say anything about where we are?"

She shook her head. "I can ask him as soon as he finishes."

Holverd nodded and then left to join the other lancers over near the entrance, pausing on the way to check on how his injured men were doing, assuring them that everything would be fine and they would be back on their feet soon enough.

Adarra hoped that was the case. They were placing all their lives in this old hermit's hands. The island was a complete mystery to them. They'd barely been on it a couple of days and had already lost over half the men that had landed with them. Belakor was probably their only hope for reaching the Tallosians, since he seemed to be the only one who truly knew where they were.

Aiden, who'd been spending most of his time at Lanmiere's side keeping the ambassador's compresses supplied with clean snow, stood and walked over. "Well, I guess I was wrong." He glanced over at Jonas. "He didn't leave after all."

"Good thing for us."

"Where do you think we are?"

"Holverd just asked me the same question." She shrugged. "Could be anywhere."

They had followed Belakor through most of the night as he led them north across the island. At least, she thought it was north. As backward as this place was, for all they knew south was north and east was west. She was just thankful to have found shelter enough for them to rest without the constant threat of being eaten. She looked over at the row of injured. "How's Lanmiere doing?"

"His fever is still up. I keep soaking his compress in melted snow, but as soon as I get one on, he sweats through it."

She sighed. She could see from here the ambassador was trembling under his blanket. "Just do the best you can. Hopefully, this tonic Belakor is making will help."

"Is that what he was showing you? Let's hope it does. I don't see Lanmiere making it through another night without something. A couple of those lancers aren't looking too good, either."

Lanmiere shifted restlessly under his blanket, causing the compress over his forehead to slip off. Aiden sighed, then headed over to replace the fallen compress with a fresh cloth.

Adarra joined Jonas on the other side of the fire, doing her best to stay far enough back to keep from getting splattered by anything that clung to his knife as he continued to dress the rather smelly creature. She wasn't sure which smelled worse, the undrained blood or the pelt.

"How close are we to your home?" she asked as he tossed the hide over near the entrance to start work on the meat underneath. His hands were covered in blood. A couple of the lancers grabbed the pieces of skin and fur and started for the tunnel.

"Bury deep to hide smell," Jonas called after them.

The lancers nodded and left.

Jonas grabbed one of the creature's flanks, then looked at her. "What was question?"

"How much farther till we reach your people?"

"Two days' hike up to Idris."

"Idris?"

"Gateway to the Five Peaks."

"Is that where the Five Houses of Tallos are located?"

He nodded and continued cutting the carcass, casting furtive glances her way every now and then. "You look rested."

She nodded. "I feel better than I did yesterday, but hardly rested." She watched him for a while, then left him to his work to check on Belakor as he prepared the medicinal tea.

Mervall stopped her on her way and pulled her to the side. "Has anyone mentioned where we are, yet?"

She almost laughed. "Jonas seems to believe we are a couple days' trek from the entrance to the Five Peaks."

"And that's where we'll find his people?"

She nodded.

"Good, good. The sooner we get this over with, the sooner I can get back to my ship." He walked away, mumbling something about wishing he'd been sick the day Overlord Barl had asked for volunteers.

Belakor's makeshift table was nothing more than a large boulder that had been chipped flat at the top. The hermit was busily chopping the roots when she joined him. As he finished, he placed them in a tin pot half filled with melted snow.

"How's it coming?" she asked, picking up one of the pieces of roots to sniff. It didn't have much of a smell.

"Very good. You will see." He carried the pot over to the fire and hung it from a spit overtop. "Must wait for them to cook through. Be patient." He sat on an upturned stump beside the stone table, retrieved the white flowers from his bag, and began cutting off the stems.

She smiled and took a seat beside him on an upturned piece of firewood. "So, you were a scholar to Overlord Saryn?"

He turned. "Who?"

"You said you worked for Overlord Saryn."

"Oh, right. Uh, yes, Saryn."

"So how does a scholar end up on Tallos?"

"The same way anyone does. Bad luck."

She chuckled. "I noticed you weren't carrying a light with you while you were out last night. Is that to keep from attracting more creatures? How do you see without one?"

"I, uh . . . when you've been here as long as I have, you find you can get along without it."

That seemed highly unlikely. He wasn't exactly giving her the answers she was looking for, so she tried a more direct approach. "Jonas called you Shayan. Do you . . ." She leaned in. "Do you have magic?"

"What? Magic, no. I don't have magic. Are you crazy?" He started to stand, but she grabbed his arm and attempted to pull him back down.

"Don't worry. I am Shayan as well."

He lowered slowly into his seat, but something in the way he looked at her said he wasn't surprised. He fiddled with his beard, which hung all the way to his lap, and waited for her to continue.

"Things are getting a little better for wielders now," she said, keeping her voice lowered. "The overlord of Sidara has just decreed that his kingdom would open its borders to those with magic."

Belakor's eyes narrowed. "I might be old, girl, but I'm not that far gone."

"No, really. The Tower sent bulradoer to Easthaven, and there was a battle. It was a group of local wielders who saved the overlord."

His face blanched. "You know of bulradoer?"

"I didn't until after they showed up. I had always thought the White Tower was hunting wielders to get rid of them."

"Hah!" Belakor spat to the side. "Ain't that the twist of the knife. The one place that's supposed to be keeping Aldor safe from us cursed wielders is using those same wielders to its own end. Curse that flaming place. The world would be better off if we pulled it down stone by stone."

Belakor sounded different. His earlier playfulness and simple speech had dropped away, leaving her to wonder if it had all been a defensive ruse. "You seem to know quite a bit about it," she said.

"I should. They're the flaming whoresons who sent me to this Creator-cursed island in the first place."

Adarra was confused. "Wait, I thought you worked for Overlord Saryn."

"I did, until he discovered I was ven'ae, then he shipped me off with the first group of Black Watch to ride through Ecrin."

"So you went to the Tower?"

He turned and looked at those sitting by the fire, then spared a quick glance over near the entrance where Captain Holverd and Captain Mervall were quietly chatting. "Yes, I was there."

Adarra's heart pounded with excitement. "Wait here just a moment." She rushed over to her satchel and pulled out one of her journals. She wanted to make sure she wrote it all down. She retook her seat and started jotting a new entry.

"What's all this?" he asked, pointing at her book.

"I'm writing what you have to say so I don't forget it. I'm a memoriae."

"A what?"

"My gift is the ability to remember everything that I see. So if you tell me something, there's a good chance I'll forget it, but if I write it down, I won't."

He scratched his head. "That's a strange gift to have. Don't reckon I've heard of that before. I'm a . . ." He paused and looked around once more before leaning in. "I'm a sensitive myself."

"What's that?" She wrote down the word *sensitive.*

"I can sense magic."

"What does that mean? You can see it?"

"No, I feel it. It's how I knew you and your friends were nearby. I could sense your magic."

"Kind of like the sniffers?"

He sneered. "I am not like those abominations. They were created with dark magics."

She had a thought and paused her dictation. "Can you sense any other magic here?"

He looked around the room, then shook his head. "No. Just us."

She smiled. "That's a pretty handy gift."

"A dangerous one," he said.

She nodded and continued jotting in her book. "No doubt one the Tower found very useful." When he didn't respond, she finally looked up.

His head was lowered as he stared at his lap. There was a sad look in his eyes. "All too useful, I'm afraid. I'm not a brave man, mind you. All it took was one time on the inquisitor's rack, and I was volunteering my services for whatever they wanted just to stop the pain. Can't say I'm proud of it, but I wanted to live."

She didn't say anything, simply recording what he'd said. "What's an inquisitor rack?"

He spent the next few minutes describing a place called the Chamber of Inquisition and what went on inside. Adarra's hands shook as she tried recording what the poor man had seen and endured. "So how did you end up here on Tallos?"

Before he answered, Belakor got up and walked over to check on his plants. He poked around inside the pot with a wooden spoon and then eventually pulled it off and carried them back over to the table, where he set it down to cool. He retook his seat. "Where were we?"

"You were going to tell me how you ended up on this island."

"Oh, right." He took a deep breath with another long stroke of his beard. "As I said, the only way to end up here is bad luck. A room in the Tower was discovered years ago, and inside, a small collection of books, most full of magic. The kind you don't ever want to read. One of the books told of a place where some of the Dark Wizard's followers would go to experiment with their craft. From all accounts, they were looking for a place secluded from the mainland, one that couldn't be easily found. More importantly, one that would ensure that their experiments were contained. What better place to do that than an island?"

Adarra wrote as fast as she could, hardly believing what she was hearing. This was extremely important information, and she was finding it hard to keep writing for wanting to sit there and just listen.

"Once it was discovered that Tallos was the island that Aerodyne had sanctioned for their experimentation, Arch Chancellor Bezaleel ordered an expedition be sent. Because of my unique gift, he wanted me to be there in case there were any strong magics to be found. Namely, he sought talismans left over from another age. I think he was hoping to find some ancient laboratory filled with stockpiles of magical weapons. At the very least, some of the ancient grimoires used by those before."

She stopped writing. "And did you?"

He scoffed. "Hardly. What we found was an island filled with monsters. Abominations that should have never been." He turned and pointed at what was left of the creature Jonas was working on. "Look at that thing. It ain't right."

"I looked in one of your journals," she said. "It appears that you've been cataloging these creatures."

He nodded. "I've been studying them. Had to, just to stay alive." He looked at the pot on the table. "Should be cooled sufficiently." He stood and tried looking inside, but it was too dark at the back of the chamber to see in. "These infernal eyes." He grabbed an unlit candle from a shelf behind the table and mumbled something under his breath as he held it over the first pail. The wick flickered to life and a small flame appeared.

Adarra gasped, her fingers tightening around her writing utensil so hard she nearly snapped it. "How did you do that?" she asked, keeping her voice low as a couple of lancers passed by on their way over to help Jonas carry what remained of the rat-turtle's carcass outside.

Belakor turned. "How did I do what?"

She pointed at the candle. "How did you light that? Was that magic?"

He looked at her funny. "Of course."

"But how? You said you were a sensitive, not an incindi."

"What kind of wielders have you been hanging around, girl?"

She started to name a few types, and he waved her off. "No, no, no. I didn't mean for you to actually tell me. You do realize that you can do more than just . . . what was it you said you do? Memorize things? Wielders are capable of performing other magics besides their gifts."

Her mouth went slack. "We can do other magic?" Her mind was racing at all the possibilities.

"Of course, what have these wielders been teaching you?"

"Nothing. We didn't know we could do anything else but what we were gifted with." She looked at the candle. "Show me."

He sighed, then snuffed out the wick. "The incantation for fire is *Voyestra.*"

He placed the candle down in front of her, and she repeated what he'd said. "*Voyestra.*"

Nothing happened.

"Why didn't it work?"

"Patience," he said, rolling his eyes. "It took me several days to get to where I could light a single wick. Try again. This time pull from your magic, from here," he said, pressing just below her chest. "It's not just the words that do it. If it were, everyone would be shooting off magic all over the place. Dig deep inside and find where your magic comes from. Find the heat."

She'd never felt her magic in that way before. She knew Ty could feel his. He described it as a warming sensation that would flood through him. Her magic was different, though. She never had to try pulling it up. It just worked. She took a deep breath and focused, trying to find the center that he was referring to. She closed her eyes, imagining herself feeling around for something warm. It was like feeling around inside a chest full of knickknacks for one specific item she'd never seen or felt before. It was more difficult than she thought. How was Ty able to—

Wait. Was that it? Yes, there was a warm place inside her. Why hadn't she felt it before? No one had ever told her to look. She reached for it and then opened her eyes. "I think I have it."

"Good, then try again."

She concentrated on the candle, pulling on her magic, letting the heat fill her. It was a strange sensation, and yet comforting. She took a small breath. *"Voyestra."*

The candle lit immediately, and shouts behind them had her and Belakor spinning around to see the fire in the pit suddenly shooting outward. Two of the injured lancers shrilled as their bedrolls ignited, setting their legs ablaze.

Adarra squealed.

"Release it!" Belakor said, shaking her arm.

Adarra immediately let go of the magic, and the flames lowered to their normal state.

"What in the fiery Pits was that?" Holverd shouted, his sword in hand as he scanned the room. Aiden and the others were too busy trying to put out the fires to draw their own weapons. They yanked off the fire-ridden blankets and quickly pulled the injured men back from the cook pit.

"Well?" Holverd demanded. "Is someone going to say something?"

Belakor looked at Adarra, and she looked at him. Her hands were shaking. How could she possibly explain this away? She couldn't tell the truth. If she did, Jonas would know she was a wielder, which could completely derail all their efforts. She didn't know what to do. Taking a deep gulp, she slowly started to stand.

"I'm to blame," Belakor said, and Adarra quickly sat back down.

"I was demonstrating some small bit of magic, and it got away from me."

"You fool! Look what you did. You nearly killed my men."

Jonas stared across the fire at Belakor, his face hard. "Shayan." He looked at Adarra. "Come away. Shayan are dangerous."

Aiden looked at her as well. "Might be a good idea," he said, sparing a nervous glance at Belakor. "He about burned Lanmiere alive."

Adarra started to stand, but one look at Belakor and her conscience overpowered her survivalist instincts. This wasn't right.

"Step away from him," Holverd demanded, and pulled out his hunting knife as he started across the room. "I've half a mind to cut his flaming tongue out."

"No! It wasn't Belakor. He's not to blame." She glanced around the room nervously. "I'm sorry. It was me."

"You?" Holverd looked astonished. "You're a . . . you're a—"

"You can say it," she said. "A wielder. Yes."

Mervall pinched his thick mustache, looking somewhat blanched himself. "Well, there's a twist for ya."

"You're a fire wielder?" Aiden said, looking just as shocked as the others.

"I'm not an incindi. Belakor was just showing me that wielders can do other types of magic."

"Wonderful," Holverd groused, throwing his hands in the air. "Just when I thought these ven'ae couldn't be more dangerous, we find out they can!"

"It was an accident," she said.

"I can fix," Belakor said, shuffling over to his table. "I make some more tonic and salve."

Adarra could feel the judgmental eyes of everyone in the room bearing down on her. This was the one thing she'd been hoping to avoid. Even Aiden seemed concerned as he looked up at her from beside Lanmiere. But Aiden wasn't the one she was worried about. It was Jonas. His opinion was the only one that mattered at that moment, and when she finally mustered the courage to look over at him, she found him staring at her as though he'd never seen her before. His eyes were hard. It was an unsettling feeling. He was afraid of her. She took a step toward him, and he placed his hand on his knife, and she froze.

Lanmiere, in his delirium, groaned and tried turning over, which gratefully caused enough of a distraction for the others to at least pretend to go about their own business, though with cautious and repetitive glances her way. She shook her head despondently. When things go around, they really come back hard. She'd done the very thing she had constantly badgered Ty about. His first attempt at demonstrating his fire magic to her had set her dress aflame, and now she'd done so much worse.

Unable to take the disapproving looks of her peers, she walked over and joined Belakor at the back. "What happened? Why did it do that?"

He shrugged. "I guess you used too much magic. Don't think I've ever seen anyone pick that spell up so quickly." He turned back to his pail of cooked roots and began to steep them. The kettle contained a couple of other herbs from one of the jars on the small shelf behind his table. "Not too tasty," he said, "but it will get the job done." He poured a cup and handed it to her. "Have them sip slowly, and make sure they drink it all."

She started to leave but stopped. "You don't know of any healing magic, do you?"

"Afraid that's well beyond my abilities." He started pulling the white petals from the flowers and mashing them together.

She nodded and took the steaming drink over and had Aiden help Lanmiere up into a sitting position.

"What is it?" Aiden asked, looking into the cup.

"No idea, but it's supposed to help him sleep." They managed to draw the ambassador out of his fever-induced state long enough to help him get the drink down, then she refilled it, but when she turned to do the same for the others, they all scooted back.

"I'm sorry," she whispered. "I didn't mean for any of this to happen." With a heavy sigh, she handed Aiden the rest of the tea to dispense.

By the time the rest of the injured had finished it off, Belakor had completed mixing a poultice and went from one man to the next, plastering it over their injuries. After rewrapping the wounds, they left the men to sleep while Jonas started cooking some of the meat he had dressed. It didn't smell the best, and tasted even worse, but it was food and they needed to eat.

After breakfast was over, it was quickly decided that they would spend the day resting and tending to their wounded. Hopefully, the ambassador's fever would have broken by then, and their men would be well enough on the morrow to continue. Of course, all of that hinged on whether Belakor's claims about his tea and poultices were accurate.

The man swore his medicinal herbs would do the trick. He said some of the plants on the island seemed to have magical properties and that they had saved his life on far more occasions than he cared to admit.

With a mercifully full stomach and eyes barely able to remain open, Adarra crawled into her blanket next to the fire and pondered over this incredible new discovery she'd found concerning her magic—and also the dangers associated with it. She cast a quick glance over near the entrance and found Jonas standing there staring. His eyes were just as hard as they had been earlier, and it hurt her to see it. The disappointment in them stung, and she worried how this new revelation would impact their mission.

Chapter 60 | Ayrion

WE NEED YOU TO LISTEN, BRIM!" Zayden said, urging the Orpa primary to see reason.

Ayrion stood to the side, watching. Behind him, on either side of the doorway, stood his father and what remained of his team—Ferrin, Myron, and Bek. The rest were either trying to recover or helping those in the infirmary with the influx of wounded. They had given everything they had, and he'd defy anyone claiming they could have done better, save perhaps Nyalis himself, which was why he needed the clan's support.

It wasn't enough to have just one of the clans join him. He needed all three, but at the moment, he would settle with a simple majority. He turned and whispered to Myron, asking him to find out if there was anything Rae could do to get Sirak back on his feet, at least long enough to get his vote on how to proceed. Myron nodded and slipped through the flaps. Ayrion caught a glimpse of white fur just on the other side of the doorway. Nola must have been standing guard. She had saved his life. Ayrion could see why Ferrin had modeled his newest creations after her.

He turned back to the two men as they continued to argue over whether to follow Ayrion's leadership. They needed a united front, and right now Ayrion had one day to convince them to pull their clans together. After the losses they suffered the previous night, he knew they wouldn't survive another without a single unified force. Ayrion had thought that after the crippling blow of this battle, the other primaries would have seen reason. Zayden had. It seemed Sirak might have, but he was still in the infirmary. However, it was Brim who was holding everything up, which wasn't too unexpected.

"You fought alongside me not a few hours ago," Ayrion said, pressing the man to give in. "What's stopping you now? If this has something to do with Flon and letting your pride and anger take precedence over your people, then you don't deserve the title of primary."

Brim pointed at Ayrion. "You don't have the right to say his name!"

"And you don't have the right to send your people to their deaths. Even you are smart enough to see what a colossal disaster this was. We had men running all over the place, tripping over themselves, clans fighting each other to get to the front. If not for Lenara and Zynora, they would have overrun the camp. Every one of those injured out there would be dead right now. We could have never evacuated them in time, and all of this was completely unnecessary."

"What gives you the right to come in here and dictate how we fight?"

"Experience!" Ayrion spat, losing patience. "When it comes to stealth, and killing, and one-on-one combat, we have no equal, but our people have never faced a threat like this. You don't know the first thing about structured warfare. And I would hope you're not too full of hatred and stupidity to listen to someone who does."

Brim reached for his sword, but Ayrion drew his before Brim got it halfway out of its sheath. "This will not end well for you," Ayrion said, pointing his own sword at Brim. "But it would certainly make my job easier."

Brim snarled but slowly sheathed his weapon.

"No, please," someone behind them said. "Don't stop on my account. Kill each other."

Ayrion turned and exhaled a sigh of relief. Sirak stood in the doorway, leaning against a spear. He didn't look ready to jump into the fray, but at least he was on his feet. Ayrion sheathed his sword and waited for the head of Kovaa to join the other primaries by the table on the far side of the tent.

As weak as Sirak was, Brim and Zayden didn't look much better. All three had ripped and torn uniforms, dried blood caked in multiple places. One side of Zayden's face was a mass of bruises, the eye swollen half shut. Brim had a nasty gash in his leg, which had been wrapped to stop the bleeding. The wrapping was already turning red.

"This is all we need to seal our fate," Sirak said, looking at the other two, "the three of us battling it out. Why not hand our home over to the khuls and wish them well?" He looked down at the map on the table, then walked over and sat in his chair. "I'm not too big a man to admit when I'm wrong." He looked at Brim. "I trust my fellow primaries are not either. Pride is for those who have nothing to lose. We have too much for me to hold on to mine." He looked at Ayrion. "Consider Clan Kovaa at your disposal. We need someone with military training to help us, and I vote to enact Ayrion as the commander of our warriors."

"I second that," Zayden said, walking over to take his seat on Sirak's left.

Brim stayed where he was and remained quiet.

Ayrion frowned. "That won't be enough."

"What are you talking about?" Sirak looked stunned. "I just voted to hand you all three of our forces."

"And therein lies the problem. We can't have *three* separate forces. This is what I was trying to say from the start. As long as those men out there look at each other as competition and not brothers-in-arms, whatever we decide in here is going to be futile. And trust me, I know this isn't easy to hear, but we need to get rid of this notion of three different clans. Unless we can come together as a single people, those fighters out there are never going to work together. Zayden took the first step, having his men remove their patches. That's a good start. But we need this," he said, holding up his newly fashioned ring with all three of the Tanveer symbols. "We need a united front."

Sirak's hands tightened on the edge of his seat as he bristled against what Ayrion was saying. Ayrion knew that if they didn't come together now, there was little hope of them surviving.

"Our people have been fighting each other for years," Ayrion said, frustration leaking into his voice. "Fighting to see who gets to claim which section of the city, fighting to see who gets the better contracts, fighting over the monthly food caravans and who gets first pick." He threw his hands in the air. "How has it helped us? We nearly lost everything during the last attack because the clans refused to work together."

Zayden cleared his throat.

"Except, of course, for Raju," Ayrion pointed out. "And did you see what happened? They became the stronger force. So much so that they were able to turn the khul advance. Unfortunately, Clan Kovaa was nearly wiped out in the process." He stared at the primaries for a moment, hoping that what he was saying was sinking in. "Are you willing to let that happen again? Because I can promise you, we won't survive another clash unless we stand together.

"Have you ever wondered why the Upaka haven't grown as a people? Why you are forced to live in this ruin of a city, which is crumbling around you. You are dying. You don't even have the ability to fix what is here. No skills besides your swords. In a few more generations, there will be no Upakans left. A divided people will never be able to stand and flourish; they will always stagnate and die. You need this, and not just for your warriors and the hope of surviving the khuls. You need to come together for our survival as a people."

Ayrion paused, wondering where that tirade had come from. He certainly hadn't intended to say most of it, but he felt like he was looking at his people for the first time, finally seeing them for who and what they were.

Sirak and Zayden looked at each other, then at Brim, who was still standing beside the table, leaning on it just to stay on his feet.

"Time is running out," Ayrion pressed. "One way or another, our future as a people is changing today. Either we die here as three clans, too stubborn to change, or we fight as one people and try to push these creatures back to the Pit where they came from."

"You have my vote," Zayden said. "To be honest, I've been getting tired of all the bickering between clans anyway." He looked at Sirak. "Well, you were about to turn over our forces a moment ago. If change is inevitable, best be on the right side of it."

"And who leads this united people?" Brim asked, giving the others pause.

"You will," Ayrion said. "All three of you, just like before. Each clan's Peltok consists of three members. Why shouldn't the head of a rebirthed Tanveer do the same?" He watched to see their reactions at his sneaking in their former name. If they were averse to the idea, they didn't say it.

Sirak hesitated, but after a brief glance over at Zayden, he eventually gave in with a nod. They looked at Brim. The head of Orpa didn't say anything, but his face was taut. Ayrion could see he was doing everything he could to think of a reason why not to. Once again, it was Zayden who was first to speak.

"If you don't add in your vote, I'm going to tell everyone out there whose greed it was that unleashed this plague on us in the first place."

Brim looked up, surprise written on his face.

"That's right," Zayden said. "My spies tell me that it was you who ordered these lower tunnels excavated in hopes of pillaging their gold. Were you going to share this new wealth with the rest of us?"

Brim snarled. "Fine. You have my consent. But I'm warning you, this will be the end of us all."

Sirak turned to Ayrion. "How do you suggest we start?" The head of Kovaa was beginning to droop in his seat. Ayrion could see pain in his eyes as he fought just to be there.

"We need to start by telling your people everything."

"Do you think that wise?" Zayden asked.

"Always best to start with the truth. Someone taught me that years ago, and it's always stuck with me." He glanced over his shoulder at his father, who was smiling proudly.

"After they hear the truth, we should start with the uniforms. We can't have the men out there balking at having to stand beside a member of another clan. Best to get rid of anything that represents one of the three factions."

"What do you propose we do about these?" Zayden asked, holding up his own Raju ring.

That, Ayrion was less certain about. Giving up their patches was one thing; telling them to throw down their rings was something else. He remembered how important his had been to him.

"I believe I can help with that."

Ayrion turned as Ferrin took a step forward and looked at the three leaders.

"But it will require a little magic," he said with a slight grin.

Surprisingly, it didn't take a lot to convince the Upakan fighters to remove their patches. Say this for Ayrion's people: they were good at following orders. However, it did take a while for the three former heads, with Ayrion's help, to fill everyone in on what was happening, including the backstory of their Tanveer heritage.

Ayrion wasn't exactly convinced that the three heads really believed everything he had told them, but by the time they had finished relaying all of the most pertinent information, the chamber was filled with chatter, especially when the revelation of who they had once been came to light, not to mention who it was they had at one time been the protectors of.

Namely, wizards.

By the time they had finished, the place was buzzing, but Ayrion couldn't make out what was being said. He wasn't exactly sure how their warriors were taking it. If it was anything like their primaries, then not well. It didn't help that the clans were still divided by clans. Even gathering around to listen to what their leaders had to say, they kept their distance from each other.

"There is still one other change that is yet to be made," Sirak said, though he sounded hesitant in saying it. "If the goal is to keep one clan from fighting another in order to find a way to work together, then it will require more than stripping the patches off our uniforms." He held up the ring on his hand. "We also wear the symbol of our division here. Apparently, these symbols once represented a united people, the Tanveer."

"Each symbol speaks to the motto of the Tanveer," Zayden added, then motioned for Ayrion to continue.

Ayrion took a step forward on the makeshift platform they had crudely constructed in front of the command pavilion. "These three symbols are engraved into the foundational stone of our former home. The motto reads: Truth In All. Honor Above All. Justice For All. It is the basis of who we are. Not three divided factions at war with each other but one people fighting side by side. We are guardians, not mercenaries. But if you're not willing to put aside your differences now, then we've already lost. Because when the khuls tear down that passageway tonight, either they'll find a divided force ready to be crushed or a united front willing to do anything to protect their home."

"Are you saying we should remove our rings?" someone called out on the right.

"No," Zayden said. "We don't want you to throw away who you are. But we are asking that you be willing to put aside what divides us for what unites us instead."

"We are having you remove your patches for a reason," Sirak said. "As long as our fighters wear them, we risk falling back into the same old contentions of clan against clan. Your rings are no different. But instead of demanding to get rid of them, we would rather change them."

"How so?" another fighter asked.

Ayrion held up his reshaped ring. "Instead of our rings bearing a single clan's marker, they will bear the markers of all three. The true crest of our people."

"And how are we going to do that?" someone from the back asked. "We don't have time to be remaking rings. We need to be preparing for what's coming."

"Lucky for you," Ayrion said, "we happen to have an extremely skilled metallurgist with us who believes he has a way to reshape all of your rings at once." Ayrion turned and looked at Ferrin, who was standing a few feet behind him on the left.

Ferrin nodded.

Ayrion wasn't sure how he was going to pull something like that off, but if he said he could, Ayrion believed him. He motioned for Ferrin to join him and the other three on the platform. "Tell them what you need them to do."

Ferrin looked out across the sea of hardened faces staring at him from around the cavern chamber and gulped. "In order for me to change your rings, I will need them to all be touching each other at the same time."

"Do you want to stack them in a pile?" Zayden asked, confused.

"They can't do that," Sirak said. "They'd never be able to figure out whose ring belonged to who. It would take hours to find ones that fit."

"No," Ferrin clarified, "I don't need you to pile them, but I will need them to be touching, so we will need everyone with a ring to line up around the chamber so that everyone's ring hand can be touching, like this." He demonstrated by opening his hand and placing it against Ayrion's opened hand, so that the back of Ferrin's hand pressed against the front of Ayrion's.

Ferrin turned to the three primaries. "We can start with a simple demonstration here at the front." He asked them to open their hands and place them together. Ayrion almost chuckled. If these three could be made to hold hands, surely the rest would be willing to follow suit.

Ferrin waited until all three hands were pressed together—Brim being the last—then glanced out at his rather inquisitive audience, who were breaking clan boundaries to get a closer look. "You see? All three rings are touching." He stepped a little closer and placed his fingers against Zayden's ring, since his was on the outside and closest to Ferrin.

"It's not going to hurt, is it?" Zayden asked, soft enough so the men watching wouldn't hear.

Ferrin smiled. "Not a bit." He closed his eyes, and Ayrion scooted to the side to see for himself. He waited for something to happen. All three men stood very still, most likely afraid that if they moved, their hands might get reshaped instead of their rings. A moment later, Ferrin's eyes opened, and he took a step back. A murmur ran among the men. It hadn't been much of a show.

"Did it work?" Sirak asked, afraid to move.

"See for yourselves."

The three men raised their hands and looked down at their rings. Ayrion could see that the single emblem at the center of each had been converted into three.

"Impressive," Zayden said.

Sirak merely nodded.

Brim didn't say a word. In fact, he hadn't said anything since they had left the command pavilion.

Ferrin turned back to the fighters strewn across the cavern. "I show you this so you understand what we will be doing. I don't have time to go from one person to the next and change each individual ring. So if everyone will line up, side by side, and make sure your rings are touching the person in back and in front of you, I should be able to change everyone's ring at the same time."

It took them a while, but with a little prodding from the men on the platform, the new Tanveer army had formed a line that wrapped around the cavern, looping in on itself until every last fighter capable of standing had managed to find a place.

"I believe we are ready," Ayrion's father called out from somewhere inside the loop. He'd been in charge of getting everyone in line and making sure no fights broke out between clans. Surprisingly, none did. Ayrion figured they were more interested in the idea of seeing some magic than battling each other. "But hurry. We can't hold it for long."

Ferrin stepped off the platform and approached the first person in line, who happened to be Ayrion's brother. Jorn kept his hand open for Ferrin to take hold of his ring.

"Here we go!" Ferrin called out, loud enough for everyone to hear. Even some of those inside the infirmary stepped out to watch. "Keep as still as you can."

Ferrin once again closed his eyes. This time the magic took longer, and Ayrion could see sweat breaking out on the smith's forehead. After a while, Ferrin's hands began to shake, and his breathing grew strained. Whatever he was doing, it was taking a lot out of him.

Ayrion was worried he'd have to stop him, but as soon as he took a step closer to see if he was alright, Ferrin released Jorn's ring and stepped back.

"Phew, that was harder than I thought it would be," Ferrin said, completely out of breath. "It's finished!" he called out and turned and slowly walked over to the side with Myron's help and took a seat.

The room filled with excited chatter as the men examined their newly formed rings.

Ayrion walked back up onto the platform with the other three heads as the fighters once more spread out across the room, though maybe not quite as separated as before.

"Now what?" Sirak asked, studying his own ring.

Ayrion looked out across what remained of their broken forces. "Now, we train."

Chapter 61 | Ty

TY OPENED THE DOOR for Narendi, and she offered him a polite nod as she walked past.

"So this is the Performance Night you told me about?"

"It is," Ty said, and stepped in behind her, just ahead of several others who were coming up the front steps behind them. Breen was already inside somewhere looking for Fraya.

"Good to hear that word of our festivities has traveled abroad," Bue said as he greeted them with a tip of his hat, offering a small bow to Narendi. "Always happy to entertain those from out of town." He noted the bulge in Ty's jacket pocket. "I hope that's your flute I see there."

Ty smiled. "It could be."

Master Aboloff grinned. "Good. Hopefully that will pacify some of this crowd."

"What do you mean?"

"Just tell Missus Aboloff to make sure to place you on the list." Bue immediately turned and began greeting those coming in behind.

"What was that about?" Narendi asked.

"I don't know." Ty directed Narendi farther into the lobby and out of the immediate doorway so they wouldn't get in the way of the growing numbers still coming in. Even for a cold winter's night like this one, it was a packed house, especially considering they had come an hour early to make sure to get good seats. But if the crowd in the lobby was any indication, they should have come that morning.

There was barely room to stand, people bumping into each other as they made their way to the common room. Thankfully, he had been able to talk Narendi into leaving her spear, promising her that the most she would have to worry about would be the odd drunk singing a bit too loudly and off-key. She was dressed in her finest outfit, deciding to wear the red cape this evening instead of the green. She had even left her sword behind, though she kept a long dagger under her cloak.

Ty wore his best tan jacket. In truth, it was his only jacket, but though the colors had faded and the leather was a little worn, it was his favorite thing to wear. He also kept his cap on to cover his white hair, still too wary of showing it in public.

They worked their way through the crowd until they reached the main room, which was nearly filled. He shook his head. "I've never seen this many people at a Performance Night before. The closest was when all three of the overlords were in attendance." He continued scanning the tables.

Narendi looked as well. "Do you see her?"

"Who?"

"The one who has your heart."

Ty turned, a little stunned she would ask. "No. But I wasn't looking. I was trying to find Father and Breen. I'm hoping one of the council might have gotten here early and saved us some seats."

Besides, Lyessa would usually wait and arrive later with her father in some grand fashion. She might have been one of the finest fighters he knew, but that didn't stop her from flaunting some newly purchased gown on occasion. It was one of the things he liked about her—tough as ironwood but still maintaining that soft core.

"She will be here, though," he said. "Can you promise me you won't try killing her?"

"I can try."

"Try hard," he said with a curt smile. "Honestly, you two really do have a lot more in common than you know. I bet you could be friends."

She huffed. "We have only one thing in common."

Ty sighed but refrained from commenting.

"There," she said, pointing toward the front on the far right.

Breen was waving at them from the side of the platform. Even though Ty ribbed his brother sometimes for his giant size, there were times, like now, when it came in handy. Ty led Narendi around the maze of packed tables and overflowing aisles as people continued to mingle, catching up on the latest gossip as though they hadn't just spoken with each other earlier that day. It was something he loved about Easthaven. The people were generally very civil, most treating you like family.

"Excuse us," Ty said as he tried pushing his way through a tightly bunched gathering of men, who'd apparently already gotten a head start on the mead.

"Pardon," one man said and thumped another atop his head. "Move for these fine people. Have you no manners?"

Ty turned to thank the man and stopped when he saw the eye patch. The image of the Bristonian boat of lancers suddenly surfaced, and the one-eyed man shouting orders from the helm. Unfortunately, other than having an eye patch, the man aboard the ship had been too far away for Ty to notice his face.

The man stared at him. "What's wrong? Never seen a missing eye before?" He pulled up the patch to reveal his empty socket, and everyone started laughing.

Ty shook his head. "Sorry."

He pushed his way through the rest of the men and kept going, pulling Narendi along with him. They finally broke through the overflowing aisles to reach the front and found that the wielder council had indeed garnered a couple of tables for themselves.

"Greetings," Ty's father said as he stood from his place at the end. He had his pipe in one hand and a tankard in the other. "Come, have a seat."

Ty turned to Breen. "I thought I just saw . . ." He looked at the table of men, but the one with the patch was no longer there, and clearly none of them had uniforms on under their cloaks or even carried themselves like soldiers.

"Saw who?"

"Nothing," Ty said. "Never mind."

He turned to his father. "Why the crowd?"

"I just asked the same thing," Breen said, sitting down next to Fraya on the right side of the table. Fraya's straight black hair was up in a new fashion, held by one of her brightly colored bows. It looked nice on her, making her look older than the nineteen years she was, the same age as Ty's sister.

"Performance Nights have grown since you two have been gone," Orlyn said from down the row.

Reloria nodded as she popped a piece of candy in her mouth. "With all the worries of what's happening with the throne and the tension with our neighbors to the south, not to mention all the rumors of a possible Tallosian invasion, this seems to be one of the few times that people can let down their hair and enjoy some wholesome entertainment." She said the latter with a wink at a couple of the other council members.

"Well, if you ask me," Feoldor said, "there's just too many people. Can't hardly breathe with crowds like this . . . or get any service." He nearly tipped out of his seat attempting to grab one of the servers on their way by but was too slow, and she got away. "Man could die of thirst in this place."

The others chuckled and took their seats.

Ty and Narendi sat across from Breen and Fraya. He made sure to scoot down far enough to leave an extra seat for Lyessa on the end of their bench. Looking down the tables, he was surprised to find Sheeva absent. Wherever his father was, she was generally close by. Then again, she could still be. He glanced over his shoulder at the front of the stage. Ty's father had talked with her after the incident in the council chambers. Ty wondered if he'd asked her to keep her distance.

Sheeva was a strange one. Not exactly what you would call sociable. The only time he'd spent with her was their excursion north into Meerwood. She had gone with him and Breen after he'd been bitten by the arachnobes. She never said much. Really, all he knew about her was that she had at one time been a paid assassin for Overlord Meyrose. Not exactly a ringing endorsement of stability.

"I'm surprised you were able to find a table," Ty said, glancing down the row of wielders."

"No need to get here early," Veldon said loudly over the noise in the room. "They keep these two here special for us." He shared a strange look with the other members.

"So how was the rest of your tour of our fair city?" Veldon asked Narendi before Ty got the chance to ask why the inn kept two tables special for them.

"It is a very nice place," she said. "I still like the sweet rolls the best."

The members laughed. The whole city, and all she really remembered was Reloria's rolls.

"You aren't the only one, my dear," Orlyn said with a wink from across the table. "Her rolls are what make getting out of bed worth it."

Ty looked at his father. "Gilly not coming?"

His father finished a puff on his pipe. "You know him. Not much for large gatherings."

"I was hoping he'd be around to show Narendi a thing or two about being a vanti."

His father smiled. "You'll probably see him at the council meeting later tonight."

"I almost forgot about that," Breen said as he snatched one of the servers before they made it past again, and they all ordered drinks. Feoldor and a couple of the others just wanted a refill, or better yet a pitcher or two left on the table. The crowd continued to grow to the point that there was barely standing room, and by the look of the numbers still coming in, even that would be gone soon enough.

"Why does no one sit there?" Narendi asked, pointing to a single empty table near the center, close to the front.

"That would be Overlord Barl's table," Breen said.

"But there's no one there."

He smiled. "I'm sure they'll be here soon enough. They usually don't arrive until right before the entertainment starts."

"Smart man," Feoldor said. "If I had known the crowd would be like this, I would have probably done the same."

Narendi looked at Ty. "Are you nervous?"

Ty's father lowered his drink. "Are you planning on playing this evening?"

"Bue requested I bring my flute, so we'll see."

"Better let Noreen know, then."

Ty looked around the room for the innkeeper's wife and found her over near the bar, chatting with several people, one holding a lute. "I'll be right back."

Leaving the table, he made his way along the front of the stage to the other side of the room, where Mistress Aboloff was busy barking out performance orders, directing the talent as to when they could expect to have their turn.

As soon as she saw him coming, her eyes brightened. "There you are! Bue said he'd seen you. I hope you're here to play."

"Unless you already have a full booking," he said, noting the growing number of performers surrounding her, "which it looks like you do." He smiled. "I can just wait till next time." He wasn't exactly looking forward to getting up there again anyway.

"Rubbish," she said. "We can make room. I'll put you near the end." She scanned her sheet and scribbled something on it. "How about right after Lady Lyessa? You two complemented each other the last time you were here." She smiled when she said it.

"If you don't think it will be an inconvenience."

"No, no. The crowd loves you." She turned and started chatting with several others.

There wasn't much else to say, so he started back. Looked like he wasn't going to be getting out of it after all. He didn't feel quite as nervous this time. He'd been spending most of his evenings at Aero'set playing his pipes in his room. He had better control over his magic now, unlike his first experience at Performance Night. He would just have to be careful not to let it get away from him.

"Well?" Breen asked as Ty retook his seat. "Did she put you on?"

Ty nodded. "Not sure if that's a good thing or not. Remember what happened the last time?"

"I think you'll find the people a little more receptive now," Orlyn said, sharing a quick grin with the other council members.

Before Ty could ask what he meant, the server returned with their drinks. She'd just placed the final tankard down when some kind of commotion in the lobby had people turning in their seats.

"Barl must be arriving," Veldon called out from the other end of the table.

Ty looked past his father, barely able to see over those still standing in the aisles. Most had begun to take their seats, but there were still quite a few circulating around the room. The crowd parted at the back, and Ty could see Overlord Barl's retinue making their way toward the front. Lyessa's father was in the lead, followed by a couple members of the Sidaran Assembly. Ty spotted Cirian's head above the rest. Darryk was there as well. And just in front of him, Ty could just make out the top of Lyessa's head, her red hair a flame in a sea of mostly brown and green clothing.

Those in the aisles moved aside, most taking their seats to get out of the overlord's way. As soon as they did, Ty caught a good look at Lyessa. She looked even more radiant than usual, if that was possible. She was dressed completely in white, from her gown to the fur-lined collar on her white cloak, which made her hair blaze even brighter.

Ty heard Narendi grunt beside him.

Barl and the other members of the Sidaran Assembly took their seats while Lyessa scanned the room. Ty stood and waved. It took her a moment, but she did eventually see him and started his way. She slowed when she spotted Narendi beside him but then straightened her back and continued coming. Behind her, one of their entourage carried her half-harp, placing it beside the empty seat Ty had saved and out of the way of the servers' feet.

Ty waited for her to sit before taking his own. The others greeted her, but most kept looking at Narendi. It was clearly an awkward situation, and no one was sure how to make it less so, least of all Ty. Hopefully, the more these two were around each other, the less awkward people would feel, but right now the newness of it seemed to be capturing the council's attention.

"I see you have your harp," Ty's father said, breaking the silence. "I look forward to hearing you play. We've missed you performing of late."

Ty turned. "You haven't been playing?"

"Not since you've been gone," Fraya said, giving Lyessa a disappointed look.

"Before we forget," Veldon said, speaking up as best he could over the noise in the room, "we are planning on meeting this evening to discuss training." He looked at Lyessa. "If you have the time, it would be good for you to be there as well."

"I can be there."

Ty groaned inwardly, not wanting to put Lyessa and Narendi back at odds all over again. Before more could be said on the issue, Noreen Aboloff took the stage.

"Welcome to our Nùwen monthly Performance Night. And a special welcome to our esteemed Overlord Barl and Lady Lyessa, as well as our honored members of the Sidaran Assembly."

Applause erupted as Barl and the members of the Assembly stood from their seats and waved. Lyessa stood as well, but only long enough to offer a simple wave and retake her seat.

Narendi grumbled some more.

They retook their seats, and the applause died down for Noreen to continue.

"We have a full lineup of entertainment this evening, which is sure to warm your hearts on this cold winter's evening. And if that doesn't work, there's plenty of ale at the bar." Her joke earned her an abundance of laughter from the audience. "We'll begin with a flute duet by the brothers Gorsy and Bevan."

A round of applause broke from the room as the two teenage boys took to the stage. They were identical twins, and only a year or two younger than Ty. Ty remembered enjoying their performance the last time and thinking how well their harmony had complemented each other.

The two bowed, their hands shaking a little, but this was only noticeable by those who were sitting close to the stage. A moment later, they were filling the inn with a soft but upbeat tune that Ty was unfamiliar with. He could tell they had been practicing, as the melody was passed between them quite smoothly. Ty wondered how many songs each performer would be allotted, since it seemed there were quite a number of people looking to reach the stage. He wasn't sure if he should plan for more than one.

His question was answered at the end of the brothers' song, as they bowed and then quickly exited the stage to a round of applause. The servers rushed out from the kitchen and the bar just as soon as the last notes were released to serve orders before the next performer took their place.

Ty looked at Narendi. "What did you think?"

"I thought it was very pleasing. And so is this drink," she said, earning her a smile from Fraya, who had ordered Narendi an apricot tea, same as her.

The next performance was by an older woman with a strong soprano. If only her ability to keep pitch had been as strong. She received a moderate applause from the audience, not so much for the performance, but for their appreciation of it being over. Next up was a traveling bard who'd journeyed all the way from Highcrest, the coastal Sidaran city where Aiden's family was from. It had Ty wondering how Aiden and Adarra were faring, whether they had reached Tallos yet or not.

The bard told a riveting tale of a young sailor adrift in the Ozrin Sea for three days and nights after his boat capsized during a treacherous storm. He had everyone on the edge of their seats as he told of the sharks that began to circle, and how the poor man was unable to paddle any longer. He painted them a picture so vivid, Ty could almost smell the salt in the air. And just as the great hunters of the sea began to bump his legs and the young sailor knew he had reached his end, the bard relieved the audience's worries with the arrival of an ocean nymph that swam up from the bottom and carried him back down to live with her.

It would have been a more riveting tale had the bard explained how the man had survived breathing underwater, or how anyone could have possibly heard the tale, since apparently the man was never seen again. Either way, it was fun to think that there could be people that lived under the water. After all the strange things that Ty had seen and heard since leaving Easthaven, there was no telling. Perhaps there were.

The bard received enthusiastic applause as he left the stage, and Mistress Aboloff gave the servers time to make their rounds once more through the crowd as she waited to introduce her next performer.

The night went about the same, though the crowd's attention seemed to wane the longer it went. The applauses weren't as strong as they normally were, and the people a little more restless with each new talent that mounted the steps. If this kept up, Ty was almost assured that by the time they got to him and Lyessa, half the crowd might have already left.

Several more performances were given, and the people continued to grow more restless. The one performer still able to break through the strange impatience they were seeing from those in attendance was Ethen and his vielle and bow. As soon as the local carpenter's name was announced, the crowd burst into applause. The spry carpenter hopped up on the stage and took his place with a wink and a smile.

"Here we go!" Breen shouted over the clapping, beaming with excitement.

No one needed to guess what he was going to play. It was the one song everyone always expected of him. It was also the one that drew the biggest response. Sure enough, Ethen lifted his bow and started straight into the chorus of "Bart the Fool." Before he was halfway through the first verse, people were already drumming their mugs on the tabletops and stomping their feet. By the second verse, they were out of their seats altogether, belting out the familiar words along with Ethen's strong baritone. By the third verse, Ty was off the bench as well, joining Breen, Fraya, and Lyessa as they danced in place to the rhythm of the music.

Narendi didn't know what to do as she watched everyone else dancing and shouting. She stayed in her seat, but the next time Ty looked back, she was clapping along and stomping her feet with Feoldor and Reloria.

The crowd erupted in applause and cheers and demands for several more verses, but Ethen finally tucked his vielle under his arm, and with one final bow, exited the stage.

Things went downhill from there, as the crowd grew surprisingly agitated. Two more performers came and went to hardly any applause at all, and Ty was just turning to ask what was going on when someone shouted from the back of the room.

"We want magic!"

Ty nearly spit out his drink, half choking on what was in his mouth. *What did they just say?*

From the back of the room, the people began to chant, and it rolled across the audience like an avalanche, the mantra building as people lent their voices to the call: "Ma-gic! Ma-gic! Ma-gic . . ."

Chapter 62 | Ty

TY WAS DUMBFOUNDED. Across the table, Breen looked just as shocked, his mouth gaping.

"Ah, blazes!" Feoldor said. "Here we go again."

"Here what goes again?" Ty asked.

"So much for me getting to play tonight," Lyessa said, looking a little disheartened.

"Why?" Ty asked. "What's going on?"

She turned with a sigh. "You'll see." She nodded behind him, and Ty turned to look.

Veldon, Feoldor, and Orlyn all stood from their seats.

The crowd began to cheer, and Ty spun back around. He couldn't believe it. They were crazed with excitement. He glanced back at the three council members as they started up the platform steps at the side.

Was this really about to happen? He looked at his father, and his father simply shrugged. "I told you, things have changed a bit since you've been gone."

Veldon was the first up the stairs. As soon as his feet hit the platform, he struck a spark on his flint, and fire flew from his hands. The crowd went crazy. Ty could hardly believe it.

They actually *wanted* to see magic.

Feoldor sent a funnel of wind into the fire and had it spinning in circles around the stage as the two men played to the crowd. The audience went from loud cheers to captivated oohs and ahhs as they sat wide-eyed in their seats, clearly enthralled by the incredible performance.

"Can you believe this?" Breen asked Ty as they stared out across the room of Easthaven townsfolk.

"Quite the change, isn't it?" their father said with a smirk. He puffed on his pipe contently as he watched their friends on stage.

Orlyn pulled out a pot from beneath his robes and placed it on the floor at the front of the platform. The runes on his staff began to glow, and a vine shot up out of the soil and started to crawl across the stage. The people cheered once more. The vine then began to produce a variety of colorful flowers along its stem and was met with thunderous applause.

Ty felt like he was going to burst with excitement. Not only did Easthaven seem to no longer fear magic, they wanted to see more. Had Overlord Barl's announcement made that big of a difference? Was that all it took—one man taking a stand to change the people's hearts—or had they been willing all along but were just too afraid to admit it?

Ty watched as the three council members continued to perform, faces beaming as they ate up the audience's praise. By the end, Veldon was juggling balls of fire and lifting candle flames from some of the closest tables to soar into the air. Feoldor floated chairs and crates across the stage with controlled streams of hardened wind. Orlyn's plant had covered the entire stage and was now creeping out toward the first tables.

It was a Performance Night to match no other. Ty suddenly wondered if he should do the same, let his music take flight. What would the crowd do then? It would certainly be an incredible way to end their show. He wondered if Noreen was going to announce any of the other performers. She seemed unsure what to do as she paced along the other side of the platform, seeming just as engrossed in the wielders' performances as everyone else.

The other performers sat along the side, their eyes glued to the scene on stage. They seemed to have given up on the idea of performing. Who would want to go up there after this?

Veldon wrapped up his act by pretending to eat the fireballs he'd been juggling, extinguishing each as he put them in his mouth. Beside him, Feoldor lowered everything on stage and finished his vanti performance by floating a tankard of ale from the bar right into his hand and taking a big swallow. The crowd banged their tankards on the tables in salute. Orlyn finished by calling the vines. He wiggled his finger, and they followed him across the stage. He then pointed at the back wall, and they scurried up the wood and stone to form a beautiful canvas to brighten the stage backdrop. That done, he picked up his pot and placed it back within his robe.

The audience sat in awed silence before someone on the right started to clap, then another, and another. Pretty soon the common room erupted in applause as the wielders slowly made their way back down the stairs.

Ty was enraptured by what had just taken place. He watched as Noreen walked down the row of performers on the other side of the stage. She was clearly trying to get them to go up, but each one shook their head. No one wanted to follow an act like that.

"Are you going to play?" Ty asked Lyessa.

"Not after that."

Mistress Aboloff looked beside herself and finally started for the platform steps herself, but halfway there she caught Ty's eye. He saw the desperation on her face, so he stood. She smiled and frantically waved him up. She was so flustered she didn't even bother going up to offer a formal introduction.

"What are you going to do?" Narendi asked.

"I'm going to play."

She smiled. "Are you going to do some Mazota Wanjenga magic for them?"

"Something like that." He left the table and headed up the steps at the side, passing the other three council members on their way to their seats.

Orlyn smiled. "Good luck following that."

He was joking, of course, but Ty kind of took it as a challenge anyway as he made his way up the steps and across the platform to the front.

A lot had changed since the first time he'd stood in this spot. For one, he was stronger now, more capable of his magic. Before, what he'd unleashed had been accidental, purely instinct; this time he could control it. The question was how far to let his magic go.

The applause from the previous performances died out, and the crowd watched quietly, waiting to see what was coming next. His pipes had been very well received the last time, and that was without the knowledge that he had accidentally used magic on the crowd. After his last performance, he had somehow made the entire audience forget what he had done. He had no idea how, or that he even could. Nyalis had told him that it was the gift of a puller. A very powerful, very dangerous gift that could allow one to extract memories and thoughts from people's minds. He'd never attempted that again.

He stood at the edge of the platform quietly, looking out across the crowd, then slowly reached into his jacket pocket. The audience leaned forward in their seats, holding their breath in anticipation. When he pulled out his pipes, there was an audible groan.

"He's just going to play a flute?" one child asked his mother.

Ty tried not to laugh.

He took a moment to look at the overlord's table. Lyessa's father had a smile on his face as he waited, but Ty noticed the Sidaran Assembly members did not. In fact, they didn't look happy at all to see him up there. He wondered if they still held him responsible for what Mangora had made him do. He guessed it was only natural for them to be at least wary. The first time they'd seen him, he was trying to kill them. For a brief moment, he hesitated. Perhaps this wasn't the best time to bring his magic to bear.

He shook it off. No, if the community was ever to accept him like they clearly had the others, then he needed to show them who he was. Well, part of who he was.

Ty lifted the flute his father had made to his mouth and took a deep breath. The notes flowed out of the instrument like water over the falls of Aero'set, cascading down into pools at his feet, forming dozens of streams that flowed between the aisles and around the table, filling the entire place with a sense of wonder and beauty.

The crowd slowly began to relax in their seats, leaning back as they let the music drift over them, covering them like a warm blanket on a cold winter night, or like a comforting blaze and a hot drink after a long day's work. Smiles began to blossom on faces like Orlyn's flowers on the vine. Eyes lowered as those listening let the haunting melody lull them into a gentle rest.

For a moment, he wasn't sure where to take them. The last time he participated in a Performance Night, he had transported them to his special place in the woods behind his house, but this time he wanted to do more.

An idea sprang to mind. Why hadn't he thought of it until now?

He and Breen and Narendi had spent hours trying to convey to the council the incredibleness of their journey to find the key, but Ty never once thought to use his gifts to show them. And even though he was getting a little weary of the retelling, the idea of being able to show his audience these places with their own eyes had his hands shaking.

He eased his magic into the music, and the room came alive. The notes flowed out across the room, snatching hold of the walls and ceiling and floor and folded them in on themselves, transporting the audience from the East Inn straight into the swamps of Reed Marsh. The people gasped as the inn disappeared. He couldn't believe how excited he was to take them on this journey, though leaving out the more crucial details that the townsfolk didn't need to see, like Douina's home inside the marsh or the traveling mirrors or the key.

The crowd tensed as he took them along the trail leading through the dense bog. It was like floating through the air just above the ground as they moved quickly down the mist-filled path. They startled as one of the razorbacks on the right turned and hissed.

Seeing the crowd's response, Ty decided to be a little more careful about how much he showed of the horrors they'd seen. The last thing he wanted was the people turning on him because he'd frightened their children so badly they didn't sleep for a week. He sent them through a thick patch of fog, and when they came out, they were floating across the river he'd nearly drowned in.

From there, he led them out across the open grasslands to the village of Karpaath, guiding them through the mountain and out overlooking the incredible maze below. Oohs and ahhs erupted at the sight. He took them through the maze, past the lumbering maze monster, and down to the wall of fire. Most gasped and covered their faces when he took them through.

When the crowd opened their eyes, they were floating out over the dunes of the Wengoby. He'd decided against taking them down into the underground cavern where the lake monster lurked. Even he wasn't all that keen on seeing it again. If the council members wanted a more detailed viewing, he could show them during their meeting later that evening.

Ty spared a passing glance down at Narendi, whose face brightened when she saw her homeland. They left the mountainside and headed out over the dunes. It was a lot of fun flying over the desert. Ty even added in a sandstorm behind them, just to let them see the force of it, even going so far as to let it envelop them for a short time.

He eventually brought them out of the storm just before reaching Narendi's home. He hadn't been awake when they had carried him and Breen into the Imbatoo village, so he recreated the image as best he could from what he could remember of the place. He took them slowly through the sea of sherakin skin tents and let them watch Narendi's people move about their daily lives. There were tears in Narendi's eyes as they passed her family's home.

Leaving the tents, he took them out across the training grounds behind the village. They passed the Mzwati dune runners as they ran through their training, some even popping up from under the sand to startle several in the crowd. He took them into the stone chambers where the Wazeri held their teachings, showing them the surrounding statues of their former leaders.

From there he took them out over the dunes toward Zwaneri a Wakale, slowing their pace as they reached the feeding grounds. He brought up several of the orm for them to see, but from a safe distance. Many in the room froze when the sand below them moved as one of the giant orms tunneled past.

Not wanting to take them through the actual temple, he let the desert fold in on itself, and they entered the Riverlands. More than one person gasped when he took them out over one of the rope bridges and they looked down and saw how high the trees truly rose.

Ty's father was smiling as he stared out across the beautiful giants. Ty took them through the shops and homes built inside the great trees and led them slowly down the circular staircases to the thick roots at the bottom. From there he took them up the Bul Isra River to Tulgava Rashuvi. After taking a moment to circle the upper palm of the great tree, leaving off the mirrors, he then transported them into the snow-covered Angoran Mountains.

He took them through Lower Wellhollow before it had been burned by the bulradoer, and then up into the pass leading to Upper Wellhollow, letting them see the town that had been carved into the side of the mountain. He took them into the tunnel at the back, past the old oracle's dwelling, and into Harok Laos. He spent a little more time there, allowing them to see the incredible pictorial histories that had been carved into the walls. He could see Breen trying to get his attention at the side, no doubt to warn him off of showing them anything further, but Ty couldn't exactly stop right there. He had to find a way to transition them back to the inn.

As soon as they had encircled the stone chamber, the Doors of Light opened on the other side to a blinding light, and he took them through. But instead of finding themselves on the cliffs overlooking the Valley of Needrin, he brought them through the northern walls of Easthaven, down River Street, and straight up through the front doors of the East Inn, stopping inside the common room, where he released the music and lowered his pipes as the room fell into place.

The audience was stunned into silence. No one moved. Probably wondering if it was over or if they were still inside his magic.

Ty was breathing a little heavier, and he could feel sweat drops beading on his forehead. It had taken more out of him than he had expected. Then again, he had just taken them from one side of Aldor to another.

He tucked his flute back inside his jacket and walked off stage. He headed over to their table and retook his seat. Even the wielder council members seemed in shock. Had he never performed that magic for them before? He was sure he had, though perhaps not to this degree. Once they were back within the council chambers, he was going to show them Aero'set.

Lyessa turned in her seat and whispered, "Ty, that was . . . wow." She kissed his cheek, and they both stared out across the room.

"You'll have to use some of that glamour magic tonight," his father said, "and show us more of what Aero'set looks like."

Ty nodded eagerly.

Around the common room, no one seemed willing to move, and the silence was growing awkward. Eventually, Noreen got to her feet and hustled up the stairs. She cleared her throat, looking befuddled. "Uh . . . thank you, ladies and gentlemen for your attendance. That concludes our entertainment for this evening. We here at the East Inn wish you a wonderful week and hope you will return soon." She cleared her throat once more and left the stage without even calling on her servers to make their rounds.

The overlord's table was the first to leave. Those sitting nearby waited for him and his guests to pass before rising themselves.

Lyessa stood also.

"Where are you going?" Ty asked.

"I'm going to speak with my father."

"Don't forget about the meeting this evening."

"I haven't. I'll meet you there." She passed a quick glance at Narendi, then turned and started across the room. Those who saw her coming were quick to move out of the way.

Once the overlord had left, the room slowly began to vacate, everyone filing out in an orderly fashion. It was the quietest and most organized exit he'd ever seen.

"That was quite the show," Orlyn said, combing through his beard.

"Aye," Veldon said. "And to think those places are actually real." He shook his head and wiped the top of his head with his hanky.

The wielder council waited until most had left, and then they started for the side door, which led out onto Lynden.

"Why are we going this way?" Breen asked.

"Because," Feoldor said, holding the door for Reloria as she tried to straighten her bonnet, "the last time we went out the front, we were mobbed by a crowd wanting to see more magic."

"I even had several of the aristocracy who wished to hire me for their dinner parties," Orlyn gloated.

Ty's father shook his head and released another puff from his pipe. "We've been reduced to sideshow attractions."

"I recall someone making a bit of a spectacle during the archery competition at the last fair," Orlyn said, and Ty's father cleared his throat.

"I'll be along shortly," Veldon said once they made it outside. "I want to check on the docks. Last time I left Jamis in charge, he forgot to lock the front doors."

The others nodded, and they cut through the back alley behind Orlyn's shop and from there up to River Street. They had to wait a couple of minutes until most of the people leaving the inn had walked past before crossing over. Once across, they started through the lesser-known shops, eventually reaching some of the residences between River Street and the Easthaven garrison.

They made it past the first two buildings when Ty stopped. "Wait."

"What is it?" his father asked, causing the others to turn.

"We're not alone." Ty left the others and walked up to the next alleyway. As soon as he stopped, he turned and crossed his arms. "I know you're in there. What were you planning to do, jump out and scare everyone?"

"Something like that," Kraea grumbled as she stepped out of the shadows and into the street where the others were waiting.

"I don't like you coming into town like this. You take a risk of being seen."

"You'd be surprised how few people are out after dark."

"Let's not linger here in the cold, shall we?" Orlyn said with a shiver. "We risk her being seen even more."

"What was all the magic I felt earlier?"

"I was playing my pipes," Ty said, using their link so he didn't have to keep explaining what the two were talking about.

"Figured as much. The magic felt familiar."

They followed the others around to the back of the Harbor House, where Orlyn tapped on the back door with his staff and waited on Eliab to open up.

Ty could hear the chains being unstrung from inside before the door cracked and the old Harbor House gatekeeper peered out. As soon as he saw Orlyn, he opened it fully. "Didn't ecthpect anyone thith evening," he said, placing his crossbow on the table. He waited until they had all entered. Ty and Kraea were last.

"Is Gilly here?" Ty asked.

"Not yet," Eliab said, then took a look outside. "Ith that all of you?"

"For the moment," Ty's father said. "Veldon went to check on the docks, and I believe Lady Lyessa will be along shortly."

Ty couldn't get used to hearing his father call her *Lady* Lyessa. It sounded so formal and strange coming from him.

"She's not here yet, is she?" Ty asked Eliab as the older man shut the door and threw back the bracer.

"Not that I've theen." He turned. "Thould I walk you down?"

Feoldor chuckled. "I think we can find our way."

"I think I'll stay up here and wait for Lyessa," Ty said. He turned and looked at Breen, Narendi, and Kraea. "You can go on down if you wish."

They did, leaving Ty to sit in the kitchen with Eliab. The room hadn't changed much, or at all, since he and Breen had left. Stove in the corner, hutch on the back wall, the shelves beside it stocked with a variety of food items and old dishes. Ty sat quietly, watching Eliab as he rubbed a cloth across the wood of his bow. The gatekeeper wasn't much for conversation, and the longer Ty waited, the more uncomfortable the silence became.

"So," Ty said, looking over at the gatekeeper, who was now sitting quietly, staring at the door, "what do you do around here for fun?"

Eliab looked up.

Ty smiled. "Surely you do more than just sit here all day."

"I read."

"Oh?"

Eliab pointed over his shoulder to one of the shelves behind Ty. Stuffed between some stacked plates and a couple of teapots was a small selection of books. They were too far away to read the spines.

"I see. My sister likes to read."

Eliab nodded but didn't say anything, and Ty stared at the top of the table, tapping it lightly with his fingers. He looked back up. "Where were you born?"

"Here."

"Here as in Easthaven, or here as in this very home?"

"My family hath owned thith plathe for generationth."

"Oh, that's very . . . interesting." He went back to staring at the table, then at the door. Where was Lyessa? Had she decided not to come after all? Perhaps her father needed her, and she went home instead. He finally stood. "You know, I think I'll see what they're doing downstairs." He quickly left the room and made his way into the next and through the door leading down into the cellar.

"That was uncomfortable even for me," Kraea said before Ty even got to the

door.

He stepped inside to find the others quietly chatting amongst themselves. Narendi and Fraya were sitting at the back talking with Breen. Ty was glad to see her getting along with some of the others.

Ty took a seat on the left side, near his father. Sheeva was there as well. He had no idea when she'd arrived or if she'd been there waiting. Knowing her, she'd been at Performance Night the whole time. At least she wasn't locked in battle with Narendi or Kraea. In fact, strangely enough, Kraea was sitting beside her, letting the golden-eyed assassin rub the top of her head.

"Strange how both of you have such similar eyes," Ty noted.

"We were just discussing that," Ty's father said. "Or at least we were trying to, but since we can't hear Kraea, it made it a bit difficult. Ask her what she thinks."

"*Something does feel familiar about her,*" Kraea said. She turned and sniffed the nightwalker, who scooted back in her seat when she did. "*Something about her smell.*"

"Kraea says that there is something about Sheeva that is familiar. Something about her smell." He shrugged. "But other than that, she doesn't really know."

"Do things look different through your eyes than what the rest of us see?" Orlyn asked, looking at both Sheeva and Kraea. No one had thought, or dared, to ask Sheeva that before, or anything really.

Sheeva looked at Kraea, then back at Orlyn. "I don't know. What do you see?"

Orlyn laughed. "That's a fair point." He thought a moment. "I guess I was just wondering if everything seemed sort of—"

The door to the council chamber burst open, and Veldon rushed in, completely out of breath.

"What's wrong?" Ty's father asked.

"It's Lyessa."

Ty stood. "What about her?"

"She . . . she's been kidnapped."

Chapter 63 | Ty

HAT DO YOU MEAN kidnapped?" Ty asked. "Where? When?"

"Give him a chance to catch his breath," Ty's father said as everyone gathered around the front of the table where Veldon was panting heavily.

"I just ran from the docks. There were men loading a boat out of schedule." His eyes narrowed. "In fact, it was the same boat you had me check on yesterday."

"Get to the part where you think they kidnapped Lyessa," Ty said.

Veldon nodded and took another deep breath. "They had men watching the platform and the warehouse, but I was in the office and didn't have a light on, so they didn't see me. I saw them carry someone from their wagon down to the boat, but the person was wrapped in a dark cloak, so I couldn't see who it was. As soon as I stepped out onto the porch and shouted for them to stop, they attacked. Three charged me, while the rest ran down the pier for their ship. I struck my flint, and as soon as my hands ignited, the men coming for me scattered."

Ty grabbed the back of the chair. "Then how do you know they had

Lyessa?"

"Because she managed to fight them off long enough to get free of the cloak they had her wrapped in. She was bound and gagged, but I could see her red hair and the white gown she was wearing this evening. I ran for the pier as fast as I could, and she tried to fight them off, but there were too many of them for her to make it off the ship. By the time I reached the end of the pier, the ship was already halfway into the river."

Ty raced for the door.

"Where are you going?" Breen asked.

"To stop them."

"How?"

"Maybe we can catch them at the bridge." He ran through the door.

"You'll never get there in time," Veldon shouted after him.

Ty kept running. He raced up the stairs and found Eliab in the process of relocking the chains. "Open the door!" he shouted as he ran into the kitchen.

Eliab startled and quickly fumbled with the chains to get them off. As soon as the bracer was free, Ty flew out the door. Kraea was barely a step behind him. He heard footsteps thumping behind him and glanced over his shoulder to see Breen, Narendi, and his father shooting out the door after him. He couldn't wait for the others. He needed to get to the East Bridge before the ship passed.

"What are you going to do when you get there?" Kraea asked, running alongside him.

"I don't know." He looked at her. *"Run ahead and see if you can find them. You can move a lot faster than we can."*

Kraea took off and disappeared into the alleyways ahead.

Ty could feel her racing through the back streets, his own legs moving as fast as he could force them to try catching up. Why would a ship of Bristonian lancers disguised as rivermen kidnap the Sidaran overlord's daughter? What was Overlord Meyrose thinking? Was he trying to start a war?

Ty reached Wood Lane and headed east toward the square. Behind him, Breen and his father were just catching up, their longer legs giving them the clear advantage. By the time they hit the center of town and Ty glanced over his shoulder, Narendi was just reaching the main thoroughfare behind them.

She saw them and kept running.

Leaving the square, they raced south down River Street for the bridge. He could feel Kraea ahead, but she wasn't saying anything. He tried thinking about what he could do when he got there. If they reached the bridge before the ship, how could he stop them? He guessed he could try using the water to hold them in place, but the river was fairly wide around the city, with a strong current, which meant even if he could hold them there, it would be difficult to get out to them.

They rounded the bend. The bridge was ahead. *"Where are they?"* he called up to Kraea.

"I think we're too late."

"Where are you?" Ty couldn't see her anywhere.

"I'm down on the walkway under the bridge," she said.

Ty's father and brother had now pulled ahead of him as they raced down toward the guard towers on the city side of the bridge.

"Under the bridge!" Ty shouted to them.

As soon as they heard, they headed off the road to the right of the gatehouse, and from there they took the steps down to the boardwalk underneath the bridge that ran along the edge of the river. Ty stopped long enough to point Narendi to where they were going, then ran down the steps after them, staring out at the water ahead. He didn't see a ship large enough to have sails. He glanced up the river toward the bend leading to the dockworks, but there was nothing there. He reached the edge of the walkway and leaned out over the rail to look the other way, but it was shrouded in darkness.

"Ru'kasha Kor." The night brightened, and Ty spotted a ship farther down with a single pulled sail. "There!" he shouted, then hit the top of the rail. "We're too late!"

"Ru'kasha Kor." Breen stared down the river as well. "I see them."

"How?" their father asked. "I see nothing."

"Show him," Ty said to Breen, and then started running back up the steps, meeting Narendi on her way down.

"Well? What happened? Did you find them?"

Ty shook his head. "We were too late." He stopped halfway up and turned. "Wait! If we can get home fast enough, we might still have a chance to catch them at the narrowing in the river." Ty bit his tongue. "But our horses are back at the inn." He turned and looked at Kraea. "Please."

Kraea snorted. *"Fine. But only this once."*

Ty turned to his father and brother, who had joined them halfway up the stairs. "See if you can get the horses and come behind us as fast as you can. I'm going to ride Kraea back."

"Can she carry me as well?" Narendi asked.

Ty looked at the draakar, and she bared her teeth.

"Can you?" he asked. "It's important." Ty didn't know if Kraea could carry him, let alone both of them. She wasn't much taller than one of the miniature ponies he'd seen at the city fair, but she was very strong.

Kraea finally nodded. *"I can try. But I make no promises."*

Breen and his father took off up the stairs and disappeared over the top as they ran back to the East Inn. Ty turned and looked up at the bridge. "Now, how do we get you across without the guard towers seeing?"

Kraea grinned and walked over to the underside of the bridge and started climbing up the pier. Ty and Narendi watched in awe as the draakar used her claws and tail to work her way up to the undercarriage and then start across. Ty had seen lizards crawl upside down before, but he'd never pictured something as big as Kraea being able to do the same.

"Come on," Ty said to Narendi, and they raced back up the stairs and over the bridge. He thought he could hear Kraea's claws scraping along the stone underneath them at one point, but it was quickly covered by the wind and water below.

They reached the other side and waited, but Kraea didn't show.

"Where is she?" Narendi asked. "You don't think she fell in, do you?"

"I'm over here."

"This way," Ty said, and he and Narendi left the road in front of the bridge and started into a small stand of trees growing along the cliffside, which overlooked the water below. Kraea was sitting in the shadow of the tallest tree, which happened to hang partway over the edge of the steep embankment.

"So this is how you've been sneaking in."

She nodded, and they followed the trees until they were far enough away not to be seen by the guards in the towers. He took a moment to examine the draakar.

"Well, what are you waiting for," she asked, *"an invitation?"*

"I'm just trying to see how best to get on without poking anything. You don't exactly have a saddle here. Are you sure you can carry both of us?"

"No."

"What did she say?" Narendi asked.

"She said no problem."

Kraea growled, and Ty carefully climbed on her back. He had to nearly lie prone to get his feet high enough not to drag on the ground. Narendi climbed behind him and had to practically sprawl on top of him.

"This feels strange," Narendi said.

"Speak for yourself."

Ty wrapped his arms around Kraea's neck. "Let me know if I'm choking you." He looked behind him. "Hold on to me."

Narendi nodded and wrapped her arms around his chest.

"Alright," Ty said. "Let's go."

Kraea started slowly at first, then picked up speed once she was sure the two of them weren't going to fly off. The draakar was swift on her feet, but the ride was anything but smooth. Ty was bounced all over the place, the wind repeatedly knocked from his lungs every time she clawed the ground. They'd barely made it over the rise when Narendi lost her grip and flew off the back, pulling Ty with her. They both rolled across the snow, forcing Kraea to stop and come back for them.

"This isn't going to work," Ty said, patting the snow from his front as they crawled back to their feet. He looked at Narendi. "Maybe you should wait for Breen to get here with the horses."

Narendi's face hardened, and she looked at Kraea's back. "Why don't you make a saddle?"

"What?"

"With your wind magic. You can make shields and pole hooks, why not something to ride?"

Ty looked down at Kraea. He hadn't even considered it. He'd never tried to create something that complex before.

"I'll try." He gathered the wind and pictured a saddle in his mind as he tried shaping it around Kraea. He'd barely gotten to the stirrups when it fell apart. He huffed in frustration and tried again, this time keeping it as simple as possible, basically nothing more than a seat with a strap. Kraea jumped when the wind hardened around her underbelly.

"Don't crush me," she said, and Ty loosened the strap's hold.

"It's not exactly pretty, but I think it might work," he said and carefully climbed on. It was certainly more comfortable than her scales.

"It doesn't need to be pretty," Narendi said. "It's not like we can see it."

With the wind cushioning their undersides, they were able to sit a little straighter. As soon as they found their seats, Kraea wrapped her stubby wings around them to hold them in place.

Ty patted the side of Kraea's neck. He hoped they were ready. "Run!"

Kraea took off. Again, she started slower at first, but after the first half mile, when she saw they weren't going to fall off, she opened up. This time, they seemed to move as one. Ty and Narendi lowered themselves as close to Kraea's back as they dared to keep the wind out of their faces and to help her move a little faster.

It was exhilarating. It was also freezing.

Ty thought about raising a shield in front of them to block the wind, but he was afraid that if he tried, he'd lose his hold on the saddle and they'd both go flying again, so he resigned himself to the cold.

Thankfully, it was the middle of the night, so they weren't likely to pass anyone on the road. Kraea didn't seem to have any problem navigating in the dark. *"How are your eyes?"* Ty asked. *"Are you able to see? I don't want you catching a hole and laming yourself."*

Kraea growled. *"You worry about hanging on. I'll worry about the road."*

He didn't ask again.

They passed the East Hill Orchard and took the immediate road to the right, leading back toward the house. He hoped Breen and his father weren't too far behind. If they did manage to reach the narrow section of the river before the Bristonians, Ty was going to need all the help he could get. He still wasn't quite sure what he was going to be able to do once they got there. His best option was to try building that air bridge.

He could feel Kraea's unease about that decision. She didn't want to end up in the water if the bridge failed. Still, it might be their only option. If they didn't stop the ship there, Ty wasn't going to get another chance. Just a few miles down, the river merged with the outer edges of the marsh, which meant it would be impossible to reach them without a boat.

Ty chewed on his lip. Of all the days for Gilly to show up late, why did it have to be today?

The icy wind burned his face as Kraea continued to pound through the snow. His nose ran and his eyes leaked at the cold. Worse, the wind was already hardening them to his skin.

"How are you doing?" he called back to Narendi. If this was bad for him, he knew it was ten times worse for her. Her body was used to warm, dry climates, not the freezing cold of a snowy winter.

"I'm alright," she said, her voice quivering.

"Not much farther," he said.

A few miles down the road, Ty pointed to the turnoff ahead. "There," he said, and Kraea took it. They headed through the woods back toward the house, breaking from the tree line and into the yard. Kraea started to slow, but Ty waved her on.

"Don't stop," he said. "We've got to get to the river before them."

Kraea groaned.

"Unless you need to rest," Ty added quickly. He was so focused on getting to Lyessa, he didn't stop to think about the fact that Kraea had just run several miles full on without a break.

She snorted but kept going. They passed the barn and the house and headed over the small bridge spanning the creek behind. From there, they tore into the woods. He wondered how far behind his father and brother were and whether they'd be able to catch up in time. Ty sent out a web of his magic ahead, but they were still too far from the river for him to tell if the ship was there. His magic came back with nothing but the odd owl, a couple of foxes, and a few dirt diggers just waking to begin their nocturnal activities.

Ty ducked and dodged as many of the low-hanging branches along the trail as he could, missing a few, and they slapped his head and arms. He was too numb for them to complain much. He sent out another web, and again it came back empty. He started to panic. What if they'd been too slow? What if the ship had used oarsmen to flee? He couldn't afford to lose them. The next city large enough for the ship to stop was Riverton, which was south of Reed Marsh. But even if Kraea was willing to try running that far, they'd never outpace a ship, especially one that was moving with the current.

"She'll be there," Kraea said, and Ty squeezed her neck gratefully.

His fingers were so numb as they sped along the trail that he was afraid of losing his grip and tumbling off. Still, he knew they were getting close and forced himself to tighten his grip. If Kraea could run all the way from Easthaven, the least he could do was bear the cold.

They broke from the trees, and Kraea took them down the embankment to the churning water below. Their father's boat was still there on the left, just under its canvas. Ty half climbed, half fell out of his makeshift saddle, and by the time his feet hit the ground, the hardened air had dissipated. Kraea was panting hard behind him as Ty stumbled down to the water's edge to see if there was any sign of the riverboat. There was no ship coming from the direction of Easthaven, and nothing to the left either. Had they missed them?

He balled his hands into fists and looked around for something to punch.

"Don't look at me," Kraea said sarcastically.

Ty turned and stared out across the quick-moving water. All the incredible hardships he'd overcome, bringing an entire city back from some hidden pocket between the realms, and he wasn't even strong enough to catch a riverboat. A hand rested on his shoulder, and he turned.

Narendi smiled. "Maybe they just haven't gotten this far? If she's as strong as you say, then I'm sure she will be doing everything she can to try to stop them. If she saw your friend Veldon on the docks, she knows you will be coming for her."

She was right. Lyessa wouldn't give up, though Ty didn't know what she could do, surrounded by a ship full of armed Bristonian lancers. But he couldn't give up hope. He sent another web to the left, out along the southern waterway, away from Easthaven. He pushed it as far as he could, and when the web broke apart, it came away empty.

He turned to do the same in the other direction.

"Wait," Kraea said, having joined them along the riverfront. *"I think I . . . Yes, there's something out there."*

Ty walked down nearly into the water to get a better angle. His heart raced. Kraea was right. He could see something. It had to be them. The trees lining both sides of the river made it difficult to see, as their branches blocked out any chance of moonlight getting through, but his night sight helped.

Pretty soon, there was no mistaking it. He could see the white sail of the ship as it made its way toward them.

"Now what?" Narendi asked. "How are we going to stop them?"

Ty looked out across the river to the other side. "I could set a wind net." He turned and scanned the top of the embankment. "I might be able to attach it to some of the trees on the sides of the river and use it to stop the ship." He turned around. "Of course, I'd risk the ship getting caught in the net and the current pushing it sideways and flipping the boat."

"That doesn't sound good," Narendi said. "What about your air bridge?"

He grimaced. "That might be our only option."

"And you wouldn't have to create one across the entire river," she said. "Only halfway."

That was true, though it could actually make it more difficult, since he wouldn't have something to directly anchor the other end to. Ty quickly gathered the wind just to see what he could manage. Creating a saddle was one thing; creating a bridge large enough to span half the river and stable enough for them to walk on was another. He turned. The ship, which was no more the tip of his finger in size when he'd last looked, was now nearly the full length of his finger.

He had to hurry.

He gathered the air and started shaping the bridge. He used the East Bridge as a reference, with its walls and piers and archways, but quickly found that because he wasn't planning on expanding it all the way to the other side, instead stopping somewhere in the middle, he was going to need to add some supports below to hold it in place over the water. Unfortunately, the current was swift, and hardening enough air to build a pier that sank to the bottom of the river was proving difficult and time-consuming.

"I see the bridge," Narendi said, and started toward it.

"No! It's not ready."

She stopped at the edge of the water and waited.

Besides it not being all that stable, it also wasn't nearly long enough. So far, he'd only managed to build it about a quarter of the way out from the shoreline. The ship was looming out of the shadows on the right. It was now the full length of his arm in size. He gritted his teeth. This was taking too long. He just wasn't proficient enough with this kind of magic to do what was needed.

"Hurry!" Narendi said, Kraea echoing her in his head.

"I'm going as fast as I can." He fought to keep his concentration as he continued to extend the bridge. He looked up. "It's too far away from shore!" The ship was sailing closer to the other side instead of straight down the middle of the river.

"Are you going to be able to make it or not?" Narendi asked.

Ty ignored her and poured all his efforts into getting the bridge out to the ship. He looked up. The ship was already on them, hardly a hundred feet away, close enough to see men gathering along the side. "Hurry!" he shouted at himself.

"Arrows!"

Ty looked up to see several archers running up to the side rails and drawing. "No, no, no!" He wasn't ready. It wasn't stabilized. He released his hold on the bridge in a desperate attempt to raise a shield, and the bridge collapsed as the arrows ricocheted into the surrounding woods. "No!" he screamed and raised his hands, driving his magic down into the river itself. A wave of water struck the front of the ship, and everyone aboard was thrown forward. The archers dropped their bows and grabbed for handholds as the entire ship began to turn in the water. The current spun them around, pushing the stern toward the far bank as it did.

"They're going to capsize!" Narendi shouted, and Ty immediately released his hold on the water. As soon as he did, the ship began to right itself, and not a moment too soon.

He watched as it started to pass. Desperately, he flung out a pole hook and grabbed some of the rigging in hopes of climbing out over the water, but one shift of the boat and he was yanked off his feet. He would have gone headfirst into the river if not for Kraea and Narendi snatching him back.

He turned and gathered the wind and threw it at the mast. The hardened air hit it like a battle-axe, and the silence was split with a thunderous crack as the thick beam was sliced in two. It smashed into the main deck, scattering men as they leaped to get out of the way. Ty nearly bit his tongue off for not thinking about the fact that Lyessa might have been on the deck.

His fear about the crew employing their oars proved true, for even without the mast, the men didn't stop rowing, and the ship continued moving. He drew the air again and lashed it to as many trees along their side of the bank as he could, and then sent out another hook to grab the back of the ship, but before he could get even halfway, a cracking noise at his feet stopped him, and he looked down at the water.

It was freezing.

The water hardened into a sheet of ice for yards along the bank to either side, then raced out across the river and wrapped itself around the boat like a lasso, holding it firmly in place. Ty turned to find Narendi kneeling at the edge of the river with both her fists planted in the water. She pulled them out and stood.

"I had to try."

He almost hugged her. Turning, he looked out across the ice to the ship. "Is it safe enough to walk on?"

She shrugged as she raised her dagger. "I hope."

He took a deep breath and stepped out on it.

Chapter 64 | Ty

THE ICE CREAKED AND GROANED, and Ty could hear the river underneath lapping against the bottom, sending chills up his spine that at any moment it could shatter and take him through. His boots slipped on the slick surface. As soon as he got his feet under him and stomped a few times to make sure the ice would hold, he waved Narendi and Kraea to follow him out.

The moon was rising just over the trees behind them, casting its pale light across the ice and the trapped ship ahead. Ty glanced over his shoulder, back toward the forest trail. They didn't have time to wait on his father and brother, but he hoped they were close.

"Ty!"

Hearing the warning in Narendi's voice and the sense of danger flooding from Kraea, he turned, instinctively conjuring a shield between himself and the ship. Before he'd even completed his turn, he heard the thumps of arrows hitting the shield and bouncing off.

Anger flooded through him, and he brought blue flames to life in both hands as he took off, running straight for the ship.

The men near the back shouted and scurried away from the side. As badly as Ty wanted to burn those responsible for Lyessa's capture, he realized how completely stupid it would be to release his flames and set the ship on fire. He shuddered at the thought and instead lobbed several balls of blue fire just over the top, not close enough to strike the ship, but low enough to keep the archers ducking for cover.

They were about halfway across the ice when he realized they still had to figure out a way to get aboard, especially since the lancers had pulled up both of the rope ladders from the side.

"I think we could use one of your bridges now," Narendi shouted, echoing his thoughts.

He gathered the wind as they closed in on the ship, deciding to create a simple gangplank. He had two firm objects to hold the ends, and it wouldn't have to be all that long. Keeping his shield up, he shaped the wind in front of them, gluing it to the ice first and then stabilizing the other end to the railing of the ship.

"Keep just behind me," he called back as he started up the long plank. He sent a fist of air up into the main deck, scattering lancers who were waiting to cut them down. He also deflected another volley of arrows on the right. He wondered what the men aboard were thinking, seeing the three of them running up the side of the ship on an invisible bridge. Then again, the sight of Kraea alone was probably terrifying enough, but add in some boy who could toss blue fireballs around and a girl who could freeze over a river with a touch, and what did it matter if they could seemingly walk on air?

Kraea roared and jumped onto the deck. Ty hit another group with a wall of air and sent them rolling across the planks toward the other side, his head swiveling as he tried to locate Lyessa. Some of the downed lancers went over the rail; others ended up tangled in the rigging. The stern end of the main deck was blocked by the mast Ty had brought down, and all the ropes and netting splayed made footing treacherous. Twice, Ty nearly fell from getting his boot snagged in the mess.

Lancers swarmed toward them, and Ty held his shield high to safeguard against the archers up on the forward deck. He couldn't extend it too much, or he'd lose his ability to fight back. He still hadn't spotted Lyessa. A couple of men had been crushed under the weight of the mast when it came down, but he didn't see anything that resembled a white gown.

"I don't see her!" Kraea said, then jumped out from behind his shield to snatch one of several lancers approaching from behind. She tore into his neck and left him to bleed across the deck, then scrambled after the next. Ty tried to extend his shield for her, but she flitted all over the place, and he was forced to give up and focus on keeping it around himself and Narendi. He sent another fist of air into a small group coming down the stairs on the left.

Like Kraea, Narendi found an opening and left the protection of the shield to rush a couple of men near the galley doors. She stabbed the first in the chest with her dagger, then ducked the second's sword and opened his neck. Both went down, and before Ty could get to her, she slipped through the doors and disappeared inside. He needed to do the same, but as soon as he turned, another volley of arrows forced him to stay where he was.

He conjured fire and sent a ball toward the stern, where it caught several of the archers and some of the loose sails hanging across the back of the ship from the mast. He decided against throwing more. The last thing he needed was to set the ship ablaze and risk burning them all alive. Spinning around, he pummeled two more lancers with a fist of air, sending them over the side. Out of the corner of his eye, he caught a group of lancers trying to creep up behind him where they thought the mast would block his view.

He turned and drew another fist of air to slam them against the cabin bulkhead, but a loud crack broke through the night, and the ship lurched and sent him tumbling forward.

The ice was breaking.

Ty tried to shout a warning to Kraea, who was on the foredeck holding back several lancers, but before he could get the words out, the current shoved the boat sideways and the stern swung free, sending the ship into a spin. It struck another patch of ice, and the jolt threw everyone across the deck. Ty rolled until he struck the portside rail and managed to pull himself up.

The lancers on the starboard side shouted, immediately stopping their pursuit in order to find something to hold on to as the ship continued to flounder in the crumbling ice. They now sat broadside in the current, pushed against the keel hard enough that the starboard side began to rise.

They were about to capsize!

Ty released his shield to grab hold of some rigging and pull himself up the deck. "Get to the top!" he shouted at Kraea. He could see the water creeping closer to the portside rail. The ship groaned as its hull scraped across the ice.

He needed to get below deck and find Lyessa and Narendi. Kraea roared and knocked the legs out from under two of the men she'd been locked in battle with. They rolled down the deck, bumped across the rail, and landed in the river, screaming and clawing for a handhold as they sank below the ice. Kraea dug in her claws and slowly started up the deck, trying to keep as far away from the encroaching water as possible.

The boat was nearly on its side and beginning to sink. The water was halfway up the deck and nearly to the galley door, which meant if Narendi and Lyessa were still down in the hull, they might not be able to get back out. Ty pulled himself up with the rigging until he was directly across from the door and got ready to jump. If he missed, he'd drop into the river below and be swept underneath. He crouched and aimed for the handle.

About the time he was ready to jump, the door opened, and a lancer stepped partway out, holding onto the sides of the doorframe. Ty blinked, realizing the man had a sword sticking out of his gut.

A moment later the piece of steel disappeared, and he was kicked sideways out of the door, where he plunged into the freezing water below. Behind him, Lyessa stumbled sideways onto the doorframe, with Narendi's arm around her, holding her up. Lyessa's face was cut and bruised, her white dress ripped and stained with blood. Lyessa had a sword in one hand and the other wrapped around Narendi's neck.

They looked at him and then down at the water.

"Hold on!" he said, and quickly gathered the wind to build a small walkway from the door to the rigging, lashing it to the mast behind him. "Come on!"

Lyessa was first to climb out the sideways door and step onto the bridge. Narendi was just behind her, holding her balance. Lyessa scooted carefully across, hardly able to see from the swelling on her face.

"A little closer," Ty shouted. "You're almost there." He clung to the rigging with one hand and leaned forward to grab her.

She reached out from a few steps away, and their fingers brushed when a lancer leaped down from the rigging above and slammed into them, knocking Ty into the mast and flinging Lyessa back across the air bridge. She collided with Narendi and knocked her off the bridge. Lyessa spun and threw out her arm just in time to grab Narendi's hand before she dropped into the freezing waters below.

Lyessa screamed as Narendi's weight pulled her arm from its socket, but she didn't let go. She lay prostrate across the bridge with Narendi holding on for dear life.

Ty recovered and spun to kick the lancer off the bridge, but Kraea had already skittered down the rigging and snatched the lancer in her jaws. She flung him away from the ship into the water, and he disappeared under the ice.

"Ty!" Narendi screamed, her grip on Lyessa slipping.

Ty gathered the wind and formed a shield large enough for Narendi to stand on and lashed it between the foredeck and the mast, easing the strain on Lyessa's wounded arm.

"Hold on!" he shouted, and crawled out onto the bridge, where Lyessa fought to keep a grip on Narendi, tears streaming down her face from the pain. With Kraea's help, Ty managed to pull them both back onto the bridge and over to the rigging before the ship sank any lower.

Lyessa's arm hung limp at her side, so Ty put his around her to keep her from falling away from the ship, which was now standing sideways in the water with the starboard railing straight over their heads. "We've got to keep climbing," he said over the roar of the water and ice crashing across the doomed ship. He grabbed a handful of rope and heaved, using the rigging to hold his feet in place as he lifted Lyessa up with him.

He hoped when the ship hit the bottom, it didn't flip on top of them.

Narendi was just above them, pulling herself up along the mast toward the railing above. Kraea was already waiting for them at the top. The ice gave a low groan, which was followed by a scraping sound that sent tremors through the ship. Ty quickly tightened his grip on Lyessa and the rope just before they were swung away from the deck.

Ty's worst fears were coming true. The ship was going to flip and carry them under.

He looked up at Narendi. "Can you do anything?"

She looked down and shook her head. "It took everything I had with the ice."

"Climb, you fools!" Kraea shouted above them.

Ty looked down. The water was only a few feet away. He wrapped Lyessa's good arm around his neck. "Hold on." She gritted her teeth and gripped him as best she could.

One of her eyes was swollen shut, and the other looked in the process of joining it. Pretty soon, she wasn't going to be able to see at all.

He grabbed the rope and pulled, only gaining a few inches at a time. He suddenly found himself thankful for the grueling physical training they had been forced to endure over the last several weeks in Aero'set.

The ice gave another loud crack, and the boat shuddered again, but instead of dropping them all into the water, it slowly began to rock back the other way.

Ty glanced over his shoulder. What was happening? Had Narendi managed to control the ice after all? Before he could find the shoreline to figure out where they were, the ship leveled off enough to drop them back onto the deck. Water rushed off the portside as the ship righted itself. Kraea climbed off the rail before she ended up in the water herself.

Ty looked at Narendi.

"It's not me," she said, looking just as baffled.

The riverboat leveled off, and Ty helped Lyessa to her feet, then started across the deck for the other side to see what was happening. Torches lined the bank behind them as a small group of people gathered on shore.

Ty was surprised to find he could still see his father's boat. The ship must not have been pulled all that far down the river after all. Below them, the ice shattered across the water, and the ship began to move once again, but instead of floating with the current, it was being pulled against it toward the shore.

Gilly stood at the front of the gathering, his small hands out over the water.

The sound of boots running across the deck had Ty and the rest turning to find what was left of the lancers diving over the opposite side, no doubt in hopes of swimming to the far shore and escaping. Ty was too exhausted to go after them. If they made it through the ice, it would be a miracle, but apparently they preferred taking their chances with the river than a group of angry wielders.

The four of them watched from the main deck as the ship was slowly guided across the water and over to where the others were waiting on shore. Ty was too tired to even attempt another bridge to get them down, but thankfully he didn't have to, as Feoldor was there to do it for him. The vanti placed a slide from the railing down to shore, and they each took their turn.

"We feared we'd missed you," Ty's father said, looking Ty over. "Are you okay?"

"I'll survive."

"I can't believe I wasn't there for it," Breen said, his arms crossed. "I don't like you three running off without me. That's the first time I haven't been around for a fight since we left last year."

"Sorry," Ty said. "If we would have waited on the horses, we would have never made it in time." He looked around, surprised to find the entire council present.

"When we made it back to the inn," Breen said, noticing Ty's confused look, "they were collecting their horses from the stables. So we all rode out together."

"And it's a good thing," Orlyn said, leaning against his staff. "Looks like you were about to go under for good. How did you flip the entire ship like that?"

"Not on purpose, that's for sure," Ty said.

"You made the ice?" Gilly asked excitedly, looking up at Ty. "That is very difficult."

"Afraid I can't take credit for that," Ty said. "That was all Narendi's doing."

Gilly turned and looked at Narendi and waved with one of his special smiles. She looked confused but waved back.

Fraya looked Lyessa over carefully. "What did they do to you?" She grimaced and then gently laid one hand on her friend's face and another on her arm. Lyessa gasped as the chill of Fraya's magic worked its way inside her and her arm snapped back into place with a pop. The bruising, cuts, and swollen eyes faded away, until she was once again her normal self, apart from the ripped and bloody clothing and the red hair plastered to her face.

"They intended to hold me for ransom," she said.

"Ransom?" Ty's father asked, frowning.

"It seems Overlord Meyrose is not happy with my father's decision to allow wielders free rein in Sidara. Apparently, Meyrose was going to use me as leverage to round up the wielders and send them to the Tower."

"That doesn't make much sense," Veldon said.

"It does if Meyrose is in league with them," Ty's father added. "As corrupt as that man is, I wouldn't put anything past him."

"I can kill him," Sheeva said. "I worked for him. I can get in and out before they can stop me."

Ty would have laughed if it weren't for the fact that Sheeva probably wasn't joking.

"That would be a terrible idea," Orlyn said. "An overlord assassinated by a wielder? No need to guess who would catch the blame for that, especially right on the aftermath of Sidara opening its borders to wielders. That would ignite a war for sure, and turn the rest of the kingdoms against us."

Feoldor fluffed his side whiskers. "Which at the moment, it seems, is only Keldor."

"Regardless," Ty's father said. "It's not our decision to make, but Lord Barl's. We will tell him what happened, and the rest will fall to him."

The others nodded, and the group began to split.

"Who's next?" Fraya asked, waiting to heal whoever needed it, and Ty motioned for Narendi to go. He followed just after. Most of his injuries were limited to abrasions on his hands from holding on to the rope.

Even Kraea walked over and held out her tail for Fraya to heal, but Fraya shied away.

"She won't bite," Breen said with a chuckle. "At least, not you."

Fraya smiled at the draakar and slowly reached out and placed her hand on the cut near the tip. She closed her eyes, and her magic seeped inside. Soon enough, the wound had resealed, and Kraea sauntered off up the trail.

Ty turned to see how Lyessa was doing and found her walking down to where Narendi was standing at the edge of the water. He started to go down, but Reloria grabbed his arm and shook her head. "Best you let those two talk alone."

Ty nodded but kept an eye on them. He didn't know what they were saying, but he wanted to be ready in case something happened. They talked a while, and then Narendi held out her hand, but Lyessa didn't take it. Instead, she stepped forward and hugged Narendi. Ty smiled as he watched. He caught several others doing the same.

"Seems they have finally found some common ground," Reloria said with a wink at him as she popped a piece of candy in her mouth and walked over to where Feoldor stood quietly conversing with Orlyn.

Ty quickly turned when Lyessa started back his way, pretending not to have been staring.

"Is, uh . . ." He looked down at where Narendi was now talking with Gilly at the edge of the water. "Is everything alright?"

Lyessa turned and looked at Narendi and smiled. "I think it will be." She grabbed his arm and pulled him back up the trail. "Take me home."

Chapter 65 | Ayrion

AYRION STOOD AT THE FRONT of the line of newly reforged Tanveer and stared into the darkened tunnel ahead. It was long since time for the khuls' arrival, and the fact that they hadn't had everyone anxious as they quietly listened and waited for any sign of the pending attack.

"Where are they?" Davin asked. The young man had insisted that he stay with his uncle this time.

"I don't know," Ayrion said.

So far, none of the watchers had returned to let them know the khuls were coming. It had the men all the more anxious as they stood in formation behind them—archers at the sides, polemen at the front, and their main force just behind, ready to take over after the initial charge. But so far, there'd been nothing. Most of the night had come and gone, so where were they?

Behind him was every able body capable of holding a sword, many still bearing injuries. Rae was physically incapable of doing more, completely burned out. Zynora was doing everything she could to help the injured and get Rae back on her feet, but there was only so much her Dar'Rhivanni prayers and Isha's cream could do.

It had taken everything Ayrion had to get the Upakans to the point of being able to at least stand side by side. Having their clan patches stripped and their rings changed had helped quite a bit, since most were unsure who they were standing alongside. Still, it had taken all three heads to reinforce Ayrion's commands.

Once the organization of the troops was in hand, Sirak had retired back to his cot in the infirmary, barely able to stand. It was a testament to his will that he had lasted as long as he had. That left the other two primaries to support Ayrion in tonight's assault. Brim waited with the main force behind them, while Zayden stood with the archers.

Ayrion's team was at the front waiting—even Elson, who looked about as fit as those standing around him, which wasn't saying much. The man did seem capable with a blade the few times Ayrion happened to pass him in the main chamber running through drills with Ferrin, but being able to swing a sword was a far cry from being able to stand against the charge of a khul horde.

Lenara was there as well, Nola a solid presence beside her. The two had clearly formed a bond. Ayrion wondered if the wolf could sense the change in the bulradoer and was protecting her. He'd asked Lenara not to get directly involved in the battle itself unless absolutely necessary. He wanted her to save as much of her strength as possible in case they needed another shield at the last minute to safeguard a retreat.

He hoped it didn't come to that, but with their numbers dwindling, he couldn't see many other possible scenarios.

Zynora, Tameel, and Rae were the only members of their company to stay behind, not including, of course, Myriah and Suri, who were still up top with Ayrion's mother, sister, and niece.

"I don't like waiting," Ferrin said, shifting from one foot to the other. "If they are to come, then get on with it."

The longer the men waited, the edgier they became. Ayrion finally walked down the left row to where Jorn and his father were holding position. "Have the khuls ever been this late in attacking before?"

His father shook his head, and Ayrion studied the dark passageway ahead. "I'm going to take a look. Send word to Zayden and Brim. I don't want them trying to bring the entire force in after me in case this is some kind of trap."

They nodded, and Ayrion walked back around to where those of his company were waiting. "Let's go take a look."

Lenara and Nola started up through the ranks toward them, but Ayrion shook his head. "I need you two to stay here. If something happens to us, they'll need you more than we will."

Lenara looked almost relieved at not having to venture down the corpse-filled tunnel and withdrew to her place behind the polemen.

Myron grabbed a torch from one of the fighters, but Ayrion waved it off. "We won't be needing that."

Elson cleared his throat. "In case it's escaped your attention, oh wise and fearless leader, not even you can see down here without light."

Ayrion smiled. He had come prepared. "We'll have light."

The others looked at each other curiously and shrugged, then followed him down the tunnel. The Upakans had taken up a position earlier that day that was deeper into the tunnel network than where they had been the previous night, since the prior battle had pushed them clear back to their own encampment. They were now somewhere around halfway between the camp and the chamber holding the stone doors. It was also one of the narrowest spots in the lower tunnels, making it a better choice for a defensive.

Being able to gain this much ground from what they had lost was important, giving them at least a small reprieve from the fear of running into another situation like the one they faced the previous night, when they were very nearly overrun.

Ayrion found himself breathing through his mouth more often than not. The way ahead reeked of dead khuls. Usually, the khuls would leave about half their dead, retrieving the rest each morning as they retreated back to their den. Ayrion wasn't sure how they intended to bury them in all this stone, the only other alternative being one he didn't wish to consider. However, this time, there had been no retrieval. In the aftermath of Zynora's blast, there didn't appear to be much in the way of survivors.

They crossed behind the second turn in the tunnel and ran into a couple of Upakan watchmen standing on either side. It was dark enough that the others didn't notice them pressed against the rock, but Ayrion nodded at them as he passed. The group rounded a third bend, and Bek finally spoke up, keeping his voice to a whisper.

"It's getting a bit hard to see in here. If you've got a light, might be a good time to—"

"Oomph."

Ayrion turned to find Myron picking himself up off the ground from where he had tripped over one of the khuls. The others had their hands in the air, trying to feel their way ahead.

"Give me a minute," Ayrion said, and reached into his shirt and pulled out the crystal Nyalis had given him. He held it up by its chain and spoke softly. "Luminate."

The crystal sparked to life, and a soft white glow filtered across their section of the tunnel. It wasn't bright enough to light the entire channel or harsh enough to leave strong shadows, but it was enough for those behind him to keep from tripping over any more dead khuls.

"What do you see?" Ferrin asked, hands tightening on his swords as he tried scanning the darkness ahead.

"Nothing but empty rock and corpses."

"Perhaps we scared them off," the smith said, the smile in his voice indicating he didn't think that likely.

"Wouldn't that be nice?" Elson agreed, his sword trembling in his hand. At least this time it wasn't because of his drink.

"Let's keep going," Ayrion said, moving forward.

So far there'd been not a peep from their enemy, not even the faintest trace echoing back through the corridor ahead. As much noise as these creatures made, he figured they would have heard something by now. Ayrion was starting to wonder if Ferrin was closer to the mark than they thought. Perhaps Zynora's magic had frightened them into a retreat.

No, if the creatures had been fearful of magic, they would have pulled back at the first ball of fire Lenara had sent their way. That hadn't deterred them in the least.

"I can't believe we are still finding dead khuls," Bek said. "I wonder how far back Zynora's blast went?"

"It was probably compounded by the close quarters within the tunnel system," Ferrin said, staring at the far-right wall. Several veins of gold ran down the side near head level.

"Maybe she managed to kill the rest of them," Myron said. "Perhaps there weren't as many left as we thought."

Ayrion hmphed. "One can only hope." Still, the farther in they went and the more dead khuls they found, the more that hope began to build. "I wonder how far back we have to go before we reach the doors." No sooner had he asked than his question was answered. They rounded the next bend, and he quickly brought them to a halt.

Just ahead, the tunnel opened into another chamber. It wasn't nearly as large as the one where they had set up camp, but larger than any of the others they'd passed through on their way down from the city above. The two stone doors on the other side were even bigger than the ones in Harok Laos, but the runes on these didn't wrap the entire casing and seemed more decorative in nature.

"It does look similar to the cavern at Wellhollow," Bek said as they slowly started toward the tunnel's entrance, stopping at the mouth to examine the inside of the cave for any living khuls.

There were several fire pits scattered around the room. None had been used recently. Ayrion didn't know if they were from the khuls or if his people had been camped here while trying to excavate through the doors.

"That's disgusting," Elson said, his face blanching as he stared at the half-eaten carcasses lying around the fire pits.

Ayrion grimaced. "I had a feeling."

Along with the dead khuls were several piles of human remains that the creatures had been feasting on. Ayrion tried pushing through the stench, but the smell was enough to cause even the strongest of stomachs to turn.

Cautiously, Ayrion started into the chamber, keeping one eye on the hole in the bottom of the doors ahead. He also took some time to study the drawings carved into the walls around them. From the accounts he had heard by the primaries and from his family, the images did appear to tell a story, covering some great battle from centuries past.

"Could be the Wizard Wars, don't you think?" Bek asked, wiping his mouth as he walked over.

Ayrion nodded. "I was just wondering the same."

He let the soft light from his crystal brighten a section on the left, depicting two sides locked in battle—one human, one that appeared to be khul. Behind the khul hordes stood a large cloaked figure whose hands and feet appeared to be made of wisps of smoke. Ayrion wondered if that was supposed to be a representation of the Dark Wizard himself.

"Over here," Ferrin whispered, his voice echoing around the open room.

Ayrion followed the others over to take a look at another section of wall, just right of the two enormous doors.

"I think this is a depiction of this chamber," Ferrin said once they made it over. "What do you think?"

Ayrion studied the carvings with the rest. It did appear similar, showing a chamber with two doors. On one side was a group of humans. Those in front wore robes and carried long staffs, while those behind stood poised with raised swords. He stared at the runic lettering and paused. *Is that . . . ?* He thought perhaps his eyes were playing tricks on him, and he leaned forward to look again.

"I don't believe it."

The others turned, some walking over to see what he was looking at.

"What is it?" Ferrin asked. "Did you find something?"

"I'll say." Ayrion pointed to a small grouping of symbols just above the armed warriors standing near the back of the room. "Look! Is it just me, or do those look an awful lot like—"

"The symbols on your ring?" Ferrin said.

Ayrion took a step back to see the image as a whole. "It's been under our noses all along. Proof the Tanveer existed. They stood here in this very room."

"And I'm guessing those are the wizards in front of them," Bek said.

Ayrion smiled. "Our history has been here for us to see the entire time." He now had undeniable proof. Not only did it show Tanveer warriors from the time during the fall of the Dark One, but this proved they were indeed linked to the wizards.

"What are they doing?" Myron asked, staring at the men in front with their staffs aimed at the two doors.

The staffs were encased in runes and seemed to be glowing, indicated by the lines pointing from them toward the two doors. The doors themselves were half-open, or perhaps half-closed, as the carving also depicted a line of khuls being marched through. The next illustration in line showed the robed humans still aiming their staffs toward the doors, but this time the doors were shut.

"Do you think one of them could have been Nyalis?" Bek asked.

The thought hadn't even occurred to Ayrion. But from what Nyalis had told them, the wizard had been around during the fall of Aerodyne. This could very well be a retelling of something he had taken part in. The hairs on Ayrion's arms rose just thinking about how incredible that was, to have spoken with someone who had taken part in Aerodyne's fall.

"Clearly this chamber was created as a holding place for the creatures," Ayrion said. "I wonder if the old city above even knew it was down here? No one might have ever known this place existed if not for Mount Ash erupting."

"Makes you stop and think," Ferrin said, turning to take it all in. "Maybe that eruption wasn't just a coincidence."

"Are you saying you think the Defiler had something to do with it?" Myron asked.

Ferrin shrugged. "Or his followers."

"Regardless," Ayrion said, turning to look at the hole in the bottom of the two doors. "We have more important things to worry about than a quake that happened almost two hundred years ago." He started for the doors. "I want to see what's in there."

"Do you think that's wise?" Elson whispered. He was last in line behind the others as they made their way across the chamber.

"We need to know whether there are more of these creatures or not." Ayrion could feel air moving through the large crack at the bottom as they drew closer to the massive entryway. The smell wafting in from the other side wasn't much better than the one in the chamber. He stopped just in front and looked up. The doors were even bigger up close. So much so that he couldn't see the tops.

"What have you found?" a voice behind them asked, and everyone turned.

It was Brim with a couple of his men. "Where are they?" the primary asked.

Ayrion raised his finger to his lips. "Lower your voice. We were about to take a quick look inside to find out."

"I'm coming," Brim said, this time keeping his voice to just above a whisper. He headed across the room with his men in tow, not even bothering to look at the artwork covering the walls. Then again, he'd probably been down here for weeks studying it as they burrowed their way through.

That had Ayrion wondering, and he motioned for Brim to follow him over to the side. The others came along, no doubt wanting to see Brim's reaction to this new revelation.

"What is it?" Brim asked. "I thought we were going to go take a look through the doors?"

"We will," Ayrion said, slowing as he approached the carvings on the wall that depicted the existence of the Tanveer. "But first, I have something to show you."

"What? I've seen these before."

"But how closely did you look?" Knowing Brim, not very, considering the chamber was laced with gold, which had clearly been the only thing on the primary's mind at the time, not thousand-year-old cave scribblings.

Ayrion pointed at the two images showing the wizards sending the khuls back within the doors.

Brim shrugged. "What of it?"

"Do you see what is happening here?"

Brim looked again. "Yes. We already know that this is the same chamber with the doors—"

"And that those are the khuls being sent back through."

"I gather as much."

"Do you see who is sending them through?"

Brim leaned forward, his eyesight clearly not what it once was. "I gather you're going to tell me those are wizards."

"You would be right, and do you see who is standing with those wizards over a thousand years ago as they banished these creatures for the first time?"

Brim stared at the image a moment. "I see men with swords." He then turned and swept his arm around the room. "You'll find pictures like that everywhere."

Ayrion gritted his teeth. "Not like this one," he said, pointing to just above the image, where the runic symbols had been placed over the heads of the soldiers. "Notice anything familiar about the depiction of these paladins?"

Brim leaned in once more, but this time there was no snide remark. His face went slack as he stared at the three Upakan symbols carved into the stone.

"You wanted proof that what I say is true. You've had it right here all along. The Tanveer stood within this chamber over a thousand years ago and banished the khuls from Aldor. Our people played a vital role in overcoming the Dark Wizard himself."

Brim stood, taking a step back to get a fuller glimpse of the image. He cleared his throat. "It would appear so." He looked around, noticing the others staring. "Little good it does us, though, if we don't survive this. So if you don't mind, I'd like to go take a closer look at what lies beyond the doors."

Brim and his men left Ayrion and the others at the wall and headed across the room for the doors.

Ayrion snorted. It was probably about as close to an apology as he was ever going to get from the man, but he'd take it.

Brim waited at the crack in the doors for Ayrion and his team, no doubt not wanting to be the first to venture in himself.

Ayrion cupped the lume crystal with his free hand to dim its light, then motioned them forward as he started into the crack. Those from his company followed him in first, with Brim and his men bringing up the rear. It wasn't exactly roomy inside, the quarters tight enough that it made swords useless, with barely enough room to thrust. The stone on either side was caked with matted fur and blood, where the creatures had cut themselves apart trying to break free from their prison.

The doors were incredibly thick, or perhaps he'd missed where they stopped and the mountain continued. Either way, they had been walking for several minutes and still hadn't reached the other side. The only sounds were the soft gusts of stale wind filtering through from whatever lay beyond, and their boots against the stone. Ayrion kept the crystal lowered. Even with its soft light, he didn't want anything to hinder him from seeing what might be ahead.

He slowed when he saw the end of the narrow passage looming, listening intently for any sign of a khul army waiting on the other side.

So far, nothing.

He stopped on the cusp of entering the darkness beyond. Whatever was on the other side must have been massive, because his eyes couldn't pierce through it, even with the faint glow shooting out from between his fingers. He waited and listened. But there was nothing to make him think an army of creatures was waiting to attack.

Still, he needed to get a better look, so he risked his first step out from the doors. Quickly, he turned and looked up, but all he could see was the wall of a cavern so enormous he couldn't see where it ended. He cautiously took another couple of steps out from the crevice but found nothing but stone.

Off in the distance, he thought he could hear the rushing of water, but he couldn't be sure. Where were they? Was this the end, or could these tunnels possibly travel all the way under the Northern Heights?

"I can't see anything," Brim mumbled behind them as they followed Ayrion out from the crack between the doors, cautiously keeping close to each other in case of an unexpected attack. "Are they all dead?"

Ayrion loosened his grip on the crystal to let out a little more light. The cavern was massive. He couldn't really see how far back it went. There were pillars running in rows along the floor leading all the way into the darkness beyond, pillars that had clearly been cut by hand.

"Incredible," Ferrin whispered, staring up at the first column. "How did something like this ever come to be this far underground? Reminds me of some of the columns I saw in the lower reaches of the White Tower. Very similar in design, actually. Wonder if that means anything?"

The others gawked as well, turning in circles to take it in, what little they could see. It was certainly a testament to some ancient civilization long past, perhaps back during the time of the Fae. Ayrion couldn't imagine anything like this being built without the aid of magic.

He tempted a little more light, then a little more, finally releasing the crystal altogether. Unfortunately, it did very little to help them see what was there. The crystal wasn't bright enough to light the tunnels behind them, let alone fill a place this vast.

"I don't see any khuls," Bek said.

"You don't think we killed them all, do you?" Myron asked.

"We should have brought a torch," Brim griped. "Can't see anything in this darkness."

Ayrion walked several feet to the left, but as far as the light would let him see, there was nothing but stone. He did the same toward the right, finally coming back to where the others were still clumped just in front of the entrance. "Brim's right. We can't see enough of this place to know anything."

"I might be able to help with that," Elson said, stepping through the others to the front.

Brim looked at Elson doubtfully. "Got a torch hidden down your trousers?"

Elson grinned. "Something like that. Now stand back."

The others stood there a moment, judging whether Elson was being serious or not, before Ferrin finally ushered them back. Ayrion took a few cautious steps away from the former drunk. Elson was a wielder, after all, at least he claimed to be, though no one had actually seen him wield anything but his flask.

Elson undid the buttons on his jacket and pulled it off, then started to undo the front of his tunic as well.

"What do you think you're doing?" Ferrin asked.

Myron shook his head. "Have you been drinking again?"

Elson grinned sheepishly as he stood there bare chested in front of the others. "You might want to shield your eyes for this."

Ayrion was as confused as the rest, but he held his hand up in front of his eyes just in case. He was starting to wonder if Myron was right. Suddenly, a searing light broke in front of them, and Ayrion was nearly blinded by the intensity. He grabbed the shaders hanging from his neck and quickly pulled them on, but even that didn't protect against the sheer amount of illumination coming from Elson. Ayrion held up his hands once again, but all he could see was a piercing blare of light in the vague shape of a man.

"It burns," Brim said, trying to pull his own shaders on.

The light suddenly dimmed, and Ayrion slowly lowered his hands to find that the light was coming directly from Elson's skin. Every part of him was glowing, sprouts of it even shooting through his hair. It was one of the most bizarre sights Ayrion had ever witnessed. He'd never heard of anyone with a gift such as this.

After staring at the strange phenomenon, Ayrion and the others turned to get their first glimpse of the vast hall. The cavernous room was filled with pillars. Veins of gold ran throughout each, along the floors, and even up the walls. All Ayrion could do was stand there and gawk. The sides of the room were lined with open archways and tunnels leading off the main chamber into other reaches of the incredibly vast network.

Stone staircases ran along the walls, leading from one tunnel opening to the next, like an immeasurable hive of passageways. Chill bumps ran across Ayrion's body. Each of those passageways were filled with sleeping khuls.

Where were these creatures coming from? How were they surviving down here? Ayrion wondered if these tunnels did indeed burrow all the way under the mountains and into the Frostlands beyond the shroud. Was that how they were surviving? He couldn't imagine how they would otherwise; there was no food source, save eating their own. And why sleep during the day? So many questions needed answers, but none that seemed capable of helping Ayrion reverse the damage his people had done.

A roar filled the chamber, and everyone froze. The hair on Ayrion's arms stood on end as the howling rumble began to grow.

They were no longer asleep.

"Blood and ash!" Brim said as they stared out at the growing horde of khuls looking down at them from their dens, screeching their anger and hunger. "We're doomed. Look at their numbers."

Ayrion couldn't disagree. There was no stopping an army like this.

"We don't stand a prayer's chance," Bek said, though right after saying it, he quickly offered a short one.

"There's not enough magic in Aldor to stop something like this," Myron said, the horror on his face mirroring that of everyone else. "This war is already lost."

Elson pulled on his shirt and jacket and turned. "I think we need to run."

Behind them, Brim and his guards were already heading for the crack in the door. At least they had the right idea.

"Run!" Ayrion said just as the khuls started pouring out of their tunnels after them.

Ayrion was the last through the doors, waiting for the others. He stopped to take one last look behind, but now that Elson's light had been dissolved, he could no longer see what was coming. He could certainly *hear* it. The growing crescendo of khul cries rising from the chamber behind him sent a chill running up his spine as he turned and ducked into the crevice.

He still had no idea why the khuls had refrained from their ritual skirmish on this particular night; perhaps Zynora's damage had been enough to force them to regroup, or restrategize, if they did such a thing. Then again, after seeing their true numbers, he highly doubted it.

Their only hope now was the swift arrival of morning. He prayed they could hold out until then.

Chapter 66 | Adarra

ADARRA CUT A PIECE of meat from the half-rat, half-turtle creature Jonas had dressed the previous night and walked over and placed it on Ambassador Lanmiere's plate. He took one whiff and turned his nose up at first but eventually took a bite.

They had slept through the night and then rested all the next day. Belakor's tea was definitely working. Whatever herbs he was using had brought about an almost miraculous change in the health of those injured, including the burns some had received at her hands. However, Lanmiere and a few of the others were still too weak to attempt a trek up into the mountains, so Captain Holverd agreed to give them one more day.

The sun had gone down a few hours ago, and Adarra withdrew to her usual spot in the back corner to work with Belakor on her use of magic. Even after what had happened, she still wanted to learn. It was her blessing and curse, the desire to know more, to gain knowledge she might one day put to good use. To justify the risk, she told herself the magic could come in handy as they moved forward with reaching the Tallosians and setting up a viable truce. If she could have mastered her link with the fire earlier, who knows if that could have made a difference with the sniffers or the jingas, and thereby saved lives.

The others stayed as far from them as possible during their discussions, most clearing back from the pit or the torches lining the outer wall.

Belakor had told her that even though she was capable of wielding other kinds of magic, she would never be able to have true mastery over them like she did the gift she was born with. Still, she wanted to learn as much as possible while she had the time.

So far, she had learned how to wield fire, water, and even the air, but only to a very small degree. She was much more cautious with the amount of magic she used.

Jonas, unfortunately, was still keeping his distance. The couple of times she had tried to approach him, he turned and walked outside.

"Try again," Belakor said, demonstrating once more how to hold the air in his hand and harden it. Adarra wasn't sure how much she liked the idea of learning from someone who had been taught by the White Tower, but her desire to learn overtook her caution of where it came from.

She let the warmth of her magic rise as she held out her hand and brought the air to her. The first time she'd attempted it, she sent a gust through the cavern, forceful enough to knock a cup out of a lancer's hand and earn her another strong reprimand from Holverd.

The air gathered around her hand. She could feel it moving across her skin as she tried to hold it in place. For some reason, she was having a difficult time attempting to shape it. Belakor wasn't exactly the most proficient with magic himself, which might be part of the problem.

Aiden walked over and sat down beside her, his presence causing her concentration to waver, and the semi-hardened ball deflated in her hand. She looked at him and sighed.

"What are you working on?" he asked, staring down at her empty hand.

"Same thing I've been working on half the day."

"Still trying to harden air?"

She nodded.

"I still don't see how something like that is possible," he said.

She frowned. "Apparently, me either." She looked at Belakor. "I had better stop for now. I need to rest, I think."

"We could try the water once more," he said.

She shook her head. "I think I've had enough for now."

The old hermit nodded, then stood and walked over to tinker with some items on his table at the back. Adarra didn't like failing, but they were planning on leaving at first light, so she was going to need to get some rest. Learning magic had been a fun distraction from the horrors of what they had survived, but their mission wasn't complete, and from what Belakor and Jonas had said, it seemed they didn't have too much farther to go.

"Come," Aiden said. "About time we turn in for the night, isn't it?"

Behind her, Ambassador Lanmiere had apparently finished his meal and was already crawling under his blanket next to the other injured lancers. She guessed it wouldn't hurt to turn in early as well, so she stood and followed Aiden over to their spots by the fire. She started to sit when she noticed Jonas sneaking out of the tunnel. "I need to talk with him."

"But I don't think that's—"

She didn't wait for Aiden to finish, waving for him to stay where he was as she headed around the fire and over to the exit. She passed Captain Mervall, who was standing at the mouth of the tunnel, chatting quietly with his remaining men.

"I wouldn't go wandering off," he said, catching her on the way by. "Easy to get lost out in those trees, especially after dark."

"I'm just stepping out to have a word with Jonas."

He nodded, and she headed into the tunnel, which led around to the mouth of the cave. It was dark outside. No torches had been lit to mark their whereabouts, and the surrounding trees held back what little moonlight there was to be found. A twig snapped, and she turned to find Jonas, or at least a silhouette of him, sitting on a boulder about a dozen feet from the entrance. He had a small stick in his hands, which he tossed into the trees when he spotted her.

Taking a brief moment to make sure no one else was out there, she walked over to join him. He tensed the closer she got, like a trapped animal about to bolt. "Why won't you talk to me?" she asked, stopping a few feet away. She didn't want to risk getting too close and have him leave once more. "I've missed our talks."

She waited for him to respond, but he simply sat there watching, his eyes dropping to her hands as though worried she might hit him with a spell.

"I'm still the same person."

"You are not same. You are Shayan."

"I am the same," she said, her jaw tightening as she took another step forward, which had him tensing even more. "See, why do you act like that? We've sat together for weeks talking, and you never feared me then. You saved me from drowning aboard the ship. You protected me from the sniffers. You came for me in the reeds." She took another step forward. "Can't you see I need you?" She felt awkward admitting the fact.

He didn't move, his eyes intense as he held her gaze.

"Just because I was born with this inside me doesn't change who I am. Please, stop looking at me like that." Why did it matter what he thought? Why was she letting him get to her? This was foolish. He was a Tallosian. He'd taken part in the attack on her family, and yet there was still this connection that had formed. "I don't want you to be afraid of me. I would never hurt you."

He turned his eyes away. "Shayan always hurt. Magic is evil."

She sighed. "Magic isn't evil, Jonas. I'm not evil. You know me. Look at me. Do you think I'm evil?" Jonas stood to leave, and she reached out and grabbed his arm. "Please don't leave."

He pulled his arm away and then vanished into the woods.

She started to go after him but stopped. If she did, he might decide to leave altogether, and they couldn't afford to lose him. She balled her fist and sent air down into the snow. It flung powder all over her. Why couldn't she do that inside?

Angrily, she wiped off her face and marched back into the cave. The stubborn man was going to be the death of her.

Most of the others were already in their beds when she walked around the fire and over to an empty spot on the other side of Aiden. There weren't enough blankets to go around, so she lay down beside the fire and closed her eyes.

"What did he have to say?" Aiden asked.

"Not much, apparently. Wants nothing to do with me now that he knows I'm a wielder."

Aiden grunted. "Maybe that's for the best."

She didn't know what it was about Jonas that drew her so. He was nothing like Aiden—the complete opposite, in fact. Where Aiden had a soft delicate beauty, Jonas was hard and rugged and scarred. Aiden was learned and well spoken. Jonas, on the other hand, could barely speak their language, and when he did it was generally coarse and direct. So why did she keep finding herself staring at the man?

Gritting her teeth, she fought to get him out of her head. She needed sleep. They had a long day ahead of them, and she wanted to be at her best. Yet with every little noise, she'd open her eyes to see if it was Jonas returning. In the back of her mind, she worried that she'd wake to find he had abandoned them. She was mad at herself for having approached him. She should have just let well enough alone. By the time sleep had finally taken hold, Jonas still hadn't returned.

She woke to a hand on her shoulder.

"Time to get up," Aiden said, and she slowly opened her eyes and rolled over. The fire had died down, and she realized her arms were shivering from the cold. She sat up and looked around. "Did he come back?"

"Who?"

"Jonas."

Aiden shook his head. "I haven't seen him, but I just woke myself."

The tunnel leading out was still dark, which meant the sun had yet to rise. Behind them, Belakor fiddled with some pots and pans on his table. There was a kettle hanging over the fire, and one of Holverd's lancers attended it while another added a few more pieces of wood from the pile against the right wall.

"Morning," Lanmiere said.

Adarra turned, surprised to see the man on his feet.

"I don't know what was in that brew you were forcing down our throats, but I haven't felt this good since leaving Easthaven." He stretched his back and then moaned. "Well, almost as good. Clearly, it doesn't seem to cure old age."

"Have you seen Jonas around this morning?" she asked.

Lanmiere shook his head, and a sinking feeling began to build in the pit of her stomach.

"What about Jonas?" Holverd asked, apparently listening in on their conversation. He walked over from the tunnel.

She turned. "I was just asking if anyone had seen him."

"He never came back last night according to my men. Do you know where he is?"

Adarra stood, panic setting in. "I tried speaking with him last night, but he seemed agitated and then walked off into the woods. I figured he would come back. He always has before." What if she had driven him away? They couldn't make introductions without him. A searing chill shot through her. What if he told them she was Shayan?

This could be a disaster.

"What did you say to him?" Holverd demanded. "We need him to guide us up the mountain."

"He didn't seem to care much for learnin' you was a wielder," Captain Mervall said, joining them at the fire. "I hope that didn't frighten him off."

"Frightening him off is the least of our worries," she whispered.

"How's that?"

"He knows I'm a wielder."

"And Shayan are not allowed inside the Five Peaks," Belakor said on his way back to his table.

She hoped Jonas hadn't gone to warn the Tallosians. "Perhaps he's scouting ahead."

"All night?" Belakor asked behind them. "I highly doubt it."

She turned and looked at the old wielder. "Do you think you can lead us up to Idris?"

Belakor stopped his breakfast preparations and turned. "I could, but I won't. They know I'm Shayan, and as long as I don't come near their home, they tolerate me. But if I were to lead a bunch of outsiders up into Idris, they'd kill me for sure. Get your Tallosian to take you up."

"Didn't you hear? He's missing."

Belakor laughed. "And you're surprised? He's a Northman."

Adarra turned and looked at Holverd. His face was set in a hard mask.

"We require your help," Holverd said to Belakor.

"And I'll be happy to point you in the right direction, but I'm not going up into those mountains. I'll wait here and pray for your safe return." He turned back to his food.

"You leave us without a guide, and you better pray we don't return," Holverd said angrily. "Either you take us up there, or when we leave, you won't be coming with us."

Belakor spun. "You gave your word!"

"We said if you help us, then we'd take you with us. That didn't mean just giving us shelter for the night. We need to find this Idris place, which means we still need your help."

Belakor fumed, then turned back to his table, banging his pots and pans.

"Let me talk with him," Adarra whispered. She left them to the fire and walked over to the back. Blast Jonas for putting her in this position. "We really do need you," she said as she sat down on the stool beside the large stone.

"So you side with them over one of your own kind?"

"There are no kinds here. We're all human. But Holverd is right. Without someone to guide us, we don't stand a chance. If you hadn't saved us from the jinga, none of us would be alive today. We do need your help."

Belakor glanced over his shoulder at Holverd and the lancers. "Would they really leave me here?"

She sighed. "I haven't known him long, but I can say that he is a man of his word. He doesn't threaten idly."

Belakor growled. "Fine. But as soon as I see the gates of Idris, I'm gone."

She nodded. "I'll tell them."

She left Belakor to his work and relayed what he had said to the others. After a quick and somewhat quiet breakfast, the group gathered their meager belongings and waited outside. The sun was just beginning to rise, casting soft rays through the trees as the sky began to shift from pale grey to blue.

Adarra pulled on her gloves after strapping her sword belt back around her waist. She patted her tunic to make sure the pouch of Orlyn's special seeds was still there.

"Keep your eyes open for wolves," Belakor said. "They aren't like any you've ever seen. They have two heads—one in the front and one behind. They can run just as fast backwards as forwards. Though, I guess if you think about it, they don't really have a back, do they?" He shrugged. "Anyway, the land between here and the passes leading up into the peaks is their territory. You also might want to keep an eye in the trees as we get closer to the mountains.

The talarin have been known to fly down and perch there from time to time."

"What exactly are talarin?" Aiden asked.

"They are a predatory creature that live in the upper cliffs with wings powerful enough to snatch a man right off the ground. It was said that back during the height of magic, the talarin were actually saddled and ridden, and their riders were known as the Talari. They aren't as big as the dragons of old, but certainly swifter."

Adarra and Aiden shared a worried look with Lanmiere. Adarra wondered how Belakor had come by this knowledge and figured it must have been during his time spent at the White Tower.

Belakor handed out torches. "Keep these with you at all times. The wolves don't care much for fire, but if they're hungry enough, even that won't stop them."

"Do ya have somethin' positive to say?" Mervall asked, looking quite forlorn after Belakor's warnings.

Belakor thought a moment, then tilted his head. "Looks to be a lovely day." With that, he turned and started into the woods.

Chapter 67 | Adarra

HE MARCH THROUGH THE snow-covered trees was slow but surprisingly pleasant. No birdsong filled the air, but Adarra did spot a few red-and-grey tree rats gathering nuts. It was the first sign of normal life she'd seen since stepping foot on Tallos. All the other animals they had come across had been corrupted by dark magic. For a brief moment, it seemed as though she were once again traipsing through the forests behind her home.

Behind her, Lanmiere and the other injured seemed to be back to full form, though the ambassador moved a bit stiffly from the cold. Lanmiere made use of a fallen limb he'd found on the trail to steady his stride, but that was a concession of age rather than his injuries from their encounter with the jinga. Belakor's tonic and poultice had worked miracles.

The wind picked up speed the closer they got to the edge of the mountains, and stronger gusts spilled into the trees below. The farther they went, the steeper their climb became, and the more wild the terrain, slowing their ascent. There were times they were forced to skirt large stands of rock or crevices too wide to leap, but the direction never seemed to waver, continuing ever upward.

Every now and then they would reach a flatter area, and Belakor would stop to rest. He was every bit as old as Lanmiere, judging by the white in his beard and the wrinkles around his eyes, and he wasn't shy about showing it as he bent over to catch his breath before starting back up again.

Adarra wondered how far up the pines went, as they didn't seem to be thinning in the least.

After another couple of hours of climbing, Belakor brought them to a stop at what looked to be the edge of a path, one clearly not animal made, as there were wheel tracks from a hand cart or small wagon. Somewhere ahead, the sound of wooden chimes filtered down through the trees, a very unexpected thing to find in the middle of the woods, but enjoyable.

But Belakor's eyes widened when he heard them, and he quickly put his finger to his lips and backed quietly into the woods, motioning for them to do the same as he led them away from the trail. They traveled west for at least a good quarter hour before he brought them to a stop inside a small nook in the rock's face.

"What's going on?" Holverd demanded.

"We traveled too far east," Belakor said, his breathing heavy as he glanced around nervously at the surrounding woods.

"What does that mean? It looked like that was where we would find Tallosians."

"Oh, you'd find them there, alright. But you wouldn't like what you found. That trail leads up to House Dolzag. They are the most brutal of the five houses. Their first—which is what they call their leader—is the second head of the Dogar."

"That's the Tallosians' ruling body, isn't it?" Adarra asked.

Belakor nodded.

"How do you know that was Dolzag?" Holverd asked.

"Didn't you hear the dead calling?"

"The what?"

"You mean the chimes?" Aiden asked.

"Those are the bones of their enemies," Belakor said. "They leave them to hang as a warning to those who would dare pass through their territory." Belakor gulped. "They've been known to hang some of them out there before they're dead. I've even come across a few that had been nailed to the trees."

Adarra shivered at the image that invoked. These were the people they wanted to strike an agreement with? The people they wanted to help? A thought struck her. "Which house does Jonas belong to?" *Please don't let it be Dolzag.*

Jonas hadn't been all that forthcoming when it came to himself and how he fit into the Tallosian hierarchy. All she knew was that he had been sent as one of the members of his house to join the team coming to Aldor.

Belakor shrugged. "I have no idea which house he belongs to. Couldn't see any markings. If he had been Dolzag, though, you would have known it."

"Why's that?" Lanmiere asked, still trying to catch his breath from the hike up.

"Because he would probably be wearing your scalps right now, or floating in the sea after you threw him overboard for trying to slit your throats. He would have never agreed to guide you anywhere, and as soon as you freed his hands, he would have gutted most of you."

That certainly didn't sound like Jonas. She didn't remember any visible markings on him other than the ugly scar on the side of his face. Perhaps his face paint had been some kind of house crest.

"My guess is he's from one of the smaller, weaker houses like Orlig or Warnog." Belakor cocked his head. "How much do you even know of these people?"

"Only as much as Jonas has told us . . . which, granted, isn't much. We know they are governed by the Dogar," Adarra said, "which is made up of the heads of each of the five houses: Ulgrim, Dolzag, Mitgal, Warnog, and Orlig. They pride themselves on showing force instead of diplomacy. The strong rule over the weak. Rank inside the houses is taken, not earned."

"Glad I wasn't born here," Aiden said with a shiver.

"Be very glad," Belakor said. "Soft boy like you, they would have culled you long ago."

Aiden scowled at that.

"Ulgrim is the largest of the houses," Belakor said. "It's also known for being the most cunning. Second to them is Dolzag, which as I've stated is the most brutal. Third is Mitgal. They are known for their skill with wood and stone. Warnog is fourth, and they are known for their work with the soil. If you are here to help the Tallosians with their crops, then Warnog is the house you will want to deal with. Last is Orlig. They are the smallest of the five. Most they are known for is their weaving."

"And Idris leads into the five peaks, correct?" Adarra said.

Belakor nodded. "From Idris, there is a road that runs all the way through the five peaks, ending at the conclave. It's seen as neutral territory. It's the main road leading in and out, and it intersects with all five territories."

"Jonas spoke of other, smaller passes leading down from each house," Adarra said.

"Yes. Each house has their own back ways off the mountains, which are heavily guarded."

"Then why don't we find the pass leading up to that Warnog group?" Holverd said. "Sounds like that might be a better option than going to Idris. Better to let just one house know of our presence than all five, especially if they are the ones who tend to the crops anyway. I'd rather deal with them than this Dolzag you mentioned."

"Afraid it's not quite that simple. First, I don't know where the Warnog pass is, and second, if your goal is to keep them from mass migration over to your fair kingdom, then it will require the vote of all the houses, which means a meeting of the Dogar at the conclave."

"What is this conclave?" Lanmiere asked. "Is it an official hall of sorts?"

"It is the meeting place of the Dogar." Belakor shrugged. "Thankfully, I've never been there. Those who end up in front of the Dogar usually leave in pieces. At least, that's what I've been told."

Adarra and Aiden both gulped.

Holverd turned and looked out at the trees surrounding the face of the rock. "So, you're saying we are in Dolzag territory?"

Belakor glanced behind him. "Possibly. Dolzag territory borders Ulgrim's. And ever since this plague of bugs showed up, skirmishes between the houses have grown, as the houses cross lines in order to find food. I've even spotted warriors as far down as the sand pits, which has me very worried, since that isn't all that far from my own place."

"Do you know which of the peaks happens to be Warnog's?" Holverd asked.

"I think it's somewhere on the other side, but that could take us another day to get there."

Holverd looked at Lanmiere. "Seems that would be the safest option."

Lanmiere looked at Adarra. "What do you think?"

"I wish Jonas was here. This is why we brought him." She looked at Holverd, then back at Lanmiere. "Warnog does sound like—"

"Wait," Belakor said. "Something's coming."

"Another wielder?" Adarra asked, turning to look, remembering Belakor was a sensitive.

The older man shook his head.

"Wolves!" a voice behind them called out.

Everyone spun to find one of the lancers drawing his sword at the edge of the rocks, pointing down the side of the embankment. They all rushed to the edge. Flashes of white and grey moved through the trees below. They were too far away to see clearly, but Adarra shuddered as she saw that Belakor had been right. They *did* have two heads.

"They've caught our scent," Belakor said, staring down at the encroaching pack.

Mervall drew his sword. "We should run."

"If you think you can outrun a wolf, be my guest," Belakor said. "I'll say a prayer for your corpse." He turned to the others. "Quickly, back against the rock."

Adarra moved with the others as they scurried away from the edge and back into the recess in the cliff face. Belakor grabbed their torches and began placing them on the ground in a half circle across the entrance, walling them off from the oncoming pack. He looked at Adarra. "I'll need your help."

"What are you doing?"

"I'm going to try to keep the fires high enough to hold them back."

"What do you want me to do?"

"I can't keep them all burning. I'm not strong enough. You'll need to take half."

"I don't know if I can."

"Then you better figure it out. Just try not to burn us in the process.

Remember, start small."

She nodded and watched as Belakor held his hand out to the torches and the flames of those on the left side began to grow. She did the same, pulling on a small amount of her magic, letting it warm her insides. She whispered the incantation *"Voyestra"* and reached out to the torches on the right. She connected, and their flames began to flicker, then grow. Her heart raced.

She was doing it.

The wolves reached the lip of the rock and started over. Her concentration wavered as she stared through the flames at them. They were magnificently misshapen, continually turning in circles to allow both heads to see. It was a strange symbiosis.

Their barks and growls had her sweating as she fought to maintain her grip on the rising flames. The wolves' eyes glowed in the light of the fire, their fangs glistening as they spread their jaws hungrily, drool hanging from the sides of their mouths. There were at least a dozen of them, and right now the only thing keeping her and those with her alive was her hold on the flames. She hoped their hunger didn't outweigh their fear of the fire.

A couple of the wolves tried to sneak around the outside between the last torch and the rock wall, but Adarra willed the flames to stretch out and cut them off, startling even her. She didn't know something like that was possible until she had done it.

Beside her, Belakor's hands shook, and his face shone with sweat as he concentrated on his torches. He didn't look well at all. He had admitted to not being very capable with magic. She hoped he could maintain his hold. The wolves held their ground on the other side, back near the edge, and watched them through the flames. She knew they wouldn't be able to hold the fire forever; eventually, they were going to expend too much magic, and the fires would snuff out.

Adarra kept the heat burning inside her as she drew on whatever was there. She hoped she had enough to hold as well.

A loud screech filled their alcove, and an enormous black shadow fell over them as something swooped down from off the cliffs above and snatched one of the wolves right off the ground. Its wings were over a dozen feet in length or more; one flap blew their torch flames perilously close to the huddled company.

Adarra and Belakor quickly released their hold on the torches before it scorched them all.

It was a talarin, Adarra realized, staring upward. Somehow Jonas hadn't managed to convey the sheer size of the bird.

Half the pack loped off at the first sound of the talarin's call, but the others stayed, and as soon as they saw the opening in the ring of fire, they attacked.

Adarra barely had time to get her sword out of its sheath before Holverd and his lancers flew past. She stumbled to the side and grabbed Belakor and pulled him back as one of the wolves leaped for him. She swung and managed a small cut to the wolf's side, but not much more. She quickly grabbed one of the torches and raised it. "Voyestra!" The flames shot out and engulfed the wolf, and it took off running.

A lancer went down, one of the beasts dragging him away. Holverd fought to reach him, but before he could, the rest of the pack returned. The lancer's screams followed him into the trees, and Adarra tried not to imagine what was happening to him.

Two of the returning wolves skirted Holverd and Mervall's men and made their way to the rear of the group, looking for easier prey.

"Get behind me!" Adarra shouted to Lanmiere and Aiden. Belakor was already behind her, his sword drawn, though his hands were shaking. He'd expended too much magic and was having a hard time catching his breath. Adarra held up her torch, her magic still connected to the flames as she watched the two-headed beasts slowly work their way deeper into their nook in the rock. The wolves were too close to their men. If she were to release the fire, she'd very likely send it right into the back of Holverd and Mervall.

She raised the torch and let the flames glow brighter. It was all she could think to do. She hoped Aiden was ready with his sword.

The wolves studied her, hackles raised, eyes glowing as they crouched.

"Get out of here!" she shouted, waving her torch.

A cry was all the warning they had before another shadow dropped from above. This one didn't have wings.

Jonas landed on top of the two wolves, slamming a dagger into each.

She was so shocked by the unexpected arrival that she nearly unleashed her magic on him. Quickly, she lowered the torch.

Jonas kicked the first wolf back, one of its heads lolling to the side, and buried his dagger in the second wolf's other neck. The wolf released a mournful wail and slumped to the ground, but before Jonas could turn, the first wolf leaped on top of him, and they both went rolling across the stone.

Jonas grabbed the thick fur around its neck and held it off while the creature fought to get its jaws around him. Aiden ran to help, but Jonas managed to kick the creature back before he could. Jonas reached for his dagger, but Adarra sent flames into the wolf, killing it before it was able to get back to its feet.

She ran to help Holverd and Mervall, drawing on her magic, letting it fill her. It was more than she had ever called up before, and she released a stream of fire across the front of the pack. The wolves howled and fled back into the woods. By the time she released the flames, she was feeling lightheaded as a bout of dizziness washed over her. She leaned over as the world spun, forcing her to take a couple of deep breaths until it stopped.

Holverd, Mervall, and the remaining lancers helped the other injured back into the safety of the alcove as they waited to see if the wolves would return.

Adarra remained near the edge, clutching her torch in one hand and sword in the other, keeping an eye on the trees. Belakor joined her, also holding a torch, keeping his eyes on the rock ledges above.

"Do you see anything up there?" she asked.

"No, but that doesn't mean much at my age."

Aiden walked out to join them. "Are they gone?"

"For now," Belakor said. "Do you see any of those flaming big birds up there?"

Aiden turned, and after a moment of searching the lower ledges, he shook his head. "Not that I can tell. I've never seen something so big."

Muffled cries from a couple of the lancers had all of them stopping their search and turning. Two men's legs had been mauled, and the arm on the third looked to have been nearly torn off. She glanced at Belakor. "Do you have any more of that poultice?"

"A little."

"Then do what you can for them. I can watch from here."

"And where were you?" Holverd spat, looking up at Jonas from where he knelt beside his men. "Just left us to die."

Jonas looked down at him but didn't answer. Instead, he turned and walked out to the front where Adarra and Aiden were standing. He looked at Adarra, then at Aiden, and cleared his throat. Clearly, he wanted to speak with her alone.

She looked at Aiden and nodded. "I'll be fine. Give us a minute."

Aiden's jaw tightened as he stepped away and headed over to sit with Ambassador Lanmiere, who was resting quietly off to the side.

Jonas stood beside her in silence, staring out at the trees but keeping one eye on her torch.

"Why did you leave?" she finally asked, growing impatient with his unwillingness to speak. She kept her voice low. "I told you we needed you. *I* needed you."

He didn't reply, standing there like one of the mountain pines, silent and unwavering. There was blood running down his left arm, and she laid her hand on it. "You're hurt." He jerked back at first but then allowed her to inspect the wound. That was something at least. Last night, one touch from her and he'd run off into the woods.

"You hurt me, you know, leaving like that." She looked up at him. "I was afraid you would . . . sell us out."

He sneered. "I have honor." He spoke in his native tongue, so she switched to it as well.

"How is it honorable to break your word? You promised to lead us to your people. You promised to protect me."

His mouth tightened. "I did protect you."

"Barely. We've lost another man, and three more are severely wounded."

He turned and stared out at the woods once more. Something was clearly weighing on him.

"What? Why won't you look at me? I don't know how many times I can apologize for what I am. I should have told you sooner, but I didn't want you to—"

"I had things I needed to prepare for, before I brought you up."

"What things? You didn't mention anything about that before."

His face tightened once more. "It's complicated."

"What is? What are you talking about?"

Jonas raised his hands to his mouth and released a loud call that sounded like a red pinepecker.

She turned. "What are you doing?"

The trees below began to fill with Tallosians, all armed, all wearing face paint. Where had they come from? Had they been there the whole time? She backed away from the edge as they raced up the hill toward them. There was nothing her torch could have done to stop so many. She turned and looked at Jonas.

"What have you done?"

Chapter 68 | Ayrion

OW ARE WE SUPPOSED TO hold off an army like that?" Brim said dejectedly as he slumped in his seat across from Zayden, who looked barely able to stand, himself. "We cannot hope to win against such numbers. I don't care how many patches you pull or rings you change. And depending on how deep and filled those tunnels were of khuls, I doubt all the armies in Aldor combined could stand against such a force."

"Which is apparently why they were sealed away by wizards over a thousand years ago," Ayrion said, angry at himself for having actually hoped they had indeed beaten the creatures. "We should have never been down here." He tried not to look at Brim when he said it, though everyone got the meaning. He also noted that he said *we* instead of *you*. He had only been back a few days and had already started considering himself one of them, as though the last twenty years had never happened.

Ayrion sat next to Ferrin inside the command pavilion on a couple of chairs facing the two primaries, while the rest of those that had followed him down—including his father, brother, and nephew—sat on the ground near the back. Tameel, Zynora, Elson, and Rae were busy inside the infirmary, helping where they could.

They had managed to hold back the khuls' advance, but only just. Thankfully, the sun's rising hadn't been that far off, and with the Upakans now fighting in single rotating formations—even with the limited training they'd received—they had been able to withstand the brunt of the khul attack, but at this point, they knew they were only prolonging the inevitable.

"He's right," Ferrin said. "No amount of strategy is going to win us this war. Our only option at this point is a full retreat."

Ayrion groaned. "That's not an option we can consider." He raked his hands through his hair as he struggled to find a solution that wouldn't leave them all dead. "To retreat at this point would be to give these creatures free rein of Aldor. It's the same problem we faced in Belvin with Argon. If we hadn't stopped him when we did, he would have spread so far, there would have been no way to contain him."

"But in Belvin, you had a single source," Ferrin said. "Here, there is no source. You kill one and there's a hundred more waiting to take its place, perhaps a thousand, and they have no regard for life, not even their own. How do you fight against an enemy that has no fear of death?"

Ayrion turned, and a twinge of pain shot through his arm where he'd been cut during the battle. He winced, doing his best not to move it. It was wrapped for now, and there were others in more dire need of Rae's gift than himself. Taking a deep breath, he tried looking at the dilemma from all sides but kept coming to the same conclusion. Ferrin was right. There was no spelled crystal to smash that was going to suddenly see all the khuls disappear. And from the endless numbers of khuls they had seen beyond the stone doors, Brim was right as well: all the armies in Aldor might not be enough to stop them.

So what was the solution?

"We need to reseal the doors," Zayden said desperately, as though it hadn't been mentioned more than two or three dozen times in the last few days.

Ayrion looked up. "If only it were that simple. Even if we had a way to rebuild something that was created and sealed by wizards, how would you plan on doing so with khuls charging through?"

"We wait till daylight?" Zayden said.

Ayrion almost laughed. Thankfully, Ferrin spoke before he did.

"How long did it take you to dig through that bottom crack?"

Zayden turned and looked at Brim, and Brim frowned.

"It took us weeks."

Ferrin looked at Zayden without saying more, his facial expression saying enough. There was no way they could rebuild in a single day what had taken weeks to destroy.

"And even if the creatures took a week or two off from their attacks," Ayrion said, "those doors were cut straight out of the mountain. No amount of mortar is going to hold the pieces back in place. Once you broke through, that was that."

"Then what do you suggest?" Brim groused. "So far, all we've heard is how nothing we do is going to make a difference. Please, tell us, *oh wise leader*, how you are going to save us. That is what you've returned for, isn't it? To come back as the great hero of the Upakan people."

Ayrion's jaw tightened, and he squeezed the seat of his stool. Brim's words hurt because of the truth buried inside. He *had* hoped to return and earn back his people's respect by saving them from the khuls. But he had not been prepared for what they were truly up against. And even after all that he had accomplished in getting them to come together as one people, to fight side by side, it wasn't enough. It wasn't nearly enough. In fact, there was nothing he could do that was going to make a difference. Curse that wizard. Why had Nyalis sent him here in the first place?

His mind raced. How could they stop an insurmountable force? A force that apparently not even the wizard council of old had been able to destroy completely. If they had, there would have been no need for this place.

"We use the mountain," Ferrin said, momentarily redirecting Ayrion's thoughts.

"What do you mean, use the mountain?" Zayden asked, straightening in his seat.

"I mean we seal them in."

Brim harumphed. "I thought we just established that wouldn't work."

"I said we seal them in. I didn't say we re-seal the doors."

Ayrion looked up. "The tunnels."

Ferrin nodded.

"But will that be enough?" Brim asked. "Couldn't they just dig through? Most of these lower tunnels were collapsed when we found them, and we were able to clear a path."

"They were only partially collapsed," Ayrion's father corrected, earning a harsh glare from Brim. "Most of the tunnel's structure was still there. We just had to remove the loose rock."

"And how do you plan on collapsing the tunnels?" Lenara asked, which was the first time she'd spoken since before the battle yesterday evening. Nola, who was sitting next to her, lifted her head. "The last time, it took Mount Ash erupting. I doubt she'll be as accommodating this time."

"What about that old tinker woman?" Brim asked. "Can she use her . . . whatever it was to shake the rock free?"

Ayrion shook his head. "She expended most of what she had to kill the khuls the first time. Even if she had recovered enough to try again, you saw what happened. The blast basically followed the tunnel itself. It didn't do that much damage structurally."

"What if she were to direct it at one of those stone pillars on the other side of the doors?" Brim asked. "That would bring the place down."

"It wouldn't be enough," Ferrin said. "I've seen her magic used twice now, and I think most of it would disperse around the pillar. And even if she could focus it enough to bring one down, I don't think one will be enough to bring everything down. You saw that place. There were scores of support columns. And if by some chance she did manage to collapse the place, being that close to the focal point, she wouldn't have enough time to get back out. You would be sentencing her to her death."

The tent went silent, mostly because they knew he was right. Even if Zynora had the strength, there was no way Ayrion could ask it of her. He'd sent men to die in battle before, but this was different. Being in the military was a risk every soldier voluntarily made, at least in Elondria. They risked their lives every day in its service. Choosing to be a lancer was a noble calling. But Zynora wasn't a lancer. Asking her to give up her life to save his people was not something he could do—or would. He would have given his own life gladly, but not hers.

"So," Brim said, pounding the arm of his seat with his fist, "we're right back to where we started. With nothing."

"Not exactly," Ferrin said. "I might have another way."

Ayrion twisted to stare at the smith. Ferrin radiated a confidence that gave Ayrion hope.

"Well?" Brim said. "Are you going to tell us what it is or wait till the khuls arrive?"

"I think it would be better if I showed you." With that, he stood and started for the tent flaps.

"Whatever we do," Brim said, "we need to do it quickly. The day is wasting, and we won't last another night. There's too many injured to hold the line."

Ayrion and the others followed Ferrin up, and they left the pavilion in single file, then made their way through the camp, skirting clusters of soldiers as they huddled dejectedly around their cookfires. Most bore battle scars, though the true injuries lay somewhere deeper. Internal scars that couldn't be fixed by salve or balm. Ayrion could see it on their faces. It was the look of defeat. Ayrion would have lied if he said he wasn't feeling it himself. Whatever Ferrin was about to show them, he prayed it worked.

It was nice to be able to walk through the camp without being forced to break up a fight or two. Apparently, Ayrion's efforts had gone a long way in healing some very old rivalries. He knew it wouldn't fix everything, but it was a start.

Ayrion followed the smith through the camp, making their way through the last of the fires, then started into the tunnel. They didn't walk far before Ferrin directed them over to the left wall. "There," he said, pointing to several veins of gold that ran along the stone. He placed his hand over the largest and closed his eyes.

Ayrion stared at the deep yellow line running down the length of the wall. "You're not thinking what I think you are, are you?"

Ferrin smiled but kept his eyes closed.

"Thinking what?" both Brim and Zayden asked at the same time.

A few moments later, Ferrin opened his eyes and took a step back from the wall. He nodded. "It might be possible."

Brim balled his fists. "Will someone please tell me what's going on? What's possible?"

"I think I can use the mountain."

"You said that before," Bek said. "But what did you mean?"

Ferrin turned. "I think I can collapse it."

Ayrion's brother huffed frustratedly. "We already said that wouldn't work. They could eventually dig their way out."

"I don't plan on collapsing just the tunnel. I plan on collapsing the mountain."

"The entire mountain?" Myron asked, eyes bulging.

"No, not the entire mountain, this section of it."

Ayrion stared at the gold a moment. "How?"

"This gold runs all the way through the tunnel system, and as we've seen, the largest deposit of it is found within that chamber beyond the doors." He frowned. "Though, now that I think about it, I can't seem to sense the gold inside that chamber. Something is stopping me from seeing beyond the doors."

"Could be warded," Ayrion said. "The doors in Harok Laos were. Without that key, there was no way through. Perhaps there are some lingering threads of that magic still left here."

Ferrin shrugged. "Could be."

Ayrion looked at the wall. "Is there enough gold here, without using what's beyond the doors, to collapse it? I can't see how pulling out some veins of gold is going to destabilize the surrounding rock enough to make a difference."

"Oh, it's not just the gold. There are very large deposits of ore all through here, most of it intersecting. If I can connect with it all at once, I should be able to shift the surrounding rock." He turned and looked back at the camp. "Does anyone know how far up the tunnel the gold runs to the city above?"

"About halfway," Brim said. "Why?"

"Because I have to physically be touching the gold in order for me to link with it. And I'd prefer to be as far away from the main deposit as possible."

"So you think it's possible?" Ayrion asked.

Ferrin thought a moment, then nodded. "I do."

Ayrion turned to the others and smiled, feeling almost hopeful. "Then I guess we better start breaking camp. We need to transport the injured up to the city square. It's the largest central location we have available."

"That won't be enough," Ferrin said, and Ayrion turned. "I don't think you realize the devastation this collapse will cause. If the entire city of Rhowynn sank into the ground from the shaking of Mount Ash all those miles away, what do you think will happen if we bring down part of this one right over our heads?"

Ayrion's brows rose as the gravity of the situation began to dawn on all of them.

"Are you saying we have to leave our home?" Brim asked, his fists tightening. The two primaries looked like they'd just had their hearts ripped from their chests. They had been fighting all this time for one purpose—to protect their home. Now it looked like the only way to save it was to destroy it.

"I'm saying that if I do this, there will be no home left to come back to."

Ayrion's mind raced. This could be exactly what he'd been needing all along, a way to force his people from the Lost City. As long as the city survived, convincing them to leave would prove impossible. But if this worked—

He stopped himself. Now wasn't the time to be thinking of that.

"Maybe . . ." Zayden said. "Maybe there's another way?"

"And what other options do you believe we have?" Ayrion's father asked. "We aren't even sure of this one. The one thing we do know is that if we don't do something right now, none of us will survive. I say if the outsider thinks he can stop these beasts, we let him try."

The primaries remained silent.

Ayrion looked at Ferrin. "How far will we need to go to be safe?"

Ferrin thought a moment. "At least to the rise we stopped at behind the city."

"That far?"

"That's a long way to transport all these people," Myron said.

"Not to mention belongings," Bek added.

"We don't have time for belongings," Ayrion said. "Our focus should be on the people and an immediate evacuation of the city. I'm not even sure that's possible in the amount of time we have left. However, if they want to grab something, tell them to grab all the food they can carry, and some warm clothes and blankets." There was no sense in escaping a falling city just to starve and freeze to death up top. They had a long way to go and needed whatever provisions they could manage in a short amount of time.

Brim bared his teeth, then turned and marched back into camp, disappearing into the crowd.

Zayden followed soon after, looking completely crestfallen. This was not the news they had been hoping to hear.

As soon as Zayden was out of earshot, Ayrion turned to Ferrin. "How sure are you of this? I can't very well order our people to leave and then find out it's not going to work. This is a huge risk."

"You heard them," Ferrin said, pointing after the primaries. "We aren't going to last another night regardless. At least this way there's a chance your people survive. If this doesn't work, there's no chance for any of us."

Bek looked up at the ceiling of the tunnel. "I'm suddenly feeling rather enclosed down here. Just don't go touching anything until we're gone."

Ferrin smiled.

Ayrion took one last look down the tunnel in the direction of the doors. There were two guards waiting at the next bend, keeping watch. "If we are to get all these people out, especially the injured, then we need to move fast. We have less than a day to evacuate."

He looked at Lenara. "Do you think you and Nola can move one of the excavation carts up to the city? Might be the best way to get as many of the injured out as we can." He looked at Bek and Myron. "See if you can help them. I know Rae and Zynora will be too weak to move anyone themselves. Tameel as well. And grab Elson while you're there."

"We'll stop by the house," Ayrion's father said, "and get your mother and the others."

"I can get them when I take Rae up top," Ferrin said.

"No." Ayrion shook his head. "I need you down here with me. The others can look after Rae and Suri. I need you to find the spot where you think you can do the most damage."

Ferrin's lips tightened, and he looked at the others, who were still standing there waiting. Apparently, they didn't want to leave without first making sure Ferrin was fine with it.

"I'll make sure your sister and Suri get out with the rest," Myron said.

Ferrin bit his lower lip but finally nodded. "Fine. Keep them safe."

"You know we will."

The others turned and headed back into the chamber. Brim and Zayden must have already ordered the evacuation, for the camp was already fast becoming a cluster of chaos as soldiers scurried to get the wounded up through the tunnels.

"Is there anything else you need from us before we go?" Ayrion's father asked as he, Jorn, and Davin stood waiting quietly at the side.

"Just watch over the girls," Ayrion said. "And keep an eye on Brim. He's anything but happy about this, and with Sirak down . . ." Ayrion shook his head. "You never know."

"I can deal with Brim," his father said. "He's greedy, but he's not completely stupid. Whatever you showed him in the tunnels seems to have changed his mind about certain things. I've never seen him so compliant in my life."

"I showed him proof of his heritage."

His father nodded. "Still, it's Zayden who's going to need help. Most of this is going to get dropped on his shoulders."

"Just make sure they get the people out. Make sure they understand we don't have time to gather possessions. If they aren't out before the sun sets, they'll be buried with them."

His father nodded, then he, Jorn, and Davin headed back into the camp.

Once he'd lost sight of them amongst the rest, Ayrion turned to Ferrin. "Let's get to work."

Chapter 69 | Ferrin

FERRIN WAS NOT HAPPY with leaving Rae, Suri, and his sister's evacuation in the hands of others, but as much as he hated to admit it, Ayrion was right. He needed to find a good location far enough up the tunnels that he had a reasonable chance of escaping once the cave-in began. He honestly wasn't sure whether the destabilization would affect what remained of the Lost City—truth be told, he wasn't sure he could even cause enough of a shift to collapse the tunnels—but it was better to err on the side of caution.

He released his magic, letting only a tiny trickle remain. He could still feel the ore around him, a mountain of it, more than he'd ever felt in his life. It beckoned to him. He'd never felt his magic so alive. He could almost hear it humming in the back of his mind, calling to him. It was exhilarating and frightening at the same time. It was strange to be standing in such a place, surrounded by so much potential wealth, knowing he could pull it straight from the walls and not even consider the possibility of leaving the Upakans to face the mess they had made for themselves while his little band fled with as much gold as they could carry.

His sister was now quite wealthy from selling off her late husband's estate, but the amount of gold in these tunnels could make Ferrin the wealthiest man in the Five Kingdoms. Weeks ago, his first impulse would have been to take what he could and get out of there, but here he was, standing under a mountain of rock, fighting against creatures out of the Pit to save a people who had originally shunned their help simply because they were outsiders. What had happened to him? Why had he dragged his family and friends into this?

He watched the weapons master head back into camp and couldn't help but wonder what sort of spell the man had over him. Ever since meeting Ayrion, it seemed all their decisions were based on helping others. It was a great way to get yourself killed. Still, there was something to be said for the way it felt. Running and hiding was a good option, but sometimes the cost left a rather unpleasant taste in one's mouth.

While Ayrion went to tell those standing watch to evacuate, Ferrin went to check on Rae. He'd make sure she was okay, then focus on the task ahead of him. He could hear Zynora shouting orders clear across camp as he pushed his way through the throng of Upakans. Most of their gear was being left behind. They carried little but food and weapons. Ferrin hated thinking about the smithy and its tools being buried under a mountain of rubble, but like Ayrion had said, the people were their only concern.

He reached the far side of the chamber, just left of the infirmary, and was stopped by the flow of those trying to make their way into the tunnel. Ferrin worried that the injured lying outside the tent would be trampled as men rushed to make their escape, but the closer he got, he realized the injured were no longer there. Had they already been carried out?

Ferrin finally reached the tent and found Bek and Myron standing outside, diverting the throng far enough around to keep the wounded moving, who with Elson's help, they were placing in a hauling cart. Lenara was struggling to hitch the cart to Nola, but the wolf didn't seem all that keen on having a harness strapped around her. She shifted back and forth and bared her teeth but allowed the bulradoer to work.

Sirak was there as well, somehow on his feet, though using a spear to lean on. He shouted orders to those passing by, making sure they didn't leave without helping one of their fallen brothers. His legs wobbled, but not enough to stop him from grabbing passing warriors and dragging them back toward the front of the tent, where Bek and Myron were waiting to hand off the next injured in line.

"Is Rae inside?" Ferrin asked.

"Yes," Myron said, helping a man with a bandaged leg limp out to those waiting.

Ferrin squeezed by and headed through the flaps, grimacing as he did. The smell of blood filled the air, strong enough that he could taste it. The tent flaps were tied open, but it wasn't enough to circulate clean air inside. The ground was covered in makeshift cots and bedrolls, stacked so tight they were nearly on top of each other.

He found Rae sitting on a stool at the back, but she stood when she saw him coming.

"How are you?" he asked, hugging her, then forcing her back into her seat. Her face was pale and her eyes gaunt. It hurt him to see it. It reminded him of the way she had looked inside the Tower, though at least she had a little more meat on her bones now.

"I'm tired," she said, looking up at him fondly, squeezing one of his hands.

"What's happening out there?" Tameel asked, taking a moment to walk over from where he had been helping one of the soldiers with a cup of water. "Heard something about everyone needing to leave."

"We're evacuating the city."

"Why? Are the khuls coming?"

"No. Well, yes, eventually, but that's not why we're evacuating. I'm going to try to collapse all the tunnels and lock the creatures away for good."

Tameel scratched the top of his head. "How are you going to do that?"

Ferrin briefly explained his plan, everything he had told the others.

"That sounds dangerous," Tameel said.

Rae stood. "You won't be hurt, will you?"

Ferrin smiled and helped her back down into her chair to rest. "No."

"But how will you get out?"

"I will start by collapsing the rock farthest away, which will set off a reaction that should work its way through the entire tunnel system and possibly the city itself. If it's a big enough shift, it might bring everything down, which is why we need to evacuate. And we only have until the sun sets, which means we don't have much time." He glanced around at the half-filled cots. They still had quite a few people to move.

"What about Suri?" Rae said frantically, tugging on Ferrin's sleeve.

"Myron said he will make sure she and Myriah get out. Ayrion's father and brother are already on their way up to get them. They will be safe." He looked at her and frowned. "You need to get something to eat and drink or Lenara will be loading you on one of the haulers."

"I'll make sure she does," Zynora said on her way by. She stopped long enough to place her hand on Ferrin's arm and look him in the eyes. "You be safe, you hear me?"

Ferrin nodded. "Keep your eye on this one," he said, nodding toward Rae. "She tends to have a mind of her own."

Rae kicked him softly in the foot. "I don't like you being down here," she said. "What if the creatures come back?"

"They haven't so far. As long as we can get everyone out of the city in time, then everything should be fine."

Ayrion stuck his head in the tent. "Are you ready?"

Ferrin looked at Rae and smiled. "I promise I'll be fine. Just make sure you stick close to Myron and the others, and before you know it, we'll be leaving this place for good." He leaned over and kissed her, and she clung to him. He had to unwrap her arm from his neck to step back. "We'll be in the tunnels leading up to the city, looking for the best place for me to work, so I'm sure I'll see you on your way up."

He offered her one last fond smile, then turned and headed back out into the main chamber, where Ayrion waited. They got in line and started into the tunnel just behind Lenara, who was directing Nola and their hauler up through the passageway, toting over a dozen men up to the city above.

Ferrin studied the walls, stopping every so often to feel along a specific vein. The gold wasn't always prominent; some of the veins veered off and didn't return until farther up the shaft. "It's strange that the tunnel doesn't follow the gold," he said. "It's like it wasn't dug for that purpose."

Ayrion was watching it too. "Maybe it wasn't." Ayrion turned and stared down the passage behind them, where the gold suddenly disappeared into the wall. "Perhaps it was built specifically for reaching those doors."

"I don't think any of these passageways were here when whatever that place down there is was created," Ferrin said. "Those pillars were carved out of the mountain by incredibly skilled stone masons, using an extensive amount of magic, I'd wager." He slapped the wall. "These passageways are nothing more than crudely dug holes in the ground."

Ferrin turned as Lenara and Nola's cart squeaked around the next bend ahead, with a line of fighters trudging along behind. Ferrin and Ayrion kept to the side of the tunnel to stay out of their way.

"Should we keep going?" Ayrion asked.

Ferrin nodded, and they moved back in line with the others.

They reached a smaller chamber farther up and stopped. Ferrin circled the room but couldn't find, or even sense, another vein, so they continued on. After a while, Ferrin finally stopped. "I think we've gone as far as we can. I'm not sensing any of the ores up here. We need to head back down."

They left the small chamber and moved back down through the oncoming fighters, keeping their eyes peeled for any more flickers of gold caught in the torchlight.

"There," Ferrin said, pointing to the right. A thin line was buried in the side, hardly noticeable save for the contrast against the darker stone. He walked over and placed his hand on it. Closing his eyes, he let his magic flow up through him and out into the gold. He reached forward, letting his mind move along with the vein as it branched outward and down, thickening the farther in it went. It seemed these outer edges were little more than a remnant of what lay deeper in, which had him worried. The farther away from the source he was, the harder it was to sense, and the more magic it required to manipulate.

He was forced to spread his magic quite thin to attempt to connect himself to the ore inside the chamber with the stone doors, which meant attempting to manipulate it from here was going to prove difficult at best. He might have committed himself to something he wasn't capable of doing.

His hands began to shake, and sweat beaded across his forehead by the time he'd finished. He supposed using magic this way was similar to how Rae's magic delved inside the human body, branching out to find disease or injury. Ferrin was just working with a much, much larger body. By the time he released the magic, he was quite winded. He'd never tried to stretch it so far before. He was used to manipulating ores he could hold in his hand, not ones located nearly a mile away.

"Well?" Ayrion asked. "How does it feel? Is this a good spot?"

Ferrin turned and smiled. "Good as any." Truth was, this was the only safe place he could attempt it. Any farther in and the odds of getting out before it collapsed were almost negligible.

Ayrion looked at him skeptically, no doubt trying to read his face.

Ferrin ignored him and ran a hand along the gold, using a little of his magic to remove some from the rock. He held it up to the light of the passing torches. It sparkled beautifully. He closed his eyes, picturing a delicate bloom of a flower. He could feel the gold reshaping in his hand, and when he opened his eyes, a golden water lily rested in his palm.

"Remarkable," Ayrion said.

"There they are," someone behind them said, and they turned to see Rae and the rest of their group walking up the tunnel, just in back of the last of the soldiers. Myron had an arm around Rae, supporting her, while Tameel and Zynora made the climb with assistance from Bek and Elson. They all stopped to take a breather before heading the rest of the way up.

Rae walked over to where Ferrin was standing beside the wall and leaned against him. He put his arm around her to hold her in place and then handed her the golden flower. Her face brightened when she saw it, and she cradled the blossom carefully in the palm of her hands.

"That is quite stunning," Zynora said as the others gathered to take a look at his latest creation.

Ferrin had an idea, and he reached over and pulled a little more of the gold from the wall and then took the golden flower and attached the new gold on the bottom to form a simple bracelet. He placed it around her wrist and then resized the gold so it fit, then hardened it so it wouldn't break. The deep yellow bracelet shone against her caramel skin.

She smiled. "It's beautiful."

"Is this where you plan on collapsing the tunnels from?" Myron asked curiously, staring at the thin vein of gold in the wall behind Ferrin. When Ferrin nodded, Myron turned and looked up the tunnel where the evacuees were still making their way. "I thought you would be closer to the city."

Rae looked up at Ferrin. "You aren't going to be down here in the tunnel, are you?"

Ferrin gave Myron a stern look before addressing Rae's concern. "We are a long way from the doors. I'll have plenty of time to get out."

"How? Not only do you have to run back up these tunnels, but then you have to get across the under city, then you have to climb up through those tunnels and out across the over city. You can't run that far!" Her fingers dug into his arm, and he felt her tense.

"I'll be waiting for him up top with horses," Ayrion said. "I can get him through the upper city quick enough."

Ferrin caught Elson staring at him quizzically. Ferrin wondered if his friend was sensing his own hesitation.

Zynora cleared her throat. "Regardless of where he chooses to collapse the rock from, if we don't get ourselves out of here, he won't be doing anything. These old legs don't move like they used to. Let's get a move on."

Tameel patted Bek's arm, which was wrapped around his waist. "You heard her. Hyah, my good man. Onward and upward."

Elson handed Ayrion one of their torches, and Zynora handed Ferrin a biscuit with a slice of meat between and an apple. "Here, I almost forgot. You'll need to keep up your strength."

Ferrin thanked her and placed the small meal down on one of the larger rocks near the side of the tunnel and then turned to Rae. "There is nothing to worry about, I promise." He pulled her close and gave her another kiss.

"Be careful," she said, running her fingers over the golden flower on her wrist. "Suri and I still need you to show us Aldor. You promised."

He smiled, his chest tightening. "I will. We can talk about where to go next tonight after all of this is over." He kissed her once more and then watched her and the others make their way slowly up the tunnel passage. Ferrin stared after them until they had rounded the next bend and their torchlight faded from view. He listened quietly to the echoes of their footfalls until he could no longer hear them.

Ayrion tucked the torch into a small crevice along the left wall to keep from having to hold it.

"So, how long do you reckon until nightfall?" Ferrin asked.

"We still have some hours, I hope."

"How will we know when everyone is gone?"

"I've instructed one of the scouts to tell us as soon as they get everyone out."

"And when you say out, you mean over the rise behind the city, correct?"

Ayrion nodded.

This section of the tunnel was quite a bit narrower than what could be found farther down. Ferrin took a seat on the right side and Ayrion the left, both facing each other. After several minutes of awkward silence and uncomfortable glances, Ferrin was wishing he'd told the swordsman to head up with the rest. The two had never really been close. Ayrion seemed to keep most everyone at arm's length, though there was clearly a special bond between him, the tinkers, and Bek, no doubt forged by all they had shared the past months.

Ferrin had never found that same connection to the man. Even though they held a unique link with Ayrion's blades, conversations between them felt forced. Ferrin stared at the dragon hilts, just visible over Ayrion's shoulders. He was amazed to have been rejoined with his creations after all these years. He had always wondered who he had made them for. He had imagined the king himself using them, but the Guardian Protector was certainly the next best option.

"I wanted to thank you," Ayrion said, interrupting Ferrin's thoughts.

"For what?"

"For being willing to travel across Aldor and risk your life to save a group of people most consider irredeemable. It says a lot about a man's character to be willing to do something like that, even more to be willing to lead others in the process. You have a very strong group of friends who clearly care a great deal about you and respect you. There aren't many who'd be willing to follow someone into danger like that."

Ferrin was a little stunned by the swordsman's frankness. What's more, Ayrion's thoughts had been running along similar lines as his own.

"They are the closest thing I've got to family," he said, staring at Ayrion a moment. "You seem to have acquired that same loyalty with Tameel, Zynora, and Bek. Most tinkers, from what I know, tend to shy from society, preferring the open road. They would be the last people I would ever expect to be rushing into harm's way, especially the kind you've spoken of. That's more than friendship if you ask me."

Ayrion smiled. "They are a special breed, that's for sure."

They waited again in silence with nothing but the occasional flicker of the torch to keep them company. Somewhere in the distance, Ferrin could hear the faint dripping of water.

"How are you feeling?"

Ferrin looked up.

"Do you feel strong enough to pull this off?"

"I'll be ready." He looked down the tunnel. "No real reason for both of us to sit down here. You should probably go see if they need help getting the rest out."

Ayrion stared at him a moment. "I don't like leaving you down here alone."

"There's not much you can do at this point. If the khuls were to attack before nightfall, it's not like you'd be able to stop them—and I need the solitude to prepare," he said, pointing to his head, "which will be much easier without someone sitting there staring at me." He gave Ayrion a lopsided smile. "To be honest, I'll feel much better knowing you are up there waiting with those horses. I'm going to be coming fast, and I want to make sure you're ready for me."

Ayrion finally nodded and stood. Ferrin stood with him.

"I'll send someone down when everyone is out." He paused, studying Ferrin's face. "Are you sure?"

"I'm sure."

Ayrion turned to leave but stopped. He reached up and pulled a chain out from around his neck and walked over and placed it around Ferrin's. "Here. *Luminate* conjures its light. *Luminor* extinguishes it."

"Won't you need this?"

"I'll take the torch," Ayrion said, grabbing it from the wall. "We don't need this thing to go out and leave you blind down here. At least with the crystal, you'll know you will always have a way to see."

Ferrin looked down at the piece of translucent rock. He pulled on his magic and spoke the incantation. "*Luminate.*" The crystal brightened, and the tunnel filled with a soft white glow.

Ayrion smiled and put his hand on Ferrin's shoulder. "Good luck to you, my friend."

Ferrin smiled. "To us all." He watched the swordsman turn and head up the passageway after the others, listening as his steps echoed in the distance. As soon as they had faded completely, he sat, a chill washing over him as he stared into the darkness below. It almost seemed to be staring back like a living thing, watching quietly, waiting to see what he would do.

He took a deep breath and exhaled. Maybe asking Ayrion to leave had been the wrong decision. He drew his new blade and held it up into the light, admiring the way the wolf seemed to be looking at him, its gold eyes hungry. He drew the long dagger as well and laid them both across his lap, feeling a little safer knowing they were close at hand.

He had thought these tunnels eerie before, but now they were ten times worse. He leaned back against the rock and tried not to think about it, turning his thoughts instead to Rae and Suri and the others. He wondered how far they'd made it. Were they still in the tunnels or had they reached the underground section of the city yet?

He picked up the biscuit and started to eat as he thought about the trek up, remembering the building above where they had stashed a lot of their personal gear before entering the underground city. He wondered if Myron and the others would grab some of it on the way out or if they would feel too embarrassed after telling everyone else to leave their possessions behind. Ferrin lifted his weapons and stood, sliding them back into their sheaths. He didn't need to be sitting there thinking about whether they left their gear or not. He needed to focus on making sure he was able to do what he said he could.

Right now, it wasn't looking too promising. He wondered how far he was from the city above, how far he might have to run. He'd never done anything like this before. He had no idea how long the collapse would take or if it even would collapse. His palms started to sweat, and he rubbed his hands on his trousers. It was the only chance they had. The Upakans would not have been able to hold the khuls back another night, which meant it would have been a complete slaughter, and then the creatures would have been released on the world regardless.

At least now, if his attempt failed, the Upakans would still be alive, and perhaps they could keep ahead of the horde long enough to warn the Five Kingdoms. From what he had seen, it would take their combined armies to stand a chance. He took another deep breath. He couldn't dwell on what hadn't happened yet. He needed to keep his full attention on the now.

He placed his hand against the gold, the cool rock underneath drawing the magic from him. As he feared, he was too far away. He was going to have to move closer. Sparing a quick glance back to the bend in the tunnel that led up to the city, he listened to see if he could hear anyone coming. The tunnel was silent, so he turned and started down, letting his hand run along the stone as he did.

The light from the crystal let him see enough to keep from tripping over any of the jutting rocks at the side of the passage. A few twists and turns farther down, he found a thicker source of the same vein and placed both hands against it. His magic connected better here than where he had been. He wondered if he should have left a marker on the wall to let someone trying to find him know he had moved farther down.

What time was it? He couldn't even guess. Time down in the tunnels seemed to change at a whim. Where he thought an hour had barely passed, an entire afternoon had come and gone, and there were times that a few minutes felt like hours, especially while engaging the khuls.

He released his hand from the stone and sat down. This was it. This was the farthest he dared go. The vein was thicker here, which helped. He hoped it was enough. He drew his sword once more and placed it across his lap before leaning back against the rock and closing his eyes. He needed to rest. He needed to prepare for what was coming.

Chapter 70 | Adarra

ADARRA STUMBLED AGAIN and dropped to her knees in the snow, only to be jerked back to her feet by one of the Tallosian warriors. Most of the Northmen's faces were painted in white and black, just like Jonas's had been during the raid on her family's home. Others wore painted human skulls as a mask. Their hair was long like Jonas's and braided in various fashions, some using human bones as decoration.

However, even behind the paint and the bone masks, she could see gauntness—skin stretched tight, sunken eyes, thinning limbs. The famine was certainly taking its toll.

Adarra's hands, like those of the rest of her party, were bound in front of her. The thick leather cords bit into her wrists until they bled. She struggled to keep her feet moving.

Beside her in line, Belakor whimpered like a frightened child. They had him gagged to prevent him from casting any dark magic. Twice he had tried to bolt and make a run down the mountainside. Both times he'd been caught and beaten. His face was bruised and swollen.

Thankfully, they hadn't gagged her. She wondered if Jonas hadn't told them yet that she was a wielder. And if not, why?

Behind her, the ambassador was having a difficult time keeping up. His legs were too feeble to maintain the strict pace the Northmen had set around the mountains. Holverd tried to help as much as possible, but he had his hands full with the men who'd been injured during their fight with the wolves. Belakor had managed to get some of his poultice on their legs before the Tallosians arrived. Hopefully it was enough to keep them going.

She didn't want to think about what might happen to any who fell behind. To the Tallosians, they were nothing more than additional mouths to feed, which under the circumstances would be cause enough to execute them all.

Aiden and Mervall were farther back, and the couple times she'd managed to turn and look, they seemed to be keeping up. The remaining lancers brought up the rear, guarded by the majority of the hunting party that Jonas had brought with him.

She wondered which house they belonged to, which house Jonas belonged to. More importantly, why would he have ambushed them? Why were they being carted off like animals and prisoners? Was this retaliation? Hadn't he told his people why they were even there? She couldn't help but notice the irony. When they left Easthaven, Jonas was in cuffs, and now that they had arrived, it was they who were bound.

The warriors down the line didn't speak as they marched the diplomatic party along the rugged terrain. She could see Jonas up near the front, but she hadn't been able to say a word to him since he had turned them over. Why wasn't he coming back to talk with her? Her skin crawled as she began to wonder if she'd been wrong about him all along.

She had a bad feeling they had all been played for fools. Still, if this was just about getting free, Jonas could have left them to die several times, but he hadn't. Was there something else he wanted?

The seeds.

No, he could have just taken them from her. She ground her teeth. Why was he doing this? She hated being so helpless. She hated not knowing.

They'd been on the move for most of the day. The Tallosians took them back down into the foothills before heading west around the base of the five peaks. Coming down off the upper reaches at least made the trails easier to walk, certainly easier than those up on the crags near the top.

She had no idea whose territory they were possibly crossing, or which of these mountains belonged to Jonas's house. For that matter, she didn't even know where Idris was. Were they trying to sneak them into their own territory without the others knowing? The farther they went, the greater the chance grew of them running into a rival house. At this point, Adarra didn't know if that would be a good thing or not.

One of the men in front lifted his hand, and everyone stopped. Adarra glanced over her shoulder to see Lanmiere bent over trying to catch his breath.

"Why are we stopping?" Lanmiere asked when he caught Adarra looking his way.

"I don't know," she whispered.

Pain erupted on her cheek, and she was knocked sideways into Belakor.

"Keep quiet," someone growled in Tallosian. She looked over at the warrior who had slapped her. He still had his hand up, a clear warning that more blows would follow if she didn't listen.

She helped Belakor back up, then moved back into line. Her face burned, and white dots swam in her vision for a minute or two as the throbbing slowly lessened. She caught a brief glimpse of Jonas looking her way, his face unreadable, but as soon as she spotted him, he turned around.

The man in front began to wave his arm, and everyone suddenly dropped to their knees. Adarra tried to help Belakor down, but it wasn't fast enough, and the warriors beside them yanked them both to the ground. Adarra fell forward, barely catching herself before she landed face first in the snow.

Belakor wasn't as lucky, and by the time he got back to his knees, his face and beard were coated in freezing slush.

She stared up the line, trying to see what was happening. There were too many people in front of her to tell, so she looked out through the trees at the sides, trying to spot movement. Had they come across another house's hunting party? Maybe the two-headed wolves had returned. She strained to listen, but other than the wind whipping down through the trees from the peaks above, she couldn't hear if there was something out there or not.

If there was, this might prove their best chance at escaping. While the

Tallosians were locked in battle with another house, they could make a run for it. She was half tempted to make some noise and give away their position, but with her luck, whoever was out there was from House Dolzag, and the thought of being nailed to a tree told her it wasn't worth the risk.

They waited long enough for her legs to start going numb in the snow. If they didn't move soon and get some of the blood back in her legs, she was going to topple over as soon as she stood.

Someone in the front signaled, and everyone stood. Adarra and Belakor had to lean against each other to make it up, and once on her feet, she shook her legs to try getting some feeling back in them. They had begun to prickle by the time the man in front waved once more and they started forward.

Several more times, they stopped and dropped into the snow, only to climb back to their feet and start again. She was surprised to find Lanmiere still managing to keep his legs under him. Fear of what the Tallosians might do to those who couldn't keep up clearly had the ambassador giving everything he had.

A slight buzzing noise caught her attention, and she cocked her head to see if she could pick up what it was between the heavier gusts. It wasn't like anything she'd heard before. The closest she could describe it was a swarm of bees. The farther they went, the louder and more pronounced the buzzing became.

They reached a clearing, and Adarra caught her first glimpse of where the buzzing was coming from. The opening in the trees wasn't there by accident. It was a small field that had been cleared for planting with empty rows of turned soil. The snow had been shoveled back, and a heap of brown vegetation was stacked to the side: the remains of what had been growing.

Now, the only thing left were the stalks, an odd smell of decay—out of place for just a pile of dead plants in the snow—and a swarm of black bugs crawling over the mound. It seemed even cold weather didn't bother the insects plaguing the Tallosians. They should have been dead or at least hibernating from the cold, but here they were as active as if it was the middle of summer.

She couldn't help but wonder if magic was involved.

A large black beetle with pincers landed on Belakor's shoulder, and he hopped around until it flew off in the direction of the field. The wind changed, blowing the stench toward them, and it turned Adarra's stomach. She tried breathing from her mouth, wondering what it was about these bugs that made them stink so badly.

Another wave, and the Tallosians continued. They'd made it about halfway across the clearing when shouts rose on their right and more Tallosians rushed out of the woods on the far side of the field. They were armed, and by the angry looks on their faces, were the field's actual caretakers. Men and woman alike raced across the clearing, straight for their party. There weren't as many of them as there were in Jonas's group, but they looked more determined.

Half of the warriors accompanying them were ordered to meet the oncoming fighters, Jonas included. The man standing on the other side of Belakor was one of those to go, but the one standing next to Adarra remained, his hand resting on the hilt of a nasty-looking spiked bludgeon at his side. There were still too many of the Tallosians left for their party to try overpowering them. Even if they managed to make a run for it, where were they going to go, and how far would they get before running into another house?

Without even taking the time for civilized discourse—to explain that they were just simply passing through—the two sides collided and went straight to killing.

The battle was brutal. Limbs were severed and heads bashed in. When it became clear those defending their land were not willing to back down and Jonas's house was unable to gain an advantage, another third of those watching Adarra's group rushed to help. Jonas was on the left, fighting three at once. He moved much swifter than a man his size should have been able to, driving his dagger three times into the first, grabbing the man's bludgeon and caving in the second's head, then going after the third.

Adarra glanced behind her. There was less than a quarter of Jonas's house still standing guard. She caught Holverd's eye, and he nodded, then turned and looked behind him to his lancers.

Before she had a chance to turn back around, Holverd and his men rushed the Tallosians. The Northman next to her drew his bludgeon, and Adarra reached for her magic, desperately trying to pull the wind to her as she had inside Belakor's cave. The guard grabbed her arm, and she turned and thrust her hands at his chest.

"*Avienda!*" A gust of wind hit the man and threw him backward into one of the trees. He hit hard enough for his sword to be thrown free, then he slumped to the ground unconscious.

Adarra looked down at her hands. She couldn't believe that worked. She'd seen Ty use that trick once during their battle with the Tallosians outside their home. She looked behind her and found the rest of the guards had been subdued, and without thinking twice, she grabbed Belakor, and they all took off running into the woods on their side of the clearing. Most of their party still had their hands bound, but it didn't seem to be slowing them down any. Holverd and a few of his lancers had procured weapons from some of those they had fought and had already cut their bindings.

Adarra didn't have time to worry about doing the same. Belakor tried grabbing her arm and pulling her to a stop, but she grabbed his instead and pulled him along, doing her best to keep him from tripping over his own feet. His eyes were swollen enough that he couldn't have seen much of where they were going. Behind her, she could hear the battle still raging between the two houses. Sparing a quick glimpse over her shoulder, she saw that some of those fighting had just realized their prisoners were escaping and had turned to pursue them.

"They're coming!" she shouted as they fought their way down the side of the incline, underbrush reaching out to cut at their hands and faces.

They were momentarily shielded by the trees and the thick undergrowth between, and Holverd used the opportunity to change course. He headed left, doubling back, no doubt hoping to throw the Northmen off their trail. They kept running, sliding, rolling down the steeper section at the foot of the mountains until they hit a ravine at the bottom edge and quickly slid to a stop. The drop over the side was dizzying.

Holverd spun to Belakor. "Where do we go?"

Adarra turned and realized for the first time that Belakor's gag was still in his mouth. She quickly yanked it out.

He gasped for breath. "I tried to stop you," he said, barely able to get the words out. "This is a dead end. There's nowhere to go."

Holverd snarled and then turned and started back up the rise. They'd barely made it back into the tree line when they were met by what remained of Jonas's house. All armed, all covered in blood. Their own group had maybe three or four swords among them, while the rest were still bound. It was obvious they wouldn't be fighting their way clear, so Holverd ordered his men to lower their weapons. They were escorted back up to the planting field, where they found a pile of dead bodies, including several from Jonas's house.

The dead of Jonas's house were not left with the others. They were lifted and carried along. Adarra wondered if they did so for some form of burial rite, or because they simply didn't want whoever's house they had just picked a fight with to know who it was that had been in their field. One of those they were carrying was the man she had hit with her small gust of wind. Had she killed him? She tried looking at the body, but she couldn't tell from all the jostling whether he was breathing or not.

A sudden rush of panic struck, and she momentarily hoped she had killed him. If he wasn't dead, he could identify her as Shayan.

Jonas left the front and moved back beside her. It was the first time he'd been close enough for them to speak, and she certainly had a lot of questions, starting with—

"That was very foolish," he said softly in his native tongue as the hunting party started back down the trail.

"After what you did, do you blame us for trying to escape?" she hissed back at him.

"No. Using your Shayan magic."

How had he known she'd used magic? "I didn't exactly have much choice, did I?" She tempted a quick glance back over her shoulder at the body. "Will he . . . will he live?"

"No. His neck was slit in the struggle."

Her head lifted. "What? I never—" She suddenly realized what he was saying, and blanched. That's how Jonas knew. The man must have told him what happened, and Jonas slit his throat. He'd killed one of his own to keep her secret. But why?

"Does anyone else know?"

He shook his head.

"Where are you—"

"Quiet. No more questions."

She bit down, exhaling sharply. She wanted to know what was happening. Her wrists were burning, and she looked down to see even more blood caked around the outside of the leather bands. Apparently, she had opened the wounds even further in her run down the mountain.

Jonas knelt and grabbed some snow and covered the wounds. He didn't say anything to her, just wiped the cold slush up underneath the leather and kept walking.

They reached what looked like a small roadway, which had been traveled enough that there was nothing much there but two wagon-wheel-sized indentions where the weight had packed the ground hard enough that nothing would grow. It had also been traveled enough that even the snow had been ground down into the soil and rock.

The head of their caravan waved them forward, and they started onto the road, which ran farther up into the mountains.

"Does this lead to your house?"

"No," he whispered. "Stop asking questions." He spared a quick glance behind him to the next Tallosian in line. Apparently, he didn't want the others seeing him conversing with the prisoners.

They kept on the road for a good half hour, slowly climbing toward the upper reaches of the mountain chain. They crossed through another section of woods, and the man in front waved everyone over to the right side of the road, practically in the ditch. She tried standing on her tiptoes to see what was going on but couldn't see anything above the shoulders of the men in front of her.

Jonas squeezed in beside her, his hand resting on his dagger. She was about to ask, but as soon as she got her mouth open, another caravan of warriors passed on the opposite side of the road. These weren't wearing face paint, but they were carrying axes and saws and tools for what Adarra figured was felling trees. Belakor had said that House Mitgal was known for their skill with wood and stone. Perhaps that was who these were. If so, then it was safe to assume by the way the two groups behaved that Jonas wasn't part of their house.

The men passing stared at her and the others, even going so far as to stop their descent to watch as Jonas's house passed by. She couldn't see what the other group did once they had passed, since Jonas's house spread back out across the road.

She was surprised the two groups hadn't attacked each other. Was the road considered common ground like Idris? Was this the road into Idris?

Her questions were quickly answered as the road made a sharp turn ahead, and the last of the trees fell away to reveal a mountain of rock rising in front of them, barring their way. Between the rock stood an incredible stone gate, every bit as tall as the Sidaran Assembly building. The walls were covered with statues of strange, deformed creatures, no doubt based on experiments performed by followers of the Dark Wizard.

Two enormous wooden doors lay open between, though from her vantage point, something about them looked off. There was something on them, but she couldn't tell what. They reached the gates and started through, and Adarra quickly realized what it was about them that looked out of place.

Both doors were covered in human skulls.

Chapter 71 | Adarra

ADARRA STARED UP AT the wall of skulls. Some near the top still had their flesh, empty sockets staring down on those who dared pass. It sent a shiver up her spine. This was who they thought to negotiate with? These people were little more than animals.

Belakor started whimpering, this time loud enough that one of the guards backhanded him across the face. Adarra put her arm around him to keep him on his feet and to try comforting him to keep his whimpering to a minimum.

"It'll be alright," she said softly.

He looked at her and shook his head.

The hairs on her arms rose as they started through. She could feel the weight of the dead looking down from their lofty perches, and she wasn't embarrassed to admit that at the moment she would have been fine leaving the Tallosians to starve. If it wasn't for the possibility of them coming to her shores, she wished they had never come to this place. Belakor was right. It was cursed.

The road leading in through the gates of what must have been Idris was much wider than the wagon trails leading out and down the mountain. It was also cut from the surrounding stone—and by the smooth surface, magic was probably involved—and followed a winding creek bed through the center of all five peaks. The melting snow seemed to keep it filled and was apparently used by all, as there were a number of people drawing from it.

Apparently, Belakor was correct. Idris was considered neutral territory. Not a single Northman fought another.

Looking around, Adarra wondered if this entire place had been built by Aerodyne's wielders all those centuries ago. The outside gate's decor showcasing their work suggested it had.

After all, she didn't see these rugged, uncivilized Northmen having the skill to build something to this kind of scale. Their ingenuity seemed to peak at making cloaks out of each other's scalps, which meant that if these gates had been built by ancient wizards, then how much of what was up here had been as well, and did the Northmen even realize where it had all come from?

The Tallosians' sole reason for having left the mainland in the first place was to escape magic, and yet they ended up settling in one of the most magic-ridden places in all the Five Kingdoms. Worse, *dark* magic. A place so dangerous that not even Aerodyne and his wizards wanted to risk their creations being released.

She figured it was probably best not to bring something like that up in their negotiations. Her skin crawled as she stared up at the lonely mountainsides, feeling them closing in around her. Who was she kidding? There were clearly not going to be any negotiations.

The road through the five peaks filled with traffic the farther in they went. She wondered where it ended. They passed an opening on the right, a smaller road that branched off the main and followed a narrow pass leading back to what she guessed was one of the Tallosian houses. There was a single archway carved out of the stone that crossed over the opening of the new road, with writing at the top that she couldn't decipher. If her guess about the builders of this city was correct, then it was probably written in the old tongue.

There were Tallosians coming and going from the passageway, and those who happened to see them stopped and stared. Some appeared to follow after them. In fact, everyone they passed who happened to see them stopped whatever they were doing to join the others in following them up the main causeway. She couldn't exactly see behind her very well, but what she could gave the impression that their group was gathering quite the entourage.

Most of the people inside Idris didn't have their faces painted like those of the hunting party, revealing even more the extent of their starvation. They were every bit as frail and sickly looking as the warriors escorting them in. These people were dressed ruggedly, and surprisingly few wore cloaks made of scalps. Perhaps that was reserved only for warriors. One thing was certain, no matter what they wore, Adarra and the ambassadorial team's clothing set them apart as outsiders and was quite the spectacle.

Perhaps that was why Jonas's people had brought them up this way instead of in secret through whatever back channels led up to their house. It was a way to gloat, to show their prowess in front of the other houses. From everything Jonas and Belakor had said, a house's strength and standing meant everything to them. No doubt capturing a group of outsiders would only bolster Jonas's own standing.

They passed three more branches leading off the main road, each with its own arch, each with its own set of rune lettering that she couldn't translate. By the time they reached the fifth branch, she didn't need to try looking behind to see how many were following. The crowd was so big they filled the road, no doubt stretching quite a ways back.

Word of their arrival was spreading fast. She wondered what that meant for them.

Up ahead, the road through the peaks ended at the base of a wide set of stairs. The stairs led up to a large construct that had been cut into the side of the mountain. It didn't appear to be part of one of the five houses, as there was no archway or branching road that led off from the main thoroughfare. The road simply ended at this final peak. It seemed to be part of Idris. Before they could get close enough for her to examine it, their caravan turned right and started through the final arch.

Belakor grabbed Adarra's arm and pulled her close. They must not have retied the gag quite as tight because he managed to get it down far enough to whisper, "They are House Ulgrim." His voice was riddled with fear. "It's the largest of the five and the most cunning. Be careful what you say. Sheegwa is as ruthless as she is beautiful. You can't trust a word she says."

The Northman guard saw what he was doing and quickly yanked him away from Adarra before he could say more, then tightened the gag over his mouth. She remembered Belakor mentioning the name Sheegwa but didn't remember under what context. It was one of those pieces of information she hadn't been close enough to one of her journals to jot down. Whoever this Sheegwa was, Belakor sounded as though he had had a run-in with her before, and it hadn't gone well.

At least they hadn't been captured by House Dolzag.

Behind them, it looked like those who'd been following had stopped just outside the stone gateway, not willing to cross into House Ulgrim's territory. The mountain edifice disappeared behind them as they were marched through a pass that led away from Idris. Ribbons of snow slid down the rock in places, others holding long javelins of ice. Above them, watchers on ledges stood at the ready, bows nocked as they studied the convoy below.

The passageway leading through the rock was only wide enough to fit maybe two wagons side by side, and the farther in they went, the more the walls felt like they were closing in around her. She tried to control her breathing, but it was hard to concentrate with Belakor's whimpering as a constant reminder of where they were.

She spared a quick glance up at Jonas, but his eyes stayed focused on what lay ahead.

The rock face began to slowly widen, and eventually it opened into a large canyon surrounded by rock on all sides, with scores of homes having been built in and around the face. On the other side of the canyon was another set of stone stairs, though nowhere near the size of those she'd seen back in Idris.

These steps led up to the largest of the stone buildings, no doubt the one being occupied by this Sheegwa person. As they started across the opening, it quickly became apparent that was where they were being taken. If the head of their clan was known for her cunning, then perhaps she was smart enough to realize the importance of an alliance with Sidara and Easthaven. Though, if what Adarra had seen thus far was any indication, she wondered whether these people were capable of allying with anyone. If their sole way of surviving or increasing their own place within their community was taking from others, then Adarra's chances weren't looking very promising.

Doors began to open as people came out to see the outsiders. Two lines formed on either side, leading all the way to the main structure, as they stared at the prisoners being marched across their home. Children stood near the front, pointing at Adarra and the others as they passed. She caught fragments of what they said—they were asking who the outsiders were, why they looked so different. Some of the children looked frightened.

They reached the other side and started up the stairs. Adarra had to steady Belakor after he slipped on the second step. She wasn't sure if it was because his legs were too weak or because he didn't want to reach whatever awaited them at the top.

She counted about twenty-five steps in all before they reached the veranda. Stone pillars rose to either side, half cut out of the surrounding mountain. She could see a set of thick wooden doors over the heads of those in front of her. It wasn't long before they were passing between them.

As soon as they stepped through, each of them was thoroughly searched once more for weapons. Jonas was the one to search her, which she thought he did mostly for show. He didn't make eye contact.

Not finding any weapons, they let them proceed.

As they crossed the threshold, the Tallosians parted to the sides. Jonas stepped away as well, leaving Adarra and Belakor at the forefront of what remained of their diplomatic team. They stood just inside a central room. It, too, had been cut from the surrounding stone. The inside was quite dark compared to the sunlit canyon they'd just left, and it took a moment for Adarra's eyes to adjust.

Torches lined the walls, and a healthy fire danced in a pit near the center of the room, keeping the place livable. The place smelled of smoke, sweat, and cooked meat. She prayed it was animal and not human. The thought had her heart racing and stomach turning.

The room was filled with warriors in painted faces and bone masks, dredging up bad memories of the hunting party that had raided her home. There was an opening on the other side of the room directly in front of a small platform with a single chair. On it sat a woman close to Adarra's father's age. Her dirty-blonde hair hung in many braids down over her shoulders, reaching all the way to her waist. She had markings on her cheeks and forehead. It wasn't like the paint worn by their warriors; hers seemed decorative or symbolic.

This had to be Sheegwa. She was a handsome woman, and something about those markings, especially the ones around her eyes, made her seem almost regal, but also devious.

Belakor whimpered when he saw her, and Adarra grabbed his hand and squeezed. Adarra's knees were trembling nearly as bad as his as she tried imagining what they would say to the person sitting on the other side of the room. She thought it best to let the ambassador do most of the talking and only translate.

She wondered if they were even going to get a chance to speak. Surely Jonas would relay why they were there. She turned and looked at him over at the side, but he didn't return her gaze, keeping his eyes on the front.

"Bring the outsiders forward," the woman on the chair called out in the Tallosian tongue.

"What did she say?" Captain Holverd asked.

Adarra turned. "She said to bring us forward."

Belakor started trembling, and Adarra tightened her grip on his arm.

It looked like the only way to reach Sheegwa was through a narrow split between the warriors, leading from where they stood to the front of the platform on the other side of the room. The narrow opening was lined with spears—which were topped with human skulls in various stages of decomposition. She tried not to look at them and instead kept her focus on Sheegwa.

"I'll go first," Captain Holverd said, no doubt seeing the fear in Adarra's eyes, and he and Lanmiere moved past.

Aiden and Captain Mervall moved up along with the lancers.

"How are you?" Aiden whispered, but before she could answer him, the Tallosians along the wall moved forward and started forcibly shoving the entire group toward the row of piked heads.

"I'm nervous," she whispered back.

"Me too."

Adarra reached the first of the spears and cringed at the half-decayed skull on top. The eyes were missing, but he still had most of his hair. She averted her eyes from the dead man's rotted face and stared at the feet of the person in front of her, which happened to be Lanmiere. He was barely limping through the narrow corridor, and at one point nearly tripped, but she was close enough behind him to keep him up.

She clenched her hands to keep them from shaking as they stepped out from the last of the heads into a small opening in front of the platform. Sheegwa's eyes were hard but curious as she looked each person over. Adarra had tried looking for Jonas, but he was nowhere to be seen. She hadn't seen him since they stepped into the corridor of skulls. He might have waited back near the entrance with the others, or maybe he had left altogether.

She balled her hands. The thought of Jonas's betrayal hurt worse than everything else that had happened on this disaster of a mission. The fact that Holverd had been right all along made it even harder to bear.

As soon as the last lancer entered the circle, it was closed around them, blocking off all chance of escape. Adarra and the others stood quietly in front of the throne—if that was indeed what it was supposed to be—waiting to see what would happen next. The torchlight sent the Northmen's shadows filtering across the walls, giant shapes looming over them, reminding Adarra of how insignificant she was.

Adarra drew on her magic, afraid of what was about to happen. She wanted to have some small way of defending herself. She almost laughed at the ridiculousness of it. What was she going to do against an entire room of Tallosian warriors, let alone five mountains' worth? Still, feeling the magic's warmth gave her a small sense of strength, something she needed now more than anything.

Ambassador Lanmiere looked around, then finally cleared his throat and spoke, his voice cracking. "My name is Ambassador Lan—"

Lanmiere was struck from behind by one of the Tallosians and thrown to the ground. Holverd and Mervall were there to quickly pick him back up. He rubbed the back of his head, and his hand came away with a little blood.

The woman on the platform looked down at their group, once again studying each. No one spoke, which put Adarra even more on edge. Sheegwa stopped when she saw Belakor, and her face twisted. "How dare you show your face here again, Shayan?"

Belakor raised his head from where he'd been staring at the floor.

"I told you that if I ever saw your face here again, I would remove it."

Belakor's eyes bulged, and he dropped to his knees, almost pulling Adarra over, as she was still holding his arm. He began to mumble something through his gag, but no one could understand what he was saying.

Sheegwa pointed at one of the warriors on the right, and the man drew an axe from over his shoulder and stepped forward.

Adarra panicked as Belakor shook his head, trying to talk through the gag. She tried to think of what to do to keep them from killing the old man. What had he done to deserve this? She quickly drew more of her magic but hesitated. If she did this, they were going to know who she was, and then it would be her head on one of those pikes.

The Tallosian with the axe started for Belakor, and he shrieked and started crawling backward.

"What's going on?" Lanmiere and Holverd kept asking, but she didn't have time to explain. Everything was happening too fast. She'd promised the old wielder that everything would be alright.

"Stop this!" Holverd shouted, and his men tried to get in front of the man with the axe, but as soon as they tried stepping out of line, the armed Tallosians grabbed them and pulled them back.

One of the Northman grabbed Adarra as well and pulled her back against him, holding one arm around her shoulders. She couldn't let this happen. She frantically cast about to see what she had to use and dove inside herself, reaching out to the first thing she could sense and whispered, *"Voyestra."*

The fire from the pit behind them burst into the air. The Northmen standing closest leaped out of the way, knocking those in front of them down, sending part of the room into chaos.

"He wishes to burn us all!" Sheegwa roared. "Kill him, now!"

Adarra's breath caught in her throat. She'd made it worse. Quickly, she drew the wind and tried to focus it like she had back in the woods, but she was too panic-stricken to control it, and with the big Northman holding her arms in place, she couldn't even aim.

One of the Northmen grabbed Belakor, who was now trying to squeeze between their legs to hide, and threw him down on his stomach on the stone and knelt on his back. Belakor's arms and legs flailed as he tried to wiggle free. The Tallosian with the axe stopped at the side and lowered the blade just over the wielder's neck, to make sure he hit the right place. Tears streaked the old man's face as he twisted around and caught Adarra's eyes.

She focused on her magic, pulling up the heat. It was her only chance. It had to work.

"*Avienda.*"

The wind whipped around the room but did little more than yank a few of the skulls off their pikes and bounce them off the wall. No! Tears burned her eyes as she looked down at Belakor. She'd failed the old man, just like she'd failed Sergeant Finnly.

The Tallosian raised his axe.

She couldn't watch. She closed her eyes.

"Wait!"

Adarra opened one eye and peeked through the lid, then opened the other. Jonas was up on the platform with Sheegwa. He was whispering into her ear as she held one hand out toward the man with the axe.

Jonas finished whatever he was saying, and Sheegwa turned and waved the man with the axe off. She then looked down at the quivering wielder. "It appears you have an advocate who believes you might be of some use. But if I sense even the slightest bit of magic moving about my house again, I won't just kill you. I'll make it last for weeks."

Jonas turned and looked directly at Adarra, and she quickly released her hold on the magic. As soon as she did, the wind died and the fire receded.

Sheegwa stood from her seat and looked down at Belakor, who was still too frightened to even raise his head. "You have my son to thank for sparing your life. Make sure he doesn't regret the decision."

Adarra gaped up at Jonas. *Son?* He was the son of the head of the most powerful Tallosian house? Why hadn't he said something before? He looked at her briefly and then turned and left the room.

Sheegwa waved to the guards. "Put them in the pit. I'll deal with them later." The head of the house rose from her seat and marched off in the direction Jonas had gone, taking a doorway on the left.

"What's happening?" Aiden asked. "What did she say?"

"She said we owe our lives to . . . her son."

"Her what?" Aiden and the others turned and looked in the direction Jonas and Sheegwa had taken. "Are you saying that—"

"Yes. Jonas is next in line to be head of the largest house in Tallos."

Chapter 72 | Ferrin

ERRIN STARTLED AWAKE. "What was that?" His eyes were groggy as he looked around the tunnel. The soft pale glow from the crystal lit about ten or fifteen feet in either direction. There was nothing there. Had he imagined it? Perhaps he had been dreaming. It had sounded like a rock skidding across the stone, but he couldn't tell from where. The passage was all but silent now.

How long had he been asleep? It felt like days since he'd gotten any. He sat up, a chilling running through him. What if he'd missed whoever Ayrion had sent down to warn him? What if they'd called, but he hadn't heard?

"I'm down here!" he shouted back up through the tunnel, hoping by chance if there had been someone, they might still hear his echoes. He doubted it was the khuls. They weren't shy about letting you know they were coming.

His call was answered with silence.

"Pull yourself together. There's nothing down here but you." He laughed, though it sounded forced. "I'm losing it."

He grabbed his sword from his lap and stood. He paced a few times to relieve some of the soreness and let the blood flow back into his legs, then returned to his seat.

Doubts rushed in to fill the silence. What if they had tried to warn him while he was asleep? What if he was supposed to have already started and they were all waiting on him? What if the sun had set and the khuls were on their way?

He started to sweat as he listened intently for any sign that the khul horde was coming. He didn't think he heard anything. Then again, as flustered as he was, he didn't trust his own senses.

"No, Ayrion would make sure that whoever came found me," he told himself firmly. He stood once more. "I need to go put a mark on the wall, just to be sure."

Another rock rolled across the ground, its echoes reaching his section of the tunnel, and he stopped. There'd been no mistaking that. He thought it had come from the tunnel leading up. Maybe it was the guard coming to tell him everyone was out. He drew his dagger and quickly ran up the tunnel to the first bend and hunkered down next to it, pressing his body against the wall.

He looked down. *Idiot.* He'd forgotten to darken the crystal. *"Luminor."* The white light vanished, leaving him to the darkness. It was the kind of darkness he felt, one that stirred his imagination in ways that made him feel as if hands were reaching out of that blackness and sliding their fingers up his arms. He shivered at the thought.

Another rock moved, and this time it sounded closer. There was definitely something out there. His fingers tightened around both hilts as he waited for whatever was coming. He stood poised to call up the crystal, his mouth open and ready. Then a flash of light flickered off the wall in front of him. It brightened, eventually revealing the shadow of a man floating along the wall. Ferrin released a small sigh of relief and stepped out from the corner.

Elson screeched and nearly dropped his torch as he grabbed his chest. "Are you trying to kill me?"

"What are you doing down here?" Ferrin shot back. He held up his crystal. *"Luminate."* The tunnel brightened even more.

Elson bent at the waist, his hands on his knees as he tried to slow his heart. He finally stood back up. "I thought the khuls had gotten you. I was about to give up and turn back around. What are you doing so far down?"

"I have to be where the gold is," Ferrin said, pointing at the wall. He looked past Elson and back up the tunnel passage. "Why are you even here? What time is it? You need to get up top with the rest. They could be down at any moment to tell me it's time."

Elson walked over and took a seat on one of the rocks jutting from the side. "I was already on my way down when one of the Upakan fighters found me. I told him I was coming to see you, and I'd give you the message. He seemed eager to let me. So consider the message received."

"What message?"

Elson stood from his seat. "That everyone is out and the rest is up to you."

"Wait, why were you on your way down to see me?"

Elson shrugged. "Call me crazy, but I think I've known you long enough to know when you aren't telling me everything. The others might have believed you when you told them there was nothing to worry about, but I could see it in your eyes. You're not so sure."

Ferrin hated that his friend knew him that well. "I'm worried that I'm too far from the doors for my magic to work."

Elson pursed his lips and nodded. "Not going to lie. That's not exactly great news."

Ferrin rolled his eyes.

"And if it doesn't work?"

Ferrin stared into the darkened tunnel leading down to the encampment. "It has to."

"Well, not to rush you, but you might want to get a move on. As fast as that Upakan runner was moving when he found me, I don't reckon he thinks you have much time."

Ferrin took a deep breath. "Then here goes nothing."

"That is such a stupid expression," Elson said. "Whoever came up with it should be horsewhipped. How does *nothing* go anywhere? It should be, here goes *everything*."

Ferrin sheathed his blades and walked over to where the gold was reflecting the light of Elson's torch. *Please work.* He wasn't sure who he was asking, but if there was someone up there listening, he could really use some help right about now. He placed his hands against the cold stone and closed his eyes.

"Here goes *everything*."

He drove his magic into the ore, feeding it along the veins as they dissected and intersected and branched out all along the tunnel's passage back toward the awaiting doors below. He fed his magic into the system, spreading from one ore to the next as they began to culminate back near the final chamber that sealed the khuls off from the rest of Aldor.

The magic forced him to go deeper than he had before. He could feel the ore, feel it all. It was like a living entity spreading its way through the mountainside. Sweat beaded once more across his forehead, and his hands began to tremble as he felt himself reaching the end of what he thought he had to draw upon. He could feel the ways of the mountain, its ancient life, every twist and turn underneath as the veins of ore carried him throughout.

He had no idea how long he'd been at it. Time seemed to have stopped. He could feel his heart pounding, his blood rising. He finally sensed what he was looking for.

This was it.

He had to draw it to him.

Focusing his mind on what he wanted, he imagined calling the ore to him, starting with what lay just inside the walls surrounding the two doors. He couldn't reach what lay beyond them, but he didn't need to. He just needed to collapse what lay on this side.

The rock under his feet began to quake. He could feel the heat inside him rising, and he gritted his teeth, concentrating everything on seeing that chamber collapse. He could feel the iron shift, the gold sliding from its resting place, and he fought to keep it moving.

His arms and legs began to shake, and it was growing hard to breathe. He was close. The tremors became even stronger as they worked their way toward them.

Suddenly, his legs buckled, and the darkness took him.

". . . errin."

"Ferrin!"

Something slapped his face, and he jerked awake. "What happened?"

"I don't know. You tell me," Elson said as he helped Ferrin up against the wall. "One minute the mountain is shaking, the next you're lying on the ground unconscious." He looked down the tunnel. "Did it work? Do we need to be running?" He grabbed under Ferrin's arm and helped him to his feet.

Ferrin shook his head. "I . . . I don't think it worked." He reached out to place his hand back against the gold and realized half the wall was covered in it. "What happened?"

"Well, the gold started coming right out of the rock and sliding straight down the wall. Was that supposed to happen?"

"I don't know."

"You don't know? Again, not filling me with confidence here."

Ferrin bit down. "It might surprise you to know that I've never tried to collapse a mountain before." He placed his hand on the gold and sent his magic inside once more, but instead of letting it branch out and follow all the hundreds and thousands of minute trails, he followed only the main course leading back to the chamber with the doors.

His magic slid inside the room, flowing around the walls and over to the stone doors. His heart sank. "It didn't work. I couldn't bring it down."

Elson stared at the gold. "What does that mean?"

"It means I'm too far away from the source. I need to be closer."

"How much closer?"

Ferrin's expression stiffened.

"Oh, that much closer. But that would mean . . ."

Ferrin nodded. "I know."

Rae's face flashed in front of him, reminding him of his promise to her. To protect her and Suri. He could see his sister as well, and how angry she would be if she knew what he was contemplating. But if he didn't, and the khuls were loose . . . He shook his head. If he had a chance to stop them, he had to take it.

"But what about the khuls?" Elson said, glancing down the tunnel. "They could already be on their way. I would think if they weren't awake already, shaking the mountain probably did it."

"Which means I need to hurry." Ferrin turned and took his friend's hand. "Tell Rae and Myriah I love them. Oh, and make sure they write a ballad of my heroism." Before Elson could say anything or even get his mouth open, Ferrin took off down the tunnel, following the flow of gold, his feet carrying him to whatever end fate had in store. *So much for my prayers*, he thought as he raced toward the camp below.

At this point, it didn't matter how far back he thought he could be to collapse the mountain. There was no outrunning it, so he might as well try to get as close as he could, even if it meant walking into the very chamber itself. He couldn't believe it had all come to this. Everything he'd endured in the Tower, everything Sylas had put him and his friends and family through, all for this. If there was a Creator, he had a twisted sense of humor.

He could have kicked himself. Why had he ever agreed to help Ayrion? Why hadn't he just kept to the plan—a quick stop in Easthaven and then found some remote village on the edge of nowhere to live out his days. But no, here he was, about to bring a mountain down on his head in order to stop some ancient flaming army of the flaming Dark One himself. It better be a glorious ballad, with bards recounting the tale of how Ferrin the Powerful brought down a mountain to save the Five Kingdoms. He smiled at the thought.

He was out of breath by the time he reached the encampment. Embers were still burning in dozens of remaining fires. Gear, bedding, and clothing were scattered throughout. He raced across the chamber, dodging cookfires as he went, and then charged into the tunnel on the other side. So far, there'd been no sign of the khuls. Perhaps it wasn't quite as late as he thought, or perhaps the trembling of the mountain had given them pause. One could only hope.

No matter the reason, he was thankful to have made it this far. The gold was thicker here in the lower tunnel, the veins more spread out along the walls, and even the ceiling and floor in some places. Still, he kept going. He needed to get as close as he could to the chamber to make sure he could cause the greatest impact. He thought he heard something behind him, and he spun around, his sword and dagger still in hand.

The light from his crystal shone only partway across the tunnel since the lower tunnels were much larger than those above. There was nothing there, so he turned and kept going. The stench was horrific as he raced through the river of dead corpses, doing his best not to trip on their remains. He made it around three bends in the corridor before he heard the first signs of something ahead.

He recognized the echoes as they filtered back in his direction. "Not now.

I'm so close." All it took was a single time on the front lines to know the sound of a horde of khuls coming your way. Their growls and barks, and the scraping of their claws against the stone, flooded the tunnel ahead. He wasn't going to be able to reach the chamber.

"Why can't just one thing go right for me?" He sheathed his weapons, since they weren't going to do him much good anyway. Either he was able to bring it all down from here or he'd just wasted his life for nothing. He ran to the side of the tunnel, not caring how many khul corpses he had to climb over, and thrust his hands against the largest vein he could find.

His magic was on the tip of his fingers, waiting to be released, and he drove it inside. He pushed it as hard as possible. Once again, it branched out, intersecting from one collection of ore to the next, and he worked to find them all. He focused and forced the magic deeper. Faster.

The cries of the khuls were getting close. The ground shook beneath him, and it wasn't from anything he was doing. He dove as far as he could within himself, forcing his magic to find what he was looking for. He was close to the chamber, but he wasn't there yet. He could feel himself weakening, his magic thinning.

The khuls were nearly on him. His entire body was shaking as he fought to beat them to it. Why now? Why did they have to come now? If they would have waited just a few minutes longer. The first of the wave broke around the tunnel's corridor on his left, but he didn't open his eyes. He didn't need to. He could feel them. He could hear them.

His mind screamed as he tried to shove his magic closer. He was out of time. Perhaps, at the very least, he could bring down what was here and stop the immediate threat. Perhaps that would give Aldor time to prepare. He reached out to the ore and—

Someone shouted behind him, and the tunnel burst with light. It was so bright, Ferrin could see it through closed eyes, so bright he could feel it pressing against him, pushing him against the wall.

The khuls roared and screeched, and then ran . . . but not at him. They turned and raced back through the tunnels they had just come from, scrambling over each other to get away from the light.

"Come on!" Elson shouted on the way by.

The light faded, and Ferrin saw Elson running like a crazed man straight for the khuls. Ferrin held his hands in front of his eyes and chased after his lunatic friend, his head dizzy from the expending of magic.

"What do you think you're doing?"

"You didn't think I was going to let you have all the glory, did you?" Elson shouted back over his shoulder as he continued to chase after the creatures. His light was only half of what it had been, but it was still enough to keep the wave of khuls fighting to stay ahead of it.

They ran all the way back to the pictorial chamber, reaching the end of the tunnel just as the last of the khuls went shrieking inside the opening at the bottom of the stone doors. Elson ran across the chamber and over to the doors, then stuck his arm through the opening and sent a beam of light through the crack. More shrieks rose from the other side.

Ferrin dropped to his knees near the entrance of the chamber, barely able to keep on his feet. "Why did you do it? You shouldn't have come down here."

"Well, that's gratitude for you," Elson said. "You're welcome, by the way. Feel free to thank me later."

"And how am I going to do that after I bring the mountain down on our heads?"

"Good point. Didn't think of that." He stared at Ferrin from the other side of the chamber. "At least now you can reach the source," he said, looking up at the ceiling and some of the veins of gold along the surface.

Ferrin looked up. Elson wasn't wrong. This was the most ideal spot for his magic to connect. It was too bad it wouldn't reach beyond the doors. It was one thing to seal the creatures in, it would have been another to collapse the mountain down on top of them and make sure they never hurt anyone ever again. Unless . . .

"What's going on?" Elson asked. "I know that look. You're up to something."

Ferrin pulled himself back up to his feet and slowly started across the chamber. "How much of that light do you think you can give me?"

"How much do you need?"

"I need enough to get me in there."

Elson looked inside the hole he was standing in front of and laughed.

"Well, if this is our end, guess we might as well make it a good one. This was a poor time to give up drinking. Where's my flask when I need it?"

Ferrin chuckled.

"Perhaps they'll sing a few verses of me in this ballad of yours," Elson said.

Ferrin sighed. "Idiot. You were the one who was supposed to let people know to pen it. Now no one does."

Elson frowned. "Right. Didn't think about that either. Oh well. Nothing for it now. He turned and looked into the hole. "We best get on with it, then." He raised his arm and sent another beam of light ahead of them as they stepped into the opening. "You don't believe Lenara will think any better of me, do you? Knowing what we've done down here and all?"

"Probably not. Why does it matter?"

He shrugged. "Just wondering."

They kept going until they reached the end of the door and moved into the ancient cavern beyond. The chamber was booming with the sounds of thousands of khuls as they packed the enormous chamber, waiting for the light to dissipate so they could make another break for it.

Ferrin motioned to his friend. "You first."

Elson smiled, then unbuttoned his coat and shirt and pulled them off. His body was already glowing, but not quite as brilliantly as it had before. He stepped out from the doors, and the room brightened. Half the khuls fled back into their dens, the other half moved toward the back.

The chamber was massive, each pillar standing the height of a full pine and nearly five times its girth. Ferrin stepped out behind Elson, his hands in front of his face as they slowly made their way deeper into the cavern.

"We need to get to one of the pillars," Ferrin said, pointing to the closest on the right.

Elson nodded and shifted directions, keeping the main part of his light beaming straight ahead. The khuls moved back, parting to the sides to keep away from the light. The creatures roared, whipping themselves into a frenzy, beating on the ground, on the pillars, on each other, desperate to get their hands on the two of them but too fearful of the light.

Ferrin hoped Elson had enough magic to give him time to finish what he needed to do.

The room glowed in amber waves as the light reflected off all the gold. Ferrin was almost afraid to connect with it, afraid his magic would be pulled to the breaking point. Of course, what did he have to lose? For a split moment, he paused, thinking about those on the surface. He knew how hard Rae and Myriah were going to take this. He was glad they had Myron there to help.

"What are you waiting for?" Elson asked.

Ferrin shoved the thought aside. "Nothing. Here we go."

He walked over to the pillar and placed his hands over the gold marbling that ran throughout. He released his magic into the ore, and it shot straight up the pillar, across the ceiling and down the next. There was so much gold. He couldn't help but wonder who had created such an astonishing place. How long had it taken? And to think he was about to destroy it in a single moment.

The khuls' cries grew, and Elson was forced to brighten the light, sending directed beams into those creatures trying to inch their way forward. They roared and barked but moved back.

"Have you got it?" Elson asked. "Getting a little tired here."

"I've got it. This feels so . . . I can't describe it." He concentrated all his efforts and pulled the ore to him.

"Then don't describe it. Just warn me before you—"

An enormous clap shook the back of the chamber as the last row of pillars shattered, sending thousands of pieces of stone and gold flying into the khuls.

The next row of pillars broke, and the back quarter of the cavern dropped on top of the creatures.

Ferrin looked up. It had begun.

Light or no light, the entire horde stampeded forward at once.

Ferrin's entire body shook as he released the pillar and turned to Elson. "Time to run!"

Elson threw his arm around him, and they charged for the doors. Behind them, Ferrin heard the next row of pillars shattering and the next section of mountain collapsing. The cries of the khuls grew as everyone raced to escape the destruction.

The doors were just ahead.

Elson fired another beam of light back into the coming horde, but it didn't seem to be slowing them down in the least. Ferrin and Elson reached the doors as the next two rows shattered, barely glancing back over their shoulders before racing inside. The magnificent structure was crumbling behind them, half of it already gone.

Ferrin's one quick glimpse revealed that the khuls were running for their dens. Those not close enough headed for the only other exit, which was the doors. Like Ferrin and Elson, however, there was nowhere the khuls were going to be able to run to escape.

"Keep going!" Elson shouted, doing his best to keep Ferrin running. Ferrin's heart was pounding so hard it felt like it was about to rip through his chest. He gasped for each breath, but his will to survive—even knowing his death was imminent—kept his legs moving. He could feel the blackness coming for him, but he willed it off. There was no escaping, but he kept running for Elson's sake.

The khuls were already heading through the corridor behind them, and Elson shot a blinding beam of light back to slow their approach. The creatures were ripping each other apart trying to get through. If they were lucky enough, the khuls would cause a big enough pile that it would completely block them from reaching the other side.

Ferrin and Elson broke free of the stone and started across the intricately carved chamber with all its stories etched into the walls. The ground under their feet shook hard enough that it nearly had them stumbling to their knees more than once.

"Watch out!" Ferrin shouted as rocks fell from the ceiling of the cavern.

They dodged them as they fought to reach the other side, hoping to get into the tunnel before the entire thing collapsed.

There was a loud crack, and the ground rumbled so hard it threw them forward and sent them rolling straight into the tunnel on the other side. Ferrin's legs and arms were scraped from the fall, and he turned in time to see dozens of khuls clambering through the two massive doors behind them. They'd barely made it into the room when the doors split apart, and the ceiling dropped on top of them.

Ferrin looked at Elson, and they jumped to their feet and started running once more.

The tunnel around them shook as multiple splits along the rock chased after them. Cracks formed around them, racing up the stone ahead. Most split along the veins of gold, leaving crevices, some wide enough they had to leap over them. Sections of rock jutted from the sides as parts of the ceiling collapsed in different places, all of it creating a maze that made their run even more difficult.

Ferrin's body felt numb as they tore around the final bend, tripping over corpses the entire way. Up ahead, he saw the encampment, and for the first time he felt a slight ray of hope. Maybe they could somehow make it out. Then he thought about how far they still had to go, and that hope was quickly snuffed out.

They would never make it.

Ferrin tripped on a dead khul and went down. His legs were too tired to lift him back up. His chest was on fire. Shallow gasps of air were all that was keeping him going, that and refusing to give up for Elson's sake.

"Get up!" Elson screamed, hauling him back to his feet.

They stumbled on, reaching the mouth of the cavern holding the Upakan camp as half of the left side of the ceiling collapsed, the other half about to go. Behind them, the tunnel at the last bend disappeared in a pile of rock. The mountain shook so hard they were both thrown into the wall to the right.

Elson scrambled to his feet and helped Ferrin to his.

Ferrin smiled. "It's been an honor, my friend. I can't think of anyone I'd rather be standing beside here at the end."

Elson grabbed Ferrin's arm. "The honor is—"

A barking howl on the other side of the chamber had them both spinning around.

Ferrin's breath caught in his throat. "Nola?"

The giant wolf tore into the chamber, racing across the fallen boulders and leaping over the cracks in the floor that were already forming.

Ferrin stared in awe as the giant wolf lumbered up in front of them. "I don't believe it."

Elson helped Ferrin onto Nola's back and then climbed on himself.

Ferrin barely had time to grab a handful of her fur before she leaped back into the chamber. The tunnel behind them collapsed, shaking loose what remained of the ceiling in the main chamber. Ferrin and Elson both looked up as the entire mountain began to fall.

"Run, Nola!" Ferrin shouted, and the wolf tore ahead, leaping from one boulder to the next. Ferrin gasped as the ceiling plummeted toward them. They weren't going to make it. The frostwolf raced across the final boulder and leaped into the air and through the tunnel's mouth as everything came crashing down behind them. Ferrin hung on for dear life, and he could hear Elson howling his fear and defiance behind him as Nola raced forward, her powerful legs pulling them up, somehow keeping just in front of what was coming.

Cracks split the walls around them, chasing them all the way up to the underground city itself. They broke free of the tunnel to find parts of the roof over the city already collapsing. Stars shone through the upper reaches of the cavern.

Nola flew down the side street running along the edge of the cave's face until they reached the main thoroughfare leading back toward the center square. She took it, then cut down another side street before they reached the Justice Hall. The street was narrow, but so far there didn't seem to be any debris blocking the way.

Elson tapped Ferrin's shoulder and then pointed up at a wide section of the roof that seemed to be barely holding on. Ferrin nodded that he saw it as Nola broke from the street and over to one Ferrin recognized. It was the road they had traveled on when first climbing down to the underground section of the city.

"Hurry, Nola!" Ferrin urged as another loud crack behind them signaled the arrival of the coming collapse.

Above them, the failing section of ceiling split from the rest and dropped.

"Stop!" Ferrin shouted, and Nola skidded to a halt. "Get off the street!"

They raced to the left between two buildings just as the enormous plate of stone collapsed across several homes in front of them, turning them to instant rubble, sending pieces of stone flying in all directions.

"Now," he said, and Nola left their hiding place and took off across the top of what had dropped. Strangely enough, it was covered in snow and sand. It almost felt as though they were already aboveground.

Ferrin wondered how much longer Nola could keep this pace while carrying two grown men, especially when one was as big as Ferrin. He remembered her carrying him before and leaping from the end of a dock all the way aboard the *Wind Binder*. She had extremely powerful legs, but she'd been running for some time. They reached the mouth of the tunnels and took one quick look behind as the rest of the dome over the underground city crumbled.

"We've got to move," Ferrin said, and rubbed Nola's neck like he would a horse. "Hurry. We still have a long way to go."

Nola turned and raced back up through the final tunnel leading to the top. He hoped the wolf had a good enough memory to be able to navigate across the back half of the city without them going through one of the sinkholes. He wouldn't be able to remember something like that, not after dark and on the run.

Ferrin was just beginning to gain a little bit of feeling in his extremities when Nola tore out of the tunnel and into the building where they'd left their gear. It was all still sitting in a pile on the other side, but there was nothing they could do about it now. The building they were in was already shaking itself apart. Ferrin urged Nola to keep going. The door ahead was beginning to sink below the surface.

"Down!" Ferrin shouted at Elson and they both hunkered across her back as she dashed through the entrance just before it disappeared behind them.

"Where have the two of you been?" someone shouted on their right, and they turned to find Ayrion atop his giant warhorse. He was holding the reins to a second horse pacing about skittishly.

Ferrin gawked. "You're still here?"

"I told you I would be. Though I was giving up hope." He turned and held out the reins, glancing at Nola. "Elson, I guess this one's for you."

Elson half climbed, half fell off Nola's back as his wobbly legs stumbled toward the brown stallion. He somehow managed to pull himself up, barely getting his leg over and grabbing the reins. Ferrin was glad to be able to take at least part of the weight off Nola's back.

"Follow me!" Ayrion shouted. He spun his warhorse around and took off through the city. Ferrin's crystal was still glowing, giving him and Elson enough light to keep up, not that Elson needed it, as his hands were still glowing. Behind them, buildings were dropping into the city below. Loud cracks and rumbling shook the ground as they raced ahead, doing their best to keep to Shade's hoofprints.

Ferrin glanced behind him to see the city slowly sink beneath the surface. Spouts of snow and debris shot into the air as the crust collapsed. He turned back around, hardly able to believe they were still alive. Even thinking back on it, he had no idea how. He dared a quick glance upward, not too proud to acknowledge that perhaps his earlier cry for help might not have gone on deaf ears after all. Though, it would have been nice if the help hadn't waited to arrive until the last possible moment.

They raced over the snow-covered sand and rock up to the ridge ahead, where rows of torchlight lined the rise. Apparently, the entire Upakan nation was standing there watching as the three of them came riding over the edge.

Ferrin hadn't exactly expected a fanfare, but at least some applause would have been nice. Instead, the entire assembly stood there somberly, watching what was left of the former capital city of Keldor drop below the surface and finally earn its name: the Lost City.

For this time, it was truly lost, once and for all.

Chapter 73 | Ayrion

YRION STOOD SILENTLY with his family, watching as their home continued to crumble and sink below the surface. Grey light brushed the sky over the eastern peaks and soon kissed the plain below. Fading echoes of the destruction washed back off the surrounding mountainsides, as far back as Howling Gorge. He wished it hadn't taken the near destruction of his people to accomplish the task Nyalis had given him, but now it was time to move forward, to take that next step.

It was time to bring the Tanveer home.

Whatever Ferrin had done in those lower tunnels, he certainly hadn't gone halfway. There was nothing left. Ayrion couldn't believe how close the swordsmith and his friend had come to perishing with the city. Ayrion glanced to his right and found Ferrin and his companions standing farther down the row, just beyond Tameel and Zynora, their eyes on the devastation below.

Ferrin hadn't told him yet what had taken place below and why it had taken him so long to return, or why Elson of all people had been down there with him. All Ayrion knew was that he could have never accomplished any of this without their help. He was grateful their paths had crossed when they did and that he and his friends had been able to help Ferrin and his beleaguered company. It really showed how helping others could come back to you in a positive way.

"Now what?"

Ayrion turned to find Sirak hobbling over with an arm around Zayden for support. Brim was nowhere to be seen. Ayrion's brother and sister moved to let the two primaries through. They stopped beside him and watched as the last remnants of their home sank below the surface.

"I don't know what your man did," Sirak said, "but the khuls won't be getting out of there anytime soon, if at all." He looked at Ayrion. "What do we do now? We've lost everything."

"That was hardly everything," Ayrion said. "It was a hole in the ground, one we've been hiding in for so long we'd forgotten what it was to be a people. The Upaka have always relegated their work to the shadows. It's time that the Tanveer step back into the light where we belong."

Sirak cleared his throat. "You mentioned a place in the Angoran Mountains, one we once called home. How secluded is it?"

Ayrion wanted to shake his head, or shake the primary, whichever worked best. Was that all they cared about, keeping as far from the rest of the world as possible? "It is more secluded than this," he said, nodding toward the empty valley below.

"And how would we provide for our families there? What sort of work would we be engaged in?"

"It won't be contract killing," Ayrion said. "I don't know what all duties we will have once we get there, but I can say that keeping our people fed will not be a worry. Your needs will be provided for. We were guardians and paladins. I suspect our routines will be much the same as they were here—days filled with training and patrols."

"That's all well and good," Zayden said, "but how do you suggest we get there? We left the city with little more than the clothes on our backs. What provisions we managed to grab won't last a couple of days. We aren't used to conditions like this," he said, kicking at a pile of snow, "and we have injured and elderly to carry with us."

They were all good questions that needed answering before they could decide what to do next. He wished they'd had more time to prepare.

"We need shelter and food," Sirak said. "But no one is going to go out of their way to help us."

"They have a point, son," Ayrion's father said from his right, his arm around Ayrion's mother. "You have an entire people who now find themselves homeless. From what I've seen, listening to those gathered, most are still in shock. But once that wears off, you had better have some answers ready, or you'll wish you were back down in the tunnels with the khuls."

"Agreed," Ayrion said. "Food and shelter are our first priority." He glanced eastward. "Most of the passes through the Northern Heights are lost to us. It would be too dangerous to attempt crossing over unstable ground."

"There are some smaller ravines to the south," Zayden said. "They don't span from one side to the other, but they are large enough for our people to shelter for a night or two."

Ayrion nodded. "It's a two-day journey around the mountains to the forest south of Norshag. We should be able to make a temporary camp there until we decide where to gather provisions."

"We could try sending riders west to Chorazin and Pinnella," Sirak said, "to see if they have food to sell. Because of the khuls, we weren't able to meet them when they came with their shipments a couple of weeks ago."

Ayrion shook his head. "We don't have time to wait. It would be at least a half-week journey there on horseback, and a full week for wagons laden with food to make it back."

"Then what do you suggest? We'd never be able to forage enough food to feed this many."

"There is one place we might be able to get provisions, but I have a feeling it will take some convincing." Ayrion smiled inwardly as he pictured the look on Magistrate Sirias's face when he showed up at Oswell with an entire population of Upakans. "It's at least a week's journey east, so for now our only concern is finding shelter for tonight, and food to last."

"We'll send riders south," Sirak said, readjusting his grip on Zayden's shoulder. His face tightened against the pain. He needed to be on a stretcher, not limping his way all over the rise. "While they ride ahead to look for somewhere to set up camp, we'll start our people moving in that direction. We can't just stand here staring at nothing while we freeze to death." He slid his shaders over his eyes with one hand as the sun breached the peaks in their direction.

"Anyone seen Brim?" Ayrion asked.

"Last I saw, he was helping to load some of the injured on wagons," Zayden said. "I think he's with his family on the other side."

Ayrion nodded. "Make sure he knows what we're doing." He looked at Sirak. "And as soon as Rae is strong enough, have her see to your wounds. We need you capable enough to walk."

"Agreed," Zayden said loudly. "I'm getting tired of hauling his heavy backside around."

The two primaries smiled, which was one of the first times Ayrion had seen that happen. Things were moving in the right direction. And Brim had been spotted helping the injured. He shook his head with a smile. What was the world coming to?

"I'll leave you to it, then," Ayrion said, and headed over to join the rest of his companions, who were now gathering behind Ol' Lerra, along with Shade and Nola. They turned and waited as Ayrion joined them.

"So, what's been decided?" Tameel asked.

"We are going to send riders south to search the mountains for a suitable place to set up camp for tonight, then we start the journey south around the mountains and find shelter in the forest south of Norshag."

"Sounds reasonable," Tameel said, scratching at his feathery white hair.

"Any idea how we will be feeding all of these people?" Bek asked. "It's a long way to the Angorans."

"I do, but I can't say it's a good one."

Myron blanched. "Tell me you're not about to suggest we take them all back to Oswell, because that will likely kill that magistrate friend of yours."

Ayrion shrugged. "You have a better way to feed everyone?"

Bek patted Ayrion's shoulder and smiled. "Just make sure I'm there when you break the news to him."

Ayrion couldn't help but chuckle as he turned and looked down at Zynora and Rae, who were seated on the back step. Rae's eyes looked drawn, and her face pale. "How are you two doing?"

"We will survive," Zynora said, handing the young healer a piece of dried meat to chew before taking one for herself. Suri stood beside her mother with Tippi tucked under one arm. Nothing much seemed to affect the little girl.

"As soon as you're feeling better, I need someone to see to Sirak. We're going to need his help keeping this caravan together. The other two primaries look to him, and right now he'd be on his face in the snow if not for Zayden doing everything he can to keep him on his feet."

Rae looked up, took a shallow breath, and nodded. "Perhaps I'll be feeling better by this evening."

"And not a moment sooner," Zynora said, giving Ayrion the eye.

Ayrion nodded that he understood and turned to Lenara, who was leaning against the side of the wagon, rubbing one of Nola's ears. "How are you feeling?" He tried not to look at her stomach. "You expended a lot of magic in the tunnels. Are you feeling up to traveling?"

She looked around at the others, noticing they were all staring. Her face hardened. "As capable as the rest of you."

The others quickly turned around.

Ayrion turned as well, then took a step back to admire the rather eclectic group. "I wanted to offer you my deepest gratitude once again. If not for your willingness to risk your lives, my people wouldn't be here today. You didn't just save them; you likely saved the lives of many thousands more. I dread to think what would have happened to Aldor if those creatures had been released." He turned to Ferrin, who had moved to stand on the other side of Suri. "Once we get the people settled this evening, I'd like to hear what took place in the tunnels. From the looks I've seen you and Elson sharing, I have a feeling it will be quite an interesting tale."

Ferrin half smiled, half grimaced, and Ayrion left it at that. He spotted his family working their way out from the back of the Tanveer and walked over to meet them. "You are welcome to travel with us," he said, about the time Suri ran past to grab Ava's hand and drag Ayrion's niece back over to the wagons, chattering about wanting to show her something inside.

"We were just coming to see if you had room," his father said.

His mother put her arm around Ayrion and squeezed. "It's been a long time since I've been able to do this. You better get used to it because it's likely going to happen a lot."

Ayrion's father chuckled. "I'll try to restrain her."

She released Ayrion, stepped back, and nudged her husband in the side.

"So, I hear you are taking us to some place in the Angorans," Jorn said, though it sounded more like a question. Ayrion's brother hadn't been there when Ayrion had told the rest of his family about Aero'set. Of course, he hadn't exactly told the rest of his people all that much about it either.

"What's it like, Uncle Ayrion?" Davin asked, standing beside Jorn. He tended to stick close to his younger uncle. Ayrion was glad to see Jorn watching out for him.

"It's a place that is truly without words to describe," Ayrion said. "But I'm sure we'll find plenty of time between now and our arrival to try." Ayrion noticed his sister glancing back over her shoulder toward the rise. There were tears in her eyes. "I know we didn't have time to bring much," he said, "but I promise we can replace what was lost."

She looked at him and shook her head. "You can't replace everything."

His chest tightened, and he stepped forward and wrapped his arms around her, and she buried her face in his chest. "I'm sorry," he said.

"We never even got the chance to bury him," she sobbed.

Ayrion's mother walked over and pulled Rianna away, wrapping her own arms around her.

"I know it's not a consolation," Ayrion said, "but you can be proud of your husband's sacrifice. Of all their sacrifices. If it wasn't for their willingness to give everything, your daughter and son, and likely everyone here, would be dead. I promise, as soon as we reach Aero'set, we'll find a way to commemorate Lorn and the others. Their lives will be remembered. I'll make sure of it."

He knew it wasn't much comfort now, but he hoped it would be later. Records needed to be written of the deeds that had taken place here, and the costs that were required.

Shade walked over, sensing Ayrion was ready to be on the move, and Ayrion swung up into the saddle. He rode out to the front of the large caravan of people spread out along the roadway and patted the warhorse's neck. "Well, boy, looks like we made it through another battle in one piece."

He turned in his saddle and stared out over the mass of people as they spread across the roadway as far back as the edge of the rise. The hard part was over. They'd defeated the khuls, or at least stopped them, and in the process left themselves with no other options but to follow Ayrion back to Aero'set to once again take their rightful place.

Three clans had now been united into a single people. He pulled off his glove and held up the ring, letting the early-morning sun brighten the emblems.

Three symbols: Raju. Kovaa. Orpa.

One motto: Truth In All. Honor Above All. Justice For All.

The End of
Book Four of
The Aldoran Chronicles

Dear Reader,

I HOPE YOU enjoyed this fourth book in the Aldoran Chronicles series. If you found the story entertaining and would like to see more, then please consider helping me reach that goal by leaving a quick review on **Amazon**.

Reviews are very important. They help encourage other readers to try the book while at the same time showing Amazon that the book is worth promoting.

> > Thank you in advance!

Where To Find Me

Stop by and say hello!

« michaelwisehart.com »

« facebook.com/MichaelWisehart.author »

Books

STREET RATS OF ARAMOOR

(Starts 20 years prior to the Aldoran Chronicles)

Book 1 | Banished

Book 2 | Hurricane

Book 3 | Rockslide

Book 4 | Sandstorm

Book 5 | Wildfire

THE ALDORAN CHRONICLES

Prequel | Shackled

Book 1 | The White Tower

Book 2 | Plague of Shadows

Book 3 | The Four-Part Key

Book 4 | The Tunnels Beneath

Acknowledgements

I THANK GOD for the doors and windows He's allowed to open in order for me to reach this point.

I want to thank my parents, *Mickey and Julie Wisehart,* for their unending loyalty, encouragement, and support over the years. None of this would be possible without you. Love you both.

I want to thank my Author Team, whose endless talent, time, and dedication have made this project possible:

AUTHOR TEAM

I want to thank my cover illustrator for working with me on designing our first look at Ayrion's famed Upakan ring — *Dongjun Lu "Russell"*

I want to thank my concept artist for bringing Ferrin's frostwolf blades to reality. They are more beautiful than even I had envisioned — *Dongjun Lu "Russell"*

I want to thank my cartographer for working with me to create a location I had not even yet described in my books. In fact, her initial concepts, based on my descriptions and early sketches, helped me complete *The Tunnels Beneath,* as it gave me a visual reference for the things that were happening in the book. Beautifully conceived — *Elwira Pawlikowska*

I want to thank my content editor for picking apart my story, and in doing so forced me to craft a better one — *Nathan Hall*

I want to thank my line editor, who managed to take a semi-readable script and turn it into a book to be proud of. I've never seen so many red marks — *Danae Smith*

I want to thank my copy editor, whose vigilant eyes have made my books worthy of print — *Crystal Watanabe*

I want to thank those on my Beta Team, who took precious time out of their busy schedule to suffer through an unedited draft in order to make sure I was delivering something worth reading. — *Joshua Parker, Leigh Herring, Kenneth Harvey*

About the Author

MICHAEL WISEHART graduated with a bachelor's degree in business before going back to school for film and starting his own production company. On April 14, 2014, he incorporated his love for cinema into the written word and began typing what would become two epic fantasy series: The Aldoran Chronicles and the Street Rats of Aramoor.

He currently lives and writes in Northeast Georgia.

Glossary of Terms

Months of the Year

1. **Aèl** [*ay-el*] First month of the year.
2. **Sòl** [*soul*] Second month of the year.
3. **Nùwen** [*noo-win*] Third month of the year.
4. **Manù** [*mah-noo*] Fourth month of the year.
5. **Toff** [*toff*] Fifth month of the year.
6. **Kwàn** [*quon*] Sixth month of the year.
7. **Nor** [*nor*] Seventh month of the year.
8. **Èldwin** [*el-dwin*] Eighth month of the year.
9. **Kùma** [*koo-muh*] Ninth month of the year.
10. **Akòsi** [*uh-kah-see*] Tenth month of the year.
11. **Èshan** [*ee-shon*] Eleventh month of the year.
12. **Zùl** [*zool*] Twelfth month of the year.

New Character Glossary

Introductory characters not mentioned in prior books

Ava - *aye-vuh* - Daughter of Rianna and Lorn, and Ayrion's niece. Tall, stunning, strong features, long straight black hair.

Belakor - *bell-uh-kor* - Half-crazed man living on the Isle of Tallos. Former scholar to Overlord Saryn. Considered by the Tallosians to be Shayan, which in Tallosian means "cursed one." He is a wielder.

Bevan - *beh-von* - Twin brother to Gorsy. Known for playing a flute duet with his brother at Performance Night in Easthaven.

Bismont - *bizz-mont* - Sidaran river captain who transports the Tallosian food over to the Isle of Tallos. Ship was lost in the Bay of Mist.

Brunella - *broo-nell-uh* - One of the oldest women in Easthaven. Mistress Peyla's grandmother. One of the original founders of the Easthaven bakery, which shared a wall with the Sweet Shop.

Davin - *day-vin* - Son of Rianna and Lorn, and Ayrion's nephew. Sixteen. Brother to Ava. Taller than Ayrion, thinner, with strong features, dark hair like all Upaka.

Gorsy - *gore-see* - Twin brother to Bevan. Known for playing a flute duet with his brother at Performance Night in Easthaven.

Hinkle - *heenk-lee* - Magistrate of Minotha. A tall, lanky man with a horseshoe hairline.

Holverd - *hohl-verd* - Captain in the Sidaran Lancers who is sent to lead the expedition to the Isle of Tallos. Holverd is a large man with a shaved head and thick goatee that hangs a few inches below his chin.

Ilban - *ill-bun* - Magistrate Sirias's rival in Oswell. Head of the city council. He was the one to put a bounty on Sirias's head by hiring the Upaka to kill him.

Jamis - *jay-miss* - One of Veldon's underlings who works for him at the Easthaven docks. Last time Veldon put him in charge, he forgot to lock the front doors before leaving.

Marak - *maer-uck* - Magistrate of Lower Wellhollow. A distant relation to Ozlin Beartooth. Neither have spoken to the other in at least a decade.

Mervall - *mer-vaul* - Captain of the ship taking Adarra and the Sidaran ambassadorial team to Tallos. One of the only captains willing to risk the Bay of Mist.

Matti - *mă-tee* - Name that Belakor gave his whistle, which he used to scare off jingas.

Minkle – *meen-kul* - Friend of Sirias who gave him the news of running Ilban out of town.

Nobis - *no-biss* - One of Douina's razorbacks that she has carry her through Reed Marsh. It means "a thick fog" in the old tongue.

Oriss - *or-iss* - Ship's navigator aboard Captain Marvell's ship, which sailed to the Isle of Tallos.

Shayan - *shay-yan* - Means "cursed one" in the Tallosian language. It represents someone found to have magic.

Sirak - *sir-ack* - Head of Clan Kovaa. Not quite as tall as Brim but just as thick in the chest and arms. He bears several scars across his face.

Trunken - *trun-ken* - Ferryman in Aldwick.

Zayden - *zay-den* - Head of Clan Raju. Shorter and thinner than the other two clan heads, with grey hair cut short enough to not cause a distraction to his vision. Relies on speed and agility rather than brute force and strength.

Stop by and visit:

www.michaelwisehart.com